SANDSTORM

STEPHEN FRANCIS MONTAGNA

Printed in the United States of America
Published by: Stephen Francis Montagna

ISBN: 978-1-970301-14-4 PAPERBACK
ISBN: 978-1-970301-15-1 HARDBACK

PROLOGUE

The long years that followed the collapse of the communist Russian Empire, were stormy times of reconstruction and hardship. The trying times that followed while turning over to a freer and more democratic Russian government, were confusing times for the Old Russian elite. The Russian government turned its back on many important Generals and scientists, causing many to resort to the black market and Russian Mafia for their survival. Thus began years of turbulence, selling and back stabbing of Russia's vigorous military might and machines. The Russian government was aware of the bleeding off of its military hardware to a number of Arab nations.

The Russian leadership was at a loss on how to place a stop to the thievery of its nation's assets. Soon, many radical nations found themselves in the position of being offered T-80 Main Battle Tanks, advance attack fighter aircraft, and Russia's guarded military secrets at a fraction of what they should sell for on the open market. Although the United States and other industrial and free nations as Japan, England and France did their best to block Libya and Iraq from acquiring the Russian military equipment. Nevertheless, it continued to be siphoned off unchecked. The world threatening war machines and weapons of mass destruction filtered out of Russia, no matter what and how the Russian government and other nations tried to stem the flow.

Many leading Russian Generals and lesser military officers made their modern and advanced aircraft and equipment available to the open market. By smuggling them out of Russia, and then placing them on the open market for sale to the highest bidder. The Russian President was not fully aware of the depth of the situation rapidly developing in his military, or he would have reacted swiftly to place a stop to it. Especially in light of the recent military action that was carried out against the renegade Russian Officers, Colonel Mikhailchenko and Major Evnostropov who stole six of Russia's mobile nuclear missile launchers and warheads. The Russian rebels were successful with moving the missiles into what was left of the nearly destroyed North Korea nation. They had the missiles aimed at China in hopes of starting a shooting war between Russia and China, and pulling the United States into the war on their side. The renegade Russian Officers threatened China in hopes of making it possible for the Communists of Russia to make a move against the President Vitaly Kvantrishuili Administration, and takeover power in the USSR once again.

The Communist Colonel's plan was to make their move on the Russian government, by using the pandemonium created by their unprovoked attack on China with nuclear weapons. The Communists were going to move to assassinate the Russian leadership, and then they planned to come to Russia's aid and lead the war against China. Once defeating her, the Russian rebels would then assume complete control of the fractured government. They planned to drive out America's influence from Russia, and refuse to repay the massive debt accumulated by Russia, and use the monies to make Russia a country to be feared again by nations, militarily.

The plan had a chance of succeeding if it was not for the swift actions of the American Special Forces, who deployed a rapid response force to Russia, and these soldiers destroyed the missiles and Communist Officers, before they had a chance to carry out their plan.

In the Middle East, there was the destruction of Israel, Jordan, and Iraq, and the limited destruction of Saudi Arabia, Iran, and Syria, that occurred when Iraq was prompted to attack Israel by Libya, who was locked in a war with the American forces occupying the Sudan. Iraq was ordered to attack Israel with nuclear weapons to get the heat off Libya's neck. This plan did not work out very well, and Libya suffered the complete destruction in the end, to conclude the war raging over clean drinking water for Egypt.

Although Iran suffered the destruction of its capital of Tehran, it left much of Iran still intact, and a powerful Persian nation in the Middle East. The destruction of Iran's capital hurt the ruling Islamic party, leaving the nation open to takeover by anyone who displayed leadership over the torn country. It did not take long for a radical leader to step forward. Sheik Hassan al-Suhail al-Tamini took command of the leaderless nation of Iran, and moved the seat of power to Kerman, that he proclaimed the new capital of Iran. Sheik al-Tamini was in power for a week before he claimed himself Ayatollah, and spiritual leader of the Iranian Islamic people. His grip of power tightened when the Ayatollah ordered the deaths of all Iranian citizens who did not believe in him, or his distorted religious beliefs.

The bodies of hundreds then thousands of civilians fed the combustible heap of humanity that assured the new Ayatollah of Iran of a steadfast and fanatical support for his extremely violent and radical Islamic regime over Iran. Through selected assassinations, the Ayatollah decimated what was left of Iran's old leadership, and plunging the divided nation in revolt, and allowing himself the power to completely take over the troubled nation.

The Ayatollah's first order to his military was to make Iran the feared military country in the rapidly rebuilding of the war torn Middle East, and most Arab nations. To ensure Iran of this great feat, Ayatollah Sheik Hassan al-Suhail al-Tamini ordered his followers to get their hands on multi-nuclear tipped, submarine launched long range missiles for his fleet of five Russian built nuclear submarines. These five boats were moved to Iran's safe ports during Iran's devastating war with Iraq. The Sheik placed his military advisors on this nationwide proclamation, to ensure this command became a reality for his terribly unstable government. He needed these missiles and nuclear warheads to enforce his death grip he wanted to hold over the heads of the civilians of Iran. Then the Middle East and then the world.

CHAPTER ONE

NOVEMBER 2nd, 1998

From the protected Iranian harbor of Bander Beheshi on the Gulf of Oman. Twelve huge fuel tractor trailer tanker trucks started their powerful engines. The machines then headed out into the vast desert heading for the border separating Russia from the Persian nation. The tanker convoy was instructed to make their way to the Russian border using the Dashte Kavir Desert as their cover from the ever prying eyes of the American satellites.

The convoy traveled at breakneck speeds over the rough roads made of hard compressed sand, and in some cases, makeshift roads carved out by the wide wheels of the machines themselves. The stifling temperature of the deep desert was nearing one hundred and twenty five degrees, enough to heat the remaining fuel in the tanker trucks to a dangerous and highly combustible range, making the threat of an explosion a real possible.

Ignoring this, the Iranian drivers pushed forward. In a half a day's harsh travel, the twelve vehicles make way from Bander Beheshi past Bampur, and they progressed to the small desert town of Rigon, where the drivers took on water for the grumbling machines and themselves. A distance of three hundred miles had been traveled in the early morning hours.

After allowing the machines to rest for twenty minutes while being refueled and the water in the engines topped off, the drivers ate and drank, and then they set back on their ordered mission. The drivers bypassed the new Iranian capital of Kerman, and made their way to the Iranian town of Shahdad. From there, the drivers hoped to make it to the city of Bafq, where they would take on more fuel and their final meal before entering the vast and extremely dangerous Dashte Kavir desert. The drivers hoped to travel most of the desert during the cool of night.

It was a grueling trip, with the weary drivers reaching speeds of one hundred miles an hour plus. As they strove to reach the safety of the vast desert before darkness set in. The sand plain was over nine hundred miles from their point of origin.

Once the trailers entered the Dashte Kavir desert, backup drivers took over while the first drivers got some sleep. The trucks bounced forward, making it nearly impossible for the main drivers to sleep. The second crew used the vehicle headlights with secondary headlights mounted on top of the rigs, to light their way through the pitch black of the endless desert. Everything seemed identical as the drivers headed forward, guided by compasses mounted on dashboards to ensure they went in the right direction. Mile after endless mile, the trucks headed on.

At one point, the convoy of Iranian fuel tanker trucks was forced to stop as a long caravan of Nomads slowly made way before the machines. The drivers took this slight break to get out and stretch their legs, and relieving themselves on the soft sand. Some of the Nomads offered the driver's goat's milk and pita bread which they gladly accepted.

**SEVASTOPOL UKRAINE,
HOME OF THE BLACK SEA FLEET.
NOVEMBER 3rd, 1998**

Russian Admiral Yevgeny Proushinsky, stood along with Iranian Colonel, Muhsin Abu Marzuk, as they waited for the arrival of the twelve tanker trucks. Colonel Marzuk was instrumental in brokering the deal creating the transference of twelve Russian made SS-N-23 submarine launched nuclear tipped missiles. The ten MIRV (Multiple Independently Targeted Reentry Vehicle) warheads, with a two hundred and fifty Kiloton yield, and four thousand, five hundred nautical mile range, the missiles were propelled by a liquid propellant.

Admiral Proushinsky stood with the Persian Colonel by the Delta IV submarine from which the missiles were scheduled to be removed from. The Russian Admiral excused the removal of half the submarines nuclear capability, stating a sudden radiation leak was detected from the discarded missiles when inspected. With the endless cutbacks in the Russian military, to classify the nuclear missiles as leakers meant they were earmarked for immediate destruction. This command made it possible for a Russian Officer to sell the twelve long range missiles to Iran without explaining where the missiles and warheads ended up. Admiral Proushinsky had to state the missiles were sent to Taldy Kugran in Kazakhstan for their destruction.

The Russian Command was stockpiling nuclear waste near the Chinese, Russian border, had the dump mined with heavy explosives. If China ever dared to attack Russia through this area, the Russian Command was prepared to destroy the nuclear dump, sending a cloud of radiation over a huge section of both China and Russia. This would occur without a nuclear explosion by employing explosives and not a nuclear reaction. Thereby staying well within the perimeters of the Start III arrangement with the United States. It would also protect Russia's border from any possible invasion by the yellow plague in the southeast.

The excuse the Admiral offered to Russian Command, ensured no one would bother to search for the missing nuclear missiles, and pleased the government because it meant they destroyed more missiles that made it easier for Russia to adhere to the Start Agreement with the United States. Even though the destroyed missiles were an act on paper, no inspectors from the United States bothered to check to see if the missiles reported demolished, were truly destroyed.

Colonel Marzuk stood with his hands locked behind his back while watching the workers place the SS-N-23 missiles on their transport trailers. The wait for the fuel trailers began with the Persian leaned closer to the Russian Officer and whispered after covering his mouth. "Admiral Proushinsky, my trucks should be near the border with Russia about now. I have no reports of them being detained at Azerbaijan. It'll take them the rest of this day to arrive at this port, sir. May I suggest we have something to eat?" Colonel Marzuk smiled at the Russian Admiral.

Admiral Proushinsky replied confidently. "Da! Then we'll speak of my svinaya (fucking) money. Shall we go Comrade Marzuk?" the Russian Admiral bowed because he was pleased to get out of the glaring sun as he waved his hand to the side, and allowed the Persian Officer to lead the way to the mess building. Once inside, they headed for a lone table, the Persian placed his attaché case on it and opened it enough for the Russian Officer to get a good look inside.

Colonel Marzuk smiled, enjoying the look on the Russian Admiral's face as he offered politely. "Admiral Proushinsky, it's as we have agreed, no? Two million American dollars for each of the missiles. Maybe we can discuss a transaction where my government might buy the technology to construct the missiles on our own. I've been instructed by Ayatollah al-Tamini to offer you ten million American dollars for this information." The Persian smiled at the Russian.

"Mudnya!" Shit! "Ten million Amirikanskaya dollars you offer!" Proushinsky exclaimed.

"In cash might I add to you, Admiral Proushinsky?" Colonel Marzuk added with a grin.

"Cash. Hummm... I believe there's a way your government might end up with the technology you seek to build the missiles. Yes Comrade, I might help you get the technicians your country needs to build these missiles. But I fear the cost might be more than even you're willing to pay."

Colonel Marzuk's sneer instantly left his lips as he stared at the Russian Admiral with cold, calculating eyes, and he remarked. "Admiral Proushinsky, my country's willing to pay no matter the cost, if the information's worthwhile to my government's needs." Colonel Marzuk slowly spread his hands apart while resting his elbows down on the table.

"Comrade Colonel Marzuk, it'll cost your government fifty million Amirikanskaya dollars for the information you have just request from me. I'll also make the technicians available, but you'll have to make your own deals with them though. I'll have nothing to do with them or the deals you make with these people once they leave my country. I have enough trouble dealing with my soldiers and these foolish Russian politicians, sir." Admiral Proushinsky smirked at the Persian.

"By the sacred gray beard of the prophet Mohammed. The vast sum of money you ask me for is far greater than my government had planned to offer, Admiral. Surely, there's some neutral ground we can come to stand on to make this deal a reality, Admiral Proushinsky. A ground let's say, a little less expensive to my nation of Iran, sir?" Colonel Marzuk offered.

"Comrade Colonel Marzuk, perhaps you don't appreciate the extreme risks I take for the sake of your country and the deal we speak of. Or the many other people we'll be forced to pay to make this transaction come to fruition for us. The trail I'm forced to deal with, extends all the way to Moscow. All I need is for one of my people to become unhappy with my arrangements, and we could find ourselves spending the rest of our lives in jail, or worse. Be stood before a firing squad, and life ended. No Comrade, it's as I have requested. Fifty million Amirikanskaya dollars if your country's truly serious in their crusade for the technology to enable them to construct their own nuclear warheads and missiles to deliver the weapons to their targets."

"Praise Allah's will, fifty million American dollars, I pray Allah will forgive me for agreeing to this great a sum. But if I must, I'll request another bit of information, Admiral."

"Da! (Yes!) What's this other information you need from me, Comrade Colonel Marzuk?"

Colonel Marzuk did not mind the Admiral using the Communist term when speaking to him, even though he was well aware more of the Communists of Russia were either killed, and the survivors are in hiding in the country "AnsnAllah, If God wills it Admiral Proushinsky, my government will need the information to enable us to turn the four nuclear reactors we brought from the Russian nation, into breeder reactors. With these we can produce our own weapon's grade Plutonium, so we can develop our own nuclear arsenal after that time, Admiral Proushinsky." Iranian Colonel Marzuk glared angrily at the Russian Admiral.

"Comrade Colonel Marzuk, I see no problem agreeing to this request. But you'll have this information at your finger tips once you make your deal with the technicians I'll make available to your nation, Comrade." Admiral Proushinsky announced with little concern over his words.

Colonel Marzuk decided to use the same term in his reply to the extremely dangerous Russian Officer. "Comrade Admiral Proushinsky, in that case I'll agree to your stipulated sum. I'm prepared to turn over the twenty four million American dollars. Once the missiles are loaded inside my trailer trucks, and the foul machines have crossed the border back into my land..."

"What's this treachery you're perpetrating against me, Colonel Marzuk? You're going against our original agreement, Colonel. We had agreed to turn over the fooking money and missiles at the same time. We never agreed to wait until the god dom trucks crossed back into Iran. Nyet! This is totally impossible, it means I'll have to afford you security, and escorts until the fooking trucks cross the god dom border, something I'm not prepared to agree to. It'll be far too dangerous to offer such security to your trucks." Admiral Proushinsky snapped at the Iranian.

"Then I fear we no longer have a deal between our countries, Admiral. You can do what you wish with the warheads and missiles you stored on the carriers." With this said, the Iranian Agent snapped the locks closed on his attaché case, and made an effort to stand before the Russian.

Admiral Proushinsky's hand reached out and he roughly grabbed the Persian's wrist, and he pulled him back to his seat as he snapped. "Comrade Colonel Marzuk! You have placed me in a very compromising position. What do you suggest I do with the fooking missiles I just ordered pulled from my god dom submarine for your fooking country? I cannot reinstall them, it'll cause too much of a commotion, and someone will surely report the change to Command, and it'll cost me my life, fool. If you don't take the fooking missiles, I'll kill you and report to my Commander I was carrying out a subterfuge against your country to draw a black marketer to surface. This report will force my government to report your government to the Security Council, and then severe sanctions will be instantly leveled against your government, and I'll be a hero."

"Admiral Proushinsky, I care not one grain of worthless sand what you do with your god cursed missiles. If I had my way, every nuclear warhead on the face of the earth would be destroyed. As for your threat against my country and my person Admiral, you're free to do whatever gives you pleasure with them. One thing Admiral Proushinsky, what you threatened me, is already set in place with one change in the equation, sir. We have placed people to make it known you offered to sell me nuclear tipped missiles. It's I who went on with the deal to expose your plot to the rest of the world. Either way, you'll end up dead, Admiral Proushinsky. So I suggest you afford me the security I'll need to get the missiles safely into my country, or the deal and your life will be over." Colonel Marzuk pulled his hand free of the Russian Admiral's grasp, and then he put his attaché case on his lap and attempted to stand for a second time.

Again, the Russian Admiral reached out and held the Persian's hand, this time he did not pull him back to his seat as he replied. "Comrade Colonel Marzuk, take your seat. I'm certain we'll be able to work something out that'll satisfy the both of us. We went too far to pull out of this deal now. Comrade Colonel Marzuk, let us continue to speak, we can work this out I'm certain."

The Iranian Colonel Marzuk allowed himself to be pulled back to his chair by the Admiral again. Once seated he placed his briefcase back down on the table, and he permitted a weak smile to cross his lips, while crossing his hands and rested them on the table and he asked. "What do you plan to work out with me, Admiral Proushinsky?"

Admiral Proushinsky did not reply, and the silence caused the Iranian to offer. "Comrade Admiral, think of my position. If I give you money before my trucks reach Iran safely, it'd be easy for anyone to have them ambushed, and the missiles removed and I'd be out everything, even my foolish life. It's not to say I don't understand your position. I agree you should have something in possession to say, err...seal the deal between us, a good faith agreement. Comrade Admiral, I'll do this, I'll give you half the agreed monies to settle the understanding. Here are ten million American dollars. You have two million paid in advance to begin this transaction. I'll give you twelve million American dollars when my trucks cross the Iranian border." Colonel Marzuk sneered as he slid the briefcase with the cash slowly across the table to the Admiral, who shook his head while he took the case and quickly left for his office to count the money.

Once in his office, Admiral Yevgeny Proushinsky dumped out the stacks of hundred dollar bills in packs of fifty thousand dollars each, and quickly counted them as his smile grew. He had already established his escape route out of Russia by means of friends in Poland. He planned to live the rest of his life in South America, changing his residence once every year to keep the KGB searchers off his trail so he could live in peace.

ON THE BORDER BETWEEN IRAN AND AZERBAIJAN

The twelve massive tanker trailer trucks waited at an idle at the border for their turn to enter the Russian controlled nation of Azerbaijan. The Iranian markings were proudly displayed on each side of the large vehicles. The machines idled, and constantly spewed a cloud of heavy black exhaust. The drivers revved the engines in an effort to irritate the Russian guards, hopefully making them move their trucks along with the minimum of inspection and friction.

The driver of the lead machine thought how easy they successfully traveled through the vast Dashte Kavir Desert, losing only one rig that he ordered to be towed to the first town outside the desert. There the driver, a Commander in the Iranian Guard, and carried the necessary papers and ID to enlist the aid of any Iranian villager. When the convoy came out of the desert, they stopped at the Iranian city of Qum, where he removed a horse rig from a flat bed truck, and then ordered it hooked up it to his trailer, and again traveled the sand packed road for the Iranian, Russian border. The Commander smiled as he thought of the owner's face when he woke, only to find his rig missing, and his name painted on the trailer rig left behind.

The thing angering him the most was, this rig had no air conditioning. Now, the Commander found himself being boiled alive inside the confines of this stolen rig, waiting for his turn to be inspected by slow moving Russian border guards. Again, he revved the powerful engine, raising another thick cloud of eye burning black smoke. This time the move caught the attention of one of the guards who turned and then glared down the long line of vehicles.

Iranian Captain Malika Nabeel Elmasry closed his eyes and rubbed them with the palms of his hands as he took a swig of warm, almost hot water. He grunted at remembering how much time they made once the rigs reached the paved road leading to the border. At the early hour they traveled, there was very little if any civilian traffic in their way. Captain Elmasry was to be in control of the loading of the missiles inside the five nuclear powered submarines. Once the missiles were installed, he was to be in control of construction of the missiles, once they received the technology to construct their own missiles from the loathsome Russians. The responsibility to make the weapon's high grade Plutonium was someone else's problem to solve.

A car was allowed through the border gate, and the other vehicles moved up. The Captain revved his rig and moved forward, followed by the eleven other machines. Captain Elmasry was sure the American satellites had successfully picked up his convoy. He was banking on the Americans placing little if any value on his rigs traveling the desert for Russia. It was known Russia was in such a state, the country was unable to produce its own fuel oil needed to heat homes, yet keep their vehicles on the road. He cursed the

Great Satan that controlled so much of the earth. The United States' control was going to be hampered once Iran had the power to deliver nuclear warheads to the very shores of the United States.

Once Iran could produce her own nuclear weapons and missiles, she would no longer need help from any other nation of the world. He cursed the Chinese for not coming through with the deal to sell them missiles that could carry warheads, and launch from their submarines. Never in Captain Elmasry's wildest dreams did he ever figure on dealing with Russians for these weapons of mass destruction. He looked towards the Heavens as if trying to see the United States satellites he was certain were reporting his position to the American military authorities in that country. The line of vehicles moved forward again and he followed them.

NORASATCOMOB, NORTH AMERICAN SATELLITE COMMAND AND OBSERVATION HEADQUARTERS AT NORASAT COMMAND CENTER IN MARYLAND. NOVEMBER 2nd, 1998. 2010 HOURS EST

The Iranian Military Officer did not know how right he was, one satellite was constantly tracking their progress through the desert. In the heart of American Command of NORASAT, Keyhole 113 lit up and transmitted a low level information report, complete with pictures to the console. The extremely bored Airman Sergeant manning the screen, dropped his feet from the table and sat up as the report came in. As he read it, the Sergeant called out. "Hey Williams, I have a Level Three Alert coming in from Bird 113 covering Iran, sir."

Lieutenant Williams, who was enjoying reading the latest Playboy magazine instantly leaped up over hearing his name being called out, dropping the magazine on his desk and he rushed over to the concerned Sergeant. As he rested his hand on his back and read the report.

"Hmmmm... twelve fuel trucks heading for Russiaville. Wonder what those sneaky bastards are up to with the damn things. Any time those ragheads move their shit around, they give me a fucking hardon. Betta sends a low level warning to CIA HQ, I'm sure them fucks are interested in anything happening in sand land. Betta mark it a Level Four, I don't want them getting any gray hair over these tankers heading for Russia. Sure wish I knew what these sand fleas were up to.".

"Got'ya Lieutenant, transferring the report over to CIA HQ now, sir. This should wake some ass up over there and give them something to do besides slugging down some damn coffee and eating donuts all the time, Lieutenant." The Sergeant's hands moved over the keyboard with lightening speed as the report was instantly shifted over to CIA HQ.

CIA HEADQUARTERS, LANGLEY WEST VIRGINIA
TWENTY THIRTEEN HOURS EST

The officers reporting for work, were responsible for running the graveyard shift. They were speaking to one another when the low level report from NORASAT came in, and the teletype screamed to life. The agent leaned over the console and saw the yellow edge on the page and remarked. "Relax Paul, it's only an information gripe. Shit, it's Iran; it looks like the goat ropers are moving a number of trucks around. Damn, they're heading for Russia. Interesting. Better let the Chief know about the report STAT. I'm sure the

Director would be concerned about anything happening in and around Iran, what with the riots since the command structure change."

"Billy, you don't want me to move the damn report up to a grade Three Level, do ya sir?"

"Naw, you better leave it down at a Level Four Alert for the time being. I don't want to go through an alert, I got plans with a hot one tomorrow, and I don't intend to be stuck in this damn office just because some lousy Arabs are screwing up agai..."

"But they're Iranian trucks we're tracking." Paul corrected as he gave the other worker a look.

"Who gives a shit. Arabs, Iranians, Persians, they're all the same fucking A-rabs to me, and I don't want to be stuck here sucking up to these boring ass machines. When I could be fucking the shit out of Lucy Wilson."

"Whoa boy! You got a fucking date with Lusty Lucy? You lucky little bastard you! The last guy who got in her pants, ended up in the hospital for a week while suffering from severe lack of strength, man. I was told she sucked his energy right out of the end of his dick on the poor fella. Damn, how the hell didja ever land a date with her." Paul moaned.

"You got that right, I heard all the damn stories about her. I'm sure going to enjoy lying in the hospital bed, proving all the scuttlebutt about her right, my friend. You better keep the report down to a Level Four, or I'll kill ya if you fuck up my date with that bitch, buddy."

"Okay Billy, it's marked down at a Level Four Info Alert. When you leaving, Lieutenant?"

"As soon as my shift ends I'm gone. Lusty Lucy got the day off tomorrow, and I'm taking full advantage of it and her. I've been eating oysters, and taking a mess of iron pills all week long."

"Fuck you, I hope your damn dick falls off on ya." Paul griped with a smirk as he shifted the report over to the CIA Director's main feed. CIA Director John Raincloud was expected in house at Twenty Hours, his usual arrival time for the evening work.

CIA Director John Raincloud arrived at his office at eight p.m. sharp. The full blooded Sioux Native American entered his office carrying coffee and his briefcase for a late night at the office. His eyes instantly picked up the light, and knew he just received a report from a satellite station. He dropped his briefcase by the desk and placed his cup down, and then went over to the lock box. He smiled as he let out his breath when he saw the yellow edge, and knew it was a low level report. He read it and was unhappy as he pressed the button on his intercom, and bitched. "Brenda, you better patch me through to General White, I have to speak to him please."

"Good evening Director Raincloud, I'll get the General on the line for you right away sir."

Seconds later, the growling voice of General John White was on the receiver. "Yeah Director Raincloud, you working late tonight I see huh? Whatdaya have for me John?" General White was a large, sixty year old black man and the second black Chairman of the Joint Chiefs of Staff.

"Good evening John, I just received a low level gripe on Iran."

"Arrr... crap, you betta get over here with the damn thing. I don't want anything happening over there, without my knowing about it first. Should I call for a meeting with the Boss?"

"Naw, you better read the report first and then decide. I don't think it amounts to very much. I read the communiqué ordering us to keep our balls to the wall on anything happening in the Middle East. Especially in Iran." Director Raincloud mumbled as he took a sip of his coffee.

"How soon can you be over to my office?" General White asked as he yawned.

"Forty minutes at the least, if the traffic's with me, General." Director Raincloud replied.

"I'll be waiting for you, coffee's hot and plenty of it John."

CHAIRMAN OF THE CHIEF OF STAFF'S PRIVATE OFFICE, THE PENTAGON, TWENTY, ZERO TWENTY TWO HOURS EST

Director Raincloud entered General White's office in a huff with the report in hand and an empty cup, and he plopped down in the chair as his secretary took the Director's cup and she automatically filled it for him. As strong minded as Mary was, she did not mind when one of them needed coffee. When Director Raincloud had his coffee, Mary left so the two men could speak in private. She would hold all calls until they were finished. The only time she would interrupt them, was if the President was on the phone, or an emergency cropped up.

Director Raincloud threw the report on the General's desk, and John scooped it up and he quickly read over it. When he was done, he leaned forward and clasped his hands together and asked the Director with concern in his voice. "Whaddaya think? Are the Iranians and Russians up to no good here or what? In the interest of time, give me the short version will ya John."

"Bet the bank on it. These ass wipes are always trying something that'll definitely go against our best interests in the Middle East and elsewhere, General." The powerful full blooded Native American snapped, his demeanor grown worse since the unexpected death of General William Weidenbacher, the former Chairman of the Joint Chiefs. General White took over the office after his death, and lately there were many complaints lodged against Director Raincloud because of his rather abusive language and nasty phrases and attitude.

"I agree with you there Chief, and I'm gonna call for a special meeting with the Boss and his cabinet. I want to stay on top of this one before it gets outta hand on us, sir. It's tough to get the shit back in the horse once it's out, if you know what I mean Director Raincloud."

"Got ya John. I'll stay on top of this garbage for you as well."

"Can you do that for me John?" General White asked the CIA Director.

"If I can't I'll eat a bug, General." The Director replied with a smirk, making General White laugh. "When will we meet with the President and his people, General?" the Director added.

"Tomorrow afternoon if I bet right. I know he's got some other shit set up for the morning, I got word he planned to get in a little golf if possible. Sure hate to fuck up the President's game, he's a real shit when I do. I hope that pain in the ass Manning's not gonna be there, dammit."

"Arr... crap, that muthafucka's a turd that just won't flush, General. I wish the President would dump that sonofabitch, he's always fucking up every god damn meeting we have. One day he's going to wise up and shitcan the asshole." Director Raincloud griped as his drained his cup.

General White enjoyed a quick laugh as he pressed the button, and then he asked Mary to set up a meeting with the President for the next afternoon with his White House staff. He waited to find out when the meeting was a go. General

White offered Director Raincloud another coffee, just as the phone rang. "General White, who's this?"

"It's the President, that's who it is mister! What's this crap about you wanting a powwow with me tomorrow afternoon, General? You know damn well I made plans for tomorrow. Christ sake General White, I can't get a minute to myself." President Cole griped at his military officer.

"Terribly sorry for the disruption Mr. President, and yes, I'm aware of your plans for tomorrow sir. But we just received a low level communiqué concerning Alpha, Juliet, Delta Three. I was only following orders to keep you informed of anything taking place in that region." General White had to wait until the President located his call letters, and the area he was speaking about.

"Oh Christ! Please don't tell me we're going to start having some god damn trouble from the Iranians now for the love of God, General White?"

"Nothing's hot as yet Mr. President Sir, but we're tracking a convoy of twelve trailer trucks heading for Russia from Iran, sir." The General offered to his Commander in Chief.

"General White, you just messed up my god damn plans, so you better get hold of that partner in crime pal of yours, and the both of you chaps get over to the Office by three thirty tomorrow afternoon, sir. I'll have everyone set in place by the time you arrive at the White House, sir. I hate to ask this, but what's the situation with the RRF?" (Rapid Response Force)

"With all due respect Mr. President, you seem to forget, it's now being referred to as the MNRRF sir. The Multi National Rapid Response Force. They're scattered all over the nation, mostly on leave Mr. President. The Russian soldiers are in the States, and the French and English soldiers are at home in their respective nations, sir. The Japanese soldiers are heading for the States to linkup with our troops when they come back from leave, Mr. President. I can have the force organized and ready to go in action in twenty four hours time at the latest, sir."

"What about the madman you call Road Kill and his group of nuts? Where are they General?"

"Mr. President, the last word has it they're on Marathon Key enjoying their leave sir."

"John, I don't know what this crap's about, sir. But you better be ready to cancel all leaves in case we have need of these specialized soldiers of yours, sir. Christ, I really hate this shit. These little pain in the ass wars keep crippling me ever since I took over the Presidency, General White. I have no time to worry about what's troubling my country, because I'm trapped in these wars. I wish another country would step up to the plate and take some heat off me for a change."

"Mr. President Sir, I don't see that happening any time in the future, sir. Besides, I wouldn't want another country in command of my people. That's what makes our nation great."

"Yeah, yeah General White, stow the commercial and make certain you're in my office by three thirty tomorrow afternoon, sir. Since you have messed up my day tomorrow, I'll see what I can do about messing up your evening, mister. All kidding aside sir. Thanks for keeping me abreast of this current situation, sir. I hate it when I don't know about something until it comes up and bites me on the damn ass. I'll see you and your friend at three thirty General."

President Cole placed a call to his staff advisor, and ordered him to get in touch with the other members of his cabinet, and he ordered the aide to have them all to report to the Oval Office before three thirty tomorrow afternoon.

THREE THIRTY P.M. EST. THE OVAL OFFICE, THE WHITE HOUSE, WASHINGTON D.C.

The President of the United States was seated, along with Secretary of State, Maria Hernandez, National Security Director, Norman Griffin, Secretary of Defense, Jerry Levenhagen, the civilian advisor, Raymond Manning, and Deputy Secretary of Defense, Harold Clifton. President Cole waited for the Vice President, Mary Hirshfield to arrive for the special meeting. He was hoping she would be there before both General White and Director Raincloud arrived for the meeting, so he could brief her about the events unfolding in Iran. He was wrong because the two powerful men came strolling into the Oval Office and Mary was still out of place.

General White appeared with Director Raincloud in tow minutes before the Vice President arrived at the Oval Office. The President gave out with a deep sigh as he waited for Mary to be seated almost right behind the two men and then he bitched. "Christ sake Mary, I was hoping you'd beat General White here, so I could've brought you up to speed on the situation currently facing us. I'm afraid you have to pay attention and what you don't know, work out for yourself. I'll allow you to ask questions, so long as they don't get out of hand and delay this meeting on us." The President nodded politely towards his Vice President and she returned it.

The President then turned to General White and gave him the slight nod and offered. "General, you're the man who pushed the panic button for this damn meeting; so it's up to you to straighten out the machinery for the rest of us here, sir."

General White stood sharply; and then he removed a file folder from his briefcase and laid it on the desk as he began. "With all due respect Mr. President, Vice President Hirshfield, Secretary Hernandez. Gentlemen. I requested this meeting because something was picked up in Iran."

ON THE BORDERS OF IRAN AND AZERBAIJAN

Iranian Captain Elmasry's lead rig finally reached the KGB Border Guard who glared angrily at him because of his constant revving of the engine of the machine. Even though Azerbaijan was no longer under the direct control of Russia, KGB guards maintained border security, policing and military elements of that nation. It was a way for Moscow to allow Azerbaijan believe they were no longer under the suppressive Russian yoke. Russian President Vitaly Kvantrishuili was heard saying on occasions. 'What is freedom but an illusion that makes one feel he's free? Try and exercise that freedom and I'll snap your fooking neck and end the illusion quickly'.

The fuming KGB Sergeant actually jumped on the running board of the truck, and then he stuck his face right in the Iranian's face and barked savagely at him. "Filthy desert dog, rev your god dom fooking engine again and I'll have you shot as the lowly dog you are."

The smug Iranian Captain just smiled back at the guard with rotted teeth as he said. "Russian General, forgive me, but we're but a poor nation, and don't have the mechanics needed to keep our engines running properly. I'm sorry if I caused you displeasure, but I fear you would be more displeased if one of our engines stalled and it did not start again. You would have to supply guards, or the thieves in the night would steal our fuel oil. Fuel oil your government needs to keep its mighty military equipment running to defend Russia against the great Satan..."

"Silence that miserable hole of yours before I put my foot in it, dog. Russia no longer possesses a powerful military, it has been sold to the highest bidder lately. If you're having trouble with your fooking machines, pull through the gate and park by the side of the building while I check your papers out." The angry border guard snapped at the driver of the truck.

"Alhamdulilah. Will this take long my young Russian brother?" the Iranian Captain asked.

"Yes it'll take all the time I deem fit, why? Do you have a date with one of the filthy bitches that sell themselves to the lowlife animals who cover themselves with camel piss of your foul country, fool?" the Russian laughed as he jumped down from the running board.

"Yes my brother, you see Russian General, your country is not the only one who has people selling their prized assets to the highest bidder." The Iranian driver sneered at the KGB guard.

The Russian guard's anger rose as he aimed his weapon right at the driver's face, fuming over the way the Iranian just spoke to him. The Iranian Officer stared back at the guard, as if daring him to shoot him. The Russian had all he could do to stop from pulling the trigger, and ending this savage's life, and dumping his body back in his own country for the jackals to feast upon.

The Iranian spoke through his sneer. "Go ahead Russian General and shoot me. Then it'll be you who'll have to answer to Admiral Proushinsky, as to why you have done so."

A cold sweat instantly broke out on the guard's face as he moaned aloud. "Is that Admiral Yevgeny Proushinsky,

Commander of the Black Sea Fleet, you filthy dog of the desert?"

"Yes General, he's the one expecting my trucks at his docks so he can fuel his mighty Navy. I believe it's to be used in his ships. Submarines I was told before I headed for your country."

"You svinaya idiyot. (fucking idiot) Why did you not inform me your fuel was for Admiral Proushinsky's Navy. It would've saved you time and me from allowing my blood pressure to climb, fool. Let me check your papers, and then you can get on your way, lowly Iranian dog."

"Alas, I'm sorry great Russian General. I pray to Allah you did not give me a chance to explain who my fuel was to be delivered to." The Iranian was actually taunting the guard with his reply as he continued to sneer, knowing he had the Russian guard pissing his pants over his orders.

"I'm no god dom Russian General, you great desert fool you. I still have to work for the little money my government pays me, if it pays me at all lately Iranian dog." The guard had no idea the Iranian Captain desperately was trying to insult him by calling him 'General'. The driver knew the guard was a mere Sergeant, and a Sergeant in the Russian military was nothing more than a low paid worker, who had his neck stuck in a noose constantly. Because he was responsible for everything that went wrong in his Unit for his officers.

The Iranian Agent shoved his crumpled up papers at the Russian Sergeant. They were written in Iranian and the Sergeant was not going to admit he could not read the Persian scribble. After looking at each page not understanding one word printing on them, he handed the papers back to the grinning Persian driver and then he hissed savagely at the driver. "I'll check your load before I allow you to precede any further into Russia, fool."

Now it was the Iranian driver time to start sweating as he moved the truck where he was ordered to move it to. Once his machine was parked, the Russian guard ordered the driver nastily. "Open the god dom scuttles one, three and five for inspection."

The Iranian driver got out of the truck and then complained at the Russian soldier. "Sergeant, you're causing me to lose much driving time fishing in my fuel oil. What do you think I carry in of my cursed trucks and cargo? Remember Russian Gen... err... Border Guard. I have a Russian Admiral waiting for my fuel to arrive for his ships. I'm certain the Admiral would not think very kindly of you wasting my valuable time with this very foolish inspection of my cargo."

The guard did not reply, instead he unshouldered his AK-47 Kalashnikov Assault Rifle, and then he again aimed it at the Iranian's face. Then he trained the weapon at the side of his tanker and warned the Iranian in no uncertain terms. "Worthless camel eater, open those fooking scuttles as I ordered. Or I'll just shoot enough holes in your rig to dump the contents on the ground and then inspect it. It's you who's wasting my time, and I'll place a quick stop to it."

"Very well Russian General, if you insist on this time wasting search of my vehicle and contents, please enjoy yourself." The Iranian bowed slightly at the angry Sergeant, and then he climbed on top of his rig and opened the three requested scuttle hatches. The strong pungent odor of stale fuel oil instantly assaulted his nostrils. The Russian Guard leaned his head over the first scuttle and was forced to hold his breath as his eyes began to water from the burning fumes. He went over to the second scuttle and peered into the bowels of the tank.

Nothing but fuel oil so the guard moved to the last scuttle and looked for a small stone on the ground. He saw a pebble and ordered the Iranian driver to pitch the stone up to him. He held it over the scuttle and then peered in it. He dropped the rock, it splashed in the thick liquid and instantly disappeared. He had no way of knowing the oil was only eight inches deep, and the thick liquid stopped the rock from sounding its report as it struck the inner shell of the water tight compartment it encircled. The guard then jumped down from the truck's compartment as if it burned him, and he ordered the driver to close and secure the three scuttles. Then he waved him on and turned his back on the Iranian Officer as he past him.

"Great and fearless Russian ally, does this mean all my trucks are free to follow me to your great country? Or will I be forced to waste even more of my time waiting for you to inspect each of my trailers?" the Iranian tried a smile on the Sergeant, but it was wasted on the soldier.

The guard hissed back at the smug acting Iranian without turning to him and he barked at the driver. "Svinaya sabaka! (Fucking dog!) Neither I, nor my country are fooking allies of your worthless country. If I had my way about it, I'd eliminate all Arab speaking fools from the face of the earth, dog. You're nothing more than a nation of lowly thieves and liars."

The Iranian Captain instantly glared while wishing he had the power to attack the nasty Russian soldier for what he just said to him about his country and people.

The Russian guard easily picked up the anger from the Iranian and he tightened his grip on his weapon as he warned the driver in an angry tone of voice. "You dare much to speak to me in that god dom manner fool, you better move your fooking trucks before I order you to transfer your god dom fuel over to good Russian made trucks which run properly all the time, and they don't emit such a black cloud of exhaust, and we take your fuel with no pay for your god dom cargo, and we drive you back into your worthless god dom country."

The fuming Iranian lead driver climbed back in his rig and then he revved the powerful engine three times, raising another thick bellowing cloud of eye burning black exhaust for spite. The other Iranian trucks followed their Commander's lead and they all started revving their engines, and the trailing vehicles then pulled up behind the lead truck. In seconds, the long Iranian convoy of tractor trailer tanker trucks were traveling at sixty five miles per hour. But the trucks had not traveled very far into the nation of Azerbaijan before pulling off the road and onto a dirt side road, and the twelve rigs parked in a thicket of trees. There, the exhausted Iranian drivers were met by a number of other Russia soldiers who immediately set to work changing the Iranian marking on the twelve large trucks over to those of the Russian Navy marking, while the exhausted and hungry drivers quickly changed into clean Russian Naval uniforms. Each driver spoke fluent Russian and they knew how to act like the always angry Russian soldiers.

Once this exchange was accomplished, the once Iranian marked trailer trucks pulled back onto the main road and they again headed directly for the Russian port city at Sevastopol in the Ukraine. Because of the Russian Naval markings now painted on the sides of the tanker rigs, the machines would not again be inspected by the closely controlled border between Ukraine and Russia. It was the only way for the rebel Russian soldiers working with the Iranian drivers to ensure the rigs would pass the inspection at the Ukraine and Russian checkpoint without much if any trouble by the border guards on station there. The trucks increased speed up to seventy five mph. No one in Russia would dare stop a Russian marked truck, no matter what speed it traveled on the road.

CHAPTER TWO

SEVASTOPOL UKRAINE, THE HOME PORT OF THE BLACK SEA FLEET

Russian Admiral Yevgeny Proushinsky took great pleasure over counting the massive amount of money the Persian Agent gave him. He was overjoyed burying his hands in the mountain of cash. Once he was finished playing with it, he placed the cash back in the attaché and then stored it in his safe. The Admiral then emerged from his private living quarters, and he immediately started to look for Colonel Marzuk. The Iranian Officer made him wealthier than he had ever dared hope for in his entire life. He picked up the ugly

Persian staring down the road leading onto his major naval base. The Admiral headed for him, but not before ordering one of his men to head for the mess, and retrieve two glasses of Russian Vodka for him. He laughed as he remembered the terrible face made by the Iranian when he first downed the harsh liquor.

Then he grunted over the foolish people who did not enjoy a glass of good Russian Vodka. It proved to him that all Persian fools would never become civilized people. He walked up to the Iranian Colonel at the same time as his assistant arrived with the drinks.

"Ahhh... Comrade Colonel Marzuk, all is in order as you have offered, my friend. I thought you might care to join me in a special salute to our great success, Comrade Colonel Marzuk." Admiral Proushinsky handed the Iranian the glass of Vodka, and then he held his glass high. He smiled over the horrible expression made by the Iranian as he tipped the glass back towards the Russian Admiral in his own salute.

"Das fidaniya my Iranian friend!" Admiral Proushinsky bellowed while downing his drink in one gulp. The Iranian did not reply as he looked for a place to spit out the vile tasting liquid.

A young Russian soldier walked up to the powerful Admiral, and then he waited to be acknowledged by the Naval Officer. Admiral Proushinsky noticed him and allowed him to whisper his report. "Da! Kaneshna Da." (Yes! Of course yes) The Admiral then turned back to the Iranian and remarked. "Comrade Colonel Marzuk, it seems your Captain has created a slight problem with the Border Guards while crossing the border. That was not a very wise thing for him to create, it could have cost the great fool his worthless life, and also led to the discovery of our plan. I hope the fool behaves himself for the rest of the fooking trip."

"I'll speak to my fool and I assure you he'll behave once I have communicated with him, and point out his errors to him. You'll excuse me for a moment. Admiral, how far are my trucks reported to be?" Colonel Marzuk asked as he fingered the transmit button of the hand radio.

"Your trucks are five hours from my base and making good time, Comrade Marzuk."

"Good, excuse then Comrade Admiral. Marzuk to Elmasry, come in."

THE LEAD IRANIAN RIG

Captain Elmasry was enjoying a quick nap in the passenger seat of the speeding rig when the radio woke him. The Captain took the radio while letting out his breath in a hiss, angry his sleep was being interrupted by his Commander as he replied to the Colonel's call. "Yes Marzuk, Elmasry! What is it you want of me; I was trying to catch up on some of my rest."

"Elmasry! You better take better care when addressing me, fool. This is why I wish to speak with you. It was reported to me you gave a border guard some problems. I order you to stop these most troubling and foolish actions, or you'll suffer my wrath coming down on your worthless head. Our mission must be successful if Iran is to become a nuclear power, and curb the Great Satan. If you do anything else to halt this dream, I'll blot out your life, but not before you witness the death of your wife and children. Do you understand what I'm warning you of, fool?"

Captain Elmasry had to bite back his rage before he responded to his Commanding Officer. "Forgive my poor lapse of judgment, it shall not happen again I assure you sir."

The Iranian Captain squeezed the mike with enough force to make the plastic creak in his hand.

"That's much better fool. You're reported five hours from your destination. Is this not true?"

"Yes, I'll be standing by your side in the time limit you have just stated sir."

"I'll be waiting at your destination for you to arrive, safely fool!" Colonel Marzuk growled angrily, hearing the underlying tone of sarcasm dripping in the Captain's voice.

"I'll arrive by your side safely Colonel." With this, the Captain broke off the connection.

THE OVAL OFFICE,
THE WHITE HOUSE, WASHINGTON D.C.,
NOVEMBER 3rd, 1998, 4:30 P.M.

The meeting lasted much longer than was expected, mainly because Director Raincloud was known to be rather long winded. When he finished his report, no one was alarmed over his information. As the CIA Director wrapped up his report, a call came for him in the Oval Office. After hearing the information, he reported to the President and others attending the meeting. "President Cole, I just received word the Iranian trucks had entered Russia, sir."

The President shot to his feet and began to pace behind his desk after sending the pencil he was twirling between his fingers, flying across the room. No one spoke again as the President walked off his sudden anger. Stopping, he rested his hands on the back of his chair and stared at Director Raincloud before commenting. "Director Raincloud, no, correct that please, General White. You're the one who'll watch this shit from here on out sir. I'm authorizing the use of an operative in Iran. You'll work out all the particulars with the Director. I'm not interested in that end of your mission General. If there's any teeth in this possible threat, I want to know about it before it comes at me. I'll leave the details up to you on how you get your operative in Iran and activated. I'll expect a full report in forty eight hours, thank you gentlemen, and ladies." With this said, the President loudly clapped his hands and shoved himself away from his chair.

"Mr. President, a moment of your time please sir." General White moaned exhaustibly.

The President spun around and barked at the military officer. "Yes, General what is it now? I knew you'd have something else to add, bound to stop me from sleeping tonight, huh General?"

"With all due respect Mr. President Sir, should I call in all leaves and start organizing the Rapid Response teams, sir?" The General asked his Commander in Chief.

"Oh boy here we go. The moment anything is happening the troops are always called for." Manning grumbled as he stood and he stared at General White.

"Don't screw with me, you little turd! Or I'll chew you up and spit you out in the shitter." General White snarled as he turned to the civilian advisor. Allowing his hatred of this man to surface. He balled up his fists and hunched his shoulders, preparing to attack the civilian.

The President crossed the distance between him and his desk in three strides, and snapped. "Gentlemen, I warn you I'll no longer put up with these childish outbursts. General, I order you to stand down. Mr. Manning, take your seat. The question was directed at me and didn't require a response from you, Mr. Manning. General White! I don't want you pushing any panic buttons quite yet sir. We'll play this one close to the vest. I don't want any news reporters picking up we're worried about any crap happening in Iran. Allow the soldiers enjoy themselves, if we need them, they'll be organized in twenty four hours. Nothing too severe could happen in that short a time. I authorized the use of the operative in Iran, and that's the way it'll stand until something comes to the surface. How long for you to get your command in place, General White?"

"Mr. President, my team's always in place and good to go sir. I could go hot in ten minutes, calling up air wings, getting the Navy moving, and ground troops humping for an invasion…"

"Did I miss something here? I didn't know we're planning to invade Iran for any reason, Mr. President?" Manning moaned as he stood up and looked at the President.

"One day I'm going to rip your head off and shit down your damn throat, Manning!" General White savagely snapped the civilian's name out as if it were a four letter word, as he pointed his finger at Manning's chest so threateningly it made the civilian take a step back.

"General White! You'll keep a civil tongue in that filthy mouth of yours, or I'll have you thrown out of my god damn office, mister. In case you have not realized it, I have women present, and they don't need to listen to this battlefield smut. Sit down Mr. Manning, General. I have no intention of calling out our forces unless there's a world threatening incident. Calm down! All I want you to do is bring your people up to speed, and make certain anyone you need is at your finger tips General White. Just in case they're needed."

"Understood Mr. President." General White nodded to the American Leader.

"You have orders, I suggest you carry them out, General. That's it for now, I expect a detailed report from your office within the week. Now, I have a second meeting to attend, thank you. Have a safe trip home." The President did not wait for anyone to speak as he rushed out.

General White nodded to Ms. Hernandez, and he bowed politely to the Vice President always friendly to his cause. As he picked up his briefcase, and rushed out of the office with Director Raincloud on his heels. The two shared a car to General White's Pentagon office. During the trip back, they dumped on Manning and complained about why the President put up with the civilian appointee. As they entered General White's office, John snapped at Mary. "Coffee!"

"It's hot and waiting in the office sir. I'll hold all calls unless an emergency arises, General." She announced to the back of General White, knowing he had not heard a word she said.

General White threw his briefcase at the extra chair, and paid no attention as it tumbled and landed on the carpet. Director Raincloud plopped down in a chair and waited as General White poured coffee for them. General White dropped in his chair with all the grace of a sack of potatoes dumped off the end of a truck. He then sipped his coffee and announced. "Ahhh... that's good. That damn Manning gets my ass going every time dammit. No matter how hard I try and control myself, the little bastard always gets under my skin. Even his smile burns my ass."

"I hear that John, he's a pain in the ass. How do you want to work this out between us General?" Raincloud replied as he stared into the concerned eyes of the military officer.

General White sat forward in his chair and offered with a snap in his voice. "Director Raincloud, get your operative moving in Iran, sir. Even though this alert warning was sent out as a low level warning. I'm reacting as if these damn Iranian shits are up to no good in Russia. Better send a memo back to NORASATCOM, and have them man the satellite for the next few weeks. I don't know why, but I'm getting a real bad read on this one John."

"No problem with NORASATCOM. I sent a keep watch order out already General. But I'm a bit confused about your order." Director Raincloud offered as he sipped his coffee.

"Zat so, how come Chief? I never seen you so confused."

"I don't understand why you want to activate an operative in Iran. The trucks are heading for Russia. I figure you would've wanted to activate one in Russia." Director Raincloud shrugged.

"Normally I'd go after Russia, but I believe the damn Iranians are picking up, not delivering if there's anything to this trip. Director Raincloud, what could the Iranians have Russia wants?"

"Fuel, General?"Director Raincloud offered seriously.

"In a pig's fucking ear fuel! If the damn Russians needed fuel so desperately they had to have the crap shipped to them in a number of Iranian rigs. They would've picked a fight with Iran, and then just went and invaded the damn country and take what they wanted or needed. As strong as Iran's grown militarily lately, and how weak Russia has become. Iran doesn't have the capability to stop the Russians if they decided to attack them in force. You know the damn Russians suffer from a lack of tact whenever they want something from someone."

"I see the reason for your madness, General. Lemme see, yes, I'll activate a sleeper, which area of Iran do you want to have him concentrate his efforts on? Iran's vast, with little in the way of civilization in most desert areas." Both men's eyes went to the wall map. General White hit a button and the region covering Iran lit up. "That's a good question. Let's pick the likely place the trucks will head once they reenter Iran. Did the report state the start off point of these rigs?"

"Yes General, the report stated the rigs left from the port of Bander Beheshi…"

"Bander Beheshi! Bander Beheshi! Why does that name ring a bell with me, dammit?"

"Simple General, it's believed the new Iranian government had the six nuclear submarines they brought from Russia sail to Bander Beheshi from Bandar-e-Abbas, until the latest revolution ran its course. At one point, we even considered attacking the complex at Bandar-e-Abbas and sinking the damn submarines before they became a serious threat to our security in the Middle East sir. That was before the damn Russian rebels moved missiles into what was left of North Korea. Personally, I think we…" The same thought hit both men at the same instant.

"Submarines!" General White snapped as he rushed to his desk.

"Right. Of course, that's the missing piece of the damn puzzle General White." Director Raincloud offered excitedly to the Chairman of the Joint Chiefs of Staff.

"What's with the six submarines, I thought the Iranians only had five submarines? Shit! What's keeping the damn Iranians from becoming a world threat? Missiles, nuclear missiles for their damn submarines. Can you imagine the problems Iran could cause to the oil lanes if they ever get their hands on Russian sub launch SS-N-20 or 23 missiles? The bastards will run our asses ragged detecting them while trying to figure out which of the six are loaded with missiles."

"That's what we figure, six submarines in all General White." The Director replied.

"Six, dammit! Trying to figure out which of the six fucking submarines has missiles stored inside it." General White moaned as he let out his breath in a rush.

"You're taking a helluva large leap in fate with very little information to go on, General White Sir. We don't even know for certain if the god damn Iranians are going after any Russian nuclear tipped submarine launch missiles, sir. What we're following here might be nothing more than just a simple sale of some damn fuel oil. We don't even know where the damn rigs are going in Russia at this point, General. They might be heading for the capital well away from any possible military installation in Russia, General." Director Raincloud offered, he watched in silence as the General started tearing up his desk while looking for something he was after.

"What the hell are you looking for John?" The Director asked with a smirk.

"Say Raincloud, I remember reading a report a few months ago about how it was believed the damn Russians were moving their missiles around to try and avoid detection and sabotage. What the hell did I do with that damn report anyhow for crap sake? Don't just sit there looking dumb, help me look through this mess for the damn report, will ya huh."

"General, I can make this much easier on you if you give me access to your computer, sir. I can access my computer and then simply pull up the report you're looking for a lot easier than you can find it in this mess you call your office, sir."

"For Christ sake man, what the hell are you waiting for? Do it John." General White ordered.

SEVASTOPOL, UKRAINE, THE HOME PORT OF THE POWERFUL RUSSIAN BLACK SEA FLEET

When the Iranian Colonel Muhsin Abu Marzuk finished speaking with his driver, he reported to the Russian officer.

"Admiral Proushinsky, my driver's terribly embarrassed by his childish outburst at the border crossing, and he has assured me it'll never happen again sir. He has also informed me they should arrive within four hours. Maybe you should get your people moving? Have you given any consideration as to affording my vehicles safe escort to the Iranian, Russian border as I have requested of you, Admiral?"Colonel Marzuk refrained informing Admiral Proushinsky that he had a full battalion of military vehicles and soldiers waiting just over the border to safely escort the rigs to the installation they were earmarked to travel to.

The specially constructed building stationed at the Iranian Naval Base Bander Beheshi, was designed for the transfer of the missiles into the submarines Iran just bought from Russia. The nuclear powered submarines were undergoing a complete overhaul while waiting for the Russian missiles to arrive at the Naval Base. The building spanned much of the port that would enable the submarines to actually be moved inside the structure one at a time to receive the missiles. The covering would protect the transfer of the missiles from satellite observation.

Admiral Proushinsky grunted at the soldier, and he ran inside the tent covering the missiles resting on tracks. The Admiral turned to the Iranian and remarked. "Yes Comrade Colonel Marzuk, I gave consideration to escorting your rigs safely to the border. I'll release six BMW armor vehicles for your escort. I'll log it as guard duty, reporting we uncovered information concerning a threat against the leaking missiles. My armor will stay with your rigs until they reach the border in Azerbaijan. No one will question my orders, and since the vehicles will not be crossing into Iran, no report should be filed about their presence with your tanker rigs. I have my people standing by in Azerbaijan to remove the Russian markings from the trucks, and replacing them with the markings of your country. I hope this is most satisfactory to you sir?"

Colonel Marzuk replied. "Comrade Proushinsky, this escort will be most satisfactory to my needs, I thank you for this consideration. Err... there's one more request that must be answered before I leave your country. Have you given thought about making the construction of your missiles and warheads available to my country?" Marzuk wrung his hands waiting his reply.

"Da I certainly did consider that request Comrade Colonel Marzuk! I see no problem with my handing over the blueprints of the construction of the SS-N-23 missiles to you. As long as the Amirikanskaya cash is here before you leave my country with the blueprints. I have sent word out to a number of dishearten technicians I know are very unhappy with their work here in Russia. Let's say I know these people are looking for other employment, and would be most interested in working for your government if given half a chance to. A few of these technicians are schooled in the construction of long range missiles and warheads. Others have knowledge to transform the nuclear reactors over to breeders, needed to produce weapons grade Plutonium sir.

"These breeder reactors will produce enough weapons' grade Plutonium to make six to ten warheads per year. I'll arrange for the sale of six more Delta IV Ballistic Missile Submarines, this sale will include twenty four missiles stored in each submarine under the covert sale of the boats. It'll be the last sale I'll setup with your country. Then I'll make my escape from Russia before all is discovered of the missing missiles and their warheads. This sale will be made between you and me. Each submarine will be sold at the cost of one billion Amirikanskaya dollars to your country. The transaction will be carried out in the Arabian Sea. But this will be worked out once the sale of missiles and schematics has taken place, and the monies changed hands. I trust you have access to the other twelve million dollars in cash?"

Colonel Marzuk's smile remained as the agent for Iran replied confidently. "Comrade Admiral Proushinsky, one phone call from me, and a aircraft will be overhead within twenty minutes sir. The cursed American money will be air dropped before I leave your country, if I feel everyone can be trusted that is, sir. If not, the American cash will wait for us at the border, and I'll turn it over to you when I shake your hand and take control of the said schematics for the missiles. I like to have the exchange take place at the border though if I had my way about it, Admiral."

"Ahhh... Comrade Colonel Marzuk, I see you still don't trust me in the least sir. I thought after the deal we have just closed between us, the both of us would be able to trust one another to stay to their word when given. I see I was in error to believe in the manner I was thinking, sir." The powerful Russian Admiral offered as he cautiously eyed the Iranian Agent.

"No it is not that at all I assure you Comrade Admiral Proushinsky. It's just that it'd be much simpler for me to have the money waiting there at the border for us. Anything can happen to a plane in-flight. It could be intercepted by your fighter planes, or suffer mechanical difficulties and crash. Or the pilot could have a change of allegiance and make off with the money himself. Many things can take place that is beyond my control, but that's for Allah to decide. I..."

Admiral Proushinsky held up his hand and offered with a smirk. "There's no need to explain any further, Comrade Colonel Marzuk. It's a wise man who does not trust the one he's dealing with illegally, no? I'll wait for the Amirikanskaya cash at the border, Comrade Colonel."

Colonel Marzuk bowed politely to the Russian Military Officer as they settled in to watch the seamen working on constructing the tents, and preparing the missiles for transfer into the trailer trucks when they arrived on the base. The Admiral turned to a seaman and asked. "Is there any word when the next Amirikanskaya satellite will make its pass over our fooking base?"

"Yes Admiral Proushinsky, it's scheduled to pass over our area in the next three hours, sir."

"Mudnya!" Shit! He snarled as he raised his hand to the Heavens, cursing the Amirikanskaya and their technology. "That's when the Iranian trucks are to arrive. Captain Olishchuk, you have to camouflage the missiles. The Amirikanskaya eyes will arrive at the same time as the trucks."

The Ukrainian Captain stopped what he was doing, and he turned towards the Admiral and responded. "Aye sir, I have everything set and ready for use, the fools will see nothing but the tops of our tents with their spy satellites." The Captain suddenly hawked and sent a honker flying and where it landed, it stuck onto the side of a board.

"That's all they better see Captain if you know what's good for you, or I'll have your fooking head hanging from the yardarm, and the seagulls feeding on your eyes, mista." The Admiral warned the Captain, shaking his head at the uncouth actions of the hated Ukrainian Officer.

THE PENTAGON, WASHINGTON D.C.
FIVE TWENTY P.M. EST. NOVEMBER 3rd, 1998

General john White paced in his office while Director Raincloud worked on the computer. After a few moments, he made contact with his computer and had the information he needed transferred to the general's machine. He pressed the print button and looked at the printer. General White read it as words appeared on the paper, he let out with a low whistle.

Director Raincloud whistled also as he remarked. "Now I know what they're up to General White. You better call for another meeting with the Boss, and the rest of his merry men sir."

General White ignored the Director's remark, as he read the report. He snapped his fingers as he complimented himself for remembering the memo, and filing it in his mind. "Christ sake Director Raincloud, I can't believe we had this information, and no one was on the ball to call it up. How long have we known about this trick the Russians are pulling, for crap sake?"

"We picked this information up three years back when one of our satellites happened to make a routine pass over one of the Russian Missile Bases. At that time, the bird detected a number of fuel tanker trucks; much like the ones we're trailing here, General. Sitting in the yard, and one of our operators decided to keep the bird's eye in position long enough to see what all of the hubbub was about on the base sir. The operator nearly shit his pants when he picked up the tail end of the trailer truck open up, and a ballistic missile slid in the tanker like it was made for the damn thing.

"The tail end hatch was replaced after the missile disappeared inside the truck, leaving it looking as if nothing was out of the ordinary with the damn thing, General White. The truck then pulled off the site like this was an everyday occurrence. Dammit John, you don't think the damn Iranians are picking up some twelve nuclear missiles from the Russians, do ya? How could the damn Russians dare to do it, especially after what just took place in North Korea, and the god damn war that mess could have started. Christ sake John, do you think Russian President Kvantrishuili would've called for a detailed inventory of his damn missiles and warheads after that one, and clamp down a heavy security lid on the damn things at the same time, sir. I don't think his Administration could withstand another such nuclear fiasco General."

"Director, I don't give a rat's ass about that damn Russian Administration, sir. I'm only concerned about a number of possible nuclear missiles ending up in the hands of the Iranians. We have to find out which ones they're going after, and report to the President before he finds out about this shit from someone else in his Administration, sir. Can you find out when our bird's scheduled to make its next pass over this section of Russia?" General White asked the Director.

"No problem General, I'll contact NORASATCOM." Director Raincloud placed his call to an airman who snapped in the phone before thinking who he was speaking to. "NORASAT HQ."

"Yes, this is CIA Director John Raincloud! Who am I speaking to, and what's your problem, mister?" The steaming Native American bellowed angrily in the phone.

The NORASATCOM operator instantly snapped to attention and replied. "Yes Director Raincloud, this is Lieutenant Edward Williams, sir. I have no idea what you mean by having a problem, sir. I have no problem, everything's fine over here sir."

"Then why the hell did you answer the phone in that, arr... never mind that crap for the time being. Look Lieutenant Williams, I need to know when the next bird's scheduled to pass over the section of alert in both Russia and Iran, mister."

"I'll check that information out for you immediately sir. Hold the line, it'll take a few moments to accumulate the information you have just required, Director Raincloud." The Lieutenant placed the phone aside, and he moved his hand as if he was masturbating and cocked his head as he worked the computer terminal.

Director Raincloud slid his glasses up so he could massage his eyes. It did nothing to relieve the ache pounding in his skull. The Director turned to General White as he placed his glasses on his nose. "General, one of these days you're going to piss off the big guy about that damn civilian advisor of his, and you're going to come out of his office with your crank nailed to your forehead, and then you'll be pissing out your damn ear, sir." Director Raincloud laughed.

"I know, but the scumbag gets under my skin. It's so bad lately, I even hate the looks of the sonofabitch. Something I never felt before about anyone dammit." General White griped.

"Yeah, I know what you mean. Huh, yeah Lieutenant, I'm here, what do ya have?"

"Director Raincloud, I have a bird scheduled over the area within the next two hours, sir."

"Great. Okay Lieutenant, can you transfer the feed over to my office in real time sir?"

"Simple Director Raincloud Sir. I can have the feed go directly to your private terminal, and you'll see it as it takes place, sir. I'll also send you a hard paper report with pictures and video. SOP sir." The Lieutenant smirked, he knew he was wasting the Director's time.

"I know you have to send a damn report. Don't fuck with me or you'll not like the outcome Lieutenant. I suggest you go someplace and get laid before your mouth gets you in more trouble than your dick can handle mister. If you can transmit a real time report to my office, can you transmit the same report to General White's office?" Director Raincloud growled as he tried to strangle the receiver in his hand, fuming he allowed this snotty Lieutenant to get his goat.

"No problem with that request sir. The General has a 3A-R1 clearance rating sir. Which means he's able to receive any report through HQ, sir?" The Lieutenant began to sweat, fearing he might have gone a bit too far with trying to bug the Director for snapping at him moments before.

"Fine, I want the report transferred over to General White's office also, mister. I'll be at his office when the report comes in. That's it, and I warn you again mister, you can bet the bank on it you'll be hearing from me once this crap's over with, Lieutenant."

Now the Lieutenant knew he was in trouble, and tried to smooth things over with the Director angry as he offered. "Director Raincloud, I can have the written report sent over to General White's office. I can have a pair of reports sent over to you, one to your office, the other to the General's office, if this would make it any easier on you, Director Raincloud Sir."

"Ahhh... that's much better, I see you can be a professional after all mister. That'll be fine, have one of the long versions sent over to General White's office, and the second over to my lock box. It might be a wise idea to have a duplicate on my person, I'll probably be forced to leave it with the President when we next meet mister. Thanks, make sure I get that damn report the second it becomes available to the office." Director Raincloud warned the Lieutenant.

"Yes sir, you'll get a live time report and long version as soon as the main feed ends, sir."

Director Raincloud did not reply as he hung up and complained. "These damn kids are getting too big for their pants. I remember when I shit myself when an Officer called. Now, these kids want to play mind games with ya, and they aren't afraid to challenge ya either, General."

"Never mind that crap John. When's the next flight scheduled to take place sir?"

"Within the next two hours to be in the flight window, General." Director Raincloud replied.

"Fine, we'll know for sure where these damn trucks are heading, and what they might be up to, dammit. In the meantime, I'm going to make contact with the President, and fill him in on what we're tracking here so far John. Might as well have him prepared when the shit falls, sir."

SEVASTOPOL UKRAINE, HOME PORT OF THE RUSSIAN BLACK SEA FLEET

The Russian Admiral Yevgeny Proushinsky finished off his third glass of Vodka. A mosquito whined about his head, and for the umpteenth time he swatted at it and missed it again. He watched his workers preparing the missiles when he heard a roar from the twelve large rigs as they rapidly closed in on the Naval Base. He smiled with the knowledge he was a rich man. Richer than he ever dared to believe and hope for.

Colonel Marzuk pointed down the road leading to the Russian Naval Base.

The rigs were just about to enter his base. A seaman rushed to the Admiral. "Admiral! The American satellite is about to break over the horizon and pass over our base. What shall we do?"

"Seaman, start the diesels and begin the smoke screen, pop the flares off, in case the god dom Amirikanskaya satellites try to burn through our cloud cover using their infrared systems. This is nothing new, we have done this countless times in the past, and we shall do it countless times again in the future. Get to it before the fooking rigs are parked in place, and we give the dom Amirikanskayas a show of it?" Admiral Proushinsky placed his hands on his hips.

"Yes sir." He barked, saluted the Admiral and then screamed orders at the workers. "Start the generators, launch the flares, we have the filthy Amirikanskaya eyes overhead again."

Hundreds of flares were set burning in the complex, with more launched in the air. The smoke making generators cranking over then burst to life as the motors raised clouds of thick white smoke drifting over the entire complex. The seaman moved closer to Admiral Proushinsky and offered. "Admiral, do you believe this defensive action seriously blinds the satellite, sir?"

"Da! It has to help, if it does not, what the devil do I care? I'm following orders to help confuse the god dom satellite. If it works that's great, if it doesn't, I fulfilled my obligation to Command. I doubt if this trickery is an effective cover, from what I read about the satellites and their capabilities of seeing through rain clouds, fog and heavy mist. The Amirikanskayas are capable of looking down a woman's blouse to discover if she's wearing a bra."

The twelve grime covered filthy trucks pulled onto the Naval Base as the man made fog covered them. The fog forced the Admiral to station a seaman every fifty feet, to direct the trucks through the maze of buildings until they reached the tent area. The rigs were led through the tents with the fronts of the trucks protruding outside the long tents. A horde of workers immediately descended on the trucks. Bolts were quickly undone, exposing the inner stainless steel tank of the machines. A crane was moved by the truck between it and the nuclear tipped missile.

The crane strained from the staggering weight of the missile as it raised it and sled with steel wheels still attached. The crane then carefully swung the missile around as the workers kept the swing of the missile under control with a number of tag lines, they attached to the sled. The workers then pulled to get the point of the missile properly aligned with the void of the trailer.

As the point of the missile housing the ten reentry nuclear warheads began to slide inside the truck, hands of many workers grabbed the carriage and cautiously guided it inside the truck. As the wheels took hold, the sliding grew easier for the workers. The tail of the trailer dropped due to the added weight of the missile. When the balance point of the missile was achieved, the led cables of the crane were released, and the crane moved the missile deeper in the trailer, using the boom of the machine. The metal wheels screamed in protest as the missile slid deeper inside the truck. When the boom moved until the last of the cables were stopped by the tank housing, the cables were released, and then sheer man power was used to horse the rest of the missile in until it was fully seated inside the truck. Three technicians crawling in the tank and secured the missile to the sides of the truck with chains connected to lanyards welded in placed.

It took the horde of Russian technicians over half an hour to get the chains and tie downs properly set in place from the missile to the sides of the tank. Once satisfied the missile would not shift as the truck drove on the road, the workers crawled out of the tank green from the smell of old oil. The group of technicians checked each other's work to make certain the missile was properly secured and would not move an inch inside the trailer truck. Those base personnel not involved in the Admiral's plan, were told the missiles were leakers and set for destruction. This was more economical than trying to save the missiles. The technicians believed the twenty four drivers were Russian soldiers, they were dressed and spoke perfect Russian.

The horde of workers paid no attention to the truck drivers as they headed for the second truck to begin placing a missile inside this machine. The Russians were working on one truck at a time to avoid any possible mistakes with the missiles or their work. The man made thick cloud cover made the worker's eyes burn, and breathing labored. The workers understood the smoke was necessary to keep the security of the movement of the missiles from the American satellites, it was a fool hearted mistake on their part.

CHAPTER THREE

NORASATCOM HEADQUARTERS MARYLAND.
NOVEMBER 4th, 1998. 0230 HOURS

The Lieutenant started his eleventh straight hour of work when the satellite reached its position that allowed it to tape where the twelve Iranian tractor trailer trucks were heading. He leaned closer to the fuzzy screen as the video recorded every mile of land as the satellite slowly worked its way over the end of Iran, and then it entered Russia. He carefully studied the area the satellite floated over, looking for the twelve missing Iranian tanker trucks, determined to locate them so he could get his ass out of the frying pan with the powerful CIA Director. He smiled as he thought of the Director and General in the office waiting for word on the trucks.

For the first hour and a half, he found nothing out of the ordinary, just Persians doing what they did to make a living in the desert. In Russia, it was a different story, tanks and other vehicles were gathered near the border. The American Lieutenant stared at the screen as the satellite turned to other sections of Russia. The first decision he made was when the satellite communicated an interest request. The computer requested to divert its attention and flight path.

The Lieutenant opened his log and checked the areas this satellite covered. The first target was the Naval Base housing the Black Sea Fleet in the Ukraine. The second target was two missile bases stationed in the Russian city of Novokuznetsk. These housed missiles once installed in the country of Kazakhstan, but when it pulled away from Russian influence. The Russian missiles were moved to these locations for storage and future use if needed.

The young military officer checked the map locations of the targets, and knew the satellite could not cover both positions on the same pass, without expending on board fuel, and a ton of in-flight corrections. These corrections would have to be cleared by the Pentagon first, before he could possible move the satellite from its ordered flight path. The soldier cursed over being forced to make decisions on his own. Guess right and he would come out smelling like flowers. Guess wrong, and he would stink like dog shit stuck on the bottom of a soldier's boot.

The Lieutenant cursed as he went over the target the twelve trucks would surely be heading for. Logic ordered him to divert the satellite over to the second target where the missiles might be from. But something about that region did not sit quite right with the young officer. Something he heard or felt, told him he should head the satellite for the massive Ukrainian Russian Naval Base. Something he remembered made him consider this target as the one he should obviously concentrate all his efforts on. He suddenly snapped his fingers and mumbled to himself, 'Yeah, the Russian submarines are stationed on this base, sure as snot the trucks had to be heading for the Ukrainian Naval Base if they're after any god damn missiles.' He tapped the keys to divert the satellite to the position he wanted covered. He did not have to do much controlling the bird, because the satellite was preset to cover the Russian Naval Base as part of its original orders, unless otherwise instructed to divert to any secondary targets.

The satellite started the turn to place it on the heading directly for the Ukrainian Naval Base at Sevastopol. Different areas of Russia then the Ukrainian landscape came up on the screen. The Lieutenant knew the satellite would hover over the military base for three hours if needed, and he planned to make a detailed mapping of the base, until he located the missing Iranian trucks.

The Sergeants manning the NORASATCOM HQ desk moved over to the Lieutenant when the satellite began its pass. The first thing they saw were the blue waters of the Black Sea.

"That's the final correction the Sat will need to make. It's perfectly lined up with the center of the Naval Base at this point, Lieutenant." Sergeant Peters said as he pointed to the screen.

The two soldiers leaned a little closer to the screen as the shoreline of the massive base finally came in view. "Wow, it sure is cloudy as hell over there Lieutenant." The Sergeant moaned as they both stared at the manmade mist blanketing the entire naval base.

"Don't be such an asshole. The damn Russians are trying to block our vision of their base by releasing smoke and flares. The screwy Russians will never learn they can't stop us from spying on their damn asses. With this bird, we can burn right through this shit they're sending up. Damn, they're really putting the cloud cover to us today Sarge. They must be up to something." The Lieutenant grumbled as he shifted the satellite cameras to enable them to burn through the manmade smoke screen. The base came in clear as a bell after the few minor corrections.

"What's that shit in the lower section of the Sat screen, Lieutenant?" The Sergeant asked.

"I bet my dick on that's a fucking tent, and I'm certain it's hiding the missiles and trucks we're looking for. See the end of the tent, that's the trucks, and you can bet the bank they're sliding the missiles inside those suckers as we speak Sarge." Lieutenant Williams pushed the keys to transfer what they viewed to a secured receiving head stationed in General White's office at the Pentagon. At the same time, he called the General on the scrambled secured phone.

After the third ring, the General picked up the phone himself and said. "Yeah Lieutenant, we're receiving your transmission fine sir. What do ya make of what you're seeing son?"

"General White Sir, the damn tents are obviously housing the missing Iranian trucks, with Russian missiles being stored inside the damn vehicles sir. The sonofabitches are taking possession of submarine launch ballistic nuclear tipped missiles, sir."

"You can confirm this from what your satellite is picking up?" General White asked.

"Errr... well, not exactly sir. But what else can those damn ragheads and Russians be doing under those tents, General? Why the tents, and why are they shooting smoke and flares at..."

"Lieutenant Williams, there's no need to be disconcerted over this mess. The damn Iranians are people who should be respected at all times mister. One thing, what did you mean they're shooting off smoke and flares? Did our satellite come under attack sir?"

"Sorry General White, it'll not happen again, I'm just excited and that's all sir."

"Yeah yeah, okay kid, just answer my damn question will you please sir."

"Sorry General White, the Russian workers on the base are firing off great numbers of flares. They're hoping it'll upset the infrared systems on board our bird sir. All I have to do is switch the taping systems to the next step up, and everything comes in clear as a bell and burns right through anything they try and throw at us from the deck, sir. The Russians are also dumping a ton of smoke to cloud over the entire base and stop us from viewing their actions, sir."

"Their plan isn't working I take it, am I right to think in this manner Lieutenant? Because I can see everything they're doing on that fucking base clear as if there was no smoke screen being employed by the base workers. Let me ask you another question while I'm at it Lieutenant Williams, is this tactic ordinary, or is this something special they're doing against us today, sir?" General White paused to allow the Lieutenant to respond to his last question.

"General White, the only time the Russians try this shit against us, is when they're doing something they don't want us to witness, sir. I'd say they're up to something shady under those damn tents of theirs, General White. I make it out to be a transfer of the missiles, sir."

"You stake your god damn career on that statement, Lieutenant Williams? Before you answer, allow me to say. If you're right, you'll be a Major by tomorrow morning. On the other hand, if you're fucking wrong and you make me look like a sack of shit. You'll find yourself counting god damn polar bears at the North Pole while dressed in a damn bathing suit mister."

"Yes sir. I sure do, General White. I'm positive of what I just offered to you sir."

"Then answer Lieutenant!" General White barked at him.

"General White, it's my opinion the Russian workers are transferring nuclear capable, submarine launched ballistic missiles into Iranian owned trailer trucks, sir."

"Good Major, cause that's exactly what I see as well mister. You'll get confirmation of your new rate increase by morning, sir. You see nothing strange about Russian servicemen loading the missiles inside those god damn trailer trucks?"

"They're not Iranian trucks, General." Director Raincloud moaned from his chair.

General White turned to the Director and groused at him. "What the hell are you talking about Chief? These fucking machines aren't the same trucks we were tracking all yesterday John?"

"Oh yes they are General White, but somewhere along the way the Iranians evidently changed the markings on the sides of their vehicles. Look, see the Russian Red Star painted on the side of this truck they just finished working on, sir?" Director Raincloud actually touched the screen with his finger as he pointed to the tanker truck just slowly pulling out from under the tent, and then he added. "Something else

I was able to pick up, General White. See the smoke from the horse, the truck's obviously a helluva lot heavier than when it was traveling on the roads yesterday. Yes General, I'll agree with the Major. The trucks are loaded with missiles, judging by that Delta IV submarine moored at dockside, I'd say the Iranians are now in control of SS-N-23 submarine launch missiles. Look, that's a missile being stored on a carriage where that tent flap just blew open from a gust of wind. We got the sonofabitches dead to rights now sir. Lieutenant... err... Major, did you get all this shit down on the damn tape, mister?"

"Director Raincloud, everything you're viewing is being taped and logged in, sir."

"Good. General White, I think I'm going to push the panic button here sir." With this said, Director Raincloud picked up the phone and he quickly dialed the White House. The phone rang four times before the White House Chief of Staff answered and the Director said. "Hello Paul, I have to speak with the Boss STAT sir."

"Jesus Director Raincloud, do you have any idea what time of night it is, sir? The President just turned in for the night from a late night meeting with certain members of his cab..."

"I don't give a rat's ass about any meeting the Boss was attending. I have to speak with the President at once, mister." Director Raincloud barked, and then he added, "again, sorry Paul, but this is extremely important, and the President has to be briefed immediately."

"It's I who am sorry Director Raincloud. I didn't realize it was so important sir. Do you want to hang on, or would you rather hang up and I'll get back to you when I wake the President, sir?"

"How long will it take you to get to him and back to me, Paul?" The Director asked.

The White House Chief of Staff aide laughed on the other end of the phone.

"Call me back then Paul. But you have to keep in mind this is extremely important I speak with the Man as soon as possible." Director Raincloud offered giving into the aide.

"Yes sir, by all means Director Raincloud, I'll do that sir. I believe it shouldn't be any longer than ten minutes at the most, sir." Paul found himself speaking to a dead phone.

Like walking with the weight of the world on his shoulders, Paul headed for the elevator to the third floor, the private living quarters of the President while in the White House. The doors of the elevator opened to the hall, and he breathed a sigh when he picked up the light under the door from the bedroom, and heard the TV. He rushed to the door slightly ajar and tapped on it.

"Yes. Who is it please." It was the President's wife speaking.

"Excuse me Barbara, but I must speak to Albert, I'm sorry, but it's most important Ma'am."

"Just a minute please and I'll get him for you Paul." She offered politely.

Paul heard Barbara whispering, warning the President to hurry up. He heard the rustle of sheets, and knew they were enjoying themselves in bed. He was pleased they were still so much in love. His thoughts were interrupted by the President's angry voice as it barked at him.

"For Christ sake Paul, this better be pretty damn important, or you're going to find yourself counting blades of grass in the Rose Garden for disturbing me at a time like this, young man. I just got comfortable." The President appeared at the door, his hair mussed and one arm in his bathrobe while the other searched for the elusive sleeve, he had on pajama bottoms but no top. Barbara was lying in bed with the covers pulled up to her neck, smiling at the aide in the hallway.

"Allow me to help you with that please Mr. President Sir." Paul offered.

"Do you need me Albert?" His wife asked from the bed warmly.

"How the hell do I know? I don't know what got Paul up here yet. It better be good though. Remember where we left off. Now for you mister, what's so damn important Paul."

"Mr. President..." The aide began, but was cut off by the President.

"It's Albert, I'm not that angry with you, yet." The President warned the young man.

"Sorry Mr. Pre... err... Albert. I'm sorry for disturbing you, sir. But I just received a call from Director Raincloud, and he requested to speak with you immediately, sir. He stated it was imperative. I asked him if it couldn't wait until morning, and he insisted. I must say the Director wasn't quite himself this evening sir."

"Yes, and how is that Paul?" the President asked the young man.

"He was most insulting, and very demanding of me at the same time sir."

"Do you know where was he calling from?" the President asked the young man.

"He gave me the number and I checked it. It was from General White's office, sir."

"Uh-oh, those two birds are burning the midnight oil tonight I see. I better see what's got my Director so damn excited tonight, son. I'll place the call from the library."

"Fine, a glass of brandy sir?" the aide asked the President with a slight smile.

"Yes, warm please Paul." The President replied as he tied his robe closed, and rushed down the hall to the second floor to the library that was being warmed from the fire in the marble fireplace. He sat in the chair supposed to be President Grant's favorite chair. Albert reached the phone just as Paul returned with his brandy.

"Will you need anything else for the night, Albert?" Paul asked politely.

"Naw, and it's Mr. President to you mister, disturbing me at such a crucial time, my friend. I'll get even with you for this one." The President snorted with a laugh and a waving finger.

"I can't wait sir." Paul replied as he smiled, and left the President to his privacy.

President Cole placed his call and the General answered it and the President offered. "Ahhh... General White, I believe Director Raincloud's waiting to speak with me, and I was informed he was at your office with you, sir. Kind of burning the midnight oil aren't we, General White? May I speak to the Director if he's available, General white?"

"Yes Sir Mr. President, you told us to keep you informed of any new developments involving those damn trailer trucks from Iran into Russia, sir." The General retorted.

"Good, getting right to the damn point are we I see, I like that because I really don't have the time to chew the fat with you, General White Sir? I was just turning in for the night when you jumped on Paul's ass, and we have to talk about how you speak to my aides, sir. General Weidenbacher did the right thing with picking you to replace him as Chairman, sir. Now don't go and tell me that minor Iranian truck incident has suddenly escalated into a world threatening situation? Not even General Weidenbacher could make up an international incident this quick."

The President smirked as he allowed his mind to drift to the debacle of the General's funeral. It turned out to be nothing short of a complete disaster, with newspapers dumping on the deceased General for allowing the Russians to get so far with their plan to destroy a vast area of China from North Korea, in hopes of getting China to attack what was left of North Korea. No one knew it was the President's hesitation that allowed the Russian rebels to get as far as they did with their plans to start a shooting war with China. If it wasn't for General Weidenbacher and his good judgment. The plan would have surely succeeded. But the President being a politician, and known to be quick on his feet, allowed the General to take the full brunt of the punishment in the newspapers and on the air waves.

Albert did not come away from the fighting in one piece either though. The news reporters turned their wrath loose on him and his cabinet, for not committing enough military forces to ouster the Communist plan. He was crucified in the papers everyday for over two weeks straight. Ever since taken office, there had been one small war after another, or one world threatening situation after the other, and the last one might have caused a nuclear exchange between the three nations of the United States, Russia, and China.

As terrible as these accusations were, they were true, and the situations were allowed to get rather hurtful. Because the President was cautious to err on the side of peace, not war until he had no other alternative, and he was forced to finally react militarily against the situation. He had no idea his caution would be taken as a sign of weakness by his favorite adversaries. The egotistical white supremacists of South Africa should have been stepped on from the start, instead of him trying to negotiate a peaceful solution with them, and allowing them to take over the United States Embassy stationed in Namibia.

The President cursed at his civilian advisor Manning who allowed the situation in South Africa to get out of hand on him, and caused him a major military engagement because of his uncontrollable mouth. There was the mess starting the destruction of Asia, with China invading North Korea, and forcibly taking over Hong Kong and stealing cash, invading Taiwan. Then the mess in the Middle East that greeted him after he was part of the decision to attack Cuba.

'Yeah, the news people were correct when they moaned about the wars the United States was involved in over the last few years of his Administration. What was he to do about them, allow the bad guys to take over countries while he watched. It was better to meet the enemy head on their soil, rather than allow the enemy to get established first, and be forced to fight from the trenches to drive them out of power. President Cole made up his mind he was no longer going to try a peaceful solution to any bad situation. If some ass tried the might of the United States, he was going to find the full weight of the United States on his neck. Yeah, whoever said being the President was the best position in the United States, was talking out of his asses.

The exhausted President's thoughts were suddenly interrupted by General White as he offered to the President. "Mr. President Sir, Director Raincloud's sitting by me, if you'd like. I can brief you on what's transpiring in Russia and he can take over when I'm done, sir."

"Excuse me General White, I guess I was kind of daydreaming there for a moment, it's awfully early in the morning, sir." The President complained at the military officer.

"Yes Sir Mr. President, I was offering to brief you on what's taking place in Russia, sir."

"Where's Director Raincloud dammit? I thought he wanted to speak to me General White?"

"He's with me Mr. President Sir." General White offered a second time.

"And he doesn't mind you delivering the briefing for him, General White?"

"No sir not at all, we've been keeping a close eye on Russia together by means of a live satellite connection and feed to my office, sir."

"Christ sake General, don't tell me we have another situation developing inside Russia again. What the hell could those pain in the asses be up to this time, dammit?" The President grumbled.

"Fraid so Mr. President Sir, as we speak, I'm watching a number of Russian Seamen loading nuclear tipped ballistic missiles inside the Iranian fuel carriers we were tracking on the satellite for the past two days, sir." General White remarked, as he watched the tape running, and spoke with the President at the same time.

"Inside the damn trucks you're offering General White, I don't understand this, sir. How can tanker trucks carry nuclear missiles inside them? That's impossible. Why not carry the damn things in plain sight of the world? Why not use box trucks to transport these damn things around, General. I don't mean to question what you're telling me, General. But are you absolutely certain of your information you're viewing, sir?" the President moaned at his military officer.

"With all due respect Mr. President, the Russians have taken to transporting their extra, or any missiles for that matter by means of these fuel rigs, sir. They have a false interior, and the tail end of the tank opens, so the workers can easily load the missiles inside the trucks. No terrorist ever attacked a fuel carrier sir. I guess any would be terrorist wouldn't give these targets very much attention. Not enough bang for the buck I'd say, and the damn Russians think they're fooling us by this sneaky move, Mr. President Sir. We have allowed them to believe they're fooling us, so they wouldn't change to another method of transporting these god damn missiles around, and we can keep a pretty good track on the damn missiles being transported for destruction."

"This is normal actions for the Russians to employ I take it then, General White Sir? I sure hope the damn Russians are not up to something that might end up threatening the peace for the rest of the world, General White."

"Yes Mr. President, we've known of this procedure for some months now, sir."

"You have all the information we need to prove this new threat coming from Russia at hand, if we need to react against this latest situation developing in Russia that is General?"

"Yes sir, it's all down on tape, and by other means of accumulating intelligence on any situation we're still tracking inside Russia, Mr. President Sir." The General replied.

"If that's a fact then General White, we're going to go after these damn assholes with guns a blazing this time around I assure you, sir. No more pussy footing around with these damn asses who want to take over the entire world. General White, I feel you have proved to me we need to meet pronto over this rapidly developing situation in Russia sir. Err... I want you and your sidekick at my office by six o'clock sharp, you got that General?"

"Yes Sir Mr. President, we'll be at the meeting with all the intelligence we have gathered so far over this new mess, sir." General White replied to the President.

"General White, I'm warning you and your partner in crime who seems to always be standing by your side lately, sir. You better be damn ready, and fully able to prove everything you just told me with absolute and foolproof evidence and intelligence reports, sir. Or I'll be serving your balls up for snacks at this damn meeting, sir. I want all your tapes with real time pictures and photos and any other intelligence you have developed on this damn situation, sir. All your written reports as well from both you and Director Raincloud, General White. I further want more than enough proof if I'm going to commit my troops to another god damn military action overseas. General White, are you ready to wake up your crew of elite soldiers, wherever they might be lurking about in the States and elsewhere sir?" the President bitched at the General.

"I take it you're speaking about the Rapid Response Force we have developed for this type of situation under General Weidenbacher's Command, Mr. President Sir?" General White was unable to hide his grin over the fact his specialized troops were going back in action.

"That's the soldiers I'm speaking about, General White Sir. How soon do you think you can have them damn gun bunnies of yours reporting back to base, so we can better prepare them for this next possible military action, sir?"

"My troops will be ready for any military action you need them sent out on, Mr. President Sir. On a moment's notice might I add as well, sir. All you have to do is say the word, and the soldiers will be foaming at the mouth to carry out your orders, no matter what they might cover sir." General White boasted proudly, as he gave the thumbs up to Director

Raincloud along with a wide grin, and then he turned his attention back to the President.

"If what you say is true General White, I have a bad feeling I'll be needing your specialized troops on this mess if it turns into a serious situation on us, sir. God, I hope we won't need the troops, General." The President broke off the connection.

General White glanced at Director Raincloud and then he bitched at the lead CIA Agent. "Dammit, I really like this President. He said he was going to react if some dopey ass try to screw around with us again, no matter where the action's occurring, and he seems to means what he says. It looks like the United States is on their way up the meat scale again with this President standing at the helm of the United States, Director Raincloud."

MARATHON ISLAND IN THE FLORIDA KEYS

Many members from the MNRRF (Multi National Rapid Response Force) took up residence on the Island of Marathon and the surrounding Florida Keys. All followed Lieutenant Robert Walker, Sergeant Dorothy Ramirez, Lieutenant Frank Hall, who was branded by the other soldiers as the Mutt, because he had a white mother and a black father, and his girlfriend Sergeant Barbara Meyerhoff, tagged Fun Bags because of the size of her breasts, moved down shortly after. Other members of the MNRRF followed them down to Marathon with many newcomers. After the fighting in Russia ended, the old RRF was changed to MNRRF, to include soldiers from Russia, Japan, France, England, Italy and Spain. Three Russian women soldiers, and two males joined the group before it left Russia, with soldiers from Japan, one male, the other female. The soldiers were waiting for troops from the other nations to join up.

Lieutenant Walker and Sergeant Ramirez were a thing and have been for three years now, the same with the Mutt and Meyerhoff. The two women warriors were having fun with the female Russians, the latest to join their elite group of soldiers. It was Ramirez who pushed to have them join and was happy when they did. The Russians fitted in fine. Sergeant Taras Zarugnaya was a Ukrainian, Sergeant Leonid Maslennikova, also a Ukrainian, was the only male, and had a narrow sense of humor. Corporal Sevtlana Dostoyevsky, a woman who had her motor running all the time, and tried to conquer any male she came across, sexually. The last Russian soldier to join the group was Corporal Lidiya Stepashin.

Taras was constantly after Walker, always trying to get his goat any chance she got, offering him sex for any reason, and then pulling back when Road Kill was drooling all over himself over her. Together with Ramirez, the girls drove him absolutely crazy. The group of soldiers were expecting a second Japanese soldier to arrive later that day. Though they had never met the new soldier, there was advance word he was a hell of a fighter.

Today was Saturday, and the specialized group of soldiers rented a half day charter to go after some dolphin commonly referred to as Mau Mau. If Marathon was noted for anything, it was the great fishing and people came from all over the world to fish in the clean blue waters around the Keys. Walker chartered On The Hook, a thirty three foot World Cat boat Captained by a female, one of the only female Captains on the entire Island, and she was known to be the best, never coming in without fish. The joke was she was part Native American, and if anyone could find fish, she sure could.

As expected, the fishing was fantastic, with Walker's group catching twenty dolphins weighing between twelve to thirty five pounds each. When they got back to shore, Walker let the soldiers spread the word there was going to be a fish bake at his home. Each member of the group carried a handheld radio so the soldiers could maintain a constant communication linkup with Walker, he would be the first to be notified if the group was needed by Command.

Marathon was one of the only Keys to have an commercial airport, and the Japanese soldier was due to land that afternoon on U.S. Air. Walker ordered a few guys to wait for him, Corporal Nasayoshi Nakamura, already tagged Nintendo, was there in case this guy only knew Japanese.

The soldiers waited at the main building, killing time watching women waiting for their planes to arrive. Private Clifford Saldinger, called Sun Tan because he was black as the Ace of Spades, and was the Unit's main complainer. It was said he would complain about a blow job, along with Private Vincent Lombardo, branded Buckethead because of the size of his head, and Corporal Milton Pettibone, tagged CoCo-G. The soldier's plane was announced and they went to meet it on the tarmac as it landed. A U.S. Air plane with ten passengers on board landed. The new guy was the only Japanese looking guy on the plane. He noticed the men looking like soldiers and headed right for them. Nintendo immediately put out his hand who barely looked Japanese as he remarked. "Konnicha wa, Tomo." (Good day friend.)

"Huh?" the soldier snapped back at the stranger speaking to him.

"Hey man, you understand English huh?" Nintendo said with a grin.

"What the fuck's with you man? You some full blooded Nip or what? Of course I understand English, I had an American mother, bird brain." He snapped as he flung his duffle bag at CoCo-G, who stepped aside and allowed it to fly by him, and that soldier growled at the new soldier. "Hey fucker, what the hell do I look like, your stinking boy? Here, every grunt carries his own weight or he goes home with a foot up his ass, Homes. What's your fucking name rude dude?"

"David Nirajima." The new guy said with pride in his voice as he retrieved his bag.

"David Nirajima, man, that's a fucking tag if I ever heard one said, Homes. The last part of your name's definitely fucking Japanese pal. But David, that's a real change what's wit the first name buddy." Nintendo squawked with a grin at the soldier.

"Yeah, my father's Jap and my mother Irish." Nirajima mumbled as he hoisted his bag on his shoulder, and fell in line with the rest of the soldiers were waved off the tarmac by security.

"What a fucking mix that is buddy, the stinking Mutt's gonna be dipped in shit when he finds out he's not the only mutt in the group any longer. Hey guys, we gotta brand this rude dude before we get back to the rest of the guys at Walker's place." CoCo-G offered to the other soldiers gathered with him.

Nintendo moved nearer to the FnG, (Fucking new Guy) and eyed him before announcing. "Hey FnG I hereby dub you McNip in honor of your mixed up blood man. Accept the tag before someone else comes up with a name a helluva lot more demeaning, rude dude."

Nirajima stopped; looked at Nintendo and smiled. "I like it. It'll do. McNip, I like that."

The group shared a laughed as they closed ranks and stopped at the side of the Mutt's beater Chevy pickup truck. CoCo-G drove while the other soldiers piled in the rear of it. As they sped for Tingler Island, any woman they passed was abused with whistles and hoots. The women enjoyed the attention as they waved back. By the time they reached Walker's place, the party was in full swing. Some of the local police officers were invited to keep an eye on the drinkers and cook for the soldiers. The soldiers mingled in with others while Nintendo walked McNip over to Walker, who was standing with the Mutt and Ramirez and introduced him to them.

"Say Road Kill, here's the new shit you sent us out to get hold of man. We dubbed the dick McNip, because he's got a Jap father, and Irish mother, Homes. Another mutt, hey Mutt?"

Walker offered his hand. "McNip huh, you speak fucking English buddy?"

"I don't know, do you speak Japanese, pal?" he snapped back sarcastically.

"Who is this guy I don't like already. A wiseass huh sucka? Well we know how to deal with wiseguys around here. We eat the shits and crap them out in new born shits." The Mutt growled as he tried to get around Walker, as McNip squared off to intercept the nut threatening him.

The Mutt saw McNip take a threatening stance and warned him. "You wanna dance fucker? I'll put you down for the stinking count slick as snot, asshole. I'll send you to meet the man. If you fuck with me, you'll wish your father never dicked your mother and shitted you outta her ass. I'll beat the snot bubbles outta your buster. It's gonna be Friday night at the stinking fights, sucker. Yeah Homes, look at me like that fucker that's right man, I'm laying a little brother down on your little yellow ass. You got the damn balls to do something about it other than just mad dog my ass, sucka? I'll smack you so hard your first born will come out with a black eye." The Mutt roared as he tried to get around Walker. The commotion the Mutt was causing, drew the attention of the cops. One Deputy motioned the other, and they both started for the Mutt.

Walker placed his hand against the Mutt's chest and ordered him. "Back off some both of ya dicks before I kick the shit outta ya both. Mutt, cool off will ya man, you know you can kill this new spudhead until we get to know him betta. McNip, the Mutt didn't mean nuthin, you know, he's like Guido from the village. Everyone's gotta have a stinking Mutt in the group."

The Mutt turned to Walker and bitched at him this time. "Fuck you Charlie and the horse you rode in on. I want this little fuck, his ass is grass and I'm the fucking lawn mower, Homes."

McNip pointed his finger right at the Mutt's face, but before he could say anything. The Mutt was roaring at him again. "You keep waving that fucking finger in my stinking face, and I'm gonna bite the damn thing off on ya sucka. C'mon Homes, let's mix it up some pal."

"Christ Mutt, talking to you is like trying to talk to a fucking foreigner lately man. I told you once to back off Homes. Look shithead, you got the heat coming at ya ass now. Relax, will ya."

"Walker, some guys are alive because it's against the law to kill them." McNip offered.

"Now you did it Homes. I'm gonna stomp a fucking mud puddle in your face and walk it dry." he Mutt bellowed as he pushed Walker, only to be grabbed by the cops who pulled him down.

"Take it easy with him buddy, he'll be fine once he cools off some." Lieutenant Walker warned as he pulled on the cop's arm. Mother Flanagan moved in to grab the other cop when Walker warned him off with a quick head movement. The Lieutenant did not want this mess to escalate. He jumped up and barked at the new soldier. "hey asshole, see what you did? That fuck under there's a stinking Lieutenant, you should be saluting his fucking ass."

"My business is shooting, not saluting. I've been in a bad mood for the last couple years now. So why don't you leave me alone. How the hell was I to know the fish was a damn Lieutenant. If you want me to know these things, have the fool wear his rate tattooed across his damn chest, man." McNip snapped as he placed his hands on his hips, but he would not back down.

Sergeant Ramirez saw things were starting to get rapidly out of hand and she knew she had to do something before fists started to fly. "Walker, this dude has balls, and balls are enough to make him accepted to the group, no?"

Someone else called out. "Yeah Homes she's right, I think we should change the cock stiffeners name from McNip, to Gonads. Serves the shit right for screwing with us man."

This broke the tension and the Mutt laughed as he called out from under the two cops sitting on his chest. "Yeah, it'll serve the ass right. He's not the sharpest knife in the drawer, but he has balls. Hey guys, you wanna get offa my ass, I can't breathe good under here. I'm cool."

"You sure friend." The Sheriff Sergeant growled as he loosened his grip on the Mutt's arms.

"Yeah sure, everything's cool pal." Lieutenant Walker replied to the cop.

The two police officers released their grasp of the Mutt and he quickly wiggled out from under them. He stood, stared at McNip and then he smiled as he offered him his hand. They shook, the music began and the others went back to what they were doing before the heat began to boil.

"Beer pal?" the Mutt asked the new guy.

"Yeah thanks. Where can I dump my shit off?" McNip snapped.

"Right there's good enuf. It's safe, no ass would dare steal anything round this place, it'd cost the fool his life." Walker offered as he took a beer and popped the top. "Where you from pal?"

"Osaka, but I was schooled in the United States for my last three years of school on the east side of Manhattan. Never made it to college though, mom got sick and we moved back to Japan, I helped dad out. I joined the service when everything was cool, well as near normal as it can get without mom's help. Did good in the service though, showed initiative and the higher ups took an interest in my ass. When the government informed me they were setting up this new Multi National specialized troop thing. The higher ups searched for the right people, and someone offered me up on a silver platter to the bastards, and voila, here I am Lieutenant."

"Sounds like the same way most of us guys got stuck with this bullshit duty, man. Someone wanted to get rid of us, and served us up in this Unit man." Buckethead added and then belched.

"Yeah, enuf of this shit, you're fucking up my drinking time on me, Homes." Wacko, (Sergeant Salvatore Tomassi) yelled out as he turned to one of the Russian women he was trying to talk into serving him a topless beer. A few of the female soldiers were running around without tops, and the other girls were under pressure from the male soldiers to take their tops off.

"Hey guys, we gotta brand the new Gorkie hens if we're gonna adopt them Ruskie bitches into the group." The Roach suddenly announced while swaying slightly from drink.

"You're right Homes, but do the Russian chicks know what the other girls hadta do to come up with a name for the hens?" the Mutt grumbled with a sneer as he turned from McNip, and aimed his attention at the three Russian women being circled by the other members from the group.

Sergeant Taras Zarugnaya placed her hands on her hips and gave a sigh as she glared at the men gawking at her with lust in their eyes. She spoke the best English of the Russian women, and knew what the men were hedging at. "Okay hot hero shots, what we do join you misfit?"

"Strip and fuck the shit outta the lot of us at the same time, baby." Someone called out.

Sergeant Ramirez held up her hand and warned the other soldiers quickly gathered around the three Russian female warriors and she warned the male soldiers. "No one's going to take on this lot of uglies unless they agree to do you shits first. Taras, you and the other girls have to strip so these filthy pigs can get an eye full of your bodies, and they see what part of you they want to use as your tag names for the outfit, sorry."

"You do this get when what you say, tag name Sergeant Ramirez?" Taras asked.

"No, it wasn't that simple for us. We had to fuck and suck the noncoms to be accepted into this crazy ass group of madmen, who make the best warriors of any Army." Ramirez said, trying to make light of her actions, though embarrassed by them.

"If as you say, fuck and suck bunch we do same thing, better than American woman do. We no want be treated different from anyone else. If we come part group, we do what you to accept by them. You think America babies keep up with Russian sexy women. I fear live be danger."

"Hey bitch, don't worry about our health, just spread them purdy legs and open your mouth, and we'll do the rest fur ya." Someone called out as he grabbed his crotch and pulled on it.

"Hey Raz, don't fuck this up on us with that woman's lib shit. If the damn Ruskies wanna screw the lot of us, let them have at it and keep your mouth shut." The Mutt snapped at Ramirez.

Ramirez looked at Walker grinning at her from ear to ear, and she hissed. "There's no sense in my asking what you think about this mess. Where do you want the girls to set up housekeeping?"

One of the cops tapped Walker on his shoulder and then whispered at him. "Hey Walker, if these three women are going to fuck the rest of these shitheads here. I think you better have them set up in the house sir. If I don't see it, I don't break it up on you guys."

"You're not going to join in on all the fun and games Sarge? It's gonna be open season on the Gorkie babes, so you might as well get in on some of the fun man." Walker remarked.

"You know better than that sir. I'm stretching the limits by turning my back of this pack of animals as it is, Lieutenant. If it's going to be done, it has to be carried out inside the house, or I'll be forced to stop it on you, sir."

"Okay Sarge, inside it'll be then I guess. Hey Raz, we gotta get the Russian babes set up and ready inside the dump..."

"They gotta strip out here first Walker. I wanna see what I'm getting before I get involved with this Gorkie ladies, man." A male voice called out from the group of grinning male soldiers.

Taras looked for the voice calling out against her, not seeing the speaker she said a few words in Russian to the other two Russian woman warriors, and the three of them began to strip. They were making a big thing out of getting their clothes off and driving the men wild, and charging up some of the women from the outfit at the same time. Meyerhoff even offered to help the Russians with the male soldiers. Baby Tee, (Corporal Teri Dorland), also offered to help with the men. Ramirez whipped off her shirt and she announced with a wide grin on her lips. "I'm not going to allow a few of my girls to tow the line all by themselves, girls."

A cheer rose from the group with Lieutenant Walker adding while slurring his words from all the dink he consumed. "You're getting involved in this thing too my lady?"

"Bobby, if you're going to tap the Russian girls, I'm going to be humping a few of these stiff dicks around here. I got first pick of this mess." Ramirez called out as she entered the house first.

"Not if I help it." Taras offered, getting caught up in the all excitement of having sex with so many of the male soldiers inside the home. The fun and games went on without trouble with some women taking care of two and three men at the same time.

CHAPTER FOUR

SEVASTOPOL, UKRAINE THE HOME OF THE PROUD RUSSIAN BLACK SEA FLEET

The Russian Admiral Yevgeny Proushinsky kept his attention glued to the workers as the last of the SS-N-23 nuclear tipped missiles slowly disappeared inside the bowels of the remaining tanker truck. When the workers started bolting the end plate to the truck back down, Admiral Proushinsky rested his hand on the Iranian Agent's back and announced. "Comrade Colonel Marzuk, I believe it's time for you to come up with the rest of the monies you owe me."

"Comrade Admiral Proushinsky Sir, I understand and remember we had an arrangement where you were to provide me with a safe escort back to the border sir. Then I was going to turn over the rest of the money I still owe you Admiral."

"Ahhh... that was for the Amirikanskaya cash and blueprints for the missiles, Comrade Colonel Marzuk. I want the twelve million dollars for the god dom missiles that was the last missile placed inside your trucks." The Russian stopped speaking and held out his hand flat.

The Iranian though for a second and the grin reappeared, he snapped his fingers and the driver handed him a briefcase. Colonel Marzuk knew the Russian was supposed to wait until they reached the border before getting the rest of his money. He was willing to throw the twelve missiles away if he got his hands on the blueprints as he replied. "Admiral Proushinsky, you're correct in your request for the American cash now sir. A bargain is a bargain between friends is it not? You have fulfilled your end of the deal properly sir. So here's the last of the money for that part of the deal we made together sir." The Iranian Agent handed the Russian Admiral the second briefcase and then he added. "I'll be most pleased to wait until you count the money."

"In due time I shall count it. I have no fear of you trying to deceive me. Comrade Colonel Marzuk, is it not a fact you're still remaining in my country and at my disposal? Cheat me and neither you nor your men or their god dom trucks will ever reach the border, and I'll have my missiles back with the cash you already gave me." It was the Russian's turn to grin.

The Iranian bowed politely to the Russian while his mind laughed. Colonel Marzuk knew he paid the Russian military officer in counterfeit American dollars printed in Iran.

"You'll have all the rest of the money waiting for me at the Russian border when we arrive there, am I correct to believe this true Comrade Colonel Marzuk?"

"If you're in possession of the schematics needed for the construction of missiles and nuclear warheads, the money will be waiting at the border. I promise Comrade Admiral Proushinsky."

The Admiral lightly patted his breast pocket as he replied. "Comrade Colonel Marzuk, I have everything you requested in my pocket. You worry about having the money waiting there."

The first rig pulled on the road, it was followed by the other eleven machines.

"Comrade Colonel Marzuk, I believe it's time for us to leave for the border."

"Yes Comrade Admiral Proushinsky, you're correct, shall we leave then sir?"

The Russian armor vehicles pulled out and mingled in with the convoy, with one taking the lead, another taking position in the center of the column, while the third at the rear of the column.

Admiral Proushinsky went to great pains to point out the armor machines waiting to the Iranian Agent as they headed for his vehicle. "Comrade Colonel Marzuk, we'll drive to the border in luxury, no? I have air conditioning in my car." The Admiral was right, but it did little to cool off the vehicle. In minutes both were sweating as the car bounced down the unpaved road.

THE WHITE HOUSE, WASHINGTON D.C., 6:01 A.M. EST. MONDAY, NOVEMBER 4th, 1998. THE OVAL OFFICE

Everyone waited in the Oval Office for General John White and Director John Raincloud to arrive. General White's eyes instantly met Ms. Maria Hernandez, the Secretary of State, and he smiled at the older woman suffering terribly from the crippling disease. She put up a great front, but General White noticed she was in constant pain as the President moved her wheelchair a little closer to him. She locked eyes with General White and smiled, acknowledging his concern for her condition. Hernandez was a military soldier's best friend. If she thought he was right, she would go down in flames while backing him to the hilt all the way. But if she thought he was wrong, she would sway everyone against him and his ideas.

"General White, Director Raincloud, I believe you know everyone seated here. So I'll refrain from the usual amenities of introducing everyone and save us some time. Shall we begin the meeting? We have a lot of ground to cover and no one's going home until we're finished with everything we have to go over at this meeting. Who's first to speak General White?" the concerned President asked as he loudly clapped his hands, and as habits dictate, he immediately picked up a pencil and began to twirl it slowly between his fingers.

"Mr. President, I hoped to have this meeting take place in the situation room, sir. So I'd have better access to video players and projection screens for the still pictures, sir."

"I understood the message from our conversation, General. So I took the liberty of having a portable tape player and projection machine set up in my office for your convenience.

Larry, you can take the tapes and pictures from the General, and display them when he calls for them."

Larry was the security guard in charge of this section of the White House. A young man appeared and he put out his hand. General White handed him the tape and pictures.

"Okay General, you may begin with your report for us if you please."

"With all due respect Mr. President Sir, as everyone attending this meeting is aware of, the day before yesterday we had received an information alert sent from Satellite 113, stating it had detected a number of tractor tanker trucks heading from Iran to Russia. Since that time, we have discovered the mission of these Iranian trucks, and it made my blood run cold, sir. I need the tape marked A-3 to begin at this time Mr. President Sir."

The President shifted his weight and allowed the pencil to drop to the desktop as he snapped. "Larry! If you'll start the tape just requested by General White please."

The eleven curved windows inside the Oval Office instantly darkened as the curtains closed automatically, and a screen instantly appeared between the two farthest windows from the President's desk. The screen went from a stark white to a multi colored conglomeration in seconds. Then the first sign of the trailer trucks traveling on a dirt road appeared.

"These are the twelve Iranian trailer trucks the Satellite had detected before they crossed the Iranian, Azerbaijan border into Russia..."

"I thought Russia no longer had control over the nation of Azerbaijan, General White Sir." The civilian Manning moaned from his seat.

The General shot a hot glare at the civilian before he spoke. "In the eyes of the world, it doesn't. But make no mistake about it, if anything happens to threaten the old Russian satellite nations, you'll see who controls those nations that once made up the old USSR, Mr. Manning. As I was saying, these are the twelve Iranian trucks crossing into Russia..."

"How do you know they're the same trucks General White?" Manning interrupted again.

"Because we plotted their course through the Dashte Kavir desert with each pass of a satellite. The trucks gave us the slip as they came out of the desert. But we relocate them when they hit the highway heading for what we believed to be their final destination. The Azerbaijan border..."

"General White, how can you be certain these are the same trucks you were tracking before you lost them in the desert?" Manning asked unpleasantly, knowing he was starting to get under General White's skin by his constant interruptions. He figured if he could not get at him without upsetting the President, he would drive the General crazy in any fashion he could think of.

General White let out a deep disgusted sigh, and then he angrily placed his hands on his hips and glared harsher at the civilian. Before he was able to respond, the President took the initiative and he warned as he stood, snapping the pencil he was again playing with and sending one piece flying across the room. "Mr. Manning, you're forcing us to stay here all day with your constant interruptions of the general's presentation, and I'll have to have the General back track a bit because someone might have missed something important he said. Mr. Manning, you'll remain seated with your mouth closed until the General completed his briefing. If you find you have an important question to ask of him, write it down and ask the General at the end of his briefing.

Larry, I believe Mr. Manning needs a pencil and note book pad please."

No one spoke until Larry handed the pad and pencil to the civilian. The President waited until Manning was comfortable again, and then he offered. "General White, please excuse the few interruptions sir, they'll not happen again sir. Please sir, proceed with your presentation General."

General White nodded to the President and went on with his words. "Ladies and Gentlemen, pay attention to what happens to the trucks after they pass into Azerbaijan. Here, we can see the Iranian markings painted boldly on both sides of the rig, and the rest of the trailers behind them as they're being checked by the KGB guards, and here, now crossing into the Russian satellite nation. Here they're shoving off, keep watching as the trucks move from the border. Here we go, see they left the main highway headed nowhere. We lost the rigs for a few hours because of this turning off the highway, but bare with me until we pick the machines up again."

The tape fuzzed out here, and the operator advanced the film until the next image appeared.

"Hold it there, no, back it up a second yes that's it Larry. Please start the film again when we picked up the rigs on the highway again. Yeah, that's it, hold it there, start it again, good, thank you. As you can see Mr. President, we have picked up the twelve tanker trailer trucks, but there's something different about them this time around sir."

Everyone, including the President sat forward in their chairs, and stared at the screen. "I don't see anything different about the trucks." Vice President Mary Hirshfield interjected.

"I see something has indeed changed with the once Iranian machines General White Sir." Security Director Norman Griffin sighed.

All eyes drifted to him as he pointed to the Red Star painted on the side door of a truck. "The trucks now have Russian military markings painted on the sides of the machines."

"Sonofabitch, he's right." The President griped as he moved a little closer to the screen and he added. "You're right Norman, but I find myself asking the same question Mr. Manning just asked. General White, are you certain these are the same trucks you were following all along?"

"Yes Mr. President, allow me to prove the point to you sir. Can I control your operator?"

"Sure General White, all you have to do is call out and he'll hear you, unless you have to speak to him personally, General White Sir?" The President offered.

"No sir, all I have to do is direct him with the tapes from here Mr. President."

"Then call out Larry's name when you want to communicate with him, he'll hear you sir."

General White nodded, and then called out. "Larry, if you'd display the second tape please."

The screen went dead for a few moments then new images appeared. General White moved until he actually touched the screen and traced the truck with his finger. "If you'll follow my finger, I'll show you these are the same trucks with different marking. We feel this is why they turned off the main drag during the last satellite pass. Here, you can see where someone spilled a can of silver paint on the roof of the second rig. The truck marked with silver paint is forced to remain in the second position during the entire trip. There's a second way to make positive both sets of trucks are the same. The fifth truck is no longer an American made International truck, they obviously replaced the horse with a Mercedes rig. Evidently they had trouble with the truck, and replaced that rig with this one. Okay, Larry, advance the tape to frame one, one, two."

The numbers on the bottom of the screen flew by until the requested frame was reached.

"With all due respect Mr. President, here we see the Russian markings. Now, the satellite's going to pull in until it's singling out each truck for close inspection. The first truck shows nothing out of the ordinary except for the Russian marking. Here comes the second truck, and you can see the silver paint splattered on the top of the truck in the same pattern. There's the Russian markings, wait a moment, there's the third, now the fourth, both are International trucks. He comes the fifth, there's the Mercedes with the red strip going down the sides, and the Iranian markings have been removed, and replaced with the Russian ones, Mr. President." General White stopped speaking to allow this information to sink in on everyone sitting in on the meeting.

"Okay General white, you have proved your point to me well enough, sir." President Cole answered weakly and then offered. "Please continue with your presentation General."

"Very well Mr. President Sir. We tracked the rigs through Russia to the Ukrainian border. We believe the Iranian markings were changed to allow an easier inspection at the border station. We know the KGB Agents running this outpost are real sonsofbitches to deal with, and Iranian trucks this far into Russia would require special inspection. Changing the markings made us leery, and we kept a close eye on their progress. See how easy they went through the inspection stop at the Ukrainian border. The machines went on and we continue trailing them, we were forced to alter the satellite's flight path on three separate occasions, to enable us to keep an almost constant vigil on the rigs until we knew what they were up to. He we see them heading for their final destination, headquarters of the Russian Black Sea Fleet stationed at Sevastopol in the Ukraine."

Everyone in the meeting remained silent as they continued to watch the screen, viewing the trucks as they were shown pulling onto the massive Russian Naval Base, still kicking up a dust cloud behind them, and the machines instantly disappearing beneath the tents waiting for them.

"Do you have any idea what the tents are being used for, General White?" The Secretary of Defense, Jerry Levenhagen called out, remaining in his seat while staring at the General.

"Yes Mr. Secretary, we believe it's a lame attempt on the Russian military's part, to try and hide their criminal actions being carried out with the Iranian trucks. While they transfer the SS-N-23 submarine launch nuclear tipped long range missiles inside the false inside of the twelve tanker trailer trucks for transport back to Iran sir." The General allowed his words to linger in the air like the threat the missiles posed to world peace.

The President was instantly on his feet and pacing. Then he stopped and turned back to the General and growled at the military officer this time. "You're sure about this god damn information General? How reliable is this shit you're bringing up at this meeting, sir?"

"Absolutely positive about it Mr. President." The General replied calmly to the President.

"Jesus Christ Almighty General, here we go again, dammit." The President moaned angrily.

"Yes, I'm afraid so Mr. President Sir." General While offered in a calm voice.

"General White! Where the devil do you think they'll be transporting these damn missiles to inside Iran, sir?" Vice President Hirshfield asked, and then she quickly added as if it was an afterthought. "Are you quite certain the missiles are stored inside these damn trucks? Couldn't it be as simple as the Russians buying needed fuel from the Iranians, sir?"

"Ms. Hirshfield, we have known the Russians were moving certain numbers of their missiles around their country inside these same type altered tanker trucks for quite a while now, Ma'am. We believe it serves a two point reason for their actions being carried out by the Russian military Ma'am. One: is to stop a possible terrorist attack on one of their transported nuclear missile system. The Russian Mafia or black market would stop at nothing to get their damn hands on one of these little babies here. Two: we believe it was a wasted effort on the Russian military's part to try and keep us off step from discovering what they were up to, and when they were moving any of their damn missiles around inside their own country Ma'am.

"If you pay close attention to the screen and the film as it continues Ma'am, you can easily see the thick columns of heavy smoke the Russian base workers were laying down in their failed attempt to try and block our satellite's vision of their sneaky moves from our satellites Ma'am. The Russian base workers fired off hundreds of flares to try and block our satellite infrared systems, but we countered every one of their wasted efforts, Ma'am."

"General White, you have answered the second part of the Vice President's question. But I believe you were going to inform her where the damn Russians were transporting the missiles to, sir?" The President said to his military officer with concern in his voice.

"I beg your pardon Ms, Hirshfield. Larry, start the third tape please." The General remarked as the screen went dead momentarily, and then the new set of images appeared on the screen.

Once the tape was running, the General went on with his report to the members attending the meeting. "Right here Ms. Hirshfield, it's the large Iranian Submarine Base stationed at Bander Beheshi on the Gulf of Oman in the Indian Ocean Ma'am. We have strong evidence that the Iranian Navy had moved its complete compliment of six nuclear powered but outdated Delta I Russian made ballistic submarines to this base for safety reasons from the Bandar-e Abbas Port. The Iranians moved the submarines to this base during the revolts that occurred since the nuclear attack on Iran by Iraq during the recent Middle East war, Ma'am. We believe the missiles are earmarked for one of these submarines ported there, to keep us guessing and give Iran a nuclear capability at the same time, Ma'am." General White stopped speaking to allow Mr. Griffin, who looked like he had to go to the bathroom, ask his question.

"Thank you for that explanation General White, but unless I'm wrong about what I was informed about this situation. Does the Delta I submarine system have the capability of launching a nuclear tipped ballistic missile from its launch tubes, sir? If I'm not mistaken, I seem to remember something about these old sewer pipes were only able to launch the shorter range SS-N-6 or 8s with a single nuclear warhead capability, General White." The worried Security Director used the slang word of sewer pipes for submarines.

"Correct Mr. Griffin. The Delta I submarine had the capability of launching the SS-N-8, during the past few months the submarines sat idle at port, we believe they underwent a complete refit, and now they have the capability of launching the more powerful SS-23 missiles, sir."

"Shitttt!" Director Griffin hissed through clenched teeth as he stared back at the General.

"Shit nothing Mr. Griffin! I say we load up and then go in there and bomb the shit out of that god damn Iranian Base before the damn missiles arrive at the base and they're installed in the submarines. If we destroy the damn submarines, what the hell good will the damn missiles do the sand nigg...? I sorry General White, I meant nothing against you, sir." Secretary of Defense Levenhagen offered, thoroughly embarrassed for using the slang phase for the Arab people.

General White waved it off with a flick of his hand, he sometimes called Arabs names.

Director Raincloud took the ball and he responded for the General this time because he was the one who knew more about this than the General. "Secretary Levenhagen, we couldn't move in and bomb the, as you say, shit out of the base until the missiles reached their destination, sir. We have to destroy the missiles as well as the submarines in one action. We're going to be confronted by world opinion, with everyone living in the Middle East trying to reconstruct the havoc from the recent war. We have to be concerned over reaction from our Arab allies. I don't think Saudi Arabia would think very highly of us if we go in Iran in force, and blow parts of the country apart without absolute proof of what we say is there, is the truth. We'll be involving Russia in this mess, and I wouldn't want the damn Russians going against us and..."

"Going against us on this one! For the love of the Christ Child, it's because of their god damn lack of security that these fucki... please excuse me ladies, these damn nuclear missiles are heading for Iran in the first place, General White Sir." Secretary Levenhagen stormed as he assumed a threatening pose against the CIA Director who smiled it off.

"Quite right, but we have to proceed as if we're walking on eggs. Too many nations are dependent on the Middle East for oil. We could come out bloody if we react to carelessly."

"Come out bloody?" Secretary Levenhagen responded as he held the back of his chair and then added. "Come out bloody you say General! Why don't you tell that to the poor souls who lost loved ones on that damn plane bombed out of the air over Scotland? Or the other souls who lost their lives in the TWA crash I think was a bombing? How many more of our civilians are going to be bombed out of the air before we go after the throats of the lousy bastards killing our children and parents? For Christ sake General, Director, I remember when there was a time in this country when we were considered the backbone of the world, the sleeping giant. Now we became the underbelly of the same beast. The Jews have it down pat. Kill our children, and you and your country will pay dearly for your actions. All we do is give news coverage, and watch parents and loved ones crying on the tube over their children blown away all over the earth, sir.

"Dammit to hell General White, Mr. President! It's time we make these sonofabitches pay for daring to attack our children. I saw Presidents in action in my past, FDR, Eisenhower, Kennedy and yes, especially Nixon, Reagan and Bush. Bush was tagged as RamBush for the action he employed against Iraq. When these Presidents were in power, no one dared to mess around with us. For too many years now we had weak Presidents and leaders afraid, or too damn passive to go after the damn throats of the terrorists. Look at what they done to us in the States, we force our people to stand in lines for up to two hours waiting to board overseas flights.

"We made the price of flying on our civilian carriers double, and some say it'll go up next year, because some nuts killed our children. We subject our civilians to time consuming and terribly embarrassing searches of their bodies and luggage, before we allow them to board the aircraft. We treat everyone who lives or visits the United States as criminals for what I ask you? We allowed the damn terrorists to win their rotten little game of death, poison and destruction. If a nut decides to get a bomb on board a civilian aircraft, the nut will do it no matter what we do to try and stop them. So all we done is punish the civilians of our country while the damn animals that kill our women and children, live life of kings in both Libya and Iran. No, it's time we do something about this backasswards situation, and we do it right dammit.

"It's time we punish the killers of our children, and eat their guts instead of punishing the ones who lost their children in a terrorist attack against our country dammit. Any country that doesn't go along with this way of thinking, should be forced out and shunned by the other civilized countries of the earth. It's time we not only punish the damn criminals, but punish the countries sending these damn jackals out to do the killing of the innocent, or punish any country giving safe haven to any of these damn international criminals and murderers.

"Public opinion be damned to hell and back. Where was public opinion when our women and children were bombed out of the sky, their bodies burned beyond recognition. What the hell type of nuts are we putting up with? No wonder the world's in the state it's in Mr. President. What kind of people would kill innocent women and children in the name of their God? Muhammad must be rolling over in his grave to know these animals killed women and children in His name. God, I'd be afraid Muhammad would come down from Heaven and strike me dead, because I took an innocent life in His honored name. God, to kill anyone in the name of religion goes against the teaching of that religion for God's sake. In the Qur'an, Muhammad preaches it's terrible to take a life, murder appalled Muhammad to no ends and He states so in his Writings.

"To believe Muhammad would open the Gates of Paradise and offer these murderers a bushel basked full of virgins to please their lust to murderers is ludicrous, ludicrous to believe. What a world we must live in when nuts run free to attack women and children of any nation. Then the terrorists are given a hero's welcome in the host country, and we sit on our damn thumbs while watching them on TV dancing in the streets, and shooting their guns in the air and burning our great flag as if they won a victory over us, dammit. What world leaders would applaud these animalistic actions? How would they feel if we blew their women and children out of the air, or killed their children in the streets of their countries as if they were shit? I say we load our missiles and level these radical countries that send these lowlifes out to kill. If they hate us, let them hate us for a real reason. Let them stop dealing with us, ignore us. Stay away from us.

"We don't need any of them, and they don't need us. The bastards think nothing of taking money we offer them, yet they try and eat our hands off up to the elbow while taking the damn money from us. No more I say. If you kill our women and children, you have to pay with your damn life. There'll be no Paradise for killers of our women and children, only the fires of hell. Any country that doesn't join on the search for these animals should be sanctioned. We should turn our backs on them! It's time we declare a real war on terrorism, whether the terrorist be bombers or drug runners, they're no better than the damn terrorists, either way, they're killing our children. I'm tired of seeing children loaded in body bags and then being dumped in ambulances as if they were slabs of meat!" The secretary stabbed the desk with his finger.

The President allowed his Secretary to vent his anger. He was only guilty of speaking the words no one else attending the meeting dared to speak on their own. The President finally offered to try and calm his secretary. "Jerry, I hope you weren't referring to me when you spoke of the weak ass Presidents, mister?" the President tried to make a little light of the conversations.

"No sir, you're the only one who has the balls he was born with…"

"Jerry, I must insist you try and keep a civil tongue in your mouth. Or I'll stop you right here, sir." The President warned, "in case you might have forgotten, I have a number of women attending this meeting, and I don't think they enjoy your colorful interpretation of current affairs presently facing our nation sir. If you wish to keep speaking to this assembly, I want you to clean up your act a little better or sit down. I never seen you react this way before sir."

The Secretary's face turned red as he looked at the Vice President, and then to Ms. Hernandez as he apologized. "I'm sorry ladies, but I feel what I'm saying had to be said though. I'm sorry if I might have insulted you when I dumped on the other Presidents, ladies. I was speaking of our past Presidents only. They were the ones guilty of allowing the United States to become the unfeared giant. We're the last super power on the face of the earth, and we're being stepped on by shit countries that would be no more than a fart in war against us. Look at what we did to Iraq under the Command of President George H. Bush. But the other countries forgot what power we control, and they no longer fear to come to our country and burn our women and children.

"Who blames them when we change crimes and give them romantic names such as pedophile, and home invasions, instead of calling them what they are, child molesters and burglars? I'm waiting for the day to come when we make murder, self defense. We removed disgust from the crime, the fear of retribution and threat of devastation to commit an act of terrorism against our country. For Christ sake, we should elevate terrorism as an act of war on the attacked nation, and every nation should side with that attacked nation, and go after the attackers. It's time to act."

"My God Jerry, you sound like war dogs of our military." Manning complained at him.

"I resent that remark buster, especially coming from you. I'm offering what I feel in my heart is right, Mr. Manning. These bastards have no fear of us, and until we make examples of the bastards and their countries, they'll never fear us. We have allowed these little shits to attack our bases in Saudi Arabia and Lebanon, and do jack squat about the deaths they caused to our people, our soldiers. Is it any wonder these shitheads planted bombs in Centennial Park at the Olympics a few years back? It was a show to prove to us they could do it, no matter how many security personnel we engage to try and protect our civilians. Our law enforcement agencies done a super human effort, but the bastards had to prove they could kill Americans anytime they chose. We have to hit the terrorists and their damn bases, their training centers with evil intent."

"Are you suggesting we resort to using nuclear weapons on the terrorist countries, Jerry?"

"No sir, not at all Mr. President. Conventional bombs yes, and many of them at that, sir. If I had my choice over the matter Mr. President Sir. I'd rather lose my son on the field of battle where he stood an equal chance against the lousy bastards, allowing him to fight for our women and children. I'd rather this than have him blown out of the sky where he was absolutely powerless to defend himself, or do anything about it."

"What about Israel and the other countries destroyed in that war?" Vice President Hirshfield asked, deeply concerned with that nation because she was Jewish.

"Israel's starting to breathe again and getting back on her feet Ma'am. Iraq, who we were relying on as a sort of buffer state, a sort of nuisance in the side of Iran to keep that Persian country occupied militarily, is down and out for the count. I don't think Iraq will ever have the ability to rebuild her nation into a world force to be feared again. No country's willing to help Iraq. Iraq's out of the equation, and this enabled Iran to come out as one of the more powerful nations in the Middle East. Outside of Saudi Arabia where we're rebuilding the crippled nation. Christ sake Mr. President, I wish Iran would put her energies into making herself a much more understanding nation, instead of a military might in the destroyed Middle East. I thought she was starting to come out of the stone ages when she joined forces against Iraq and Libya, sir."

"What's the state of the rest of the Middle East? So many of the Arab nations were ripped apart in that Middle East War." President Cole asked his Secretary of Defense, and then added. "It's been so long since the last time I even thought about this region of the world, what with all the problems going down in Asia and Russia of late."

"Libya's getting together pretty well, Mr. President. I was sorry about the assassination of Qaddafi though, that one really hurt, and it served to destabilize that entire region." Director Raincloud added as he picked up on the conversation from Secretary Levenhagen as he went on with his words to the American Leader. "I'm sorry to inform you Mr. President, lately we've been picking up some rather disturbing information suggesting the new Libyan party is starting to screw around with constructing chemical weapons. We've been able to amass intelligence about this situation, dictating the Libyans have activated two or their chemical processing plants again. The twin plants were constructed in secluded areas of their vast desert, Mr. President."

"Dammit!" The President vented angrily as he shifted his weight, distressed over the information he just heard offered by his Defense Secretary over the condition of Libya.

"Then we should settle their hash at the same exact time when we go after the god damn Iranian submarines and missiles, Mr. President Sir." The Secretary of Defense offered in an angry tone to the American Leader.

The President gave a slight chuckle as he replied to his rather upset Defense Secretary. "You seem quite certain that we're planning to go after the Iranians this time, Jerry."

"Knowing you like I do Mr. President. We're surely going to do something about this latest developing threat, and we're going to do it real soon at that sir." The Secretary replied.

"You're quite right in this case that we're planning to go after the damn Iranian submarines and nuclear tipped missiles, and we might also do something about those two god damn chemical weapon plants in Libya while we're at it at the same time. I must be honest with everyone attending this meeting though. I'm getting real sick and tired of waiting until the situation's out of hand before we act on them. This time we're going to jump the gun and hit before being hit by anyone threatening the peace of the world. We're not going to do anything until we hear from Director Raincloud's operative in Russia. Right now, time is on our side, and I'm going to use every second before I act. I want to be positive the Iranians have the damn Russian missiles in their possession, and where they're storing them before we go active against the damn things."

The upset President turned to General White and voiced at his military officer. "General White, I'm ordering you to activate your entire Rapid Response Force, sir. I'm putting the soldiers on full alert, General. You better get the troopers ready to go in action at a moment's notice, General White. We're going to act on this Iranian and Russian missile mess rapidly developing on us. Pull in the troops from the countries who offer to supply their elite soldiers for this specialized unit. What you need General; you'll have at your disposal upon request, sir. I won't be holding anything in reserve this time I assure you sir. Planes, armor, ships, whatever the hell you need sir, and you'll have it at your disposal for this possible action, General White.

"I want this damn situation ended as quickly as possible with as little loss of life as possible to us or any other nation working with our troops who are involved with this latest damn situation, sir. General White, I'll expect daily reports from both you and Director Raincloud on his operative working inside Russia as it progresses. The second we discover where these damn missiles are located in Iran, we'll jump off do it sir that quick. Okay people, let's get the gears in motion, I'll instruct Ambassador Walters to set up a special meeting of the Security Council with the United Nations. I want everyone on my side before anyone steps off on this possible upcoming operation. I don't like crossing swords with Iran, because it's going to cause some serious problems between us and Saudi Arabia and a few of the other Arab nations we once classified as our allies in the Middle East and Northern Africa."

The upset President took a quick breath for himself and then he went on with his orders to his military officer. "General White, you know what you have to do on this one. So get it done for me General. Director Raincloud, I want up to date intelligence reports on this mess as they come in by err... let me see, today's Monday, by Wednesday morning at the very latest, sir. I'll scheduled the requested meeting with the Security Council on Friday, November 8th, in the a.m., and I want to be perfectly clear on everything I'm talking about at this requested meeting. If anyone asks me a question and I don't know the answer to it, you'll pay dearly for my embarrassment with what you have hanging between your legs, mister. Is this understood Director Raincloud Sir?" the President stopped speaking and he stared at his CIA Director.

Director Raincloud smiled as he nodded slightly, knowing the President was only kidding by threatening him if he got stumped at the Security Meeting he'd request. "Mr. President, I'd rather activate an sleeper operative stationed inside Iran, sir."

"Good Director, Iran it is then so let's get down to business and get things hoping over this latest situation gentlemen, time is of the importance on this operation." The President said as he returned Director Raincloud's smile with one of his own, and then he turned to the women attending the meeting to make certain he included them in his words.

The President cringed when he used gentlemen when addressing his people attending the meeting moments before. He stood and suddenly clapped his hands loudly together in the same motion. Then everyone attending the meeting stood and snapped to attention, while waiting for the President to leave the Oval Office, so they could set out on their orders they just received from the Commander in Chief.

The meeting broke up at the same moment the President left the office; the others from the meeting went in action.

CHAPTER FIVE

THE CIA OPERATIVE KNOWN AS SAND STAR

Right in the very heart of Iran's new capital city of Kerman, the American sleeper operative stayed in a two room dilapidated flat. He was installed in Iran four years ago and went into deep sleep, waiting orders to activate. Bdellah, listening to the ordered channel at the prescribed time every day, ever since first entering Iran. He froze when he heard the song that activated him being played. He instantly took a pad and pencil, and took down every forth word of the first song, every third word of the second song, and ever fifth word of the third song, and kept bouncing back to the words of each song until he was able to construct his orders.

The suddenly excited operative ignored the sweat beading up on his forehead as he worked on deciphering the code. Bdellah's blood ran cold when he read the Iranians were thought to be in possession of twelve nuclear tipped missiles, and he was being ordered to make his way over to the Iranian city of Bander Beheshi, where it was rumored the Iranian government had its Naval Fleet and submarines stationed. As he worked the message out, he read it again, memorized it, and then snapped the sheet of flash paper between his fingers. In a flash of flames, the paper instantly ignited and disappeared to nothing, leaving no detectable sign of the code message.

Bdellah, a twenty seven year old Arab man, born in Saudi Arabia and was enlisted in the CIA at the age of fifteen. He worked for the United States government, and was instrumental in locating the scud missiles hidden in Iraq during Desert Storm War. He was a cold blooded killer and not afraid of anything, he hated Arabs against the Arab race coming out of the dark ages. He was tall, slim, and strong, and had no one in his family alive. They had been killed by a scud missile fired at Saudi Arabia by the madman once running the nation of Iraq. The operative was a long time American sleeper agent, who once worked for the department of records of Iran, and he was involved with a very beautiful young Iranian woman of twenty three years of age, and was disgruntled with the new government suddenly running the nation of Iran.

When the report was understood and destroyed, he packed, once swiping at the sweat running in his eyes in the non air-conditioned small room with one window to allow fresh air in. Bdellah reached under the lice infected bed and pulled a loose board up and removed the 9 mm Colt pistol with extra clips, and a stack of hundred dollar American bills. The agent had ten thousand American dollars hidden in his room, and twenty five thousand dollars more hidden in a metal case buried in the desert. It was more than enough money for him to be able to buy himself out of most trouble he might accidently stumble into, even if he was arrested for being a spy.

The American operative quickly finished packing, and then he picked up the phone and called his workplace. His supervisor answered, and he made his voice sound extremely upset as he explained his mother had just died and he had to see to her burial. His supervisor was sympathetic and gave him all the time he needed to take care of the final arrangements for his mother. One thing Arab nations well understood, the family came first.

As he spoke on the phone his girlfriend entered the room, the door was never locked. She saw him on the phone and stripped and then sat down on the edge of the bed and she wiggled between his arm and lap, and then began to play with his manhood. When it was hard, she drew it in her mouth, as he continued to speak on the phone. As she played with him he stuttered, and Fatima chuckled as she made it hard for him to speak to whoever he was talking to. She stopped playing with him when she heard him say his mother was his life, and her death was deeply upsetting. She knew he had no family alive and he was lying to someone over the phone. Fatima stroked him as she listened to the rest of his conversation. When he was done she asked him, "what was that all about, your mother's no longer alive, is she Bdellah? Who were you lying to and why?"

He ignore her question as he replied in a snap. "I have to leave the country for a few days."

"I don't understand, why are you leaving Iran, Bdellah?" She asked him with concern.

"Business." He snapped back at her without even looking at her lovely face.

"Bdellah, what type of business are you speaking about my love? Why are you being so secretive with me all of a sudden? What are you up to?"

"None of your business Fatima, I have things I must look after that don't concern you."

Fatima surveyed the room and she immediately spotted the pistol sticking out from under one of his undershirts on the table. "Is that a gun? Bdellah, what are you doing with a gun?"

"Who are you? Why are you asking me so many questions? I don't owe you any explanations unless you work for the police, woman." He shoved her off his lap, growing angrier at her.

Fatima sprang up to her feet, her training came in play as she moved with the swiftness of a predator, and made a move for the weapon, ignoring her nakedness and vulnerability it created.

The American operative saw what she was up to and made it to the gun first. He placed Fatima in a breath robbing headlock and squeezed with all his might until her lips began to turn blue and she stopped struggling so much, and then he roared at her. "Who the hell are you, bitch?"

Fatima struggled to breathe and speak while still locked in Bdellah's grasp. "Captain Fatima Rahimi of the Iranian Special Security Police. I was ordered to report anything you do out of the ordinary to my superiors for immediate action by them."

"And you believe you found something out of the ordinary about me to report to your god cursed headquarters, bitch?

Now you're my enemy, witch of the desert sands!" Bdellah snarled as he controlled his anger for allowing this pretty woman to outflank him so easily like she done.

"Yes Bdellah! You're acting very suspiciously." She offered between deep gasps.

"Like how am I acting suspiciously to you, bitch of the hot desert sand?" he demanded.

Fatima did not answer until Bdellah tightened his choke hold on her neck even more now, and she almost blacked out from the pain and lack of air to her body. "Like what!" He repeated in a harsh tone, ignoring her suffering.

"Bdellah, you were reported by one of your workers to my superiors as acting suspiciously of late. I was ordered to keep you under surveillance until I was certain of your intentions."

"For what reason bitch?"Again he tightened his choke hold on Fatima's neck.

Fatima coughed while pulling on his forearm that crossed over her windpipe, and answered weakly. "The man felt you might be an operative for a foreign government, Bdellah."

"Me! Working for another government! Which one bitch?" he laughed sarcastically.

"The report stated you might be working for Saudi Arabia, or the American government."

"And you stupid people believed this shit as the truth, am I not right Fatima?" he growled angrily, stunned he had been so easily discovered by her, and he hadn't been aware of it.

"Yes. In my first report I suggested you be arrested and interrogated, there might be something to the report filed against you, and..." She allowed her words trail off.

"And what?" he again tightened his grasp on her again. "And what!" he bellowed in her ear.

Fatima pulled on the forearm crossing her neck as she struggled for air. "That you should be put to death." Fatima replied in a strained voice as she coughed when he relaxed pressure.

"You people are so fooking screwed up Fatima. You were going to put me to fooking death just because some bastard said I might be a spy for another god damn government? It's so damn easy to eliminate someone you might not like or want to work with in this miserable country. What the hell's wrong with you people anyway, dammit?" he hissed as he tightened his grasp on her neck and held the pressure until Fatima's taught body slowly went limp.

Fatima did not go out so easy though, she clawed at his eyes, trying to drive her thumb in them. Failing this attempt, she next tried to get a hand down between his legs to rip at his manhood, when this also failed, her attack next focused on his throat. She could not get at it because of his weight, so she drove her fingernails deep into his forearm, trying to find a vein or artery to cut. She even tried to bite through his arm, nothing changed the outcome of her desperate struggle, she was going to die at the hands of her once lover.

He held her throat until her struggling stopped completely, and she actually pissed herself. He then let go and shoved her head down to the floor. He then placed his knee in the fold of her neck, putting his full weight down on it until he heard a sickening crack, and Fatima's body violently jerked once. After that, he knew she was dead and he leaned back and stared down at the dead, stunning beauty. He fondled her breast one last time before wrapping her body in plastic. He then rolled her under the bed and checked her clothes for anything that might be useful to him. Rummaging through them he found Fatima's secret police ID without a photo, and he stuffed it in his pocket just in case he might need it later on during his activation time. He then balled up her clothes and shoved them under the bed with her body.

The room smelled bad, so he felt another stink would not be detected so easily, and to make sure this was a fact he actually took a crap in a bowl and left it resting out in the sun from the window. All his training was in gear and he checked his room to make sure he was not leaving anything behind that would help identify him, or he might need during his operation. Then he locked the door to the flat and left. He was certain no one would bother his room for at least a week, until the smell got so bad someone would be forced to check it. He rushed down the stairs and out to the street and jumped in his car, he gunned the engine and quickly drove off.

He traveled until he noticed a car parked off the side of the road, and the driver was out of it and he was obviously enjoying the sunset. Bdellah stopped and went over to the young male driver as if looking for directions. When he was close enough to his target, he struck out with the palm of his hand, catching his victim across the throat, snapping his larynx and killing the man instantly. He grabbed the driver before he fell down to the floor and placed him inside the driver's seat of his car. He poured gasoline on the inside, especially over the face and hands of his victim, and then he started the car and aimed it directly at a stone wall. The car plowed head on into the wall, turning the vehicle into a blazing inferno as it struck the wall.

The operative made like he stopped at the accident and he was desperately trying to get at the injured driver of the burning car, as a number of other people came out of their homes to see the accident. A police officer drove up and actually pulled him away from the flaming car. The officer whispered he did everything he could possible do to try and save the life of the driver of the vehicle. Bdellah allowed the officer to walk him over to his victim's car, and smiled as he started the car and then drove off.

A number of fire trucks arrived, but the body was burned beyond recognition and Bdellah knew the government would believe it was his body that was burned to death in the crash. He understood the special police would write it up that he was killed while trying to escape his arrest and their investigation of the wanted criminal that was surely going to end now.

With a deep sigh of relief he drove to the southern coast of Iran as he fought to control his hands. The operative was heading for his other safe house to receive further orders from his controller. It took him seven hours to reach the safe house. While he drove, he cursed for being so foolish as to get involved with a woman. He could not understand how he was so sound asleep at the switch to have overlooked the possibility Fatima was working for the Iranian secret police, and came so close to uncovering him as a sleeper agent for the United States.

The sleeper agent activated from his slumber, he parked his car three blocks away from the safe house, and walked to it. After waiting an hour, he was certain no one was watching the building or his actions, and he entered using his key. He went over to the radio, keyed it to the frequency then sent his code numbers out, and immediately received the message informing him to locate the missiles and destination. He was to report the information to his contact.

Once he finished listening to the report he converted the scrambled numbers and letters into a coherent text, Bdellah completely destroyed the radio, changing the frequency before he crushed it underfoot. He ate the bug infested bread he hid with the radio while he conceived a plan of action. He knew which roads the fuel tanker trucks would travel, and it was not hard for him to figure out where to intercept and then follow the rigs to their final destination. He decided to make his way to Yazd that was the first Iranian town the trucks would pass, once they came out of the vast Dashte Kavir desert. The operative knew the drivers would be looking for water and food by the time they crossed the barren landscape of the vast desert.

He finished eating the bread and then left the safe house and crossed three different streets as he back tracked his path to make certain no one was trailing him. Once he was certain he went undetected, he headed for the stolen car. Driving, he left the main roads and traveled the rough back roads of Iran's interior, skirting round a number of small towns and villages as he headed for the village of Yazd. He knew he was well ahead of the trailer trucks that had last been reported to be just entering Iran when he was on the radio.

AT THE BORDER WHICH SEPARATED IRAN FROM AZERBAIJAN

Russian Admiral Yevgeny Proushinsky was the first to emerge from the car as the again Iranian marked tractor trailers pulled up behind them. He did not like leaving the Ukraine to enter Russia, it was giving him a track easily followed by anyone investigating what was going on, if suspicions were raised. When the vehicles first left Russia and entered Azerbaijan, Admiral Proushinsky decided to forget selling the Iranian more submarines, and he reworked his escape route from Russia in his mind. He knew it would be only a matter of time before someone picked up what he done, and he did not want to be anywhere in Russia when the KGB came searching for him. The changing of Russian markings back to the Iranian ones on the sides of the trucks went without a hitch, before they reached the Azerbaijan, Iranian border. The Russian armor vehicles pulled away from the convoy, and parked on the Russian side of the border as the powerful Russian Admiral and Iranian politician spoke privately.

"Comrade Marzuk, I believe you have something to give to me. I warn you Comrade, none of these trucks will cross the god dom border until I have my money, and it has been counted sir."

Colonel Marzuk raised his hand and a soldier from the Iranian side of the border rushed out the guard house, and headed right for him. "Comrade Admiral Proushinsky, I believe you have some papers that belong to me as well." The Iranian agent put out his hand and wiggled his fingers.

"Yes Comrade Colonel Marzuk, I certainly do, once they're paid for that is you will have them." Admiral Proushinsky reached in his breast pocket and removed a thick envelope, and handed it over to him and offered. "You may check the contents once I have my money."

Colonel Marzuk took the suitcases from the Iranian soldier and handed them to the Russian. "Comrade Admiral, here is your fifty million dollars. It'll take you days to count it, and I'm afraid we'll bring attention to ourselves if we remain on the border for that long a time."

"I assure you, you worry needlessly Comrade Colonel Marzuk. Captain Zhitarenko, front and center!" The Admiral waited for the Captain to dismount his machine, and then he rushed to his side. "Captain Zhitarenko, you have the money counting machine set up?"

"Yes Admiral Proushinsky it is ready sir." The Captain replied proudly to his Commander.

"Good, count this god dom money and let me know how much is there, Captain. How long do you think it'll take for your god dom machines to count the money, Captain?"

"Admiral Proushinsky, it was reported the machine is capable of counting one million dollars every two minutes. To count fifty million dollars will take an hour and forty minutes."

"There you have it Comrade Colonel Marzuk. You see, it'll take us an hour and a half to count all this god dom money. That should be enough time for your fooking trucks to pass the Russian inspection, and cross over to your own country. As you can see for yourself, with patience, everything works out properly for the both of us. Captain Zhitarenko begin counting and you'll try and make more speed from the god dom machine. Take possession of the two suitcases Captain. Comrade Colonel Marzuk, one of your trucks will be allowed to cross the border every time the Captain reports the machine has counted four and a half million dollars in that way we both get what we have paid for between us Comrade."

Iranian Colonel Muhsin Abu Marzuk paid little attention to the Russian Admiral's words as he searched the other side of the border for his convoy sent by his President to escort his tanker trucks down to the port city of Bander Beheshi. He issued orders before entering the nation of Azerbaijan no sign of the escort should be seen by the Russian soldiers until the last tractor trailer crossed the border into Iran. Colonel Marzuk was not a stupid man, and he knew there was no hope of the Russian coming through with an offer to sell him the advanced submarines with a full complement of nuclear missiles on board them. He realized the Russian Admiral was not going to report back to his base, he noticed the two other suitcases containing money in his trunk. He saw them when the Russian removed papers for the guards, when they left the Ukraine.

Colonel Marzuk's attention was pulled away from the Iranian border to the Russian side when the Captain came from the vehicle and gave the Admiral a nod. He gave the same signal to the guard, and ordered the Iranian to start his engine. The fence was raised and the first rig crossed.

"Ahhh... you see Comrade Colonel Marzuk. It's as I had informed you, that was the first four and a half million dollars counted, and your first truck was allowed to leave my world safely."

"Yes Comrade Admiral, it's a wonderful thing when trusting allies work so well together against a common enemy, and make both nations great at the same time. When can we work out the remaining details for me to buy the ten Delta IV submarines and missiles from you, Admiral Proushinsky Sir?" Colonel Marzuk asked, knowing he was wasting the Admiral and his time.

"I'll work out the final details on that sale when I get back to my Naval Base Comrade Colonel. I believe we can conclude the transaction within a week's time, providing your government comes up with the amount of money I demanded for my submarines."

"Do not worry about it Admiral Proushinsky, the money will be available when we're assured the submarines are ready for transfer to my country. I'll give you the amount we have agreed on once we closed the deal. This arrangement has gone through without any problems." Colonel Marzuk smiled, wondering how long it would take before the foolish Admiral discovered the cash he gave him was counterfeit. He knew the money would not be discovered until the Admiral spent quantities of the counterfeit bills. He grunted as he thought of the face the Russian would display, when he was informed his wealth was not worth the paper it was printed on.

When Colonel Marzuk was given the counterfeit money from his government official and carefully examined it, he was amazed at the fine craftsmanship. He was pleased, because he was doing a service for his country, while also weakening the United States at the same time. He was undermining their economy, by flooding the world market with a flood of counterfeit American cash. Colonel Marzuk grinned no matter what the United States did to try and secure its money and make it impossible to counterfeit, his country would do what was necessary to make their copies perfect, and release the money in poorer countries that did not check the bills closely.

It did not matter to Colonel Marzuk, a Colonel in the Iranian security guard was destroying the lesser countries by flooding them with the bogus American cash. His driving force was to harm the United States in any fashion he could, and if that meant smaller countries had to be sacrificed then so be it. Nothing mattered to him but his country and religion, and until Iran could wipe the other religions from the face of the earth, his work would not be concluded.

The counting of the American cash went much quicker than first expected, and in less than an hour's worth of time, the last tractor trailer truck finally crossed over the border back into Iran. Colonel Marzuk waited and when the last truck moved out, he shook hands with Admiral Proushinsky and then he headed for the border to link up with the Iranian truck convoy.

The Russian Admiral watched as the Iranian was given a car, then drove to the front of the convoy. Admiral Proushinsky shrugged, glad to be rid of the Iranian Agent, whose stink made his stomach turn. As the Russian headed for his car, he heard other trucks start. He saw the trucks following the civilian car, but then saw a cloud of dust rising over a wadi and stared. He watched with rage, as military trucks moved out and quickly encircled the convoy of Iranian trucks.

At first, the Russian Admiral was worried their transaction had been discovered by his government, and the military was present to capture the rigs and Colonel Marzuk as he entered his country. But when he noticed the military trucks take positions around the rigs, he knew the Iranian Agent had obviously ordered the military to escort his trailers to their home port.

The fuming Russian Admiral raised his hand in rage as he cursed the Iranian Colonel, and then his country for betraying him. He knew every American satellite board just lit up, warning them of the Iranian trucks moving away from the Iranian, Azerbaijan border. His body shook, because he knew he had no other option but to flee Russia as soon as possible now. He cursed again, knowing he would not have time to pick up his lovely young mistress. He stormed around in a circle, trying to walk off some of his anger as he quickly formulated a new plan in his mind.

Admiral Proushinsky gave a quick thought to his government, and their reaction to the Iranian machines driving so close to the border. There must be Russian aircraft and armor already dispatched and on their way for the border at breakneck speed, as he stood like a fool cursing the Iranians. As if to answer his thoughts, a Russian Lieutenant suddenly rushed out from the command post. He was out of breath as the Lieutenant saluted the Admiral; he immediately reported a battalion of tanks and armor vehicles were heading for the border as they spoke.

The machines were dispatched from KGB HQ. The Lieutenant further told him he informed Command of the Admiral's presence at the border, and HQ questioned why he was at the border. He said HQ turned Command of the border guards over to him until the battalion arrived. The officer failed to inform the Admiral that he had been instructed to place the Admiral under arrest if he tried to leave the area before the other troops reached the border, and the Lieutenant was further ordered to use deadly force if necessary to stop the Admiral from leaving the area.

"Errr... Lieutenant, I'll take Command of the border post and I'll set up my armor and have them secure the border at the same time." He pointed to the armor parked by his car and then added to his orders. "I'll Command from that position there until the battalion arrives. You're to man the border to move traffic along. You and your troops will take positions defending the border; I have reason to believe the Iranian dogs will be back, and in force. When the battalion arrives, I'll have their soldiers relieve your soldiers, Lieutenant. You have done very well to report to HQ, Lieutenant." The Admiral moaned, as he searched for any information.

The Lieutenant smartly saluted the Naval Officer as he remarked in an excited voice. "Admiral Proushinsky Sir, it was not I who contacted HQ, but it was the other way around. HQ ordered me to secure the border as you have just done sir. I informed HQ an Admiral was visiting the border, and they were rather interested in why you were over here sir. It was then Command gave you the power of Command over the border and us border guards, sir."

"That was a very wise decision on your part, Lieutenant. Anyway, I just issued you a number of new orders, so carry them out as received Lieutenant." Admiral Proushinsky ordered with a snap in his voice as he watched the soldier rushed over to his border troops, barking orders and the guards hurried to their new positions. Admiral Proushinsky moved over to his armor, and instructed the Captain to move his vehicles into a defensive circle around his vehicle. He then removed the cash from the machine, and placed it in the trunk of his car. Once the armor was moved, he moved his car behind the armor until it was well hidden from sight.

The worried young KGB Lieutenant watched intensely until he was positive Admiral Proushinsky was going to stay put as he was ordered. Then he turned to the border and prepared to defend it from any possible invasion by the Iranians.

When Admiral Proushinsky was certain the border guards had their full attention trained on Iran, he made his move to escape from the border area. He ordered the Captain to standby until he returned, and he started the car and crawled away. Once he was sure he was far enough away from the border, he put the gas to the engine and within seconds, he was traveling eighty miles an hour heading for Turkey. If he was taken prisoner, he would seek political asylum after hiding the cash in the desert, and give valuable information to the hated Americans in return for his freedom and safety. He stayed well off the main roads for fear of running into the battalion.

MARATHON KEY, FLORIDA.
NOVEMBER 4th, 1998.
LIEUTENANT ROBERT WALKER'S
HOME ON TINGLER ISLAND

Lieutenant Walker was the first to wake on this day. He strolled his property, kicking a few sleeping soldiers in their leg to make sure they were still alive and breathing. His parties were becoming well known throughout all the Islands of the Keys, and everyone tried to get invited when word was released of another pending party at his place.

The Mutt, (Lieutenant Frank Hall) staggered out of the Lieutenant's house while rubbing his eyes, and then shielding them from the glaring sun. He spotted Walker standing by the dock and headed right for him as he moaned and in a slurred voice. "Hey Road Kill, that was some friggin party we had last night, man. Them damn Russian babes have unstoppable stinking motors man. I thought they were going to out fuck the entire group on us buddy."

"In case you hadn't noticed it my friend, they did out screw us all. Christ, they even worked over some of the chicks from the outfit. I didn't think they were going to stop until everyone get their share, or they were dead. Where the hell are the two cops at man?" he asked as he continued to search for the two police officers who did all the cooking for their party.

"I saw the two dudes leave the party around four in the morning, Walker. I think they had to report to work fur today, man." The Mutt offered as he belched, and then farted and laughed.

"Who the fuck is that man?" Someone moaned from behind the two men talking.

"Mutt." Lieutenant Frank Hall offered to the unseen soldier who just bitched at him.

"I shoulda known it'd be you shitting in your god damn pants, dog man." Mother, Sergeant Richard Flanagan grumbled as he crawled out from under a palm tree. He was covered from head to toe with dried leaves and coral gravel. He was bleeding from some minor wounds the gravel caused by digging in his exposed skin. Mother Flanagan got his tag name of Mother, because he was the one in charge of any FnGs sent to their outfit, and he mothered them along until they knew what they were doing in the Unit. FnG was grunt slang for Fucking new Guys.

"Didja get any loving from the stinking Ruskie babes last night, Mother?" the Mutt asked as he scratched his balls by shoving his hand down the front of his shorts, the only thing he was wearing, and also centered his dick while he was at it.

"Yeah, I popped three times last night, once in the mouth, twice between someone's legs."

"You don't know who you boffed last night, you asshole?" the grinning Mutt laughed as he stared at Mother Flanagan while waiting for his reply.

"No, but I'm sure as hell it was one of the stinking Russian babes I was doing the dirty with, Mutt. In fact I'm positive of it man. I remember because she was bitching at my ass in her Russian garble. I guess I wasn't doing it right for her man." He offered to the man.

"Christ man I hope so, I'd hate like hell to wake up and find you were corn hogging me last night because you were too fucked up to know what you were doing and who you were doing it with man. That's real scary man." The Mutt fired at the grinning Mother Flanagan.

"You wish prick face, I wouldn't fuck your ass with Walker's dick, scummer." Mother groaned as he looked for coffee, he smelled it cooking, but didn't see where it was being brewed.

The three soldiers laughed as Walker said. "Mother, Ramirez and Fun Bags are brewing up a shitload of lifer's juice (coffee) by the damn gallon, man. We gotta get some of these walking dead back on their stinking feet before they up and friggin die on us for fuck sake."

"I agree with ya there man. Some of these stinking guys look like they're death warmed over already." Mother replied with a smirk as he looked at some of the other soldiers, and some civilians also were lying helter skelter, while sleeping on the ground and in chairs.

Sergeant Dorothy Ramirez walked over to the three soldiers and offered them some coffee. Each took a cup and Ramirez joined them.

"Where's the stinking Russian bitches at baby?" Walker asked his girlfriend.

Ramirez laughed as she replied. "I think they're still looking for a warm body to screw. They joined the group last night, I had trouble keeping up with them myself you know."

"Where the hell's Barb at Raz?" the Mutt asked her as he downed his coffee.

"The last time I saw her, she was with one of the Russian girls, they were working over CoCo-G. Ha, they had the poor slob wiggling all over the place like he had a hot rod shoved up his backside, Mutt." Ramirez laughed as she poured each soldier another cup of coffee.

"Did anyone think to name the stinking Russian chicks last night afta the party ended? That's usually when we brand any new grunts to the outfit with their tag names, man." Lieutenant Walker asked softly because he was suffering from the mother of all headaches, and he was trying his best not to move his head too much to try and avoid more pain lurking just under the surface. Everyone looked at each other and then shook their heads no.

"That's great, once we wake these pricks, we'll gather everyone and go fishing through names until we find the ones that'd best suit the new chicks. I want them tagged so they feel they belong even though I don't trust'em as far as I can throw then." He offered as he blinked the pain away.

"What about McNip? Are we gonna allow that name to stick to his ass?" the Mutt moaned.

"What? Who? Who the hell's McNip for crap sake? I don't remember any new stinking cherry showing up yesterday, dammit." Walker complained as he placed his hands on either side of his pounding head and squeezed, trying to stop his head from pounding so badly on him.

"He's the Jap FnG who joined up with us yesterday man?" Mother Flanagan laughed.

"Christ sake, I still don't remember anyone joining up with us yesterday, Mother. Shit, I think I'm drinking too much lately man. I'm beginning to forget things all of a sudden Homes."

"Don't worry about it Walker, I don't think too many of the grunts remember the FnG either, man." The Mutt laughed as he quickly scanned the rest of the scattered group, looking for the new guy to their group. Not seeing him anywhere, the Mutt turned to Buckethead, (Sergeant Vincent Lombardo), lying right on the gravel as if it was a silk blanket. He was with a naked local woman. The Mutt walked up to Bucket and kicked him on the bottom of his foot.

Buckethead stirred then turned over and looked and then bitched at the person who just kicked him. "Hey Homes, can't you see friggin I'm dying of a stinking alcohol overdose, mutherfucker. I need some more stinking sleep or I'm gonna bleed out through my damn eyes."

"My fucking ass bleeds for ya man. C'mon big guy, we gotta get the rest of these damn pukes moving, Homes. Some of them hafta get inside or they're gonna get a bad sunburn man." The Mutt growled as he kicked Buckethead once more on the foot.

"You kick me again scumbag, and I'm gonna fold your ass up until you fit in a fucking envelope, and then I'll mail your can to hell, fucker." Bucket warned the Mutt as he rolled on his back, causing the sleeping girl to complain as he moved away from her.

"Who's the fucking chick, dickhead?" the Mutt asked the big man.

Buckethead sat up. Your mama." He snapped back, he sniffed the air suspiciously and then barked. "Okay man, who's got one going? Who's got the blunt burning?"

Wacko, burning a joint crawled out from under a bush. "I shoulda known that fucking bloodhound of a nose of yours woulda found the slightest hint of grass cooking off man."

The Mutt added, "even though he has a nose like a bloodhound, the rest of his face is okay."

"Gimme a fucking hit from the damn thing will ya man. I need something to get my blood flowing again, Wacker." Buckethead grumbled as he stood and struggled into his pants and then put his mitt of a hand out to take the offered roach from Wacko.

Wacko handed him the joint and Buckethead's hand completely covered Wacko's as the half joint disappeared between his thick fingers.

"I'm next big man. I need a hit from that damn thing myself man." Mother grumbled as he waited for the joint to be past over to him.

"For what?" The Ghost, (Sergeant Walter Casper) asked as he joined the growing group of elite soldiers next. He was known as Casper, the unfriendly ghost, because he was the type of guy who could walk up behind you, and you would not know he was there until it was too late, and you were history to the real world. This uncanny ability won him and his sidekick, the Hunter, (Sergeant Frank Whitcomb), to pull the most dangerous point duty for the outfit during any operation they were out on.

"A fucking joint go round Ghost." Mother announced to the man with a smirk.

"Kinda fucking early for that some of crap, isn't it man?" Casper snapped as he snatched up the joint from Bucket exhaling the smoke. "that's some damn good shit man. It'll put the hump back in a stinking camel's back, man." He moaned as he coughed up a lung.

Mother took the next hit, as the Mutt bitched at him this time. "Hey man, you're fucking up the stinking rotation, Mother. It's puff, puff and give it up, Homes."

Mother Flanagan ignored the Mutt's complaint as he took another pull on the smoke, and then he asked Walker. "Hey man, what are we gonna do today, Homes? Man it's already hot today."

"We're trying to decide on names for the Ruskies." Walker bragged as Meyerhoff joined them.

"Yeah man, them damn Gorkie bitches were good last night, real hot man. I had a couple of helpings of them babes." Mother smirked as Roach, (Private David Burgwald) joined the group.

"I had some of them girls myself." Meyerhoff grinned proudly to the men.

"Along with CoCo and the rest of these pukes standing here baby." The Mutt snapped at her.

"Ohhh... whatsumatta, you getting a little jealous because I humped another swinging dick other that you, buster?" Meyerhoff growled as she made her breasts jingle softly before his face.

The Mutt glared angrily at his girlfriend as he quickly digested her words.

"It's alright for you to plug the Russian girls and have a good time with another girl. But it's not okay for me to do a little exploring on my own with the other men from the outfit? You're getting to be a real stick in the mud lately, dog man." Meyerhoff turned and stormed away.

"Yeah, yeah, keep bitching at me Barb." The Mutt called out after her.

"You better watch your step with that one, buster. Or you're going to end up losing her to someone else if you can't keep her happy with you, stupid." Ramirez warned the Mutt as she took a drag from a second joint going around.

"Lose her shit Raz, I'm gonna ask that girl to marry my ass, baby."

Everyone stopped what they were doing and they all stared at the Mutt, trying to see if he was really serious with what he just told them.

"When are you going to ask her to marry you, dog man?" Ramirez asked excitedly of him.

"Probably sometime later today I guess is as good a time as any to ask her. Mama told me not to put things off." The Mutt announced as he smiled back at the group staring at him.

Everyone shook hands with the Mutt while patting him on the back as Sergeant Ramirez moved over to Walker's side, and then she purred just loud enough for him to hear her words. "Does that give you ideas, mister?"

"Like what honey? I didn't hear nuthin going on here that mean nuthin to my ass, baby." Walker asked Ramirez, not giving into what she wanted to hear from him.

Ramirez did not respond with words. Instead, she punched her dangerous soldier in the guts, catching him off guard as she glared at him. The stunned Lieutenant did everything in his power to try and cover up the damage she just done to his guts as he growled in a squeaky voice at her. "You trying to hurt me baby? Give it up it ain't gonna happen."

"Looks like she already did if you ask me, Homes." The Mutt laughed and he was joined by the other soldiers standing in the group.

They made so much noise standing in the group and talk loudly that soon everyone began to stir and wake. The girls polled together and then they all headed off for the bathroom to wash and brush their teeth. The guys popped beers and then slugged down the brew to wash out the terrible taste of the party. It was a hot morning with the temperature already hovering near eighty, the weather allowed the women to remain topless. Two Russian babes were topless and the third had just a sheet draped over her shoulders. They saw Walker and headed for him and the other soldiers standing with him.

Sergeant Ramirez automatically hugged Sergeant Zarugnaya as she asked her. "How did you sleep last night honey? You girls were fantastic last night you know."

"Wonderful, I like what you call air-condition contraption Raz. Between cool breeze and good sex, I sleep better here ever than in Russia, sister. But in Russia, we no need air-condition thing like you need here. Weather always fine for sleep with window open or closed."

"Yeah, it's great if you want to wake up looking like a stinking snowman, bitch." Poncho Villa, (Sergeant Robert Lopez) laughed as he added to the conversation, his arm still bandaged from the wound he had received when Walker's group went up against the rebel Russian Commander, Colonel Otto Mikhailchenko, and his renegade soldiers in Russia a few months ago.

Taras spun around so she could confront the soldier who made the crude remark against her country. "What you mean remark, mista? You no like Russian women to sleep with, stupid?"

"Hey baby, don't get your tits in a stinking uproar. Poncho didn't mean nuthin by his last remark." Ramirez warned the angry acting female Russian fighter.

"What about the naming thing? Let's get back to naming the stinking Russian babes if we're gonna allow them to linkup with our Unit guys." Someone called out from the growing group of soldiers as more of them gathered around Lieutenant walker and the others.

"Yeah the dude's right, let's get back to naming these Gorkie bitches." The Mutt griped.

Lieutenant Walker held up his hand and everyone stopped bitching so they could hear his words. "Okay you Squids; the Russian babes did what was expected of them all last night to make them more than welcome in our outfit. So I say we draft the lot of them in the group and accept them as fellow and equal soldiers."

Everyone agreed, calling out their yea to the offer of enlisting the Russian women to the specialized group of mixed elite soldiers.

Again, Walker held up his hands and waited for everyone to quiet down and then he stared. "Okay you animals; no one's allowed to join the group unless he or she has a tag name to go with the soldier. I'm opening the offerings, any good name will be considered."

"Have the babes step forward so we can remember what they look like. I was so drunk if I was forced to describe their bodies, I couldn't do it man." A new voice called from the group.

"Good idea." Walker moaned as he turned to the Russian chicks and mumbled at them. "Hey Sergeant Zarugnaya, have your people move over to the fountain so the grunts can see ya. That's the only way we'll be able to pick out names for the lot of ya."

Without saying another word to the milling troops, the beautiful Russian soldier sashayed her way over to the decorative water fountain right in the middle of Walker's backyard, and she was followed by the other two women warriors and one Russian male soldier. When she reached the fountain she placed her hands on her hips, making her breasts point out further. The men cheered her actions as they stared at the three pretty looking Russian women fighters.

"Who's first with a name for this Russian chick?" Walker yelled out to the group.

"Me, pick me, pick me." The Roach bellowed as his paced, and raised his hand over his head.

"What the hell's wrong with you shithead? This ain't no fucking school, you don't hafta raise your stinking hand to be noticed by any of us, stupid. You got a stinking name picked out for one of these foreign hens here then spit it out man." Mother bitched at the other soldier.

"Yeah, I got a name picked out for the short Russian babe with the light brown hair and evil fucking eyes." Roach offered as he pointed at one of the three beautiful female Russian soldiers.

Walker pointed at Corporal Svetlana Dostoyevsky and asked the Roach while trying not to speak much because of his pounding headache. "This one stupid?"

"Yeah man, that's her, I want to dub her Caviar." The Roach cried out to the group.

"Caviar? What the fuck kinda stinking name is Caviar for a fucking soldier, screwball? You pissed off at her for somethin or what Homes?" Mother Flanagan called out as he threw a hand full of gravel at the soldier branded the Roach.

The group broke up as Walker gave the 'fuck you' look at soldier and then bitched at him. "Hey Roach, you better start laying offa the stinking grass a little buster, cause your stinking brains are starting to get fucked up on ya real bad, buddy. I gotta agree with Mother on this one, why the fuck do you wanna tag her little purdy ass with Caviar for, man?”

“What's wrong with you pack of dumb shits, you guys still high or what man? Don't any of you pukes remember that old slogan, people. 'If it smells like fish, it's a fucking dish. If it smells like cologne leave it alone.' Well let me tell ya something man. I had my head down between her legs last night more than a few times, and one thing I can tell ya for certain is, she smelled like fucking fish man. Besides Homes, she sucked my dick as if she were a drowning person, and my balls was the only oxygen left in the whole friggin world, man.”

The soldiers laughed, with some dropping to the ground, because they were laughing so hard.

Walker, wiping a tear from his eye, and then offered to the rest of the soldiers standing with him. “It seems like you people dig the tag Caviar. I agree. I like the way the stinking Roach come up with the stinking name for this one.” He turned to the female Russian soldier and asked her. “Svetlana right?” He had to wait for Taras to translate his words for him. She nodded and smiled back at Walker. “Great, we had a vote and we picked Caviar. Is this name okay with ya? No gripes with it?” Again, he had to wait for Taras to tell her what he said.

Svetlana smiled back at Walker as she shook her head yes to his question. She was well pleased with the pick of the name even though the soldiers didn't explain to her how they came up with the name because they were worried she might not like how they picked it.

Taras informed Walker in heavily accented Russian English. “I told Svetlana how big stupid soldier came up with name he pick out her, she thought it fine name to be what you say, tagged with. I like name me self, what my name go to be American soldier you?"

"Okay Squids, it's time to tag this one bitching at my ass." Walker pointed to Taras.

"I got her tag name all picked out already." The Mutt said more in anger than in jest.

"What's wrong with you Mutt? Your stinking nuts tied up in a friggin knot on ya Homes? You sound pissed off at the little Gorkie hen." The Lieutenant asked his lifelong friend with concern.

"Huh, I screwed that one last night, and all the while I was doing the dirty with her, I felt like she was really pissed off at my ass, and that was when I thought of the name for the Russian bitch, Walker. I wanna dub her Siberia." The Mutt growled almost on an angry voice.

"Oh brother, I gotta hear how you came up with this name buddy. Why the fuck do you wanna brand the Russian chick Siberia for, Mutt?"

"Because she's as cold as a friggin ice cube man. She wouldn't show she was enjoying herself last night for nuthin man. Christ sake, I felt like she was fucking to hurt me and not enjoying herself in the least while we did the deed man. I thought she hated my stinking guts all the while she was doing me and..." the Mutt's words were cut off by the Russian female Sergeant.

"You got right, big stupid American soldier you. Next time you want make love to good Russian woman, you take shower and brush you filthy teeth first, stupid. If Svetlana smelt like fish, you smelt crud like under rock by seashore in Mother Russia, big stupid man you." Taras barked back almost as nastily as he was talking at the Mutt as she glared at him.

"Hey Mutt, she got your number down pat man. I've been meaning to tell ya to take a stinking shower a little more myself, buddy." One of the women from the group called out covertly.

The Mutt turned and bitched at the female talker. "Fuck the lot of you sleazbags."

"I like the name he picked out man." Buckethead called out to the other soldiers.

"Well if the big guy likes it, it's a done deal then I guess. Taras, you're here by dubbed Siberia to the Unit, sister." Walker announced to the second of the three Russian female fighters.

She nodded to Walker's offer for her tag name for the unit.

"We got another one left to name from the group of Ruskies." Walker announced to the group.

"I got her name picked out Bobby." Sergeant Ramirez offered as she grinned at the Russian.

"Yeah?" the Lieutenant asked his girlfriend as he returned her smile with one of his own.

"Yeah, I want to call her Mink, because she's as soft as the fur is, Homes."

"And you know this personally I take it, Raz?" Buckethead grunted out from the group.

"Yes I do big guy." Ramirez purred sexily as she wiggled her hips and smiled at him.

"I'd like to know how you found that name out for her, Ramirez." Casper yelled with a smirk.

"Eat your stinking heart out Ghost. It hurts your feeling I know something you don't I guess, mister." Ramirez smirked back at the scary and extremely dangerous soldier. She again wiggled her hips while running her tongue slowly over her lips at him.

"Well that's it for the naming thing then. We're done with the naming of the Russian chicks." Walker announced, still not trusting the Russian soldiers in the least. He did not like the idea of have them being part of his group as well. He was stopped from ending it when the male Russian soldier asked. "What about me Lieutenant Walker, what name be me given to sir."

The soldiers chuckled, and someone called out from the group. "Who did he fuck last night?"

The group laughed as they waited for someone to offer a name for the Russian soldier.

The Lieutenant felt bad he forgot about the only Russian male to join his group of elite soldiers and he announced. "I'll tag him myself; he's AK after the Russian weapon."

Leonid Maslennikova grinned and nodded, proud to be named after a Russian weapon.

The group slowly began to break up, with most of the specialized soldiers leaving the area while joking and laughing as they searched for some coffee and food.

Walker entered his home just as his small handheld radio went off on him. The military radio was supposed to be carried on his person at all times n case something went wrong in the world, and Command needed to get in touch with him in an emergency situation. It was someone from Command trying to get in touch with him. Ramirez saw the flashing red light and her heart skipped a beat as she cried. "Do you think it's another mission so soon, Robert?"

"Beats the farts outta my stinking ass on me baby. But there's only one way to find out if it's another stinking mission or not, baby. I don't think it could be another operation this quickly. I didn't see anything happening that would cause us to be pulled in form our leaves. But just in case it might be another mission you betta stop anyone from disappearing from our place until I find out for certain what the fuck's up in Washington." The upset Lieutenant warned her as he answered the radio call in order.

"Walker here, who's this and what's going down up there?" the Lieutenant actually hissed in the radio in an angry tone.

"Lieutenant Walker! How are you today, Lieutenant? General White..."

CHAPTER SIX

THE SMALL TOWN OF YAZD, IRAN

The American operative rapidly made his way to the Iranian city of Yazd without any problems, and he was now sitting in a cafe while enjoying a cup of bitter tea and warm pita bread, when a stroke of luck crossed his path. While sipping his tea, Bdellah happened to overhear a conversation being carried out between three Iranian men in the café.

The Iranians are hard workers, but if one of them is trusted with a secret, he can't wait to share it with someone else. The worker tried to give a number of subtle hints of what he was doing in the desert outside Yazd. But as luck would have it, the other two men were not the least bit interested in the worker's bragging over his supposed secret work outside of town.

At first, the operative listened casually, suddenly he stopped to listen to the words of the worker dressed in rags more clearly. He heard him brag he was employed in the construction of a secret building. But the other two men still showed little if any interest in the boast. He knew the others were not going to fall victim of the third one's bragging. When he had enough waiting for the other two men to ask questions, he walked over to the three Iranian workers. Displaying an air of confidence always displayed by a member of the secret police, he sat down uninvited and then stared angrily at the three men, daring any one of them to question him.

After what seemed like an eternity to the three men seated at the table, Bdellah suddenly grinned at the men staring at him with fear in their eyes. He looked at the older men, and then hissed. "You have no work to perform today? If you do not, I believe I can always find a job that needs to be carried out by two strong looking men such as you two fools."

They both jumped up and bowed towards what they believed was a police officer, and then they rushed from the cafe without paying for their food. The cafe owner did not challenge them, he too thought this stranger was secret police, sent to spy in his village. Many in the cafe took this to pay for their half eaten meals and then leave. The owner busied himself in the backroom, ignoring the two men sitting uncomfortably at the only occupied table in his establishment.

The worker suddenly scared to death tried to leave the café with the others, but Bdellah reached out and grabbed his wrist and applied pressure, forcing him to take his seat again without even looking at the man. Once he was satisfied there was no one else within ear shot of him, he hissed angrily at the stranger. "What is your god cursed worthless name, fool?"

"My name is Bader Jiyad al-Kanani, sir." He replied, while trembling with fear and staring.

"I believe you know who I am, am I not correct, fool. If you don't know who I am then you are even stupider than you fooking look, son of a lowly jackal." The American operative snarled, displaying little interest in the man as he took one of the cups half filled with tea and sipped it.

"You are secret police sir?" Al-Kanani replied in a shaky and scared tone to him.

"You are much wiser than you look, young fool." He snapped as he let go of al-Kanani's arm, and then he slid the ID he took from Fatima across the stained table at him.

Al-Kanani barely took notice of the weather beaten leather ID case, and took his eyes from it when he noticed the black emblem of the Iranian Secret Police. He was sweating as he wondered what he had done wrong to gain the interest of the secret police officer. Whenever an Iranian officer showed interest in a person, that person usually ended up dead within hours.

Bdellah knew he had the kid right where he wanted him, and he hissed again at the young and obviously scared to death man. "Your papers fool!"

Al-Kanani gave them to his inquisitor without question. Bdellah quickly unfolded the faded, crumpled identification papers and merely glanced at them, and then he placed them in his pocket. He turned to the worker and barked at him. "You seemed to be trying to tell the other two fools of your supposed secret work. It was wise of them they did not question you about your work. Or I would've had to take all three of you in custody and have you interrogated, fool."

"I'm under arrest?" Al-Kanani asked, feeling a weight of despair descend on his shoulders. He heard stories of what happened to those arrested by the police, many were never seen alive again.

"I don't know yet, young fool of the desert." Bdellah replied as he gave him a half smile.

"You don't know? Thank you, I don't have much money on me, but what I have I'll happily give you if you could find it in your heart to forget and forgive my foolishness sir. I have a wife and two young children to care for. I'll pray Allah for you and your family every day of my life, sir." The young worker offered while wiping some sweat from his brow.

Bdellah's smile grew wider as he grumbled at him. "You offer me much fool. It's not money or prayers I'm after, fool. It's information you possess in that foul head of yours, jackal. I been assigned to keep an eye on all workers from the, err... secret base you're working on at err..."

"I was working on the new base at Iranshahr. I don't know if this is the place you're investigating or not, kind Officer sir." Al-Kanani announced in a shaky tone.

"Yes, that is the base I'm interested in, fool of the hot desert sands. Iranshahr, I have to keep an eye on the security at that fooking base. To carry out my surveillance, and to also observe the trustworthiness of the workers there. I've decided to compile a list of where they work, and make certain they didn't do anything to jeopardize the project's security, young fool. You can avoid your arrest by convincing me you have not sabotaged the project with your foolish words you told the other fools you were with. If you tell me what your duties are at this god dom base, and how you carry out those duties, I'll judge your work for myself. If I feel it meets with my satisfaction, you'll be with your wife and two children before nightfall."

With a deep sigh, the worker shifted his weight as he told Bdellah what his duties were. He spoke rapidly and without fear, holding nothing back as he told Bdellah everything.

The operative intensely listened as al-Kanani spoke, when the worker explained what was hidden under the tarps he saw being stored by the site, his attention sharpened and he asked with concern in his voice. "Al-Kanani, what do you think was under that tarp you saw, fool?"

"I don't think I know what it was, sir. I know they were missile housings, another worker and I had to go under the canvass to measure the width of the housings, sir." The worker said, actually bragging as he felt he was telling this officer something he did not know.

"How many of these fooking tarps were on the base, fool?" he asked him seriously.

"I never thought to count them, they were all over the area sir. Other plant workers at the base worked in labs of the complex, and word nuclear warheads were to be constructed on the site. Many times military officers would brag, once Iran was able to build their own nuclear warheads, they would own the Middle East, and the West would dry up from lack of oil, sir."

Bdellah was stunned but able to hide it from the young man. If this worker was correct, Iran was constructing a building to develop nuclear warheads, and the United States had to know about this situation immediately. Where was Iran able to get their hands on the technology to enable them to begin constructing nuclear warheads and missiles? It clicked as he remembered why he was sent to Yazd. Russia. His mind was spinning as he quickly formulated his next question, he had to know how many missiles were being constructed at the secret complex.

"Al-Kanani, you have no number on the missile housings you saw at the plant site, huh?"

"No sir, as I said I never thought to count them sir."

"Would you say ten were there, fool born from a camel's arse?"

"Many more than that number were hidden under the heavy tarps I saw."

"More than twenty five then I ask you, fool?" he asked again as he glared angrily at the young worker who looked more scared than ever now.

Al-Kanani took the warning of the glare and he replied. "There were more than twenty five missile housings that were being stored under the tarps I saw, sir. I'd say I saw up to fifty missile housings held in special containers, or under the tarps Officer."

"Special containers? What are these special containers you offer to me, jackal?" he snarled, angry he had to pull the information from the worker.

"Yes sir, someone told me they were submarine launch missile tubes, sir. The missiles were to be constructed at the site, were going to be for submarine missiles in our Navy, sir."

"What was the distance across the missile you measured, fool?"

"If I remember correctly, I believe it was twenty seven inches across the middle, kind sir."

His blood ran cold as he understood the meaning of the inches. There was only one Russian made missile that wide, it was the SS-N-23. "Have you seen any warheads at the base?"

"No, but I was often told ten of them would fit inside the nose cone of one of these missiles the workers were in the process of constructing at the complex, sir."

Bdellah stared at al-Kanani as he quickly collected his thoughts.

Al-Kanani suddenly became suspicious because this officer's questions were centering more on one subject, and they were drifting away from what this officer should be interested in, the security of the secret base. He stuttered and then he nearly whispered at who he thought was a secret police officer. "Excuse me sir, but may I see your ID papers again, please sir?"

Bdellah knew the worker was not going to answer any more questions for him so he barked at the young man as nasty as he could speak. "Bader Jiyad al-Kanani! You have failed your security test, and you're under arrest, fool. Stand up and walk before me. Don't try anything stupid against me or I'll be forced to shoot you dead where you stand, fool." The operative slid his hand inside his jacket to warn al-Kanani he was armed and ready to kill him if necessary.

"You said if I answered all your questions, I'd be free to go home to my wife and family, sir." Al-Kanani cried as he stood on shaky legs, and then waited for Bdellah to stand.

"Fool, I wanted to see if you would spill any secret information, and you did without thought or hesitation. You have compromised the security of the special base and our country, you son of a lowly scorpion. I'll send a car out to arrest your entire family, I'm certain they're just as guilty as you are of betraying your country, fool." He shoved the worker forward towards the door.

The café workers heard the worker was under arrest and they put their heads down, not wanting the officer to pay any attention to them. The owner saw the policeman shoving the man towards the door and he ducked back in the kitchen. No one wanted to be seen by police.

Once outside the cafe, Bdellah shoved the worker until they were by the alley. He pushed him down the deserted alley, drawing his weapon and pointing it at al-Kanani as they walked.

"Why are we going in the alley sir?" Al-Kanani began begging, fearing for his life now.

"Because fool, this is where my car is parked. Keep moving and ask no further questions of me. Talk again and I'll kill you where you stand, traitor." Again, Bdellah shoved al-Kanani.

Once the pair was at the end of the alley, al-Kanani looked for the officer's car.

Bdellah saw him look and he warned him from behind. "Here al-Kanani is my fooking car, fool." He aimed the gun right at his forehead.

Al-Kanani instantly dropped down to his knees and began to cry, begging for his life. It did him no good. He was a dead man because he saw Bdellah's face and ID, and it was impossible for him to leave the man alive, to be interrogated by a real secret police officer later.

"Al-Kanani, what do you think they'll be doing in this building you work at fool?"

After a slight hesitation, the worker replied in an effort to try and save his life. "Building Russian missiles." Al-Kanani looked at Bdellah with pleading eyes and added. "Sir, I have two young children and a wife, a home and I have worked all my life and am a trusted..."

Bdellah ignored the pled as he hissed. "I thought so fool. Al-Kanani, pray to Allah to open the gates of Paradise for you, and forgive you of your sins. You have one minute, so don't waste it begging me. Pray fool. I give you time." He gave him a minute to pray and then an unsilenced shot rang out, splitting al-Kanani's forehead as the slug ripped through his brain.

Everyone in the restaurant heard the shot and knew the worker was just executed. It was not the first time someone was arrested, only to have his body found the next morning, dead lying in the street. A warning for anyone who might think of betraying Iran or her beliefs.

The operative rushed out of the alley to his car. He checked his watch, and looked down the road towards Yazd for any sign of the trucks. Off to the end of the city, a huge cloud of dust was bellowing. He knew the trucks were coming, he climbed in his car and sped off.

After ten minutes of breakneck driving, he came across the first truck, he was shocked to see it was a military vehicle. It came at him and crossed the road and cut him off. The driver got out and cursed Bdellah, warning him to pull off the road and wait until his convoy passed. He warned him if he tried to drive on the road before the convoy passed, his life will be forfeited.

He nodded at the man cursing him. The driver disappeared back in his vehicle and the car dashed down the road. In seconds, truck after truck passed before him at a high speed. In the middle of the convoy he saw a lone civilian car, followed by more trailers. Bdellah snapped pictures of the rigs with a miniature Kodak camera, when he took a picture of each truck he hid the camera in the compartment by his stick shift he found driving to Yazd.

Once the last machine passed, he pulled on the road and headed out in the desert. He used the Global Positioning System to find the radio use when he had information to report to his control. His track took him around the new capital city of Iran, Kerman towards the Afghan border though he remained in Iran at all times. It was the right direction, he was certain he would be ordered to Iranshahr to investigate this supposed secret base.

It took the young American spy a little over three hours to reach his second safe place, a crumbling mud hut built right in the middle of nowhere. He slammed his car in park and then he ran behind the dilapidated building and paced the feet off. He then dropped down to his knees and began to dig in the soft sand and discovered the radio was still there. He pulled it out of the sand and rushed inside the building. After kicking the wood door off the hinges, he immediately pulled the radio out of the protective covering and turned it on. It took a few seconds for it to warm up, and then he transmitted his message via SATCOM. Satellite Communications off Bird 11. He sent out his report at nine p.m. sharp for the headquarters of the CIA.

NORASATCOM. NORTH AMERICAN SATELLITE COMMUNICATION CENTER, MARYLAND. TUESDAY, NOVEMBER 5th, 1998. 1300 HOURS EST

The Airforce Lieutenant manning the console was on his third straight day of work, sleeping in the center now. He was enjoying his umpteenth cup of coffee when the CIA Bird transmitted a communication. "Holy shit, Sneaky Eye 11's bitching, you better patch it right through to HQ." He barked at the Sergeant working by him.

"I'm on it right away sir. Sending it there now sir." The Sergeant snapped back at him.

CIA Director John Raincloud was in his office going over the latest intelligence on the tractor trailer rigs traveling through Iran. He studied the pictures of the machines rumbling over the Russian border and entering into Iran, paying close attention to the Iranian military vehicles linking up with the convoy of rigs. He was startled when communications from center buzzed his office. Director Raincloud snapped at his aide. "Sam, what do ya have coming in for me, sir?"

"Director Raincloud, I have a communication coming in from Operative Sand Star, sir."

Director Raincloud bolted up, realizing something important was up as he grumbled at his aide. "Sam, pipe it to my office at the same time." Same time was slang for information to be transmitted directly to Director Raincloud's office.

"Yes sir, you should be receiving it ...errr... about now sir." Sam warned the Director.

At the time Sam said now, Director Raincloud's lockbox received paper. The Native American broke the connection and went over to his lockbox and tapped his foot. He had to wait until the message was completed. If he tried to open the box before it ended, there would be a flash fire, and nothing could put out the furnace, until every trace of paper was burned off, and ashes blown apart. It seemed to take a short lifetime before the paper stopped. John opened the box and tore the paper from the machine, he unrolled it and began reading from the top.

/\/\/\ SAND STAR TO SAND HOLE /\/\/\
/\/\/\ HAVE IMPORTANT INFORMATION. DISCOVERED WORK
CARRIED OUT IN DESERT AT OR NEAR IRANSHAHR.
BREAK... HAVE RELIABLE INFORMATION IRAN CONSTRUCTING
SS-N-23 SUBMARINE LAUNCH MISSILES AND POSSIBLE NUCLEAR

WARHEADS TO GO WITH SAID MISSILES, WILL
CONFIRM. BREAK... /\/\/\
/\/\/\ CONFIDENCE HIGH IRAN IN POSSESSION OF
TECHNOLOGY NEEDED
TO CONSTRUCT SAID MISSILES AND WARHEADS.
BREAK... /\/\/\
/\/\/\ WITNESSED TWELVE MACHINES TRAVELING
DUE SOUTH. BREAK...
HAVE TAKEN PICTURES OF SAID MACHINES AND AM
IN PROCESS OF
TRANSMITTING SAID PICTURES BY PROPER MEANS.
BREAK...
AM CONCERNED OVER INFORMATION OF IRAN'S
CAPABILITY OF
CONSTRUCTING MISSILES AND WARHEADS. BREAK...
/\/\/\
/\/\/\ WILL WAIT FURTHER ORDERS. BREAK...
STANDBY FOR TWO HOUR
HOLD DOWN BEFORE MOVING FOR SECURITY
REASONS. BREAK... /\/\/\
/\/\/\ SAND STAR OUT. /\/\/\

Director Raincloud opened the link with his operative, and then typed in his new orders. The clicks and static his transmission was turned into came out as a complete and readable message to Operative branded Sand Star.

/\/\/\ BIG BOY TO SAND STAR /\/\/\
/\/\/\ ORDERED TO MAKEWAY TO IRANSHAHR AND
CHECK ON GATHERED
INFORMATION AND CONFIRM SAME. BREAK...
REPORT MOMENT, EXACT SECOND CONFIRM OR
DISCREDIT

INFORMATION SENT. BREAK...
AM ALERTING MNRRF FOR POSSIBLE INCURSION
INTO IRAN TO
ERASE COMPLEX ONCE POSITIVE MISSILES AND
NUCLEAR
WARHEADS ARE CAPABLY OF BEING CONSTRUCTED
AT SAID SITE. BREAK...
REPORT AT NEXT SAFE POSITION. BREAK...
REPORT ONCE INFORMATION CONFIRMED. BREAK.
/\/\/\ BIG BOY WORKING WITH EAGLE ONE'S
UNDERSTANDING AND
PERMISSION TO CARRY OUT SAID MISSION. BREAK.
/\/\/\
/\/\/\ SAND STAR, BIG BOY OUT. /\/\/\

Bdellah was impressed Director Raincloud replied personally to his report as he lifted the radio over his head, and then he send it crashing to the floor. He realized the code name for the American President was Eagle One, and Director Raincloud's code name was Big Boy and CIA headquarters was code named Sand Hole as he finished destroying the radio with his foot, not before he spun the dial to change the radio frequency settings. Once the radio was completely destroyed, he was back in his car heading for a gas station and then Iranshahr.

CIA HEADQUARTERS LANGLEY VIRGINIA

Director John Raincloud placed his report in a blue border file, which gave it the highest top secret security standing. Once he finished, he dialed General John White's office, and quickly informed the General he was heading to the White House after informing the White House Chief of Staff, he demanded a level one meeting with the President. General White whistled in the phone when he heard a Level One meeting was being declared by Director Raincloud. He immediately informed the Director he would meet him at the White House when he got there.

Director Raincloud sent the warning to the White House, and went to the North parking lot for his car. He snarled at the driver. "The White House, use the siren I have to get there PDQ."

"Yes sir." The driver grunted, in seconds they were heading on Arlington Highway.

THE WHITE HOUSE, WASHINGTON D.C. TUESDAY NOVEMBER 5th, 1998, 1350 HOURS EST

Director Raincloud's car pulled on the White House circle drive a second before General White's vehicle. Both men hopped out of their cars and shook hands as Raincloud briefed General White of his report from Sand Star as they entered the White House. They were met by the aide, and informed the President was waiting for them in the Oval Office. They were allowed to walk unescorted down the hall to the Oval Office. Director Raincloud banged on the door.

"You two better get your backsides in here, and I warn you two this better be damn important or else. I was on the ninth hole when my staff yanked me off the damn course. Embarrassing me like hell might I add." The President bitched as General White and Director Raincloud entered the Oval Office and headed for the second couch in the office. Secretary of State Maria Hernandez, along with

Defense Secretary Levenhagen and Director Griffin were already seated in the office on the other couch facing each other and the President was seated behind his desk.

General John White nodded to Secretary of State Hernandez, who suddenly looked much more weaker than usual. Just as Vice President Mary Hirshfield strolled in the room behind them.

"Seats everyone." President Cole growled as he nodded at Mary, and barked. "Not you Director. You report while I get my knife and fork out, in case this meeting's a hype, mister."

When Director Raincloud removed the blue bordered report from his briefcase, everyone in the office quieted down and they paid close attention to the large Native American as he started his report for the members. "Mr. President sir, I have received a communication from my Operative Sand Star, recently activated in the nation of Iran sir. Evidently, he was in the right place and at the right time, and he transmitted some rather disturbing information, sir."

Director Raincloud quickly handed out the duplicates of his report from Sand Star he had printed up for the other members at the meeting.

Secretary Jerry Levenhagen let out with a low whistle as he quickly scanned the report.

President Cole lifted his eyes and asked, "can your Operative confirm this report, John?"

"Not at the moment sir. I ordered him out to a new position in the Iranian desert, Mr. President Sir. Lima, Echo, Foxtrot, Four, Four, One, Whiskey, Delta, Charlie..."

The President waved his hand as he shook his head no and complained. "Don't give me any of that crap Director. Just tell me where the hell you sent your damn Operative to. I hate that military jargon you people keep relying on when you guys are making a report to me, John."

"Yes Sir Mr. President Sir. I forgot and am sorry for confusing you Mr. President Sir. I ordered my Operative to make his way for the Iranian city of Iranshahr, and he's to report back to me the instant he uncovers irrefutable evidence on whether or not the damn Iranians are in possession of the capability of constructing submarine launch long range missiles and the nuclear warheads for the damn things, sir." Director Raincloud drew in a breath and let it out slowly.

"Where the devil did the Iranians ever get hold of that information?" Hernandez asked him.

"Evidently, Admiral Yevgeny Proushinsky sold the Iranian Agent the schematics to the warheads and missiles, Ma'am. We're speaking of submarine launch long range nuclear tipped missiles, the ones the Iranians brought from the Russian Admiral, just yesterday in fact Ma'am." Director Raincloud added before being asked about the missiles from anyone at the meeting.

"Jesus, I'm going to get hold of the Russian President Vitaly Kvantrishuili, and let him know what his god damn Admiral has done to the security of the world. Could you imagine what Iran would be like if she ever launched six nuclear capable submarines into the damn Persian Gulf? I shudder to think what the Middle East would look like. General White, we're forced to act as if this information is confirmed, and we're going in and wipe this crap out before the damn Iranians have a chance to load their damn submarines with these god damn Russian made missiles and nuclear warheads. What's next? Did you speak with your people in what was that Island?"

"With all due respect Mr. President Sir, it's Marathon Island sir..."

"Did you make contact with them? I don't want them running the last moment to assemble."

"Yes Mr. President, I spoke with the Unit's leader, Lieutenant Robert Walker, and ordered him to prepare his Unit for immediate action, sir. I placed the soldiers on a forty eight hour alert."

"Raise that to a twelve hour alert status, I want the soldiers ready to go at the drop of a fucking hat, General White Sir. What's our next move now sir?" The obviously upset President Cole growled as he sent another pencil flying across the office.

"I intend to order the entire Rapid Response Force Unit to assemble tonight. I believe the only position we have, is to go in Iran on foot to make certain the damn missile and nuclear warhead information is correct. Then order the troops to confiscate the information and then destroy the rest of the crap in position. What else can we do about this present situation Mr. President Sir?" General White said as he hunched his shoulders and then slowly spread his hands apart.

"Mr. President, I think we might be jumping the gun a little here, sir," Security Director Norman Griffin offered as he stood, and then continued with his remarks. "where the hell are the Iranians going to acquire bomb grade Plutonium from? From thin air? Each warhead requires up to seven to ten pounds if it's going to make a bomb. Even the damn Russians aren't going to sell the Iranian enough Plutonium to construct active nuclear warheads, sir. They know well we're monitoring their supplies closely, for them to bleed off enough to make the Iranians happy."

All eyes went back to General White, who showed he did not have the answer to that last question. He breathed a deep sigh, he knew how the President got when a question was asked and it could not be answered. He noticed Director Raincloud raising his finger as he offered. "Director Griffin, I can answer that question for you if you would like sir."

All eyes went back to Director Raincloud as they waited for him to reply.

"How can they get their hands on enough of that crap to make the warheads for these god damn Russian missiles, sir?" the fuming President snarled at his CIA Director, showing him he wanted an answer right now.

"Mr. President, as you're aware that just two years ago the Russians were in the midst of a staggering monetary depression, and they went through with arrangements to sell three RF-145 Steam Pressurized Nuclear Reactors to the Iranians. Remember how we fought against the sale, and when they moved to Iran to construct these damn reactors, we actually convene a special Security Council meeting to try and block the damn sale of these reactors to the Iranians. As usual they went against us when China refused to vote against the reactor sale in err..."

"I'm well aware of that god damn mess, I have a very long memory Director Raincloud. Please get on with your explanation for us, Director Raincloud. I assure you I'll revisit this sale with the new Russian Administration after this meeting is over with sir." The President interrupted.

"With all due respect Mr. President, we have detected a number of Russian engineers going to Iran over the past few weeks sir. A few technicians were reported to be nuclear smart. I had a report two days ago that alerted me to the possibility of the Iranians converting one of the Steam Pressurized electric reactors into Plutonium breeding reactors, Mr. President."

A snap from the President's pencil echoed like a gun shot in the Office, silencing everyone as they looked at the upset

American Leader as he sprang to his feet, and began pacing the office while cracking his knuckles. He marched until his temper cooled down, and then he rested his hands on the back of his chair and stared directly at the CIA Director and asked him. "Director Raincloud, how long did you say you were in possession of this god damn information, sir?"

"For the past two days Mr. President Sir." Director Raincloud replied in a low voice.

"Two fucking days! And I'm just becoming aware of this damn information now, mister!" President Cole raged while jumping back away from his chair, and then he looked at Director Raincloud as if he was going to attack him.

"I'm afraid so Mr. President Sir. This information hasn't been confirmed positive as yet and that's why it wasn't brought up to your attention until now sir. So I didn't think to burden you with it, until I was able to confirm the information as correct or not, sir. With all that's been taking place lately, I didn't think you needed something else to load your mind down with, Mr. President. My office is continuing to working to confirm the information as fact, and once we're positive. I planned to make an extremely detailed report about the findings to you, Mr. President." Director Raincloud replied confidently, not feeling threatened by his actions.

"I'm pleased you're so damn concerned about my frame of mind. I remember sending a memo demanding to be informed on anything taking place in and around the Middle East, especially Iran, Director. I expected a reaction from Iran, after the raid when the former President received information Iran was involved in the attack on our base in Arabia in '96, this could be it."

"Mr. President, with all due respect, I hoped once Iran joined forces with us in the Sudanese, Libyan war, further aggressive actions towards us would be forgotten, sir."

"You willing to place your career on the line for that rather foolish assumption, Director?" The President snapped nastily at the Commander of the CIA.

Director Raincloud did not reply. General White picked up the ball as he stood and waited.

The President turned his harsh glare at him as he growled at his military officer nastily. "Do you have something you wish to add to this god damn conversation, General White?"

"Yes Sir Mr. President, I believe we have already massed enough information to know that Iran's up to something that isn't in the best interest of the United States, sir."

The President could not believe what he heard and had to laugh to control his anger.

General White continued on with his report to the American Leader. "Mr. President, Director Raincloud and I have worked out a certain scenario of the best possible course of action to be employed against Iran, if and when we have to react against them if..."

"I take it you believe we'll be engaging in military action against Iran, General White?"

"Yes Sir Mr. President! By all means I certainly do at that sir." John replied sharply.

"Christ sake! Okay General White, run this scenario by me and I'll see if it floats."

Director Griffin stood and asked to be heard before General White explained his plans.

The President looked at his Security Director and then he nodded politely at him.

"Mr. President, I was wondering how your conversation went with the Russian President?"

"Not very well I'm afraid Norm, President Kvantrishuili's away from his office, and he wasn't expected to return until after the weekend. I requested he place an immediate call to me at his earliest convenience, his secretary informed me he was unable to be contacted. This means he won't be at the United Nations meeting Friday mooring. I believe the man's in the hospital because of his heavy drinking. I planned to contact the Russian Leader the first thing Monday morning as I have offered earlier at this meeting if you remember correctly, Norman."

"I take it you'll question him on these items, the turning over of technology for the construction of SS-N-23's, and Russian technicians in Iran to convert reactors to breeders. General White, how much weapons grade Plutonium could one of these reactors produce in a month's time?"

"That's a good question, I do have the information with me." General White said as he thumbed through his briefcase, and then groused. "Ahh... here we go Norman. Each reactor could produce up to fifteen pounds of high grade Plutonium each month of operation sir."

"That's enough for two warheads. Multiply that by three, and the Iranians could crown one missile with six warheads every god damn month, General White Sir. Christ Almighty, we have to do something about this god damn situation, and we have to do it as soon as possible sir. This is ten times as bad as what the damn Russian Colonel Otto Mikhailchenko tried to pull off against China a couple of months ago, dammit. I'm sorry for interrupting you at this time General, please continue with your report sir." Secretary Griffin nodded.

The powerful Military Officer nodded at Director Griffin and then he picked up with his report where he was interrupted. "Mr. President, we're trapped in a rather sticky situation sir. If we go after Iran without positive evidence to convince the Saudis of the seriousness of this latest situation. We stand a good chance of losing them as allies in any action we'll be forced to take against Iran. We can't stand to turn any Arab nation against us at so crucial a time. Let alone having the damn Russians and Chinese go after our throats at the same time sir. I'd like to send my entire MNRRF force into Iran to have them amass undefeatable evidence about this nuclear processing plant where the Iranians plan to build missiles and nuclear warheads.

Once we have this evidence in hand then I'll have our people destroy the entire damn supposed secret complex, but not before removing all the damn information on the warheads and missiles. Once we have this and prove to the world what was going on inside Iran, we'll employ Secretary Levenhagen's term and, 'Bomb the living shit' out of the submarine pens and the three nuclear breeder reactor sites at the same time in Iran, sir."

"Let me get this right, you want my permission to allow you to get your people in motion am I correct General White?" the concerned American Leader remarked to the military officer.

"Get your people in motion for what Mr. President Sir?" Manning barked as he entered the Oval Office unannounced and headed for his usual seat in the Oval Office. He allowed his face to display the displeasure at seeing they had already started the meeting without him being present. Manning was on the other side of Washington when he received word, ordering him to report for a Level One meeting with the President and his staff, it took him this long to cross Washington.

"Sit down and be quiet Mr. Manning! We have an extremely serious situation rapidly developing on our hands, and I don't have the time to bring you up to speed on what we've been discussing at this meeting, sir. Pay attention and see if you can catch up sir. General White, I believe you're correct with this last request of yours, sir. You have my permission to assemble your specialized soldiers, sir. Get them going, and have them prepare to enter Iran at a moment's notice, sir. How long do you think it'll take you to prepare the soldiers for immediate action, and how soon before you can get them in the air and heading for Iran, General White?" President Cole asked his military officer.

"Wait a minute Mr. President Sir. What's this all about sir? Why the hell are you allowing General White to assemble his despicable covert specialized Paramilitary Army for sir? Then get them in the air to attack Iran!" Manning snapped as he stood and placed his hands down on the President's desk. He actually glared at the grinning Chairman of the Joint Chiefs of Staff General John White, who he interrupted while giving a report to the President and other members of the meeting when he first entered the Oval Office as if he owned it.

"Mr. Manning, I told you to sit down and be quiet, and take your hands off my god damn desk and sit down as I ordered you, mister. We have a situation that needs a possible immediate military solution. Unless you'd like to go to Iran and try your hand at negotiating with the Iranian Leaders this time sir?" the President smirked as he stared in the eyes of the civilian advisor.

"Err..., no thank you Mr. President Sir. I don't have any interest in becoming a negotiator, and especially dealing with the Iranian nation Mr. President." Manning complained as he quickly sat down, remembering what he went through in South Africa when the President sent him over there to try and deal with the white supremacists of that country.

Many, including Hernandez, gave a slight chuckle over Manning's embarrassment.

"I didn't think so Mr. Manning. General White, you're operating on a clear channel for this one. Anything you need or want just request it, and you'll have it sir. I want those damn troops of yours ready to go in action within two weeks at the very latest sir. Allow me remind you of something General White, no one, not one of your soldiers is going to do a god damn thing until we get a complete report from Director Raincloud's spy working inside Iran, sir. When he gives us the exact location of this supposed secret complex by the Iranian city of Iranshahr, and he confirms what the Iranian's are doing at this miserable Iranian complex. Then and only then we'll go after the site if what you offered, is true sir."

General White rose from his seat, but the President immediately waved him back to his chair as he offered. "General White, I'm afraid you might be raising some demons here sir. General, Director Raincloud, you have the White House's permission to redirect any satellites to keep this region under constant surveillance at all times. If you're good, you might even be able to talk me into launching a shuttle to help with the surveillance of Iran, gentlemen."

"That was my next request, Mr. President. How do I go about trying to woo you into a launch of err... three shuttles." General White offered as he shot the president one of his best smiles.

"Three shuttles!" President Cole and Manning griped at the same time as they both leaped up from their seats and looked at the General. The President shot a hot glare at the civilian who resumed his seat. Then the President turned to the Chairman and warned him. "You sure do know how to get what you want from me, General White. I'll do this much for you sir.

"I'll give you one launch as soon as the technicians can load the damn shuttle with equipment we need, and get it on the launching pad. Next week, I'll give you a second shuttle launch, but three. I'll never get Congress to swallow a triple launch without the news declaring world doom. Two General, no matter how much you cry, only two sir!" the President held his fingers up to drive his point home as he added. "I can get away with two launches, but three and even my wife would be standing on my tongue trying to get information from me, sir. General, you have your controls set in place. No action's to be taken until Director Raincloud's operative reports with information. You have the Officers you need to control these crazy soldiers of yours, sir?"

"Yes Sir I sure do Mr. President Sir. Everything's already set in place on my side as we speak sir." The General offered to his Commander in Chief.

"Very good General White, get going on this then sir. I have no intention of waiting until the damn Iranian's get as far as the Russian rebel troops did with their plans to conquer the world's people. I'm not waiting for anything to be confirmed this time General White. I intend to meet any and all threats leveled against the United States head on, and if Iran gets in the position of controlling the entire oil production in the Middle East. It's definitely a serious threat to the United States, and every other nation of the world. I won't allow the news people to question me on why I waited so long ever again, General. Now, they're going to question me why I jumped off so quickly this time around sir. At least I'll be ahead of anyone who thinks he or she's going to hurt the United States, dammit. Get going on this mess General

White, you too Director. I expect updates from you and your operative working in Iran, Director Raincloud."

They both stood, but they both stopped dead in their tracks by Secretary of State Ms. Hernandez as she asked the military officer. "General White many I have a second of your time please sir."

General White nodded and smiled at her as he waited for her to ask him her question.

"Thank you for that consideration General White, these young soldiers under your Command are children and our nation's treasure, our children General, and you must remember this at all times when dealing with our nation's sacred treasures. The second I feel you forgot this; for one second you'll lose my support for your office, General. Do I make myself perfectly clear on this subject of our nation's soldiers, General White?" Ms. Hernandez gave her best effort to stand, but her affliction forced her back in her wheeled prison.

General White turned to his favorite, and grinned at her again.

"General White, I knew you'd understand where I was coming from with what I'm telling you at this time sir. You'll enjoy my complete support for your soldiers on this and any other military operation you and they are sent out on sir. Please remember General White, I want our children to be fully supported on this, or any other mission they're dispatched on by us sir. I'll have your hide hanging from my office if I ever hear these children our soldiers needed support from our military, and it wasn't there for them when requested or needed sir. We've given you everything you need for a successful mission here and in the future, even personal IFF units. So you'll protect these our fine young soldiers under your Command as I protected you and your predecessors at any meeting we attended together, or else. You're now dismissed to carry out your orders, sir." Ms. Hernandez smiled at the General.

General White gave one last look at the President, who nodded as he left the office. The General smiled as he heard Manning yelling to be heard over the other members at the meeting, and the President snapping for him to take his seat again and shut up.

The General knew the civilian was going jump on the President for clearing him for action in Iran without having evidence to convince the world this was a must. The General wished he could have remained so he could defend himself and his troops against Manning's attacks.

CHAPTER SEVEN

General White rushed back to his office with Director Raincloud in tow, he dropped in his chair and checked his watch, it was four twenty p.m. The meeting with the President lasted two hours plus. He pressed the intercom and his secretary Mary answered. The General had the option of replacing her when he assumed General William Weidenbacher's position of the Chairman of the Joint Chiefs of Staff after he died of a heart attack, but chose to keep her on.

"Mary, get Lieutenant Robert Walker on the horn for me please. When I finish with him, get Captain Bruce

Leadbetter, and then Colonel Joseph Salsiccia in that order. Buzz me when you get through to Walker please." General White turned to Director Raincloud and asked. "Drink?"

"Yes. Fire water will do just fine, John?" the Director offered.

"Of course, what else is there." He pulled two glasses and a bottle of homemade White Lightening from his bottom drawer, and began to pour. "Say when Chief."

"When your finger gets wet." Director Raincloud replied with a smile.

"Christ sake John, I said a damn drink. I didn't say get your ass plastered with this crap, Chief." General White offered with a smirk, but he was not prepared for Director Raincloud's response at his attempt to be funny.

The Native American glared angrily at General White as he snapped at him. "You above all people General White, should know what it means to be stereotyped, sir. Blacks were believed to be lazy and criminals until men like yourself stepped forward. Native Americans, despite the misbegotten belief aren't a bunch of drunken wife beaters sir. That's something a past government tried to make everyone believe about us, so they could steal our lands, our beliefs with clear minds, General White. There are many Native Americans in top positions, positions like Congressmen, Representatives, and CEO's. I resent you still think us as a bunch of drunken naked savages sir." Director Raincloud sent the drink flying across the room.

"Whoa, hold on a minute there John. I didn't mean anything by what I said, I was just trying to make a joke. Seeing how lame it was, I'm thoroughly embarrassed by my remark sir. I stand corrected, sir." General White said as he bowed towards the Native American.

The confrontation was interrupted by the buzz of the General's intercom. "Yes Mary."

"General White Sir, I made contact with Lieutenant Walker, sir. He's on line one sir."

"Thanks." General White asked. "Is everything okay John? I don't need you pissed at me."

Director Raincloud allowed his shoulders to relax as he unclenched his fists, he then smiled.

"Thanks." General White said as he turned his attention to the voice on the phone. "Ahhh... Lieutenant Walker, I trust you have everyone on full alert as ordered mister?"

TINGLER ISLAND, MARATHON ISLAND
THE FLORIDA KEYS
5:10 P.M.. TUESDAY, NOVEMBER 5th, 1998

Lieutenant Walker was swaying from drink and tiredness as he answered the General's question. "Yes sir, I notified everyone they're on forty eight hour alert, sir. Why General?"

General White noticed the slur in his voice, and demanded. "You drunk mister!"

"Is there any other way to be in this stinking world, sir? My ass has been on the front line so many times this is the only way I can handle it any longer, General White."

"God dammit, are you trying to Section Eight out of the service on me, mister?" General White snapped angrily at him and then waited for his reply.

"No way in hell General White Sir. I don't Section Eight on nothing I'm in sir."

"What the hell does Sergeant Ramirez have to say about you being drunk, son?"

"She's threatening to dump my ass in the washing machine to dry me out some, sir."

"That's a damn good idea there Walker. You tell her if she needs a hand, let me know."

"Yes sir. I certainly will General White Sir." Lieutenant Walker fired back at him.

"Walker, cut the drinking and drugs out as of this moment, mister. I have a mission rapidly forming up on us, and you have to organize your entire Unit sir. I don't need you, or any of your other swinging dicks and bouncing tits falling down drunk, or thinking they're seeing monsters in the damn dark, because they got their hands on some bad shit to drink or smoke, buster. Dry them out starting now Lieutenant!" General White growled at the young officer.

"Yes sir, err...General White, but I'm sure you didn't call me to find out if I'm drunk or not, General. What's the fucking latest deal, sir? You mentioned something about forming up the Unit for a possible action sir. Does this mean we're gearing up for anuther operation sir?"

"Your entire Unit's going hot Lieutenant." The General snorted at the arrogant soldier.

"How soon we jumping off sir?"

"Ten minutes ago, and you better start assembling your Rambo and Pambo warriors by the damn numbers. They're ordered to report to Camp Lejeune STAT. Officers and stripes first, no written orders, they're to report by word of mouth. Zip Lip on this one, I don't want any damn reporters picking up orders to report to base over the radio, and meeting us as we disembark."

"I can pull in the entire Unit easy enuf from where I'm standing, sir? You want all the Units to report to back base, sir?" Walker retorted.

"Everyone and more is needed for this one I believe Lieutenant. Walker, you better prepare them for desert duty on this one sir." The General warned his lesser officer.

"Can you give me an idea where we might be heading on this upcoming mission, General?"

"Err... crap on it. I wish this god damn communication was on scramble and secured, sir. I'd feel much better about this damn conversation. Walker, you're going to know soon enough I guess, so I might as well tell you that you're heading for Iran. The Iranians got their hands on a certain number of Russian missiles with nukes, and your group's going to supply us with irrefutable evidence of the damn missiles, so we can level the damn complex. That's about the size of it, sorry you got the shit duty again, but that's what you've been trained for, son."

"We gonna get the support we need on the stinking mission, sir?" Walker growled.

"Yeah, the President's got a real bug up his ass about this one, and the way he's going to scratch it, is by rubbing it on the rubble of these damn missiles in Iran mister. Err... Walker, I don't think this one's going to be the only operation in the Middle East. While we have the Unit there, we're combining two missions together. When you finish one, you might be heading right for the other one, sir. This all depends on if we get information on the second situation in time before the first mission's completed by your elite troops, sir. Either way, plan on a possible double operation on this detail, soldier. We heard some scuttlebutt about another god damn country screwing around with some weapons of mass destruction, and I think the President's going to clean this one up, before it becomes a major situation against..."

"Let me take a stab at it sir." Walker griped as he interrupted the General.

"Take a shot at it Lieutenant if you think you're so smart, mister."

"I believe we'll be heading for Libya next, right General White!" Walker offered.

"You're smart, perhaps a little too damn smart mister. You just won the damn cigar for that guess Lieutenant. Get your people hot. I expect to hear from Captain Leadbetter that your troops are arriving on base later on tonight, sir. Good luck on this one sweat warrior."

Walker set the receiver and turned to Ramirez. "We gotta dry the asses out; we got a mission. We became the cleanup crew every time some country gets their hands on missiles or nukes."

"Oh Walker no, I was hoping we could have a little extra time to settle down, maybe even start a family together before we had to report back to base for another damn mission." Ramirez cried exasperated and then went on with her complaint at her soldier and lover. "God, I can't believe we're heading out on another god damn mission so soon, Bobby. We just got home from one for mission Pete's sake, and we haven't even had time to and enjoy unravel our new home. It's been one mission after the other lately. I'm tired of this shit, I want to stop..."

"Stop what? I never knew you to say you had enough of anything." The Mutt snapped as he came walking in the living room, along with Buckethead and Mother Flanagan close behind him. The three elite soldiers stopped walking and stared at Ramirez.

"We're going out on another mission, Mutt." She cried as she ran for their room.

"What's this shit all about Homes? Another fucking mission this soon man? Where? When dammit?" the Mutt growled as he popped the top of a Bud, and took a pull from the suds.

"She's right, and you gotta stop drinking until we get the scuttlebutt on this mission."

"I'm not going on it this time Walker." The Mutt snarled as he threw his beer across the room.

"I hope you're gonna clean up that fucking mess you just made, pal." Walker warned angrily.

"Didn't you hear me man? I just said I'm not coming on another mission this time. I had my stinking full of this shit, I'm so short time I'm suffering from STS, (Short Timers Shakes), I'm a SDM, (Single Digit Midget) I have less than ten days left to my fricking hitch, Walker. I'm so short time when I'm standing on the ground, my balls are dragging on the fucking floor, man."

"You gonna clean up that stinking mess, right dog man?" Walker repeated at the other soldier.

"Didn't you hear me man! I just said I'm not coming with ya on this mission this time and I really mean it man!" The Mutt bellowed as he hunched over.

"Who the hell are you threatening with that stinking stance, shitbird? I heard you loud and clear, and I told you we gotta dry out for the upcoming mission, buddy. You betta inform the other spudheads we got an operation coming up." Walker warned the Mutt hotly.

"It means nothing to you I said I'm not going this time does it Walker?" the Mutt hissed.

"It would if I thought you really meant it Homes. Mother, you betta get ready, all Officers and NCO's are ordered to report first. The rest of the shits got until the end of the week to report."

"When do we go active Walker?" Mother Flanagan asked with concern in his tone.

"We're already active as far as it goes now Mother. Most of us will report to Camp Lejeune later tonight. I just got word from General White, Captain Leadbetter and the other Officers are heading for base as we talk. Let's get going, I got a shitload of crap I gotta handle before I can close up shop, and then leave for fucking base." Walker ordered the other soldier.

"Any stinking idea where we might be heading on this one Walker? I'd sure like to know our fucking destination before reporting for active duty again, Homes. It helps to know this shit man." Buckethead grumbled as his hand closed over Mother's shoulder.

"None, but you betta be prepared to do a shitload of sweating this time around, Homes."

"I thought you didn't know where the fuck we're heading for buster?" the Mutt snapped as he suddenly flung his arms in the air. He then turned to Mother Flanagan and Buckethead and complained at the two soldiers. "Look at the lousy sonofabitch, he knows damn well where were heading, and he won't be square with us, dammit." The Mutt turned to back Walker and finished his gripe. "C'mon Walker, if you know where we're heading, be right and clue us in man."

Mother stepped up and added his voice to the Mutt's bitch. "I gotta side with the dog man on this one, Walker. If you know where the fuck we're heading, do the right thing and clue us in on the shit, man." Mother stared at Walker as he waited for his reply.

"C'mon you shits, you know how it works around here. We're on a stinking Zip Lip order. The less people who know, the less likely word will get out on us." Walker bitched at them.

Mother Flanagan showed anger in his face as he hissed. "What's this shit Walker? All of a sudden you don't fucking trust us?" Mother pointed to himself as he glared at Walker and added. "Fuck you where you breathe from man! You can go on this stinking mission by yourself for all I care. You can bleed with me, but you can't trust me with our fucking destination man? What a chicken shit outfit this one's turning out to be. What the fuck happened to brothers, same blood, same mud, you watch my back and I watch yours, man? You wanna shit on me, and then expect me to watch your fucking back? I'll frag your damn ass, that's what I'll do." Mother warned.

"Okay Mother be cool will ya man. I see we're a bit testy this morning." The Lieutenant tried a quick smile on the excited soldier, but found it was wasted on his friend as he went on. "Don't look at me like someone just took your fucking crayons away from ya, Mother."

"C'mon Walker, I'm getting moist with fricking anticipation here man. You know you're gonna tell us, so you might as well get on with it, man." Mother smirked at him.

"You gotta tell us. It's the only right thing to do Walker." Buckethead added.

Walker shot a glare and hissed. "I don't gotta do nuthin but stay white and die man!" he turned to Mother, saw his look and knew he had to give in, with a sigh he offered. "Iran."

Mother gave out with a triumphant smile. "There, I knew that'd get your ass Walker."

"Fuck you Mother, didn't you hear what the lousy cocksucker just said to us man? We're heading for fucking Iran. That's a country loaded with a bunch of shit filled angry Persian bastards who'd rather eat your ass, than make peace with us." The Mutt complained as he stomped around Walker's living room swinging his arms up in the air and shaking his head.

Mother Flanagan's smile immediately disappeared when the Mutt's words sank in, and he vented his anger also.

"Christ sake, we're heading for the armpit of the fucking world man?"

"Not to fucking worry. This time it's mostly a stinking recon mission, and once we find the information we need, we're gonna be E-vaced, and the fly jockeys are going to do our act. The way I see it, we'll be taking a little walk in sand, snap some stinking pictures of the bastards, and be outta there by noon drinking suds on that recovery ship, while the Birdmen, (pilots) do their stinking act. Playing with their high priced toys, employing their famous PGMs, (Precision Guided Munitions) while carving up this backasswards nation in eatable little pieces. C'mon people, we're gonna blow the shit outta the place then beat feet the fuck outta there and be back here for breakfast, slick as snot." Walker smiled at the lot, but none of them were pacified by his words. The Mutt was still hot, he wanted out of the mission and was not backing off.

"Fuck this crap man! I'm fucking outta this shit. I'm gonna keep my ass on this stinking rock popping tops and screwing my damn brains out. While you sand fleas trudge through the stinking desert on your way to hell. Christ sake people, I'm just getting over the nicks and cuts I got from the Russia mission. Poncho Villa's still not healed up good and proper, and a few uther guys are down and they'll never be ready for this one, which means we'll be stuck with a shitload of FnG's. I don't like the idea of getting my ass dumped in fucking Iran with a bunch of stinking cherries (new guys) for backup. Like I said, I'm outta this one champ."

Walker glared at the Mutt, steaming he was giving him so much flack about the mission. "All a sudden, you getting hit by a stinking conscious attack, huh dog man? Back off, I'm getting tired of this constant bitching of yours every time our number comes to the top of the deck. If you don't like what you're doing then get the fuck outta the outfit, and I'll find someone else to pick up your slack for ya, fucker." Walker flipped his hand at the Mutt in a dismissive motion.

"That's cold as the uther side of the stinking pillow man. The stinking Mutt's got a right to voice his fucking opinion you know. No one hadta pick up his slack before, it comes with the territory. Everyone knows what's expected of them in this outfit. I'm siding with the Mutt on this one, man. What the hell happens if the brass in Fort Fumble (Pentagon) pulls the same crap they did in Russia? I don't mind telling ya man, it was touch and go there for a while. I thought they were going to leave our asses hanging out in the breeze. If that happens in Iran, we're gonna find ourselves being roasted alive over open fires then feeding a shitload of fricking wild ass dogs. I don't mind working for the Gov, but I have to know they're backing us to the stinking hilt, or I'm not going either man." Mother Flanagan complained as he moved nearer the Mutt.

"Dammit, I see I'm gonna have some stinking trouble with you too now, huh Mother? Look, I'm not gonna wipe anyone's ass for them. I got word the President's gonna back us, the Boss had his fill of nations threatening world security. I think he finally found his stinking balls swinging between his damn legs, and he's gonna swing them over his shoulder this time around." The Lieutenant replied angrily as he glared at his friends and fellow soldiers.

"If that's a fact pal then you can count my ass being in on it." Mother grunted at Walker.

"Me too Walker." Buckethead added with a grin on his face as he stared at him.

All eyes went over to the Mutt, and they waited for him to announce he was in also.

Walker stared at him for several moments, and then he bitched at him. "Hey pip squeak, you're gonna force me to ask ya? Are you in, or are out Mutt? You gonna unass yourself?"

"Pip squeak, pip squeak! I gotta good mind to plant my pip squeak foot up your stinking ass fur ya, Homes." The Mutt let out his breath and then spoke again. "You think I'm gonna trust these dopey ass shits with my girl for this stinking mission, man?"

"I thought so, glad to have you on my side Mutt." Walker offered as he put his fist out. The Mutt immediately pounded it with his then the others hit the top of Walker's then the Mutt's with their own. "It's good to have everyone in on this one, I don't like going against the Iranians."

"Huh? They can't be any betta than the stinking Russians were, and we kicked the shit outta them stinking assholes." Buckethead grumbled as he stepped forward with a grin.

"Yeah shitcan, but we didn't go against all the stinking Russians. We just went afta a small group of Commies. Here, we're going up against the entire Iranian nation. Every mother's son will try and kill us on this one. Even their women will be coming after us with evil intent."

"What's our first move then?" the Mutt asked as he plopped down on Walker's couch.

"We gotta get our asses' hot and moving people. We'll take all here to Lejeune with us whether they're officers, NCOs or uther crap. The more we get back to base, the longer we'll have to prepare everyone for the damn mission. Mutt, you betta get out there and close up the stinking bar, and tell anyone they're to sober up. I'll send the assemble code order out over the handheld. I believe Captain Leadbetter's gonna transmit the assemble code on the universal, the moment he gets word to do so. Betta get a move on it gentlemen."

The Mutt headed out the door first. Mother Flanagan remained where he was standing.

"What's up your ass, Mother? Your feet stuck to the fucking floor all of a sudden man?"

Mother made a quick head movement, using his nose to point over Walker's shoulder. It made Walker turn and he saw Ramirez staring at him. "You okay baby?" He asked her with concern.

"Yes, I'll close up the house and notify the police the home will be empty. They'll keep a eye on it for us. Walker, I hate this." Tears rolled down her cheeks and she went weak in the knees.

Walker opened his arms and she rushed in them. He wrapped her up and gave her a hug and whispered. "I know baby. Who knows, maybe this one will be our last. Maybe this one will fix the world." he kissed her on the forehead as she stared at him from the safety of his arms.

With a deep sigh, Sergeant Ramirez pulled away from his arms and offered. "I have a lot to do, tell Mutt I'll fix sandwiches for everyone. I'll call Barb, and she'll help. Where are the Russian soldiers? They better stay close, they don't know their way around or where to go, and they understand little English, Bobby. I don't want them to get lost on us Walker."

"They're by the pool and they understand more English than you think." He warned.

"Maybe so Walker. Nevertheless, I want them to stay close until we're on base."

"I'll get them." Walker offered, glad to be out of the house. When he walked outside, he saw everyone cleaning up. Many walked around like robots, and knew the word was out. He looked for the Russians they were by the dock. He headed for the Russians, Taras saw him coming and moved to the front of the group to intercept him. "What mission?" She demanded hotly.

"Dunno, all I know is we have orders to report to base, and that means you guys too baby."

"We follow hell if order by you, American big shot soldier you." She stared at Walker.

"Funny you should choose that fricking phrase there because that's where we'll be heading on this mission honey." Walker shot back at the Russian.

"What you say, big American soldier shot you?" Taras asked as she stared back at Walker.

"Nothing baby. Fugetaboutit will ya. You or your Gorkie sisters need anything, extra clothes, some extra underwear? You betta get the crap now for yourselves."

"Everything need have in equipment with us, American soldier you." Siberia pointed to their heavy bags sitting on the patio where they dropped them the night before.

"Stay ready and stay tight. We're moving out within the stinking hour. I have to order a number of cabs to transport this mess out to Miami Airport. I'll have charter planes on standby there as we arrive." The Lieutenant went to leave the female Russian soldiers, but he was stopped when Siberia asked him. "Where head once reach this Miami place of you, sir?"

"Camp Lejeune." He grinned at the good looking Russian female soldier.

"Is this Army Base in you American country, Lieutenant Walker?" Siberia asked Walker.

"Yes, sort of, A Marine Base to be exact, baby." He replied with a grin.

"Is base beautiful this place is, what you call Marathon Island, Lieutenant?"

"No way in hell baby, Lejeune is pure toe jam, a real hell on earth sister. Made that way, and meant to be just that for training purposes, baby."

"Huh, I believe big shot American soldier you. Long live, never see blue water all time, breathe clean air, and see friend people in life like here. I wonder United States so nice, if all America people friend as here. I worry everything told me United State not right. I order believe America people hate good Russian people, I find attitude wrong on Marathon. Everyone friend here, help, it America people can no do enough you. It same all across America, no American soldier you?" Sergeant Taras asked bewildered of the Lieutenant's words.

"Pretty much so I guess." He grinned again at the pretty Russian female.

"What is I hear crime all time, murder all time in you country too, big shot American soldier you?" Taras stared at Walker, while she waited for him to explain this fear to her.

"That's a bunch of hype the stinking news reporters dump on us assholes to sell their damn papers, and fill their news. But crime and murder's only a small part of what makes America tick. The United States got the greatest people in the stinking ever loving world. It's the few bad apples who fuck it up for the rest of us. You'll see the greatness of the United States when you move around a while longer." He again smiled at the female Russian soldier.

"I see ready, but America mistake. It Russia has greatest people." Taras replied with pride.

"That is a load of crap too, bitch. Arrr... that's just more propaganda tripe your stinking leaders put out during the cold war years baby. Every country in the world has great people."

"Arrr... youself big shot America soldier you. It no how you say propaganda. It truth I say you, I know truth, I witnessed many time me self in person." Taras growled as angrily at him.

"Yeah, right, okay whatever you say honey. Russia's got the best people in it. Anything you say, as long as you stay close and pay attention to any orders issued you Gorkie soldiers. I have no intention of locking horns with you at this time, baby." The Lieutenant griped as he headed away from the Russian female. He had not traveled ten feet when he felt someone walking on his heels, he turned to find himself standing face to face with Taras and the rest of her crew.

"What's this shit about bitch?" he snapped as he placed his hands on his hips.

"You order me stay close you all the time I do as you order me. We all do as ordered by you, we stay close you all time Lieutenant Walker." Taras offered with a smile.

"Back off for crap sake, I didn't mean for you to follow me like a stinking little puppy dog, dammit. Look, I want you to keep me in constant eye contact until we leave for base, that's all I want from you people for shit sake." He bitched angrily at her.

"I no understand, you speak word quick to fast understand right, Lieutenant. My English no so good as you, big foolish American soldier you." Taras shrugged and shook her head no.

Walker put up his hands and made a motion of shoving her back as he said. "Keep me in your eye, but back off some from me okay." He pointed to his eyes. "Understand?"

Taras smiled as she rapidly shook her head yes as she announced to her new Commanding Officer. "Understand big American soldier you."

"Good, then fucking do it for me will ya bitch." He complained as he shook his head and then grumbled at himself. "Fucking foreigners for crap sake damn."

IRANSHAHR, IRAN.
NOVEMBER 6th, 1998 2:30 P.M. (6:30 EST.)

Bdellah not only pushed his vehicle for all it was worth, but he pushed his body to the limit to ensure he would arrive where the secret base was supposed to be constructed in the desert. For the past two hours, he had not passed another living thing. The paved roads ended five hours earlier, and the hard packed sand roads, or anything even resembling a road, ended an hour ago. It was hell driving in the desert at night without headlights. His eyes were fatigued by the time he ended his travels for the day. He remained in the desert hidden from view of the locals, and only dared to venture to the town as the sun rose, when he knew everyone was heading for work. For the rest of the day, he made like the invisible man, drawing little attention to himself as he scouted the town out, looking for any signs of the workers employed at the secret base.

The day was hot as hell, and by the early afternoon he started looking around for someplace to get some food and drink and hopefully cool off a little. As he walked through the small town, he spotted a small cafe on a side street, and he growled at himself for not checking the cafe life out a lot sooner. He headed for the only place he was sure of picking up any loose information. He aimed himself at the Iranshahr Cafe, with the torn canvass overhang and broken front window and filthy storefront and chairs all over the front of the place.

As he cautiously entered the café that was as filthy inside as it was outside, and he instantly drew the attention of everyone sitting, or working inside the structure. They all stared at him as he walked across the dining room as if he owned the building, and then he sat at an empty table. No one in Iran trusted another, especially a stranger to their town, anyone could be working for the government. That worker could make anyone disappear from the face of the earth, for so mere an infraction as eating at a table he wanted to be seated at. At this time, the cafe was full of customers, and he glanced at his watch, it was two thirty p.m. Iranian time, and he let out his breath in a deep and exhausted sigh.

The American operative acted like all the Iranians, arrogant and non caring, he glared at anyone who displayed terrible manners by looking at him as if he were a criminal. After plopping down in a broken chair haphazardly repaired by rusted wire, and a few slats of scrap wood wrapped around the damaged leg. He leaned forward on the filthy table that wobbled under his weight. The small oil lamp resting in the center of the table flopped over, and he stood it back up without showing the slightest bit of concern for the debris suddenly burning on the filthy table as he waited to be served by someone working for the cafe.

A thick cloud of cigarette smoke mixed with the fog of burning food, hung heavy in the room that stank of body odor, rotting food, liquor and broken bathrooms. Bdellah picked up the sloppily hand written menu, while the burning debris slid down the wood table. With a sign, he settled for nibbling on some dates, and a side order of pita bread and bitter black tea Iran was well noted for. With a slight nod, he summoned the waiter who walked over to him as if he disturbed his sleep. A cigarette dangling from his mouth, the waiter dropped a wet dish towel on the burning mess on the table, putting out the fire threatening to engulf the table. The waiter then barked at him, while asking what he wanted to eat. After ordering, the waiter remained and added up the cost of the order and then he snapped at him. "By Allah's great breath, you'll pay now or you'll not be eating here stranger." He put out a filthy hand and waited.

He sneered as all Iranians did as he fished for his Iranian cash, he did not dare use any of the American money, it would have immediately drew the attention of the secret police. Something was taking place near the rear door, but he ignored it as he waited for his food to arrive. He saw his waiter hovering near the commotion growing in its intensity. It made him pay a little more attention to what he thought was the owner ripping someone apart. The owner was cursing, spitting and threatening to beat some old man showing absolutely no fear to his threats.

Finally, the old man flung his hands in the air and then he turned his back on the owner of the establishment as he tried leave. The owner rushed his back and as the beggar entered the walkway he shoved him on the back, sending the old beggar tumbling head over heels and slamming in his table and almost knocking it over. Bdellah had to put out his foot to stop the older man from rolling over on top of him. The old beggar stood, and then smoothed out his filthy clothes as if they were made of the finest material, and then he glanced at him.

Out of politeness, the operative bowed politely at the older man, and the beggar smiled pleasantly at him, but the friendliness was cut short by the owner nearly roared at Bdellah. "By the strength of Allah's great will; don't offer this son of a lowly camel's whore any politeness. He's nothing more but a poor follower of the Islamic religion, a weak believer who chooses to have faith in only what he chooses, and he ignores the rest of the writings of the great prophet Muhammad. Allah should see fit to make this filthy non believer eat dogs, and become infested with fleas and lice, and suffer open sores. You be gone from my establishment Ahmed Hussein al-Shamarral, before I call the police and have you arrested for being a non believer, filthy old one." Again, the café owner shoved him hard on the back, forcing him closer to the front door.

When the beggar was outside the cafe, the owner stood before Bdellah, staring at him before apologizing for disturbing his meal. The operative smiled as he remarked to the owner. "Allah Akbar, I'm a faithful believer of Islam."

The owner bellowed with laughter as he slapped Bdellah with a crushing blow on the back, and then he stormed back to the kitchen while screaming at the waiters this time. Soon his food arrived, and he realized just how hungry he was as he quickly devoured the dates and bread. The air was growing worse inside the cafe, because the front door was closed when the owner pushed the old beggar outside the structure. Bdellah stared outside, wondering why the doors were still remaining closed and his question was answered quickly.

Many Iranian military trucks suddenly roared down the main street of the small village heading out towards the vast Iranian desert at the south end of the town. The massive dust cloud raised by the speeding trucks made it so Bdellah could no longer even see the street. The waiter appeared and asked the stranger if he wanted anything else to eat or drink. He shook his head no, and then he looked outside of the cafe window again.

"By the great Allah's Mighty hand and unending mercy, I must beg you to leave my establishment immediately if you're not going to order anymore to eat or drink, stranger. No one is allowed to remain inside my establishment unless he's eating or drinking. No one is allowed to loiter and waste their time in this town." The waiter waited for Bdellah to stand and then leave.

He angrily stared at the waiter for a moment and then he stood. A loud backfire from one of the large truck made both men flinch, and he decided to press his luck and asked the waiter why there were so many military trucks about and ripping through the streets of the town.

In an obvious state of relief, because the waiter knew Bdellah was not working for the police, he replied as he lowered his guard. "Our military is building some structure near our town."

"Where?" he asked as he stared at the older man who seemed angry with the world.

"To ask that question is to die, to answer that question is to die a very slow and extremely painful death, stranger." The waiter said as he walked Bdellah to the door. Once there, he bowed and warned him barely over a whisper. "Stranger to my town, be very careful of the questions you ask in our town. They could cost your foolish life, no matter how innocent they might be to you. There are many ears, listening to hear any treachery aimed against our government, whether it be there or not. We're a very peaceful lot of people here, but our government is working in the area, and when they're around, their ears are listening to everything said by all and no one is safe. Leave the way you have entered my establishment. It's late, and the ears of the secret police will be plenty on this night. May Allah give you a safe journey to your final destination."

"My name is..." Bdellah offered, but he was instantly cut off by the upset waiter.

"I'm not the least bit interested in your name. Be gone from my establishment, the less I know of a stranger to my town, the safer I am."

Bdellah smiled as he slipped the waiter a worn Iranian bill as a tip and then left. Outside he was forced to turn his back to avoid the thick cloud of dust hanging heavily over the town. No windows were open, and no one was milling around outside as the last truck passed at speeds too fast for safety. He remained with his back towards the street as he struggled in his pocket to find his cigarette lighter, and then as he was lighting his cigarette a voice suddenly called out to him. "Kind stranger, you would not have another cigarette to offer one of no use to anyone?"

Bdellah looked around until he saw the old beggar standing at the head of the alley speaking to him. He smiled at the elderly beggar as he fished out a cigarette and he flipped it to him.

"I fear I have need of a light, if you would be so kind as to offer me one, stranger."

Bdellah gave a disgusted sigh, and then he snorted at the old man. "Do you want me to smoke the damn thing for you also, old man?"

The beggar laughed as Bdellah lit his cigarette for him, and he blew the smoke over the stranger's head, paying little attention to the insult just leveled against him.

Bdellah studied the older man intensely as he puffed away on the cigarette. He looked haggard and famished. "When was the last time you ate any real food, my father of endless time?"

"Who knows, who cares to eat any longer, my most caring son of the hot desert sands." Al-Shamarral, the beggar smiled when Bdellah gave him the honor of calling him father.

"Praise Allah's Grace and kindness, I'd be both pleased and honored to buy some food and drink for you to enjoy, father of time."

"Save your praise for a woman who will offer herself up to such a kind man as you obviously are, sir. I don't want or need any food, but I'd be glad to take the money you would've spent on the food for me, my son." The beggar grinned again at Bdellah.

"You live here, old man of the desert?" Bdellah asked, trying to keep the conversation going.

"Too many years to count and admit to, my faithful son of the Holy ways of the Qu'ran. At one time in the recent past, this village was a fine Paradise to live and work in. But with the foolish leaders of our country we had, the beauty of it has been stolen from our towns and hearts and minds. Iran is rapidly dying, and we're too proud and stupid to realize it's future fate. We have concentrate our anger at the Great Satan, and we have ignored our own evil selves and how we treat each other in our own country. We have allowed our religion to be mired in the past times.

"Iran has to come out of the dark ages, our religion has to change as all religions of the world do. We have to understand there is no true Paradise for anyone who kills another soul for any reason. The days of terrorism are over, we have to start to worry about Iran, or Iran will cease to exist in this world, my son. We have deluded ourselves with the thought the one who controls the oil, will rule the world. There's a far greater danger threatening the world, and we're too blind and foolish to read the warning signs written upon the sacred sands of the vast deserts, my son."

"What is this great threat you see and fear so much, old man?" Bdellah asked as he took out his cash, and peeled off a few bills of lesser denomination, and handed them to the old man.

"Water my foolish son of the endless desert sands! By Allah's all knowing wisdom, what good will all the oil of the world do for a nation, if that nation has no pure water to drink? You cannot drink oil, nor grow crops in the filth. We Iranians have to take preventive steps to secure drinking water for our future, and the hell with the want for oil and riches. Once, a long time ago, the United States offered to help us find drinking water in our vast deserts. I remember the many ways the American engineers told us on how they could get clean water supplies for our nation. But when we killed the Shah of Iran, the mighty United States turned its back on our country. Even when we held their people hostage, we could not force America to help us.

"Then the black years of terrorism entered the lives of the faithful Iranian peoples and their hearts, years of forcing the world to turn their foul back on our nation of Iran. Now we work so hard at making Iran strong, by military means rather than by leadership and understanding. We are foolishly guilty of turning our cursed backs on our own people, and we allow our children to starve, or die of thirst so we can buy another rifle, another bullet for that cursed rifle and another missile to kill a person or a nation. All so we'll be armed for the black day when the Americans come and invade our faithful lands. We're so wise a people, yet we're too blind to see through those eyes that still refuse to see the future. We remember not what the United States has done to Iraq in ten days of battle. America's so powerful a nation, if they come for us, nothing outside of nuclear weapons and judgment day would successfully stop them." The old beggar reluctantly flipped the cigarette from his crippled fingers to the ground.

The beggar picked up Bdellah looking at his deformed fingers and he replied. "Another great gift from my kind government, my son." He held up the smashed fingers so Bdellah could get a good look at how the secret police interrogate their captives.

The American operative saw this and offered the old man another cigarette out of kindness.

"Ahh... may Allah bless you for your future years my kind son, with a horde of uncountable and polite children to fill your tent, and a good woman to spend the long nights in joy with."

"He has, but are you not taking a chance of speaking to me like this, my wise father? I could be working with the secret police, and you could find yourself being interrogated in a most unpleasant way again." He grunted as he lit the cigarette for the old man a second time.

"Allah knows well I fear no one man of this world, my foolish son. I can smell the hated police in a herd of a thousand filthy camels. Besides, I trust you my new son, you have an honest face and a very kind heart and eyes. You are no threat against me my son."

Bdellah nodded at the old man as he offered while keeping his tone polite. "By Allah's wide heart and great wisdom, I believe as you obviously do my wise father of the vast desert and time everlasting. Iran should modify its great religion and beliefs to be equal with the modern world."

The old Persian beggar stopped smoking and stared at the young man for a moment before offering. "By Allah's endless mercy, I see there is still a chance after all for Iran's future. You believe what you have just offered to me my son?"

"My Allah take His wrath out on my worthless head if I dare lie, my father of the gray beard. I believe as you, I'm working to bring Iran to the way of the new beliefs to secure Iran's future in the coming age. In this world of constant changes, we have to change or be left behind, staring at the arsis of all those who have passed us in the future years who are enjoying the grapes of production and freedom that Allah has placed out before us to enjoy, my wise father."

"Allah be praised for His great wisdom my son. I see I'm not the only one in all Iran who believes in this new manner of thinking and beliefs, err...?" The beggar put out his hand to shake with Bdellah.

"Please forgive my poor manners, my worthless name is Bader Jiyad al-Kanani." Bdellah shook the mangled hand of the old beggar as he offered the name of the worker he killed back in the Iranian city of Yazd. Although he trusted the old man, he never use his real name whenever dealing with someone he intended to kill in the near future.

"Ahhh... by Allah's wisdom, a proud name it is, but it's not an Iranian name I see. My name is Ahmed Hussein al-Shamarral of the Fifth Tribe of Hajfarah. Why have you come to my little town of Iranshahr? I can tell you're not local, you have lived many years near the water. I know you're a stranger here, because I know everyone who live in the village."

"You're correct my all seeing father of time everlasting, I'm not Iranian my father of the desert wonders. I came to Iran five years ago, to explore the ancient archeological find outside Tehran, but they were destroyed by Iraqi god cursed nuclear weapons and hatred of this country." He skillfully led him away from the cafe front, in case the police were around and noticed the commotion he created inside the cafe. As they walked, Bdellah decided to trust his luck and he inform the old man what he was doing in the village. He leaned closer to the old man as they walked, allowing the noise of the village returning to normal to drown out his whisper.

Car engines revved, horns beeped, and women yelled at young children not obeying their parents and music played, merchants began to again hawk their wares to anyone walking the town. Pleasant odors soon filled Bdellah's nostrils, as merchants cooked chickens, fish and other Iranian dishes in coal pits, to sell to the passerbyers who could afford the asking price. Bdellah's stomach growled in anticipation of the wonderful delights it would soon encounter.

The concerned operative carefully led the old man towards the most noisiest section of the small village, as he whispered to the beggar who stank like old boots and unwashed hair. "My wise father of the dunes, I have worked my way to this village, because I heard Iran was in the process of constructing a secret military complex to build rockets, to carry the curse of the new world to the United States heartlands, my honorable father."

Al-Shamarral's first thoughts were to flee this young stranger while calling out the alarm, but there was something about Bdellah and his presence that stopped him from turning him over to the secret police. The beggar looked deeply into Bdellah's eyes as if to look into his very soul, and then he smiled as he thought he saw the future of Iran written within the twin pools of blue liquid, a future depending on this stranger's shoulders. Al-Shamarral nodded as he pushed Bdellah on the arm. "My son, this is not the proper place to speak of such subjects I fear. I'll lead you to a much safer place where we can speak without fear of being overheard by the wrong people." The beggar took the lead and he rushed Bdellah towards the basement of an old building that looked like it would crumble if someone dared coughed within twenty feet of it.

Al-Shamarral led Bdellah through the basement, moving some debris out of his way with his foot. They came out in a wide secluded courtyard surrounded by other crumbling building. Al-Shamarral stopped and flipped over a rotted door, and then he removed a flask of warm clean drinking water. He turned over a wood box that looked as if it would not support his weight, and he sat down on it. In a booming voice, he suddenly announced to unseen people of the shadows. "I'll speak with this man undisturbed and in peace. I leave it up to my children to warn me if danger approaches us as we speak together, so we'll remain safe while speaking. This is your new mission, to protect our lives." The old beggar cocked his head, and then he listened as if trying to hear the wind speak the words he was seeking to hear.

A low mumble replied. "Yes my father, we'll keep you safe in Allah's light."

Bdellah stared at the old man with questioning eyes until he turned his attention back to him.

"Ahhh... I see you still don't understand what's happening about you, my foolish son. Those who answered my call, will make certain no one dare tries to listen to us while we speak together. My children of the shadows will warn us in advance if the police are once again snooping around our village. Most police are wise enough to avoid this certain section of town. Because they understand it'd cost them their worthless lives to dare enter this area uninvited. The children of the rubble will keep us safe from all harm, it's a minor convenience offered to all who live on the street, by those who live on the streets as well, my son."

Bdellah scanned the rubble covered courtyard that once held the beauty of Iran within the walls, and was unable to locate a single person in or around it. But he could feel the presence of so many lurking about the crumbling buildings. He knew this was the slum area, the ghetto.

Al-Shamarral offered the bottle of water to Bdellah, but he waved it off. The beggar's arm did not move away from him as he held the bottle out in the younger man's face.

Bdellah did not understand what else to do, so he took the bottle and removed the cap and took a drink without wiping the top free of the beggar's germs.

"That was a very wise move on your part my young friend. Because if you did not share a drink with me, my children would not trust you, and they would have attacked and killed you and removed me from possible harm, my son." Al-Shamarral took the bottle and replaced the cap and hid it back under the rubble of broken blocks and other building debris. A rat suddenly darted out over his foot, but al-Shamarral did not flinch a muscle as Bdellah stood and got out of the rat's way as it shot back under the mound of rubble.

"Ahhh... my young new friend, I see you worry much about the things that do you no harm. But you'll allow yourself to dwell within the world where anything you do could cost you your very life. Praise Allah's vast wisdom my son, I believe you were saying before we came here to speak in private and safety, my new son?" The old beggar silenced himself from speaking again, and then he waited for Bdellah to speak more of what he was offering him moments ago.

The American operative was surprised at how smart this old beggar truly was. He was probably well schooled, and he realized he must have been a politician in the time of the old Shah. Again, he decided to press his luck with the old beggar as he went on with what he was speaking of before. "Did you work on the personal cabinet of the old Shah of Iran?"

With fear suddenly blazing in his eyes, the beggar stood, and took a threatening stance against the stranger staring at him as if he had suddenly done something wrong. Other beggars appeared from out of the rubble of the courtyard, and were ready to leap in action at request of the beggar.

"Who are you, and be truthful with me this time if you know what is good for your worthless life, stranger from the vast desert sands. Or that rat you were afraid of moments ago, will be dining upon your lying tongue and deceitful eyes, young master of a thousand flees." Al-Shamarral removed the tooth shaped Jambiya blade from his worn and ripped robe, and he aimed it right at Bdellah's heart and then he waited for his reply.

"By the power of Allah I am right, you did work for the old Shah of Iran, my ancient father of times past." Bdellah asked, ignoring the threat from the knife locked in al-Shamarral's hand.

"Yes, and you obviously work for the cussed Americans? You're a spy for them, am I not right my new found son?" The beggar snapped at Bdellah as he held him in his angry gaze.

Bdellah knew he had to be completely honest with the elderly beggar, or all was lost to him, even his life. "Yes, as did you once I'm certain my all seeing father."

"By Allah you assume much, too much my reckless young son with a wagging tongue and dancing eyes." Al-Shamarral replied as he slowly sheathed his knife, and then retook his seat on the wood box and relaxed as he waited for the stranger to tell him why he singled him out.

"Do you still work for the Americans old man who has the wisdom of the old ones locked within his mind?" Bdellah asked the Persian beggar with concern in his tone.

"No my brash and very daring son! I have lost my contacts with the Americans when the new Ayatollah took over power in Iran. All I once relied upon, has dried up and died when the missiles from Iraq fell from the afternoon sky. By the grace of Allah's merciful will, I was lucky to be out of the capital on that terrible day of death and destruction falling from the sky. I hid in this village when this so called savior of Iran, this self proclaimed Sheik Hassan al-Suhail al-Tamini, this trash from hell on the side of Satan. Had crawled out of the vast desert like a lowly jackal he is to take Command over all of Iran. The fool had even dared to take the time honored title of Sheik, as if it was going to give his worthless meaning credit and true worth to the pulse of the world. He's no man of the religion to call himself Sheik.

"Then once this torturer of the truth took control of the weaken Iran, he had the audacity to proclaim himself ruling Ayatollah. My eyes bear witness to the fools of my country who have flocked around this evil man as if he was the messiah coming, basking in his false strength. Yes, I dwelled in the Shah of Iran's circle of close friends, and yes, I once worked for the Americans. Now you my son, do you work for the Americans, and what is your mission in Iran?"

"Yes al-Shamarral, I work for the Americans, old father of kindness. My mission's to locate this military complex, and observe the going ons there. Then I must report to my contact and explain what I had observed, so they can decide whether or not to destroy the building, and the terrible items held within it, my father." He shrugged at the old man as he stared at him.

"And al-Kanani is not your real name I take it, my son?" the old man said to Bdellah.

"No." he said, knowing he had to be absolutely truthful with the old man now, or chance losing his assistance and future need of the old man.

His last word hung heavy in the air, with al-Shamarral refusing to speak again until he found out this American agent's true name. It was important for him to know it. Bdellah gave out with a deep sigh, knowing he needed this old man and could no longer put him to death as he offered. "Al-Shamarral, please forgive my minor deception, I did not trust you readily my wise father. My name's Mohammed Boua Bdellah, and I was trained in the United States."

A grin slowly crossed al-Shamarral's parched lips, exposing his rotted teeth that added to the stench being emitted from the old beggar's grotesque body. But the grin disappeared as quickly as it had appeared as he said. "Praise Almighty Allah and this mission for the Americans? Your foul lips might lie, but your eyes speak the truth to me my son. What do you think the Iranian military is building in the vastness of the great desert, my new son?"

"I don't remember saying anything was being constructed at this complex, father."

"Ahhh... I have, how you place it, ahhh... yes. I made a slip of the tongue. As old as I am, I'm no fool either my son. I noticed all the activity and military personnel arriving in the area of late, and I dared to venture out to the desert to examine what might be happening there myself." Al-Shamarral announced, knowing he had the information the young American spy wanted.

"Our mouths have been shut by the sands of a thousand years. Perhaps, you would not mind telling me what you have observed on one of these ventures of yours out to the vast desert, al-Shamarral?" Bdellah smirked with a reassuring and pleasant smile.

"Ahhh... you think yourself that much my friend I should accept you so easily into my trust, my heart and my tent, Bdellah? You have the tongue of a liar, and the honor of a fool, my son." Now it was al-Shamarral's turn to smirk at the younger man.

"I see your fear make you foolish my father. Al-Shamarral, if you don't share your information with me. Then I'll be forced to venture out to the deep desert myself to amass the information that is already in your possession, my wise and kind father of the desert sands. Which I feel would be a terrible waste of time, and would show me who truly does not trust whom with their life, old man." He shifted his weight, reaching under himself and he removed an offending pebble from his rearend. He tossed it in the direction the rat had disappeared in.

"By the all seeing eye of the Almighty Allah, I see your point and yes, it's as you have just stated to me my son. Yes, it'd be a waste of your time to search the endless desert especially because you don't know your way in this desert. I'm sure once I tell you what I observed, you'd be forced to the desert to see for yourself, to make certain I'm not speaking for self-satisfaction. Yes, I visited this supposed secret complex, and I saw the hated missiles under various construction stages. I knew immediately it was only a matter of time before an American Agent would turn up, and when I first laid eyes upon your face, I knew instantly you were that agent. It's my duty to help you, I owe it to the late Shah. I'm your honorable servant my son Bdellah." Al-Shamarral bowed politely to Bdellah before he added to him.

"I'll most happily accompany you out to the endless desert, and would be as proud to show you of this secret complex I have discovered out there, and all of what they build at this cursed place of evil, my son. I don't believe the mere presence of these hated missiles in Iran would cause your country this much concern, my son. Is there more to this drama that I have not discovered for myself, my son?" al-Shamarral asked him cautiously.

"Yes al-Shamarral there is much more to this drama than your eyes have discovered. We were informed the nation of Russia sold the instructions on how to construct nuclear warheads for these hated missiles, to the Iranian military. It's my responsibility to locate this complex, and take infrared pictures of it. To get the evidence of these missiles and warheads existence in Iran. Then send it to my country so they can send in the planes to destroy this foul building."

"Much like the attack the Americans had carried out against Libya so many years ago am I correct my foolish son?" Al-Shamarral replied confidently to Bdellah's last words.

"Yes al-Shamarral a surgical strike, one that shall only destroy the complex, along with the foolish technicians working there. The rest of the village area will not be attacked, my father."

"This is good for my old ears to hear, because I have many friends living near Iranshahr. But what would happen if I were to inform you many of our young men were arrested, and they were pressed into slave labor at the site? What happens to these friends of mine, my son? Would we get them out before the attack begins? Or would they perish beneath the American bombs?"

Bdellah returned the stare of the old beggar just as intensely as he answered his question weakly. "I'm sorry for these friends of yours, and their soon to be deaths, al-Shamarral."

"Yes, yes, yes, I understand this as the wise course of action to adopt, and I too am very sorry, for the soon to be deaths of some of my closest friends and neighbors. I'll pray to Allah's mercy for their souls to keep safe for eternity. I shall dearly miss my friends, but I understand this is necessary, attacks on aggression have their share of Martyrs to be offered."

"Yes al-Shamarral, Martyrs are what makes nations strong and free." Bdellah replied sadly.

"Shall we go over what I have observed of this installation constructed in the desert?" Al-Shamarral announced as he waved his arm out before him, and the horde of rabble standing at the ready to attack him in the yard, instantly disappeared. Then he took out a weather beaten map and stabbed his finger on the paper and announced proudly. "Here is where we shall meet, and then we shall travel alone out to this position in the desert, my son."

"This is good, because I must make contact with my control before we head out to the desert, my father of the great sand desert born with the wisdom of the centuries. I want them to know I am working on their orders, and I also want them to know where I am in case something happens and we need help. If they don't know where I am, they can't help us if we run into any trouble." Bdellah replied as al-Shamarral's finger remained pressed down on the well aged map.

"Yes Bdellah, it's most wise of you to make contact with your people back in the United States and let them know where you are when we venture out into the vastness of the endless desert. As it is as wise for us to travel separately into the desert at night. One never knows when the Iranian police might appear. Be prepared tonight, for the desert's a very unforgiving place to wander about. Observe the sky, and read the signs about you. Tonight, the desert will be most unpleasant I fear. I have studied all the signs, the winds will be aroused and blowing with anger on this dark night.

The sand will be cutting, so dress protectively or the sands will blast you to dust. Then your soul will follow the forever blowing grains of sand to the end of the earth and time itself. Bring water to drink and wait for me to appear before you."

"You'll not be waiting for me at this position when I arrive there tonight, my father?" Bdellah questioned with concern, as he stared at the old man preparing to leave him.

"As I warned you before when we spoke, I'm no fool my young son who has obviously not retained the wisdom your parents have instilled within your foolish head. I'll watch you from a safe distance as you walk upon the soft sands of my desert. I'll stay well out of sight until I'm quite certain you're not being followed by anyone we don't want knowing of our business in the desert on this foul night, Bdellah. It's most wise of the both of us to take certain precautions, when dealing with the hated secret police of Iran. They're a ruthless bunch of camel eaters and cutthroat murderers." Al-Shamarral warned cautiously.

Bdellah let out a sigh of relief as he replied to the beggar's words of warning. "Father of the gray beard, what time do you want me to arrive at this position you ordered?"

"Can you read a compass faithfully and correctly, my foolish son from the land of the Americans? Be truthful with me so I know for certain if you can read a compass."

"Yes, of course I can read a compass my cautious father." Bdellah replied proudly.

"In the dark I add, young bragger of a fool who does not take what I offer him very seriously I'm afraid?" The old beggar snapped nastily at the American Agent.

"Yes I can read a compass even in the dark, my wise father of time." Bdellah snapped just as proudly back to the grinning beggar who was staring so intensely at him.

"Good, this is very good for me to understand. Then we should meet at this position at the high moon. (twelve midnight) It's a good time to be out an about in the deep desert, wandering in the darkness with the angry wind protecting us from any who we don't want to come across in the desert. The wind will also work out very well for us by covering our tracks in the sand almost as quickly as we make them. It'll furthermore keep the ones who we don't want around us, resting in their cursed homes and fortifications for the night's time, no?"

"Yes, all you tell me of I understand perfectly and agree with it all as well my father. Shall we start my father of great wisdom and kindness? I have to locate my radio and make contact with my people as soon as possible." Bdellah offered as he stood and stretched.

"Yes my young son with much responsibility, you must remember to bring water with you in the desert tonight, and dress against the biting of the harsh wind and blowing sands properly. Although it'll be cold in the desert at night, the winds will make it as dehydrating as the day's blazing sun, my foolish son. Be well prepared for anything, are you armed by any chance of good luck, Bdellah?" Al-Shamarral warned and asked the young man at the same time.

"Yes my father, I am with protection." Bdellah said with caution in his tone.

"This is good for me to know as well, my young wild one. For any fool to walk in the middle of the night on the dangerous and ever shifting desert sand without arms to protect himself with. Would only end up with their worthless bones being bleached white by the unforgiving and burning angry eye of Allah in the morning sun's harsh glare. Once the desert dregs have killed you for what little you might carry upon your worthless person, my son." Al-

Shamarral admonished the young man as he turned, and then he walked away from Bdellah towards one of the other members of the group standing out in the open, while waiting for the old man to finish speaking with this stranger to their group of survivors. But before he could walk off, Bdellah called the old man back to his side.

CHAPTER EIGHT

The American spy Mohammed Boua Bdellah wanted to know more of what they had planned for the night, and he Ahmed Hessein al-Shamarral continued to go over all of what he had observed in the desert, and when al-Shamarral finished, he moaned aloud to the young man. "I'll see you at high moon in the vast desert tonight as I offered, my new son."

Bdellah knew he had to make contact with his control, and he asked the old beggar. "Al-Shamarral, I have need of my radio, and once I pick it up I'll need a secured place to leave it.

It's my last radio, and one I'll need throughout the rest of this mission here in Iran."

"Allah knows that I have such a place for it to be stored safely for as long as needed. There are many such places discovered when you live out on the street, my son."

"Fine my father of the vast desert sands, I shall leave now and retrieve my radio, and then I'll make contact with my people in the United States. Then I'll return to this exact place with my radio to hid it until I have need of it again." Bdellah offered cautiously.

Al-Shamarral grabbed Bdellah by the wrist, and warned in a curt tone of voice. "I'll accompany you as you travel to your radio. You'll not leave my sight, if you wish to remain alive long enough to complete your mission for the sake of yours and my nations, fool."

"That'll not be necessary my father of the vast desert, I can look after myself very well, al-Shamarral." The American operative looked deeply into the staring eyes of the old man.

"Please Bdellah, I'm but a foolish old man who suffers from many fears, indulge me I caution you wisely, son. Praise Allah's will, it's for your own safety that I speak, unless you no longer trust the old al-Shamarral to guide you with my wisdom of many years of age?"

Bdellah shook his arm free of al-Shamarral's hold. He looked at the old man and then smiled as he offered kindly. "Yes al-Shamarral, I'd be honored if you accompany me to find my radio. Although I'd move more swiftly if I work alone, nevertheless you'll come with me."

"The desert is a dangerous place to be about during the daylight, but it's late and I fear by the time you find your god cursed radio. It'll be dark and you might lose your way, or be attacked by the ones who own the night's darkness. I'm certain once you spoke to your people, they'll demand you go to the complex with me, to make certain all I told you is correct, and you'll need someone to show you the safe way to the site, my son." Al-Shamarral smiled at Bdellah.

"Yes my father of the truth and justice, shall we go al-Shamarral?"

"Yes, lead the way for your foul radio, for I'll stop you if I feel you're heading towards danger, my foolish son. I know where the night people stay, and I'll stop you from stumbling into them. You must remember, if I tell you to stop you must stop, or you'll find yourself alone, and I'll be sitting in the filthy café causing the owner more grief, while you're being tortured my friend."

"I understand, shall we go then my father?" Bdellah replied to his words of warning.

CAMP LEJEUNE, NORTH CAROLINA. NOVEMBER 6th, 1998 OH, SIX FIFTY FIVE HUNDRED HOURS EST

Lieutenant Robert Walker was able to make contact with ninety percent of the soldiers in his group, before leaving the tiny Island of Marathon the night before. He checked in with Captain Bruce Leadbetter, and informed him of the few soldiers he was unable to make contact with.

Lieutenant Walker had the grunts closest him, the ones he trusted the most. The soldiers settled in barracks twenty eight which Walker took for his own. It was a good mixed crew with the Mutt at Walker's side, No Neck, McNip, Roach, Wacko, Mother Flanagan, Boot Camp, Repeat, Hardon, Snatch, Shot Gun and Blood Clot, the Unit's medic. Ali Baba, Suds, Danko, Scrap Iron, Payback, Chevy, because all Antonio Alvarez did was talk about Chevies. The Ghost, Hunter, Sticks, CoCo-G, Poncho Villa, Short Round and

Stainless, Geronimo, Dead End, Prowler, No Finger, Short Cut, and Smith and Wesson. The Goat who got his tag because he ate anything, whether it was fit to eat or not if he was hungry.

Stalker the outfit's SATCOM, or Satellite Communications man. Nintendo and Diaper Man, like Mother Flanagan, always got stuck with the new recruits. Dock Rat, Lipman, Plus Ugly, Hard Core and Gas, Zippo, Griper, Wild Card and Buckethead. Jungle Bunny and Sun Tan, and the Russian male, AK. These soldiers made up most of the elite specialized troopers Walker wanted surrounding, and fighting with him. The list included women warriors he felt were equally as good fighters as any males. Sergeant Ramirez, Fun Bags because of the size of her breasts, Fire and Ice, Baby Tee, likewise named because of the size of her breasts. Foreplay, One Night, Moss, Bouncer, Jail Bait, Breeze, Hipster and Hand Full, named for breasts, Cabbage, her name was Cabot. The three female Russian soldiers, Siberia, Caviar and Mink rounded out the rest. All the tag names were chosen to highlight a particular deformity, a personal mannerism or idiosyncrasy, or odor as in Walker's case, Road Kill, or a personal character trait.

The names bestowed on the soldiers, would not thrilled their parents because they would be shocked to know what their fellow soldiers called their children. But in the tight knitted world of the specialized soldiers, a chosen name meant he was accepted into the ranks of the elite and close friends. Each soldier were as proud of their tag name, as they were of their given names. This name was an honor sought after by recruits the world over and not given lightly, nor was it treated with disrespect no matter what the name represented. It was a name given to a soldier to make it easier for the other soldiers to put up with their business, a business included legalized murder. The name enabled the soldier to detach him or herself from their grizzly actions. It allowed them to kill using the Unit's given name, dirtying it up while keeping his civilized name free from marring stain created by the death he or she caused.

Captain Bruce Leadbetter sent the 'report to base' Command over the radio, and he received confirmation from the still missing soldiers. He was furious the few soldiers were obviously not carrying their communicators on their person as instructed. This was something they were ordered to do when they were on leave, after returning from the action in Russia. The Captain made note of the ones who failed to follow orders, vowing he would have his revenge on them.

"Are your people settled in yet, Lieutenant?" Captain Leadbetter growled at his officer.

"Yes sir." Walker grinned back at the Captain as he responded.

"Fine, I have fifteen walking around without their damn ears on, sir. They're mine when they finally turn up. I'll transmit the report signal all day, any fucker who doesn't report in by Twenty Four Hundred is out of the Unit, period. I'll teach these assholes not to follow fucking orders."

Walker shrugged as he leaned forward, he opened the small icebox and removed a Pepsi.

Captain Leadbetter stared at Walker for a moment and then he went to the icebox and checked and then mumbled at the young Lieutenant. "Whatsumatta, no more damn Buds in here?"

"Yeah, but I'm cut off until after training's completed, and we reached our assigned target, sir. Then, I'll drink if I want one, Captain." The Lieutenant took another pull from the ice cold Pepsi.

"That's good thinking on your part mister? You really like that shit, huh Walker?"

"It's only second to fucking beer, Captain." Walker smirked back at the officer.

"I bet it is. Assemble your damn people, let me see." Captain Leadbetter looked at his watch. It was Zero, Seven Ten Hundred Hours. "Err... you better have your pack of screaming eagles assemble on the grinder at Zero, Eight Hundred Hours. I'll brief them on the upcoming operation at that time, sir. Did you tell any of the dumb shits about the fucking mission?"

"Just a few of them sir. They know we're heading for Iran for a picture taking session, sir. I told them the plane jockeys will carry out most of the burden on this mission, sir."

Captain Leadbetter stared at Walker for a few long seconds, and then he bellowed at the young military officer. "Who the hell clued you in on this fucking target, mister? Brother, have you got your nuts twisted up in a god damn knot now, shithead."

"Whaddaya mean by that load of crap Captain?" he snapped back, getting angry himself.

"Walker, your troops are going in to take over this damn Iranian complex, mine the missiles and labs. Before you do any of that destroying shit, you have to secure the complex for however long it takes to locate the crap on their nuclear warheads and missiles we want. The Boss wants paperwork on this crap. I believe the President's going to use it to club the damn Russians over their head with it. The President wants to prove to Russia and the world what Iran was up to in the desert. He's got intentions of hitting Libya after this mission has been completed. I heard scuttlebutt about this being a double edge mission." Leadbetter glared at Lieutenant Walker.

"I heard the same fricking thing myself Captain Leadbetter. I was led to believe this one was nothing more than a stinking cake walk on the wild side of life, sir. Snap me some damn pictures for the flyboys, an in and out mission and I'll be home by Sunday." The grinning Lieutenant snapped his fingers to show the Captain he believe the mission would be over in a flash.

"You're living in a fucking dream mister. How the hell long were you in the service anyway buster? Lieutenant, have you ever known any god damn operation we ever been sent out on to be a fucking cake walk for us grunts, or being completed just like that, asshole." Captain Leadbetter mimicked Walker's move and he snapped his fingers back at him.

"Yeah, I got your stinking point Captain." The Lieutenant snapped at the other officer.

"Walker, just assemble your damn people at Zero, Eight Hundred Hours, and I'll brief them at this time mister. Better get out there and inform the flaming assholes I'll eat alive any mother fucking Squid that shows up late for muster. Them Russian bitches show up yet?"

"Yes sir, they were with me on Marathon, and I dragged them up here when I reported in sir."

"How do they look Walker?" the Captain asked with a smirk on his lips.

"Hot as shit I tell ya sir!" Walker grinned back at the Captain.

"I don't mean that shit, dip stick. I meant, how do they look? Do you think they can handle themselves okay on a mission, I mean when the fucking crunch time comes-a-knocking?"

"Yes sir, they proven themselves pretty well during the Russian operation, Captain."

"Yeah, I know they did good in their own fucking country, Walker. They had no other stinking choice but to do good in Ruskieville, or their damn President would've had them drawn and quartered and fed to their dogs. I was referring to how you think they'd do working in our Unit, as a team member Walker." Captain Leadbetter asked as he watched his Lieutenant quickly finished off the Pepsi, and then dunked the can in his waste basket as if it was a basketball.

"What's this shit about, you suddenly one of them damn Harlem fucking Globetrotter shits? If you're trying for that team, I got news for ya ass, mister. You're the wrong color and you have a long way to go for it buster." Captain Leadbetter gave a laugh at the Lieutenant.

Walker ignored the barb fired off at him as he replied to his Commanding Officer. "Captain Leadbetter Sir, I believe the Russian chicks will hold up their end of the party when we start dancing with the bad guys, sir. But I just can't bring myself to trust them completely yet, sir."

"I don't either, but I'll take your word for them new Russian pukes, Walker. Hmmm... you say they're hot to look at, huh? You birds party with them damn Russian hens yet, mister?" Captain Leadbetter asked the young Lieutenant with a sneer crossing his lips.

"Yep, like I said, they're hot as hell sir." He replied proudly to the other officer.

"Why you lousy shit you, you could've at least invited me to one of these god damn parties of yours, mister. I heard they're damn good and wild, didn't it occur to you I might be interested in joining your little den of sin and do some partying with the rest of you guys?" Captain Leadbetter snapped as he opened his center drawer, and he removed a file folder and slammed it down on his desk in front of him, he knew he would never really party with anyone from the outfit.

Walker did not reply to the Captain's words as he leaned back in his chair.

"I didn't think so, thanks for nothing Walker. I'll remember this shit. I'll file it next to that stunt you and your sidekick, did when you birds set my damn tent on fire. The Mutt still like playing with matches?" Leadbetter hissed as he removed a few sheets of paper from the file.

"Yep. We almost changed his damn name to Matches, Captain. Zippo's was already taken by one of the explosive ordinance people of the unit sir. What's this crap sir?"

"It's the name of the fucking new pukes linking up with our little family, mister. It's the list of some soldiers from Italy, Spain, and France arriving shortly. It's my responsibility to bring these birds up to speed after they arrive. The English soldiers are here, and I put them in barracks twenty seven, right next to yours. Better get going, and get your people in motion Walker. It's late, and we have a shitload of crap to cover, and little time to cover it in mister."

"When do you think we might be shoving off for action?" Walker asked, turning serious.

"That's a good question there. We might be jumping off by the end of next week I figure."

"Next week! That doesn't give me a helluva lot of time to prepared my people." Walker growled as he stood and leaned over and rested his hands on the desk, staring at the officer.

Captain Leadbetter stood and he put his nose just inches away from Walker's face as he snarled right at him this time. "Prepare for what grunt? As far as you're concerned, you pack of shitbirds are to be prepared for action at a moment's notice, that's why the Boss branded you shits the Rapid

Response Force, mister. Get your fucking hands off my god damn desk, before I have them lopped off and fed to you for fucking breakfast, buster."

Walker did not back down an inch as he hissed back at his Commander. "I want to know what this fucking mission's about. So I can betta prepare my people correctly for it Captain."

Captain Leadbetter completely ignored Walker's demand as he fired back at him just as nastily. "I ordered you to remove your fucking hands from my desk, and that's what you'll do buster! Or I'm gonna apply a little size eleven education to your fucking backside mister."

Walker removed his hands and calmed down a bit and then offered. "Look Captain, I hafta protect my people. I hafta know what the hell they're getting themselves into in this mess."

"What are you an insurance company now, buster? If they want insurance, let them deal with Allstate. You can't protect everyone's ass you know mister. Someone has to pick up the tab, it goes along with the fucking territory we dance in, Walker." Captain Leadbetter said as he retook his seat and then tried to dismiss Walker with a mere wave of his hand.

"That may be so sir, I'm no insurance shit, but I can stop as many of my troops from dying as possible. And the only way to do that is to make sure they're prepared for the mission."

Captain Leadbetter stared at Walker and then barked at him. "You're right, your troops have to be prepared properly for their next damn mission buster. So why are you wasting your fucking time barking in my god damn face like this, when you should be working with your damn troops mister? Get the fuck outta my office before I have your ass removed by force. I don't have the time for this macho man bullshit you're trying to lay down on my ass, buster."

"I want to know a little more about this upcoming mission we're heading out on Captain, and I wanna know it now!" Walker demanded as he slammed his fist on the Captain's desk.

Captain Leadbetter jumped back to his feet and bellowed at Walker as angry as he could speak. "Whatsumatter buster, you getting cold fucking feet or something on my ass?"

"The fucking ink don't run when you mix a little GI blood with it, sir." Walker growled back.

"In combat Walker, you better be quick, or you're going to be dead. There's no in-betweens in our line of line of work. Get out of my damn office, now!" Captain Leadbetter barked again.

Walker prepared to fend off an attack from the fuming Marine Captain, but he was smart enough not to allow this confrontation to go to where his ass was placed in more trouble than a little bit. He finally stood, his body shaking with anger, and he thought better of it and snapped to attention, ripped off a sharp salute to the Captain and then he left his office. Lieutenant Walker showed the Captain he was still pissed by not waiting for Leadbetter to return his salute as he called out. "When is Major Frank Pizzorusso due in Captain?"

Captain Leadbetter stared at the back of Walker and then growled at him. "Forget about his fucking ass on this mission, he's assigned to other duty at this time mister. Muster's at Zero, Eight Hundred Hours, any Squid late will eat his own damn dick for fucking breakfast."

"Who the fuck's gonna be running the stinking Op then, sir? I need to know who the commander is gonna be sir." Walker griped as he flinched at the word Squid, it was used for the trainees and boots. He felt the Captain was calling him a trainee and was insulted.

"Don't know for sure at this time mister, get the fuck out of my office I told you fucker!"

As Walker closed the door the phone rang, it was Chairman of the Joint Chiefs of Staff and Captain Leadbetter offered. "General White sir, the troops showed up as ordered sir. I have a few stragglers, I guess they were caught out of position. Everyone should be on base by Twenty Four Hundred Hours or they'll be dead, sir." Captain Leadbetter added with a chilling tone.

General John White knew Captain Leadbetter did not truly mean his last threat, so he ignored the remark as he offered calmly. "Captain Leadbetter, I have Colonel Joseph Salsiccia reporting for duty, and he's to be an important cog on this mission, but you're the one who'll be in Command of this entire operation sir. Errr... Captain, there's a promotion in it for you because of this leadership. As of today you're now a Colonel, sir."

"Is that a full bird Colonel, General White?" the Captain asked smugly.

"Colonel, I never saw a fucking eagle that can fly with only one wing, have you sir?"

"No sir, thank you for the bump in rate sir." The new Colonel Leadbetter replied proudly to the powerful and well liked Chairman of the Joint Chiefs of Staff.

"Don't thank me Colonel Leadbetter, you earned it during that action in Russia, sir. Sorry I didn't get back to you before this time sir. You did a bang bang job there Colonel. Well, that's about it for now, I have nothing new to report, not until my operative reports in. I wanted to tell you Colonel Salsiccia was going to help run this damn mission with you sir. I'll be back to you the moment I get anything new. Good luck on this mission, I believe you're going to need all the luck you can possibly muster on this one, Colonel Leadbetter Sir."

The new Colonel could not hide the grin plastered on his face as he replied to the Chairman. "Thank you General White Sir." He then slammed the phone down, and he bellowed out for his aide. "Sergeant Kirkpatrick, get your fucking ass in here on the double quick mister."

Sergeant John Kirkpatrick rushed into Colonel Leadbetter's office. "Sir, I was ready to land on Walker's ass if he went too far with you sir. He would've never got to you sir."

"I know that Sergeant." Colonel Leadbetter smirked at his Sergeant.

"I wanted to assure you I had your back sir. That one's an excitable chap Captain."

"He's concerned for his fucking troops as he should be, he's a damn good soldier and Officer mister. Sarge, head over to the PX and pick me up a set of pigeons for my collar."

"You're shitting sir, you got a raise so long overdue from Brass Hat, sir." Kirkpatrick announced, genuinely happy for his Commander.

"Yep, and I can hardly wait until I see the expression on the Squid's faces when they see the big birds standing on my fricking neck, Sarge." Colonel Leadbetter replied proudly.

"A full bird Colonel, that's great new Colonel Leadbetter." The Sergeant added.

"It had to be a full bird Colonel. You ever see an eagle that can fly with clipped wings?"

Sergeant Kirkpatrick did not reply, he could not because he was already out of the door by the time the new Colonel finished bragging about his rate increase.

Colonel Leadbetter walked over to the mirror and quickly removed his Captain bars. Then he pressed down his uniform, buttoning his pockets and straightening out his jacket. Sergeant Kirkpatrick rushed back in the office with the blue box clasped in his paw. "Here they are sir, the assholes wanted to see authorization before they sold the damn things to me, sir. I told them they were for Colonel Albanio visiting the base. I told the ass he lost his eagles and needs a new pair. That did the trick and they couldn't sell me the damn things quick enough to me, sir."

"You're lucky, you knew what I would've done to your body with a fucking rusty nail, if you turned up without those there babies." Leadbetter complained as he took the small box.

"I shudder to think about it, sir." Sergeant Kirkpatrick joked as he helped Leadbetter place the eagles on his collar. "Here sir, allow me to do that for you. A full bird Colonel shouldn't be messing around with the little things sir. Hold still, there, you look like a new dollar bill sir."

Colonel Leadbetter looked in the mirror and smiled at his reflexion as he remarked to his Sergeant. "You got that right mister, let's flaunt these little babies in front of the rest of those damn Squids. I can't wait to see Walker's puss when he sees these hawks staring back at his ass." Colonel Leadbetter checked his watch and saw it was nearing eight and announced. "Let's go, you control the assembly. I don't want Walker to think he's in charge of anything."

"Got ya sir." Sergeant Kirkpatrick replied as they rushed out of the office.

THE DESERT OF IRAN.
NOVEMBER 6th, 1998 8:30 P.M. IRANIAN TIME

The American Operative Mohammed Boua Bdellah fumbled around in the desert where the HF-43 radio was supposed to be hidden. It was a small handheld solar powered portable unit employing a high frequency anti jam system, using the new SHINCOM technology incorporated in the advanced digital switching system for the secured burst transmission. It was difficult to see what he was doing in the twilight using the locator no larger than a pack of cigarettes. For three minutes the buzzer moaned, informing him he was very near the missing radio.

Finally, he found it buried in a foot of sand and pulled it out and pushed the button, the indicator warned him the batteries were very low, and he would have to charge them before transmitting his report back to his control in Washington. He aimed the solar collector at the remaining sunlight and the batteries quickly charged up. The agent watched the indicators climb rapidly. As he waited for the batteries to be completely charged up, he assembled the umbrella aerial and stuck it in the sand, and then hooked the wire to the center and locking block that properly aligned the aerial with the satellite uplink setup.

Bdellah carefully scanned the area around him; he was in the perfect position to remain unobserved by anyone. He smiled when he realized whoever hid the radio for his use, picked the best possible position for it. One offering the user advantage of spotting any possible pursuers before they had a chance to spot him and what he was doing. This assured him the time needed to destroy the radio and defend himself, or flee. He checked the indicator, his batteries were nearing ninety percent charged already. He lightly tapped his foot in the sand while waiting for the needle to climb to the fully charged indicator level.

Finally, the radio was ready for his use, he hit the transmit button and the unit sent out a high pitch whine, it was broadcasting his call name. Instantly, a reply whistle returned, and Bdellah watched the four inch monitor screen. The words appeared in a rush, giving him enough time to read them, before they disappeared in the void of electronic death.

/\/\/\ SAND STAR, NORASATCOM.
BEGIN TRANSMISSION NOW. OVER /\/\/\

The American operative known as Bdellah quickly tapped out his message on the miniature keyboard of the radio in a rush, his words were sent the instant they were typed out on the tiny radio pad. It was hard to send a message without seeing what he was sending out, because of the darkness of the night rapidly closing in on him and the words disappearing almost as quickly as he typed them. The glare from the tiny screen did not help his typing either.

/\/\/\ SAND STAR TO BIG BOY... /\/\/\

A stop transmit was broadcast, and Bdellah thought his position might have just been compromised until the explanation came in over the monitor.

/\/\/\ SAND STAR TRANSMISSION
TRANSFERRED TO BIG BOY'S LAIR.
RESUME TRANSMISSION IN
FIFTEEN SECONDS. OVER. /\/\/\

CIA HEADQUARTERS, LANGLEY, VIRGINIA, WEDNESDAY, NOVEMBER 6th, 1998. ZERO TEN HUNDRED THIRTY HOURS

CIA Director John Raincloud was scanning over a stack of reports when his scrambler machine suddenly screamed to life on him. He immediately read the call in numbers and he knew instantly it was a communication coming from his Iranian operative. He rang General White, the phone rang three times before being answered.

"General White's office, what can I do for you please?" General White's secretary asked.

"Mary, Director Raincloud here, is the General in please?" the Director asked politely.

"Director Raincloud, how are you this morning sir? Yes the General's in, but he's currently engaged at the present time, sir." Mary purred sweetly into the phone.

"I'm fine, but you have to do me a favor and interrupt him, young lady."

"The General left strict orders he was not to be disturbed, Director. Sorry sir."

"Mary! Arr... tell him it's a Class Two Alert that should do it and keep you out of trouble."

"Thank you Director, that's all you had to say sir. Hold the line please." Mary buzzed General White and informed him Director Raincloud was on the line with a Class Two Alert.

"Yeah Raincloud whaddaya have for me sir?" General White barked in the phone.

"A message from Sand Star coming in the next few seconds, sir. I thought you might want to know about the report coming in sir." Director Raincloud offered to the military officer.

"I'll be right over John." The General broke off the connection and was observed running through the halls of the Pentagon to a staff car.

Director Raincloud stared at his monitor as Sand Star's words appeared as a hard copy print out, as the type was printed out at the same time, and sent over to his lock box. As well as on the hard drive of the main computer for future reference.

/\/\/\ SAND STAR TO BIG BOY. BRAKE... /\/\/\
/\/\/\ HAVE RELIABLE INFORMATION MILITARY
COMPLEX EXISTS. BRAKE...
AM PREPARING ENTER DESERT TO HAVE MARK ONE
EYEBALL ENCOUNTER WITH SAID COMPLEX.
BREAK...
WE WILL BEGIN FIRST EXCURSION TO IRANIAN SITE,
THEN
BEGIN SURVEY OF SAID INSTALLATION AND REPORT
YOU MOMENT SURVEY
COMPLETED BY US. BREAK...

General John White rushed in Director John Raincloud's office and sat in a chair and watched the agent working on his computer. The powerful CIA Agent was stunned the General reached his office so quickly, until General White mouthed the words between gasps.

"Marine Corps HMX-1 squadron." General White offered with a grin.

"How the hell did you ever wrangle one of those babies from the President, General?" Director Raincloud marveled, knowing the private helicopter fleet stationed at Quantico Virginia, was the personal fleet primarily used by the

President and Vice President of the United States, and some of the other members of the President's staff.

"The President was visiting at the Pentagon and he gave me permission to take his machine, because some of his security agents had me blocked in tighter than a virgin's ass at the parking lot, Director. What's coming in for us John?"

Director Raincloud pointed towards the monitor as he replied to the Chairman. "What's this about a Mark One Eyeball encounter sir?"

"How soon we forget John, that's a military term meaning he's going to eyeball the installation himself. To make certain it's a complex, and the Iranians are constructing the missiles and warheads at the site like we believe they're doing." The General smirked at Raincloud.

"What's he sending us, John?" General White grumbled as he read Sand Star's report over the Director's shoulder on the computer screen. He stopped reading when he came to a confusing part, and bitched at the Director again. "What' the fucks this shit about we're going to the complex? What the fuck does your Agent have, a turd in his fucking pocket John?"

Director Raincloud laughed as he replied to the Genera's question. "Evidently, my Agent must have located a friend to help him through the desert. This isn't an unusual thing for him to do, General. My Agents are instructed to enlist the help of any locals, but only if he's positive the local can be trusted. We learned a long time ago to use this tactic, and it saved us a helluva lot of time. Besides, it stopped one of my Agents from stumbling into a trap more than once sir."

"How many times did one of these so called trusted locals lead one of your god damn Agents into a fucking trap that cost that damn Agent's his life, John?"

"That happened more times than I care to remember and admit to, General." Director Raincloud grumbled as he turned back to the monitor until the report from his operative working in Iran ended without adding much more information for either man.

Director Raincloud looked at General White and then he offered. "John, if you have any needs, wants, or further wishes. Now's the time to make the requests known while I'm still in contact with my Agent in the field, sir. I don't want this operative making too many contacts with us. Every time he reports, his chance of being discovered increases a hundred fold, sir."

General White slowly rubbed his chin as he went deep thought of the vital information he needed for his troops when they go active against the Iranian complex. He knew the troops were going to attack even if the missiles were not being constructed at the site as suspected. A thousand thoughts instantly flashed across his mind, making him sigh with exhaustion. The General could not get everything he wanted, so he decided on the most important items he needed from this agent working in Iran. "Err... John, I need a detailed map of the entire area in question, covering as much of the complex as he can possibly get for us sir."

"That shouldn't be too much of a problem for him to accomplish for us sir. My operative's going to hang around the complex for a certain period of time, until he can confirm what's going on at the site. While he's there, he should have no problem compiling a detailed map for your troop's benefit and our future needs General. I'll send out your request to my operative with my sign off message to him, General White Sir."

"Now your operative finished transmitting, how long will he remain on the open key before signing off himself, and disappearing to wherever the hell the damn spies hide, Director." General White asked as he watched Raincloud's fingers dancing on the keyboard.

"My Agent's ordered to remain on key for twenty seconds after finishing his report to us sir. If no response from me begins in that amount of time. He'll immediately break down his unit and then he carries out his ordered responsibilities, or he moves over to next safe spot in which he'd transmit from, if I was using him for an ongoing info gathering mission, General." John said as he punched the keys, knowing he had a few seconds left before the operative would break down his equipment and disappeared again. He knew each letter transmitted to his agent, was stored inside the computer. The only thing that would stop this message from reaching the operative, was if he was arrested, and the enemy confiscated his communication unit, or he had to break down to avoid detection. The message was going through, so Director Raincloud knew neither fears were taking place, and his operative was still on the key.

Mohammed Bdellah was just about ready to break down his radio aerial when Director Raincloud's message crossed his monitor screen. The startled agent stared at the screen that shined brightly in the twilight.

/\/\/\ BIG BOY TO SAND STAR. OVER. /\/\/\
/\/\/\ YOU ARE INSTRUCTED TO GO THROUGH
OBSERVATION
OF SAID INSTALLATION. BREAK... YOU ARE
INSTRUCTED
TO SUPPLY DETAILED MAP OF SAID AREA,
INCLUDING ARMED
FORTIFICATIONS, MACHINE GUN STRUCTURES,
MARKING POSITIONS

TANKS, ARMOR VEHICLES, NUMBER TROOPS GUARDING SAID
COMPLEX, NUMBER WORKERS AND TECHNICIANS.
BREAK...
INCLUDE NUMBER ROADS LEADING TO COMPLEX, VILLAGES OR
TOWNS NEAR COMPLEX WHERE HELP MIGHT COME WHEN BEGIN
ATTACK ON COMPLEX. BREAK... INTERESTED LOCATION OF NEAREST
AIRPORT, OR ROADS ABLE SUPPORT WEIGHT OF C-17 TRANSPORT
AIRCRAFT FOR EMERGENCY EXTRACTION IF NEEDED. /\/\/\
/\/\/\ YOU ARE INSTRUCTED TO KEEP EYES OPEN FOR INFORMATION
DEEMED NECESSARY FOR SUCCESSFUL COMPLETION OPERATION. BREAK...
EXPECT MAP AT END
EXCURSION OF SAID COMPLEX, SHALL REMAIN THIS POSITION UNTIL NEXT CONTACT. OUT. /\/\/\

Director Raincloud ended this communiqué as he just snapped off his radio receiver to serve more as a warning than a signoff for his operative working in Iran. In essence, he warned the operative he would remain in his office until the next contact time arrived. It was no secret that Director Raincloud was not very fond of working late, and when forced to, he always let the offender know he was upset with him.

THE DESERT OUTSIDE IRANSHAHR, IRAN

Bdellah smiled as he read the last statement from Director Raincloud. Then he quickly broke down the antenna and radio. Once it was unassembled, he replaced it in the protective container and then slid it back under the sand. He decided to leave the radio where it was and he attached the locator to a fresh, one year battery to ensure his location of the radio next time it was needed by him. He removed all traces of his presence in the ancient wadi, using his shirt to remove his foot prints, by filling them in with brushed sand. He surveyed the area, and when he was pleased no one would be able to discover he used this wadi for a communications pit, he climbed up the side of the depression. He dragged his shirt behind him, using it to cover his tracks in the sand.

Bdellah walked on the same exact footprints he made heading for the wadi, covering his old tracks with his shirt as he moved along. The agent covered them until he lost them in a maze of other foot prints once he ended up on a well traveled path leading to the Iranian town of Iranshahr. It was here he checked his compass to get his bearing. He was fifty seven degrees from the direction he was to travel for his reunion with al-Shamarral, who finally agreed and allowed him to communicate with his people by leaving his side. He checked the star studded sky and located the North Star. He walked in the void that made up the great desert.

The bag containing the protective desert robe called a Howli, an extra shirt and one three liter bottle of warm water was tossed over his naked back. For the moment, the warm night air was refreshing and Bdellah continued to drag his shirt along the sand, but the calm of night quickly changed on him. Soon, the star filled sky was covered by ominous black clouds, and the wind blew in from the east and picked up as the temperature dropped rapidly around him. The warm water did little if anything to quench his thirst, as he took a pull while trudging on. Without thinking about it, he put on his shirt after shaking the sand free of it. Deeper, he walked into the desert, using his compass and miniature flashlight to see where he was going.

The American operative used the pen light held in his mouth to check his watch in the pitch darkness, and the compass every fifteen minutes. It was late and he figured he was still at least five miles away from the linkup spot with al-Shamarral. Each time he checked his watch or compass, he would drink another swallow of actually hot water. The wind was blowing hard and he was forced to put on the heavy Howli. He wrapped the heavy outer cloth around his face, covering his nose, mouth and head. He folded the cloth in the manner of the ancient desert travelers, with a small slit opened across his eyes. The Howli drastically cut down his vision, and he was forced to slow his pace down to avoid tripping his way out to al-Shamarral.

He gave up all efforts to try and cover his trail, the wind was blowing so hard at this time his footprints were being covered by the blowing sand almost as quickly as he made them. He checked his compass and figured he was now two miles away from position. He shook the bottle, it had less than three swallows of water left, and he cursed because he committed the first sin of desert travel. Not making sure to have enough water for his entire journey. The want of life giving water quickly started to consume his thoughts, he knew he was not in any danger of dying from thirst, but his mind knew he was out of water, and it screamed it was thirsty at him.

As Bdellah climbed and stumbled what seemed like the millionth tall sand dune. He drank the last of his water, the remaining few drops did little to quench his thirst at all. He then threw the container over his shoulder and trudged on. He no longer needed his compass, he locked on the only stars still visible in the growing storm, marking his way south. The wind blew with the anger of a small tornado, whipping up clouds of blinding, stinging sand that acted more like tiny needles stabbing any of his skin left bare.

When he finally reached the rim of the sand dune, he was cursing the United States, Iran, its people, and his mother. His throat burned from the lack of water, and having to breathe through his mouth added to his thirst, and the soreness of his throat. The sand made his throat raw as it mixed with what salvia was left in his mouth. The sand was clinging to his boots and making them heavier to walk in. He could not help tripping, every step he took the sand constantly moved under his feet and caused him to lose his footing with every step. At one point, he actually tumbled down the side of a twenty foot sand dune because he lost his footing.

As cool as the night was, he was suffocating under the heat of the heavy Howli and excursion caused by walking on the soft sand. The combination of not being able to see where he was going and not able to breathe properly, and no water to drink, robbed him of his strength. He dragged his feet like an old man up the side of the sand dune he just tumbled down, striving to reach the top where he was to meet the old beggar. He did not realize he was a quarter of a mile away from the position. When he reached the top of the dune, he dropped down as if shot and then hunkered down, pulling his feet under him, and completely covering himself with the Howli. He pulled the desert robe over to where the last of the slit allowed only one eye to see from the tent like Howli as blowing sand threatened to cover the mound of black cloth resting on top of the dune.

He desperately tried to watched as the sand moved, sometimes resembling an ocean tide, as waves of sand tumbled down the side of his tall dune. The wind constantly changed the face of the sand, disorientating his judgment. He was stifling under his heavy cloth cover, the howling of the wind caused him much concern, he could not see or hear anything outside the wind. Forcing his senses to go on full alert, he strained to see any threat coming at him. It was a useless attempt at self preservation, mainly because he could not see a foot before him. He understood he was at the mercy of luck and the desert, he would be unable to detect anyone coming at him.

Al-Shamarral smiled to himself as he watched the clumsy Bdellah struggle up the side of the dune he just stumbled down. The well aged beggar was comfortable and secure under his Howli, as he sipped warm water from the goat skin container. For the past two hours, he watched in amusement as the American wandered and stumbled around through the desert. He even stopped and buried the discarded bottle Bdellah used for water, hiding all traces of them being in the desert on this night. Al-Shamarral knew Bdellah was out of water, but he decided to check his mettle before coming to his aid. The beggar was a veteran of the desert, sometimes remaining in the ocean of sand for weeks on end, living off what the desert offered for survival.

The once extremely influential Iranian politician now thought to be nothing more than a lowly beggar, cursed Bdellah for the terrible way he wrapped the life protecting Howli around his foolish body. A skilled desert traveler would never allow any air to escape the heavy covering as

Bdellah has done, for each opening allowed sand to enter the protective world of the heavy garment. Al-Shamarral checked his watch, it was fifteen minutes away from the time he was scheduled to meet with the American operative. The rest of his people were ordered to wait by the fifth stone, an ancient sand dune hard as rock. The old beggar would never be allowed to travel through the desert alone, his age and worth to all who depended on him, forced his many followers to protect the old man's life as if he were a God to them.

Al-Shamarral's horde of followers knew it was only a matter of time before Iran depend on the help of the United States, and they believed it was al-Shamarral who would strengthen the ties between the two nations again. Many children of the old beggar tried in vain to talk him from keeping this appointment with the American spy, because no Persians trusted the Americans. They argued if they were forced to help the Americans, the young ones wanted to deal with them, and not with an unworthy spy who was despised by all.

Despite all their efforts, al-Shamarral voted them down and he headed off for his scheduled meeting with Bdellah. For most of his trip, the young ones led the way and keeping al-Shamarral safely tucked in the middle of the Nomadic caravan of desert travelers. It was when the caravan moved within a mile of the position he was to meet with the American spy, that al-Shamarral was finally allowed to move to the head of the caravan and then take Command of everyone involved.

The wind howled even harder, almost knocking the elderly al-Shamarral from his perch, and with a quick head shake, he took a swallow of water. With a groan depicting his age, the beggar struggled to rise to his feet in the hard blowing storm, using his hand to shove his weight from the sand. Handfuls of sand poured out of the many folds of the Howli as he shook his body as does a dog after taking a bath. As he had done many times in his long life, he headed down the side of the sand dune, making sure of his footing as he traveled. He aimed his body right at the black shape some three hundred yards away from him and off to his left side.

Quite on purpose, al-Shamarral made enough noise to wake the dead of Iran's ancient ancestors. No matter what he did, the beggar could not raise the attention of Bdellah. He was unsure of the American operative or his reactions, he did not know how he was going to react when he picked up al-Shamarral walking out of the blowing blackness towards him. He looked up towards the sky, the stars and light from the slit of a moon, was completely black out by the bellowing clouds of churning sand above him. He was not going to get any help from nature, or from the gods who prowl the desert looking for poor wandering lost souls.

With a deep sigh of pure exhaustion, the elderly al-Shamarral made up his mind to walk right up to the foolish Bdellah while employing extreme caution, he placed his foot on the sand dune where the foolish American was waiting sat. For a second, he thought about causing a sand tide. With his foot, he knew he could easily move tons of sand with one swift movement. But he quickly decided against this, because the whole sand dune could shift with one foolish move in the desert. With the ever shifting sand, it could cause Bdellah to tumbled down the side of the dune, and be cover over by a sea and tons of sand. Al-Shamarral witnessed this happen a number of times in his life, with the same result. By the time they dug out the buried soul he was dead, crushed from the massive weight of the sand crushing down on his body.

Al-Shamarral cautiously worked his way up the sand dune, planting each foot very carefully in the soft sand before him, using his hand at times to help keep him upright as he worked his way towards Bdellah. When he was within twenty feet of the American spy, he called out loudly to him. "Bdellah, it is I, al-Shamarral. Praise the Almighty Allah, do you hear me my son of the desert sands? Open your worthless ears and hear my words and let me know you hear me, fool."

No response came from the spy as he stared at the fool sitting on the sand.

"Bdellah, it is I, your friend al-Shamarral. Do not shoot me fool. I have water to end your thirst my son." Al-Shamarral held his goat skin out at arm's length for him to see. He feared Bdellah, he was worried if the unknown one would jump up and shoot at his form when he came out of the darkness and made his presence known to the foolish American spy.

"Bdellah, for the love of Allah answer me, or I'll stop and allow the desert to cover over your worthless body." Al-Shamarral was worried if this stranger died wrapped so poorly in his heavy Howli, in what was fast becoming a feared sand storm born in the pits of hell. He had no idea of Bdellah's stamina, or if he could survive one hour in the harshness that made up life in the desert.

CHAPTER NINE

The old beggar stopped and called out one last time to the American operative. "Bdellah! If you don't respond to me, I'll leave your god cursed foul bones out here for the night children of the desert to pick clean in their never ending hunger, and the sun will bleach them white, a death no one would envy. Answer me before I leave you out here alone my son!" Al-Shamarral bellowed in the blowing sands. He knew his words were being knocked right out of the air before they reach Bdellah's ears because of the howling wind. He was aware he would have to climb right to where

Bdellah sat and tap him on the shoulder, if he was to let the American know he arrived.

Al-Shamarral allowed his howli to open, the opening let the barrel of his prized possession on the earth to protrude. It was the barrel of the ancient Kashmiri rifle. A gift given him by the late Shah of Iran. An impressive gift respected by all, even the Ayatollah. It was a badge that could get the possessor out of trouble. Al-Shamarral lifted the weapon and aimed it at the mound of black seven feet in front of him as he took a few steps back. A sigh escaped the his lips when he spotted a soft moving glow under the Howli. He now knew Bdellah was alive as he called out. "Praise Allah you live Bdellah! It is I, your friend al-Shamarral. Look my friend, I have water." Again the beggar called in the howling wind, only to have his words blown back in his face.

When al-Shamarral received no response from the agent, he dared to move closer to him. Slowly, the old beggar closed the gap separating them until he was standing within a few feet of him. He reached out with his loaded Kashmiri rifle, and he placed the barrel up against Bdellah's shoulder, and then he gave him a hard shoved him with the weapon.

The American operative was startled when he received the sudden shove and he immediately sprang to his feet as he fumbled under the folds of the Howli while looking for his 9 mm pistol. He cursed himself for not having the weapon held it at the ready at all times while out in the desert. His movement caused him to tumbling down the side of the sand dune.

Al-Shamarral quickly gave chase to the tumbling American spy, at first cursing him and the gods of the desert. Then his luck for allowing himself to hook up with this American operative in the first place. By the time he finally reached Bdellah who was sprawled out at the base of the sand dune partially covered over with sand, he laughed because the American spy was trying to stand. But he was so dizzy from the roll, it was making it impossible for him to get up on his feet. He looked foolish as he crawled around on his hands and knees on the soft sand.

The beggar reached the American just as he got on his knees his arms was still trying to pull the Howli from his shoulders, so he could see who just shoved him. Al-Shamarral reached out and helped him get his head out of the heavy fabric. When Bdellah saw the smiling face of al-Shamarral, he laughed with the desert traveler. The old Persian leaned close with his lips just about touching his ear as he offered excitedly. "Praise Almighty Allah for your life young fool. I thought you knew the desert and its harsh ways of surviving in the world of sand and danger."

"I do father, but I was ill prepared for the awesome power the desert controls during the time of the wind. I wish you would've warned me of the pending Shammal (sand storm)." The American yelled back at the old man while licking his lips in the early stages of splitting.

"Young fool, you have failed to remember my words before you ventured out to the desert on this foul night? I warned you of the pending storm my foolish son." Al-Shamarral replied.

"Huh, you told me the night might have a slight blow to it, father. This is a lot more than just a little wind. It's a fucking hell born sand storm my father." He cried angrily.

Al-Shamarral's face flushed over the obscenity Bdellah just used, but he chose to ignore it given where the Persian man received his training. It was no mystery every man and woman of the Middle East knew the Americans had foul mouths, cursed their God every chance they got, enjoyed naked women and left no dignified behavior to the secrecy thought sacred by Arabs and Persians between a man and his woman as he replied. "Fool, this is not a sand storm at all, if it was a mighty Shammal, we would not be speaking in this manner. Allow me to prepare my Howli properly for you, and then crawl under it with me and we shall speak of our next move."

Mohammed Boua Bdellah nodded as the old man knelt and then he quickly spread his Howli out, until it looked more like a tent than a protective cover from the blowing sand. When al-Shamarral was done, he signaled Bdellah who crawled under the tent like structure with him.

"If we're going to have room needed to be comfortable under my protection Bdellah. You'll have to remove your Howli, young fool of the desert." Al-Shamarral offered as he spread his hands, and then smiled at the younger man in an effort to get him moving again.

Bdellah crawled outside the protect the old had just created and quickly removed the covering. Then he crawled back under al-Shamarral's cover.

"Where did you leave your Howli resting, young fool of the desert night winds?"

"I left it lying outside this protection on the sand my father. What else was I to do with it?" Bdellah replied, not knowing what he did wrong again.

"By Allah's wrath, never leave your prized possessions to the desert's desires or to the ones who travel on its sand at night. If you lose your garment, you'll find yourself at the mercy of the desert's angers. The desert does not understand mercy, my son who knows not the ways of the desert. Bring your garment underneath and use it to sit upon, fool." Al-Shamarral waited until Bdellah pulled the heavy fabric under his protection. The beggar shook his head as he watched the uncoordinated and very sloppy American struggle with his Howli loaded down with sand. Once he had it folded properly under al-Shamarral's directions and sitting on it, the old man began speaking. "Bdellah, not only do you not know the many ways of the desert. You have not read your compass correctly. You missed the position by a number of yards." The old man was being kind to the spy, not telling him he was a quarter mile off his reading as first agreed upon.

"What difference does it make my father? A number of yards is no big deal, we're together, no al-Shamarral." He growled at the old man using his Kaffiyeh draped head as the center post of the makeshift tent. Kaffiyeh was the typical Arab head dress.

"You're correct my son, what difference does it make? I have not traveled this far into the desert just to argue with a very combative young soul." Al-Shamarral ran his hand over the sand and smoothed a section between his feet. Then, with the tip of his deadly Jambiya blade, he made a map. Bdellah used his penlight so he could see what he was doing in the sand.

"My young American fool of a friend, we are sitting here," he dug the tip of the tooth shaped knife lightly in the soft sand and then he continued with what he was telling the American operative. "the secret complex I have discovered and you wish to visit lays here my son." Al-Shamarral dragged the tip of the blade lightly across the sand, and then he dug it in at its new location and added to his explanation. "It's three kilometers from where we are resting, due south. It should take us no longer than an hour to reach the site you seek my son."

"I beg Allah, what is wrong with you, father? Do you think we can travel three kilometers in this shit in one hour's time?" he snapped, angry this old fool chose to place his life in danger, as to head to the complex with terrible atmospheric conditions existing.

Al-Shamarral was taken back at Bdellah's sudden hostilities being displayed against him, and he found himself staring at the young man in disbelief, and complained. "Foolish American child, I pray to the Almighty Allah to forgive you of your foul sins you have committed against His great laws. Have I upset you in any manner I am unaware of on this night, my son?"

"Upset me, why you old sonofabitch you. I don't take it very lightly when an old fool like you, places my damn life in danger as you have done on this terrible night. Why the fuck could we not waited until this weather passed? All we needed was the night to cover our actions, we didn't need this fucking blowing sand and crap." Bdellah bellowed as he spat sand particles from his mouth, and ran his fingers up his nose to try and clear sand from it.

Al-Shamarral was fuming over Bdellah's string of obscenities, more than being called an old fool as he warned the American spy in no uncertain terms this time. "Praise Allah's great mercy, was it not you who came and searched out my help, young fool. It's not my fault that you don't know the many way to wear one's Howli correctly, or you foolishly drank all your life giving water wastefully while out in the vast desert sands, Bdellah. I'll not listen to your vile mouthing a moment longer, fool born from a camel's arse. If you wish my help any further, you'll not dare to use such vile words within my presence again, or I'll react against them if you dare to employ them again before me, fool." Al-Shamarral drove his knife deeply into the sand, as he glared angrily at the agent until he was sure Bdellah understood his threat.

Bdellah swallowed, the parchness of his throat hurting him. The agent was embarrassed by the strong rebuke from al-Shamarral, and all he could do to make it better was nod at the beggar.

"Praise Allah that is much better fool. Now we understand each other, I'll continue with my words. But first, there are important matters we have to look after before we cloud each other's mind with words. Here, you look like you can use this." Al-Shamarral held out his goat skin.

Bdellah took the container and removed the cord holding the stopper in place, pulled it from the neck, raised it under al-Shamarral's covering. The water was hot, and it actually stank from being held in the skin. He did not know if the water was pure, nor did he care as he drank. The water tasted like the finest wine as he allowed a trickle of it run down both sides of his face.

"Here here young fool, you cannot allow such precious liquid to be wasted such as you are doing, fool. You have drank enough water for ten men traveling in the desert." Al-Shamarral complained as he pulled the container away from Bdellah's hands. He then slammed the wood stopper back in the neck of the animal skin, and quickly tied it in place as he slid it around until it disappeared behind his back and he grumbled at the American operative nastily. "By the sacred will of Allah, in the desert water's more important than a man's blood, and it must be protected more cautiously than one's own life." He warned as he stared at the American.

Once again, Bdellah nodded dumbly towards the much wiser old beggar.

"Now, I'll try and answer all your worries and concerns with my words. Yes, it's true tonight is not a very pleasurable time to try and travel through the vast desert, even our enemies will understand this. That's why I chose this night to visit the foul place you wish to see. This is something you're not aware, but if you were a true son of the desert, you would've foreseen this. Then my explanation would not be necessary, and I'd not be wasting my words, and we'd be traveling for the complex. If you could read the desert and stars, you would've understood, this wind will not blow all night. If you listen closely, you'll know it has already slackened young fool." Al-Shamarral stopped speaking to allow Bdellah listen to the sounds of the desert.

The American operative was easily able to tell the wind had truly died down quite a bit. Again, he nodded to the old man.

"My son, here in the desert you have to see not only with your foolish eyes, but you must also see with your ears, your mouth and most of all, your heart young fool." Al-Shamarral pounded his chest with his fist to emphasize his point to the agent, and then he went on with his words of wisdom for the foolish American. "May Allah protect me from all evil, I wanted to be at this position when the wind stopped blowing tonight. You see my son, the complex has roaming bands of security guards traveling through the desert near this complex.

"Mostly, these security guards are nearer the villages, and if they start their rounds after the wind had stopped and they find fresh footprints in the sand leading for the foul building. They'd immediately notify their friends, and we'd not get within twenty kilometers of the god cursed structure. This is why I chose this night to travel upon the desert sands, young fool. The winds shall erase all traces of our wandering through the sands, and there are no patrols this near the complex. I'm certain this is so no attention is drawn to the foul buildings. To your spy satellites these structures must look like abandoned factories built many years past. I'm quite certain this is the effect Ayatollah al-Tamin had searched for in the construction of this evil complex. Vehicles are hidden from view, and there are no sign of life near the complex.

"From the air, the few buildings able to be seen must give the appearance of crumbling and long ago abandoned structures. There are no cared for roads leading to the complex to finish the picture of these buildings being abandoned. The roads were dug up and destroyed by the engineers. There are only hard packed sand roads used, and the winds of the night completely erase all evidence these roads are still traveled upon, young fool." The old man took a quick breath before continuing explaining why he chose to travel on this stormy night.

"There's little electrical power used above the foul ground, the power plants are constructed below the sand, and the exhaust is piped away from the structures to confuse your satellites. This is an attempt to mask them from your infrared detection systems, water and food are stored below ground with the foolish workers. There are tons of sand on the roofs of these buildings, and no one is ever seen walking on the sand, everything's carried out below ground. It was by just luck I happened to stumble across this cursed place. One of my sons was in charge of my worthless camels, and his stupidity allowed my prized breeder to wander away from his control in search of a detected bitch in heat. I spent three days searching for this breeder, and I found him with his bitch that I added to my herd. As I was leading them home I noticed a helicopter land in the middle of nowhere. At first I believed the pilot of the machine was in trouble.

"I sat down on the sand dune and watched as the pilot got out, and then he opened the door of the machine in no great hurry. He helped a few men out, and others appeared from the ruins of the buildings, and they led these men into what I thought were abandoned buildings. The helicopter then quickly disappeared to the north. The pilot was in a fast hurry to leave the area. From that day forward, I had this region constantly under watch by my many desert children. It was my son who allowed the camel to escape his watch, who reported trucks carrying cylinders. He sent his brother to fetch me, and what he believed to be cylinders, were indeed missile housings. For three full days, we watched as a steady stream of military trucks appeared, and unloaded machinery and obvious missile parts." Another breath was drawn in by the old man.

The American operative suddenly shifted his weight on his Howli while waiting for the elderly beggar to continue informing him of what he observed at this secret Iranian complex.

"Next to appear at this once secret complex were countless technicians and lab workers. These new men and women were treated with great respect. Some were identified as Soviet workers, I myself heard their ugly language being spoken, as they ordered my people as if they were dirt under their cursed feet. As I told you, many of our young men were taken in the middle of the night, and they were forced to work at this foul site of lowly jackals. I have not seen this, but heard my people complain about it. It's been said a number of women were kidnapped in the nights, and forced to relieve these filthy Russian jackal worker's foul, and animalistic needs.

"I angered the Mighty Allah for allowing this to happen to his faithful children, our women are our lives, to see them defiled so by these Russian camel eaters is more than I can bear. This is why I'm so willing to help the American soldiers. No matter how depraved they are, they would never rape our women, nor forced them to please them unwillingly, my foolish son. It's a very ugly world we live, and it's only a matter of time before Allah comes to earth, and with one wave of His Mighty hand, erases all the ugliness from the face of the earth. Leaving only the true believers and followers of His sacred word alive to start the world anew, my son."

Bdellah held up his hand to stop the beggar from complaining as he offered the old desert wanderer in a calm tone of voice. "Al-Shamarral, now is not the time to begin a holy war against the world entire. We're here to observe this secret complex. Then I'll make a very detailed map of the place, and my people will come in the middle of the night and return the favor to these bastards, err... please excuse my poor choice of words, my father."

The old beggar smiled, pleased the American spy showed the respect demanded from him as he replied. "I pray Allah you are correct with your swaggering and bragging, my son."

"My people will erase these evil people from the face of the earth. My country's soldiers will remove these cursed weapons of mass destruction from the soil of Iran, and return the sacred land to its rightful people. Al-Shamarral, I swear my government will not forget those who help them in their time of need. What you want from my government, just ask me and I'll make sure you receive it. It can be like it was when the old Shah was once ruling Iran."

Al-Shamarral protested lightly. "American, it's a fool who wishes to return his thoughts to the useless ways of the ancient past. This is why my country's in such bad shape, because Iran's new leaders want it to remain mired in the days of the past, to use the outdated ways of the old to control the modern young of Iran. It's time for Iran to move forward, to allow the new ways of thinking and believing to enter our life. I don't wish to forsake the sacred ways of the past by any means, but we have to be open-minded to accepted the new ways of living, and respecting our God, and our country to enter our way of thinking. Ahhh… Iran's in need of help my son." Al-Shamarral moaned disgusted as he threw his free hand through the air of the enclosure.

"Al-Shamarral, there are uncontrollable forces in the world, that control the destiny for all of us. What we have to do is concern ourselves with these cursed weapons of mass destruction, the military of Iran are trying to develop. We have to stop this evil effort on their part. We cannot possibly allow Iran to control nuclear weapons, and the submarines to launch them. I fear these leaders of Iran will use them to start a war between the United States and Russia. I believe they suffer from the illusion they believe Iran will survive such a devastating exchange, giving them control of what will be left of the world, after the exchange where two countries destroy each other, my wise and faithful father. Al-Shamarral, any exchange between the two great powers, will destroy the world, and no one will be left to pick up the pieces."

"Praise Allah mercy, I understand this to be true as you spoke the words, this is another reason I have decided to help your country in its quest to destroy these god cursed weapons in Iran. Although I must admit, I'm not overjoyed to provide this help, mainly because I don't trust the United States, I don't like America, and I see the United States as the lesser of the two evils to threaten Iran and her faithful children. Thus, I chose to help you and your country my son. I believe there's hope America will be held in the loving arms of Allah, as it once was in long ago past times." Al-Shamarral offered as he wiped some sand from the corner of his eye.

"Al-Shamarral that's a political problem, and believe me I'm no politician my father. My concern's to protect the young warriors of my country, and what I do is for her safety,

America's freedom and liberty, my father. Nothing more than that I assure you, al-Shamarral." Bdellah replied to the old man as he looked him dead in the eyes.

"As it should be when one is concerned for their fellow brothers and sisters my son. One should be honored to sacrifice himself for his beliefs and country. Paradise is filled with the great Martyr's of one's honored country, no Bdellah?" Al-Shamarral asked the American operative.

"I don't believe in becoming a Martyr for any reason whatsoever my father. I'll not sacrifice myself needlessly for any goal, any aim in my heart and mind. I'll never strap a bomb to my waist, and use it to kill innocent women and children in the name of Allah. My war is not aimed against the innocent of the world, I don't kill women and children or working men of good nations. My war is with the government of Iran, before it becomes a war between our two nations, possibly involving the world in war as wel..."

Al-Shamarral suddenly interrupted the ravings of the American operative as he held up his hand and then remarked to the young man. "Please, I did not wish to get involved with a political complaint raging between us my son. Because it's as you have stated, we're both not politicians. We're our country's faithful warriors, and as such we must be focused on what is at hand. We must head out if we wish to be set in position while there's still enough darkness to hide our movements from the searching eyes of the security people of this cursed installation. I have no idea if the security guards might change their evil habits, and send out a night patrol on such a dark and stormy night. The ways of the cursed thinkers are different than mine."

The American smiled as he replied to the old man's words. "You say an hour is needed to get us over to this position and secret complex, father?"

"Easily, the wind has stopped blowing all together as I had planned it would on this foul and most dark night." The old man offered with a mouth full of rotten teeth.

"When did you think the wind would stop completely?" Bdellah asked.

"Twelve midnight y young one." Al-Shamarral announced proudly.

Bdellah mumbled as he smiled at the old desert wanderer this time. "It's fifteen minutes past twelve. You were almost correct to the very minute, my wise father of the desert lands." Bdellah felt he caught him in a slight mistake, and he was enjoying rubbing the mistake in on him. He wanted al-Shamarral to know he did not know of all the ways of the vast desert.

Al-Shamarral smiled back at Bdellah as he questioned him cautiously. "What makes you believe I missed the time I had offered you, son who thinks me wrong. We spoke longer than I had planned. If we stopped speaking at exactly midnight, you would have seen the wind had stopped blowing at that exact time, foolish jackal of a son. Come, we have to move while there's still some wind left to cover over our tracks in the sand. One never knows if these sons of camel eaters might change their ways and send a patrol out because of the storm. The wind is a desert traveler's best friend, if it's used correctly in their times of need, my son."

"So you admit it was a sand storm after all I see, my wise father." Bdellah remarked with a grin as he felt he might have found another mistake committed by the old desert wanderer.

"Forgive me for using your term for a friendly little wind blow in the desert, my son. Shall we go now?" Al-Shamarral stood and in doing so he dumped the sand filling the folds of his Howli.

"How are we going to see where we're going, and how will we know when we finally get there, father?" Bdellah asked the beggar as he prepared to follow him in the desert.

"Ahhh... my son without any good manners and knowledge of the many dangerous desert ways, you're not born to the ways of the desert wonder and vastness. I fear you spent too long living in the underbelly of the beast. The United States, and its soft ways of life have successfully robbed you of the all seeing desert eyes one needs in order to survive in the world of sand and endlessness, my Persian son. If you take the time to look to the east, you would've see the stars glowing brightly on this endless night. They'll light our way to our destination my son."

Bdellah followed al-Shamarral's lead in silence, and he stood and then struggled back in his heavy Howli, he was stopped by the old man when he suddenly yelled at the American spy. "No Bdellah, don't put that on with the black side out, this time young fool. Yes, that's correct, make certain all the sand is out of your faithful Howli. But this time you shall turn it inside out for our night time travel over the sands of my ancient ancestors."

Al-Shamarral skillfully removed his Howli in one swift motion, and then he spun it high over his head like a matador trying to torment the angry bull would fling his cape, until the garment was perfectly inside out. He then brought it down evenly on his shoulders like he had obviously done countless times throughout his ancient life. It seemed like the Howli actually had a life of its own as it took the shape of the old man's form resting on his body. The old man then wiggled his body slightly until his Howli fitted his body like a second skin. Once he was again dressed perfectly in his heavy desert robe, he looked at the American and then gave him a huge victorious smile as he waited for him to get in his Howli so they can begin the trek to the secret complex.

Bdellah shrugged and then he began his battle to force his garment as if it was fighting his every move while he was trying to cover himself with the robe, and complained at the old beggar at the same time as he continued to struggle with the heavy garment. "Why are we doing this for old man of the desert sands? This thing is so hard to work with, walk in and it makes the desert even hotter than it really is, my father."

"Ha my young foolish ally from across the Ocean, that's because you're not very friendly with the unending ways of the vast desert, and you're also unfamiliar with the life giving equipment that one needs whenever he's traveling upon the ever shifting sands of the endless desert. The reason why I want you to turn your Howli inside out for our next travels, is because we'll be traveling in extremely dangerous areas. As you see with your foolish eyes, this side of the Howli closely resembles the sand of the desert.

"If we detect any possible Iranian military patrols coming at us, we'll just simply drop down to the sands, and then quickly cover ourselves with the Howli, and no one will be able to pick us out from the sand as we lay, and we can then watch the great fools continue their search for anyone traveling upon the desert on this black night. To live in the endless desert, one must know its many ways of survival and existence in the desert, if he truly wishes to see another rising of the unforgiving Eye of Allah and the start of his next day of living on this earth." The old man stopped speaking and then he just kind of stared at Bdellah, as he continued to work with the garment giving him so much trouble getting it on his body correctly.

"The Eye of Allah, al-Shamarral? What do you mean by the Eye of Allah, my father?" Bdellah asked with concern in his tone of the old man.

"Praise Allah's great wisdom and guidance for his faithful children of the land of sand." Al-Shamarral cried as he suddenly raised his hands up towards the heavens, as if looking there for an answer that never came as he continued with his explanation to the confused looking American operative. "You who say you know the countless ways of the vast desert and its survival in the lands of endless sand, is a very stupid man indeed I see and fear my son. The angry and always unforgiving Eye of Allah is the sun that bathes the hot oceans of sands with its greatness and anger every day the earth's blessed by the Eye of Allah, and the Breath of Allah are the great sand storms that cleanse the vast sand of the desert to set the desert right again time after time." Al-Shamarral snapped hotly at the American.

Bdellah was finally able to get the troublesome protective garment laid correctly on his body, and then he followed the old man closely. Looking behind him every once in a while, to see the remaining wind that was still blowing the lose sand over their footprints they were leaving in the sand almost as quickly as they have made them.

With each step they took forward, the footprints beyond them almost instantly disappeared in the sea of ever shifting and blowing sand of the desert. The American smiled to himself as he watched the wind do what he was doing with his shirt before he linked up with the old man, as he dragged the shirt behind him as he walked the sands heading for the position he was to meet with al-Shamarral.

CHAPTER TEN

THURSDAY, NOVEMBER 7th, 1998.
0105 HOURS IRANIAN TIME.
THE DESERT SURROUNDING THE TOWN
OF IRANSHAHR

The American operative Mohammed Boua Bdellah increased his pace in order to try and stay up with the old man walking at a quick pace over the soft sand. He was amazed the old man could move so swiftly on the soft sand. With a quick wave of a hand, al-Shamarral signaled Bdellah to drop down and once they were lying flat on the sand, the beggar waved him over to his side. He waited for the agent to crawl up to him and then he pointed off to his right.

The wind died down to less than a slight breeze now, but every so often the wind would kick up enough to send sand stinging in his eyes. Bdellah focused his eyes to see a building some five hundred yards ahead of them. When his eyes adjusted, he saw three buildings in the center of the large complex, with a number of smaller building surrounding the larger ones. The buildings looked as if they were about to crumble in on themselves and then be reclaimed by the ever blowing sand. As they moved over to a better position to observe the secret complex, Bdellah noticed the buildings had five large garage doors, each easily capable of swallowing up a tractor trailer truck. On closer inspection of the complex, he picked up and heard the heartbeat of the building, and workers laboring inside the structures. He listened to the constant whine of machinery and heard someone in the complex yelling, though he was unable to tell what he said.

A jeep suddenly shot out from the building and it darted into one of the smaller building. The men struggled as they rushed inside while carrying a large box between them. A tractor started and the back of the machine dug a hole, and the box was dropped inside the pit, and then the front of the machine was used to cover the box over with sand.

Al-Shamarral leaned closer to Bdellah and moved the fabric from his ear and whispered. "Praise Allah, we have reached the position I seek. There's the building I discovered where the rockets are being constructed." Al-Shamarral shifted the goat skin container and took a quick swallow of water. He sloshed it around in his mouth before swallowing the tepid liquid, and then he offered the grotesque thing to the American Agent to drink from.

Bdellah took it and drank, copying al-Shamarral by sloshing the foul tasting water around in his mouth first. He then replaced the wood stopper, tying it in place and he handed it back to the old man and then he mumbled at him. "Sure is right in the middle of no place in the desert, father." He noted as he looked around the complex.

"When one breaks the laws of mankind and nature, one does not want many witnesses around to observe the crime that he's committing against the earth of our true religion, my son." Al-Shamarral offered as he looped the skin over his shoulder.

Bdellah laughed as he replied. "You're wise beyond your ancient years I see old man."

Al-Shamarral ignored the compliment as he added. "As you see my foolish young son, whoever is in charge of making this building look abandoned, has succeeded his task wisely."

"True father." He smirked as he searched the outer rim for any military defenses.

"Huh foolish one you must stay real close to the foul sand or someone will detect you and then your life will be a very short one for you to enjoy. What are you doing young fool?" Al-Shamarral snapped as he pulled on Bdellah's wrist, drawing him down closer to the sand.

"Al-Shamarral, I must locate any military defensive systems. I have to pin point them on my map for my troops when they come and destroy this nightmare born from hell, father."

"This is rather simple to accomplish, but first you must stay close to the sand young fool. There are soldiers stationed on top of the roof of the taller buildings ready to part you foolish brains for you, my wayward son. I'll point out the military defenses of this building to you to make it easier for you to locate them. This will leave you free to make the map for your proud soldiers when they come to free Iran from this yoke of nuclear weapons she's laboring under."

"Please al-Shamarral, my life and the lives of my soldiers are in your hands." The American operative offered as he bowed slightly to the old man, and then he waved his hand out before him, motioning the old man to take the lead. He cursed the forces that led him to this place. He was angry he did not have a pair of infrared glasses to make his observations easier.

Al-Shamarral was correct, the sky was covered with flickering specks of light, the moon was nowhere to be seen, and the stars did not light the earth any. He complained to al-Shamarral who warned if the night was bright, their enemy would see them easily.

Bdellah cursed the beggar under his breath as he followed the aged man on his hands and knees as they crawled along the sand. He asked the old man how long they were going to stay in the desert. He told al-Shamarral he had to make contact with his control as soon as possible.

Al-Shamarral flashed a harsh look of anger as he groused at him. "By Allah's Almighty hand foolish one, we must spend the day observing, and noting what takes place here. It's time to plant the body of the goat in the Circle of Justice, and place fate to the test. We'll move again tonight, perhaps waiting until almost morning before fleeing this foul area. We must be as skillful as the snake, or we'll be discovered and suffer a most unpleasant experience before being allowed to die very slowly." Al-Shamarral smiled as he crawled out before Bdellah, moving to his left. The old man slithered like a snake using his arms and feet to propel him forward on the sand.

His reference to the Circle of Justice was the age old Arab test of strength employed by them since Arabs first walked the earth. They put the body of a goat in a circle, and the riders picked it up and rode twice around a field to deposit the body back in the circle. It was an extremely dangerous test called Buokashi for each rider, sometimes a hundred strong whipping and kicking each other, trying to get the goat from each other, and then carry it and deposit it in the Circle of Justice. Many times, the riders would lose their lives in this test.

Bdellah nodded, and then he shoved off thinking he should have brought the small radio with him. But he understood that would have been a serious mistake, and quickly dismissed the thought from his mind. It was wise to have reverse the Howli, for when al-Shamarral crawled ten feet away from him, he seemed to disappear in the sand. Time passed slowly for the two.

CAMP LEJEUNE, JACKSONVILLE, NORTH CAROLINA. WEDNESDAY, NOVEMBER 6th, 1998. ZERO EIGHT HUNDRED HOURS

The new Colonel Bruce Leadbetter marched out of his office and he angrily looked over the warriors assembled on the marching and training grinder. He walked to the head of the formation of soldiers carrying his clipboard. He remembered the name someone once tagged him with on the last mission, and it still really bothered him, Clipboard Charlie. He tried to remember the offending soldier's face as he nodded at Lieutenant Robert Walker standing at the head of the formation. He made certain Walker noticed the eagles pinned on his collar.

"Okay you shits, I'm not going to waste my god damn time screaming at you group of shit bags, because I believe it'll do me no damn good whatsoever. I trust you know why you're here."

There were a couple of negative responses that caused the Colonel to barked at the group of elite soldiers. "Put a fucking lid on it, and I'll explain to you screaming squirrels. Iran got her lousy hands on a number of Russian nuclear missiles for their submarines." The Colonel noticed a few squirming. "You!" He pointed to a man. "What's you malfunction, who are you?"

Snatch pointed to himself as if shocked the Colonel was talking to him over the rest.

"Yes you, you fucking idiot you! ID yourself on the double quick, asshole."

"Yes Sir Colonel, I'm Private George Weaver, sir." Snatch offered to the angry Colonel.

Someone from the ranks called out his tag name for the new Colonel. "He's Snatch, Homes."

The Colonel glared at the formation as he growled at the lot of them this time. "I see I'm going to have some fucking trouble with you pack of pissants after all. I don't remember addressing anyone but this P.O.S. standing here before my ass." (P.O.S. was slang for Piece Of Shit)

"Yes sir." Weaver replied smartly.

"Okay Snatch what the hell's bugging your ass anyhow, mister? You were squirming around in formation like you had to take a fucking crap, mister!" the Colonel asked him.

"Sir, Iran always gives me the stinking heebe jeebies, Colonel Leadbetter. I heard they cook and eat ya if they don't like ya, and they don't like anyone, even themselves I hear Colonel." The soldier flashed a quick smile after noticing the Eagles pinned on the Colonel's collar.

The group laughed until Colonel Leadbetter snapped at the group of specialized soldiers. "The next P.O.S. who laughs in formation will be eating my fucking boot for breakfast." He turned back to Snatch and added. "Iran gives the world the fricking heebe jeebies, soldier. That's why we're going in there and rip them new assholes. Give them a manner's lesson sort to say." Then the Colonel turned to the other soldiers and added. "Each and every one of you shitbirds, by the time we head out for Iran, we'll know everything there's to know about these damn slugs to defeat them. Our mission's not complicated as the one in Russia this time around. Mainly, we're heading to Iran to take a crap load of pictures, set a few explosive charges, and then bug the hell out of there toot sweet." As he spoke, he noticed one of his men holding onto something.

As the Colonel headed for the trooper, he immediately recognized the soldier and he flipped a few papers on his clipboard looking for the soldier's name. As he searched, Colonel Leadbetter forced his mind. It was Wako, Mako, something like that he remembered as ran his finger down the long list of soldier's names.

The Roach, standing alongside the soldier the Colonel was heading for, urged him to drop the string. But his words were ignored, so the Roach stared ahead and waited for the explosion to take place. He did not have to wait long before all hell broke out with the new Colonel.

"Ahhh... as I live and fucking breathe, the famous Corporal Salvatore Tomassi, fucking Wacko, right tag name for your ass I must admit, mister?" Colonel Leadbetter snarled while trying not to look at what Wacko was holding on to.

There was a loud sigh from the soldiers when they heard Wacko's name yelled out.

"Yes Sir Colonel. Wacko it is sir." Tomassi replied proudly with a grin to the angry officer.

Colonel Leadbetter allowed his stare to wander to the string the young soldier was holding on to, and then he growled when he saw Wacko had no intention of dropping it. "What the fuck is this shit about mister? Why have you brought a fucking rock on a god damn leash to my grinder? There better be a damn good explanation for this crap, or I'm going to eat you alive."

Wacko was grinning, and he pulled on the leash as he offered. "Sir, he's my pet rock, his name's Fido, Colonel Leadbetter. It was sent to me by my girl. I take it everywhere I go sir."

Another sigh went through the ranks of soldiers as they waited for the Colonel to explode.

"A pet rock you say huh? There's something seriously wrong with your fucking brain, mister. Too many damn drugs I guess huh buster? You operating with half your damn brain cells working. A pet rock, now I seen everything soldier. You better get rid of that damn thing, or I'm going to shove it up your ass, and see if your pet can find its way out of your shit hole."

The soldiers standing in formation laughed as Colonel Leadbetter really ripped into Wacko. Suddenly, he screamed at the group. "I don't remember giving any of you other P.O.S.'s permission to laugh. Stand at attention while I cure this asshole of his fucking illusions evidently he's suffering from." He waited for silence, and then the Colonel resumed his assault on Wacko as he pointed his finger right at his chest, knowingly driving it between a set of ribs to cause him some pain. "Wacko, you had your fricking little joke, ditch the god damn rock mister."

Wacko picked the rock up by the leash, and then he dangled it out before him for a second, and then he drop kicked it and sent it flying twenty yards into the empty field near the grinder.

Colonel Leadbetter pointed his finger right in Wacko's chest again and warned him in no uncertain terms this time. "Okay you mixed up bag of nut, as of this minute no more fucking poko loco for you, mister. You're cut off of the crap until further notice soldier. Am I perfectly clear on that last order to that thing you call a friggin brain, Squid?"

"Perfectly clear to my ass Colonel Leadbetter Sir. It's what you say that goes in my book, sir." Wacko snapped back while still standing at attention.

"Good, I don't know why they ever legalized that crap in the first place, dammit. I'm cutting orders to the PX not to sell you any of the shit to you Screaming Spudheads. As for the rest of you shitbirds, if I catch any of you jerks supplying this asshole with any grass, I'm going to plant you and see if I can get you to grow a new god damn brain for yourselves."

"That's okay with me sir. Lately, the crappy pot's been so watered down with stinking regular tobacco that it's getting harder to get off on the shit from the PX anyhow, Colonel."

"You're fucking impossible shitbird." Colonel Leadbetter snorted at the young soldier.

"Pardon me sir, obviously you have me confused with someone else who gives a shit, sir." Wacko smirked as he looked to where his pet rock landed over Leadbetter's left shoulder.

"Yeah sure, I bet. Let me warn ya, if I catch you smoking that crap. I'll cut your dick off and have it dried, and I'll give you something real to smoke." Leadbetter snarled at the soldier.

When the Colonel ended his attack on the soldier branded Wacko, he turned to the other soldiers in formation and barked at them. "Everyone to the gym, take a seat and pay attention. I'm going over the area we're to hit in Iran. We'll have to go over this shit quick, I don't think we'll have the luxury of time to prepare properly for it on this upcoming mission. Left face." The Colonel waited for the group to turn, "double time it, go." The group headed off as one.

The Colonel smiled, knowing the soldiers had their edge set in place, they were going to need it on this mission. Once they were in the gym, seated and quiet, the still upset Colonel had the map of Iran opened in his hands, and he started to go over their attack scenario.

CIA HEADQUARTERS, LANGLEY VIRGINIA, ZERO SIX HUNDRED THIRTY HOURS, THURSDAY, NOVEMBER 7th, 1998

CIA Director John Raincloud was in his office manning the computer, he was trying to get a communication opened with his operative working in Iran from NORASATCOM. He was told the operative was not transmitting, making it impossible for them to make contact with each other. The Director was fuming as he ordered the Lieutenant to interrupt him when any new communication from his operative came through. He slammed the receiver down and cursed. General White came in the office and saw the anger in his friend's eyes and asked him with concern. "What's up John? You look like you could take a bite out of a junk yard dog's ass."

"Arrr... my damn operative's out of position, and you know it's only a matter of time before the Boss is on the horn demanding any new information for the damn upcoming

United Nations meeting tomorrow morning." The Director moaned as he poured coffee for them both. It was decided yesterday General White would meet Director Raincloud in his office this time.

"Yeah, and he'll be really ticked off at you if you have any new intelligence to lay down on his ass." General White added with a grin as he took the cup and sipped the steaming liquid.

"Yeah, my operative must be in the damn desert with that new friend he picked up from somewhere dammit. I told the sonofabitch I needed to hear from him every eight hours, unless it was impossible for him to transmit a message to me. I sure hope the ass didn't get captured, or his friend didn't turn him in for Pete's sake." Director Raincloud hissed angrily.

"C'mon John, you have enough shit to worry about as it is sir, without you adding to your own stress level by getting on your operative's ass. I'm sure as hell he's safe, and he's carrying out his orders as received. He'll make contact with us when he gets back to his damn radio, John."

"Yeah, but by then it'll be too fucking late, and the President's going to take some large chunks out of my damn ass for breakfast at the meeting sir." Director Raincloud griped.

At that very moment the intercom screamed to life, scaring them as the CIA Director's secretary informed him the President was on the line and he was requesting to speak with him. General White glanced at the exhausted looking Director with a look that felt the President knew what they were just talking about. Director Raincloud picked up the receiver and offered pleasantly to the Boss. "Good morning Mr. President, how are you this morning sir?"

"Don't give me any of that damn nicely nice shit, mister. What's the status on your operative in Iran? You know I have that damn United Nations meeting tomorrow morning, and I don't have enough information to lay out before them to prove my point to the Iranians, and anyone else who'll stand up and back the sonofabitches against us. What the hell's happening John?"

General White saw Director Raincloud's expression change, and he knew the President was in a bad mood, and he smiled at the Director who gave General White half a peace sign.

Director Raincloud waited for the President to finish his bitch at him so he could respond to his anger. "With all due respect Mr. President Sir, I have a number of pictures and other irrefutable evidence to support your position at the United Nations meeting tomorrow, sir."

"Well, where the hell are the damn things at John? Strange, I don't seem have them lying on my damn desk at this time, sir. Director Raincloud, I want you to locate General White, and I want the two of you over at the Oval Office ten minutes ago, sir. I want everything you have of Iran for my damn presentation tomorrow morning's."

"Yes Sir Mr. President." Director Raincloud said into a dead receiver.

Director Raincloud looked at General White and then asked the military officer. "Did you hear the man on the damn horn, General?"

"Enough, I think everyone in the office heard him." General White smirked as he waited for Director Raincloud to get his briefcase. He waved his hand before him and bowed. "Shall we?"

"Yeah, I want to do this shit like I want to have my damn balls beaten flat with a wood hammer, General. This meeting isn't going to be very pleasant I tell you sir."

General White placed a hand on the large Native American's back and they left his office together. They headed off for the White House and when they got out of the car, they were immediately greeted by the White House Chief of Staff. "How's the Big Guy today?"

"He's as angry as a wet cat, he has everyone hunting a hole to hide in, sir. I never saw the President this upset sir. This Iranian thing's really getting the best of him, Mr. Director."

"I hope what I have will calm him down some today." Director Raincloud offered as he fell in step with the Chief of Staff as they entered the corridor leading to the sequestered Oval Office.

Phil waved Director Raincloud and General White into the Oval Office and he remained out of the office because he was not invited to sit in on this meeting.

As General White passed Phil he bitched at him with a smirk on his lips. "You chicken shit you." Causing the young man to chuckle as he followed the two powerful men.

The President remained seated as he pointed to chairs as Director Raincloud and General White entered the office. The Vice President was seated to President Cole's right, and sitting by her was the Secretary of State. The Security Director was seated to the left, and he was next to the Secretary of Defense. General White automatically looked for Manning.

The President saw the look and immediately snapped at the military officer. "Can I help you any General White? You seem like you're looking for someone sir."

"Sorry Mr. President. Is everyone present for the meeting already sir?" The Chairman of the Joint Chiefs of Staff asked the seated American Leader.

"This is it. Why, were you looking for someone else to be attending this meeting, General?" The President snapped as he spread his hands apart and then stared at the General.

Director Raincloud plopped his briefcase down on the table, breaking the slight confrontation going down between the President and General White. President Cole turned his attention to the CIA Director and asked him with some concern in his voice. "Are they the same pictures I saw the last time when we meet over this same damn situation over Iran, Director Raincloud?"

"Yes sir, but any new information from this region is rather hard coming by as of yet sir. I can't push my operative without forcing him to take some serious chances, chances that might compromise his entire operation and his life, Mr. President Sir." Director Raincloud remarked as he removed the 8x10 pictures, and then he handed them over to the upset President.

"What the hell are these damn things you have here, Director?" President Cole grumbled as he dropped the stack of pictures down on his desk.

"They're the pictures of the Iranian trucks entering Russia sir. Then getting the Russian missiles loaded inside the false tank trailer. Then the trucks heading back to Iran, Mr. President."

"Have I seen these pictures before John? They look rather familiar to me sir, like I saw the damn things before, sir." The President asked the CIA Director again.

"I believe so Mr. President, I took the liberty of writing a paragraph explaining everything on the pictures for your benefit, Mr. President. I also have the pictures numbered, along with the corresponding text backup sir. I hope this will make it somewhat easier for you to compile a speech for the meeting tomorrow morning, sir." Director Raincloud offered the President.

The President handed them to his Security Director Norman Griffin, who quickly thumbed through them, and then he nodded to the President who turned to Raincloud. "Director, you made it much easier for my staff, for this I'm pleased. But I need more than this for my presentation, and since you don't have it. I'm ordering you to accompany me to the meeting in case I get stumped, and I need help to get my foot out of the mud." The President looked at Raincloud.

Director Raincloud smiled as he offered to the American Leader and commented. "President Cole, I'd be honored to accompany you to the United Nation's meeting if you'd like, sir."

"Fine, we'll be leaving tonight for New York City then, Director. I want to be in New York by say nine p.m. tonight at the latest sir. So I can get a good night's sleep before the damn meeting tomorrow. How much time do you need to get ready to leave with me, Director Raincloud Sir?"

"I can leave immediately if you'd like Mr. President." John offered kindly.

"That won't be necessary, you'll be accompanying me on Air Force One, and my secretary will make all the arrangements. Be here eight o'clock tonight. You'll be able to receive messages from your operative. I hope we can get confirming information before the meeting tomorrow."

"Mr. President, I'll be carrying a portable scrambler machine that allows me to remain in constant contact with NORASATCOM, sir. I'll be able to communicate with my office and General White if needed if anything comes in from my operative working in Iran, sir."

"Fine, I'm done with you then sir, take a seat while I speak with General White."

Director Raincloud sat down and General White immediately stood as he began to address the President and the other members of the meeting. "Good morning sir."

"Good morning General White. I want to know what the present status is on your specialized troops, sir. Will they be ready to move out on a moment's notice, General?"

"Mr. President, my people are ready to move out as of this very moment sir."

"I hope so, for all our sakes General White. We're going to need them on this one sir."

CAMP LEJEUNE, JACKSONVILLE NORTH CAROLINA. ZERO SEVEN THIRTY HUNDRED HOURS, THURSDAY, NOVEMBER 7th, 1998

Most of the previous day was spent in class rooms getting the soldier's familiar with the terrain and climate of Iran. Colonel Leadbetter was feeding the information to the soldiers as fast as they could possible absorb and retain it. He cursed the lack of intelligence from HQ, he was angry with the idea of using Pakistan as the jump off position for their possible invasion of Iran. He did not breach this subject with the other soldiers. Colonel Leadbetter was stunned when word from Command filtered down that his troops would assemble in the Pakistani village of Panjgur on the Iranian, Pakistan border some thirty miles away from their target of Iranshahr. Although he did not like Pakistan in the least, it was the most logical position to use as a safe zone to operate from, providing they could keep the area a safe zone before jumping off.

The new Colonel was largely upset because he did not trust any Islamic nations, and he did not trust Pakistan any better. One day Pakistan was the United States' ally, only to get what they wanted from us. Then they were at the United States' throat, just daring any American to enter their country, and threatening Americans working in the country. When Colonel Leadbetter received word, his suggestion was to allow the Islamic countries kill each other off. The Colonel did not trust Saudi Arabia or Kuwait any better either. The only Islamic country he sort of trusted in his mind was Egypt, and this was because of the dead President Sadat, and President Hosni Mubarak, letting the opposition know where they stood at all times.

Colonel Leadbetter found Egyptian President Mubarak to be a good leader steering Egypt down the right path for the future and well being of his country. For the umpteenth time, he sent out a 'request for information' to NORASATCOM, and for the umpteenth time he received the same exact answer. "No new information available at this time."

THE WHITE HOUSE, WASHINGTON D.C.

Director John Raincloud left General John White manning the computer while he went to the White House. He and the President were ushered to Marine One and whisked to Joint Andrews Airforce Base where Air Force One was waiting. They boarded the cloistered aircraft surrounded by a horde of security agents who completed their sweep of the plane using dogs and bomb detection devices. The President was not allowed to board until the sweep was completed.

The President entered the aircraft first followed by Director Raincloud. President Cole headed for the overstuffed wing chair, sat and then buckled in. The CIA Director sat by him as the President stared out window while waiting to take off. Director Raincloud did not speak, he allowed the President his few moments of peace.

Once in the air, President Cole unbuckled his seatbelt and asked Director Raincloud if he wanted anything to drink. The Director waved the offer off, and engaged in conversation, going over what the President was going to say at the United Nations meeting. The Director carefully went over the intelligence he had accumulated of Iran, and the movement of the Russian nuclear missiles into that country. The President gave a deep sigh and then moaned. "Christ sake John, I wish you had more compelling evidence Iran planned to construct copies of the damn Russian submarine launch missiles and nuclear warheads, sir. That's the only way we'll force Saudi Arabia and other Coalition members to reunite against this latest threat in the Middle East."

"With all due respect Mr. President..." The CIA Director offered to the American Leader.

"For the love of Pete, Albert, please John. There's no need to stand on formalities here when we're heading for New York City together, sir."

"Yes, thank you Mr. President. Albert, I have pictures of what we believe is the secret complex some seven miles from Iranshahr. We sent out an X-117 to snap some pictures of the place..."

"What do they look like John?" the President interrupted the Director a second time.

"Not very much I'm afraid, Mr. President Sir. The damn pictures show three main buildings, surrounded by seven smaller ones, and the place looks like it's one step from collapsing in on itself. If you were to display these pictures to the members of the United Nations, they'll draw the same conclusion, the buildings are abandoned. It'll weaken the impact of your presentation if you try and use them at the meeting, Albert." Director Raincloud stopped speaking and dug in his briefcase. Finding what he wanted, he removed the pictures and handed them to his Boss.

The President quickly thumbed through the small stack of pictures and then he dropped them down on the table and complained. "I see what you mean John, I want to take those pictures with me. But I'll use them only as a last resort sir. That's all you have for me, John?"

"Fraid so Mr. President." Director Raincloud offered as matter of fact to the seated President.

The President did his best to try and control his anger as he stared out the window again. Both men were silent as the plane cut through the night air. It took an hour for the aircraft to arrive at John F. Kennedy International Airport in New York. Upon landing, Air Force One was immediately ushered over to the penalty box where it was parked. A column of New York police cars instantly surrounded the aircraft as the ramp was moved into position. Three agents were the first to leave the plane, guns held at the ready as they cautiously surveyed the entire area. Other police officers were seen on top of the terminal building with SWAT teams.

Three black limousines pulled up to the side of the 747, each displaying the great seal of the President. The agents checked the cars, once they were satisfied there was nothing inside that could compromise the President's life, he was allowed to disembark the aircraft. Both he and Director Raincloud were rushed into the lead limo while the rest of his entourage piled into the other vehicles. They were whisked into the night before any reporters got near the caravan.

Six cars of New York City's finest were in front of the President's car, clearing the road. The police cars cut off side roads, blocked main roadways and highways as the President's vehicles sped for the very heart of New York City. Another six cars and two SWAT trucks took up the rear of the convoy. One police car actually bumped a car of reporters who came too close.

Fifth Avenue was sealed off as the President's limousine rushed down the avenue, and pulled up to the Trump Plaza and came to a full stop in front of the building. President Cole had the Presidential suite covering the fifteenth and sixteenth floors, and overlooked Central Park.

Donald Trump was standing outside, and he greeted the President as he stepped out of the limo. President Cole introduced Director Raincloud to Trump who he knew, and they entered the Trump International Tower and Hotel that was spotlessly clean and decked out in all its beauty and splendor. The manager and staff stood before the empty foyer as Trump ushered the President and his people towards the elevators. The operators were standing outside the lifts while a horde of security agents checked out the elevators. They bowed politely to the President as he rushed in the lift, the operator followed and brought the President up to his room.

Donald Trump showed the President to his room and was invited in a bottle of Dom Perrignone was chilling. President Cole headed for the bottle freshly opened and poured himself, and then Trump and Director Raincloud a glass. He raised the glass and toasted the two other men in the room with him. "To New York gentlemen."

"To New York City and State and also to the United States of America gentlemen." Mr. Trump replied proudly and knew it was time to leave, and he made his excuses. He shook the Presidents hand then Raincloud's and left the room.

"There's a damn good man and one day that man is going to end up as the President of the United States." The President offered as Trump closed the door behind him.

"Yes sir, I like how he paid the mortgage for the man who stopped to help him when he was broken down. A class act sir." Raincloud offered as he put the half glass of champagne down.

"I didn't hear about that one John." The President replied with confusion in his tone.

Director Raincloud explained what happened, when he was done, both men picked at the snack of shrimp. It was a snack that could have fed a third of New York City.

When finished, the President suddenly clapped his hands together and then announced. "Gentlemen, ladies, it's getting rather late and I suggest we turn in for the night. We have a big day ahead of us tomorrow, and I want to be well rested if I'm to be at my best before the members of the United Nations." The President checked his watch and saw it was after twelve.

IRANSHAHR, IRAN, FRIDAY, NOVEMBER 8th, 1998. ZERO FOUR TWENTY HOURS

The American operative Mohammed Boua Bdellah, used most of the night to get near the once secret Iranian complex, while compiling an extremely detailed map of the entire place. Al-Shamarral helped him with the map, but his patience was growing rather thin. He wanted to be out of the desert before the sun was high, and if they did not leave presently, they would be coming out of the desert at the busiest time of the day.

Ahmed Hessein al-Shamarral worked his way over to Bdellah's side and he lightly tapped his foot with his hand, making the spy jump. He turned to al-Shamarral and snapped before he realized what he was doing. "Don't do that, you nearly made me shit myself, al-Shamarral."

The old beggar laughed, and then he pointed at his wrist and Bdellah knew what the elderly man wanted. He nodded and then crawled over to the low dune they were using for cover. When they were behind the sand mountain, they pulled their Howlis down to enable them to talk easier. Al-Shamarral leaned closer to Bdellah and then warned him. "We have to leave this area now my foolish son, or we'll be forced to spend another full day and night in the desert to wait for the cover of darkness to hide our approach to the town." Al-Shamarral's Kashmiri rifle sticking out from under his Howli, in the way as they spoke together.

Angrily, Bdellah shoved the barrel of the weapon away from his body, it was actually poking him right in the ribs as he complained at the old man. "For the love of Allah, I hope that damn thing is not loaded al-Shamarral."

Al-Shamarral laughed as he replied. "Of course the weapon is loaded, son of a camel. What good would a rifle be in the hostile desert, if it was not loaded? As I warned you since Allah chose to place you within my footfalls. The desert's not a very friendly place to wander about. Bdellah, there are many things here that wish you harm, and not all are of the human variety."

"I heard," Bdellah replied as he worked the Howli back over his head then added. "you're correct al-Shamarral. We better leave now, because I have to make contact with my control and get this latest information to him. I'm sure he's eating the rug, screaming why I have not made contact with him as yet." The American operative tried to calculate how many contacts he missed. What difference as long as he got the requested information to them.

While Bdellah made the finishing touches to his map, he crawled around the complex for the last time. Al-Shamarral spent his time pointing out a number of tanks, machine gun bunkers, Army barracks and mortar installations. He covered their tracks as they pulled back, or changed positions. The beggar dragged a cloth behind to avoid raising dust as he covered their footprints.

Bdellah stood, and then he joined al-Shamarral and they shoved off. Leaving the desert went much easier than entering, especially with al-Shamarral leading the way for the two of them. They were starving and thoroughly exhausted, neither one of them planned to be out in the desert so long, and the food disappeared the night before. There was a light breeze blowing in from the south, helping to cover their tracks as they walked the endless sand plains.

The two desert wanders traveled at a good steady pace, with the breeze picking up in strength. Al-Shamarral folded the cloth he used to smooth their footprints and made it disappear under his Howli. They came out of the desert near nine o'clock, this was a bad time to appear in the small Iranian town. Everyone was out and about, either going off to work or shopping before the heat of the afternoon drove everyone indoors.

Al-Shamarral stopped just outside the village and he took a few moments to observe the town, there were too many people moving around to just walk into the village. In the town he knew there had to be police, or military personnel mixed in with the population, and the sight of them coming out of the desert was sure to draw attention to them. The old man backed down the low sand dune and ran his hand over the sand and used his finger to make a map and he explained. "We are here, here is the village. There are many people about, so I plan to move here." He stabbed the sand with his finger and added. "This is the back of the cafe where we first met. We'll walk out of the alley, and I'll beg a cigarette, and you'll curse without giving me one.

"You'll go into the cafe for a morning meal, I'll try to follow you into the establishment. I'm certain the god cursed owner will stop me from entering his establishment, and the commotion will cover our coming out of the foul alley, it'll help to hide we came out of the desert. Any police officer will figure I spent the night sleeping with the garbage in the alley, and you, a poor passing villager was being assaulted by the hated village beggar."

"Great al-Shamarral, I agree, all I have to do is get to my radio and report to my control."

"Ahhh..., I fear that is impossible." Al-Shamarral smirked as he erased his map with his foot.

"Why is that al-Shamarral?" Bdellah snapped defensively at the old man this time.

"Because, while I observed the village, I happened to notice a military truck parked near the center of the market square. It was one of the machines with the listening devices mounted on top of the machine. You see, there are laws against listening to American propaganda stations on the radio. Especially those who take a stand against our leadership. Once a week, the military trucks enter our village in search of illegal radios. Anyone found in possession of one of the cursed things, is immediately arrested and never seen again by their loved ones." Al-Shamarral shrugged and then he slowly spread his hands apart as he walked away from Bdellah.

The American pulled the old man by the arm and forcibly spun him around by it.

In one motion, Bdellah was dumped on the sand sitting on his rearend and staring up at the ancient barrel of the Kashmiri rifle. Then in the flaring eyes of al-Shamarral as he snarled at him. "By Allah's great will, you will never lay hands upon my person ever again and live to breathe in another breath. To do so will cost you your worthless life, son of the lowly desert scorpion. I'll destroy you if you dare to touch me ever again." Al-Shamarral actually pushed the barrel of his ancient weapon into the belly of Bdellah as a finally warning.

Bdellah stared at the old man and then asked. "You're a priest old man? A Sheika."

Al-Shamarral did not reply to Bdellah's last words, but he did relax his weapon slowly. Then the old man put it up when he was sure Bdellah was not going to approach him any further. Nevertheless, he held the American operative in his cautious glaze.

"Yes, of course, I'm right al-Shamarral. You're a priest? A Sheika."

"By Allah's great wisdom and kindness, what does it matter to a lowly infidel who slithers on his belly on the sacred sands of Allah's Garden. We have to leave this area immediately, or we'll find ourselves being forced to spend another full day out in the burning desert sands."

"I have to get to my radio and make a report to my control as soon as possible, father of the desert sands." Bdellah cried as he struggled to his feet and followed the old man down the ancient, long ago dried up stream bed that nearly circled the village of Iranshahr.

"I know this my foolish young son, but as I have just said Bdellah. You'll have to wait until this military truck has left the heart of the village. If you don't wish to do this then allow me to know and I'll part company with you right here and now, fool. Only a fool destroys a wise man, if you have a wish to be captured by the military, and experience their very persuasive ways of gathering information from your lips. Go find your worthless radio, but I have no such wish to experience my death. You must decide, choose to speak on your radio, and I leave you forever. If you're willing to listen to my words of caution, allow me to keep you alive, for you to be able to report to your government later. I'll stay." Al-Shamarral stared at the American Agent.

"It's imperative I speak to my control as soon as possible, father of the desert." Bdellah cried, not wanting to put off his conversation with his control in the states.

"By Allah's glory, it's imperative you remain alive also my foolish son. Does your cursed control expect you to give up your worthless life to report to him? Bdellah, the military are not like the dog eating fools of Iraq. They know what they're doing, and they're good and well experienced at what they do. What good will it do you to start your report, knowing you'll be discovered before you had a chance to complete your foolish report to your control, son."

Bdellah sighed and then gave into the beggar's demand he wait before chancing to make contact with his government, and he offered. "What other choice do I have, my father?"

"Your choice open to you is to trust me with your worthless life, fool. I'll keep you alive despite yourself, so you can make contact with your control. After that, we'll see what's to become of our fostering friendship. You'll follow me and do as I say." Al-Shamarral snapped.

Bdellah silently fell in step with the old man and they both walked towards the small village. They ended up coming out behind the cafe as loud speakers planted in the village were turned on. They knew this was happening because the speakers made an ear piercing crackling, and then a loud disturbing hum while the speakers warmed up and waited for the priests to begin their morning prayers for the faithful of their Islamic religion.

The call to prayers was echoed loudly from every minaret dotting the skyline of the small Iranian village. The daily prayers were enhanced by the many loud speakers. As the priest bellowed out the prayers, everyone in the village laid out their prayer rugs and dropped down on them. All facing to the Saudi Arabian village of Mecca, believed to be the birth place of the great Prophet Muhammad himself. The priest belted out his incantations, making them more musical and compelling to listen to. Everyone from Iranshahr stopped what they were doing, and they prayed as the words demanded of them, most of them were of the Sunni belief.

Bdellah was surprised to see al-Shamarral kneeling and answering the priest's calls. He did not know where or how the old beggar produced the prayer rug. Al-Shamarral ignored Bdellah as he prayed all his life. Bdellah felt embarrassed that he invading al-Shamarral's privacy. Without knowing it, he went down to his knees and faced west, and responded with words of prayers.

When it was over, Bdellah found al-Shamarral smiling at him pleasantly as he offered the much younger man. "It's a true believer of the sacred words who'll bend a knee without the softness of a prayer rug to help protect his bones from the painful gravel. Yes I like you my son, and I'll protect you from all harm." Al-Shamarral did not inform the agent they were being shadowed by the caravan of his well feared desert fighters who had orders to stay out sight.

The pair of desert wanderers stood with Bdellah helping the old man up to his feet, and then they both walked out of the alley by the filthy cafe. Everyone from the village returned to what they were doing before the call to prayers, so the two emerged from the alley unobserved by anyone from the town.

THE UNITED NATIONS BUILDING, NEW YORK CITY, NEW YORK. FRIDAY, NOVEMBER 8th, 1998. 9 A.M. EST

The United Nations meeting was having trouble organizing, it was not every day the American President requested permission to address the members. Many had no idea why the American Leader requested permission to address the meeting. It was followed if the United States, or any other nation had a gripe, it was to be aired before the fifteen permanent Security Council members. This was usually done behind closed doors, so councils had a chance to iron out the problem secretly. Once the problems were corrected, the subject was then released for public consumption, and the public was allowed in the Security Council to observe the politicians activities. To make it seem the Security Council was doing its job preserving world peace.

Before the American President entered the great hall, he waited in the office of the American Ambassador. Every nation represented at the United Nations sent a memo requesting a special audience with the American Leader before the scheduled meeting began. They were trying to find out the reason behind the President's request to address them. But President Cole kept a low profile, and he refused to meet with any representative privately before the meeting started. The President was pleased when the special memo from the Russian Ambassador, Nicholas Antich arrived. He showed it to American Ambassador Walters.

"Sure, now the damn Russians want to meet, but this paper doesn't say I tried to reach Russian President Kvantrishuili, since I first discovered the Russian missile sale to Iran. Then I find out President Kvantrishuili's at a retreat and he couldn't spare me the time of day. Now, he can cool off his heels while waiting for me this time, dammit." President Cole crumpled the request and sent it flying across Ambassador Walters office.

Ambassador Walters left the bunched up piece of paper where it landed as he offered. "Albert, not trying to side with the Alliance States, sir. But you know the Russian Leader's health is in question lately. We know the by-pass surgery didn't have the desired results, and there's talk the Russian Leader needs a heart transplant if he wants to live. I heard that's what's taking place. I don't expect to hear from the Russian President for three weeks if this is true, Mr. President." Ambassador Walters picked up the crumbled paper and threw it in the basket to be burned later.

"I heard this myself a while ago Ambassador Walters. You think there might be some truth in it or could it be just a ploy by the Russian Leader?" the President asked.

"Yes sir Albert." Ambassador Walters replied as he smiled at the President.

"Then he had an excuse to dodge me. While I'm addressing the members of the meeting I want you to contact the Russian's office and set up a private meeting for after my address. I'll see the Russians, Saudis, and the other members of the old Coalition Forces. I plan to spend the entire day and most of the night in New York attending to these meetings. I'm not against spending tomorrow in the City, if the meetings last longer than I expected. So don't be afraid to set up as many meeting as you can, Ambassador." President Cole took a second to catch his breath.

"Then I'm lead to believe this is a very serious situation we're talking about here, Albert." The suddenly deeply concerned Ambassador asked, searching for his own bits of information as to why the President was waiting to address the United Nations members in his office.

"I was under the impression you were brought up to speed on the situation we're facing in Iran, Ambassador. I guess I had better fill in the missing blanks for you then, Ambassador Walters Sir." The President was extremely embarrassed Ambassador Walters was not informed of the reason why he sought to address the United Nations meeting. He made a mental note to head hunt when he returned to the White House and blast the one who failed to report to the Ambassador why he was heading for New York. But the President's explanation was placed on the back burner, because as he was about to begin, the Ambassador's intercom buzzed.

Ambassador Walters eyes went to the machine, and. "Excuse me for a moment please Albert. This message has to be important to interrupt us, Mr. President Sir."

"Sure go ahead and answer it Ambassador." The President said as he busied himself.

It was the Ambassador's secretary and bodyguard, her voice purred sexily over the intercom. "Ambassador Walters Sir, they're ready for President Cole to begin addressing the members at the meeting, sir. Everyone's already seated and the hall's quiet as a church, sir."

"Good Helen, inform the Master at Arms we're on our way for the meeting. Inform security to standby." He let go of the button and he said to the President. "Looks like I'll find out with everyone else what this is about Albert. There's no time to explain now, they're waiting for us.?"

"You're leading the way for me to enter the hall, Ambassador Walters? I want you to lead me in the hall." President Cole asked and sort of demanded at the same time.

"Yes sir, it'd be my pleasure, Mr. President."

The President followed the Ambassador to the hall. He was stopped from entering the room, and Ambassador Walters entered the hall and he quickly took his seat. President Cole waited to be announced by the Master at Arms that the American Leader was heading for the podium. He lightly tapped the mike and it screamed in resentment over the intrusion. The Master at Arms waited until the squeal subsided, and for conversations to end. When there was silence in the room, he addressed the representatives. "Ladies and Gentlemen of the United Nations, Secretaries, and all who have business before the States. I'd like to take this time to introduce to you the President of the United States, President Albert John Cole." The Master at Arms then waved his arm towards the unseen President.

Everyone attending the meeting stood and started to clap while President Cole slowly walked and waved on the stage to the podium and sea of microphones. Blinding flash bulbs fired off one after the other as reporters took pictures of the American President. Other reporters spoke in their microphones and tape recorders, as they explained what was transpiring at the meeting. The standing ovation would have continued unchecked, if it was not for the President raising his hand to ask the emissaries for silence. Even after this request was repeated a second time, the clapping went on. This was the first time the President requested to address a meeting in person.

The Master at Arms saw the President wanted to begin his speech, and he stepped to a side podium and bellowed. "Ladies and gentlemen, the President of the United States. Please allow him to address the members." He repeated as he raised his hands to silence the dignitaries.

Slowly, the gathered Ambassadors took their seats and quickly quieted down. Even after all of this, it still took at least another ten minutes for silence to return to the meeting hall.

President Cole smiled and he continued to wave at the many of the dignitaries while scanning the countless faces staring at him, and making eye contact with certain Ambassadors who were allies of the United States. The American President was being extremely patient while waiting for the commotion his presence had caused the diplomats attending the meetings, to finally calm down enough for him to begin his speech to the members.

When it was finally quiet enough for him to speak, the President of the United States suddenly cleared his throat and then began speaking.

CHAPTER ELEVEN

The America President began his speech. "Ladies and Gentlemen, I have requested permission to address this, the two thousand five hundred and fifty forth meeting of the peace loving nations of the United Nations. Because I have certain information of a world threatening situation rapidly developing between Iran and Russia, and the rest of the world."

The American President's words were instantly cut off as mumbling from many of the gathered Ambassador's began, and all eyes drifted towards the two Ambassadors from Iran and the Alliance States. The Iranian Representative sat undisturbed by the President's words, acting like he was barely even hearing them. The Russian Ambassador was caught completely off guard though by the American Leader's stinging words aimed at his country, because he had no idea of the deal struck between Iran and Admiral Proushinsky, the Commander of the Black Sea Fleet. He stood in stunned disbelief the American President spoke against Russia, and no one in Russia done anything to upset him as far as he was aware of.

The Russian Ambassador slowly spread out his hands in totally bewilderment as he mumbled. "Mr. American President Sir, I don't know what you think you might have discovered against my nation of Russia. I know Russia has done nothing to be ashamed about. I resent you're attempting to chastise my nation of Russia before the gathered members of the United Nations, sir." The Russian Ambassador stared at the American Leader with shock etched on his face.

President Cole smiled pleasantly at the Russian Representative as he added to his words. "Ambassador Antich Sir, I believe your leaders are guiltless in this situation, sir."

"Then why are you bringing bad feelings against my country before the members of the council Mr. President?" the Russian complained as he stared at the President standing by the podium.

"I beg your pardon Ambassador Antich sir if I lead you and the other members of this meeting to believe I was attempting to chastise your great nation of Russia as a whole, sir. What I should've said in my opening speech was, my Representatives have amassed irrefutable evidence that one of your Admiral's has sold a number of SS-N-23 submarine launch nuclear tipped ballistic missiles capable of launching up to ten independently warheads...”

“Mr. American President Sir! I must protest this conversation in the strongest possible means, especially being aired in a public meeting forum such as this one is, sir. I assure you that my government has no idea of what you speak of, Mr. President. What missiles do you speak of sir? What Russian Admiral would dare sell Russia’s nuclear tipped missiles to any other nation of the world? I’m sorry to utter these words to such a well respected National Leader. But this is sheer nonsense I believe. Mr. President, your words are not true I fear sir! You have not offered the name of this so called traitor Admiral you say sold missiles to Iran.” The Russian Ambassador turned to the Iranian Ambassador with disgust in his eyes. “Mr. American President, Russia would never sell the smell from our waste plants to Iran. We don’t like the nation as a whole.”

A roar from a number of Islamic nations rose as each one protested the Russian Ambassador’s ugly words as he remained standing and ignoring the mild protests. The Iranian Ambassador rose as if he was going to reply to the Russian, and then he obviously thought better of it as he retook his seat, and again stared in nothingness. Showing he was not only bored over the words being bantered about, but he held complete disdain for all who attended the meeting.

Frantic conversations threatened to upset the entire meeting. President Cole stepped away from the podium allowing the President of the Council, French Ambassador Gene Bartlett to get control over the meeting rapidly unraveling around him. The French Ambassador had to pound his gavel down many times, to get the angry Ambassadors to quiet down so the American Leader could lay out his evidence before them. Not until the French Ambassador had the Master at Arms move out to the platform did quiet finally return to the meeting hall.

When everyone was seated again, Ambassador Bartlett turned to President Cole and he offered to the American Leader. "Mr. President, you were offering to the assembly sir?"

The Russian Ambassador angrily called out this time. "The American President tried to make the Ambassadors believe a Russian Admiral sold missiles to the Iranian nation. But he has failed to mention this Admiral's name he's implicating falsely, as a traitor to my nation sir."

Again, Ambassador Bartlett banged his gavel down as he openly glared at the angry Russian Diplomat and he replied with a snap in. "Please Ambassador Antich Sir, I know this is unbearable to hear, but you have to allow President Cole to finish delivering his evidence before us. So we may weigh, and then correct what I believe is a terrible situation the American President is trying to alert us to. Please, you must allow the American President to continue his words uninterrupted if we're to get to the bottom of this present situation he's speaking of." Again, Ambassador Bartlett turned to the American Leader and offered. "President Cole, please."

President Cole stared right at the Russian politician and he began anew. "Ambassador Antich! The name of this Russian Admiral I speak of is Yevgeny Proushinsky." The American President stopped speaking as he allowed his words to sink in the mind of the Russian Representative.

Ambassador Antich could not hide his shock which forced his face into a mask of consuming bewilderment as he heard the well respected name Admiral Yevgeny Proushinsky mentioned as the coconspirator in this tale of astonishment the American President was weaving at the meeting. He swallowed before finding the strength to rebuke the American's accusation. He shook his head and then remarked. "No, this is completely impossible sir. I know the Admiral for many years, and his reputation is beyond reproach, beyond reproach I say. This is totally impossible to believe, your spies are terribly mistaken about the Admiral I assure you, Mr. American President Sir. You must dig much further into this fairy tale you offer, and I'm sure you'll realize your spies are wrong. I don't understand how you possibly brought this Admiral's name into a web of lies and accusations." As his words came out, they increased in tempo.

Ambassador Bartlett picked up the fact the Russian Ambassador's temper was getting a little out of control, and he got involved before the Russian went too far with words of anger aimed at the American President, who was also obviously getting noticeably angry himself. He brought down his gavel and when the Russian Ambassador was quiet, Ambassador Bartlett asked him. "Ambassador Antich Sir, is this man an active Admiral in your country's military service?"

"Is this Admiral Yevgeny Proushinsky in my country's service you ask of me? Ambassador Bartlett, Admiral Yevgeny Proushinsky is in Command of the mighty Black Sea fleet. He has the power to send our Armada of warships out to defend the shores of Russia against any threat aimed at my country or our allies. I'm absolutely convinced the American President's confused with his accusations aimed against the good Admiral. I resent them vehemently, and I must protest their continual use. I further demand the American President apologize to the Russian people, and to the Admiral for these horrendous remarks he has just offered us. I cannot believe after all of what has taken place in my country. The Americans would try and make the world believe this nightmare is being revisited on them. I believe the Americans are seeing ghosts hiding behind every tree, and are using the good Russian people as their evil spirits."Ambassador Antich's shoulders hunched as he rested his hands on the table and stared at the President.

In a low hiss, the Russian Ambassador snarled at the American Leader. "President Cole! I, as well as everyone here, wait for your evidence against the Admiral to be offered before us, or you must apologize for besmirching the good Admiral's name and reputation. Evidence I trust is in your possession and will be displayed before us, or I again must demand an apology from you, sir." Ambassador Antich growled 'President Cole' with as much sarcasm and venom as he could possibly muster to show his utter contempt for the American President's latest words.

President Cole did not take offense to the insult being delivered against him by the Russian as he allowed a slight smile to slowly cross his lips, and then he replied. "Ambassador Antich Sir, I have monumental and irrefutable evidence that'll clearly show beyond a shadow of a doubt, the traitorous transaction, and the transfer of said nuclear tipped submarine launch missiles between this said Russian Admiral, and the Iranians who have already transported these missiles to Iran." The President motioned with his fingers towards the Russian Diplomat accusingly.

"American President, you expect me to believe this transfer of Russia's missiles was carried out beneath our very noses, and we were not aware of this happening? Impossible! Impossible I say! You're obviously mistaken sir." Ambassador Antich snarled as he glared at President Cole.

The American Leader let out an exhausted sigh and then began speaking again. "What are you saying to me Ambassador Antich? Russia must have been aware of this illegal nuclear missile transaction with the Iranians, sir? That would be most disturbing to me, and to the other Ambassadors attending this meeting. Up until now, I was willing to give Russia the benefit of the doubt that they were unaware of what this renegade Admiral was doing with their nuclear arsenal. But if you want me and everyone else attending this meeting to believe nothing happens in the borders of Russia, that's carried out without the blessings of your government's leadership.

"Then I'd be forced to demand to know why your government's going against every agreement signed between the United States, Russia and every other nation who has signed their name to the NNPT-Nuclear Non Proliferation Treaty sir. I further demand to know why your government's selling nuclear, long range submarine launch missiles to Iran, and I further demand to know how many other nations your government has chosen to sell these weapons of mass destruction to, now, and in the future." President Cole openly glared at the upset Russian Ambassador this time.

For a breathtakingly long time, there was no response from the angry Russian, prompting the President of the assembly to ask. "Ambassador Antich, I believe there was a question put forth that demands a response from you, or your country's President, sir. Please Ambassador Antich, we're waiting your reply to American's accusations aimed against this Russian Admiral, sir."

The Russian politician barely took any notice of Ambassador Bartlett's request as he turned away from him and placed his full attention back on the waiting American

Leader. In a low almost contrite tone of voice, Ambassador Antich finally mumbled like he was trying to make only President Cole hear any of his words. "Mr. American President Sir, if you have this what you refer to as irrefutable evidence, why have you not chosen to bring this situation up to my government's attention, before leveling these most terrible accusations before the rest of the world sir? If your words are true as spoken sir then my government would've done everything under its power to correct the situation and place a stop to it immediately, sir."

RUSSIA

No sooner were the words of the Russian Ambassador spoken at the United Nations meeting, than did the Russian government go into action. All leaders of Russia were glued to their TV sets listening to every word spoken by the American President doing battle with their Ambassador. The Russian Leaders were stunned by the American Leader's words, and the calls started. Many calls were placed to the KGB Directorate, Valery Shohekochihkin. But the one that stirred the wheels of the KGB in action, came from President Vitaly Kvantrishuili's hospital bed.

"Directorate Shohekochihkin, you know god dom well who this is I trust, sir?" Russian President Kvantrishuili asked in an exhausted and extremely angry tone.

"Yes Mr. President I know who this is sir. How are you doing sir?" The KGB Directorate replied with a little concern in his tone of voice.

"My health is not your concern to worry about Valery! I'll not waste my god dom time demanding you pay attention to my words. I demand Admiral Proushinsky be placed under immediate arrest by the time I finish speaking with you.

Bring him back to Moscow alive, so I and the Council may question this god dom traitor before having him publicly executed."

"But President Kvantrishuili, the American President has not given us the proof to accuse our Admiral of any wrong doing, sir. I know this Admiral well for many years, and I don't believe for one moment that he would ever, or dare become a traitor to Mother Russia and the military he so proudly served for over twenty years faithfully, sir." Director Shohekochihkin offered weakly.

"Don't be such a ignoramus when speaking to me Directorate Shohekochihkin! The god dom American Leader is far from being a fool sir. Believe me Directorate Shohekochihkin, if he takes time to stand before the United Nation Council, complaining that this god dom Admiral Proushinsky has sold a number of long range missiles and nuclear weapons to that hated nation of Iran, he must be correct sir. He must have the evidence to back the position his worthless country has adopted against us sir. Directorate Shohekochihkin, I want this god dom Admiral Proushinsky in custody wherever he hides, and brought back alive! To Moscow!!!" President Kvantrishuili's body was wracked by a wave of pain and he stopped speaking on the phone.

Directorate Shohekochihkin heard his President's sudden moan, and he waited for the Russian Leader to gather his strength back. The powerful Directorate cursed the old man who survived two coup d' tats and an assassination attempt organized by him, in his effort to try and take back power in Russia. He cursed the endeavors by the Communist backed military officers who had failed to attack China with nuclear missiles launched from North Korea. It was an attempt to force the leadership of Russia to come to North Korea's aid, when China retaliated against North Korea for the unprovoked attack on their mainland.

Directorate Shohekochihkin knew once Russia responded with aid to North Korea, the Communists of Russia would make their move against President Kvantrishuili's worthless leadership of Russia. The powerful KGB Directorate was surprised how close the Communists came to taking power over Russia again, and if it was not for the intervention of American soldiers, Russia might have been taken over by them. That was why he attempted to have the Russian President assassinated while addressing the rioting Communists, he hoped to place the blame for the assassination on them and whip them out before they carried out their plans.

The cunning KGB Directorate cursed the American special operations troops sent to Russia to help the loyal Russian troops defend their own country against the rebel Russian soldiers. Most Russian troops were loyal to President Kvantrishuili, but they still refused to fight the against the Communist troops being led by Colonel Otto Mikhailchenko, as he attempted to take over a secret long range nuclear missile complex constructed outside the capital city of Moscow. His dream of power rapidly fell apart when the American soldiers were given permission to enter Russia, and then help this old fool retain his seat of power over Russia.

The angry KGB Directorate remembered how he fought tooth and nail against the Russian President not to allow the American soldiers to enter Russia. He tried to convince the leader the American troops were guilty of invading Russia, and should be treated as an armed invading Army and attacked and then destroyed as all such invaders should be to Russia. Directorate Shohekochihkin tried to actually will the weak President to die before he got back on the phone. The sound of President Kvantrishuili's raspy voice informed him that the Russian President had survived another bout with death. The Directorate cursed this old fool who had more lives than Rasputin as he replied. "Yes Mr. President, you were saying before you took a breather, sir?"

"Directorate Shohekochihkin, I want this god dom Admiral Proushinsky arrested immediately, and brought back to Moscow alive so he can be questioned about this sale of our nuclear missiles to Iran and then stand trial for his crimes." The Russian Leader demand of his KGB Commander.

"You have already stated that President Kvantrishuili Sir. How is your health? Better I trust sir." Directorate Shohekochihkin repeated while not really meaning his concern for his life.

"My health is just fine so don't bring it up to my attention again Directorate Shohekochihkin. I'll have a new heart by later this afternoon if all goes right. The Doctors have assured me I should be back on my feet within three day's time, and be back at my office for a full day's work by the end of two weeks. Chairman Zbigniew Angelyuk is a very competent and most loyal replacement for me, and will have complete run my office until my return to duty sir. Directorate Shohekochihkin, you'll bring me this god dom traitor Admiral Proushinsky alive!"

"Yes my President, I'll return Admiral Proushinsky to Moscow, alive as you have just ordered me, sir. No matter where he might try and hide, I shall find him and bring him before you sir."

"Good, I must go, the Doctor's are here to take me to the operating room now sir. I'll speak to you the first moment I can speak again. Thank you again Directorate Shohekochihkin for your many years of loyal support to me and my Administration sir. I'll remember your loyalty when I return for duty, and you'll be well rewarded for your faithful service to our country."

There was a slight commotion heard over the phone, and then the banging of the receiver down then a new voice offered. "Yes, this is the Doctor, you must excuse my ward for he has fallen asleep sir." The doctor hung up without asking who was on the other end of the line.

Directorate Shohekochihkin squeezed the receiver, wishing it was the neck of the old Russian President locked in his strong hands. The KGB Leader smirked, comfortable the doctors searched the length and width of the Motherland for a donor's heart that would be compatible with the President and once found, he was nurtured to the best of health. The donor was given the very best foods, a medical and a detailed exercise routine to fill the days while waiting to die for his President's sake. Directorate Shohekochihkin knew the heart had come from a very healthy twenty five year old Ukrainian man who enjoyed the best of health, never smoked or drank.

On the man's death report, it was to state he died in a terrible car accident. In reality, he was going to be killed by the doctors in such a way, as not to cause any harm to the much needed heart for the ailing Russian President. Directorate Shohekochihkin smiled to himself because he was responsible for finding the heart donor needed to save the President's life.

The young Ukrainian man was aware of what was about to happen to him, but understood his death would ensure his family would live a very good life in Russia, protected from danger and have enough to eat and respected by Russia. The young man was willing to die for his family's sake, and for his ill President. But that lie ended with the man's death, and his family was scheduled to die in the same supposed car accident he died in. Directorate Shohekochihkin grinned as he thought what a terrible tragedy for an entire family to perish in the same accident. But in his heart, he knew the leadership of Russia did not want anyone alive, to let out the story of how the heart for President Kvantrishuili was acquired. No one in Russia wanted the world to believe they would kill a human and his entire family, to save the life of their ailing President.

When the Russian doctor hung up, Directorate Shohekochihkin immediately placed a call to his headquarters, and he ordered the arrest of Admiral Proushinsky. Every police officer, KGB Agent, and anyone else attached with the military, was placed on full alert with orders to arrest the wanted Russian Admiral no longer the Commander of the Black Sea Fleet. His next call was placed to the Naval Base in stationed Sevastopol, where a Captain answered the phone, and when he was informed to place Admiral Proushinsky under arrest. The Captain instantly informed Directorate Shohekochihkin that the Admiral was no longer on the base.

Directorate Shohekochihkin ordered the Naval Base to be placed on full alert, and he further placed all border crossings closed, and all airports placed under tighter surveillance, along with all railroads watched and shipyards searched. In effect, Russia was now a massive a prison for the missing Admiral, and it was only a matter of time before he was surely arrested, and the KGB would get their hands on the traitor, and begin his interrogation. There was something that brought great pleasure to the Directorate whenever he got the chance to interrogate an always arrogant Russian Officer. He drew pleasure breaking a strong minded person's will and body.

When Directorate Shohekochihkin felt he done everything in his power to completely close Russia down, he placed his forces on alert, and was certain the Admiral would not be able to escape the net he placed over Russia's vastness. He then sat back in his chair, and placed his feet up on his desk and tried to will the death of the Russian President going under the knife at this very moment, as he lit up an American made cigarette. Directorate Shohekochihkin wished he could have gotten to the doctor operating on the old fool. Then he would be certain the Russian President would not have lived through the dangerous operation. He slowly shook his head while he waited for word of the Admiral's arrest, and the outcome of the Russian President's operation.

THE UNITED NATIONS MEETING

The American President continued to stand before the podium as he quickly mulled over his next words. He had to gather his thoughts together and refrain from attacking Russia, his lesser target. His main concern was the nation of Iran, although he was fuming and his guts were churning. At the moment, he needed Russia's cooperation if he was to take on Iran. President Cole knew he would receive some flak from the Islamic nations as his eyes shifted to the Saudi Arabian Delegate, and saw the set of his jaw, and snarl for a stare. The Saudi stared at him with unblinking eyes. With a deep sigh, President Cole forced his attention to the Russia Delegate.

With an extremely exhausted and heavy hand, the American President rubbed his eyes and then spoke again. "Ambassador Antich Sir, please forgive me for breaching this situation with you at this meeting, sir. But you must be aware that I have done everything in my power to try and make contact with your President. But he was out of the capital and his aides didn't deem it necessary to inform him I needed to speak with him over this very concerning matter sir.

"The aides I communicated with were most unfriendly at that, and they were very abbreviated when they informed me President Kvantrishuili left word he wasn't to be disturbed for any reason. Ambassador Antich, I know your President's in failing health, and there's a question whether he'll return to Moscow or not. But this matter was extremely important as you can well see for yourself sir, and when he or anyone else from your country's leadership refused to speak to me over this matter. I was left with no other alternative but to bring this latest situation up before the other members of the United Nations, sir." The American Leader paused long enough to allow his words to be considered by all who was attending the meeting.

Ambassador Antich was stunned no one left in control of Russia, had the intelligence to inform President Kvantrishuili or himself that the American President wished to speak with his President over such an important matter as this one was. Ambassador Antich was barely able to hide his disappointment while shifting his weight, and cursed Chairman Angelyuk under his breath, for not reacting to the American's request to speak to President Kvantrishuili. At least Angelyuk should have spoken to President Cole, so he might have headed off this terrible embarrassing situation being aired at the United Nations' meeting and before the world entire.

He was extremely surprised the American President knew so much about his Russian President's health. He wasted his last curse on the Russian Rossiskaya Gazeta newspaper, floating articles about the President's poor health. Ambassador Antich knew he had to say something and he did not want to continue with the conversation about Admiral Proushinsky, or the supposed deal he struck with the Iranians, so he ventured down the only path left.

"President Cole, I assure you sir that President Kvantrishuili's health is not an issue at this time sir. I cannot believe because my President had decided to take a well deserved but short vacation, the world sees his pending death. Is it so wrong President Kvantrishuili had decided to look for a Dacha that is causing him to spend some time away from Moscow? No, I fear this is more of your country's jumping at ghosts lurking in the shadows, Mr. American President Sir." Ambassador Antich tried a weak smile on the powerful American Leader, but his sudden concern over the Russian Admiral and the Iranians made him fail miserably at this attempt.

President Cole let out a deep sigh as he snapped at the Russian Politician this time. "Ambassador Antich, it's world knowledge that your President's heart is about to fail, and your doctors are in search of a donor. I wish it were true the only thing your President was doing is house hunting. No, Ambassador Antich, I won't allow you to change what I know is true sir. Your President's health isn't why I have decided to address this meeting in the first place sir. Your President's health doesn't concern me at this time just as you have stated sir. What does concern me is one of your, Ambassador Antich," the American Leader pointed his accusing finger directly at him as he continued. "Officers sold twelve submarine launched long range nuclear tipped missiles to Iran, to be installed in their nuclear submarines, also sold to Iran by your nation, sir. Thus making Iran a nuclear nation and a serious threat to world peace."

"Twelve long range missiles you offer to me sir! With ten nuclear warheads apiece! By the power controlled in Allah's mighty fist, that's one hundred and twenty warheads in Iran's hands! That's enough to destroy the entire Middle East ten times over, if Iran chooses to do so." The Ambassador from Saudi Arabia exclaimed as he slowly rose to his feet, and then he stared disbelievingly at the American Leader before adding. "Praise Allah, I must protest this god cursed sale of these weapons of mass destruction to any Arab or Persian nation. May Allah protect us from such evil weapons that exist only to destroy whole nations in a single breath."

President Cole turned to the Saudi Arabian Diplomat and then nodded at the excited politician. For the first time since addressing the meeting, he felt his long time ally was on his side.

Ambassador Antich turned to the Saudi Politician and offered him with much concern lacing his tone of voice. "Mr. Ambassador, may I remind you that so far, President Cole has completely failed to offer any serious proof whatsoever that any such a traitorous transaction has taken place." Ambassador Antich was stalling for time, hoping against hope he would hear from his government with a much more logical explanation for what this svinaya sumashedshaya sabaka (fucking mad dog) of a Russian Admiral has done to and against his own country.

President Cole's patience and judgment rapidly drained as he all but screamed at the shaken Russian Diplomat this time. "You want proof you demand from me Ambassador Antich! Then you'll have all the proof you so assiduously search for sir. I hope this film proof will be enough evidence to convince you, and everyone else who is attending this meeting that everything I'm saying is the truth. I'm upset with this meeting because we're wasting so much valuable time with bantering words back and forth, rather than working on the problem at hand. That problem is Iran and these long range nuclear tipped missiles your rebel Admiral Proushinsky, Ambassador Antich, your Russian Admiral stole from your own country and then sold them to Iran, sir."

President Cole waged a war within himself, trying desperately to master his temper and yet display he was dead serious with what he was speaking about to the members of the Council. He knew he lost some creditability with his display of temper, and had to be absolutely perfect in his presentation of evidence, or no one would believe him. He turned to the officer standing on the platform with him and asked. "Master at Arms, I believe that Ambassador Walters gave you a number of still photographs as well as a set of video tapes before he left the meeting room, sir?"

"You're absolutely correct Mr. President Sir. He sure did sir." The Master at Arms replied.

"If it's possible, I'd like you to start the tapes running for the members of the meeting, sir. Maybe you can also display the stills to the side of the film at the same time you are running the tapes for us sir?" The American Leader then waited for the reply from the Master at Arms

"That's not a problem Mr. President. When do you want me to start the tapes running sir?"

"Hmmm... may I give you a simple hand signal to begin the tapes when I need them to start being displayed for us, sir?" the smiling American President asked the Master at Arms.

"Yes Sir Mr. President Sir. When you want the tape started just raise your thumb on your right hand and I'll take it from there for you, sir. By the way Mr. President Sir, if you'd like me to pause them or hold a picture in frame, raise your hand and I'll freeze frame as long as you hold your hand up, sir. This way you can keep your mind on the presentation and control the tapes at the same time, Mr. President Sir." The Master at Arms smiled at his American President.

"That's great, it'll take a lot of pressure off my shoulders for me if you can do this for me, sir. Master at Arms, please start the tapes when I nod to you sir. And I'd like you to stop them when I hold two fingers up sir." The President returned the Master at Arms smile.

He nodded and then quickly disappeared behind the thick wall of heavy curtains again.

President Cole turned back to the Russia Diplomat who was obviously growing a bit antsy and looking extremely uncomfortable at the same time. The American Leader nodded slightly to Antich and then offered him. "Ambassador, I'll, with the aid of tapes the United States satellites took when the movement of tanker trucks were detected in Iran. You'll see the vehicles travel through Iran, and when they entered Russia. Arrr... no more words Ambassador Antich. It's easier to watch the tapes, they're self explanatory sir." With this, the American President raised his thumb. The room instantly darkened and the wall behind the President became a moving picture. President Cole turned to see the screen and then he began explaining the pictures.

"Here you go Ambassador Antich, these are twelve Iranian tractor trailer tanker rigs traveling through the vast Dashte Kavir desert at some times, traveling at breakneck speeds. Notice how the trucks behave, like they're desperately attempting to avoid detection by any possible means."

No one spoke as they kept their eyes glued to the screen, and pictures.

"Ambassador Antich Sir, here we can plainly see the long convoy of tanker trailer trucks passing into Russian from the Iranian side of the border. Here they go sir, please pay close attention to this next part of the film. You see the rigs have Iranian markings painted on the sides of each machine. Here the trucks disappear from the main road for a short period of time, and the next time we see them they now have Russia insignias painted on the sides of the machines, sir."

"How do we know that these trucks are still the same machines, before they disappeared from your satellite's eyes, Mr. American President Sir?" The Russian Ambassador snapped, not able to keep the anger out of his tone of voice as he added smartly. "I did not see the machines being painted with any Russian markings sir. How do I know these pictures were not made up, or even doctored on one of your Hollywood sets in the United States, Mr. American President sir?"

The American Leader held up his hand and the pictures immediately stopped. He then turned to the Master at Arms and asked him. "Can you please back the film up to frame, err let me see," President Cole flipped through the papers until he found the frame numbers he was searching for and then he offered. "here we go, go back to frame three, three, two sir."

The tape instantly began to spin backwards, only the numbers were seen still being displayed clearly on the bottom of the screen behind the American Leader back. The spinning stopped on frame three, three, two, as was requested by President Cole.

"Here we go Ambassadors, please take notice of the paint spill on the roof of this one trailer truck here. And here, see the second rig in the line of vehicles, it's a different model from the other eleven trailer trucks. This one's a German made machine. Master at Arms, will you kindly advance the frame to where it was when we stopped it a moment ago sir."

While the Master at Arms did as ordered, the President turned to the Russian Politician and remarked to him. "Ambassador Antich sir, as for your last remark I won't respond to that asinine statement. I'm quite certain that you can plainly see for yourself, and you can easily recognize your own land that these twelve tanker trucks are traveling through at this time, sir."

When the tape resumed at its normal speed, the American President pointed out to the other members of the Council. "Here again Ambassador Antich, you can plainly see the same rigs now covered with Russian insignias, and you can also recognize the second tractor trailer by the paint spill on the roof of the truck. If you look closely, you'll see the second rig that will drop back to the forth position is the German made machine we displayed beforehand, Ambassador Antich sir." President Cole looked over his shoulder, and noticed most of the Ambassadors shaking their heads and agreeing with everything he was offering them with the tape and pictures.

"Ahhh... here we see the same twelve tanker rigs turn onto the massive Russian Naval Base stationed at the Russian Port of Sevastopol. Ambassador Antich Sir, perhaps you can recognize all the foolish precautions your base is conducting, in their failed attempt to try and cover their illegal actions from being observed by one of our satellites sir. See the thick smoke cloud and flares burning off and creating a heavy smoke screen, and the number of large tents hiding the rigs and missiles from view of the same satellites. There, you can easily see one of the exposed missiles being loaded inside one of the tanker truck. Here the trucks go, heading back to Iran.

"Ambassador Antich Sir, I want you to pay strict attention to the men we're now zeroing in on we picked up on the base. There, you can see your Admiral Yevgeny Proushinsky, and he's standing with another man we have successfully identified as an Iranian, who works for the Secret Service of that same nation. His name's identified as Colonel Muhsin Abu Marzuk, and I have his personal file here." The President held up a file folder for all the Ambassador's to see.

"Ambassador Antich, do you mind answering is that not your Admiral Yevgeny Proushinsky, who as you so proudly announced just moments ago, is the current Commander of the Black Sea Fleet, and is he not speaking with the other man on the base, that houses your Russian Fleet?" For the first time, the President asked a question demandingly of the Russian Ambassador.

"I see a man who appears to be dressed in a Russian Naval uniform speaking with another man I have never saw before in my life, Mr. American President Sir. As far as my recognizing either man, that's impossible for me to answer absolutely, sir. As I have already stated to everyone attending this meeting that I have no way of knowing if these are not just some American actors being displayed before all of us." Ambassador Antich could not help sweating, because he easily recognized the Admiral while he was speaking with the other man he truly did not know.

"I see you're still not willing to admit you recognize your Admiral Yevgeny Proushinsky who you so proudly announced moments ago you have known for over twenty years, Ambassador Antich sir. That'll not matter much longer by the time this tape is finished running and all my evidence has been displayed for everyone attending this meeting today. Here, we see the same twelve trucks heading back towards the Iranian, Russian border. Look, the Russian insignias have once again turned back to the original Iranian ones. But if you look closely, you can still see a number of

Russian armor vehicles still escorting the Iranian machines towards the border.

"Here's the border and look at that will ya, the second person we have identified as this man," Again, the American President raised the picture of Iranian Colonel Muhsin Abu Marzuk for all to see, and then he added to his explanation. "handing a briefcase we believe contains an undetermined amount of cash being passed to your Admiral Proushinsky, Ambassador Antich sir. There, the Russian Admiral's handing the briefcase containing the believed to be cash over to another Naval Officer, obviously to be counted. Here we have the Iranian marked tanker trucks being allowed to cross the border at certain intervals. We figured the soldiers working with the Admiral was allowing a truck pass the border when they counted a certain amount of the cash."

The American President turned his back on the screen displaying the Iranian and Russian border as he further explained the last part of the tape to the gathered Ambassadors. "Lastly ladies and gentlemen, we have the twelve same tanker trailer rigs heading back into the vast Dashte Kavir desert region again. We have successfully trailed these twelve rigs until they turned up at the Iranian Naval Base stationed at Bander Beheshi, where we know for certain that the six nuclear powered Delta I Russian made submarines are temporally being housed, while Iran's struggling though her new government's slow development and takeover."

Stills of the close ups and clear pictures of the Russian Admiral Yevgeny Proushinsky and the Iranian Agent Colonel Muhsin Abu Marzuk faces standing side by side were still being constantly flashed on the screen, as the tape abruptly ended in a blinding flash of bright light. Before the Master at Arms was able to stopped the camera from running.

The meeting instantly erupted into a number of excited conversations as many of the dignitaries spoke at the same time. Some of the Ambassador's were forced to yell to be heard over all the commotion. The Council President, seated across from the podium and American President, again was forced to start banging his gavel before order was finally restored.

The American Leader remained standing as did the stunned Russian Ambassador. President Cole quickly scanned the room as other Ambassadors stood and began shouting out in excited voices, while raising their hands to be heard by the secretary General. Security agents rushed to the podium and they instantly formed a tight protective ring around the American President as he waited to speak further to the members of the meeting. Everyone was upset, all but the Iranian Ambassador who remained seated and looking off into space as if he was bored to death. President Cole's eyes locked on the arrogant Iranian's face, and the both of them glared at each other before the trance was broken by Ambassador Bartlett's banging the hammer on his desk.

"Order! I must have order, I need order so President Cole may continue his with his presentation! Will the Ambassadors come to order so we can continue with this presentation please. Order please Ambassadors. I'll have order, or I'll have the room cleared at once. Order!"

After ten minutes of trying to gain control over the meeting, Ambassador Bartlett gained some sanity over the meeting. When silence was restored, President General Bartlett turned to the American Leader. "President Cole sir, I'm forced to side with Ambassador Antich. I think this matter should have been brought to the Security Council behind closed doors. I think this public meeting could have far reaching ramifications sir. I fear riots replacing good judgment, sir."

President Cole glared at the French Ambassador in charge of the meeting as he replied curtly. "I would've much rather have handled this situation with the Russians, and together we could have worked out something with Iran. But since I couldn't get President Kvantrishuili to return any of my calls, and speaking logic with the Iranians is completely out of the question. I was forced to come to the United Nations to air this problem before the rest of the Ambassadors of the world. Yes, I know I could've gone to the Security Council, but that route might have taken weeks, maybe even up to months to travel and time is of the essence over this rapidly developing situation, Ambassador. The longer these damn missiles and nuclear warheads are in possession of the Iranian military. The more possible it is for them to copy the workings of the damn missiles and warheads, and before long the Iranian's will be constructing their own god damn weapons of mass destruction to be used against the rest of the world, Mr. Ambassador Sir."

CHAPTER TWELVE

Ambassador Bartlett rose to his feet as he stared at the American Leader and remarked. "I sure hope you don't have the evidence of this Mr. President Sir. I mean of the Iranians constructing their own missiles and nuclear warheads, and using the Russian blueprints as their guide sir."

"With me sorry no! But is it taking place as we speak I assure you sir? Yes Mr. Ambassador."

The American President's words set off another maelstrom of complaints by the other gathered Ambassadors, all being aired at the same instant, and making it completely impossible for anyone to make any sense of the conversations taking place at the meeting of the United Nations.

President Bartlett shook his head sadly as he sat back and then allowed the conversations to run their course. He did not know what to say or do to try and restore some semblance of order to the meeting. He looked to President Cole surrounded by his security people, and then he shifted his eyes over to the Iranian Ambassador who he realized was being strangely quiet throughout this entire fiasco. He was stunned to find the Iranian politician seated and he was engaging in a conversation with the Ambassador from Iraq. Iraq had been allowed back into the family of civilized nations two months ago, now Iraq was undergoing major construction in an effort to rebuild the destroyed country after the nuclear exchange with Israel and the United States.

The two Middle East country's politicians totally ignored all the mayhem taking place that was once the meeting. This attitude made Ambassador Bartlett realize what the American Leader said, had to be true. He worked out what he was going to do over this situation. The French United Nations President preceding of the meeting, knew they could not possibly allow any uncontrollable Arab or Persian nations get their hands on any nuclear warheads and missiles. He knew none of the Islamic nations would control themselves, if they possessed such powerful weapons. He realized it would be a matter of time before Iran would launch them at its enemies.

Ambassador Bartlett was aware the Coalition Forces were again going to be assembled and used this time against this new Persian aggressor in the Middle East. This time, Iran would suffer their wrath if they did not come around and end their efforts to acquire these dreaded nuclear weapons and the missiles to get them to target. While formulating his thoughts, Ambassador Bartlett was unaware quiet had returned to the meeting, and everyone was staring at him. It was President Cole's sudden clearing of his throat that brought Bartlett's mind back to the meeting. He saw all the staring faces and apologized. "Ambassadors, please forgive my lack of attention, I found the American President's words most disturbing, yes, most disturbing indeed."

There was a short lived muttering of agreement with his last comment. It was at this point the Saudi Ambassador stood, and then he waited to be recognized by Ambassador Bartlett.

"Yes Ambassador Myasar Nasrallah, you may speak if you have something to add to this terribly disturbing conversation, sir." The French Leader of the meeting offered to the other Ambassador kindly, as he nodded to the Arab Politician.

"We heard from the President of the United States, and also the Ambassador from Russia. But so far we have failed to hear anything spoken from the Ambassador of Iran. I'll not make any statements about this situation at this point until I hear from him, and hear what he has to say about these stunning accusations the American President has just offered to us at the meeting."

There were many 'Yea's' uttered as everyone sided with the Saudi Politician. Every eye, every camera and human watching and listening to this meeting, all stared at the Iranian.

The Iranian Ambassador looked to all the world that he was bored to death with the American Leader's astonishing accusations as he look away from the podium and started drumming his fingers and wearing a grin that could have been mistaken a sneer. He ignored the American and his stinging words, the Persian Ambassador barely looked at the

Saudi Representative as he requested to hear from him. Calls for the Iranian Ambassador to respond quickly filled the room, as some of the Ambassadors started to stomp their feet, trying to force the Iranian to speak.

Letting out a hiss of pure disdain, Iranian Ambassador Kadhem suddenly shoved his chair back and stood. The Persian Politician completely ignored President Cole as he looked at the French Ambassador and grumbled directly at him. "All the foolish American Leader has uttered at this meeting is a complete fabrication, and if it wasn't for the Saudi Ambassador requesting I speak. I wouldn't respond to this great storyteller's foul words. It's no surprise the Americans hate Iran, they hate all Arab and Persian nations alike, and the Americans will not stop at anything to bring world opinion against them. This time America's lies fall upon Iran's head, tomorrow they shall be leveled against perhaps Saudi Arabia. Then soon Egypt, who'll be attacked next by these god cursed lies. The United States will not be satisfied until they have completely destroyed all Arab speaking nations of the world, just as it has completely destroyed our sister nation of Iraq, until that nation's nothing more than a mere shell of its once great past.

"If there's a car accident somewhere in the United States, I'm certain the American leadership would somehow blame it on we Arabs and Persians. If there's a plane crash, a fire, or even an earthquake, the United States would automatically blame each of these occurrence on the heads of Arab or Persian nations. I'm completely drained from America blaming we Persians and Arabs for all evils that befall the non believers of the world. The United States are the followers of Satan, and evil must befall Satan as is written on the great pages in the Holy Qur'an, until they, the foolish Americans are the ones erased from the face of the earth, just as they're trying to do to Arab and Persian nation. The United States will not rest at peace until it has total control of all the oil fields in the Middle East. That's the motive behind America's lies brought forth here at this meeting. I have finished speaking, neither I nor my country owes any nation, especially the hated United States, an explanation for any of our actions carried out within her own borders.

"The United States is too good at destroying Arab and Persian nations, and it's time the Arab and Persian races unite and stand against the great Satan before it's too late, and the evil bounded within the Unites States' borders are let loose on the Arab world again. America will not back off until it completely controls the entire world, as another madman once tried to do back in the forties, and we know what happened to him, and the world while he tried to conquer it. My Arab brothers and sisters who hear my words, it's up to us to prevent this from happening..."

The Iranian would have gone on if it was not for the French Ambassador interrupting his words by announcing to the Iranian Politician. "Ambassador Kadhem, we're well aware of the ill feeling that exists between your country and the United States, but you still have failed to answer the question. Are these missiles and their nuclear warheads in the borders of Iran, sir?"

"Huh, I believe I have answered that question for everyone attending this meeting moments ago." Ambassador Kadhem snapped nauseatingly at the French Ambassador. "If you were not paying attention to my words, I guess I shall be forced to repeat myself for your edification. Everything the American Leader just uttered at their meeting, is all lies fabricated against Iran to bring world opinion down against my country. It's a typical tactic the Americans employed against Iraq and now Iran's being singled out by the aggressors.

"I have finished speaking as I stated moments before, and if these falsehoods are not rescinded by the American Leader, and if America's President does not apologize to Iran. I'll walk out of this meeting and the United Nations can be consumed by the mouth and thoughts of the great Satan standing before you." Ambassador Nasrallah took his seat and resumed his stare, ignoring the commotion his words caused. The Iranian Ambassador was fuming because the American President knew what had just transpired in his nation, and was wondering if the United States had spies working in his country. He ordered himself to inform the new leader of Iran of his thought, so Iran's secret police would be ordered to search for any American spies in his country.

President Cole was called over to the side of the platform and handed the latest pictures that had just arrived from CIA Director Raincloud's office in Washington. The large Native American was grinning from ear to ear as he gave the President encouraging words. "Christ sir, when you told me you were going to upset some people here today, you weren't shitting me sir. You wanted to start the horses running from the barn and you sure did, Mr. President."

The President smiled at the Director as he asked him. "What's this stuff John?"

"Pictures of the Russian missiles being worked on inside Iran sir. Some of these pictures show a few missiles clearly being unloaded by the ported submarines being stored at the Iranian Naval Base." Director Raincloud checked his watch and then added to his words. "By this time sir, the damn missiles are probably installed inside the first Iranian submarine, sir. Mr. President, we feel the Iranian's are going to load two missiles apiece in each of their six submarines, sir."

"Shit! Any pictures of that missile factory they constructed in the desert, John?"

"Fraid not at this time sir, my operative missed his last three call ins. If I don't hear from him in the next twenty four hours sir, I'll be forced to activate a second sleeper, and start over from scratch, Mr. President."

"You think your Agent might have been captured by the Iranian secret police?"

"No way in hell Mr. President, he's too good sir. No sir, I believe he's out of position and unable to get at his radio. I'm positive he'll make contact before I activate another operative."

"John, will these pictures help me with these people at the meeting, for the love of God?"

"Just the ones clearly showing the missiles sitting by the side of the Iranian submarines, sir. Other than that, they're mostly duplications of the original pictures you have at hand, sorry sir."

"It's not your fault John, I think I'll hold back on these pictures and use them as my ace in the hold, if I get bogged down enlisting the Arab nations to form up the old Coalition Forces again. At least I feel both Saudi Arabia and Kuwait are on our side..."

"Excuse me Mr. President." President Bartlett interrupted the two men.

President Cole turned and saw the Saudi Ambassador waiting to address the meeting. He rushed back to the podium and nodded to the Saudi. "President Bartlett, I demand the Iranian Politician rebuke the accusations leveled against Iran. Although the explanation's a weak one, nevertheless, it's an explanation and I believe the United

States President will come up with much stronger evidence, if they want the full weight of this Council to be placed behind it, sir."

President Cole suddenly began to wave the large manila envelope out before him as he offered to the Iranian Politician. "Ambassador Nasrallah, I have in my hands the evidence that'll prove beyond a shadow of a doubt what I have just suggested is absolutely true." The American Leader then fished inside the envelope until he found the five still snapshots clearly showing the Russian made SS-23 submarine launch missiles resting by the ported Iranian submarines. He then handed the photos to the Master at Arms for displaying.

"Will you please deliver these pictures to the Saudi Ambassador for me, Master at Arms." President Cole offered to the aide.

"Certainly sir." The Master at Arms took the pictures from the American Leader, and he moved as quickly as manners allowed, and he handed the pictures over to the waiting Saudi Politician, and then he waited as the Ambassador quickly examined the stills.

Saudi Ambassador Nasrallah quickly fanned through the pictures. Then he sent them over to the Iranian Ambassador who barely glanced at them and then shrugged. Ambassador Nasrallah knew the Iranian was aware of the missiles in his country, and he was not going to admit to them. "Mr. President, you have convinced me these nuclear missiles are within the borders of Iran, sir. I want these pictures passed around until every Ambassador gathered here had a chance to view what I just witnessed. President Cole, we have to concern ourselves of what we intend to do about these god cursed missiles and nuclear warheads sent to us by the Devil himself."

The Iranian Ambassador jumped to his feet, and shouted nastily at the Saudi concerned Politician. "You're an old fool allowing yourself to be deceived by this great Satan, Ambassador Nasrallah. May Allah seek his revenge upon you, and all your family and country of lowly jackals." The Iranian's harsh words started a grumble of anger to pass through the Ambassadors.

"Ambassador Nasrallah, you have allowed yourself to be convinced by the cursed lies woven by the American Leader. I warned you I'll walk out of this meeting if the United States does not apologize to my country for spreading these falsehoods about Iran and her leadership. You chose to follow this American delivering your foul country into the hands of the devil. This is fine with Iran and I warn you, don't look for any help from my country once America owns your cursed country, and controls everything your people do in your own land. I warned you to be wary of America's lies." Kadhem flung his hand at the Saudi as he sat and resumed his icy stare.

The Saudi turned away from the angry speaking Iranian Politician and looked at the American and then remarked. "President Cole, you must understand that Saudi Arabia does not condone an invasion of any nation, especially an Islamic nation sir. With what America was able to do to Iraq still fresh in our minds, it's with a heavy heart that I request the Coalition of Nations be reassembled to face this new and latest threat to the Middle Eas..."

The Iranian Politician stood and requested to speak, but he was waved back to his seat by the French Ambassador, who nodded to the Saudi Politician, allowing him to continue.

"Thank you President Bartlett, because what I have to offer is most important, and I don't wish to be interrupted until I finish with my statements. As I stated, we're to reassemble the Coalition of Allied Nations, and if Iran refuses to dismantle the missiles and weapons of mass destruction, and give proof it has destroyed them along with the warheads that goes with the missiles. Proof to us Iran's not in possession, nor does she have any intentions of constructing anymore of these hated god cursed weapons of mass destruction. We'll be forced to enter Iran by force and destroy said missiles and their warheads ourselves. Destroy their God hated submarines that will enable Iran to close the Persian Gulf waters at will. President Cole, I say this to you sir."

The Saudi Politician took a quick breath to calm his body, and then he went on speaking. "Since the esteem Iranian Ambassador attending this meeting refuses to answer my questions on this subject, and since you have produced pictures clearly showing Russian constructed missiles lying beside the Iranian submarines inside the nation of Iran, Mr. President sir. I'm left with no other alternative but to commit my country's military, to assist you in the destruction of these missiles and their feared weapons of mass destruction.

"To accomplish this great feat, my country must again ally itself with the United States, and soon reorganized Coalition Forces. If they choose to again join forces with us in this just cause. Mr. President, I must warn your nation that Saudi Arabia will keep a close eye on the military actions of your fighting forces. We'll not allow this to befall Iran, the devastating and paralyzing destruction visited upon the Arab nation of Iraq, sir. If your forces get out of hand, we'll demand the fighting come to an immediate conclusion. Whether or not the cursed missiles, the nuclear warheads and the submarines are destroyed in this action. I further warn, if your forces do not hear our demand to stop the destruction carried out against Iran. We'll not hesitate to come to Iran's side." The shaken Saudi Representative remained standing as he softened his stare.

President Cole smiled at the Saudi and replied. "Ambassador Nasrallah I assure you that the United States has no wish to destroy personal property of anyone living in Iran. The only concerns we have are military targets to be attacked in this action, which are the long range missiles, nuclear powered submarines, and Iranian complex involved in the development, and construction of said missiles, or nuclear warheads of mass destruction. These targets will include the four nuclear power plants, if the reactors have been converted over to breeder power plants for the production and outgrowth of weapons grade plutonium, Mr. Ambassador."

"Mr. President, I'm afraid to offer, it'll take great amounts of proof on the United States' side, for Saudi Arabia to allow military attacks to take place against these hated nuclear power producing plants constructed inside Iran. I trust you'll share this vital information with us the first moment it comes within your possession, Mr. President Sir." The obviously stunned Saudi Representative asked as he stared at the American President with concern etched in his eyes.

"Yes Mr. Ambassador, of course I shall, the instant this information comes in my possession. I planned to have more of this evidence available before I addressed this meeting today. But as of yet, the evidence is still rather elusive. I promise to share the evidence and discuss the military targets with your country, before we dare attack said targets inside Iran." President Cole offered to the Saudi Ambassador while trying to keep his eyes on the Iranian Representative.

"Then I'm to understand there's more evidence than what you have produced today, Mr. President?" The Saudi added, concerned the American might be holding back some proof.

"Yes Sir Ambassador Nasrallah, there's much more information to come before this esteem Council. But I'll not discuss this future evidence, until I have the irrefutable proof in my hands first, Ambassador. If your nation decides to pull the plug on the fighting because it's becoming too devastating to the innocent Iranian population, or to the infrastructure of Iran. I'll order an immediate stop to my troop's where they stand, and I'll suspend all shorties, (flights) unless they're involved supporting our ground forces who might be operating inside Iran. Of course Mr. Ambassador, we'll use precision guided munitions to keep the collateral destruction to the innocent civilians of Iran down to an absolute minimum. We, my ground forces and attacking aircraft will not destroy many bridges and roadways as was had done inside Iraq, and neither will we go after the country's utility facilities. Mr. Ambassador, we don't intend to destroy Iran, only what she's attempting to produce. We will however, be forced to go after the country's Airforce, and many military installations threatening our forces on the ground..."

"Then you do plan to place ground forces inside Iran, if its agreed to allow the old Coalition Forces to destroy what we're speaking about here at this meeting, Mr. President Sir? In essence, the United States will invade Iran, with, or without our agreement at this meeting, Mr. President? I find this offer rather puzzling and extremely threatening to the security of the Middle East. The United States will invade Iran on her own with her troops. Mr. President, we're here to stop such invasions of other countries by more powerful nations." The worried Saudi Politician said and asked at the same time, speaking as if Iran was not even involved in the decision making taking place. Every Ambassador was ignoring the Iranian Politician at this point.

"Of course we will Ambassador Nasrallah. But the Coalition Forces main responsibility will be to make certain we destroyed said missiles and nuclear warheads, and the nuclear powered submarines, and any development complexes in Iran. We'll not attack other Iranian complex not involved with the construction, housing, or development of missiles, or of the nuclear side of the missiles and warheads." President Cole added confidently to the upset Saudi Ambassador.

"If it occurs as you have offered me Mr. President. I assure you that you can rely on Saudi Arabia's unwavering support on this mission." The Saudi offered to the American President.

The Ambassadors from Kuwait, The United Arab Republic, Jordan, Syria, Turkey and Afghanistan all stood, and each of them immediately informed the American Leader their nations would either side with them, or they would step aside and not intervene, or come to the aide of Iran. They all agreed Iran should not be in possession of any nuclear warheads, or the missiles need to get the warheads to their targets.

Many of the other nation's representatives, offered to lend their country's assistance and support to the United States and Saudi Arabia in various other ways and stages. Ranging from money, to added ground forces and ships, to support any and all military actions to be carried out against Iran, and the destruction of missiles and nuclear warheads Iran was in possession of. The only way this support would be lifted was if Iran stopped all their production of weapons of mass destruction on her soil.

As each nation's Ambassadors offered their assistance if the United States was forced to attack Iran, or they vowed to remain neutral in any altercation erupting in the Middle

East. The Iranian Politician stood and he slowly scanned the many faces staring at him. Everyone wanted to hear what the Iranian had to offer, hoping he came to his senses, and he was willing to head off a destructive war involving the United States and the Coalition forces against his country. All hopes were instantly dashed when they heard what he had to offered them.

Glaring at the members, Ambassador Kadhem looked away from the French to the Saudi Ambassador, and his eyes came to rest in a stare down with the American President. Their eyes remained clinched in this stare of hatred then the Iranian gave an icy warning at the American Leader. "President Cole, let your cursed country's children come, allow them to dare to invade Iran like they had done to Iraq. My country sir!" The fuming Iranian pointed at his chest with his finger as he continued with his threatening words aimed at the American Leader.

"Allow any nation be foolish enough to dare try and invade Iran and send their soldiers on Iranian soil, and the dead of their children will mount like the countless grains of sand in the vast deserts of my nation. Their nation's dead will dried up, and be blowing in the winds that wash the great sand plains pure with powerful sand storms. I remind everyone of you, the fighters of Iran are nothing like the lowly infidels of Iraq. Praise the Almighty Allah's hand, the Iranian soldiers know how to fight and defend their country against any and all Crusaders, and if need be. Iran's soldiers will die most honorably on the field of battle. The worthless American warriors will never see the hands of Iranian soldiers raised in surrender to their foul soldiers. Come, dare if you may, come and try and invade the lands of Iran and watch your dead mount.

"Come to Iran with your foolish soldiers, and you'll die the slow death of a thousand cuts delivered to keep the soldier alive until he has absorbed all the pain we wish to deliver, before we finally allow him to die. Come to Iran if you are foolish enough to dare, and your soldiers will be drawn and quartered, and their heads and hands will be lopped off, and mailed back to the wailing mothers of your god cursed country. Come to Iran, because you'll never leave its deserts alive if you dare visit my nation unwelcome." With this said, the fuming Iranian Politician stormed out of the meeting room, leaving mayhem in his wake.

The Ambassadors from Cuba, Nicaragua, Colombia, Sudan, Niger and Angola followed the Iranian Ambassador as he stormed out of the large meeting area of the United Nation's building. No one made a move to try and stop them, the Ambassador from China refrained from placing his support behind President Cole, as did the Ambassador from Vietnam.

Ambassador Bartlett banged his hammer, and called for order. He called for a vote to allow the forces from the United States, France, England, Italy, Spain, Saudi Arabia, Egypt, and the United Arab Emirates to remove the deadly nuclear weapons from Iran's possession.

The remaining representatives quickly sided with Ambassador Bartlett, all except for China and Russia, both nations had sustained the vote. The Ambassador from Japan stood after the nation's voted, and offered ten thousand of his nation's young warriors to the growing Coalition Forces. He was followed by the representative from Kuwait, who offered his country's fighters to join with the Coalition Forces as well. The meeting started to take on a much friendly atmosphere after the formalities were concluded, as many of the Ambassadors moved to the platform, and the agreeing Ambassador's shook hands with the American Leader. After waiting for a few moments and greeting the Ambassadors, President Cole made his excuses and gathered his security unit and Director Raincloud and left the hall.

President Cole was armed with the knowledge that Saudi Arabia was going to side with him, he knew this because he was in constant contact with King Fahd, and he had already briefed the Saudi Leader on the findings inside both Iran and Russia. Using the emergency hall behind the podium, Director Raincloud spoke privately with the President as they headed for Ambassador Walter's office for their own meeting.

"Jesus, Mary and Joseph, Mr. President. You don't think it was a bad idea about letting the Iranian's know we're coming after them, and what targets we have already singled out, sir?"

"Naw, not if they have the brains they were born with. Now, the Iranian's know we're aware they have missiles and warheads. They have to believe we're coming for them being we know of them, I'm certain they know which targets we'll be coming for. There's no way this side of judgment day they can stop us, let they try. It's about time we put an end to this terrorist crap, and the quest for weapons of mass destruction and the technology to produce the shit. If we spank the Iranians enough, it'll serve as a warning to the rest of these nuts who want to master the atom. Director, give our people the word we're going to put Operation Clean Sweep in motion, sir."

"The mission's going to be changed I take it, Mr. President?" Director Raincloud asked.

"Yes Director Raincloud, it has changed, we're going to clean up the Middle East whether they like it or not, dammit.

I'm very tired of getting excited every year because an Islamic nation's trying to take over the other or the world. It's getting nuts, and I'm putting an end to it with this next operation I assure you sir." The President stopped speaking as he groped the handle to Ambassador Walters office. They entered and the President rushed to the phone. He did not wait for the Ambassador to arrive before he use his office. President Cole glanced at his watch as he dialed the phone, he was shocked to see it was eleven, forty five a.m. He did not realize how long the meeting took, overwhelmed it lasted two hours. He shook his head as he finished dialing General White. The phone rang twice before the secretary answered it.

THE PENTAGON, WASHINGTON D.C.
NOVEMBER 8th, 1998 11:45 A.M., EST

"Good morning, General White's office. What can I direct your call please?"

"Good morning Mary, this is President Cole. Is General White available?"

Mary was surprised the President was calling for General White. "Good morning Mr. President. Yes, General White's in sir. I'll connect you sir. It was nice speaking with you sir. Have a nice day Mr. President." She purred in her sweetest tone as she put him through to General White, using the red button, warning General White he had a call from the President.

The Chairman of the Joint Chiefs of Staff, General John White, was preparing to head off for some lunch when the phone button blinked. He stared at the light for a second, and then he picked up the phone and responded. "Yes Mr. President, how did the meeting go sir?"

"About as expected, the Iranian Ambassador was as stubborn as we figured, and the Russian Ambassador was surprised Admiral Proushinsky sold the damn nukes and missiles to the Iranians. Most of the old Coalition members quickly lined up behind us, with Arabia warning we're not to destroy Iran like we did Iraq, or they'll pull their support. General White Sir, I'll fill you in on all the particulars when I return to Washington, sir. Place Operation Clean Sweep in gear. Get your people in motion, go active no later than Monday morning if possible, General White." President Cole gave General White a moment to respond to his orders.

"Whew Mr. President, that's cutting it mighty close to the edge. I have my troops going over the targets we have already discussed. They didn't have much time to prepare for what they might be facing in Iran. I'll change Lieutenant Walker's unit from primary to backup, and I'll have Colonel Leadbetter move his Unit up as primary attack force for this mission, sir." General White gave the President a chance to respond this time.

The President was angry as he replied. "General White! Over the past few months sir, I've been sinking enough money in this damn MNRRF force of yours to get us out of the national debt, preparing these specialized soldiers for the day when we'll need this bunch of lunatics. Now the time has arrived, are you telling me you'll need more time to prepare these god damn soldiers for action? If you are, I've been walked around by you and what I believed was a Rapid Response Unit, is nothing more than a glorified unit of ordinary soldiers, mister. General, I gave this detail of fighters more money than the Corps as a whole. If your pets can't get the job done. I expect you to repay this money to the American taxpayers' sir. I can't believe this cr..."

General White interrupted the President's tirade. "With all due respect Mr. President. I'm afraid you might have misunderstood me, that's not what I meant at all sir. My Unit can go active at this moment, all I meant was. I was hoping to allow the soldiers a tad more time to go over what they might be facing in Iran. If that time can't be given that's fine with me and my troops, sir. It looks like they'll get some on the job training on this mission that's all. Mr. President, as far as their fighting abilities, there's no fighters better on the face of the globe. My people are ready, and they can be in the air within the hour if that's what you want of the soldiers, sir."

"Huh, I thought they might be General White Sir. Now we have that little bit of trouble all straightened out between us, sir. I'll address the rest of your thoughts right now sir. General White, I don't wish to override any of your decisions, but I suggest you keep Lieutenant Walker's Unit as the primary, and allow Colonel Leadbetter's Unit to remain as the backup unit, sir."

"Why is that Mr. President?" General White asked the American Leader, concerned he was taking such an active hand with his military plans.

"Because I was looking over the records of a number of these elite troops of yours, and it looks to me like this Lieutenant Walker has surrounded himself with the better fighters from the entire group, sir. That's why I feel the Lieutenant should still remain as the primary advance unit for this full operation, General White Sir."

General White heard the chuckle on the other end of the line, and was certain the President wanted to show him he done his homework as he replied. "Hmmmm... I see what you're saying Mr. President. This Lieutenant Walker's something sir, he once shit on his neighbor's lawn because their dog crapped on his. I guess I'll keep the parameters of the mission as they were. Walker's Unit will remain the primary, and the other unit's backup and support."

"Very good General White, I'm pleased we can work together so well under these trying times, sir. I'm giving you the go ahead to put your troops in motion. Remember General, I expect your people to go active on Monday morning, period sir. The Iranian's expect a visit and I don't want to disappoint them, or keep them waiting too long, sir. I don't want them to have the time to prepare for us. The advance units will go in covert, I'll make a thing about moving the bombers and ships around, to give the illusion of more time for the Iranians to prepare for us before we attack. General White, we'll move in force on Friday the 15th, sir. I'll expect proof on this nuclear production complex by Iranshahr before that date, sir. I'll need that proof before I can attack this installation, and prove to the world that Iran planned to mass produce nuclear weapons and missiles. Do you understand my desires, General White?" The President hissed at his officer.

"Yes Sir Mr. President, and I'll have that proof for you before the attack is set in motion, sir. That you can bank on sir."

"I better have it or it's going to be your ass, along with the asses of this entire specialized MNRRF force of yours, General White Sir. Get it done sir."

"Yes Sir Mr. President." General White replied to a dial tone.

Just as the President hung up on his General, Ambassador Walters came walking in his office as if nothing was bothering him.

"Well?" President Cole asked of the American Ambassador.

"Well, it looks like everything's fine with the Saudi Ambassador for the time being, sir. I showed the Saudi the pictures of the secret Iranian complex. He was very receptive and gave us permission to send in the Rapid Response Force. The Ambassador informed me if the missiles and warheads are there, he'll allow this force to destroy the entire complex without fearing any interference from them, Mr. President. He further stated even if the missiles weren't there, he'd overlook this mission. He felt it was a just mission, one that must be taken. He was extremely concerned the Iranian's planned to mass produce the damn missiles and warheads."

"Outstanding Bob, you earned your money for the year, because I just gave General White the green light to get his units on the move. General White has assured me his elite units would have the information before the bombers and ships move in for the kill. You better keep yourself available, because when I receive any further input on the damn Iranian complex. I'm going to depend on you to get it into the Saudi's hands, and pacify them until the troops are out of Iran. I can ill afford having the Saudi King busting my horns, it's too important to world peace."

"President Cole Sir, I'll be in my office every day until I hear from you, sir. At night you know where I'll be, and I'll made arrangements with the Saudis. So I can locate the King both day or night if needed, Mr. President. I'm in a good position to handle anything that might arise." Ambassador Walters offered confidently to the concerned American Leader.

"Thank you Ambassador Walters, I have a change of plans though sir. I want to head back to Washington. I don't think it's very wise to be away from home at this crucial time, sir." The President noticed the look on Ambassador Walters face, and he raised his hand to silence his unspoken complaint and added. "Yes, I know you spent the day setting up a number of private meetings between Ambassadors and myself. You'll have to change them, keep the important ones, the Saudis and Russians and myself, inform them the meeting will take place at the White House, and then set up transportation for them. Make an excuse, you know how to do it for me Ambassador Walters." President Cole flicked his hand in the air and let out his breath.

"I see no problem with having the meeting transferred down to the White House, Mr. President Sir. I'll have the airlines make the necessary arrangements for myself and..."

"No you won't." The President interrupted and then quickly went on with his words for the Ambassador. "I'll make Air Force Two available for any Diplomat you deem important enough to send down to Washington for me to meet with them, sir. Will this do Ambassador Walters?"

"Yes Sir Mr. President, that'll do just fine with me, sir. I'm quite certain it'll also impress the hell out of the Diplomats also. That's a good way to placate the Ambassadors that'll have to get down to Washington to meet with you, Mr. President." Ambassador Walters replied as the President stood and then he stretched out his hand. They shook and President Cole slapped the older man on his shoulder as both he and Director Raincloud prepared to leave the United Nations building. Outside, the Secret Service Agents in charge of the President's security, instantly stiffened as the exhausted American President entered the hall.

Three agents went out before the President left as the controlling agent asked. "Where to sir?"

"The parking lot and then Kennedy Airport, Richard. I have to be back in Washington pronto, mister." The President smiled at his favorite bodyguard.

The special agent keyed his radio and then he issued orders. "Two and Three, check Eagle One's car, we're heading for A-5. Seven, Seven, this is Lead, come in."

"Seven, Seven, go with your orders Lead." The second agent reported.

"Seven, Seven, we're coming your way, make sure Eagle's Nest is ready for immediate takeoff, sir. Have the bomb squad go over her before we arrive on site. We're not going to have any extra time to carry out the inspection while the Boss waits for us to complete it. He's got a fire under his rear and wants to be on the move immediately."

"Got your Lead, Eagle's Nest will be ready to leave the instant the Boss arrives on site, over."

"Four and Five take the rear, the rest support, and NYPD Units get ready, we're moving out."

The gaggle of special agents moved as one, each knowing his or her areas of responsibility. A tight screen of protection surrounded the President as he headed for the United Nation's parking lot. The President's limo was pulled up to the drive leading out of the lot, New York City police squad cars blocked every port leading to the drive. Three squad cars parked before the President's car, and another three behind it. There were six motorcycles in the lead as well.

The President took a quick glanced at the AIC, Agent In Charge and nodded, pleased at how quickly the agent was able to get everyone protecting him on the move. The squad cars played leap frog blocking the entranceways to the Franklin D. Roosevelt Drive. Civilian cars were not allowed to get within twenty car lengths of the President's limo. Traffic on the other side of the parkway was completely blocked, as the long black stretch limo headed for Kennedy Airport.

CIA Director John Raincloud noticed all the civilian cars on the other side of the highway stopped, with many of the drivers getting out of their vehicles and climbing on the roofs. They were waving at the Presidential car as it passed by them and the Director remarked. "These damn New Yorkers are really something to see Mr. President Sir."

"Zat so? Why do you say that John?" The President asked the CIA Director.

"Look at them on the other side of the highway sir, here we are screwing up their entire day on the poor souls and what the hell are they doing sir? Most of them are actually sitting on top of their cars and they're waving at us as we go by them, sir. I guess this is what makes New York the cream of the crop, Mr. President Sir."

"Yes Director Raincloud, you have to be extremely flexible if you want to live in New York City and survive." The President replied as he look out of the window. Soon, he had the blacked out window lowered, and he was waving back at the drivers on the other side of the highway.

The President's caravan pulled up to the gate leading to the tarmac of Kennedy Airport. They were allowed to proceed, Air Force One was sequestered from the rest of the runways of the airport. When the President was on board Air Force One, air traffic stacked up. Nothing was allowed to land or takeoff as Air Force One taxied to Runway Twenty Seven. With a roar, the 747 shot down the runway and lifted off into the noon sun, leaving contrails to mark its course.

CIA Director John Raincloud felt like they had just taken off, when the pilot warned them to secure their seat belts, and prepare for landing as he offered to the overly tired President. "You can drop me off at the White House, and I'll find my own way back to Langley from there easy enough I guess, Mr. President Sir."

"Nonsense John, I have Marine One already waiting for me when we land at Joint Andrews Airforce Base, sir. It'll be no problem at all for the pilot to drop you off at Langley, John. You will remember to keep me appraised on what's happening in Iran at all times Director Raincloud, right? I want that report from your operative the second it comes in, sir."

"Of course I will Mr. President, I'm hoping the damn report will already be waiting for me when I get back to my office today, sir." The Director offered as he hooked his seatbelt.

"Hmmm... maybe I should follow you over to your office, just in case something has come in from your operative in Iran, John." The concerned American Leader offered as he looked into the Director's eyes, as he considered going to the Director's office with him.

"That won't be necessary Mr. President Sir. Why don't you head for the White House and get comfortable for the rest of the day. I might have to unscramble the message before I can even read it for myself if it did come in, Mr. President. If so, it'll take some time to get it unscrambled, sir. Then I'll deliver the report, so we can discuss it together sir."

"That sounds like a much better idea, I'll do that Director Raincloud. I'll have General White standby, call him when you get any information, and the both of you get over to the Oval..."

The pilot's voice interrupted their conversation as he informed the President they landed. The two rushed from Air Force One then they boarded Marine One and the helicopter lifted off.

"I take it we're heading for the White House, Mr. President Sir?" The helicopter pilot asked.

"No, I want you to drop Director Raincloud off at CIA Headquarters. Then we'll head for the White House." President Cole ordered as he took the drink offered by the Marine Lieutenant.

"Roger that you got it Mr. President Sir. CIA Headquarters it is sir." The helicopter banked to the north as the pilot altered course. Fifteen minutes later, the helicopter spooled while resting on the tarmac of parking lot North of CIA Headquarters waiting for Director Raincloud to depart.

Director Raincloud quickly disembarked the helicopter, and the President called after him. "I'll be waiting for your call, Mr. Raincloud. You better not keep me sitting on my duff for too long mister, or you'll suffer the consequences sir." The President warned in a friendly manner.

The Director ignored the friendly warning as he headed for the building. A guard saw him approaching and opened the door for him as he offered pleasantly. "Good afternoon Director Raincloud Sir, how was your meeting in New York, sir?"

Raincloud barely took notice of the security guard as he barked. "Fucked up as usual Mac!" the Director kept going to his office. He stormed in and threw his briefcase at the chair as he rushed to his computer. Then his lock box to see if anything came in from his Operative Twenty One in Iran. Nothing came in which served to make the Director angrier. Raincloud cursed as he stomped over to his desk and then fell in the chair. The intercom buzzed and his secretary asked. "Director Raincloud Sir, would you like something sent to the office to eat? It's good to have you back in your office sir. I trust everything went well for the President and yourself with the United Nations meeting earlier today in New York City, sir?"

"Just dandy Mary. Yes, have something sent up for me please, I'm starved." John realized he had not eaten anything since the night before. He closed his eyes and pinched the bridge of his nose as he leaned back in his chair and took a deep breath, and a quick moment to himself.

While John was resting, Mary came in carrying two burgers and a glass of Pepsi with no ice. Director Raincloud opened his eyes and smiled at her as he offered. "Mary, be a real doll and get NORASATCOM on the line for me, please."

"Right away sir." The secretary replied to John's request to be linked up to NORAD.

CHAPTER THIRTEEN

NORTH AMERICA SATELLITE COMMUNICATIONS, BASED IN MARYLAND

The extremely bored to death Army Sergeant on duty immediately answered the phone and he snapped to attention when he was informed it was the CIA Director on the line. He motioned to the Lieutenant who came over and covered the receiver and he asked. "Who is it?"

"It's the CIA big man himself, Lieutenant Mark."

"Relax asshole, he can't see you over the damn phone, stupid." The Lieutenant growled as he took the receiver and then replied. "Lieutenant Mark here. What can I do for you today sir?"

"Lieutenant, I was wondering if you received anything from Sand Star while I was away?"

"If you'd like, I'll check on it for you sir. I don't remember anything coming in for quite a while now, sir." The Lieutenant placed the receiver on his hip and waited a few seconds. He knew nothing came in or he would have immediately transferred the dispatch over to Director Raincloud's secured lock box. After waiting for a few moments the Lieutenant lifted the receive. "I'm sorry Director Raincloud, nothing has come in since the last report of two days ago, sir."

"Dammit, I don't want to get in a pissing contest with you over this matter, Lieutenant. You will remember to transmit any new dispatches from this damn Agent to my office the moment one comes from him, right sir?" Raincloud reminded the young military officer.

"The second a dispatch comes in you'll know about it, Mr. Director."

"Very good Lieutenant." Raincloud hung up and ate his burgers as if they were the enemy.

IRANSHAHR, IRAN.
NOVEMBER 8th, 1998. V8:35 P.M. IRANIAN TIME

The American Operative Mohammed Boua Bdellah tried his best to get to his radio, every time he went to broadcast, another Iranian military vehicle would slowly drive through or show up in the small town of Iranshahr. Finally, by eight p.m., the last of the Iranian military trucks quickly disappeared in the desert outside the town. Bdellah waited thirty minutes to make certain no more military personnel appeared near the village. When he was certain of safety, he transmitted.

Al-Shamarral sat by Bdellah's side in the one room apartment he rented in the village, as he quickly set up the small radio and the beggar grumbled at him. "May Almighty Allah protect me, I cannot believe you know how to set up such a complicated machine like that, my son."

"It's very simple to do my father of time, everything's marked and color coded." Bdellah replied as he placed the tiny keyboard down before him, and then he tapped out his message. The computer filled its memory, and then transmitted the message out in a flash burst of scrambled energy. This was so the radio key was not held open long enough to be located, each time the memory filled, it would transmit another static burst.

Lieutenant Mark cursed his relief, because the other Lieutenant was out on a date with Lillian Lust, when the first part of the burst transmission from Sand Star came in to their headquarters. His daydream shattered by the high pitch whine from the machine as it instantly decoded, and then printed out the incoming message. He read the first line then barked. "Sergeant, this is what the Director was waiting for. Get a paper copy transferred over to Raincloud's lock box, send a second copy over to the main computers, I'll take care of the hard copy myself."

"You got it sir, it's on the way as we speak Lieutenant." The Sergeant worked his keyboard, and when the computer replied it was transmitting to Lock Box Eight, he relaxed.

CIA HEADQUARTERS LANGLEY VINIGINA

Director Raincloud quickly wolfed down the last of his burger, when his lock box light shined and the first page of the report appeared behind the bullet proof glass. He wiped the corners of his mouth and walked over to the box and inserted his key. The glass door shoved aside and he pulled the paper out, his heart was pounding as he read the latest report from Sand Star.

/\/\/\ SAND STAR TO BIG BOY /\/\/\
/\/\/\ HAVE POSITIVE PROOF IRANIANS HAVE SECRET COMPLEX SET UP IN
DESERT AND ARE BUILDING NUCLEAR CAPABLE MISSILES
FOR SUBMARINES. HAVE DETAILED MAP MARKING LOCATION OF
SAID COMPLEX, DEFENSES AND ESTIMATED NUMBER ON MILITARY
PERSONNEL BELIEVED TO BE STATIONED AT COMPLEX. AM KEEPING
MESSAGE SHORT BECAUSE MILITARY PERSONNEL AROUND
IRANSHAHR. SEND TROOPS, HAVE LOCATED LOCAL HELP. /\/\/\
/\/\/\ WILL TRANSMIT EXACTLY 2200 HOURS. WILL REMAIN WITH KEY
OPEN FOR FIVE MINUTES TO RECEIVE ORDERS,
CLOSE DOWN IF NO FOLLOW ON COMMUNICATION
FROM YOU BY THE STATED TIME ALLOWED. /\/\/\
/\/\/\ MAP WILL FOLLOW AS COMPLETED. /\/\/\
/\/\/\ SAND STAR OUT. /\/\/\

The Agent Sand Star, sat back on his heels and waited for word to come in from his control, Director Raincloud as he fed the map through the scanner unit to his radio hookup. The marking on the paper instantly turned into a blur of numbers and mixed letters, and blasted through the air to the receiver stationed back in the States. There, the computer read the numbers and scrambled letters, and then instantly reconstructed them on paper to form the map. It was perfect, right down to the sweat drops and thumb print on the page. A copy went right to Raincloud.

Director Raincloud removed the map and quickly scanned the page. The Iranian complex was right where his satellites had pin pointed it. He was pleased with the number of Iranian troops being stationed at the complex for security and protection of the complex. If everything went according to plan, this mission should be much easier than the one they just carried out in Russia. He sat in front of his computer and rapidly typed out his reply to Sand Star.

/\/\/\ BIG BOY TO SAND STAR /\/\/\
/\/\/\ MAP PERFECT, HELP GREATLY. BE PREPARED
FOR COMPANY ON THE BIG M-(meaning Monday)
COMPANY WILL BE COMING YOUR
HOME AT 0600 HOUR YOUR TIME... BREAK. THE
PICTURES TAKEN,
COMPLEX DESTROYED... BREAK. PAPERS, TAPES
REMOVED
FROM COMPLEX ALL IMPORTANT FILES... BREAK.
LOCAL
HELPERS, SURE TRUST THEM? SUGGEST ELIMINATE
SAID HELPERS TO
AVOID DETECTION AND ARREST. /\/\/\
/\/\/\ WILL LEAVE DETERMINATION OF LOCALS YOUR
DISCRETION. YOU
FEEL LOCALS MORE HELP TO USE THEM, USE THEM.
WILL ELIMINATE

AT COMPLETION OF MISSION...BREAK. GOOD WORK
SS... BRAKE. WILL
EXTRACT AT COMPLETION OF MISSION... BRAKE.
YOUR DUTY
FULFILLED... BRAKE. WILL BUY FIRST BEER. GOOD
LUCK... BRAKE. /\/\/\
/\/\/\BIG BOY OUT. /\/\/\

Director Raincloud again sat back and relaxed as he waited for the burst traffic to be sent on its way to his agent out in the field. Once this was accomplished, he scooped up the dispatch and slammed it in his briefcase without putting it inside a file folder. He then dialed General White's number and held the receiver to his ear with his shoulder as he finished up in his office.

The phone was answered on the third ring by the General himself, his secretary was out of the office at the time. "Yeah General White, Director Raincloud, sir. I just heard from Double S. Do you want me to pick you up? Or are you heading for the White House on your own?"

"Pick me up." The Chairman of the Joint Chiefs of Staff requested.

"Will do, I'll be there in fifteen minutes General White." John replied.

IRANSHAHR, IRAN

The old beggar Ahmed Hussein al-Shamarral stared at the back of Mohammed Boua Bdellah who held the paper between his thumb and forefinger, and then he gave a quick snap of his fingers that sent the sheet of flash paper in a flame that instantly disappeared without leaving trace of the ash. A smile crossed the old beggar's face as Bdellah turned to him and the old man offered. "Ahh... do not take your orders to heart so my new son. Praise Almighty Allah, if I was in your place my son, how you say... ahhh yes... control's place, I would've issued the same orders to anyone working for me, my son."

Bdellah cocked his head to the side, not quite sure he understood what the old man was talking about. He still could not shake the words he read from his control from his memory. 'Eliminate local help'. How could command possibly expect him to eliminate someone he owed his life to? How could they expect him to kill someone who done nothing but help him? How could he kill someone who did not want a thing from him in return, and only offered him help and protection? Bdellah was extremely confused by his last orders, and the last words spoken by the old beggar added to the confusion clouding over his mind.

Al-Shamarral saw the look of bewilderment written on Bdellah's face that he had witnessed many times before, and he said to the much younger man. "I do not care if the great Prophet Muhammad Himself has sent you to my arms for my protection and help, my foolish son who has the look of a fool on his face. Surely he would've ordered you to eliminate your help for you own defense and security of your operation here in Iran. My son from across the unending sea, the success of this mission is paramount to both your country and mine. If you worked for me, I would've given you the same exact order as you have obviously just received from the one who controls you, Bdellah." Al-Shamarral calmly crossed his hands on his lap and smiled.

"By the Prophet Muhammad's unending love and mercy for us fools. I'm at a total loss as what to do, my most understanding and wise father. Al-Shamarral, are you suggesting I carry out the orders? I should eliminate you, one who is like own my father to me? I don't understand your words. How can I possibly bite the very hand that protects me? No al-Shamarral, my mission be damned, I'll not kill the one who helps me. I want to get you out of this place, and bring you to a country where you can live your remaining years as who you are. A true hero to my country.

"Al-Shamarral, without your help, many of my country's soldiers would be slaughtered, and I'll not repay your help with death. Am I a motherless whore who was suckled at the filthy teat of a lowly camel? No al-Shamarral, I'll not harm the one I owe so much to my father. As far as I am concerned, I have not received any such foolish report where I have to end your life of great worth." Bdellah put out his hand and offered it to the old man in friendship and respect.

"Do not torture your troubled mind so my son who is displaying great wisdom, because if you had dared to decide to follow your orders, you would not have lived long enough for you to carry them out successfully my son." Al-Shamarral smirked as he took Bdellah's hand in his.

Other beggar type people instantly poured into the room from the outer door, window, and closet, one man even came out from under the bed. They immediately assumed an extremely threatening stance against Bdellah, as they quickly circled the older man to better guard his life. Al-Shamarral refused to let go of Bdellah's hand, for fear of his reacting wrongly as he warned him. "You see my foolish young son, my life is being constantly very well protected against all harm. My children will never allow any harm to happen to me, their father of the sand." Al-Shamarral let go of Bdellah's hand and folded his arms across his chest, and grinned.

"Who are all these people and where the hell did they all come from, my cautious father?" Bdellah asked as he scanned the many angry looking faces staring at him as if they were daring him to make a move against the old beggar. They looked like they were waiting for him to do something wrong, so they could have the pleasure of killing him over his evil thoughts.

"They are my wanderers of the vast desert, my son. They're all my faithful children. They're the ones who wait for the Ayatollah's evil regimes to end. So they can resume control of Iran, and bring her into the twentieth century. We're a very patient people as you can see for yourself, my son. We understand it's a only matter of time before all world tyrant regimes end in the hatred they were produced from. We'll wait for your soldiers to arrive in Iran, and we'll help them as long as they help us. It's that simple my son." Al-Shamarral gave a rotted toothy smile to the young American spy and added. "Bdellah, when will your American troops arrive in Iran?"

For the first time, Mohammed Boua Bdellah felt suddenly threatened by the elderly beggar and the ones who were surrounding him. He stared at the old man for several long moments before he asked the old man with concern in his voice. "Why do you want to know this of me my father? Is it because of my control's thoughts that you ask me this, an ally and friend to you, a father would not dare ask this of his trusted son?"

Al-Shamarral's smile returned as he fired back at Bdellah. "My son of the vast desert sand, I have asked you this question because I must know how much work is ahead of my faithful followers. I have to know when I must order my faithful followers when it's time they should prepare for the arrival of your proud soldiers. If we're to help the American forces properly to liberate my people from this yoke we have suffered under for far too long a time."

"My wise father, is it not enough for you to understand that my country's young warriors are coming to destroy these weapons of mass destruction?"

Al-Shamarral smiled again as he added to his words. "If we intended to sit on our hands and not aid the ones who'll come to our land to help us be free, and even place their lives in danger for our benefit. Is it not the same as what you have been feeling deep within your heart? You have complained to me that you would not harm someone who has only help you. Well it's the same with me my foolish son. How can I possibly live if I don't do everything in my power to help assure your fine soldiers success on their mission. May Allah come down from His sacred cloud home and strike me with every infliction that has ever plagued the great earth and her children, if my intentions are less than totally honorable for you my son. Do you not think I could command my desert children, if the words I speak are not the truth? I have asked you when your soldiers intend to arrive in my country so I may mass my children together, and then place them where they'll be of the greatest assistance against our common enemy in Iran."

"But who is the true enemy in this country, Father al-Shamarral?" Bdellah snapped, and then added to his question. "Your soldiers or mine, wise old one of the desert sands?"

"To ask such a foolish question of me is extremely insulting to me, and it's only because you are an American, and you're trained to know no better how to properly speak to your elders, you have lived long enough to ask it of me, fool. A word of caution I offer to you my foolish son. I'll not allow you to ever insult me again, and continue to live after that insult has been delivered to my old ears that has heard all the misery and hatred that has befallen my children of the vast desert sands." Al-Shamarral hissed as he rested his hand very threateningly on the hilt of his deadly dagger. A simple motion that was not wasted on Bdellah. He noticed everyone crammed inside the small room instantly tense up, as if they were going to attack him if he dared to move a muscle or even breathe wrong. A grunt from al-Shamarral made the his desert wanderers back down and resume their peaceful stance in the room.

Bdellah stared at the old man while judging him and his words carefully. When he decided he could trust the old beggar, Bdellah replied brusquely. "Father of time everlasting, my soldiers will arrive in Iran on Monday morning. That's when we'll hit the complex in the desert."

"By Allah's Mighty bellowing breath and endless wisdom that guides His faithful children, that does not give me very much time to prepare my people to greet your soldiers who'll come to liberate Iran. I have much work to prepare for, and little time to accomplish all that must be accomplished in that time allotted." Al-Shamarral turned and ordered the others in the room.

They immediately sprang in action, preparing and opening their lines of communications between them and others of their following not present. As Bdellah listened to everything that was going on about him, he knew he had done the right thing by trusting al-Shamarral, by telling him when the American troops were coming to hit the Iranian installations.

CAMP LEJEUNE, JACKSONVILLE, NORTH CAROLINA.
THIRTEEN HUNDRED TEN HOURS EST.
FRIDAY, NOVEMBER 8th, 1998

Colonel Bruce Leadbetter returned to his office after allowing the specialized troops to break off their training to eat mess and rest for an hour. The morning briefing ran a lot longer than he expected, and the Colonel had to send a runner out to make certain the cooks kept the mess open until his troops arrived to eat. The Colonel sat in his chair and popped the top on a can of Bud, and rested his feet on his desk when his phone rang.

"Colonel Leadbetter, General White." The Chairman barked into the phone.

"Yeah Sir General White, when do we move out on our next operation, sir?" The Marine Colonel moaned as he let out his breath in a rush, and then he removed his feet from his desk. The General intruded on his down time and stopped him from collecting his thoughts so he was prepared to begin again when his troops returned from mess.

"How the hell did you know what I had on my mind, Colonel Leadbetter?" General White teased him, knowing the lesser soldiers always knew what was going on before the top brass did.

"Let's face it General White Sir it's a no brainer to be able to figure why the call from you, sir. Since when does a Pentagon control call a mud swimming grunt like myself, unless he's about to place me on the active duty list again, sir? Are we ready to ship out sir?"

"Arr... you bird dogs out in the field, dammit. I forget I can't hide shit from any of you chaps. Colonel I might as well level with you right off the bat, sir. You're absolutely correct sir, you're about to go active, sir. I'm ending the troop's training as of this moment Colonel. I decided the disadvantages to the mission outweigh the notable gratification gained, if we start a new series of scenarios on the intended targets. I don't want you to waste any time with constructing more replicas of the damn complex I sent you, and I don't want the Iranians discovering we know about this complex of theirs. Colonel, you're stuck doing OJT. (On Job Training)

"Colonel Leadbetter, the President had warned the damn Iranians we're coming after them at the United Nation's meeting the other day, but he did keep the info on the damn complex under wraps. That's why I'm ending the training the troops. I'll make certain you have all updated Intel of the Iranian site as it comes in, and the computers worked out three different attack scenarios you'll have in your possession before you ship out sir. I have your unit scheduled to get on the move Sunday afternoon. Figure to arrive in Pakistan at Nineteen Hundred Hours their time, and your troops should enter Iran by Twenty One Hundred Hours.

"Colonel, I have to level with you on this one sir, I plan to have your troops set in position on target by Zero, Twenty Three Hours. I want to gather all Intel on this god damn complex by that time, and I'll not take any excuses or delays from your troops. We'll hit the place by Zero, Four Thirty Hours, and have the mission completed by Zero, Six, Thirty Hours. I plan to catch them off guard so we can get the jump on the bastards. I'll start jamming all Iranian communications at exactly Zero Six Hundred Hours on Saturday, and then I'll continue the jamming for the week until our forces get set in positions, and then we'll hit them on Friday at Four Hundred Hours. Colonel Leadbetter, I'll knock every possible communications out of the air even TV signals, so your squad communications might be a little tough at times on your troops. The Iranians will not be able to make a god damn phone call by the time I'm done with them sir."

"Ahhh... my heart bleeds for the fucking bastards, General White."

"Exactly the attitude I want to hear from you at all times during this operation, mister. Keep it hot and heavy at all time sir. I need your pack of screaming squirrels hot enough to eat their own shit, and then beg for another god damn helping, Colonel Leadbetter. Lieutenant Walker's Unit's Primary on this operation, and the other three Units will supply support and security for the mission and backup for Walker's Unit in case anything goes wrong with..."

"Errr... excuse me a moment General White Sir, I don't mean to try and tell you your business for this operation, sir. But I think maybe the troops under my command should be considered the Primary Unit, and Colonel Salsiccia's troops should be Primary Support. That way Lieutenant Walker and Captain Wilson's troops could be held as backup support and security for the fucking operation, sir. Lieutenant Walker's Unit took a helluva beating in that damn Russian mess a few months back General White, and I was planning to cut him some slack on this operation, General White Sir. I believe he deserves some time to lick his woun..."

"Colonel Leadbetter! Are you trying to inform me that Lieutenant Walker and his god damn Unit's are too cut up to operate during this fucking mission, mister?"

"By no means am I suggest that to you General White Sir, you obviously misread what I was offering you, sir. I meant Lieutenant Walker and his Unit is as prepared as I have ever saw them to carry out his orders as received, sir. Hot, hot enough to melt butter and ready to go anywhere, and do anything that's expected of them sir. All I was suggesting was I give his team a little slack time, that's all, General White Sir. Lieutenant Walker's crew eaten enough shit for everyone in the entire Corps, sir." Colonel Leadbetter offered to his Commander.

"That's rather admirable of you Colonel Leadbetter and I respect you for the offer, sir. If you feel anyone needs any slack time, they're out of the fucking Unit, period mister. No if, ands or buts about it, mister. I don't want and will not stand for any soft dicks need time off wasting this specialized Unit's time or energies. No one remains in this damn Unit unless they can tow the fucking line, and do what's expected of them on a moment's notice without thought or hesitation, sir. That's why they're getting paid mister. Do you wish to change your last remarks, Colonel?"

"Yes Sir General White, Lieutenant Walker's Unit's a fine pick for the Primary for this operation, and the other three Units will supply backup and support and security for Walker's advance Unit, General White Sir." Colonel Leadbetter replied to his commanding officer.

"I thought you'd see things my fucking way, given enough time to think it over, Colonel Leadbetter. I might as well inform you I was guilty of the same soft feelings, sir. I'd love to cut Lieutenant Walker's people some slack time. I'd like to cut everyone some god damn slack, but it's the President who picked Lieutenant Walker to lead this damn mission. If he wants Walker, he has Walker as the lead dog. Prepare your people properly Colonel Leadbetter, I'll have the transport aircraft leaving for your base on Saturday morning. All trash hauler's (transport planes) should be there by Sunday morning, or I'll have heads if they're not. Get the Unit's gear stowed after the transports touch down at base. Take that much off of your people's asses, sir.

"Colonel Leadbetter, I'll have military bases stationed in England and Italy move their aircraft around on Wednesday. This will make the Iranians believe we're far from ready to even think about attacking them this early, sir. Colonel Leadbetter, all items we have discussed here today are subject to change at a moment's notice on the both of us, sir. If we pick up the Iranian's discovered the mission, or our time table has moved up, you'll jump your troops off sooner than first ordered, sir. I'll do everything possibly, but you're on your own on this one, Colonel. I wish I could tag along, it's been some months since the last time I got bloody in the shit, sir."

"General White, where are you going to be concentrating the jamming at sir?"

"The Iranian's are no assholes Colonel Leadbetter. They have to know we're coming after their damn submarines and soon. We'll make them believe the heaviest bombing's scheduled for the Naval Base stationed at Bandar-e-Abbas. I'll start jamming the living shit out of the Iranian communications from there, and spread it out to cover the Iranian cities of Bander Beheshi and Iranshahr. That way I'll throw a thick blanket of electronic haze over the entire area in question to better protect Lieutenant Walker's troops as they move around the damn deep desert, Colonel Leadbetter. The jamming will commence at exactly Twenty Four Hundred Hours on Sunday morning, and it'll extend until the mission had ran its full course. I'm quite certain when we begin jamming the bastards, the damn Iranians will quickly move their damn submarines, but I got them there too, sir. I have satellites stacked up over their position, and the President okayed a launch of the shuttle with that new radar syste..."

"New radar system sir?" Colonel Leadbetter cut off the General's last words as he asked his commander that question. He wanted to stay a jump ahead of everything concerning his mission.

"Yeah, something new has been added to our arsenal recently, Colonel Leadbetter. The bookworms have discovered a radar system that operates in the Blue/Green Specter, thus the name BGS-12." General White took a quick breath, allowing Leadbetter to get a question in.

"How does this new radar system operate, General White?" The concerned Colonel asked.

"Christ sake and miracles, you're getting to be one major pain in the damn ass lately with all these questions, mister." The General replied to the Colonel in a huff.

"So I've been told on many different occasions and even by my wife, General White Sir." Colonel Leadbetter remarked with a smirk.

"Look Colonel Leadbetter, I don't have the fucking time to give you a first class education on this new system. I'll give you a quick break down on the damn system. The BGS-12 operates in the blue/green specter, and as you know water lives in the blue, green zone. This damn system operates in the same specter, thus allowing it to actually see through water. I was told it negates water and makes it so to say disappear, so the system can see right to the floor of the sea, any sea. We just aim the fucking eye of the system and we can see the sea floor, and any ships or submarines are sort of suspended at the depths they travel. I don't know much more about it myself, I'm told it gives you the feeling the ships are suspended in air.

"I was also informed that we can see the larger fish swimming in water no longer surrounding them. Some shit huh Colonel Leadbetter? This damn system's more detailed than I suggested, but I'm not here to give you a fucking run down on the damn thing, sir. Anyway, we'll keep tabs on the god damn Iranian submarines, trail the sonofabitches with this new shit, and when the time comes, we'll wipe them out slicker than owl shit. Any questions Colonel?"

"Negative on that last General. I'll save my questions until we can speak better about this system, sir." The Marine Colonel said with no question in his tone at all.

"Good, that's wise of you Colonel Leadbetter, I expect your troops to begin their deportation on Sunday morning sir. Get them hot and ready."

"Yes Sir General White, my troops will be ready to rock when the time comes, sir." Colonel Leadbetter snapped into the receiver. The instant the Chairman of the Joint Chiefs of Staff hung up with him, Colonel Leadbetter jumped out of his chair, dumping his beer he searched for his aide. He found Sergeant Kirkpatrick, and ordered him to immediately assemble the troops on the grinder. The Sergeant informed the Colonel the troops just entered the mess.

Colonel Leadbetter found someone he could take his anger out on, and he puffed up his chest as he screamed at the Sergeant. Saying what he wanted to say to the General during their conversation. "Sergeant, what the hell do you think we're running around here, god dammit? A chapter of the fucking Girl Scouts? I don't give a rat's ass what the troops are doing, or if they haven't eaten in a week. Assemble the sonofabitches or I'll have you replaced, and you'll find yourself washing shit cans until the next coming of Christ, mister."

"Yes Sir." The Sergeant snapped at the Colonel as he saluted.

"Get them asses assembled, I'll address them in five minutes mister. Any swinging dick or bouncing tits late for assembly will eat his or her shit for fucking lunch. Get the hell out of my sight before I shoot ya ass for crap sake, Sergeant."

"Yes Sir Colonel." Sergeant Kirkpatrick snapped as he tensed and saluted the Colonel, who ignored him. He rushed out of the office and bellowed orders for all Head Hunter and Snake Eaters troops to assemble on the grinder in two minutes. Head Hunters was the Unit's name, to make this breed of Special Forces soldiers' independent from the civilized Corps of the service.

The Mutt, Road Kill, the Roach and Mother Flanagan, along with two of the Russian women fighters were busy brushing up on some of their hand to hand combat. The Mutt was enjoying watching Mother work on the instructor, neither man could out do the other. Siberia was standing with the Mutt when she offered him. "Big American soldier, why no you show how good are you with you hand and hand to me, big shot dog soldier you."

"I thought you'd never ask." The Mutt smirked as he cupped her breast as he smiled at her.

Siberia brushed his hand aside and bitched at him. "I no mean that way stupid American soldier you. I want see good with hand in combat, stupid you are soldier. I know Lieutenant Walker good fight, I see defeat Russia wrestler. You good Lieutenant Walker is, Mutt?"

"Hey bitch, suck my dick will ya. I can kick Walker's ass all the way to hell and back, sister."

"In your fucking dreams you can dipshit. I'd wipe up the stinking floor with your friggin ass, buster." Lieutenant Walker snarled back as the Mutt's words got his attention.

"I suck dick, only if prove me you good in fight, mista. Huh, think good that Mutt." Siberia purred sexily, knowing she just boxed the foolish American soldier into a corner.

"Betta than you think, bitch." He fired back with a wink at the Russian female.

Siberia sexually ran her finger seductively down the side of the Mutt's face as she leaned against him, and enticed him by rubbing her hips in his crotch as she offered again. "Big soldier you, you prove Siberia how good are fight, no? I want know I big hand when go out mission. Come on big boy, show what got between you legs." Siberia gave the Mutt's nuts a squeeze, and added. "I like man protect self. I no like man think I beat, err... how say... ahhhh yes, shit of."

"You got it Gorkie bitch. I'll show you honey, but what's in it for me if I win, huh baby?"

"What want from Siberia to get you show how you fight good, big boy American soldier you?" Siberia offered as she swayed her hips and rubbed his dick.

"Hmmmm... lemme see. If I dump this dopey bastard on his stinking head toot sweet. You give me your damn drawers as a badge of victory over his ass, and the only way you can get them back, is if you give me a fucking blow job like you just offered me, Gorkie. Well what do you say to that deal, little Russian bitch with the big fucking mouth?"

"What are call draw dog man? This word no known me well. Is something you made up confuse me, American dirty dog you." Siberia asked, perplexed by the Mutt's words.

"Not dog bitch, the name's Mutt, and the drawers are your underwear, your pants, your bush bag, you got it baby? And what about the blow job, head, you know, like my dick in your stinking mouth?" The Mutt grinned as he pointed between her legs and he rubbed his dick.

Siberia almost blushed, but she was set on seeing how good the Mutt was with had to hand combat, she agreed to give him what he was after from her. If he was able to beat the training instructor at his own game. Siberia nodded yes.

The Mutt could not hide the grin on his face even if he wanted to, as he called out to the female Russian. "Hey Gorkie, can I take that as a yes to both my stinking requests?"

Again, Siberia nodded yes as she gave him a sly and sexy smile.

"You got it baby. Hey Samurai I'm next up man. I wanna teach you a few things Homes." The Mutt offered the Japanese instructor, this action prompted Walker to move over and ask.

"What the fuck gives with you all of a sudden Homes? I never saw you volunteer for anything in your wasted life, buddy. You bucking for a Purple Heart, or a Section Eight out man?"

"No way in hell on either of those two remarks Homes, I'm just afta a smelly flag to hang on my footlocker for you pussy hounds to get a stinking sniff of when you pass it, and I'll get my damn blow job from her, that's all man." The Mutt fired back at the Lieutenant.

"What's the real deal with you, butt nugget?" Walker asked his long time friend suspiciously.

"Walker, this Russian bitch over here is gonna gimme her stinking drawers if I dump this little Jap ass on his damn head, and the only way she gets them back from me is she hasta gimme some stinking head, man." The Mutt announced proudly as he turned to the instructor, and then he aimed his thumb over his shoulder at Siberia behind him.

"I see there's a reason for your madness after all, Mutt. Go get the lousy sumbitch then." Road Kill laughed as he stepped aside and allowed the Mutt to move out on the practice field. Slowly, the two combatants circled each other to their right, cautiously reaching out every once in a while in an attempt to engage the other fighter. The Mutt made his first move on the instructor by grabbing the unsuspecting instructor's sleeve. He then dropped to the ground and flung the instructor over his shoulder. The instructor landed on the ground and picked up a hand full of sand and threw it to the side, angry he just got dumped on his back by this asshole. The now upset instructor leaped to his feet, and then he began his second attack on the Mutt. He was now the challenger in the struggle, a foolish move on his part because he already gave up the fight in the back of his mind to the Mutt. He was now trying to get even with the soldier for embarrassing him before the other soldiers he was trying to train in some new tactics.

Siberia moved a little closer to Lieutenant Walker and she mumbled at him. "This big dumb soldier you friend, good? How become so good with use his stupid hand sir? I no think can take shit without someone help him do it so, Lieutenant."

Walker laughed as he stared at the beautiful Russian fighter, and then he replied. "This comes from his many years of watching the stinking WWE, baby." (World Wrestling Entertainment)

"What devil WWE thing? I no never hear WWE before day. Is someplace you government send foolish American soldier to taught soldier hand combat hand good train for sir? If so, I want go WWE place to learn be so good with hand in hand combat, big shot American soldier you."

"No baby, it's a fucking wrestling program we have on the TV. It's no place my government sends any of her troops for any special hand to hand combat training sister."

"Wrestle? Watch stupid wrestle on TV make fight good you hands with? I hard believe this story you try tell me true, soldier. I believe you lie me, so I no trained good you from

WWE thing. You scared Russian soldier good, American soldier you?"

"No way in stinking hell baby, I'm being true with ya little ass sister, I'm shooting square from the damn shoulder back at you. We watch the WWE for some laughs, it's cool, and we have to admit we picked up a few interesting moves at that, that's the scoop honey." Walker grunted as he turned back to the action going down between his friend and the instructor. He smiled as he saw the instructor suddenly go flying across the sand, and land hard on his ass. The instructor looked back at the Mutt and actually cursed at him this time.

Siberia backed the instructor because she did not want to give her underpants to the Mutt, or worse, getting forced to give him some head to this ugly dark skinned American soldier she knew wanted to get in her pants. She cupped her hands around her mouth, and then she yelled out at the instructor still sitting on the ground. "Hey instructor man, you big dummy you, get back on foot before you fight me. How come you no use some WWE stuff on big dumb jerk you fight, stupid man you? He too dumb to know what do right, he no have brains blow nose on own you stupid. You beat him good, use head better, you big dummy. Beat like say beat enemy, like drum."

All the while Siberia yelled at the Japanese instructor, she made a mental note to observe the WWE. So she might learn some of the things the American soldiers knew, and using in this combat. She could bring them back to Russia to share with her fellow soldiers, so the Americans would not be one up on them.

The Japanese instructor glanced angrily at the female soldier doing all the yelling at him as he slowly got back to his feet. The Mutt immediately pressed his attack when the instructor was standing again. With a quick sweep of his leg, the Mutt brushed the instructor's legs out from under him, and depositing the instructor on his back on the ground for a third time. Then he jumped on top of the instructor and he placed his forearm across his neck and applied some strong pressure, actually choking him out until the instructor was forced to give up to him, when he realized he had no way out of the hold the Mutt had on him.

"Svinaya sabaka!" (Fucking dog) Siberia called out as she kicked dirt at the instructor and bitched at him. "You lost dumb jerk. You no instructor, you fail. You no belong train soldier."

The defeated instructor struggling to breath as he rubbed the back of his neck, and then he got on his feet and glared harshly at the Russian woman and growled at her. "Hey bitch, if you think you're so god damn good. Why don't you step up to the plate and take a couple of swings at my fucking ass? I'll tear you a new asshole, wiseass foreign bitch."

"You no scare me with you big mouth. I no fight you big dumb instructor you. I no want embarrass you more than you are already by lose to me this time. You lose one fight, now want lose one me second time big dumb jerk you." Siberia hissed angrily at the instructor and then she turned her back on him in disgust, and wiggled her ass in his face as the final insult.

"Keep shaking that fucking thing in my god damn face and I'll take a chunk out of the little thing with my fucking teeth, bitch." The instructor grinned at the female busing his horn, his words made The Mutt put out his hand, and the instructor punched the outstretched fist with his own and offered the Mutt a slight nod, recognizing he was well trained with his hands.

"Way to stinking go instructor man. You gave me one helluva trophy to place on my stinking mantle and I wanna thank you for the gift, buddy." The Mutt grinned as he headed for the good looking Russian fighter still wiggling her ass at the instructor. Mutt sashayed his way over to Siberia and then he put out his mitt and groused at her. "Hey honey, you can call me all the stinking names you wanna call me if it makes you happy, just fork over the damn drawers and I'll hold on them for ya ass until you wanna earn them back baby. I'll keep them nice and safe until you fulfill the other part of your deal you made with me, baby."

"Here?" Siberia asked as she stared up into the Mutt's burning and wild eyes.

"Yep. This is the spot I get paid baby. It's time to put your honor where your stinking mouth is, baby." The Mutt aimed a smile at her as if it was a weapon.

Lieutenant Walker heard Sergeant Kirkpatrick bellowing for everyone to assemble. "Hey Mutt, you betta get a stinking step on it Homes, or else man! We gotta assemble man."

The Mutt glared at the Russian warrior while wiggling his fingers and complaining. "C'mon bitch, you're not gonna welch out on me are ya baby? A deal's a deal honey."

"Welch? What you mean by welch, big shot American soldier? I no know this word mista. You use word I know use or no speak you no more, big American jerk." Siberia snapped as she punched the Mutt in the guts. She was sorry, his stomach made her wrist hurt.

"Welch on me, that's it bitch, chicken out and not gimme your damn drawers as you agreed to, or the blow job you promised, honey." The Mutt said, trying not to rub his stomach.

"Russia soldier no welch on any deal made, mista wiseguy fooking American soldier you. We no chicken fight, you see when we battle for sure." Siberia bitched as she angrily unbuckle her belt, and loosen her pants, dropping them on the ground and kicking out of the legs. She removed her drawers and threw them at the Mutt as she barked angrily at him. "There, hope you satisfied deal we make I no Welch on, stupid American soldier you."

"Very much, one day I gotta get in this here little safe box of yours and see how it feels, baby." The Mutt said as he caught the lacy panties, sniffed them and rubbed his hand between her legs.

"Ahhh... big stupid American soldier you, but first defeat me like do you instructor. If want from me anything mista." Siberia snapped as she shoved his hand aside and pulled up her pants.

"I see no stinking problem, Gorkie bitch. I don't mind tenderizing my meat a little before I eat on it, honey." The Mutt smirked as he again smiled at the beautiful Russian female warrior.

"There go again wiseguy American soldier you. I no understand you word again, mista big shot soldier, but assure you I no over push like that stupid instructor jerk is, mista. I beat in mush bad, and then I sit on you stupid face and make you satisfy me, instead other way round like you want from me, big and stupid American soldier you." Siberia hissed as she placed her hands on her hips, and she glared at the Mutt hotly.

"Sounds great to my ass, because either way I fucking come out the stinking winner. When do you wanna start playing around some, honey?" The Mutt grinned again.

"You no win no thing for me, big shot foolish soldier! You never win any good Russia soldier like me are, stupid

American warrior you. No American soldier ever live defeat Russia good soldier." Siberia snarled as she quickly buckled her pants.

CHAPTER FOURTEEN

Road Kill, Lieutenant Robert Walker heard the Sergeant screaming for the troops to assemble on the grinder and he grunted at his lifelong friend again. "For Christ sake Mutt, you're really a fucking dog. You always smell things you picked up offa the stinking ground like that, stupid? C'mon Homes, we gotta shove off before the stinking Sergeant has a god damn shit hemorrhage on us, buddy. Take your win and let's get going man."

The soldiers rushed as a unit for the grinder to assemble before the Colonel as ordered.

Colonel Bruce Leadbetter was getting rather comfortable at being raised from a Captain to Colonel as he remained in his office, but he stared out his window as he watched the specialized troops break their necks rushing to assemble on the grinder. Some of the elite troops were in various stages of dress, some were even caught in the showers when word to assemble was issued, and they came to the assembly area with towels wrapped around them. Others were still chewing food. The Colonel smiled as he watched the soldiers stand shoulder to shoulder at full attention while waiting further orders, knowing those orders were going to cost some of them their lives on the next mission they were going to be sent out on.

"Fine pack of god damn Head Hunters I have on my stinking hands here I see." The proud Colonel grumbled to the walls of his quarters as he slowly shook his head while picking up his cover, and forced it on his head. All the while he was preparing to leave his private quarters on the base, he wondered which one of these nuts cakes gathered on the grinder was elected to try his patience on the assembly this time around as he headed for the grinder.

As Colonel Leadbetter strolled up and down the lines of soldiers staring at each one of them, he came across Lieutenant Frank Hall, the Mutt, with the pair of women's black lace panties sticking half way out his uniform breast pocket. The Colonel stopped before the Mutt and he eyed him cautiously. Without saying a word to the young soldier, Colonel Leadbetter shifted his eyes from the Mutt's face towards the undies stuffed in his pocket, and back to his face again. Trying to elicit a response from him without being forced to ask him what this was about. As he glared at the Mutt, he tried his best to look over the Colonel's head, ignoring him. The Mutt knew what he was doing, and he was enjoying busting the Colonel's horns like he was doing.

The Colonel had enough of his little head game with the Mutt and he snarled at him. "Okay you raving lunatic you, I guess you were the fuck who was elected by the rest of this trash to bust my fucking horns today I see mister. What the fuck's this shit about, buster? Is this some kinda new sweat band you have here, mister?" he removed the panties from the Mutt's pocket, and then he held them over his head for the other soldiers to see.

Instantly, the troops broke up with some of them poking the others in the ribs.

"Enough jokers!" Colonel Leadbetter growled over his shoulder as he pulled the elastic top apart, and then he looked at the Mutt while waiting his reply. "Okay wiseguy, I take it these must be your mother's drawers. Because I know no self respecting woman in her right fucking mind would never entertain screwing your brains out, shitbird. What brains I don't know, you don't have enough brains in that damn bone dome of yours to light a bulb. I repeat buster, what the hell's the meaning of showing up at my formation with a pair of bitch drawers stuffed in your god damn pocket, stupid? Something I don't know bout you?

"Have you taken to dressing in bitches lace when not in uniform, mister? Maybe I should order you to strip down to make sure you don't have any damn woman's undies on. Are you going squirrely on me or what buster? Here, do everyone here a favor and wear these things. Show everyone how you look all dolled up in fucking lace, dog man." Colonel Leadbetter stuffed the undies in the Mutt's hand, he was doing everything to get a reaction from him.

The Colonel was actually surprised because the Mutt came so far over the past year, and he was able to control himself and his anger under his assault. He remembered the first time he ever laid eyes on the Mutt and his friend Lieutenant Walker. When he challenged him to a fight because the then Captain got on a bitch while he was preparing the unit for action in Namibia. Colonel Leadbetter put his face against the Mutt's and barked at him. "Shitbird, I just asked you a fucking question and I want a god damn answer from your ass mister. You gonna tell me why you have this bush holder in your damn pocket or what, mister? Or am I gonna be forced to reach in that pea you call a brain, and extract the information for myself, you dumb Squid."

He finally got the reaction he was searching for, when he referred to the Mutt as Squid. The Mutt balled up his fists and then he hunched his shoulders like he was preparing for a fight. The Colonel easily picked up his move and took a step back in order to give the Mutt some room to heat up, but to his surprise, the Mutt suddenly relaxed and then he merely smiled back at his commanding officer like he was not trying to get a rise out of him.

"Okay shithead, I had enough fucking around with you over this shit here. I ain't wasting any more of my stinking time on the likes of you. Mutt, you keep trying to get under my skin, and I'm going to stick a sausage up your ass and a hungry dog down your damn throat and see what happens when they meet in the middle, mister. That goes for the rest of you pukes as well." Colonel Leadbetter shot the lace undies by the elastic band into the formation of soldiers.

"Okay listen up, this is the latest scoop I have for you squirrels. I just got word from the big man in Washington. We're scheduled to move out on Sunday, we'll be in Injun country in..."

"What's our clock on this one Colonel?" Someone called out from the ranks.

"Twenty four hours, so that gives us just enough time to get to the damn target, do a detailed sweep of the damn interior of the place, and take what we want from it and then completely destroy the dump. I'm cutting the training down to preserve the mission's OPSEC. (Operation Security) I don't need a shitload of troops showing up to begin a rehearsal with all the damn eyes floating around the base lately dammit. It'll be short time before some nosy ass reporter shows up and blows our damn cover for the operation by reporting on the troops, and the asshole tips our hand to the damn Iranians. That's the last thing I need, having a lousy reporter let out we plan to insert ground troops inside Iran on this operation. Besides, you self propelled sandbags are supposed to be ready for anything coming your way at all times.

"Enough of this crap, listen up you pack of sweathogs, I don't want any of you asses screwing around with any of the local sperm garglers of either country we'll be operating in on this mission. I don't want you swinging dicks or bouncing tits coming down with a case of the drips, or worse. I catch anyone screwing around with the local color, I'll be more than happy to cut your happy sticks off, and then have them served up for lunch to the offenders. This will be a fast, hard hitting operation, and you people are expected to kill any god damn Opfors (Opposition forces) who get in your way with extreme prejudice, and take no crap from anyone you happen to trip over while you screaming squirrels are on this fucking mission.

"The paper responsible people will check file cabinets of the complex, and remove and take every damn thing you can get their grubby little hands on. The computer Geeks, you know what you have to do, I want every hard drive, CDs, thumb drives, or any other form of intelligence gathering systems found inside this damn Iranian complex we're about to erase from the face of the earth. The EOU, (Explosive Ordnance Units) you people will place your demolition charges in position to do the most possible damage to the complex.

"Making certain you guys single out every damn missile, warhead, machine, and computer found inside this damn Iranian complex. I don't want any damn thing to live through your explosions. Then you people will pull back and let the bang boys have their fun with blowing up the damn complex. But not until the photographic people take pictures to convince the world of what we found at this Persian complex. We have to make sure we hav..."

A staff car suddenly appeared on the training area, traveling faster than the usually accepted speed for safety reasons on any military base and it caused the upset Colonel to complain. "Now who the hell's this fucking nut coming at my ass, god damn?" he glared angrily at the car as it headed directly at him. The car came to a sliding stop in front of the troop assembly on the grinder and the Colonel.

"Who the fuck's this shithead, dammit? When I finish with his ass, he's gonna wish his mamma was still fucking single for crap sake." Colonel Leadbetter hissed as he started for the car in a huff, before he could take three steps, the rear door flung open and the Base Commander emerged, he was followed by a stranger dressed in civilian clothes. The Commander waved at Colonel Leadbetter, and the three huddled with the base commander speaking.

"Colonel Leadbetter, congratulations on your recent rate increase, sir. I meant to get to you before this time, but I got jammed up with the matters of this base, sir. Colonel, I want to take this time to introduce you to Doctor Joel Russbinder. The good Doctor here is on loan to us from the Energy

Department's Nuclear Emergency Search Team, or NEST for short. I want the good Doctor returned in one piece, in the same condition he was given to us once this mission's completed, sir. General White wants you to take the Doctor to sand land with the rest of your troops, he's a big wig in the nuclear weapons research field, and the President wants all the proof he can possibly amass on the weapons and warheads and missiles we find in funny land..."

"Excuse me General Peterson Sir, the President wants me to investigate the file cabinets and research documents found inside the complex, Sir. To make certain we're leaving nothing of importance behind in the way of documents and evidence and intelligence. The President wants me to check on the various stages of the missile's development, their warheads and remove a warhead for closer examination back in the States." The doctor smiled at the Base Commander.

General Peterson turned to Colonel Leadbetter and snapped at him without missing a beat. "You just heard the man, I hate to be the one to have to inform you Colonel Leadbetter. Doctor Russbinder's in control of this operation, if the Doctor wants to extend the window of time on target inside the complex, that's what you'll do Colonel. If the Doctor wants some files removed, your soldiers will remove them without hesitation. If the Doctor wants anything removed, or destroyed, you people will remove or destroy it as requested. Get the picture Colonel?"

"Yes Sir General Peterson, you painted one helluva picture for me, sir. Doctor Russbinder runs the whole show, sir. Excuse my asking you this General Peterson, but is the Doctor physically fit for this type of action sir? I mean, is the Doctor going to live through this mission, or do we have to carry him in and out of the complex on our damn backs, sir?"

Colonel Leadbetter could not help but hiss his words at the General, he was that angry over the fact a civilian was going to run his military action. Inside, he smiled, wondering how Lieutenant Walker and his band of thieves were going to take the news of a civilian running the operation on them.

"Watch your step and your tone with me, Colonel Leadbetter. I don't want anyone insulting the good Doctor here while he's on this mission with you and the rest of your troops, sir. Doctor Russbinder's well aware he's going on a tough ride, and he's prepared to carry his own weight throughout the mission. Let me warn you Colonel Leadbetter, if you have to carry the Doctor on your back to and from the god damn complex. Then that's what you and your troops will do, sir. He's the big bang on this operation, and he is not expendable. Understand your orders Colonel?"

Colonel Leadbetter stiffened up as he nodded yes to the General's angry words. Inside he was fuming, taking a civilian along on an operation went against everything he was trained for.

"Very well then Colonel Leadbetter Sir, introduce Doctor Russbinder to the rest of the troops and get your mud slappers over to statistics for an Intel briefing, mister." General Peterson saluted the Colonel. He remained standing on the grinder in the background as both Colonel Leadbetter and Doctor Russbinder moved to the front of the formation of troops.

Colonel Leadbetter turned to his people and barked at the gathered troops. "Okay you butt nuggets listen up, this crap's important people. This gentlemen standing to my left is Doctor Joel Russbinder, and he's to Command our entire operation..."

"Colonel Leadbetter, since when do we take any fucking orders from a civilian puke? Even if that butter ball's a stinking Doctor of some sort, sir. This asshole's nothing more than a damn liability on this military mission, Colonel." One soldier called out from the ranks.

"Whose gonna be responsible for the college edufuckingcated book maggot prick out to fulfill a dream of living on the edge for a stinking day, sir?" A second solder called out.

Even before Colonel Leadbetter could respond to the complaints being fired at him from some of the soldiers, General Peterson moved to the head of the formation, and then he snarled at the troops. "You asswipes better listen up and listen up real good if you people know what's good for the lot of ya! If I hear any of you shits giving the Doctor a hard time on this mission, I'll have you flogged within an inch of your life. The Doctor's smack fucking dab in the heart of the action, and it's up to each and every one of you soldiers to protect his life with your own if need be, until he's finished his work inside the damn Iranian complex, troops. The Doctor knows he's on his own once he carried out his end of the mission. Anyone reported disrespecting the Doctor will be shitting O rings out of his ass when I get my hands on him, or her. I'll fuck you people like you were never fucked before in your wasted lives. Understood soldiers!"

A splattering of 'yes sir' was mumbled by some of the bored sounding troops.

"I can't hear you shitbirds!" General Peterson bellowed as he moved closer to the formation.

A resounding 'Yes Sir' was fired back at the angry General as he responded. "That's much better! Colonel Leadbetter Sir, you have the troops back, handle them or lose them sir."

"Okay people, you have information you'll need to be made aware of. Everyone meet at M&L (Maps and Logistics) in five minutes for the latest briefing on the conditions we'll be facing in sand land. Shots and pills will follow the damn briefing. Move it out shitbirds."

Colonel Leadbetter remained standing with the doctor as General Peterson climbed in his car, and then he disappeared from the area while the troops marched towards M&L. Every one of the soldiers knew how the General despised the way the training was being carried out, and he did not want to be anywhere near the specialized training of these troops he disliked so.

"Something to eat Doc?" Colonel Leadbetter asked the new man to the group with a smile.

"No, I'm fine, thank you for asking Colonel Leadbetter." The doc replied with a slight smile.

Colonel Leadbetter smiled again at the large framed youngish looking civilian doctor as he said in a pleasant tone to the man. "Do you mind my asking Doctor, how the hell did you ever get stuck with going out on a fucking mission like this one, sir?"

"Lucky I guess Colonel Leadbetter Sir. When word first filtered down at the institute that the President needed an expert to go on a long range missiles and nuclear warheads hunt in another country. Everyone looked at me because I was the youngest Doctor on the entire staff, and I was in much better physical condition than most of the other Doctors were, sir. Some of the older Doctors had volunteered to go along on the mission, but they were unanimously voted down because of their age and physical condition. It was pointed out all the military needed was a Doctor to drop dead while out on the mission, and it'd be all for naught, Colonel Leadbetter Sir." Doctor Russbinder spread his hands and smiled.

"Well Doc, it's nice to know you damn pencil pushers volunteer much the same way us grunts usually do whenever we're called on to react to some nut screwing up the world again on us, sir. This is an action mission according to the Joint Pub. Shall we go over to M&L and see what's up there, Doctor Russbinder Sir?"

"Colonel Leadbetter, I'm actually thrilled to be going along on what you military types call a special operations mission, sir. Although I must admit I don't quite understand the difference between a special operations mission, and one of a regular military engagement our troops are usually involved in, Colonel Leadbetter." The doctor offered as he stared at the Colonel.

"Allow me to break it down a little better for you then, Doctor. A special operations mission is the most ill conceived mission ever carried out by any Military Unit, sir. It usually goes against all normal conventional wisdom and military logic of general combat conditions and rules, sir. On a special operations mission, we send in a smaller force of specially trained soldiers to defeat a much larger force of enemy soldiers, usually the enemy forces are dug in and waiting for an attack to occur against them by the Special Forces soldiers of our country, sir."

"How does a special operations mission enjoy any success with the Jack, Queen and King stacked against them, Colonel Leadbetter?" The concerned doctor asked the military officer.

"Nothing we do is enjoyable, Doctor Russbinder Sir. Absolutely nothing sir! Any mission like the one we're attempting here, takes a special breed of soldier. A soldier willing to do whatever it fucking takes to accomplish the mission for his country. When we assembled this Multi National Rapid Response Force, we search all the services for just the type of soldiers we need, soldiers whose lifestyle was in opposition to the ideal of military servicemen and women. These soldiers go against all normal accepted behavior of military life, Doctor. We need soldiers, young soldiers, crazy ass soldiers like the ones here. But not crazy enough to be uncontrollable while out on a mission, Doctor Russbinder Sir. We need strong minded troops capable of independent thinking when the crunch time comes a knocking on them. Yes Doctor, all these troops thoughts are locked on one thing, the success of the mission along with his fellow soldier's well being.

"Doctor Russbinder, we need the type of people who'll survive under the worst possible circumstances, the worst conditions to live and fight under. These selected and rare people know they might be forced to eat things a civilized person would step on, sleep where the lowest life forms wouldn't think of sleeping, and act like an animal, and be proud of it. Yes Doctor, we need thinkers, fast reacting survivors. We searched for this rare breed of soldier by examining past military and civilian history of the soldiers we're most interested in. We like a soldier who demonstrates leadership that certain je ne sais quois, living on the edge employed in his everyday life. Which is demanded from the soldiers on Spec-Ops duty." Colonel Leadbetter took a quick breath, and then he went on with his words for the concerned civilian doctor.

"Yes Doctor Russbinder Sir, we even look into their sex life on the soldiers. We're pleased when we discover one soldier we had our eye on, was classified as crazy, even when it comes down to his sex patterns. We need soldiers, warriors who like living on the edge in everything they do or say, Herr Doctor. We hunt for these special soldiers living for today, living life as if this was the last day they had on the earth. Because these specialized warriors have to understand that tomorrow, they may end up in the ground forgotten by the rest of the world. We need people, soldiers not afraid to kill, or be killed in the heat of battle. Soldiers who can work with anyone they're paired up with sir. Yes Doc, even if that somebody is the devil himself. These warriors have to be willing to do anything it takes in order to accomplish their mission successfully."

"You only need specialized soldiers who'll obey orders without question or hesitation, Colonel Leadbetter Sir?" The doctor asked, trying to understand the troops he would be working with.

"No not exactly Doc, not in the least in fact sir. As I stated, we like independent thinkers, searching these people out was only the beginning of the equation, sir. Usually Doc, we train and rehearse the selected soldiers, running countless attack scenarios aimed at a certain structure constructed almost exactly to resemble the target we plan to hit. We cover everything known about the target, going over the attack until we can shit the plans out in our damn sleep, sir. We want soldiers to understand the target inside out, so what was once a sudden action or reaction, is now a normal reflex to the soldiers involved in the operation. But on those rare occasions, such as in this case, sir. It's necessary to suspend said rehearsals.

"This is due mainly to the mission's security deemed more important than any added training. Doc, my troops are armed with the top of the line military technology, our access to latest target intelligence is a constant, this, combined with the quality of troop training and understanding, and the soldiers makes their success a given, sir. We operate under a six step rule to insure our success on any mission we are sent out on, sir. The first rule is simplicity sir, we cement ourselves to the phrase, 'keep it simple stupid'. Get in there, carry out our mission, and get out before any enemy reinforcements arrive on scene. We try to keep the number of targets down to an absolute minimum, the fewer targets the less time spend on target, sir. The second rule's security, and security's the most important rule of the trade, Doctor Russbinder.

"We don't need the damn enemy knowing what we're doing at any time, or when we're coming after the bastards, Doctor. Repetition, which as I told you we have eliminated for the purpose of the security and success of this mission, Doc. In our preparation for attacking the target, we run countless, repetitious scenarios of the objective until we know it inside out. Surprise is one of the laws we live by, and it's necessary to assure the mission's success. Doc, we attack when it's most convenient, hopefully catching our targets off guard, or on slack time. We time our attack when we believe the enemy's at its most vulnerable to hit them, sir. While they're waiting for their replacements to relieve them from duty, or especially at meal times sir."

"When are the soldiers relieved of their duties, Colonel Leadbetter?" the doctor asked.

"The target soldiers are relieved usually between hours of three and four in the a.m. We specially pick this time to attack, because we believe it's when the guards are the most tired and bored with their orders. It's been proven at this time of the day, many attacks are successful, Doctor. We add speed to the equation as well. We hit our target with lightening swiftness, because we travel light, hit hard, and gone from the target by the time the enemy has a chance to even organize a defense against our attack. The only drawback of traveling light, is it makes it impossible for my troops to get involved in a long engagement with the defenders of any targets. If we miss our window of opportunity, or we get bogged down for any reason. Or if the enemy happens to be in the right place at the right time and our Intel has let us down.

"Then there's a strong possibility we'll be forced to break off our engagement, or risk being overran and the troops slaughtered to the last trooper. A special operations action is geared to run like a fine tuned car, and if there's any screw ups on our part during any operation we're involved in. It could very well spell complete disaster for my troops, and the success of the mission at the same time. Doc, I hate to sound like a broken record and as you can see for yourself, every thought in my head is geared for success of the mission. The last equation to the puzzle is purpose, and this is a two part problem for the soldiers to deal with, Doctor Russbinder Sir.

"First off, we make certain the troops know their objective inside out, what's expected of them while the troops are on target. Even before we set off on any mission, every soldier understands what he or she's supposed to do, what's expected of them. What to look for, what to take from the target and what to destroy, and what to ignore, and what to do if the mission breaks down on the troops. Nothing's left uncovered or to the soldier's imagination for the troops involved in the operation. The last thing we need is any form of hesitation, one moment of indecision, any doubt about what he or she's supposed to do to get out of a situation, or any confusion.

"If hesitation arises, it'll surely lead to a complete breakdown of our mission, and place lives of my troopers in dire straits. The second part of purpose is to make certain our troops believe in the mission they're ordered out on. We have to impregnate an absolute positive reason for the soldiers to be on the mission, remove any doubt from their mind what he or she's doing isn't a just cause to fight for. We have to give the soldiers a sincere want to go on the operation. The troops have to think if they didn't go on the mission, the world might end.

"Purpose Herr Doctor, a mission and soldier on a mission armed with an agenda, is a soldier with a purpose, and that soldier becomes a soldier impossible to defeat with mere bullets and logic, sir. My troops operate with a single goal in focus and in their mind, and that demand is every soldier in the Unit will succeed on his or her mission, or they'll die carrying out their god damn orders, sir. We never consider being taken prisoners. There's no future in that, and each of us understands the stress of being taken a prisoner will place on the entire outfit. Herr Doctor, each soldier knows full well if they're taken prisoner, the others will place themselves in danger to try and win their release. So becoming a POW isn't an option on any mission we're sent out on, Doc. My people will do whatever's necessary to avoid becoming a prisoner at all costs..."

"Colonel Leadbetter, are you telling me that your people would be willing to commit suicide, rather than to allow themselves to become prisoners on the mission they're on sir?" Doctor Russbinder cried in stunned disbelief as he stared at the Marine Colonel.

"Yes, if need be Doc, absolutely sir. You have to understand, if the operation isn't sanctioned by the powers that be, and the troops are actually invading another country while armed. Then the country they have invaded are free to do anything to these soldiers, torture them and even stand them up against the wall and shoot them, and the Geneva Convention doesn't offer these soldiers any protections under their guide lines, sir." Colonel Leadbetter replied matter-of-factly, not giving the doctor's words much thought before going on.

"Herr Doctor, our operation works because our Special Forces troops are better trained than the bad guys, and that categorically guarantees our complete succeed on any mission we're sent on. Besides Doc, we operate on guts and pure determination. Enough, shall we join the others Herr Doctor?" the Colonel was unable to hide his displeasure, hating having a civilian going along on a military operation, and there was nothing he was able to do to hid this feeling.

"Please Colonel Leadbetter, lead the way if you don't mind sir."

Colonel Leadbetter stepped aside him and allowed the doctor to take the lead as he guided him over to the building and the other soldiers from his outfit.

"What's the matter? You want me to enter the M&L building first, Colonel Leadbetter Sir?" Doctor Russbinder smirked as he glanced back at the grinning Colonel standing behind him.

"No Doc, first off Doc we're heading for the mess, sir. You have to remember where you are at all times whether you're on friggin military base or out on a damn mission, and where you're going every second you're operating with my troops out in the field, sir. Besides, there could very well be land mines, one never knows Herr Doctor Russbinder Sir."

"Whatttt?" The doctor yelled as he pulled back behind the grinning Colonel.

"Just kidding around with ya ass that's all, Doc. But since you're coming on the mission with my troops. I think you better start thinking like a fucking soldier, and take nothing for granted, mister. If you don't Doc, your stinking ass is going to end up dead, and I'll be stuck stuffing it in a damn mummy bag before we even get started on the damn mission, sir. And, that might put the entire operation in jeopardy, and I wouldn't like that one bit, Doctor.

"Herr Doctor, you have to understand about your situation and where we're going. Everything in bad man's land will be trying to kill us. You fall asleep at the switch, and you can be screwing up the entire mission on us. Not to mention putting the lives of my troops on the line with your ass. Keep your eyes open, or I'll snatch them out of your noggin and stuff them up your damn ass, watch where you're walking at all times and we'll get along just fine, Doc. You walk around like you're out on some fucking beach resort, and I'll bleed your ass dry, and leave ya for the buzzards to pick fucking clean sir. The lives of my troops are more important than some damn book smart ass wipe civilian Doc I don't know from Adam, and I don't give a fuck that sent you on this mission with me troops. Once you're on the battlefield, I'm your judge and jury.

"Your ass belongs to me during this entire operation Doc, and I'll spend the fucking thing in any fashion I think is right, to ensure my success of the damn mission, and the protection of my troops, sir. I simply will not jeopardize this mission or the lives of my troop's, because you don't know what the shit you're doing, or because your slack ass happened to stumble into a mine field, or a damn man trap. Do I make myself perfectly clear to you on this subject, Herr Doctor?

"You can mad dog my fucking ass all you want, Doc. As long as you know your place on the mission. Remember this Herr Doctor and you just might live through this god damn mess, and see your wife and children again. Take every step as if there was a land mine under foot, like there's a cobra waiting under the sand, and he's ready to strike out and eat your ass alive, and you'll do just fine on this mission. Shall we get ourselves something to eat, Herr Doctor?"

The two walked towards the mess hall with the doctor moving like he was stepping on eggs all the way. Colonel Leadbetter smiled to himself, knowing the suddenly worried doctor was trying his best to watch himself, and what he was doing. At least now, he stood a much better chance of not becoming a casualty on the operation. With the amount of care the doctor was placing in each of his footsteps, the Colonel was forced to say to the civilian. "That's how you fucking do it, Doctor Russbinder, if you want to remain alive out in the field that is, sir."

The doctor looked over his shoulder back at Colonel Leadbetter, and he almost ended up walking into a fence running along the side of the road leading to the mess hall.

"There you go, that's exactly what I was saying to you, Herr Doctor. Because you had to turn your dumb ass around to see me and get my blessings on how you're conducting yourself, sir. You nearly ran your ass right into that damn fence, sir. You see what I mean about keeping your damn head on a swivel at all times while you're part of my group of outstanding soldiers, sir? A simple hesitation, or you not using your head on an operation, could blow apart the whole damn mission on us, Herr Doctor. I hope some of this shit's getting through and sinking into that book smart ass brain of yours sir. In the field, all the books in the world can go right into the shitter.

"It's what's in your brain that'll keep your ass alive out in the field of action, Herr Doctor Russbinder. Keep your damn eyes glued on the soldier in front of you, and do exactly what he does, and you just might survive long enough to finish this mission in one piece, Doc. We're entering a rare moment of clarity in the dust storm of violence that swirls through this inchoate movement." Colonel Leadbetter snorted as he caught up to the doctor, and then grabbed him by the arm and nearly dragged him to the building they were heading for.

"I can see what you mean Colonel Leadbetter. Just one laps in attention and I could have..." The doctor started to say, but he was cut off by the Colonel.

"Can the lip shit crap Doc, and pay attention to what you're doing about yourself, and we'll get along fine." The Colonel growled at the concerned doctor as they came up to the double doors leading into the mess hall. Already, they could hear the soldiers inside talking and laughing and bitching with each other. Everything they heard displayed to the Colonel that his specialized soldiers were confident about their mission. He smiled over his elite soldier's show of confidence, and their want to go out on this latest mission.

CHAPTER FIFTEEN

CIA Director John Raincloud picked up General John White at the Pentagon, and they rushed off to the White House for a new briefing with the President. Director Raincloud was armed with the latest intelligence reports from his Operative Sand Star working in Iran, with the map and drawing of what the operative had observed at the secret Iranian complex.

By the time they both entered the Oval Office, the President, along with a certain number of his cabinet waited for them to arrive. The President did not waste any of his time with bothering to introduce the Director and General to any of the other members of the meeting. He sat forward in his chair with his fingers clasped together and snapped at the Director. "Well, you stated you have some new information for me, Director Raincloud? Let's have it sir."

"Yes Sir Mr. President, I have hand written maps sent by my Operative working in Iran through the burst scramble system, sir. He detailed the exact location of the complex and its defenses. I have a hand drawn picture of what appears to be a nuclear warhead in its infancy stage, it's obviously designed to fit on a ballistic missile, Mr. President. We know this because it strongly resembles the warheads we removed for the Russian missiles in North Korea..."

"May I see that map you're speaking about for a moment, Director Raincloud Sir?" the President asked as he held out his hand.

"By all means Mr. President." Director Raincloud smiled as he handed the page over to him, and then he remained silent until the President had a chance to scrutinize the terribly hand sketched picture. Without a word, President Cole passed the picture on to the Secretary of Defense, Jerry Levenhagen, and he waited for his reply before getting back to Raincloud.

"Mr. President, it surely looks like the beginnings of a nuclear warhead to me, sir."

"I believe so as well Jerry. We have in our possession what we wanted, to enable us to move against Iran. Jerry, can you hand that picture over to Director Griffin before he has an apoplexy."

The Security Director smiled as he took the picture and studied it carefully, and then he replied. "Yes Sir Mr. President, it certainly is a missile and a nuclear warhead, sir."

"Glad you agree with the rest of us here Director Griffin Sir. General White do you have everything in gear with your troops as yet sir?"

"Yes Sir Mr. President, but I'd like to take this time to discuss a slight change in our attack scenario against this situation breaking out in Iran, sir."

"Jesus General White, you picked a fine time to think about changing any of the attack plans, sir. Why didn't you wait a while longer and really screw things up on us sir." President Cole let out his breath as he sat back and glared at the General as he laced his fingers together and added. "Let me hear what you want to change about the operation in Iran, sir. But I don't intend to incur any more expenses on this god damn overwhelming mission as it is, General White. If that's what you're aiming at, you better thing about shelving your gripe and let things lay as they are."

General White offered. "Mr. President, more expense is the farthest thing from my mind at this point, sir. What I plan to do will actually save us some money on the operation, sir."

"Hmmm... that'll be a sure change in policy around here, General White. If it might save our taxpayers some money then I'll all ears, General. Let me hear what you have to offer me, sir." President Cole moaned as he pushed his glasses up, and then pinched the bridge of his nose while putting his head back and he stared at the ceiling for a moment.

"President Cole, I've given our plan consideration, and came to the conclusion it's wrong sir."

"Oh Christ, I thought you said this wasn't going to cost the taxpayers' more money. If you change the plan, there'll be no end to the money I'll be forced to pour into this new idea." The President snarled as he sat forward and played with a pencil as he glared at the General.

"With all due respect Mr. President, please allow me a second to explain my reasons for wanting to change the attack plans against the complex at this time sir. Mr. President I assure you, I haven't come to this conclusion lightly, sir. I don't enjoy changing my troop's intention, especially not after they have already set their minds on a certain course of action. If we change them now, things will work out for the better for the attack teams on this mission, sir."

"Okay General White, you have my undivided attention, please continue sir."

"Mr. President, the original plan calls for us to send the Rapid Reaction Force in action on their own, while we move around a number of our aircraft and ships in the background, so as to give the appearance that we're still in the process of planning our attack on Iran and its submarine base, sometime in the future, sir. I think that's wrong for our purposes..."

"Who came up with the plan General!" The President growled as he sent the pencil flying.

"Mr. President, it was jointly agreed on because the Navy was having some problems getting some of their ships in position in the time limit decided when we expected to attack, sir."

Without taking his eyes off General White, the President bellowed. "Walter! Get in here!"

"Yes Sir Mr. President." The young man replied as he entered the Oval Office in a rush.

"Get Admiral Richardson down here pronto! I don't care what he's doing, he's to drop it and get over here. I don't care if you have to send the State Police out to find and drag him here."

"Yes sir." Walter spun around on his heels and disappeared through the door.

President Cole turned to General White and demanded. "Please General, continue with your report. We'll bring the Secretary of the Navy up to speed when he arrives."

"Yes Sir Mr. President, we originally planned to begin our attack on the Iranian installations after my troops had complete their mission on the secret complex. If we get the ships in position at the same time my forces entered Iran, they'll have a much better chance of success, and getting out of there with their skin intact, sir. Mr. President, the more confusion we can create in the first few hours of the operation, will increase the success of the mission for..."

"What exactly do you have in mind General White? How is this move going to save the taxpayer's some damn money sir?" the President hissed unimpressed as he took a sip of water and looked for another pencil on his desk to play with. Secretary Levenhagen handed him his, the President smiled as he began twirling it in his fingers.

"Albert, I think if you give the General a chance to explain, we'll get to the bottom of this situation quicker, and we'll be able to judge his plan." Secretary of State, Hernandez offered.

President Cole's eyes shifted and he smiled at the Secretary. Hernandez was the only person in his cabinet who dared to speak to him in this manner. He would allow her to curse him if she chose, he owed his seat in office to her, and she never asked or sought any favors from him in return for her tireless work on his hard fought Presidential campaign. He nodded politely to her, and then he turned his attention back to General White. "Please General, I'll try to refrain from interrupting you again, unless I feel you're getting too far out in the field, sir."

"Fair enough deal Mr. President, and I thank you for the offer, sir. What I'd like to do, is to coordinate all sea and air attacks together, along with my ground forces entering Iran..."

"What about the electronic jamming we planned to carry out against the Iranian installations before your troops enter Iran, sir? Isn't this enough to afford the cover needed for our troops protection, General White Sir?" Secretary of Defense Levenhagen offered.

The President shot a quick glare at the Defense Secretary for interrupting General White as he remarked. "Please gentlemen, ladies, no more questions until the General had a chance to finish with what's on his mind. Then we'll all jump on him at the same time and pick his brains clean."

"Thank you for a second time Mr. President Sir. If we coordinate the air and sea attacks with the ground assault, we'll move up the main attack by five full days, sir. Saving the taxpayer's a big chunk of money by not forcing the other services to be held back in check for a number of extra days, Mr. President Sir. This move will save money if everyone attacked at the same time sir, with one branch of the service coming to the aid of another who might get bogged down, or find themselves cut off during the action taking place in Iran. If we wait until Friday as planned, and my ground forces find themselves in a real dog fight, we'll be forced to step up the attack, or employ aircraft and ships we're planning to hold in reserve, to support the troops in trouble, sir. This would drive up the cost of this entire operation dramatically if they have to jump off before planned. On the other hand sir, if my troops get bogged down, and say the aircraft were in the air attacking targets, my forces would receive support much quicker on the target, Mr. President.

"I don't like having my forces heading into any military action without complete air cover over them at all times, Mr. President. Suppose the troops are discovered by Iranian soldiers, and they need immediate extraction? If I get stuck waiting for helicopters from Saudi Arabia or Russia to come in for my troops, they may get there in time to remove the troop's bodies, sir. Mr. President Sir, I owe it to my troops to protect them with everything I have at my disposal, and that's what I'll do, or there's a damn good chance this operation won't be carried out successfully."

President Cole jumped to his feet and hissed as he pointed his finger directly at his military officer. "Watch your step with me General! Your words are bordering on insubordination, mister. Any time you don't like how I run this fucking ship, you're free to jump overboard and swim for shore any time you like, sir. Taking your career with you might I add, General. I understand you feel as every Officer does, that's a given and it doesn't need any reinforcing at this meeting, sir. That's first in my mind, and in the minds of everyone attending this damn meeting, General. But if I order your troops to jump into a meat grinder, that's where they're heading, with you in Command and leading them sir. Do I make myself perfectly clear to you, General White?"

"Quite clear Mr. President Sir." The General offered to the angry President.

"Good, I'll chose to overlook this minor insurrection on your part then, sir. But if it happens again, you'll find yourself paddling your way to shore, along with your troops on a raft to Iran. Do you have anything more to add to this conversation at this point, General White?"

Secretary of State Hernandez made a motion with her hand, and it was instantly picked up by the President who turned to her and then offered kindly to her. "Do you have something to add to this conversation, Madam Secretary?"

"Yes, I'd like to address the General please, Albert. You'll forgive me for not standing sir." The Secretary of State replied as she tried to get comfortable trapped in her wheelchair.

"Please Maria, you didn't have to say that. You can address this meeting in any fashion you so choose." Vice President Mary Hirshfield offered while she covered Hernandez's hand with hers, embarrassed Maria made a comment about her affliction. Everyone in the President's Cabinet felt dreadful for Maria, struck with Multiple Sclerosis shortly after the President was elected to office, and she was asked to take the office of the Secretary of State. Over the last few months, everyone watched as her strength slowly left her body. Although she never allowed the crippling disease to hinder her in anything but walking. Lately, she began to have trouble breathing.

In a shaking voice, Hernandez snapped. "General White, since we began discussing this mission, I have allowed everyone to speak their mind as if your troops didn't matter to them, sir. I was extremely upset no one took the lives of these young soldiers of ours in consideration while speaking of the operation. It was the mission this, and the mission that, the warheads, the missiles and reactors, General White. Never once did I hear anyone stand up and say we have to do this or that to protect our soldiers, not until today that is, sir. General White, I'm very proud of you sir. As proud of you as I was of your friend, General Edward Campanelli, may God rest his soul."

"Amen to that Maria." The President added to his favorite person at the meeting.

Secretary Hernandez ignored his comment as she continued with her words. "General White, as long as I hear you worrying about your troops, I'll back you with every breath in my body. General, you know if you have me on your side, what you want, you'll get and I will see to that, no matter who I have to walk over, sir." The Secretary gave the General a quick wink of the eye.

President Cole smiled as he added to his military officer. "You heard the Boss Lady there, General White. If you have her on your side, you have me as wel..."

The conversation was interrupted by Admiral Richardson, the Secretary of the Navy, as he was ushered into the Oval Office by the White House Chief Aid, Walter.

"Admiral Richardson, take a seat and I'll try and bring you up to speed on what we're speaking about here sir. That's good Admiral, it has come to my attention the reason we plan to attack targets in Iran in separate actions, is because you're unable to get your supply ships in position to provide support when the ground forces attack. Is this true sir?"

Admiral Richardson shot a nasty glare at the General, feeling he went behind his back to gripe to the President he was having trouble supporting his mission. The President picked up the look and he added to the Naval Officer. "Admiral Richardson, there's no need to look at General White, sir! He's not asking you the question sir, I am, and I expect your answer to me, not the General. I'm waiting for your reply Admiral Richardson, sir."

"I'm sorry Mr. President, it's true as stated, sir. I'm having a number of problems with getting the Aircraft Carrier Washington to position before the ground forces launch the op..."

"What's the problem with the Washington, Admiral Richardson Sir?" the President demanded angrily as he held the Admiral in his harsh glare, waiting for him to reply to his question.

"With all due respect Mr. President, I have ordered the Washington from her station position in the Mediterranean to her homeport in Norfolk Virginia, for refit and replacement of three aircraft lost in the mountains over Yugoslavia, and to also rotate a number of her pilots for rest, Mr. President Sir. It's been hell since free elections took place in Yugoslavia, and they have overturned by that ass. I'm wasting valuable hardware in the hills trying to keep the Serbs off the Muslims' asses, sir. I can't wait until the Russians step in as they offered at the last meeting..."

"Admiral Richardson Sir, we understand life's a bitch, but I'm concerned with American lives about to enter Iran without the ability of having air support over them while they're carrying out my orders to destroy the wants of Iran to become a nuclear threat in the Middle East." The President pointed at his chest, and then went on. "I don't care what's happening in Yugoslavia. American troops, my troops need air support, and that's what they'll have, or I assure you Admiral Richardson, heads will roll. Admiral, I don't care how you do it but you will have air support in and around those troops before they step foot in Iran, or I'll expect your resignation before you leave my office, and I'll have you replaced by an Admiral who'll get the job done, sir." The President pointed his finger at the chest of the Admiral this time as if it was a weapon.

"Mr. President Sir, my Aircraft Carrier needs supplies. What the hell good will any Carrier Group do if my aircraft don't have the weapons needed to support the troops? It'd be a serious error to place my Aircraft Carrier Group in the Arabian Sea, if she doesn't have the means to protect herself, or the troops on the ground Mr. President Sir."

"It looks to me like you'll have to rearm and refit your Carrier while she's underway, Admiral Richardson. Do you have another Carrier Group you can substitute in the Washington's place, Admiral Richardson?" President Cole asked, trying to find a solution for the situation.

"No sir, the Washington was picked to be the FSG on this mission, sir."

"Err... excuse me sir, but I'm unfamiliar with the term FSG, Admiral Richardson." Secretary Griffin asked the Admiral, confused by the new term he just offered.

"Sorry Secretary Griffin Sir, the term FSG, or Floating Support Group, was given to the Aircraft Carrier Washington, because the Carrier was elected to be stationed on a twenty four hour active duty call to any trouble spot in the rest of the world, sir. She's the main ship on call as she has been for the past three years now, sir."

"This is exactly what I want from the Washington. She's to steam to the Arabian Sea to lend air support to our troops soon to be on the ground inside Iran sir. If that's what she was picked for then that's what she'll be. Admiral Richardson Sir, we wasted enough time on this god damn subject, sir. Can you supply the Washington while she's underway to her new post in the Arabian Sea, sir?" President Cole demanded while raising his voice a might as he stared at the Admiral who looked like he was trying to hide behind the Secretary of Defense.

"Yes Sir Mr. President, I suppose it can be accomplished, but it'll be a major undertaking I'm afraid, sir. The cost, I'd hate to add up what it'll cost to move the ships it'll need to accomplish this. Mr. President, everything I need is out of position, the fuelers are supplying other task forces. The munitions ships are supplying the other groups, and are miles away from the Washington. Sir, what you're asking couldn't have come at a worse time, I'm out of sync."

"Why is that Admiral Richardson?" Secretary of State Hernandez asked and then added. "I for one though you Navy people always supplied your Carrier Groups while at sea, sir."

"Normally we do Ma'am, but the Washington happens to be out of position of the resuppliers, that's why she was ordered to her homeport in the first place. I figured it'd be easier to order her to port, refit her, and order her to the Arabian Sea for support of the ground forces once she had her full complement of stores and weapon systems and ordinance, Ma'am."

"What Carrier Group's replacing the Washington's present station, Admiral Richardson?"

"The Lincoln Battle Group is moving to her old position, Ma'am." The Admiral replied to the disabled Secretary of State.

"Why not then just move the Lincoln over to the Arabian Sea if she's already fully supplied, and solve the problem that way, Admiral Richardson Sir?" Manning offered, giving his opinion of what was taking place before him.

"And leave the ground troops in Yugoslavia without any air support? That's impossible, plain crazy whoever the hell you are. That's out of the question, it's plain nuts. Who the hell's this damn civilian anyway, and why the hell is he sitting in on a military briefing for Pete's sake, Mr. President?" Admiral Richardson demanded.

"That's Mr. Manning, Admiral Richardson. My civilian advisor to the board sir."

"Mr. President, far be it for me to tell you what to do sir. But I suggest you get yourself another damn civilian advisor, before this one gets you in some serious trouble, Mr.

President." Admiral Richardson offered with more than a hit of anger lacing his tone of voice.

Most of the other members attending the meeting tried their best to hide their smirks enjoyed at Manning's expense, all but General White who openly laughed and then remarked out loud for all to hear. "Now that's the first thing I happen to agreed with all day. Admiral Richardson, I'm glad to have you on board with the rest of us, sir."

Even before Manning had a chance to protest the insult just leveled against him by the Naval Officer, the President warned. "I won't allow either of you two Officers to change the subject at the expense of Mr. Manning. Although his suggestion was ill thought out, it shows you there's always another solution at hand if you put your mind to it."

"If that's a solution to this situation sir. I might as well cancel the operation before it gets underway, Mr. President Sir." The angry General offered.

"I don't find anything very comical about this god damn situation we're discussing here, General White Sir. I suggest we get back to the issues at hand for this meeting and put personal feelings aside, people." The President hissed as he turned to face the Admiral.

Admiral Richardson shifted his weight nervous under the harsh glaze of the angry President as he replied to the Commander in Chief. "Mr. President Sir, as long as you're willing to absorb the cost of shifting any of my supply ships around, I'm sure I could have the Washington on station and refitted by the time she's needed to respond to any situation taking place n the ground, sir."

"Everything comes down to the god damn cost, doesn't it Admiral Richardson Sir? Allow me inform you of something, I'm a little tired of being forced to worry about money all the damn time whenever we have to engage in a military operation, sir. We have a world threatening situation rapidly developing on our hands in Iran. If war breaks out because we're sitting on our asses counting money then all the damn money in the world will mean shit, compared to the lives that'll be lost because we're so damn worried about money all the time, sir." The President growled as he moved away from the desk and began to pace behind it.

After walking for what he felt was a mile, the concerned President turned to Admiral Richardson and hissed at him. "Admiral, off the top of your head sir. How much would you save if you were to commit to action, say five days earlier, sir? I want you to figure in your head of course, the cost of moving these damn ships to intercept the Carrier Washington as she steams towards her new post. I want to know if it'd be feasible to move the ships around, or have the Washington port and supplied, and possibly put off the mission until she's able to sail again, sir."

General White huffed up while getting ready to complain about postponing the mission, but was immediately waved off by the President as he offered to his military officer. "General White Sir, I gave you the time to be heard, so I'd like to enjoy the same privilege before you going ballistic on me sir. I'll allow the Admiral time to do his numbers. Coffee?"

Everyone nodded yes, and the President hit the intercom. "Yes Mr. President?"

"Walter, rustle up coffee and maybe some cakes while you're at it? It looks like we're going to be here for a little while longer." The President asked and ordered at the same time.

"It's on the way to you as we speak sir. I was waiting for you to request some coffer for the member's sir, that's why I was keeping it hot sir." In moments, a cart was wheeled into the Oval Office and the members of the meeting descended on it, filling cups and taking their seat. Everyone except the Admiral who was working out the numbers the President requested from him. He did take a seat and was using a pencil and pad. When he finished, the Admiral said.

"Mr. President Sir, as near as I can figure, it'd be pretty much a wash what I'd save moving sooner, I'd spend by moving the supply ships around. I think it's a go, I'm sorry I overlooked this scenario sir." Admiral Richardson offered, embarrassed being called on the carpet, and then having to admit he overlooked something that would have made this operation run smoother.

"No need to apologize Admiral Richardson. It was only offered you today, sir. In this era of constant cut backs and penny pinching, it was very easy to overlook this solution, sir. I thank God we were able to work it out before our troops paid the price for our iffy war planning, sir. There'll be no repercussions offered against you or your staff, Admiral. The matter's closed as far as I'm concern, sir. How soon will the Carrier Group be set in position, Admiral? I believe the General plans to have his troops jump off Monday morning if I'm right. When General?"

General White replied. "Twenty One Hundred Hours Iranian time, November Ten. By Zero, Two, Thirty Hours, my troops should have the complex surrounded and collecting intelligence before commencing their attack against the complex at Zero, Four, Thirty Hours Monday, sir."

"General White please?" Griffin asked as he raised his hand, and stopped speaking. He began to stand and thought better of it, and took his seat while waiting for the President to respond.

President Cole turned to his Director and asked him. "Is this question important Norm?"

"Yes Sir Mr. President, I think it's very important sir."

"General White, it seems the Security Director has a question for you to answer for him and us, sir. Would you hear him out please and then answer his concerns, sir?"

General White turned to Director Griffin and smiled, and then he waited for the Security Director to ask his question.

Security Director Griffin began speaking the instant the Chairman of the Joint Chiefs of Staff looked at him. "General White Sir, I know we have gone over this stuff before sir, but would you mind refreshing my memory for me please? How long did you say our troops were to be on the target area while collecting this intelligence we have requested they assemble for us, sir?"

General White replied with a sort of snap in his tone of voice this time. "Director Griffin, I'll have boots on the ground on target until Zero, Six, Thirty Hours. That puts our troops on ground for two full hours, sir. I remind you sir this time schedule considers the operation running at its best possible speed. It doesn't take into account the many problems occurring..."

"Such as what General White?" This time it was the President who interrupted.

"Many things could go sour on any operation our troops were dispatched to. A vehicle crash, discovery of our troops before they reach target. When our troops engage the complex defenders, they could face heavier enemy troops stationed inside the complex than first estimated or discovered. The troops could also come under attack by enemy aircraft, we know the Iranian airforce routinely patrols the area in question we're concerned about. We're attacking this complex with only the damn Intel supplied by Director Raincloud's operati..."

"We're not relying on our satellite intelligence in this case, General?" the President added.

"Of course we're relying on satellite Intel, Mr. President Sir. But the damn satellites can't look inside the damn building, and these buildings could contain extra troops we're not aware of or not accounted for sir. There are other problems our troops could possibly face while they're on the ground, Mr. President. The troops could be forced into an extended military engagement, causing our troops to stay on target much longer than expected, and give the Iranians valuable time to reinforce their troops under attack by our ground forces. If everything went off perfectly, it doesn't mean our troops are out of the woods by any means, Mr. President Sir. Once their operation's completed, the troops are ordered to pull back, anything could happen on this troop withdrawal to create a threatening situation to develop against the troops at this point.

"During any troop pullback operation this is the most vulnerable time of the operation, while our troops are retreating from target. During engagement, retreating troops are placed in posture of a defending Army, and, open to many different forms of attacks made much easier against them by the exposure of their flanks to the enemy now pursuing them, sir. It places our troops more out in the open, and probes by trailing enemy forces could prove disastrous against our troops on the ground. If these scenarios takes place, time limits are off and amount of time and expense this operation could cost, will increase dramatically on us, Mr. President Sir.

"Then the question of whether or not we'll get our troops out of Iran alive, is up for grabs. This is why I have deemed it absolutely imperative to have a constant air cap over my troops at all times while on the ground. If the invading troops can't depend on this air support getting to them in seconds of requesting it, our troops might be learning to speak Iranian or worse. They can end up dead." General White allowed a slight smirk to cross his lips as he stared at the President.

"General White Sir, I believe we could've done without that touch of sarcasm at the end of your report, sir. That comment was uncalled for, it was a slab of meat thrown out for the benefit of my people. It served no purpose whatsoever to further this conversation along, and I resent those kind of tactics employed during any meeting I'm in command of. We got your message without you adding that crap. I told you your forces will have the air support they will need, sir."

General White bowed slightly towards the President as he flashed him a quick smile.

A slap of the President's hands startled everyone as the American Leader snapped. "Well gentlemen, ladies, it looks to me like we covered every base needing to be covered at this meeting. If there's no further questions from anyone here, I'd like to call this meeting to a conclusion. I'm quite certain no one's aware, but I'm expecting a call from Russian President Kvantrishuili today. Suddenly, it seems he wants to speak with me over what his damn Admiral Proushinsky transferred to the Iranians. Yes sir, there's nothing like finding out one of your military leaders sold you out behind your back, to make you want to call your friends. I'd hate like hell to know what's going on inside Russia at this time. You can bet the bank, it's not a very pleasant place to be, especially if you're a Military Officer in that country. Director Raincloud Sir, do you have your operatives working on this situation still going down inside Russia, sir?"

"Yes I do Mr. President Sir, I have activated fifteen sleepers in Russia, and I'll activate as many as needed to keep close tabs on Russia and what's going on there behind their curtain. I received word there's a major shakeup taking place in their military, and heads are rolling, sir. I was informed that Generals, Colonels, Captains and Majors are going through a number of rigorous background investigations, and anyone found to be harboring feelings towards the Communists, or the military overthrow, are removed from their troops immediately."

"I can bet the bank on that sir. Director Raincloud, I want to know everything occurring in Russia the moment it comes in your possession, sir. I'd like to know even before the Russians find out about it themselves, if it's at all possible that is sir." With this said, President Cole stood, his words made everyone at the meeting laugh as they prepared to leave the room.

MOSCOW, RUSSIA. FRIDAY, NOVEMBER THE 8th, 1998, ZERO SIX THIRTY HOURS THEIR TIME

Even though Russian President Vitaly Kvantrishuili was undergoing heart transplant surgery, and before the doctors began the operation on him, the gravely ailing Russian Leader was informed about Admiral Proushinsky's sale of missiles and nuclear warheads to Iran. As he was going under he ordered Chairman Zbigniew Angelyuk to gain control over the military at all costs. President Kvantrishuili informed Chairman Angelyuk he did not care what had to be done to gain this control over the military, and to maintain his Administration.

Chairman Angelyuk followed his orders to the letter. He had a number of his top ranking military officers swear a new oath of allegiance to Russia and the President. He was relentless in the search for any military officers and enlisted men with hidden agendas. The Russian Chairman ordered the powerful KGB Directorate to investigate all military officers, and any who did not make the grade, were immediately discharged and arrested and out to the swords. The purge began with the remaining Communists arrested, along with anyone who dared to state his or her beliefs, the Russian government was not living up to what was expected of it in Russia.

The feared KGB Playavick Detention Center constructed years ago within the walls of the Kremlin, was filled to capacity with prisoners, and the slaughter of them began. Hundreds, then thousands of military, politicians, civilians, and priests, paid the price with their lives for the slightest display of insubordination directed against the government. KGB Officers used this to settle old grudges with those who crossed them in the past, indiscriminately arresting them. Throughout all Russia, thousands of people met their death, and thousands of Russians streamed across the borders in their attempt to escape the murder being unleashed on the country. This caused serious problems with Russia's neighbors. Polish troops fired on the fleeing refugees, driving them back into Russia.

Chairman Angelyuk was contacted by President Cole, who demanded an explanation and was politely told to mind his own business. This prompted the American President to request a second emergency meeting of the Security Council, so as to discuss the new wave of slaughter currently taking place inside Russia. It was to be held two weeks from that Friday. There was nothing he could do to stop the slaughter of the innocent in Russia.

The next thing the acting Russian President did, was to close all the border crossings, to stop those he was searching for, from escaping his wrath. Russian border guards were doubled, and tanks were ordered to all checkpoints with China. Aircraft fields were placed on full alert. Military installations were boxed up with soldiers placed on alert. Troops in the field were ordered to protect themselves against attack from any Communist sympathizers.

Russian Officers who commanded control over nuclear missiles, submarines, and warships, found themselves sharing power with two and three other officers. Nuclear weapons, artillery, and bombs were ordered secured. Aircraft were stripped of their nuclear weapons, and stored in underground bunkers. All nuclear artillery rounds were removed from their unit's hands.

Russian plutonium processing plants throughout the country were next to feel the tightening of the security of Russia. They were shutdown while inventory of nuclear stockpiles were carried out. Weighing and categorizing stores of this substance was documented, with the plutonium turned over to the KGB Agents who took up residence at many of these nuclear sites. Word was sent out plant managers who came up light on plutonium inventory, would pay for this shortage with their lives. A detailed inventory of Russian tanks, artillery pieces, aircraft, machine guns and naval ships was ordered. Any military items found missing, the commander in charge of the base or installation was to pay the price with his life. All their nuclear reactor plants were ordered off line so inventors of the facilities could be taken.

Russian Naval Bases were taken over by KGB and GRU soldiers, blocking Russian Officers and ships from leaving port. Naval ships underway were boarded on oceans by handpicked Russian Blue Berets, Russia's elite Airborne forces, and the soldiers took command of the ships after they were sworn in. Tank commanders suffered the same fate as other KGB Officers sent out to the tank regiments, and the soldiers assumed command of Russia's war machines. Artillery Units were likewise taken under control of KGB troops. Ground forces were singled out the heaviest, with officers removed from commands and replaced by KGB Officers and known loyal Russian troops. For the first time since the days of Stalin's iron fisted rule, Russia found officers slaughtered at an alarming rate. The acting President sent two full Divisions of Black Berets to the border with Iran. Their orders were to kill anyone trying to enter or leave Russia without permission of the KGB.

Russia's politicians and Ambassadors were ordered to Russia to accept new orders. A number of these politicians and Ambassadors did not make the grade, and were never seen again. They were replaced with KGB Agents and officers whose loyalty was beyond question in Russia.

The acting Russian President turned his attention to the countless agents in the field, ordering them to return to Russia for examination. Thousands of agents streamed into Russia, with many giving up their cover to return. American Agents picking up the order, kept a close eye on all Russian airports, taking pictures of the undiscovered agents as they reported. Half the Russian deep cover agents and their sleepers were identified. This information was sent to America, where files were opened on many of the uncovered agents and their whereabouts monitored.

To live in Russia while the purge was sweeping across the expanse of the country was most unfortunate. Soldiers entered civilian homes in the middle of the night, carting off the occupants. Thousands of civilians were arrested and sent to Siberia without trial or explanation of their crimes, only to die a miserable death working in the frozen wasteland.

Once again, women of Russia cautiously walked around not daring to look up, or speak to anyone for fear of being arrested. Food stores were closed down and food supplies became a commodity, with Russian Leaders believing a hungry civilian, was one not to be feared. All forms of mass transit were shutdown. Tanks and armor vehicles replaced busses and trains in the streets of the Russian capital city of Moscow. Trusted and known to be loyal Russian soldiers lined the streets of major cities, arresting anyone who looked out of place.

The Russian police acted worse than their military did with carrying out orders, arresting civilians, beating, and in some cases, killing them in the streets of major cities of Russia. After the cities were secured, the police and military moved into the farmlands, arresting landowners for no reason, and confiscating crops and live stock.

Even the Russian Mafia was not spared in this purge of Russia, with hundreds of lesser criminals arrested. What was once sacred grounds for the Russian Mafia, was suddenly invaded by hordes of loyal KGB troops, arresting certain individuals and confiscating hundreds of millions of dollars worth of drugs and cash, and other black market items. Criminals once free of any arrest and thought to be untouchable, found themselves being loaded into wagons and then carted away with the common and poor people of Russia.

Heavy fire fights broke out between the police, military and the criminals, erupting in open warfare in the streets of many major cities of Russia. Moscow was witnessing many mini wars breaking out. Weapons fire chattered away all night just about every night, as the Russian police tried to regain control of the streets of the city. In some cases, lightweight military tanks were pressed in battle against the Russian Mafia, and when these tanks and armor vehicles came under rocket fire, they were immediately replaced by the heavy main battle tanks, the T-72 and T-80 pressed in battles raging in many cities of Russia.

CHAPTER SIXTEEN

**CAMP LEJEUNE, NORTH CAROLINA.
NOVEMBER 9th, 1998.
ZERO SIX THIRTY HOURS**

It was the first day of classes to prepare the specialized troops of the Special Forces Rapid Response Forces for their invasion of Iran. Colonel Leadbetter woke Doctor Russbinder who was sharing quarters with the Colonel. The doctor did not want any part of waking this early, and when the Colonel threatened to dump him out of the rack, he reluctantly got up.

Colonel Leadbetter enjoyed the privilege of hand picking the replacements for his force from other elite forces, Green Berets, Delta Force One, Navy SEAL Team Six and Army Rangers. Since his Unit was placed under the control of the Joint Special Operations Command, Colonel Leadbetter was concerned his once unlimited reins were about to be pulled in. The JSOC was breathing down the back of his neck, and he did not know what changes would soon be installed against his troops. He heard some scuttlebutt about forming a HRT, or Hostage Rescue Team, much like the FBI's famed unit, and he knew this was only the beginning of changes coming at him. The troubled Colonel's thoughts were interrupted by the civilian doctor when he asked.

"What are we going to do today, Colonel Leadbetter Sir?"

Colonel Leadbetter was having a field day calling the doctor 'Herr' when speaking to him. "Well Herr Doctor, first we're going to find out how good a physical shape you're really in, sir. We'll hit the obstacle course to wake us up and then we'll eat, and then hit class rooms. We'll do everything to brief the troops on the current conditions existing in Iran, and what they're to expect during this operation sir. We'll be brought up to date on the latest Intel of the area, and then eat lunch. After that Herr Doctor, we'll do some light work, pick out the Squads who'll be responsible for the security on the mission, and then locate the routes the enemy troops might use against us to try and reinforce or evacuate the god damn complex we're after, sir.

"We'll mine the shit outta the roads. Doc, we have a shitload of work to accomplish, and little time to accomplish it in. So you better hang tight and pay close attention to all my orders, or you'll be shit outta luck. A word of warning to your ass Doctor Russbinder. If you don't hear my first order then you better be able to read my fucking mind, because I never repeated an order a second time, sir. You miss the fucking boat, you'll find your ass swimming to Iran, or back to the United States. Sorry Doc for being such a hard nose about it shit sir, but you have to understand the position you're in. I can't possibly jeopardize the entire mission for one man, even if that man's the President's stinking pet. Between you and me sir, we'll be spending a helluva lot of time together, and I want you to explain to me exactly what the fuck you're looking for on this mission. This way, if something happens to you, I'll carry out your part of the mission."

"You think we'll be in that much danger on this mission, Colonel Leadbetter Sir?"

"More than you might imagined my fine feathered friend." The Colonel warned him.

"In that case sir, perhaps I better explain what my part of the mission is, so that you..."

"That has to be placed on the back burner for the time being, until I get my people's asses in gear, then we'll talk a little further about what you just brought up to my attention." Colonel Leadbetter offered as he held up his hand and started for his outer office. As he dropped down in his chair his phone rang. "What now dammit!" he griped as he picked it up.

"Colonel Leadbetter?" the voice on the other end of the phone asked him.

"Yeah, who's this?" he fired back, not knowing who he was speaking to.

"General White. Colonel Leadbetter, things changed a might for the damn mission sir."

"Kind of a little late in the damn game to start changing the puzzle pieces on me for this damn operation, sir." Colonel Leadbetter snapped at his commanding officer.

"Can the god damn ha ha's off and pay close attention to my next orders, mister! Things changed for the better this time, sir. Colonel, instead of your people being the brunt of this god damn operation, we're now combining the operation with all military assets involved in the damn thing, sir. All attacks will be carried off at the same time during this upcoming operation. I also have a commitment from the President stating we'll have an active air cap over our troops..."

"I thought we couldn't combine the attacks because the damn Carriers couldn't make it to their assigned position in time to engage the enemy forces before we go active against them, General White?" Colonel Leadbetter moaned, happy he was going to be involved in a major operation, instead of a covert deal like his past actions were.

"Stop fucking interrupting me or I'll step on your damn tongue and grind it into the dirt mister. I order you to pay attention with your ears and not your damn mouth, Colonel Leadbetter. As it stands now, the President ordered the Carrier Washington to be refitted while still at sea. This enables her to make her standoff position later on today, and be ready to engage enemy positions and targets by Sunday night, or early Monday, the time you're scheduled to jump off. This is good because if you get jammed up and need air support, you'll have it within five minutes of requesting it, sir. I'm going to give you a constant air cap overhead, so you'll have air support a helluva lot sooner. We'll pound the living shit out of the Iranian submarine docks at... whatever the fucking place is on the Gulf of Oman in the Arabian Sea..."

"Bander Beheshi I believe it is General White Sir?" Colonel Leadbetter offered, daring to correct the powerful General.

"Fuck you Colonel Leadbetter, if you know the damn place, why show off. That is it, we're going after the old submarine dump at the Iranian port of Bander-e-Abbas. We're making a clean sweep of this damn place, Colonel. We're including the three nuclear reactors supplied to the Iranians by the Russians the Persians had converted over to breeder reactors for the production of weapons grade plutonium. We'll hit them with the modified GUB-15 two thousand pound bomb with ground penetrating warhead capabilities. The X-111 Blue Light, the Naval version of the Stealth Fighter will be the delivery system for the penetrating bombs on this mission.

"Colonel Leadbetter, we picked out the Navy version to open this attack, because it has better stealth qualities for day time applications, sir. This GUB bomb was chosen as the workhorse for this entire operation, because it's a powerful explosion going off twenty feet under the damn building, and will collapse the containment building in on itself. We hope the rubble and debris of the building will keep the radiation leakage down to a absolute minimum, until the Iranians have a chance cement over the damn things and seal them up forever."

"Do you think the Iranians will take time to cover the destroyed reactor with an ocean of cement, General White Sir? From what I know of them people, they don't seem to give a flying shit about anything but going to Paradise to be with their seventy two virgins, and taking a few of us along with them while they're at it sir."

"Ahhh... if these pain in the ass camel jockies fuck with us this time around, there's going to be a bus load of them heading for Paradise none stop, sir. I'm not screwing around with the damn Persians, once we commence our action anything goes for the success of the mission, Colonel. Even if I have to commit every aircraft the Washington has on her flight decks. I'm moving the Destroyer USS Sullivans to the strike zone, she'll escort the three Missile Cruisers Long Beach, Mississippi and Texas. I'm backing up the Sullivans with the Destroyers Laboon and Chandler. Three Missile Frigates will be involved in this operation as well Colonel Leadbetter Sir. The Ingraham, Samuel B. Roberts and Vandegrift will be available for operations. Shit, I forgot to add two other ships I'm placing in this damn circus. I'm committing the Aegis Guided Missile Cruiser Port Royal, and she'll escort the Heavy Load Arsenal Ship." General White paused.

"Christ sir, you have me by the short hairs on two of these ships, General White Sir. I never heard of an arsenal ship, and this other ship the Sullivans, I think you said it was sir."

"I didn't think you would know of these two ships, Colonel. This is the first action for the arsenal ship, which contains four hundred vertical launched missiles. Some will support your ground forces, while other missiles will intercept any enemy aircraft. Other missiles from this platform are scheduled for the Carrier Battle Groups protection. It's a helluva thing to see in operation, Colonel. This arsenal ship has another four hundred missiles stored on board for instant reload of their weapon system. I didn't think you'd know about the Sullivans either, this ship was commissioned let me see, err... it was quite a while ago. Ahhh... here it is Colonel Leadbetter, she was commissioned on April 19th, 1997, she's an Arleigh Burke Class Nuclear Powered Destroyer out of Bath. She was commissioned to commemorate the five young Sullivan kids from Waterloo, Iowa, killed when the USS Juneau was sank off the coast of

Guadalcanal in the Naval exchange with the Japs during World War Two, sir."

"I remember hearing something about the five brothers, some shame huh sir? It's about time the Navy's honoring those poor kids." Colonel Leadbetter retorted hotly.

"You're a little off base here, Colonel Leadbetter. This is the second ship to be launched to honor these five kids. Colonel, the reason I'm committing so many missile platforms to this operation. Is because we're aware of the amounts of swift, small raiding water crafts Iran controls, and we believe once our operation begins, the Iranians will flood the civilian shipping lanes with these small power boats armed with rocket launchers and heavy machine guns. I'm not taking anything for granted on this damn mission, sir. If the President's allowing me to employ what I need for this mission then that's what I'm doing. I'll not leave any swinging dicks caught out in the fucking breeze. I want you guys in and out of there before the first Iranian wakes from his damn sleep. You got it Colonel Leadbetter Sir?"

"Yes Sir General White." Colonel Leadbetter replied confidently over the phone.

"Fine, oh, by the way sir. How do you like the little package I sent you Colonel?"

"You mean Doc Russbinder, General White? Yeah, he's a piece of art. Thanks for weighing me down with his ass, General White." The Colonel complained at his commanding officer.

"Never mind the smart remarks about the damn civilian puke, Colonel Leadbetter. Make damn certain you don't allow anything to happen to him, or it'll be your ass swinging from the fucking mast, and I'll be taking pot shots at it with my bee bee gun all day long, Colonel. The President likes this Doctor, and has plans for the civilian turd in the future, so don't leave him behind if you can help it, sir. What do you have in store for your troops until they finally ship out, sir? What's the security like with the damn troops, sir?"

"General White, I closed down the entire base until further notice. No one outside our world knows the troops are even on the base, and the few who do are restricted to base until our mission's completed, sir. I cut off the troops from all telephone and cell phones, and letters they write I'm having delayed until the soldiers return to base, General White. When the soldiers were ordered to report to base, I sent instruction this was a Zip Lip operation, and all actions were to be carried out as if there were spies hiding behind every damn tree, sir. I also ordered any letters sent out to my people, are to be delivered to their homes like nothing was the matter. We can't be held responsible if these soldiers are too busy to return letters or phone calls, sir.

"General White, I further notified the motor vehicle departments to hold any notifying these troopers if their licensees or plates come due while they're on this operation. I made it seem as if these people have suddenly disappeared from the face of the earth, in a pleasant way mind you sir. So as not to draw any special attention towards them from the always nose ass fucking news reporters hanging around the base and bars our soldiers use for their relaxation." Leadbetter stopped speaking to allow the General a chance to ask questions, when none came he continue.

"General White Sir, I also plan to fill the remaining hours, by having my troops attend classes on the makeup of Iran's deserts, and location of targets. Because we're restricted from running attacks on a structure, we ran a number of computer enhanced attacks on said targets. These computer workups are as real to life as we can possibly make them sir, and are designed to cover every possible problem that might arise when we jump off on target, sir.

"We have designated every route to be used by enemy reinforcements, we marked off machine gun embrasures and anti aircraft defenses, along with locations of military troops on the Iranian site for defense purposes. I feel we have covered about every possible aspect of the attack, and I'll pound these scenarios in the soldier's heads until they can run through what's expected of them in their damn sleep. I wish we had a chance to rehearse a number of real life attack scenarios against a solid structure though, General White Sir. I'm not very fond of jumping off on a mission without rehearsing the attack a few hundred times..."

"Yes Colonel Leadbetter, I understand the ideal way to train in the special operations world, is to hit a real structure. But we don't live in an ideal world now do we sir?" General White interrupted angrily.

"No way General White." Colonel Leadbetter grumbled at his commanding officer.

"You better watch your god damn tone of voice when speaking with me, Colonel Leadbetter! Or you just might find yourself remaining in Iran for the rest of your fucking life, mister. Continue with your damn report to me Colonel. What else are you doing with the damn troops while retaining them on base, Colonel?" General White barked into the phone.

"General White Sir, I'm having the troopers work out on the obstacle course, to help build up their stamina and hone them to a razor sharpness sir. Then I'll allow them to eat some..."

"Everything they want to eat, feed them well for this damn operation, Colonel Leadbetter. I remember you're quite fond of making the soldiers carry out their duties with the minimum of food and water to make better soldiers of them. I don't think this kind of training regiment will give a positive reaction, judging by the lack of time we have to prepare the troops for the damn mission, sir. I don't want any of the troops exhausted or rundown because of a fucking lack of food and water, and too much work on the preparation fields, Colonel."

"Understood perfectly General White Sir. I assure you sir, the troops will eat all they want and need, sir. I had planned to cut back on their food, but since this order you just issued me, I'll change my mind on those thoughts, General White. I believe a soldier operating on an empty belly, operates quicker than a soldier stuffed to the damn gills, sir."

"I'm well aware of your shitty ass attitude when it comes down to the training of your troops, mister. But I gave you my opinion of how I feel they should be treated for this damn operation, sir. I hope to hell I have made you understand my orders clearly, Colonel Leadbetter Sir?"

"Perfectly understood General White Sir. The troops will have access to the mess twenty four hours a day until we shove off on the mission, sir."

"Excellent Colonel Leadbetter, what about my damn Doctor friend I gave you sir?"

"I have him smack fucking dab in the middle of the troops and their training, General White."

The Chairman of the Joint Chiefs of Staff laughed as he groused at his military officer. "Jesus Christ Colonel Leadbetter sir, I don't believe you have him digging on the obstacle course with your screaming squirrels. The bastard's a damn Doctor, not a soldier. How's he holding up?"

"Better than first expected General White Sir. He's in surprisingly good physical condition for a stinking civilian puke, and I feel he might just be able to keep up with my troops for a while, before we have to start carrying his ass around like a stinking pussy he is, General." Colonel Leadbetter replied with a smirk and a trace of sarcasm in his tone.

"I don't know about you Colonel, I'm not very pleased about having the civilian training with your pack of screaming squirrels. Hell, half of them animals aren't even civilized or house broke. I don't want the damn Doctor coming back complaining to the Boss your people treated him like dirt. I'm not comfortable with this move now I think about it a bit further, Colonel. I'd rather have him sequestered from your rift raft horde than holding hands with them damn soldiers of yours, sir." General White let out his breath in a hiss as he waited for a reply from the Colonel.

"Sorry General White, but I'm forced to disagree with you on this one, sir." The Colonel replied while trying to hide the enjoyment he was having over this civilian doctor.

"Hmmm... zat so, and why is this Colonel?" The surprised General asked.

"General White, I'm a firm believer if anyone's going on a mission, that bastard better be ready to do whatever it takes to make the operation a success for the soldiers. Even if it means picking himself up a god damn weapon and fighting like his fucking life depends on it. Because it usually does General White Sir. I know the Doctor's a damn civilian, and a personal friend of the President, and he appointed this man to this mission, and all the other crap that goes along with it, sir. But if the Doc's coming on this operation with my troops. He better be damn well prepared to eat the same shit my troops do, or he's not going to make it sir."

"Hmmm... I see your position Colonel. But I'm still rather uncomfortable with the way you're treating the lousy turd though, sir. I don't need the Boss coming down on my neck, because you returned his friend covered with bumps and bruises, and smelling like dog shit, Colonel."

"General White, I'll make it a helluva little easier for you sir. You can blame it all on me, sir. Tell the President you were unaware I forced his friend to go through the same training with my soldiers. I don't give a rat's ass what happens to me after the ops completed. I'm only interested in its success, the rest of the crap can go to hell in a handbag, General. I can promise you one thing though General, by the time I'm done with this civilian puke, his friends won't recognize the Doc, because he'll be able to eat his own shit, and ask for more while fighting. His wife or girlfriend or whatever, will be pleased with the Doc's born again attitude, because of the many different ways he'll discover in the art of making his woman squirm under his dick and tongue. His colleagues will be rather surprised at how strong and willing to work the lousy little puke will be, once I return him to the real world and the rest of his egghead friends, sir."

"Hmmm... this is exactly what I'm afraid of, sir. Colonel, I don't need this pissant returned to the States as angry as the rest of your animals always are. I can't afford to have him go up to the President's office, drop his damn drawers and take a dump in the middle of the Oval Office. Then try to sexually assault some stuffed up bitch secretary in the White House. Do I make myself perfectly clear on my position concerning the damn Doctor, Colonel Leadbetter?"

"Crystal clear General White Sir, I don't believe the good Doctor will be returned in that bad a condition. But of course General White, I don't offer any guarantee's with the package when he's returned to the States. If you want guarantees, you better deal with Sears." Colonel Leadbetter laughed into the phone, and he was joined by the General, pleased the Colonel included the doctor in on the training with the troops. It was necessary, but he was not going to be the one to order it done as he added. "Colonel Leadbetter, you have convinced me of your wisdom over including the Doctor's ass in your training, sir. What else are you doing with the bastard?"

"Well sir, we're going over the reason for his coming along on the mission, General. He's going to clue me in on all he's looking for, help me identify what we need to be removed from the damn Iranian complex in the way as evidence, before we erase the complex from the face of the earth. I'll be spending every moment with the civilian until I know everything that has to be removed from the complex, General White." The Colonel informed the General confidently.

"Excellent Colonel Leadbetter, I completely agree with your plan you put forth, sir. It's out fucking standing, how did you ever get the damn pain in the ass Doctor to agree to disclose his targets with you, sir? I thought he'd be closed lip about his part of the damn mission, to sort of keep himself that important a cog to the mission. Colonel, I was concerned about the mission's outcome if anything happen to him. The President's depending on the information he might accumulate for us, sir. I know the Boss is planning to shove these papers down the throats of the damn Russians, if he finds what we're looking for at the complex, sir."

A sigh, and then the General continued with his words. "Colonel Leadbetter, I can't tell you how relieved I am you'll know what's to be removed from the damn complex. Outstanding work on your part with getting the Doctor to disclose his efforts to you. I would've taken it to the grave with me, to make sure you people protected my ass as well as you people can. I know he understands he's the main cog in this operation." General White moaned at the military officer.

"It was easy to accomplish General White Sir, all I did was ask the dopey bastard what he was after, and he informed me of every item he was in search of at the Iranian site, sir." Colonel Leadbetter replied, forcing himself to sound humble as he grinned to himself.

"You just asked him about it, huh mister? I can't believe it Colonel! Doesn't the dumb ass know he has just removed his importance to the damn mission, sir. He's now a package of dead fucking weight you can dump his ass off at any port you choose, and then continue on with the operation without him, the stupid asshole he is."

"Begging the General's pardon, is the General suggesting that I be so foolish as to dump the pain in the ass Doctor off at the next port of call, and then return the mission back to an all military action as it should be from the start, sir?" The Colonel offered, hoping he was hearing the silent order being offered to him by General White over the phone.

"I'm suggesting no such thing to your ass, Colonel Leadbetter Sir. But I happen to be in possession of the knowledge that the President was concerned with the health of the good Doctor while he was on this military operation, and he was considering whether or not to allow the civilian puke to accompany your troops on the mission, sir. I don't think the Boss would be too upset if the damn Doctor happened to miss the last plane out, and was somehow left behind. Remember Colonel Leadbetter, I'm not suggesting you make this happen sir. On the contrary, I'd have to take action against you for not ensuring he was on the plane along with the rest of your troops, sir. Hell, I don't know what form of action my anger would take, but a military action is more desirable than a mixed hazard, sir. Do you read me Colonel Leadbetter Sir?"

"Loud and clear General White Sir." Colonel Leadbetter snapped, knowing the General just gave him permission to dump the civilian doctor from the operation.

"Fine sir, I'll leave this mess in your capable hands then, Colonel. I'll handle the Boss from my side if he gets pissed off by any action you might take. Colonel, I'll remember this, and when I need an Officer in position, your name will be included in the batch. You'll be forced to eat some serious shit on this operation, but I'll make it up to you one way or the other. Well Colonel Leadbetter Sir, get back to your damn troops, sir. Good luck on this one Colonel. Although I'll not be with you, you know my heart will be there with you and the rest of your troops, sir."

"Thank you General White Sir." Colonel Leadbetter replied, he was pleased he now had the General's unspoken permission to dump the civilian doctor out of the operation, once he understood everything the civilian doctor was supposed to remove from the Iranian complex in the way of evidence for the President. The Marine Colonel dropped the receiver back in its cradle, he was deeply relieved but his happiness left quickly when his eyes picked up the doctor standing in the doorway, and he was not looking very pleased with him. The doctor was glaring at him, with his fists balled up and his shoulders hunched over to the point it looked like the doctor was going to actually attack the military officer sitting in his chair.

"It looks like you overheard a conversation you shouldn't have, Herr Doctor."

The doctor did not move a muscle as he continued to stare at Colonel Leadbetter.

"What? What's your fucking problem, mister? What, the fucking cat's got your damn tongue, buster." Colonel Leadbetter growled at the fuming civilian doctor.

Again there was no reaction from the doctor as he continued to glare at him.

"I guess you heard my god damn conversation with the General, you sneaky little pud you. Didn't your mother ever tell you it was most impolite to eavesdrop on someone else's fucking conversation, Herr Doctor? I'm stunned at your lack of consideration you're displaying before my ass, mister. Look, what the hell did you expect, this is a military operation, and there's no room for a fucking pussy ass civilian puke on board the mission." The Colonel smirked at the fuming civilian as he continued to stare at him while he was standing in his doorway.

Still no reaction came from the doctor who continued to stare at the Colonel.

The Colonel was fast becoming upset with the stance Doctor Russbinder was assuming against him as he actually growled at the doctor this time. "Herr Doctor, back the fuck off me for your own damn good, mister. You wouldn't stand a ghost of a fucking chance against me in a hand to hand fun. I'd snap you in half like a twig, and then I'll use your punk ass desk sitting body for a set of fricking oars for my damn boat, buster. What the fuck did you expect Herr Doctor? Loyalty? I thought you were much smarter than that, mister. Don't be a god damn fool Doc, and stop looking at me as if I just took your fucking toys away from you. This is a military operation from start to finish, with the god damn lives of my troopers at stake, and the last thing I needed to drag along with me on this operation, is some civilian desk jockey puke of a shit like you buddy.

"Doctor Russbinder, what I'm doing is for your own fucking good, mister. You don't need to come along on this damn mission, putting your stinking ass on the line like Rambo, think about it Doctor. Think of the shit you'll suffer through if you come along on this trip with my soldiers. Use your head for something other than a damn hat rack, and tell me all I need to know about whatever you're after in the damn complex, to enable me to carry out your part of the mission for your ass, mister. If you want, you can even stay on base, and I'll tell everyone you came on the mission and have carried out your part of it to a tee. No one needs to know any different Doc."

The doctor continued to glare angrily at the smug looking Colonel Leadbetter, who just sat back in his chair, and then he locked his fingers together and smiled at the rather upset looking doctor. One thing Doctor Russbinder understood, he did not have a prayer in the world of attacking the Colonel physically, although it was his driving force. He was so angry at Colonel Leadbetter that he had not heard most of his words.

The Colonel's patience was ebbing rapidly on him as he moved up in his chair, and then stood. He leaned forward as he rested his hands flat on his desk and bitched at the still angry looking civilian. "Hey Doc, I don't have the fucking time or patience for this pussy ass crap you're trying to shovel in my damn face, mister. I have to prepare my specialized troops for a damn mission. I believe you don't understand your position on this one mister. One thing you have to understand about me Doc, I'd stick my damn dick in a fucking grinder if I thought it'd guarantee the success of my mission, and the safety of my god damn troops at the same time, sir.

"If sticking my dick in a blender would make this mission a military one and a success, that's what I'll do, sir. I don't give a rat's ass about your stinking feelings in the least Doc, and I care even less about the President's feeling about this damn operation sir. He might've had a good reason for sending your ass along on this vacation of ours. But he's not here, so his orders are subject to change under my interpretation and need sir. All I know and understand, is I have a shitload of soldiers about to stick their necks on the chopping block, and I don't need a god damn civilian puke coming along and endangering my people more than they have to be, buster. So get the fuck out of my face before I eat you up and shit ya out later, sir."

The Colonel looked at the doctor's fists balled up, and when the civilian did not back off any against him, he growled savagely at the civilian. "Look Doctor, you find yourself stuck between the shit and the sweat on this one, sir. Either use those punk ass fists of yours, or back the fuck off and think before you try anything stupid here, Herr Doc." Colonel Leadbetter suddenly shoved away from the desk, and then took a threatening stance against the angry civilian doctor.

For several seconds, they were locked in a stare down, but it was the doctor who blinked first and unclenched his fists, and then relaxed his shoulders while casting his eyes to the floor.

"That was very wise on your part Herr Doc. You just saved yourself from finding out how good your damn government supplied hospitalization coverage is. Now Doc, if you wouldn't mind sir, I'd really appreciate you showing me everything you're after in the Persian complex we're about to go active against, sir." He waved his hand out before him to the sea of blueprint covering his desk depicting what the government believed was the makeup of the interior of the complex in question. The Colonel had the papers spread out on his desk, waiting for his help.

Doctor Russbinder folded his arms across his chest and snarled angrily at the military officer. "Colonel Leadbetter, you can go fuck yourself, sir. If you want to know what I'm supposed to look for inside the complex. I suggest you take a nuclear defense course and learn about what we need from this complex, sir. I have no intention of helping you one iota at this time sir. Need I remind you Colonel Leadbetter, I was appointed by the President to accompany you on this mission for a specific reason, sir. You, nor any soldier in this world will stop me from carrying out my responsibilities. The only Man who can stop me, is the Man who has appointed me. If you don't want me to accompany your troops on this mission then I suggest you place a call to the President, and explain your feelings to him. If he agrees with your suggestions and orders me, I'd be pleased to explain what you need to look for inside complex, Colonel Leadbetter."

"Don't be a horses ass here will you please Herr Doc. You're raising fricking demons here that shouldn't be alive in the first place, sir. Do the right thing and cue me in on what you were sent on this operation for, and my people will do the rest for you and you can remain behind safe and sound, sir. I don't have the damn time for any of this dancing around, sir. I'm not running a fucking democracy around here fella, chuck full of free thinking Squids, Herr Doctor."

"Colonel Leadbetter, I'm quite certain the President would be extremely interested in knowing how you feel about how you interpret his direct orders, sir. I thought you were under his command Colonel? I never realized Military Officers could change the President's orders to suit their own interests and needs. Colonel Leadbetter, if you'd care to dial the phone for me, I'd like to speak to the Man and see if I follow his orders, or yours mister."

"Huh, you're going to be a real fucking pain in the ass all the way, huh Herr Doctor?"

"Colonel Leadbetter, I don't know who the devil you were speaking to on the phone moments ago, but I plan to go along on this mission as I was ordered. Unless I'm ordered to do otherwise by the Man who has appointed me to go. I didn't travel here to be placed in a damn closet while someone else carries out my duties for me sir. Colonel, I happen to still agree with you knowing my part of this operation sir. God forbid something happen to me, someone else has to carry out my part of the mission. But I'll not back off my orders. Unlike you, I follow my orders from the President. So if you'd be so kind as to dial the phone for me, so I may speak to President Cole. So I can find out if I'm still an active member of this operation or not, Colonel Leadbetter Sir."

The military officer stared at the doctor for a long moment, and then he let out his breath as he plopped down in his chair. Without looking up he snapped at the civilian doctor. "Christ Almighty, you have a pair of fucking balls the size of your god damn head, Doc. If you decide to leave your profession, I'd welcome you aboard as a brother in the Marine Corps, sir."

"I take it you have changed your mind about leaving me behind, and I'm coming along on this mission as I was ordered to do by the President of the United States, Colonel Leadbetter?"

"Yeah, you win this round in the game I guess, Herr Doctor. You're still a fucking member of the mission, Doc. Judas Priest, I never met someone so crazy ass to die, sir. Specially one who only knows what the back of a desk looks like. You have a death wish, don't you Doc?"

"Not really Colonel Leadbetter, but I plan to follow my orders or die trying sir."

"Ahhh... spoken like a true gun ho Marine, Doc. Well Doc., I know I never said this to your punk ass before, but welcome aboard Doc. Now, what say we go over to the obstacle course and see if your body's as daring as your stinking mouth is, sir. Then we'll have something to eat and you can go over some of what you're after at this god damn complex with me, sir." Colonel Leadbetter smirked as he stood. Looking back, he offered. "You coming with?"

"You can bet your life on it Colonel Leadbetter." The doctor grumbled at the Colonel.

"Balls, and balls is enough to make a fucking soldier, Herr Doctor. Follow me sir."

OBSTACLE COURSE THREE, CAMP LEJEUNE. ZERO SEVEN TEN HOURS

The troops were quick marched over to the obstacle course, and were preparing to make their first run at it. Lieutenant Robert Walker stood by the side of the Mutt, Mother Flanagan, Casper, Sun Tan and Sergeant Ramirez. The Mutt Lieutenant frank Hall leaned over and mumbled at him. "Hey Walker, I feel like getting a little buzzed tonight man."

"Bullshit dog man, every time you get buzzed, you end up hitting someone and I haft end up dragging your limp ass away from the fight, or finish it for ya, Homes." Walker shot back.

"Alright, so I feel like hitting someone then Homes." The Mutt retorted with a grin at Walker.

"You'll have your chance soon enuf, man. It looks like they're going to put us through the stinking ringer on this one, Mutt. I never saw so much fucking sand shoveled around the course. I didn't know there was this much sand in the Carolina's, and it feels like it's a hundred and fifty degrees." Walker replied to his friend as he looked over the obstacle course.

"It looks like a desert to my ass Homes." Casper complained at Walker.

"Looks like the tent pegs are trying to get us used to the desert. Look at those heat lamps." Ramirez added as she pointed to the three towers with the blinding lamps pointed at the sand.

"Well, we knew this wasn't gonna be a fucking cake walk operation." Walker snapped as he wiped his face with his sleeve and then he added. "I sure hope we don't hafta wear our stinking body armor for the training crap, we'll die in that crap with this heat."

"Look over there, who's the new bitch to the group, man? I never saw her ass before, she looks hot enough to eat, man." Mother Flanagan asked as he pointed to a new recruit with his chin.

"Hey dummy, that's Sergeant Regina Raphael, she's on loan to our group from the Groupment D'Intervention de la Gendarmerie Nationale. That's the outstanding French Hostage Unit, she got in earlier this morning. I don't know much about her, but I hear she dates, man." The grinning Lieutenant replied as the other soldiers stared at the latest new member to their unit.

"I know something bout her, Homes. I went over her fitrep (fitness report) a few days ago, but I didn't know she was reporting so soon to the Unit, man." The Mutt offered to the others.

All eyes went to the mixed breed. "Whatdaya know about her buddy? Give it up to us man."

"Don't let your dick do your stinking thinking for you, Mutt." Sergeant Ramirez warned. "You know you're no longer a free agent, mister. Barb will skin your ass alive if she ever finds out you fooling around on her, stupid."

"Looks like Walker can no longer come out and play with the boys either." Sun Tan smirked.

"Oh, he can come out and play all he wants, as long as he takes me along with him, and if he wants to screw around with another woman, he has to allow me to hump anyone I want to play with, or let me join them." Ramirez purred sexily as she reached out and grabbed Walker by the balls and announced to the other soldiers with her. "These here babies are all mine, big boy."

The group roared with laughter as Mother Flanagan Sergeant Richard Flanagan repeated. "Hey dog man, what's the scoop with her ass, whaddaya know about the bitch, huh Homes?"

"I heard she's been out on so many blind dates, the national blind dog handlers of the United States have given her a free seeing eye blind dog..."

"Who'd want a blind fucking dog fur? What the hell can you do with it, drag it around man?" Buckethead asked as he walked up to the group, and caught the tail end of the conversation.

"Are you that fucking stupid Homes?" Casper growled as he punched him in the arm.

"Hey man, he musta smoked too much blunt. You know what that shit does to your head, makes it disappear on ya." Sun Tan offered with a laugh.

McNip and Jungle Bunny joined the group of soldiers as they were dumping on Buckethead.

"By the way people, drugs are out from this point on. Once we finish the mission, who cares, but for now any turds caught fucking around with anything stronger than stinking pot is gonna be shit by the time I get through with ya fucking ass. Grass, okay, cocaine is your death warrant as always, people." Lieutenant Walker growled as he stared at right at Buckethead, Sergeant Vincent Lambardo trying to figure out if the big man was screwing with him or not.

A pair of duce and a half trucks pulled up, and the soldiers inside dumped a number of crates on the ground. Walker saw the marking and knew it was their body armor and immediately ordered the rest of the troops. "Okay people, it looks like this is a full gear session, suit up before the stinking Colonel arrives, and he tries to eat us alive for not being ready to attack the course. Mutt, see to it everyone gets in their outfits PDQ. I wanna be ready when Leadbetter gets here."

The Mutt handed out the Kevlar body armor to the troops as they stood in line to receive them. As they finished dressing, Walker saw an open humvee heading right for them and he called out to the other soldiers. "Okay people look alive, looks like Colonel Leadbetter's on his way."

Colonel Leadbetter's jeep pull up in front of the forming troops. He was out of the jeep before it stopped and was already yelling at his Lieutenant. "Walker! What the hell's this shit, mister? How the hell come you don't have your fucking screaming squirrels out on the fricking field? What the hell do you think you're here for, to take up space and eat taxpayer's food? How come no one's sweating their damn guts out? How come everyone's standing here like they're waiting for a cab to take them to happy whore's fun crib, and how come you're not kicking the assholes in their tails to get them moving? Where the hell's Captain Wilson and Colonel Salsiccia at?"

"Captain Wilson, Colonel Salsiccia, front and center." Walker bellowed at the two officers.

The two officers rushed to the lead of the assembly, and they saluted Colonel Leadbetter standing with his hands on his hips, and he bitch at them. "Why have you two birds allowed Lieutenant Walker to let the troops hang around as if they had nothing better to do but bullshit and waste their damn time like this? The reason we're here is to train. Get your people out in the field, or I'll have you replaced, and you'll find yourselves doing KP for the rest of your hitch, and being pissed on from above. Get moving, Walker, get your ass over here double quick!"

Walker rushed up to Colonel Leadbetter and snapped. "Yes Sir Colonel!"

"Walker, this chap standing to my left's Doctor Joel Russbinder. He's to accompany you on the training field, mister. He's subject to the same shit you and your troops eat. Teach the puke, it's your ass on the fence if he screws up on this damn mission. Shove off, and don't forget to take your package with ya." Colonel Leadbetter shoved a thumb in the doctor's direction.

Colonel Leadbetter turned to Doctor Russbinder and growled at the civilian this time. "Doc, I have a body armor suit designed especially for you to squeeze your purdy little civilian ass into, sir. I can't allow a stray bullet to kill ya before we're on the target, Herr Doctor." The Colonel waved his arm out and a young Corporal rushed forward carrying body armor.

The civilian observed the soldiers dressing in their body armor. He copied them as best he could, he was determined not to ask any questions on how to wear the armor properly.

As he dressed, he asked Colonel Leadbetter a question that had nothing to do with the mission, or his armor. "Colonel, is that man Walker a sane person sir? He looked like he wanted to kill us."

"You got a good military eye, Doc. Lieutenant Walker's the type of guy that'd shoot at the welcoming wagon, sir. If his weapon was disabled, he'd swallow a fist full of rounds, and then fart death out his stinking ass. But he's also the type of guy you'll learn a helluva lot from, and he'll keep you alive long enough to complete your mission and return to the States, Herr Doctor. Look Doc, if you give me Bernie Williams, I can build a stinking baseball team, give me a Ronnie Lott, and I can build a fucking football team. If you give me a crazy ass like Lieutenant Walker, I'll deal a lethal blow to all terrorist operating throughout the world, he's that good a soldier, Doc. Now get your civilian ass out in the field, along with the rest of them god damn Grunts, fella. Remember Herr Doctor, you're the one who wanted this crap, hope you enjoy what you asked for. Welcome to hell, and I fucking own it. It all goes downhill from here for you, Herr Doctor." Colonel Leadbetter flashed the largest shit eating grin at Doctor Russbinder.

"I didn't think I was expected to fight anyone on this mission, Colonel Leadbetter."

The doctor's comment drew a chuckle from the troops, a few of them began to bust his horns.

"Hey Doc, you're part of Murphy's fucking law of combat now man. Your ass is in the fucking soup, and you betta do whatever the hell's expected from your stinking ass, or I'll frag your lilly white ass for ya, and leave you out there to rot and feed the worms, man."

"What did that soldier mean by frag me, Colonel Leadbetter Sir? These men use words I'm not very used to hearing or know what they are talking about sir."

"He meant if you don't pull your weight, the enemy won't be the ones after your ass, Doc."

"You have a bunch of crazy killers on your hands, Colonel. What's Murphy law of combat?"

"I wouldn't have it any other way when I'm about to go into fricking combat, Doc. I want a bunch of crazed, foaming at the fucking mouth killers surrounding me on any mission I'm out on, Herr Doctor. Hey pukes, the Doc wants to know what the ways of combat are."

"Number one, you must remember you're not superman." One of the troopers called out.

"Yeah Doc, and don't look stinking conspicuous when out in the field, it draws a shitload of enemy fire at your stinking ass."

"When in doubt, empty your magazine and reload, and then do the same again, Doc."

"Yeah Doc, you gotta remember man. Never share your stinking foxhole with someone who's braver than you are sir, if you wanna live to make it home in one piece."

A roar of laughter broke out as each soldier tried to be heard by the doctor. The confusing jumble of words blending in with the laughter made it impossible to hear the suggestions.

"Hey Doc, try and look unimportant. The bad guys might be low on fricking ammo, and they might not take a shot at your sagging ass if you look dumb enuf man."

"Remember Doc, on the stinking battlefield, never take the easy way to target, because easy ways are usually mined man." Another soldier called out to the doctor.

"Whoup, whoup, whoup, oorah." The elite troops chanted.

"If you're short of everything but enemy then you're sure as shit in combat asshole."

"Yeah Doc, any incoming artillery have the stinking right of way."

"Friendly fire isn't friendly." Another soldier called out while squeezing into his armor.

"If the enemy shooting at your ass, you're in range, and so are they asshole."

"You gotta remember this if you wanna stay alive to make a bunch of little Doctors. All field radios will fail on your sagging ass when you need the damn things the most, Doc."

"Anything you do, can get you shot in combat, even doing nothing man."

"Remember Doc, tracers work both ways, to locate the enemy both you and them."

"Hey Doc, the only thing more accurate than incoming enemy fire, is incoming friendly fire."

"Remember this one, Doc. When both sides on the battlefield are convinced they're about to lose the war, they're both right man." A female trooper called out from the ranks.

"The most important law to remember if you wanna stay in one piece is, professional soldiers are predictable, but the world's chuck full of fucking amateurs." Another soldier bellowed out.

The soldiers banged fists, and gave each other the high five as another soldier announced. "Hey Doc, remember, if you see a bomb technician running, try to keep up with his ass man."

When Colonel Leadbetter noticed the doctor was putting on his gear all wrong, he growled. "Okay you turds, enough screwing around with the civilian dude, we have a training session to run. Will someone get their ass up here and help this civilian puke pour himself into his damn armor correctly. Or we'll never get on the practice field this side of judgment day, dammit."

The laughing and good mood of the troops continued as Sergeant Ramirez showed the civilian the breast plate went on before shoulder pads were slipped over his head. She clipped the straps correctly, and released the tension between the doctor's legs, by untwisting them and snapping them correctly. When he was finished, the doctor joined Walker's troops strolling out to the mock up. The Lieutenant offered the doctor a hand. "Hey Doc, if you wanna stay alive long enuf to get back to your computers, and collect a stinking retirement check from the government. Stick close to my ass like a barnacle, and pay close attention to my orders. Let's get going sir."

Walker's group headed off as the lead squad, while Captain Wilson and Colonel Salsiccia's units did their best to pick up the security for the exercise, while Colonel Leadbetter took over command of the forth squad, and gave Walker's Unit backup support. Lieutenant Walker headed for a square laid out in the center of sand made of two by twelve lumber. There were roads shaped in the sand leading to the square. Captain Wilson's Unit broke up and took up position on three of them, while Colonel Salsiccia's Unit covered the other three road leading up to the makeshift site. The Colonel called in an over flight.

As silent as wind, a Navy Stealth X-117 bomber tore through the sky at near supersonic speeds, and the pilot dropped simulated cluster bombs on three mock up roads under Colonel Salsiccia's area of responsibility for the practice exercise. The cluster bombs dispersed with what the military had branded Lazy Boys land mines.

From each cluster unit, seventy five miniature unarmed bomb droplets no larger than a baseball, landed in and around the mined road. Each droplet was capable of disabling a medium size battle tank, or most personnel carriers by popping off a track if the machine ran over them. The small droplets were able to be set off by the weight of a man's foot. The amazing thing about this new breed of land mines was, once the American troops broke off their contact with enemy troops, they were able to keep them in check with the active mine field.

The soldiers would break off the controlling radio signal when far enough away from the enemy. When this was accomplished, each bomblett would self detonate. It gave Walker's troops the ability to set off the mine field to end a frontal attack mounted against them, or set off certain sections of the mine field, in case enemy reinforcements made a push at his troops, or make their way to the complex to root out Walker's people working inside the structure. The electronic kill switch that destroyed the mine field, proved to be the only solution the military came up with that ended the serious threat posed by active land mines, once the battle was no longer classified as such. It was a solution adopted by many nations of the world after the Bosinian war ended, and the world saw firsthand what a threat to civilian life left over land mines were.

A second, and third X-117 stealth aircraft flew over Colonel Salsiccia's position, each aircraft mining a separate road for the ground troops. Captain Wilson received the same treatment with X-117's mining roads under his area of responsibility. Within the first five minutes of action, the MNRRF Units had achieved complete security around the makeshift intended target.

It was Lieutenant Walker's turn to carry out his actions, by attacking what was to resemble the main body of the complex. Even though there were no structures in the field, the layout was a good representation of their target. The carved out square supposed to be the complex, offered no representation of interior walls and dividers. So this attack involved nothing more than merely attacking a square situated right in the middle of a large sand box. To make up for the lack of reality, the officers placed other obstacles before Walker's group. His Unit had to cross a simulated dry river bank, and get through a number of wades, and face an improved security force of the Iranian command. The other problem facing Walker's group was, the supposed security guards of the complex expecting his attack, and knew what time it was coming.

Lieutenant Walker's attacking troops worked under terrible conditions, the strong heat lamps brought the temperature around the pretentious complex up to a hundred and twenty degrees. Baking the soldiers in their heavy body armor, a strong wind developed by using powerful fans, driving the sand in the unprotected faces of the attacking soldiers, stinging and blinding them.

Lieutenant Walker's Unit moved out hitting three supposed machine gun emplacements set up just outside the simulated complex. Then the soldiers went after the five artillery displacements. In a matter of moments, his troops attacked the supposed complex doors, and breached inside the interior of the simulated complex. His troops taking over using stun grenades and simulated machine gun fire, until they had achieved total target control. One piece of reality used during the attack was, the guards and supposed defenders did not possess any body armor like Walker's troops, and they used weapons much like the Iranians would employ. It was deemed the Iranian weapons would not penetrate the armor, and only a lucky hit would result in the death of any American soldier on the attack against the complex and its defenders. So Walker's group was decided they lost only three dead, and five wounded on this military action.

Once Lieutenant Walker's team accepted control over the simulated Iranian complex, his demolition people moved in and they quickly placed charges at the base of sand piles supposed to represent computers, missiles bodies and warheads inside the complex. Walker, the Mutt and Sergeant Ramirez dragged the doctor around the area, until he said he covered his points of interest inside this supposed complex. Walker then ordered his people out of the complex, leaving the demolition team behind to finish their act. The rest of his troops took up defensive positions outside the complex, to cover the explosive ordinance team's retreat. When the charges were set, the EO teams charged out of the complex and they immediately joined Walker's group, and together they pulled back with each giving the other cover as the charges went off.

It took more than an hour for Walker's teams to complete their assignment against the complex then get out of the area and prepare for the troop's extraction. Colonel Leadbetter left the training zone in a huff, and he climbed on top of a parked humvee and bellowed out at his troops. "Okay people, get out of the fucking sand box and assemble before my sagging ass right now dammit. None of you turds are cats, so get the hell out of there on the double."

When the troops were out of the training zone. The Seabee bulldozers moved in and tore apart the structure and surrounding area. The machines completely obliterated all traces of the training scenario, as Colonel Leadbetter addressed his troops. "Walker, you and your people did well. It was a fine training lesson. But you better keep this in mind, at no time was anyone shooting at you with live fucking ammunition, and I allowed security to pullback to allow you to accomplish your mission easier. This was so you'd understand your attack lanes better. I wanted to run one more rehearsal, so you birds can get a mouth full of what you might face in sand land.

"When we go against the Persian defenders, they'll try to kill you, and eat your asses. Captain Wilson, you took longer than I wanted to get a flyover by the damn X-117s. If this was real, you afforded the enemy time to reinforce their position, or for the technicians to escape with some of their damn evidence mister. I want those god damn roads closed before Lieutenant Walker commits his people to any action. Colonel Salsiccia, you did little better than Captain Wilson did on this attack, dammit. Okay, let's leave before some damn news reporter discovers us, and the fool puts two and two together and comes out with us. Mess, body armor."

"Why? Are we going to be attacked by a bunch of stinking cooks now, Colonel Leadbetter?" A smartass soldier called out, pissed he had to remain in the stifling body armor.

"I'll give you that one wiseguy, but the next crybaby who complains out of turn, will be eating my stinking toe jam for mess. I want you bastards to get used to the weight and heat produced by your damn body armor units. It's been weeks since the you shits last wore any of this the crap, and I don't want anyone forgetting how it feels on your asses. Shove off, unless you birds don't want to eat and want to practice some more. We can always run another session."

Colonel Leadbetter walked over to the doctor who looked like a puddle of water and he asked him. "Well Doc, what the hell did you think of my training session so far, huh?"

"It was most enlightening Colonel Leadbetter Sir. I can't believe how well your troops work together. I swear they think as one, I'm very impressed, Colonel. You have trained them very well sir." The doctor remarked as he took the offered canteen from the Colonel and almost drained it before coming up for air. He watched as Colonel Leadbetter dumped the rest of the water out on the ground out of habit and he asked the Colonel. "Why did you waste it sir?"

"Because Herr Doctor, a smart fucking soldier who plans to remain alive long enough to complete his mission successfully and get back home alive, learns not to go and travel with a half full fucking canteen of stinking water, sir."

"Why is that Colonel? I can't believe you're even angry with water carried by your soldiers now, sir." The concerned civilian asked with worry in his eyes.

"Christ Almighty sir, you're a fucking real cherry I see Herr Doctor. My anger as you put it for water carried by my troops is because an almost empty damn canteen makes enough stinking noise to wake the dead, which is what you'll be if you don't empty your damn canteen the first time you use the damn thing out in the fricking field. Might as well wear a stinking bell around your damn neck, so the stinking enemy can line up his shot on your sagging ass a helluva lot easier, Herr Doctor." The Colonel snapped at the civilian doctor.

"I see what you mean Colonel Leadbetter, but what happens if you're thirsty and you don't want to finish off your water the first time you drink from your canteen, sir?" The concerned doctor asked the military officer as he stared at him while waiting for his response.

"That's where your fricking training comes in, Doc. You learn to wait as long as possible to take a damn slug of water, or you drink everything at once and go on for the rest of the lousy day without any more water to drink. You can always put a stinking pebble in your mouth and suck on it, and develop some salvia and swallow that until you really need some stinking water to suck down, Doc. On this mission, we'll carry on our person a number of small four ounce plastic bottled water. Once you drink one of them, you bury the damn thing in the sand. We don't want to let the damn ragheads know we're coming for their fricking asses. We don't need them trying to get to Paradise before it's time for them to head off for the place, Doc."

"Colonel Leadbetter, I thought you told me all rehearsals were shelved by command?"

"You're even smarter than you look, Herr Doctor. You're right as rain there sir, I was ordered to shelve all rehearsals, but I couldn't possibly send my people out on this stinking operation, without running at least one mock up for the troops, or as you have put it Doctor, rehearsal. I know I went against orders on this one sir, but our Intel boys allowed me to tailor my orders and try this one scenario on for size with the troops, sir. Doc, the machines are erasing all evidence of this little game we just enjoyed playing, ensuring no reporters will ever discover the action we just pulled off here, and blow this damn operation apart on us, sir. I can't tell you how valuable this one mock up run was to my troops, to ensure my people are properly motivated to overcome the many obstacles they'll be encountering in the Iranian desert, Doctor Russbinder Sir. The transport aircraft will be here soon, C'mon Doc, I'm hungry as hell sir."

"Aircraft, Colonel?" the worried doctor asked the Colonel.

"Yeah, the fucking transport aircraft that are assigned to carry us out to our part of this hell hole in fucking Pakistan, Herr Doctor. I hate flying in them damn trash haulers, sir. We're going in under the cover of the Army Core of

Engineers transport aircraft, using their markings as the cover for this stinking operation, Herr Doctor. Are you coming with me to get something to fucking eat or what, Doctor Russbinder? I already told you I was starving and I'm going to get something to eat even if you're not hungry, sir." Colonel Leadbetter snapped angrily at the civilian doctor as he waited for him to catch up with him.

CHAPTER SEVENTEEN

THE MASSIVE MILITARY BASE STATIONED AT CAMP LEJEUNE, JACKSONVILLE NORTH CAROLINA

As Colonel Bruce Leadbetter and Doctor Joel Russbinder entered the mess hall, the first of the four C-17 Globemaster transport aircraft began to circle the base. It was the first time transports attempted a landing at Camp Lejeune. The C-17s were able to land on rough surfaces and roads, so it was decided the aircraft would use the old training area R-7, closed after the conclusion of the Vietnam War for their landing strip. There was an asphalt road cutting through the old area, and it was a very secluded and secured zone periodically used for special training operations. It was hoped the aircraft would be free of prying eyes from the reporters hanging around the base.

The massive aircraft were to remain on the ground until they loaded all the troops and their military equipment on board the craft. The landing was not expected to draw any undue interest, because the aircraft were marked with the Army Core of Engineers insignias. Seeing the planes meant there was a boring civilian operation taking place somewhere on the military base, one of little interest to most news reporters. There was a small threat of a reporter taking an interest in the planes, and the risk of the mission being uncovered was a concern to the commander.

Colonel Leadbetter ignored the aircraft as it circled the base, and then it disappeared behind a stand of trees. He scanned the area and noticed a number of Marines glanced up at the five circling planes, and then the soldiers returned to their normal duties. Colonel Leadbetter and Doctor Russbinder entered the mess together and were instantly assaulted by loud troops in line, while others filled glasses with milk or juice. It was mild mayhem inside the mess with some of the soldiers yelling across tables to be heard by other soldiers, bad jokes and laughter.

The Colonel moved to the cooks with an empty tray, and he held it out and scrambled eggs and French fries were heaped up until the Colonel stopped the cook from placing anymore food on his tray. Five sausages were thrown on top of the mess, and then the Colonel grabbed a hand full of bacon before moving off. He filled a cup of coffee, and then he headed for an empty table. The soldiers near that table, immediately moved over to other tables as the civilian doctor joined the commander. The doctor plopped down by Colonel Leadbetter and noticed the other soldiers move away from them and he mumbled. "Huh, I guess I need a shower."

"Why say that Herr Doctor?" Colonel Leadbetter grumbled with a mouth full of eggs, as he continued to try and get under the doctor's skin by adding the 'Herr' to his name.

"I guess I stink, look at how those few soldiers moved from us as if I had a disease, Colonel."

"All they're doing is giving us privacy to talk without worrying who might be listening to us."

After Colonel Leadbetter finished his mouthful of food, he stood and bellowed. "Listen up, I want all you pukes to drink plenty of water, soup up, flood yourselves with the crap. Water, water, water, people! Drink as much as you can stand and then some more, where we're going there's not going to be very much of the crap to go around, so fill up while you can."

Leadbetter was aware all the soldiers in the mess were part of his troops, and he was not afraid to speak about their mission. The mess was closed to all other troops on the base but his, who enjoyed access all hours of the day and night, before they shoved off on their next operation. The Colonel scanned the mess looking for his two Lieutenant, Walker and Hall. He smiled when he picked them up sitting with the women warriors. He smirked because he should have known the two soldiers would be sitting with the women as he yelled at them. "Walker, Hall, get your asses over here double quick, god dammit."

Walker looked up from his meal and saw the Colonel standing and nodded.

He turned back to the doctor and groused at him this time. "Herr Doctor, I'll have you discuss everything you need to locate at the damn complex with these two birds. I'm running backup for this action, and the only way I'll get inside the damn Iranian dump is if Lieutenant Walker's troops gets bogged down by the defenders of the damn complex. So these two assholes will be the ones going inside the complex along with you and they need to know what you need."

"Makes sense to me Colonel Leadbetter Sir." The doctor remarked as he picked at his food.

Colonel Leadbetter sat back down and shoved more eggs in his mouth, and then realized the two Lieutenant were not at his table yet, and he snarled again at the two young officers. "Walker, Hall, didn't I just tell you two ball sacks to get your slimy asses over here before quick, dammit."

A chuckle filled the mess, with each soldier knowing Walker and the Mutt were pushing the envelope on the angry Colonel. As slowly as possible, Walker rose and he picked up the last sausage from his plate and placed it in his mouth like a cigar, and then he made his way over to the still fuming Colonel. The Mutt was one pace behind him. By the time Walker reached the Colonel, the commanding officer was fit to be tied, and he struggling desperately to control his temper. Colonel Leadbetter slammed Walker on his armor shoulder pad, making a noise as loud as a gun shot inside the mess as he nearly roared at him. "You're fucking with me again I see mister, and I'll remember this shit filled game of yours when we get back to the States and then I'll settle your hash with you, wiseguy. That's when I'll have my revenge on your ass nice and easy. Sit down before I boot ya in the damn can." Colonel Leadbetter shoved Walker forward and the Mutt stayed out of arms reach as he headed for the other side of the table and safety.

"What the fuck's bugging ya ass anyhow Colonel?" Walker growled at his commander.

Colonel Leadbetter suddenly reached out and he pulled the sausage from Walker's mouth, and then he bitched at him. "Forty thousand fucking screaming Chinese were born in the length of time you two assholes took getting here. You fuck with me and I'll snap your dick in half just like this, wiseguy." The Colonel broke the sausage in half between his fingers, and he allowed both ends to fall from his hand. He then ground them in the concrete floor with his heel.

The Mutt leaned over the table and looked down at the floor by the Colonel's feet, and then he moaned at the Colonel. "Yyyyeeeeoooowww, I bet that'd hurt some, Homes."

Colonel Leadbetter struck the Mutt on the top of his head with his knuckle, giving him what the soldiers called a nuggie. The Mutt dropped back down in his chair and rubbed his head.

"You two shitbirds finished screwing around with me yet? Or is there more to come?"

Walker pointed to himself. "Me? Fuck with you Colonel? Naw, never happen sir."

Doctor Russbinder laughed, drawing an angry glare from the Colonel and he grumbled at the civilian doctor. "Look Herr Doctor, that's the last thing I need, you encouraging these two Jerk Bennies who think they're so damn cute. Okay, enough of this stinking shit, we have some serious business to cover. Listen up, the Doc has something to share with you two ball sacks. He's going to inform us exactly what he's after inside the Iranian complex once we get inside the damn dump. Doc, you have the floor, I'll make sure these two asses pay attention to you, sir."

"Lieutenant Walker is it sir?" Doctor Russbinder asked as he looked at the young soldier.

"That, or if it's fucking easier on your stinking noggin to remember Doc, Road Kill."

"Road Kill, Lieutenant?" the confused doctor asked with a sort of a smile on his lips.

"Get to it for Pete's sake will ya Doc. His fucking name's Walker for crap sake." Colonel Leadbetter growled, growing impatient with the civilian speaking to his soldiers.

"Sorry, Lieutenant Walker Sir, since I was sent on this mission to see how far along the technicians were in accomplishing their goal of constructing their own nuclear warhead, and the missile delivery system to get these weapons to target. I was instructed to locate any and all reports, documents, and names of Russian technicians helping the Iranians accomplish their deadly task sir." Doctor Russbinder took a quickly breath.

"Whaddaya friggin want from my ass Doc? I'll get you inside the damn complex in one piece sure enuf Doc. But from that point on its gonna be your baby to deliver the rest of the goods you were ordered to locate inside the stinking dump, sir." Lieutenant Walker grinned at the doctor.

"That's all I want from you Lieutenant Walker. But if anything happens to me while on this mission sir. Someone else has to know what I was after, or my part of this operation will go unfinished, sir. Lieutenant, the President has ordered me to go..."

"I'm really impressed Doc. The stinking President of the United States huh?" Walker interrupted the doctor, being a wiseguy and forcing Colonel Leadbetter to get on his ass again.

"Keep it fucking up Walker, and you're not going to be in good enough fricking shape to make this trip over to sand land, mister. Enough wise cracking will ya, and keep your fucking mouth shut and pay close attention to the Doc's words."

Doctor Russbinder did not miss a step as he continued with his words as the colonel got on Walker's case. "Wants evidence he can bring before the United Nations, showing why he had you soldiers invade Iran, sir. The President will hit more targets than admitted to, and it's up to us to give him the information. He'll not look good before the other nations without strong evidence in his hand of what the Iranians were doing inside this complex, sir. I don't think I have to tell you what will happen if he looks bad before the United Nations, Lieutenant."

"No need, it's understood Doc. So what's it you want from me and my troops, sir?"

"Lieutenant Walker, listen please while I go over the many items I need to locate at the Iranian complex, sir. If anything happens to me, you'll have to complete my part of the mission for me, and if anything happens to you sir. The other soldier with you must finish my part of the operation, sir. As your operation is an all consuming thing to you, my part of this mission is as consuming to me as well, sir. My every action is geared to make my part of this mission a complete success. I, like you, do not like to fail on anything I started, Lieutenant Walker Sir."

"If I didn't know any betta, I'd swear I was speaking with a fellow stinking grunt in this friggin conversation." Walker smirked, and the Mutt laughed.

"You two shitbirds going to start that crap over again? Can the comedy act and listen up, he's not finished with you two birds yet, Walker. I'll get the rest of these shitbirds up and in gear. There's no sense allowing them to get to lazy while we speak to the Doctor." Colonel Leadbetter growled as he stood up, and then bellowed out. "Colonel Salsiccia, you're in command of this crap. March their damn asses to over Maps, and have them study the god damn terrain of our upcoming target. I want the squirrels to know the area like it's their own backyard, dammit."

Colonel Joseph Salsiccia moved to the head of the mess, and then he called his people to attention, and then he quick marched them out of the building.

Colonel Leadbetter stared at the other troopers as they quickly marched out of the mess. Once they were gone, he ordered the cooks and helpers out of ear shot. The Sergeant Major Master Cook complained he was not leaving his mess area, and he was going to clean the grease from the ovens. He was defying the Colonel. The Mess Sergeant was in command of the mess, and the power he had overrode even the Base Commander, but not with this officer. Colonel Leadbetter moved around the table and he angrily confronted the Sergeant with his arms crossed over his chest, a stain covered most of his apron.

The Colonel pointed a finger at his face as if it was a weapon at the master cook, and he snarled at him. "Now you listen to my ass you little shit you. I just ordered you to get your god damn kitchen help out of this fucking mess, and that's exactly what you'll do if you know what's good for you, and the rest of your people. Pack up your damn aprons, spoons and pots, and whatever else you want to take with you, and get the hell out of here before I stomp a hole in the middle of your fucking chest. I'm not used to being disobeyed when I give a fricking order, mister. I have no intention of bringing you up on charges, I'll settle with you right here and now, buster. Sergeant Major, are you going to leave under your own power, or do you want to be carried out of here feet first?" Colonel Leadbetter took a step at the Sergeant as he glared at him.

"It's not worth it, he has more brass than a 105 howitzer round. C'mon Sarge, let's get the hell out of here. I'll clean the ovens and grills when we're allowed back in the mess. C'mon man, it's not worth the hassle to dump the full bird eagle on his can, Sarge." One of the other cooks called out to his Sergeant, worried of him getting in too much trouble not listening to the Colonel.

The reference to being a full bird eagle made the Colonel even angrier. He shot a nasty glare at the young Corporal doing all the squawking, marking the Corporal's face to his memory. Colonel Leadbetter turned his attention back to the Master Sergeant and warned him in no uncertain terms this time. "Sergeant, you had your fifteen minutes of fame and lived through it mister. I'm getting a little tired of standing here like this, mister. If you don't want to have your cooks assigned to hazardous duty with yourself, you better make up your mind what you intend to do, bub. Get the fuck out of here before I change my mind, and have your ass shot for the hell of it, pal!" Colonel Leadbetter roared as he stepped aside to make room for the Sergeant to get past him.

The Sergeant understood he had no other alternative but to obey this fuming Colonel, even though it was an accepted fact the Master Sergeant owned the mess when troops were inside, it was never challenged before. Bucking a full bird Colonel was something new for the Sergeant, and he did not want to go too far as he replied to the Colonel. "Huh, you won this round I guess, Colonel. But I'm launching a formal complaint against your actions here, and I'll let the General settle this little fracas for us, sir. People, shut down the damn ovens and grills, let's get the hell out of here, it stinks in here anyway." The Master Sergeant ripped off his apron and balled it up, and then sent it flying across the room as he waited for his crew to finish up.

Colonel Leadbetter moved even closer to the Sergeant's face and growled at him. "If that last fucking reference to 'stinking in here' was directed at my ass, buster. I'll be forced to see how much I can make you stink out on the god damn grinder for the day, mister."

"No sir, by no means was that comment directed at you in any way, shape, or form sir. I meant I had the stink of the grease stuffed up my nose all morning now, Colonel Leadbetter Sir." The Master Sergeant tried a smile on the officer, but it was wasted.

"You're fucking lucky I'm rather pressed for god damn time here buster. Or it wouldn't be the fricking grease that'll be stuffed up your fricking nose, Sergeant. Now get the fuck out of here on the double quick, I wasted too much time on you already buster."

"Yes sir! C'mon people, the Colonel wants us out of here. Secure the ovens and move out."

When the Master Sergeant and cooks were out of the mess, Colonel Leadbetter moved a number of tables away from them, so they had room to breathe and spread out some. He pulled a chair over and sat on one, and rested his arms and chin on the back of the other as he ordered. "Doc, sorry for the slight problem with the damn cook, everyone has to be a fucking boss at least once in their wasted lives, dammit. You may continue now sir."

THE WHITE HOUSE, WASHINGTON D.C.
SATURDAY, NOVEMBER 9th, 1998. 9:30 A.M. EST

Admiral Thomas Standlund, Chief of Naval Operations, requested and received permission to address the President.

When the Admiral entered the Oval Office, he was greeted by a rather hostile acting President. Along with him was the Vice President, Secretary of State, Security Director and the Secretary of Defense. General White, Director of the CIA, John Raincloud were also attending the meeting. The President motioned the Admiral towards an empty chair, and he took it. He nodded to the others while flashing a pleasant smile at the Secretary of State.

"Admiral Standlund you have the floor sir, why have you demanded to see me sir? I planned to take some time for myself today. Heaven knows, when the troops enter Iran, my private time will be extremely limited at that point, sir. I wanted to get a few holes in then meet with General White and Director Raincloud later on today for a final briefing on the Iran situation, sir."

"I'm sorry for the added pressure I'm putting on your shoulders Mr. President. But I wanted to inform you on the mission we successfully undertook against the Iranian submarines, while they were still anchored up in the port at Bander Beheshi..."

"What?" General White growled as he straightened up in his chair and glared at the Admiral.

"John, I'm terribly sorry, but amidst all the confusion of the past few weeks, sir. I completely failed to inform you the Navy planned to mine the Iranian submarines before they left port, sir." Director Raincloud offered to the obviously upset looking Chairman.

General White ignored the Director's words, and moved towards the Admiral.

"General White, I hope you're not planning to make any trouble here, sir." The President warned, and then added. "General White Sir, I was the one who gave the green light to the Admiral's action, so if you have to be angry with anyone, it has to be me sir."

General White turned to the President and growled before realizing who he was addressing at the meeting. "Why the hell wasn't I informed an action was being planned against the damn Iranian submarines was authorized? The last thing I was aware of, we planned to track them with that new radar shit, sir. Now I find out we went after the damn submarines before they even left port. I'm plenty ticked off at being kept out of the damn loop on this operation, sir."

The President leaned over on his desk and tried to sooth the ruffled feathers of his military officer by saying. "General White, I'm equally ticked off over the way you're daring to speak to me. Need I remind you General, I'm the President of the United States, and as such, I'm entitled to the respect commanded by the office and myself, sir. I gave the okay for the Admiral to insert his frogmen in the Iranian port so they could mine the Iranian submarines while at port, General White. But I'm not in position to deliver the report. Admiral Standlund, would you please be so kind as to inform the General here on your progress with the Iranian submarines, sir?"

"Yes Sir Mr. President, I'd be pleased to report on the progress we had with mining of the Iranian submarines, sir. General White, may I tell you how embarrassed I am over the fact you weren't brought up to speed on the guts of my mission, sir. If I was aware you weren't in the loop, I surely would've made it my business to bring you up to speed about the mission, General. But since it was a Naval insertion, informing you completely slipped my mind, General White Sir." The Admiral bowed towards General White who returned it as he retook his seat.

"Mr. President, I'd like to address my comments directly to General White if you don't mind, sir." The Admiral offered, trying to get back on the good side of the Chairman.

"Fine, make sure I hear what you say, or I'll interrupt you Admiral." President Cole warned.

"Yes Mr. President, I sure will sir. General White, it was decided to prevent the six Iranian submarines from making for the open sea when your troops hit the Iranian complex in the desert, sir. In this manner, the submarines would be much easier to kill. My SEAL team came up with the suggestion of penetrating the port, and planting a series of motion fuse mines on the hull of each of the damn Iranian submarines. We call these charges the MS-167's sir."

"I believe you have me at a slight disadvantage here, sir. I'm unfamiliar with these charges you're speaking of here, Admiral Standlund Sir."

"Sorry General White, the MS-167 magnetic mine dubbed the Motion Sickness pill. It's a six kilogram shaped charge affixed to the hull of the targeted submarine, or on any other targeted ship by means of a set of powerful magnets which can even withstand a chain dragging..."

"A chain dragging Admiral Standlund?" Vice President Hirshfield asked him this time.

"Sorry Madam Vice President, a chain dragging is an old Naval procedure carried out periodically, when the Captain thinks he might be a possible target of saboteurs. A chain's fixed to ends of a rope, and then its dragged from one end of the submarine to the other, while the sailors hold constant tension on the ropes, Ma'am. As the chain's pulled along the hull, most, if not all older magnet type mines would be easily ripped from their placement..."

"Then what would stop the Iranians from doing the same chain dragging thing to their submarines, erasing all the effort by your outstanding SEAL team, Admiral Standlund? When I first agreed with this mission to mine the Iranian submarines, this subject was never breached at that meeting if I remember right." Vice President Mary Hirshfield interrupted again.

"Because Madam, the way our new and more powerful charges are designed, and strategically placed on the target boat, combined with the power of our magnets. Anything short of the explosion wouldn't dislodge the weapon from its intended target. Once the explosion occurred, their mission's to added to the success of the mission."

"There's more than one of these charges placed on each of the submarines, Admiral Standlund Sir?" This time it was the President who interrupted the Admiral's words.

"By all means Mr. President Sir. We placed five weapons on each of the six submarines. With two charges placed under the reactor, two more weapons placed under the missile storage and launch tubes compartment, and the last one was placed by the forward torpedo room, sir. Each six kilogram charge is more than enough to sink the intended target, sir. The additional charges have a reason to be placed, to completely destroy the submarine, thus rendering them totally useless to the Iranians in the future, sir."

"Admiral Standlund, how the hell do they set off the charges? Do the SEALs have to stay in the vicinity, or are we capable of setting the charges off electronically, sir?" the Security Director asked the Admiral with concern lacing his voice.

"That's the beauty of these mines, Director Griffin. Each one of the weapons are set and forget type weapons. After the charge is set, a propeller hangs down from the charge much in the same way many fish finders mark the speed of the pleasure boats. This propeller activates the detonation when the target attains a certain speed of merely five knots, sir. We know the access to Bandar Beheshi's plagued by strong currents, and the submarines are forced to stay to a very narrow channel before making it out to the open sea. In order to navigate this narrow channel, the submarines have to maintain a constant five knots speed at the minimum, but they'll not go to this speed until the craft's in the confines of the narrow channel. Here's where the detonations are marked to go off, and the submarine debris will block further shipping from leaving the port.

"Then, when our fighter and attack aircraft are overhead of the port, we'll pick and choose our targets at will, delivering a backbreaking lethal blow to the Iranian Navy in one swift operation. This action will completely block the fast attack speed boats in port from making it to the Persian Gulf, so they can attack civilian cargo ships delivering crude oil to their host nations, sir."

"Outstanding Admiral Standlund, I concur with your plan completely, sir. Hitting the damn Iranian submarines while still in port, and blocking the port to all shipping at the same time is a stroke of genius, sir. Have your SEALs been successful on their mission, Admiral Standlund Sir?" General White asked, unable to hide the huge grin on his face.

"General White, there we had a slight problem, sir." The Admiral offered.

There was a loud sigh from the President as he shifted his eyes towards the ceiling, and he began shaking his head slowly after hearing the Admiral's last words.

Admiral Standlund hesitated, and aimed his words at General White. "Unfortunately General, by the time we inserted the SEAL teams, two of the Iranian submarines had already left port, sir." The Admiral lifted his hand to hold off all questions while he went on. "We've been successful with locating the two missing submarines, and we have Crystal Eye tracking them constantly, General. Mr. President, when the time comes these two Iranian submarines will be erased before they can possibly launch any missiles, sir. I have a pair of Missile Frigates trailing each in their strike capability. The submarines will never dodge them, they are as good as dead as we speak."

Everyone in the room noticed the President relax after hearing the Admiral's assurances about the Iranian submarines. It was here the Secretary of Defense asked. "Admiral Standlund Sir, if you'd excuse my interruption please. Do you have any other means of detonating these charges you have placed on the Iranian submarines? You know, just in case something happens to one of these propeller type things, and they fail to detonate properly as designed, sir?"

"Yes Secretary Levenhagen, we definitely do at that sir. A simple coded electronic message can be transmitted to the charge by satellite means that would immediately detonate the charge attached to the submarine's hull if a malfunction happens to occur with the system, sir."

"Let me get this straight Admiral Standlund Sir, what you're telling me is. The six Iranian submarines are already as good as erased from the equation? That all our aircraft have to do is pound the hell out of the Iranian port, like shooting fish in a barrel maybe?"

"Like hooking a fish in the barrel Mr. President Sir." Mrs. Hernandez corrected.

"Arrrrrr..." The President growled as he lifted his upper lip at Mrs. Hernandez.

"Yes Sir Mr. President." The Admiral announced proudly to his Commander in Chief.

"Great Admiral Standlund, this is the best news I have received since this mess first came to light sir. I thank you for your report, Admiral. General White, I must apologize again for failing to make certain you were appraised of this pending action before it took place, sir. Please accept my apology, do you have questions for the Admiral, or can I call this meeting to a close. So I can get a few moments of relaxation in before our next scheduled meeting, General White?" The President smiled, showing he was pleased with the way the operation was proceeding so far.

General White knew when not to push his luck with the President. He had the man in a good mood at the moment, and no one had ever accused him of not knowing when to cut bait and fish. The Chairman of the Joint Chiefs of Staff decided not to ask any further questions of the Admiral at this time, but he was going to have a little chit chat with the Admiral before his next scheduled meeting with the President later on that afternoon.

"No Mr. President, Admiral Standlund has answered all my questions and concerns to my complete satisfaction at this point, sir. It was as you have stated sir, an outstanding report. Excellent in fact, and a successful mission might I add as well, Admiral. As for apologizing for clearing this mission without my knowledge beforehand, Mr. President. Sir, you're free to make any decisions you may choose without checking with me first, sir."

The President grumbled at his military officer. "Well, thank you very much for allowing me to run my office in the manner I deem fit, General White Sir. That's awfully big of you sir."

"Think nothing of it Mr. President, I'm glad I pleased you like this sir."

The most important people who ran the government of the United States laughed at the General's lighthearted comments to his Commander in Chief.

As he did every time when he concluded a meeting, President Cole loudly clapped his hands together, and then he asked everyone in the room. "Is that it for this meeting then, people?"

"Begging the President's pardon sir. But I'd like to ask the Admiral a question before he leaves us, sir." General White asked, deciding to ask that one further question after all.

With a sigh, the President snapped. "Okay, but make it quick General. Admiral please sir."

General White looked at the Admiral then he asked him politely. "Admiral Standlund Sir, when did this SEAL team operation take place, sir?"

"General White Sir, since this part of the operation was deemed a Naval action, we decided to act before notifying the other members of the Council. We inserted the SEAL team at exactly Ten Twenty One Hundred Hour's Iranian time Friday, November 8th, General White Sir."

"That's yesterday, okay Admiral Standlund Sir, do you mind if I ask you one more question before I let you go sir?" General White asked as he gave the President a sideward glance.

The President glared at the General, but allowed the Admiral to answer the question.

With a quick nod from President Cole, General White asked the Naval Officer. "Admiral Standlund Sir, how the hell were the SEALs inserted in the theater of action, and what was the operation called?" General White asked while keeping an angry edge from his voice.

"A good question General White, the mission was branded, 'Operation Prevent'. It was designed to last three hours on the scene of penetration. This operation had the chance to utilize a newly developed SEAL Team Delivery System called ASDS-1 or Advanced SEAL Delivery System. ASDS-1 is a small submersible that measures some sixty five feet long by nine feet in diameter at its widest point, General White Sir. The ASDS-1submersible's equipped with a dry and heated interior troop compartment for the insertion team's comfort, with an independent air supply system enabling the insertion team to remain stationed off the target for several days if necessary, before being pressed into action against their intended target, General White Sir.

"The ASDS-1 system comes with a ten man SEAL insertion team independent compartment. Their compartment's separated from the Captain and mate of the ASDS submersible system, by a lockout chamber and two water tight hatches. The hull's pressurized that enables it to operate at greater depths than its forerunner, the Mk-VIII SEAL Team delivery system equipped to hold a four to six man insertion team, and the hull wasn't pressurized, which gave the Mk-VIII an operating depth of only forty five feet, sir." The Admiral took this time to take a break to allow the General to ask questions, none came from the military officer so he went on with his report.

The President had lost all his anger because he was finding the Admirals explanation of how the SEAL team was inserted in the field of action extremely interesting. He was willing to give up his wanted relaxation time to hear the full report from the Admiral.

"General White Sir, the ADSD-1 system's powered by a fifty five horsepower, single propeller silent electric motor, fueled by a double bank of cadmium batteries, sir. We chose cadmiums to eliminate the possible threat of battery acid leakage. The ASDS system's equipped with four independent thrusters deployed both fore and aft the craft that are pressed into action when the submersible's operating at slow maneuvering speeds. These thrusters are retracted inside the hull to reduce hull drag while operating at high speed maneuvering, sir. The ASDS system's further equipped with an extensive array of integrated forward and side looking sonars, and a pair of optical and secured communication periscopes inside the submersible, General White Sir.

"The outer hull has a inch and a half hard faced, rubberized SAM, (Sonar Absorbing Materials) giving the submersible a detection surface of less than two square feet to detection. A detection surface this small will make a tracking sonar operator believe his machinery's having a slight malfunction, and he'll in most cases, write it off as an electronic glitch sir. A retractable snorkel, can also be raise when the ASDS system's at station, feeding the ASDS system with fresh air, if the submersible has to remain at station longer than first expected. The SEAL Team members can be inserted by means of depressurizing the separate lockout compartment, sir.

"Flooding the interior of the tail end of the submersible with sea water, the SEAL Team will then unlock the tail hatch and be released to the Ocean. Once the insertion team's released, the Captain has two options to follow. He can pump out the sea water if he feels there's a chance of detection by the enemy, so he can maneuver easier out of danger. Or the Captain can chose to allow his ASDS system to remain flooded for quick pickup extraction from the theater of operations of his SEAL Team, if he feels he's in no danger of detection. This newer version's equipped with an active ballast and trim tank capability, General White Sir. The ASDS-1 system was developed internally by a joint effort of the USSOCOM- United States Operations Command, and NAVSPECWARCOM- Naval Special Warfare Command, General White Sir."

Secretary Levenhagen raised his hand and the Admiral asked. "Yes Mr. Secretary?"

"Admiral Standlund, how do the SEAL Team members avoid underwater detection, sir? Doesn't the air bubbles from their tanks give their location away to any surface activities, sir?"

"No sir, the SEAL Team members employ the bubbleless rebreathing system that gives them three hours underwater operation time and the systems makes the members undetectable, sir." The Admiral replied as he let his breath out, pleased by answering any questions so confidently.

"I see, how does the ASDS system get to target? Is it capable of sailing the Oceans at will, Admiral?" Secretary Levenhagen asked as he smiled at the exhausted looking Naval Officer.

"Although the ASDS system has a full range of fifty nautical miles, before being forced to surface to recharge her batteries and also take on any needed supplies. We like to keep it operating at a maximum of twenty miles, even shorter distances in and around the five mile distance if circumstances allow us to operate that tightly, sir."

"If that's a fact Admiral Standlund, how does this ASDS system get to position if you only allow it to work within the five mile distance radius you just spoke of, sir?" Secretary Levenhagen asked, thoroughly confused now by the Admiral's explanation.

"Excuse me Mr. Secretary that's not what I said at all sir. I merely mentioned we preferred to operate the system within a five mile distance of the mother ship, sir. But the ASDS system's more than capable of traveling many miles when the operation calls for these distances to be employed during any mission the system is employed, sir." The Admiral grinned at the Secretary.

"Oh... what's this mother ship you speak of here, Admiral Standlund Sir? This is the first time you mentioned anything about a mother ship. Is this how the ASDS system gets to its attack position, sir?" Secretary Levenhagen asked as he sat forward and stared at the Admiral.

"I'm sorry Secretary Levenhagen, the mother ship in this case is a full size nuclear powered submarine, Mr. Secretary. The Los Angeles Class Nuclear Powered Attack Submarine the USS Jacksonville's the mother ship for this system, sir. Which was converted to an operation's platform designed specifically for this type of system, and her new port of call's stationed at Port Everglades, Florida, sir. She was decommissioned from active duty on th..."

"I remember this ship now, err... please excuse me Admiral Standlund, boat sir. I signed those decommissioning papers on her when was it now?" the President moaned as he tried to remember the exact date he was searching his mind for.

"Mr. President Sir, you signed the decommissioning order seventeen months ago, sir."

"Yes then what's this sh... err... boat doing back on the active rolls again, sir? Aren't we breaking the START II agreement with the Russians over having this nuclear powered submarine back on the active rolls again, Admiral?" the President barked as he stood and began to pace.

"No sir, not in the least Mr. President Sir. We're well within complete compliance with the START II agreements with Russia. The Jacksonville's decommissioned as for her nuclear delivery systems are concerned, Mr. President. We removed the launching tube system from the submarine, and the nuclear capable cruise missiles from her torpedo room as well. She's currently classified as a conventional warship that's nuclear powered, Mr. President Sir. The Russians are doing the same thing with a number of their nuclear delivery platforms, converting them over to other military uses. We're working on the smaller attack boats, converting a number of them over to THAAD, High Altitude Intercept Missiles Delivery Platforms…"

The President held up his hand and asked the Naval Officer. "Admiral Standlund Sir, I'm not quite following you on this conversation I'm afraid sir. After this meeting's completed, I want you to make a detailed report on this subject on hard copy for me. Then verbally to me on everything you're doing with regards to the submarines supposed to be decommissioned according to the START II treaty with the damn Russians. I can ill afford to have this crap coming up and biting me on the ass later on sir. Especially not now when I'm trying to nail the Russian's asses to the wall, because of the mistakes they're having with trying to control their damn nuclear missiles and warheads. Is this perfectly clear to you Admiral Standlund?"

"Yes Sir Mr. President Sir." The Admiral replied in a calm tone to the American President.

"Then please continue with your report so we can end this damn meeting sometime today, Admiral Standlund Sir. I'm rather pleased the General wherewithal to ask these questions of you sir. I had no idea we're doing other duties with any of our decommissioned ships, yeah I know Admiral, boats." The President corrected himself before being corrected by the Admiral.

"Yes Sir Mr. President Sir. What was the question you had, sir?" Admiral Standlund asked.

"Admiral Standlund Sir, you were about to inform us on how the ASDS systems were delivered to the point of action, sir." General White cut in and snapped, trying not to show he was very impressed with what the Navy was doing with some of their decommissioned ships and submarines, yet staying within the guidelines with the Russians.

"Yes, thank you for reminding me where I was going, General White Sir. The ASDS system's delivered to insertion point by means of the mother ship USS Jacksonville submarine. Which underwent a number of rather dramatic modifications to its hull, since being decommissioned last year. The hull of the Jacksonville had to be fitted with a water tight dry deck shelter system, needed to house the ASDS unit on its rear decking, where the Trident missiles assembly used to be housed on the submarine. The Jacksonville's more than capable of traveling at twenty five knots, which is much better than the ASDS can travel flat out in rough waters. We ordered the Jacksonville to get as near to the Iranian coast as possible, before launching the ASDS unit, sir."

"How the hell does the ASDS system get extracted from the site of insertion once the mission has been completed by the SEAL team members on board the system?" The General snapped.

"That's a good question again, General White Sir. The extraction of the submersible and SEAL Team members is simple to complete, General. The once Trident submarine, Jacksonville remains at station until the ASDS system returns from her mission. The linkup takes place at twenty five feet below the sail of the Jacksonville, sir. When launching the ASDS unit, the dry shelter serves as the place where the SEAL Team, Captain and his crew are placed inside the ASDS system, and they remain completely dry during this part of the launching of the ASDS system. Once inside the unit, the system's sealed and then the dry shelter splits in half after flooding the interior. The retaining shackles are released, and the ASDS unit separates from the mother platform. Upon returning to the mother platform, the ASDS slows down to crawl speed.

"Until becoming stationary hovering directly over the compartment that remained open the entire time of deployment. The retaining shackles are then extend, and with the help of a number of Jacksonville's divers, they're quickly secured to the mooring points on board the ASDS system, and then the unit's retrieved by merely retracting the retaining shackles. Once back inside its mooring station, the shelter's moved back in position and then sealed water tight. The sea water's then pumped out of the interior of the shelter, and the SEAL Team and crew are then taken back on board the Jacksonville. The nice thing about this shelter is, the crew can service the ASDS unit while inside the dry shelter, without being forced to return to port and working in dry dock conditions. Thus preparing the ASDS for a second, and possibly third mission as might be required by the operation at hand, while remaining stationed out in the field of action, sir.

"Mr. President Sir, we're also in the process of setting the mooring linkup on the SSN-22 Connecticut, the second of the Sea Wolf Class Fast Attack Submarines, sir. We know the shelter will not hamper the Connecticut's submerged speed capability of thirty five knots in the lease that is suffered by the weaker and outdated Jacksonville submarine, sir. It'll reduce the Sea Wolf's speed down some, but we feel the loss of speed's well worth the positive gain offered by the ASDS system working in the special operations field, Mr. President Sir."

"Admiral Standlund, I concur completely with your assumptions about the ASDS unit and its use in any future upcoming military events we'll be involved in, sir. It seems like an extremely workable synopsis that can be easily pressed into action to serve not only your specialized SEAL Team insertions members, but it will also serve my MNRRF operations perfectly if the need ever arises as well, sir." The General announced proudly to the Naval Officer.

"I think we have covered just about everything that was needed to be covered at this meeting pertaining to this new ASDS system, General White Sir." The President replied, showing he was starting to become a little impatient about being forced to remain at this meeting any longer than was absolutely necessary. Then the President repeated his usual closing ceremony by clapping his hands together loudly, and then he stood and rushed from the office before any of the other members at the meeting had a chance to stand and salute him as he left the room. But not before the President turned to the Naval Officer and he warned him. "Once again Admiral Standlund Sir, I'll be expecting those reports I requested from you sitting on my desk A-SAP, sir."

"Yes Sir President Cole Sir, and you shall have the report on your desk the first moment we have completed the interrogation of the returning SEAL Team members, Mr. President. We have to find out everything about their mission, and the success they enjoyed. Before I can possibly make any detailed reports about the mission, Mr. President. We should be able to conclude the interrogations of the SEAL Team members in the next few days, sir." The Admiral replied.

Both General White and CIA Director Raincloud linked up just outside the Oval Office, and they rushed down the long corridor and out to their waiting staff cars. Before they departed the White House compound, Director Raincloud asked General White what he intended to do after he refused to join him for a private lunch meeting. He needed to know where the General was going to be for the rest of the day in case he needed him.

"I'm getting right on the damn horn and inform Colonel Leadbetter that the god damn Iranian submarines are already out of the picture for this operation, sir." General White announced as he tried to keep up with the quickly moving CIA Director.

"What the hell good would that do him, sir? Colonel Leadbetter's part of the operation has nothing to do with the damn Iranian submarine situation, or the military bases we intend to destroy inside Iran as well, General White Sir. Or the damn ports the submarines are moored at, General White Sir." Director Raincloud offered with questioning eyes to the military officer.

"It does him no god damn good at all Director Raincloud. But it gives me a damn good reason to make contact with the damn pain in the ass, John. So I can see how his part of the mission's shaping up for the assault teams under his command, sir. I want to make certain that those damn gun bunnies of his didn't eat that poor civilian Doctor alive I sent down to him, John. That damn Doctor is an extremely important cog to this entire operation. He knows everything we need to know about those damn warheads and missile systems, John." General White explained to the CIA Director as they both headed for the cars, so they could return to their offices.

"Ahhh... I see your reasoning and your want to speak with your Colonel, General White. When do you want to meet with the President again later on today, sir?"

"Damn Director Raincloud Sir, we're scheduled to be back at the White House at four, ten p.m. sharp today, sir. I hope the Boss doesn't move back the damn meeting because of this morning's rather long session today, Director Raincloud. Say John, why the hell don't you hang out with me for the rest of the day. That way I won't have to go looking around for ya when I need you, or when we have to get back here for our second meeting with the President, Director."

"You springing for lunch then, General White?" Director Raincloud offered with a smirk.

"Sure, just give me a few minutes to speak with Colonel Leadbetter down at Camp Lejeune first, sir. You can leave your damn car parked at the Pentagon if you like, sir." The General offered the powerful CIA Agent as he flashed a quick smile at him.

"I've been meaning to ask you, General White Sir. How is your throat making out anyway, sir? Is it getting any better for you yet, sir? You seem to be talking pretty well lately, General White." Director Raincloud asked the Chairman of the Joint Chiefs of Staff with much concern lacing his voice, while remembering how close his friend came to dying just a few months ago from a gunshot wound to his throat.

"I'm not doing too bad lately Director Raincloud, getting better day by day I feel, John. Thanks for asking about the damn wound, Chief. To tell you the truth, with so much going on about me lately, I nearly forgot completely about the damn wound sir. It seems the only time it really bothers me any longer, is when I eat something and swallow it or I raise my voice, dammit. Then it reminds me in a fast hurry I was wounded recently when I was searching for General Campanelli's missing child, sir." General White replied as he absentmindedly rubbed the spot where the bullet almost ended his life. A fraction of an inch either way, and he would be lying in the ground, with General Edward Campanelli and his wife of a few days. General White allowed his mind to wander as he remember his two friends.

CHAPTER EIGHTEEN

**NOVEMBER 8th, 1998.
THE MOUTH OF THE GULF OF OMAN.
TENHUNDRED TWENTY ONE HOURS
FRIDAY NIGHT, IRANIAN TIME**

Silently, the nuclear powered USS Jacksonville submarine slid through the calm waters of the Indian Ocean, on its way towards the mouth of the Gulf of Oman. Upon reaching her assigned position, the Jacksonville then raised in the water until her sail was just twenty feet from the surface of the water. The Jacksonville then hovered at this depth amid the sounds of the dry shelter being flooded with sea water, and the walls of the shelter moved from around the ASDS system. Then came the almost silent clanks of the mooring latches being releasing. The SEAL Team operation began with the Captain of the Jacksonville giving orders to his crew members.

"Conn to Nav, blow ballast to sixty feet negative, and hold her there."

"Aye Captain, holding boat steady at sixty feet, Skipper." The Seaman reported.

"All on board SEAL Team members are ordered to the hatches, Commander of the Cigar man your post and prepare to board the ASDS system."

There was a sudden clamoring of sailors moving about the submarine as the seven man SEAL Team scurried up the ladder to the ASDS system that was branded 'The Cigar' by the Captain with the help of the crew. After a few moments of almost sheer mayhem, a voice came over the submarines intercom. "The Cigar system is manned and ready for immediate launch, sir."

"Very well, crack the seal and retract the shelter from the ASDA unit."

More noise instantly assaulted the bowels of the Jacksonville submarine as the ASDA system was released from her shackles mooring the unit to the mother ship.

"Dry shelter retraction completed and secured to the sides of the boat, Captain."

"Very well, continue with the releasing the mooring shackles one, two, three and four in that order." The Captain ordered his crew members.

"Aye sir, releasing shackles one, two, three, and four, Skipper. The Cigar's free and under her own power now, Captain." The Boatswain's mate controlling the launch announced proudly.

"Very well then, keep me appraised of the position of the Cigar at all times until she's clear of our sub. Give me constant running reports on the unit as long as she's near my Boat, mister."

"Aye sir, she's ten feet above our decking and is moving off to our portside at three knots at this time, Captain Sir. She's now fifteen feet off the decking of the boat, and is thirty feet off our stern, sir. The Cigar's completely clear of the stern of the boat sir, and the distance is increasing along with her speed at the same time, Captain. She's traveling under ten knots and opening the distance rapidly, she's seventy feet from our stern now, sir."

"When the ASDS unit's two hundred feet off our stern, dive the boat to the bottom and we'll settle down there and wait for the conclusion of their operation."

"Aye Captain, one hundred and fifty feet off our stern and opening the distance. There she goes, she's starting her dive.

That's it, she's two hundred and fifty feet off stern and dropping to one hundred feet and holding, sir." The Boatswain's Mate informed his commander.

"Good, Conn to Helm, take her to the bottom, ahead one third, down planes to full set, flood tanks three and four. Go deep, go deep, go deep. Dive, dive, dive. Quick Quiet." The Captain bellowed into his radio as he ordered the rest of the crew to go to silent running on the boat.

The Boatswain's Mate repeated the orders of the Captain as the Jacksonville responded to the commands of the Commander, and the boat pitched forward. The submarine then took three minutes to reach the bottom of the ocean, five hundred and fifty feet below her keel.

"Sonar, Conn. What the hell does the bottom look like? I don't want to bump into a any damn rocky or cluttered filled bottom and damage my boat." The Captain asked the operator.

"Clean sand below our keel Captain. Picking up no impressions resembling rocks, or other debris that might threaten the boat, sir. It's flat as a board down there Captain. Clean sand."

"Very well, level plain, slow ahead. Sit her on the sand nice and easy."

The Jacksonville slowed to no forward movement as it slowly drifted to the sandy bottom.

"Fifty feet to touch down on the bottom, clean sand, clean sand, Captain."

"Continue to call out the depth for me mister. Crew, this is the Captain, prepare for impact." The Commander growled as he looked for a handhold for his own protection.

"Thirty feet and closing slow, sandy bottom, sandy bottom, all forward motion stopped, sir."

Seconds later. "Twenty feet and closing rapidly, reporting sand bottom still Captain."

"Ten feet and the bottom is flat as a board and nice and sandy sir. Clean sand, clean sand."

"Five feet, contact with the bottom sir. We're now on the bottom Captain, clean and smooth sand sir." The Helm operator reported to his commanding officer.

The submarine shuddered then assumed a slight tilt of seven degrees to portside, as the bottom accepted the full weight of the Jacksonville submarine. Amidst the soft settling noises and hull popping sounds, the submarine slowly came to rest on the bottom and the Captain informed the crew. "We're on the bottom, you might as well make yourselves comfortable. We'll going to be here until the Cigar returns from her mission. Fire watch, look alive, Seamen, carry on assigned duties. Film Sergeant, run a movie without sound, rig for silent waiting. That is all."

ON BOARD THE ASDS, THE ADVANCE SEAL DELIVERY SYSTEM

Captain Thomas Williams, the Commander of the Cigar shaped submersible, heard everything going on about him as the Jacksonville dove. The Captain then set his course for the northeast at seventeen knots to avoid any larger boats. He checked his chart, the ASDS unit was three and a half miles away from the mouth of the Iranian channel that formed the Bander Beheshi port, and Captain Williams set his depth of the Cigar at one hundred and three feet. The ASDS unit vibrated slightly as it was flooded with noise and oscillations. The Captain looked to the mate, each SEAL Team member looked at each other as the vibrating increased a little more. The Captain checked his gauges as the mate checked his radar and sonar systems of the submersible.

"Captain Williams Sir, it looks like a cargo ship's passing over our exact position sir. It could be a fuel or cargo tanker, possibly one of those super tankers judging by the heavy turbulence she's raising even at this depth, Captain Williams."

"Better let the cargo know what the hell's happening about them before they shit themselves. I don't need them soiling their wet suits on us, because some damn oil tanker's passing over our position, mister." Captain Williams ordered as he fought for control over his small submersible.

Slowly, the massive super tanker moved off, the vibrating lessened as the mate informed the SEAL dive team what was happening. The Commander of the Cigar increased speed of the submersible to full, and the sixty five foot submersible slid through the water as silently as a whisper at twenty knots. The Commander was having a bit of a problem keeping his eye on the depth gauge while fighting the helm and turbulence from the massive ship passing over them. There was a cross current before the channel opening, and a second but lighter current bled out from the channel. Keeping the ASDS unit straight was a slight problem and Captain Williams had to use the thrusters on the starboard side almost constantly to keep the craft true to course.

"John, watch the damn depth gauge for me while I hold onto this damn thing, dammit. Let me know the depth constantly, because we're about to enter the damn channel mister."

The ASDS unit was being tossed about in the strong current as if it weighed nothing.

"Captain, the bottom's at two fifty feet, and she rising slightly on us sir."

Captain Williams did not react to the mate's information as he continued to fight the helm, hoping the heavy turbulence would diminish once they were inside the narrow channel. Overhead, sounds of high speed screws were heard throughout the Cigar. Shipping in the channel was as heavy. The turbulence slowly eased as the ASDS unit started to work its way up the narrow channel. "Depth and bottom!" The Captain suddenly roared at his sonar operator.

"One seventy feet and raising fast on us now Captain. It looks like the bottom's coming up quick Captain Williams. Reporting sandy bottom, I'm continuing to scan the bottom, sir."

"Shit, dammit." The skipper snapped as he checked the radar bounce marking his stationary targets and then he grumbled. "I'm picking up four of our targets, maybe the fifth one might have moved its registered position. I'll scan the port side again sir." The commander moved the stroke, picking up most of the civilian shipping moored to the docks inside the Iranian inlet.

"Christ sake, there's so much crap up there, I can't pick out the missing submarine, dammit. Give me direct contact with the SEAL Team."

A second later. "Tom, this is the Captain, it looks like one, maybe even two of the damn Iranian submarines have moved to a different mooring spot I take it for security reasons I'd imagine. Moving their eggs from one damn basket to another I'd suspect. I can't locate the missing two submarines up there for nothing, sir. Whaddaya want to do sir?"

"Captain, take us to the launch depth and we'll take it from there, sir. If the damn submarines are there, we'll find the damn things and end their lives real quick on them, sir."

"Captain Williams Sir, the bottom's up to one hundred feet and still raising fast on us sir."

"How far are we from where the damn submarines are moored, mister?" the Captain barked.

"Two hundred and fifty yards to the first stationary target, Captain."

"What's the depth a hundred yards ahead of our system, son?" the Captain hissed.

The mate pinning the bow reported to his commanding officer. "It raises rather quickly sir. Fifty yards reads sixty five feet in depth sir. Twenty yards after that, reads just thirty one feet, Captain. We're going to have to make a decision real quick I'm afraid, Captain."

"Any damn finger holes to the sides of this damn mess mister? I have to get out of the main shipping lanes, or someone's screws are going to rip us open like a can of fucking tomatoes. I don't need any of those bastards running a sonar pick on us, and discovering us hanging around down here, dammit." The commander growled at his sonar operator.

"I'm picking up a slight depression ten yards off to the portside of the system, sir. It looks like it might run some fifty yards or so deep, and then raises drastically, Captain Williams Sir."

"What's the width of the damn finger, mister? I need to know this so I can park her ass in the slot and wait for the SEALS to return to boat." The Captain asked as he corrected his course.

"It's pretty narrow I take it Captain, twenty feet at its widest point at least sir. The bottom's coming back as clean sand all the way in the finger Captain."

"We should fit in there like a damn glove then." The Captain then keyed the mike and reported to SEAL Team commander. "Tom, get your people ready, I'll get you to within one hundred and seventy yards of our first target, sir. Your course will be north, northeast to first target, sir."

"Thanks for the info Captain Williams Sir that should be close enough for our needs, sir. Okay, get ready people, I'll flood the interior in five minutes." The SEAL Team members ran a last minute check on their gear, and then the divers placed the mouth piece and breathed their air as all eyes went to the red light overhead. The divers waited for the light to change to green. The green light was still out, the SEAL Team felt and sensed the submersible slow down, and then drop to the floor of the channel at rest. When all forward motion ended, the Captain's voice filled the SEAL Team's compartment again, just as the green light burst to life.

"We're there gentlemen. It's now up to you guys from point on out."

A heavy rush of water suddenly flooded the compartment of the system as water rose about the team's head. In no time, the compartment was completely flooded with sea water. Tom, the leader of the SEAL Team operation, opened the hatch and then he drifted out of the submersible. It was dark, and visibility was complicated by the filth of the water. Tree branches, lumber, wood skids, fishing lines, anything that could float was about, debris kicked around by the current hampered their vision and forward progress on the SEAL team attack unit.

The SEAL Team worked towards the first submarine. When they reached it, the leader split the drivers up, sending two along with a spotter to locate the two missing submarines while the other divers set their explosive charges on the sides of the moored submarines. One spotter stayed with the leader. His job was to make sure no enemy divers appeared unannounced, his other duty was to make sure no sharks took a chunk out of any of the specialized divers.

Tom's crew split up, with the divers taking on one submarine each. Tom worked over his target, checking the barnacle encrusted bottom of the submarine for positions he was searching for. The first two positions went quick, the forward torpedo tubes were easily detected. He set his explosive charges where he was certain the torpedoes were being stored inside the Iranian submarine. Then he carefully moved down the length of the submarine until he located the reactor room area of the boat. Here, he set one explosive charge enough to break down the lead containment shield protecting the reactor. He made certain the charge was tight up against the hull after scrapping the surface clean with his dive knife. When the third charge was set in place, he made certain the propeller charge was free of any possible obstructions.

Satisfied with the placement of his charges, the commander moved down the submarine until he reached the missile compartment area, the widest point of the submarine, and the circular impressions of the launch tubs were detected. Intelligence informed him the first two missile tubes were the ones containing Russian made long range nuclear tipped missiles. He scraped off the crud from the bottom of the submarine's hull then he set the charges on the side of the boat. Once this was completed, he headed for the second member of his team, and the submarine he was working on to give him a hand with setting his charges on the second enemy submarine.

The second diver completed his part of the mission, and together the two divers headed for the third submarine to help the last team with their orders. Swimming was terrible, diver two wrote on his chalkboard he was bit by a crab he rousted while setting his charge on the side of the submarine. The water was pitch black and if it was not for the powerful dock lights, the divers would not know where they were going under the water. As the SEAL divers linked up with the third diver, the other team came over with one diver reporting on the chalkboard, the other two submarines were nowhere to be found at port. The commander asked, using a combination of hand signals and chalkboard, what they did with the charges for their assigned submarines. He noticed the divers were no longer carrying their explosive charges on their dive belts.

The lead diver reported they placed their charges, one each on ten different civilian ships dotting the Iranian harbor, the suspected ships carrying contraband supplies for Iran.

He shrugged it off, not caring what they did with the extra charges, although he was pissed they did not get all six Iranian submarines. That meant two boats made it out to sea with their nuclear weapons intact. The missing submarines were the big boy's problems now. Using hand signals, he ordered each diver back to the ASDS unit. One of three spotters had a problem with a stingray that kind of adopted him as his mother. It was constantly trying to land on him, and only when he poked it with the electrical prod, did the stingray finally take off for good.

Another diver was bleeding from the ear and corner of his mouth. He was struck by a piece of wood that was caught in the swift current of the narrow channel. As the SEAL Team made their way back for the ASDS unit, they were caught up in heavy turbulence created by a passing ship. Each diver held on to the other to get enough bulk so as not to be whisked away by the sudden heavy turbulence. But it did not stop them from being assaulted by a new wave of floating debris, and the sea bottom kicked up by the ship as it slowly passed over them.

One diver was struck by a large piece of debris that disabled him, ripping his dive suit and breaking a few ribs, one rib was sticking through his torn skin and ripped dive suit. Instantly, the little scavengers of the sea gathered around the injured man, taking little nips of his broken skin.

Tom and a second diver tugged the almost unconscious buddy along with them. A large and excited bull shark suddenly showed up, drawn in by the smell of fresh blood in the water. The spotters moved ahead of the other divers to fend off the shark. The swim back to the ASDS unit was the hardest part of the entire operation. The SEAL Team divers were suffering from exhaustion, and a myriad of minor nicks and bruises, but nevertheless the divers trudged on.

They reached the ASDS unit, and the commander shoved the injured man inside the scuttle first, and then he followed him in. Once inside the compartment, he helped the other divers aboard the unit. With the entire SEAL Team back inside the miniature submarine, he closed the hatch and dogged it down, and then he hit the lever to drained the lockout compartment of the submersible. The noise of the water being pumped out of the compartment startled the Captain as he was sort of daydreaming. He picked up the radio and barked in it. "Tom?"

After a few seconds. "Yeah Skipper, I'm afraid I have one man down, Captain."

"Shit, how the hell did it go out there otherwise than the injured man, Tom? I have to make a report to the Jacksonville Commander, sir. Did you mine all six of the damn submarines?" the Commander asked the leader of the SEAL team.

"Crappie sir. We only got four of the damn submarines sir. Two damn things must have left port. The other team used their explosives and they mined a number of civilian ships moored at the harbor, Captain. You better inform the big shots that two of the damn submarines were not home when we came looking for the damn things, sir."

"Shit, dammit. How bad is your man hurt, Tom?" the concerned skipper asked the diver.

"Bad enuf Skipper, his damn rib is sticking out of his body, I think he's going in shock, sir."

"Better wrap him up in anything you can find to try and keep him warm. I'll raise the heat as high as it'll go for ya, Tom. I'll get you home A-SAP." The Captain blew his two ballast tanks, and rose the submersible to forty feet, before heading out of the narrow Iranian channel at seven knots. When the Captain was in deeper water, he opened speed, diving while going full ahead. Then when the commander was positive he was clear of the channel, he contacted Jacksonville.

"Cigar to Base. Over." The commander was making contact with the mother submarine.

"This is Base, go with your report Commander. How did they make out sir. Over." The Captain of the Jacksonville replied and asked with a snap in his tone into the radio.

"Base, I have four babies in the soup, two babies were not at home on our little visit, sir. We were unable to play with them sir. Have one child down. Request medic standby sir. Out."

"Understood message. Hard Luck sir. Will have medic standing by for your arrival. Out."

The Captain ordered his submarine to raise to one hundred and ten feet, and hover as the ASDS unit rapidly closed in on his position as he asked sonar. "What's going on up there?"

"Captain, the Cigar's thirty feet off our portside, and she's closing quickly on us, sir."

"Get the divers in the water to lend a hand docking the damn thing."

"Divers out!" the Mate repeated the Captain's orders in the submarine's intercom system.

The loud whoosh of sea water being released assured the Captain of the submarine that the diver team was outside his boat. As the miniature submarine cautiously closed in on its mooring points. The Jacksonville's divers pulled the mooring shackles up towards the mini submarine's four lock on points. The divers helped the submersible line up properly with the hookups using their hands and arm strength. When the mooring hookups were set correctly, a diver reported 'set to moor'. The controller operating inside the Jacksonville started the winches moving. Once the mini submarine was moored properly to the Jacksonville, the walls of the dry shelter closed. When the vacuum seal's were set in place, the sea water was instantly drained off, and the hatches to the Jacksonville and Cigar were opened to each other.

The injured diver was removed from the submersible first, but he died from his injuries. The other divers were brought inside the Jacksonville, and then the outside hatches were dogged down. Instantly, the Jacksonville submarine headed for her home port in Florida.

CAMP LEJEUNE, JACKSONVILLE NORTH CAROLINA. ZERO TEN HUNDRED TWENTY TWO HOURS EST

Colonel Bruce Leadbetter finished meeting with Road Kill (Lieutenant Robert Walker), the Mutt, (Lieutenant Frank Hall) and the civilian doctor, Joel Russbinder, and then he made it to his private office so he could put his feet up while the civilian joined the specialized soldiers for a heavy workout on the obstacle course, and a long run in the heavy body armor and military equipment. A light drizzle made the exercise conditions more terrible for the exhausted doctor.

"Fuck him in the ear if he doesn't have a sense of fricking humor, or like it, the damn civilian puke anyhow for crap sake." Colonel Leadbetter growled as he popped the top on a Bud, and then he sat back. Just as he took the first sip of the brew, his phone rang. "Arrr... Christ sake, what now dammit." He moaned as he sat forward and put his beer down and picked up the receiver and snarled into it. "Yeah, Colonel Leadbetter. Whaddaya want from my can?"

"General White here, you having some problems Colonel Leadbetter Sir? Your damn phone manners leave a helluva lot to be desired you know, mister."

"I'm sure they do at that General White Sir. But I'm just as certain you didn't call to discuss my damn phone manners, sir. What's up General?"

"You'll be if you don't take better care in your damn tone when addressing my ass, Colonel." The General snapped angrily at his lesser officer.

"Yes sir." Colonel Leadbetter moaned as he looked at the ceiling while rolling his eyes.

"I wanted to get back to you to see how the training of these pissants was shaping up, and if the transports have landed." General White growled while gaining control over his temper.

"General White Sir, the trainings of my troops is going very well at this time sir. We finished an action and have the troops working out their muscles some sir. I'll have the people eat, and head for classrooms for the latest skull session of the intended target. As to the last part of your question, yes sir, the first of the transport aircraft has landed at the base, sir."

"Outstanding Colonel, by the way sir. The President okayed a surgical SEAL Team operation to mine a few of the damn Iranian submarines at port, the operation was a complete successful, sir. The original plan was good, but the SEAL's only got four of the damn submarines. Once the mined submarines get underway, they'll be pop off right in the middle of the damn narrow ass Iranian channel, blocking all shipping moored at port for a good old turkey shoot."

"That's great news, but what's that have to do with me and my part of the mission, General?"

"You better watch your god damn step and tone with me mister. I warned you once in this conversation about that shit, and I won't remind you for a second time, Colonel. If I have to remind you again, you won't like the way I'll do it I promise you, sir. There's nothing stopping me from having your ass replaced at a drop of a damn hat you understand. What this has to do with you is as follows, sir. Since the damn submarines will be sunk in the middle of the harbor, less fighter planes will be sent in to attack the damn Iranian port. That means your forces will have more fighter aircraft allocated as support for your part of the mission, Colonel Leadbetter Sir. What do you have to say to that bit of information, Colonel?" General White growled, still steaming over the way the Colonel had dared to speak to him in such a manner over the phone.

"Great, but what would make me happy as a lark about this latest operation sir, is a little more time to better prepare my troops for the damn thing, General White Sir. Maybe make a few full unit rehearsals, at least two to make sure my people are reacting like the god damn killing machines they're supposed to be, General White Sir."

"I assure you Colonel Leadbetter Sir, I'm well aware of your desires and wants, but I have already informed you that in the ideal world, we'd have all of what we desire, sir. Since we don't live in the ideal world, we have to make do with what we got at hand, Colonel. I know the military doctrines call for at least two attack scenarios completed before committing any troops to an action, Colonel Leadbetter. Since time's of the essence on this damn operation mister, and for matters of security, the usual called for workups can't be allowed to be employed.

"Your troops will have to make do with what training they have already received to this point, sir. It comes along with the damn territory Colonel Leadbetter. Your people are supposed to be a rapid response force, professional soldiers to be prepared for anything coming their way in twenty four hours to carry out any action assigned to them, mister. If you think the troops need more training then increase the workload when they're not needed. If your troops fail to make the grade, the President will look for answers, and some will come at the cost of your specialized Units, sir. Are you reading from the same page I am, Colonel?"

"I hear you loud and clear and my troops will carry out their mission as ordered, General White Sir." Colonel Leadbetter snapped, angry the General was threatening him with the breakup of his troops. A hammer he did not like hanging over his head. It was not the first time he was threatened by the General, and he was getting tired of having it used against him. He wanted to dare the General to breakup his units. The outcry from the other nations would be deafening.

"Okay Colonel, I held you up long enough mister. Get back to your troops sir. I expect to hear from you before you load up to begin your operation, sir. Good luck with it Colonel."

Colonel Leadbetter hung up and then he went back to his beer, but it was warm now and he dumped it out in the sink. Lieutenant Walker, the Mutt, and Doctor Russbinder marched into the Colonel's office as ordered. He was still hot as hell over his recent conversation with the Chairman of the Joint Chiefs of Staff, Colonel Leadbetter growled at the three. "It's about time you three shitbirds finally showed up. Walker, where the hell's the rest of the damn Unit at?"

"At the M&L building sir." Walker reported to the Colonel with a snap in his voice.

"Good, Doc, I have the hand drawn map of the entire Iranian complex. I'll show you how we intend to attack the dump, and where we believe your places of interest lay inside the damn place, sir. You can show us what you believe this crap you're interested in, might be housed Doc."

"No problem with that Colonel Leadbetter Sir." The civilian replied to the Colonel.

"Okay Lieutenant begin your damn report mister." Colonel Leadbetter ordered Walker.

BANDER BEHESHI, IRAN 0330 HOURS IRANIAN TIME

Colonel Muhsin Abu Marzuk stood with his hands clasped behind his back, as he glared at the Iranian workers struggling to repair the heavy winch system that lowered the missiles inside the launch tubes of the submarine. Moments ago, Colonel Marzuk smiled as the second Russian built Delta Class submarine carefully navigated the narrow channel towards the open sea. The special Iranian Agent checked his watch and cursed. By now, he wanted all six of his submarines far away from port as possible. He wanted them out before the American aircraft destroyed them at port. He knew the Americans were coming, but he did not know when. All he could hope for, was the workers repairing the mechanical devices in time to load the rest of the missiles, before the devils arrived in their hated warplanes of death. He cast his eyes up towards the sky.

All the while he bellowed orders out at the overworked workers, the SEAL Teams carried out their orders thirty five feet below the water's surface. With a sigh of disgust, Colonel Marzuk cursed the work being performed by the crews, as they toiled with the broken machinery. On his journey from Russia, Colonel Marzuk stopped at the base in Iranshahr to deliver the Russian technicians he secured from Russia. He dropped off the blueprints that would help enable the Russian and Iranian technicians build their own nuclear warheads and missiles that one day would deliver the weapons of mass destruction to the very shores of the United States.

Colonel Marzuk grunted over the hatred he harbored against the Americans as he renewed his vow to kill any and all Americans he came across. The smoke from the countless fires Colonel Marzuk ordered set to try and hide what he was doing on the dock from American satellites, actually made him sick to his stomach. He tapped out a cigarette and popped it in his mouth, and lit it as he glared at the workers trying desperately to fix the awry cable system of the damaged crane. His temper getting the best of him, he bellowed at the workers. "If you worthless fools cannot fix that cursed machine in fifteen minutes. I'll find someone who can, and I'll have the lot of you, your families, and their families arrested and dealt with properly. I want those cursed missiles on board these submarines, and the submarines underway before light of day sets in, fools." Colonel Marzuk flipped his cigarette at the flood of dock workers staring at him.

"Don't dare to stare at me like I'm a worthless jackal, fools. Fix the foul machine at once, you fools!" Colonel Marzuk bellowed once more as he turned and went in an office he used. Inside, there was a bottle of outlawed American rye, and a naked woman waiting to pour it for him.

When the Iranian Agent entered his private office on the dock, the woman immediately lit up a cigarette and offered it to the angry Iranian, along with a shot of the rye. Colonel Marzuk smiled as he cupped a breast and sipped the liquor as he look out the filth covered window at the clowns still desperately trying to repair the damaged crane system.

A sudden thought entered his mind, in the interest of saving some time Colonel Marzuk toyed with placing the remaining missiles on the submarine already prepared to receive the next two missiles. This way he could send three submarines out to sea before the hated Americans arrived. The Iranian Colonel turned away from the window and walked over to the stunningly beautiful young Mediterranean woman who looked so much like an American, and beat her mercilessly. While he struck, kicked, and cursed her, he roared at the Americans for all they have accomplished in their history. He beat the defenseless woman until she no longer resisted his terrible assault on her body. Kicking an unconscious woman took all his anger from him.

He quickly lost all interest in the unconscious young woman. With a final and vicious kick to her midsection, he turned towards the window with another drink in hand. He had no way of knowing, nor did he really care he had just beaten the young woman to death.

His mind was working on overtime, he vowed to himself once Islam destroyed the United States and Israel, he would take a number of Israeli women and find new ways to wreak his vengeance on their worthless bodies. He planned to do this to repay the many injustices he believed the Jews had leveled against the Arabs and Persians since they became a nation right in the heart of the Middle East. Again, he found himself cursing the hated Americans for enabling the Jews to become a powerful force in the Middle East. He blamed the Jews and Americans for all the evils that had befallen his country, not taking into account every other struggling nation suffered many of the same misfortunes. It was all part of growing, but it was much easier to blame someone else for all the problems plaguing him, rather than facing them himself.

After another drink and he left his office and walked over to the edge of the wood and oil soaked dock, to look down the narrow channel to the open sea beyond He showed little if any concern for the woman whose body he stepped over, before leaving the office. Once standing on the dock, he scanned the horizon for any signs of the first submarine that had sailed three hours ago. He was angry they were forced to sail further up channel to the civilian dock area in order to turn around safely, before the underwater crafts sailed back down the channel. With the civilian shipping pouring in the dockyards to unload their merchandise, and turn and speed out the channel before the Americans attacked, life in the port facilities was very threatening to his submarines. Bander Beheshi became an extremely hazardous place to enter or leave, with one tanker underway as one entered. Once, a pair of mammoth ships rubbed together, with one sustaining some serious damage that it was unable to be loaded with cargo.

The angry Iranian Agent was steaming that his prized submarines were being forced to sail further up channel. Then, to maintain control over the submarines maneuverability, they had to sail down the inlet at five knots or better to safely circumnavigate the sharp bends in the narrow channel, while struggling to remain in the deeper part of the channel. As he surveyed the far off horizon, he noticed the tide was starting to go out which added to the dangers facing the other submarines about to head out to sea. The Iranian Colonel glanced at the sky again, worried if the American warplanes came at this time, they would capture his remaining submarines trapped at port. Sinking them, or any civilian ships caught up in the mouth of the channel, would spell the end of all shipping inside the channel, including his submarines.

An aide walked up to Colonel Marzuk as a merchant ship steamed by his moored submarines, causing the submarines to be tossed about violently in the powerful wake of their turbulence while tied off to the docks. Colonel Marzuk bellowed at the Captain of the merchant ship for causing his submarines to be slammed up against the pilings of the dock. Workers raised their hands and joined him in his anger. The Iranian Agent glared at the aide as he bitched at him. "Fool born from a camel's arse, I cannot understand why Ayatollah al-Tamini would not allow me to keep the submarines berthed at the much larger Bandar-e-Abbas port. Does he not realize how important these god cursed ships are to our cause against the worthless United States?

"Does he not realize the countless hours and days I have worked to acquire these warships from the filthy dogs to our north? At least the port of Bandar-e-Abbas was constructed to house submarines. May Allah be praised." Colonel Marzuk moaned as he lifted his hands towards the heavens. "Look at this filthy pig sty, it's not worthy to berth even a lowly garbage scow, let alone my submarines. Look at the deplorable conditions these lowly jackals work on my machines. They treat my submarines with no more respect than they do their foul families. When this is over, I swear to the Almighty Allah that I'll have their worthless heads resting on a stick."

When not a word was uttered by the aide, Colonel Marzuk turned and looked at him to make sure he was near and paying attention to his words. His eyes leveled on the aide who, with nothing else to say, merely nodded and offered. "May Allah be with you always."

"Ahhh...., I fear Allah no longer hears my prayers. I believe what will happen in our future, will be shaped by our hands. A great destiny awaits us for the collection. With these foul submarines, missiles, and warheads we'll be constructing, America will no longer be the lead dog in the race. Our years of following them through the path of history will come to a quick end. Then it'll be they, who'll follow our arse along the trail of destiny." Marzuk sneered as he scanned the inlet.

"Did you enjoy my little present I left in your office for you, Colonel Marzuk?" The aide asked, for it was his duty to make sure all of Colonel Marzuk's needs were well looked after.

"Yes fool, the present was a fine pick, but she's of no further use to me, and I'll need another foul and worthless woman to fill the void night brings one. Make this next one from our area. Hmmm... make her a Jew so I can experience pleasure when I beat her for her cursed sins. I know our people have kidnapped a number of bitch Jews from Palestine, so we'll have a good and steady supply of hostages if the hated Jews join on the attack against our country, when the hated Americans come to attack us. Bring me a woman from this lot I speak of. She'll not be returning to the others by the time I finish with her god cursed body I assure you fool." Colonel Marzuk grinned that was more a sneer, and then he laughed as he spat in the filthy water of the channel.

"I understand and shall obey, Colonel Marzuk Sir. I'll return the beaten pig to the cell."

"Yes, you do that if she's still alive that is, you young fool you." Colonel Marzuk said, not believing the young woman was dead.

The aide instantly disappeared as Colonel Marzuk moved even closer to the submarine resting in the channel and moored to the dock with its forward launch tubes open to the air. The groan of the winch drew his attention as the mast inched cautiously towards the missile resting on the tracks. Air horns blared, sending the horde of workers and military personnel scattering.

The Iranian Colonel and Special Agent diverted his eyes from the crane to see the empty trailer barreling out of the gate of the base. He watched as the workers slung cables around the missile, and then the crane groan in protest over the massive weight of the missile on the end of the cables. Tag lines were affixed to the missile as the crane strained to lift it properly. The horde of workers held on to the rope tails, and helped guide the missile carefully inside the launch tube of the nuclear submarine. Once the tail was properly aligned with the launch tube, they untied the bottom tag lines. The crane let out more cable and the gleaming white cylinder of death slowly disappeared inside the waiting launch tube. Halfway in, progress stopped as the cables securing the mid section of the missile, and the final tag lines were removed from the missile. The only cable still controlling the missile now, was the one securing the nose cone of the missile.

The nuclear tipped Russian built missile was set in place inside the launch tube, and the workers removed the last cable, they then placed the water tight, hard plastic seal over the missile and quickly cemented it in place. Once this was accomplished, the workers helped the hatch lower by hand until it completely disappeared inside the framework of the submarine, but not before the charge that destroyed the water tight seal was connected to its wire lead. A cheer rose as the first missile was correctly secured inside the submarine. The crane spun, coming to a stop over the second missile still resting on its carrying track. The process was about to be repeated when a loud groan from the ancient crane, and then it jammed in place. With cables swinging wildly over the missile, the workers climbed over the stuck crane. Screams, curses, and orders assaulted Colonel Marzuk's ears as he stomped closer to the disabled crane in a wild rage.

He watched in anger as a fire erupted in the engine compartment of the disabled crane. The port fire department reacted and flooded the rear compartment of the crane with water pumped from the sea. The Colonel tried to stop the firemen before they flooded the engine with the salt water they were drawing directly from the canal, and ruined the engine completely. Sparks, and flames shot out of the crane as shorts quickly replaced the original fire. The Iranian Colonel jumped on the side of the machine and shoved a firemen out of his way, so he could see what was going on with the fire inside the crane. The compartment was a total mess, wires were burning and melting from many shorts the sea water caused inside the destroyed machine.

He pulled his side arm out and shot the nearest fireman to him right in the head, his actions sent the others firefighters running for their lives, as they looked over their shoulders at the commanding officer on the base as he just killed one of their own.

The Dock Master was furious that Colonel Marzuk had just fired and killed one of the port firemen as he roared angrily at the fuming Iranian Agent. "Colonel Marzuk, what the devil are you doing here? You cannot kill my men, and then expect them to work for you. Stop this foolishness at once sir! Put your gun up so I can get some help for the downed man, sir."

Colonel Marzuk glared at the Dock Master who actually reached out and grabbed his arm and push it up before he could shoot another fireman and he snarled savagely at the Dock Master. "Filthy jackal! How dare you place your cursed hands on me. I'll have you suffer the death of a thousand cuts for that foolishness. Look at the damage these fools have caused me. The crane is totally useless now. How will I get the missiles in the submarine before the Americans come?"

All eyes immediately looked to the sky as a few of the suddenly scared workers even backed away from the moored submarines. Many of the workers had no idea the Americans would dare attack a port inside Iran. Fear replaced the backbone of the workers, because burned in their memory was the terrible carnage the American warplanes had caused in Iraq. Then the latest war that had so decimated most of the Middle East, including a large part of Iran.

Colonel Marzuk saw the fear etched in the faces of the dock workers and he warned them in no uncertain terms. "Fear not the god cursed worthless American planes of war attack you fools, because I am the more serious threat against your worthless lives than any god cursed Americans, lowly fools." Colonel Marzuk then savagely ripped his arm free of the Dock Master's grasp, and he waved his weapon at the group of workers, making them move further away from him.

"Any of you loathsome fools who dares to leave their god cursed foul post, will be shot without hesitation by me. The fool's families will pay for their cowardliness as well. These god hated missiles have to be loaded inside the foul submarines, even if they have to be loaded by hand. Get back to work while you're still able to work, jackals." When finished threatening the workers, Colonel Marzuk turned to the Dock Master and warned him just as angrily. "That goes for you as well, son of a scorpion. Get back to work, old fool! No one stops working, no one rests not for one lowly moment, no one eats until the missiles are loaded inside those machines."

"My faithful Persian brother, may Allah forgive you for your terrible sins. If you'll allow me to explain sir. You might better understand the many problems we are being faced with here sir."

"Go ahead old fool and explain." Colonel Marzuk barked while glaring at the Dock Master.

"I was about to remove this aged crane from duty before it caught on fire on us sir. I feared it's too old and unreliable for fine work demanded by this loading procedure of the missiles inside the submarines. I have a more modern mobile crane moving to position, and with it we'll load your missiles inside the launching tubes of the remaining submarines much more safely, sir."

Colonel Marzuk was unable to reply, his anger was uncontrollable and actually strangling his words. He glared at the elderly Dock Master before finally stepping aside, and allowing him to get by him to help guide the new crane into working position. The older crane was dragged away from its position by a heavy track machine used to move cargo containers around on the dock.

The new crane was quickly placed in operation, and the workers slung the second missile and then lower it inside the launch tube. When the tube's hatch was secured, Colonel Marzuk ordered the submarine to get right underway. The Iranian Colonel stood on the dock as the submarine's props stirred up a cloud of silt from its powerful turbulence. The mooring lines were cast off, and the submarine made turns to four knots as it pulled away from the dock, and then headed up channel where it could turn around without becoming a problem to the other ships resting at port.

As Colonel Marzuk kept his eyes glued on the submarine's silhouette cautiously moving in the darkness. He watched his prize submarine slowly leaving the dock, a looming shadow suddenly steamed past him, while heading straight for the submarine as it was in the midst of its turn. The Iranian Colonel drew in his breath as he stared in stunned disbelief as the massive oil tanker steamed in the channel. He turned to see where his submarine was, it was carefully navigating its turn and would be hit broadside by the incoming ship. The fuming Colonel froze in place with fear that the Captain of the tanker did not noticed the outline of his submarine in the darkness.

The Iranian Agent jumped in action as he screamed wildly at the tanker's Captain. Giving no consideration that he might be unable to be heard, Colonel Marzuk continued to bellow over the roar from the ship's powerful engines. He was so angry he fired his pistol at the tanker's conning tower, trying to get the Captain's attention, or even kill him. Without warning, the behemoth ship suddenly veered off and gave way to the submarine. With a deep sigh of relief, Colonel Marzuk watched as the submarine fought the powerful wake created by the massive tanker that passed it less than thirty feet off the submarine's bow. He smiled as the sail of the submarine tossed violently in the channel as if it was a cork tied to the fishing line of a child's fishing pole.

The natural currents of the channel, combined with the heavy turbulence created by the civilian ship, produced more problems for the submarine's Captain, as he struggled desperately to try and keep his boat true on course in the narrow channel. The submarine made its way towards the sea. The Captain was forced to increase his speed, to better keep up with the turbulence, and he ordered the speed of the submarine increased to full ahead, which increased to eight knots.

The submarine's bow neatly sliced through the water, creating a bow wake. Colonel Marzuk could not hide the grin plastered on his face as the submarine came abreast of him, and then it quickly glided passed him. At five knots and one hundred yards away from the Colonel, a sudden and powerful explosion tore apart the bow of the submarine, raising what was left of the boat completely out of the water. For what seemed like minutes, the entire front end of the submarine remained above the waterline, as smoke and flames instantly replaced the bow of the sea craft.

Colonel Marzuk did not realize the charge planted by the SEAL Teams on his submarines detonated first, the charge was sufficient in strength to explode three of the boat's twenty torpedoes stored over the planted charge inside the bow of the nuclear powered submarine.

At first, everyone working on the docks ran away from the commercial shipping at port. The sky overhead was instantly being crisscrossed with heavy Triple A anti-aircraft fire, with glowing tracers lighting up the night sky on the dock workers. SAM missiles added to all the mayhem now taking place over the Iranian port. The water showed hundreds and then thousands of splashes, as the spent flack rounds returned to earth. Some of the workers pointed towards the skies, crying the American warplanes were attacking them. The workers mistaken the SAM missiles as streaking American warplanes. Since being informed by the angry Colonel Marzuk that they expected an American air attack against the port, the concerned workers were jumpy and spent a lot of their time looking more to the sky than carrying out their assigned duties.

Colonel Muhsin Abu Marzuk was stunned by the spectacle of his prized submarine being torn apart right before his eyes, as a second explosion about mid-ship of the submarine, lifted the remaining body of the submarine completely out of the water. This second explosion was followed almost immediately by a third explosion that finished off ripping the carcass of the submarine in half the long way. The Colonel's dream of revenge against the Americans, was being torn apart as if some unforeseen can opener was at work against his evil wishes.

Not for a second did Colonel Marzuk believe that any American warplanes had just acted against his base, or were at work against his submarines. He stared with disbelieving eyes as large parts of the submarine were being tossed high in the sky like they had no weight to them, and then they returned unceremoniously to the sea. A long burst of Triple

A fire brought him back to his senses, as the Iranian Colonel instinctively ducked from the powerful explosions taking place high in the sky. He was convinced the Captain of the destroyed submarine must have somehow run the submarine aground, crushing the bow on the edge of the narrow channel, and setting off an explosion inside the torpedo compartment of the submarine. He savagely cursed his leaders for forcing him to work in the narrower port, ill equipped for handling and working on his submarines. He was absolutely furious he just lost one of his prized boats, even before they had a chance to engaged any American ships on station in the Persian Gulf waters.

Colonel Marzuk surveyed all the mayhem that replaced the toil of dock workers. Fires raging out of control here and there on the dock, set off by returning flack rounds, or burning parts of his destroyed boat. The Colonel angrily shook his head as he watched a number of dock workers run away in fear. The scared men stopped the brave workers trying to mount a defense against the fires threatening to get out of control. The Colonel eyes flared with disgust as he watched other dock workers crashing into each other, many crying, others hysterical as they ran in no set direction to flee from the invisible American warplanes thought to be attacking the port.

The Colonel was marveling at the awesome power possessed by the feared American military might. A mere freak explosion, or another unforeseen circumstance had just claimed his boat, and it sent the fools of his country running as if they were a pack of women running away from a mouse in their kitchen. The scene reminded him of what once flashed across thousands of his country's TVs, as the once proud Iraqi soldiers cowered in fear under the American onslaught of their nation, and the foolish soldiers actually surrender to unmanned American observation aircraft. The fuming Iranian Colonel remembered seeing fifty well armed and obviously trained Iraqi soldiers dropping their weapons, and then they placed their hands in the air, as a news helicopter flew overhead while taking pictures of the Iraqi soldiers surrendering to them.

When Colonel Marzuk saw two of his workers drop down to their knees, and then they raise their hands in surrender, he reacted violently against them without thought. He aimed his pistol at one of the workers and fired, but a click was the only report he had from the weapon. He ejected the empty clip and slammed a loaded clip home. Then he fired at the first traitor to his way of thinking, killing him instantly with the round to the head. When the second man realized he was about to die, he tried to run from the Colonel attacking them. It took three bullets to bring him down as the Iranian Colonel roared in anger at the crying man who he just killed in his anger.

Colonel Marzuk knew he still had the other boat needing to be fitted with the remaining two Russian made missiles if he stood a chance of realizing his dream. He climbed atop the newer mobile crane, and bellowed at the top of his lungs at the fearful dock workers. When he was unable to get their attention, he fired his weapon in the air, and when this did not work, he fired right at the workers. The fleeing workers had to dodge the falling men trying to run before them.

Soldiers soon appeared and they quickly took the clue from the fuming Colonel, and they began to fire in the air over the fleeing dock workers. Their weapon fire stopped the workers from running away from the docks, and soon they began to listen to the Colonel's angry words.

"Fools born to mothers who must have mated with the lowly scorpions of the desert. This was not a cursed attack on this base by any American aircraft or military forces. It was the fault of the foolish Captain of the cursed submarine. The stupid fool must have run the submarine aground and destroyed his boat. Get back to work, I need these remaining missiles set in place in their launch tubes of the other submarines. I warn you pack of god cursed gutless jackals, if I see anyone dropping down to their knees and raising their hands in surrender. You'll not live long enough to give up to any god cursed American soldiers. As Iranians you fools are expected, and you will fight to the death with your last drop of worthless blood. Yes it's true the American troops are coming to attack us, and if you want Iran to end up like Iraq, give up to them.

"I order you worthless fools to be prepared to fight with guns, broken bottles, sticks, hammers, and with you god dom teeth if need be to defend your country against any United States soldiers. Now get back to your lowly work, fools. Soldiers, escort the foolish workers back to their work positions. You'll shoot anyone who gives you any trouble, or refuses to work." Colonel Marzuk glared at anyone caught in his sight as the soldiers pushed the workers towards their stations. A sigh left the Colonel's lips as he realized he was gaining control over the Naval Base again.

Triple A anti-aircraft fire was still being pumped into the night sky, and Colonel Marzuk had to send a soldier over to the gun installations to silence the weapons, so his workers would return to their assigned duties.

Colonel Marzuk had not realized the remaining parts of the boat, were going to severely hamper the shipping lanes of the tight access out of the narrow channel to open sea. The Colonel ordered Bander Beheshi closed, that was a main artery to supply Iran food and civilian needs, and military supplies brought from Russia, South Africa, and other ports of call, closed to civilian shipping since his submarine was destroyed inside the channel. This order blocked all shipping in Bander Beheshi from leaving port, and stacked up the civilian ships waiting outside the channel for unloading of their cargos for Iran.

Until all shipping lanes leading into the Iranian port became overcrowded and an extremely dangerous area to navigation for any civilian shipping going to other ports of call along the Persian Gulf. Quickly, the new Iranian government was being flooded with countless complaints coming from the nations of Kuwait, Saudi Arabia, Iraq, and other Arab nations bordering the Persian Gulf region. Complaining their shipping was being blocked and held up by the ships being stacking up in the Persian Gulf, while not being allowed to sail the channel leading to the port of Bander Beheshi. The Iranian government completely ignored all the endless complaints being launched from the other nations. As far as the Iranians were concerned, the Arab nations were their enemy, and were to be treated as such.

DIRECTOR RAINCLOUD'S OFFICE AT CIA HEADQUARTERS, LANGLEY VIRGINIA

Central Intelligence Agency Director John Raincloud was informed of the destruction of the Iranian submarine in the port of Bander Beheshi, it was the result of the SEAL Team action pitted against the submarines. The Director sent a request for a flyover of the port to see what was happening with the remaining submarines now successfully trapped at port. Word came back the flyover reported three of the remaining Iranian submarines still at the port were intact, and they were waiting to be loaded with the remaining

Russian missiles. The report stated there was much damage created to the port, when the first submarine exploded inside the narrow channel.

This was expected and the American military wanted as much damage as possible done to the Iranian port, before committing their warplanes to attack the dock area and what was left of the port. Although the sinking of the first boat was a big deal, the Director sent a Level Two memo out to the White House, informing the President the first Iranian submarine was destroyed.

This was the first of many attacks to be carried out against Iran and her military assets, before the main attack began against the Persian nation. American warships were ordered to attack and sink any military type Iran ships discovered on the open sea. This order included the small speed boats the Iranian command used to attack civilian shipping on the waters of the Persian Gulf.

The trailing United States Missile Frigates were ordered to move out from positions in the Indian Ocean, taking up new positions of attack, to enable the ships to come to aid civilian shipping under attack from Iranian speed boats. A second Aircraft Carrier set sail for the Mediterranean, in case she and her warplanes and support ships were needed on attacks against Iran. All American and Coalition aircraft in Arabia and Kuwait, and American bases in these Arab countries were placed on full alert, with attention turned towards the military bases, security systems. American aircraft flights over the Gulf of Oman were increased from these countries.

CHAPTER NINETEEN

Minutes before dawn on the day the American troops were scheduled to land inside Iran, Mohammed Boua Bdellah assembled his small communication radio with the help of Ahmed Hussein Shamarral. Bdellah was ordered to make contact with his controller back in the United States at midnight, and he was set moments before the transmission was to be sent out.

CIA Director John Raincloud was able to have his once sleeper operative working in Iran, Bdellah's transmission transferred over to the Chairman of the Joint Chiefs of Staff, General John White's private office in the Pentagon. So they both would be able to read the agent's report together at the same time as they came in. General White wanted to know what the agent was witnessing in Iran. So he could report the results to the President at their upcoming meeting.

NORASATCOM. NORTH AMERICAN SATELLITE COMMAND CENTER. 12 NOON, NOVEMBER 9th, 1998. EST

The Airforce Sergeant waiting for the call from Sand Star to come in, jumped up when his call name suddenly appeared printed out on his screen, and he immediately called out to his controller. "Hey Lieutenant, I have Deep Cover Three reporting in on schedule, sir."

The Lieutenant rushed over to the Sergeant's console and he read the words as they appeared, and then he ordered the Sergeant. "You better get this crap transferred over to the Pentagon A-SAP. Send a copy out to CIA HQ, and a backup sent to the hard drive downstairs. I don't want anyone coming at us later on complaining they didn't get a copy of this crap in time, Sergeant."

"Yes sir, considerate it on the way out as ordered, Lieutenant." One of the Sergeants replied.

General John White was busy enjoying a Pepsi with his feet up resting on his desk when his signal came in. Both he and Director Raincloud jumped and moved closer to the machine so they could both read the agent's report as it was being printed out.

/\/\/\ SAND STAR TO CONTROL /\/\/\
/\/\/\ TIME: MIDNIGHT, IRAN TIME SAT /\/\/\

/\/\/\ GP114 LAT BY 720 LON /\/\/\ (GP-GLOBAL
POSITION)
/\/\/\ REPORT AS FOLLOWS /\/\/\
/\/\/\ HAVE FRIENDLIES IN POSITION TO ASSIST
TROOPS WHEN ARRIVE ON TARGET. BREAK. AM IN
POSITION TO LINKUP WITH SAID FRIENDLY TROOPS
AND PREPARED TO LEAD THEM TO THE TARGET.
BREAK.
SLIGHT INCREASE IN IRANIAN MILITARY TROOPS IN
AND AROUND
IRANSHAHR TARGET. BREAK. THREE TANKS,
RUSSIAN IN NATURE
T-72 CLASS OBSERVED OUTSKIRTS OF SAID VILLAGE.
BREAK.
NO INCREASE IN MAIN MILITARY MOVEMENTS
OBSERVED AT
THIS TIME. BREAK. WILL KEEP APPRAISED IF ANY
IRANIAN TROOPS
OBSERVED ENTERING VILLAGE OR NEAR THE
SURROUNDING AREAS
OF CONCERN TO OUR TROOPS INVOLVED IN
ATTACK ON COMPLEX
IN QUESTION. BREAK.
LOOK FORWARD SEE TROOPS ARRIVE. SICK OF
SAND. OUT /\/\/\

General White pulled the paper free from the machine and then he reread the report more carefully for a second time. He then turned to Director Raincloud and said to him. "It looks like the damn Iranians are still unaware we're coming for their fucking asses, John."

"I hope you're right with that assumption General White Sir. We could sure use a damn break with this operation, sir.

What the hell do you make of the Iranian troops arriving near the city of Iranshahr, and moving those damn Russian built tanks around at the same time? I hope to hell our people won't have to tangle with any of that heavy armor on this mission, General White Sir." Director Raincloud grumbled as he took the report and read it over himself.

"It's all bullshit and bad manners if you were to ask me John. If the damn Iranians believed we knew of this supposed secret complex in this area of their desert. The entire area would be dick deep in Iranian troops and tanks. No Director, I think the Iranian troop movement's being carried out is merely to impress the locals, and keep them locked in their damn homes. The tanks could be a serious problems to our troops as you have just suggested though sir. I'm banking on them being the three machines already reported stationed by the damn complex by your operative. I sure hope the Iranians are moving the damn tanks around to charge their batteries, and lubricate the machinery. Maybe they're using them to pick up some of the local hens (women). I don't know, but I'm sure as hell going to find out. Whaddaya think, can your operative work his way out there and check on the tanks? Or should I send a satellite over for a quick look see John?"

"I think you should really send a satellite snooping around over the damn complex, General White. I don't want to send my operative back out there again and chance exposing him to possibly being uncovered and arrested by any Iranian soldiers, until he's waiting for our troops to arrive on site so he can assist our soldiers, sir." Director Raincloud offered to the Chairman.

"John, can't your damn operative check on the Iranian tanks, and you can order the Agent to also hang around the area until our troops arrive on target, and then deal with that god damn structure and the crap they're building inside the damn dump, sir?" General White asked, trying to find an easier way for him to be able to pick up new Intel than diverting a satellite.

"General White, I can't have my man roaming around the damn desert so adjacent to the target complex until it's much closer to the time of the opening attack by our troops, sir. All he has to do is be discovered by any Iranian soldiers or other Agents, and the entire operation could be placed in jeopardy and blow up under our feet." Director Raincloud smiled at General White.

"True, you have a good point there Director, I guess I'll divert a damn satellite after all sir. Either way, I'll have Colonel Leadbetter prepare his troops to take out six tanks instead of the already reported three. It's better to be safe than sorry when conducting an operation of this scale. Have your operative sit tight until tomorrow night I guess when our troops get in gear. Then I want him the hell out there with his new found friends to guide my people to target. I can't wait until tomorrow so my troops can straighten out this fucking mess by their own means, John."

"According to his latest report I have received, my Agent's already set in position to intercept Colonel Leadbetter's troops when they enter the area of concern, General White. I'll have Sand Star change his radio frequency over to the intersquad's guard channel, so he can communicate directly with Colonel Leadbetter and the rest of the troops under his command, sir."

"Good thinking on your part there John, this way the troops can set up their own linkup position with your operative out in the field, sir." General White checked his watch, it was fast approaching time to leave for the White House. One thing they did not want to be, and that was late for a meeting with the Boss, especially not before an action is about to take place.

General White stood while Director Raincloud placed the latest report inside his briefcase, and then he announced. "I guess we might as well get this thing over with sir."

CAMP LEJEUNE, NORTH CAROLINA.
SIXTEEN HUNDRED TEN HOURS EST
NOVEMBER 9th, 1998

The special ops troops under Colonel Bruce Leadbetter's command, finished a quick march of five miles with full battle gear, and the exhausted soldiers were preparing to take a break before hitting the gym to work out with the weights. Lieutenant Walker, the Mutt, and Colonel Leadbetter picked apart the brains of the doctor while the rest of the troops did their own act. Walker felt he could find most of what the civilian doctor was after inside the complex. Colonel Leadbetter wanted Walker's troops to secure the complex, and eliminate any possible Iranian troops inside, and take as prisoners any Russian technicians discovered working in the complex.

When Colonel Leadbetter thought he picked the doctor's brains clean, he growled. "Okay pukes, get out of my damn office and join the other pukes at the gym. I have other important shit to handle, and I don't need you people confusing my damn noggin. Beat it, err... Hey Doctor. You'll return to this office and sleep here. I don't want you hanging around this damn riffraff any longer than you absolutely have to, you don't want their smell rubbing off on ya ass, shove off."

"Riffraff? I ain't no damn riffraff, I'm cool Colonel." The Mutt griped as he left the office.

"You betta get the fuck outta my damn office, before I make you cooler than you think you are, by drilling a coupla damn holes in your ass. Huh, see what I mean about these slugs rubbing off on you Herr Doctor. I used to speak rather intelligently, now I'm using words like coupla and outta. You betta, huh, there I go again. Anyway, you betta be careful hanging around this shit, or they'll fuck you up bad, sir. Beat it." Colonel Leadbetter balled up a sheet of paper and bounced it off the Mutt's head as he retreated towards the door leading out of Leadbetter's office.

"Christ, can you beat that shit man? First Colonel Leadbetter calls us stinking riffraff, now he says we don't talk right, man. Next, he'll probably gripe we don't screw our women right for crap sake man." The Mutt added with a smirk as the soldiers left the Colonel's office.

Colonel Leadbetter stared at the trio as they quickly left his office, he shook his head and went to the freezer and took out an ice cold can of Bud to enjoy for a few moments of down time.

Lieutenant Robert Walker was pleased over rejoining his low lifers no matter where they were gathered. Although he was now a Lieutenant and he belonged in the officer's quarters, his heart belonged in the grunt pig sty along with the rest of the mud slappers from the outfit. The elite soldiers removed their gear and left it resting before the entrance to the gym. Some of the soldiers took time to smoke, others just enjoyed the sun, and a few more wrote letters to their loved ones even though the letters would not be sent out until the mission was completed.

Buckethead was mumbling with Dock Rat and Jungle Bunny. They were discussing the French broad. Walker and the Mutt banged fists as the doctor remained standing in the background, not sure how he was supposed to interact with these extremely dangerous men and women soldiers. Buckethead offered Walker a Bud as the others moved in to hear what Walker had to say.

Walker popped the top on the beer and then groused at the huge soldier standing in front of him. "Man that shit's fucking cold, buddy. Listen up, we hafta keep our stinking eyes open for some uther shit than just these fricking bad guys we're afta on this operation. The Doc here needs any file cabinets left secured and undamaged until he can dig through'em and find what he's looking for. Don't hit the cabinets with any stinking grenades if you can help it, McNip, you stay close to the Doc. You have the duty to pop the locks offa the cabinets if necessary for him."

Sergeant Dorothy Ramirez joined the small group of soldiers and she automatically planted a quick kiss on Walker's cheek, causing the other soldiers with him to make some cat calls and hoots and hollers' at them. The slight commotion caused the shy acting French soldier to come over and join the other soldiers. She grinned as Ramirez ran her hand between Walker's legs, and then she gave his nuts a squeeze in front of all the soldiers by them. She eyed Walker enjoying the attention from this woman, and she purred at the soldiers. "Bonjour mon ami, you must be the soldier I have heard so much about, mista. I see your reputation was not exaggerated in the..."

"Man, listen to those sweet ass sounding stinking words she's almost fucking singing at us, man. I don't know what the hell she's saying to us. For all I know, she could be cursing your ass both up and down, but if she is, it sounds sweet so enjoy the shit outta it Homes. Here, let me clear a place for you to sit down for a little while baby." The Mutt offered the pretty and young French babe as he rubbed his face with both hands, and then he added to his offer. "Hey here you go

Frenchie, come mere and place a French lip lock on this here baby of mine." The Mutt then grabbed his dick through his pants while thrusting his hips out at the female French soldier on loan to the specialized unit of soldiers and he grinned at her.

"Mon ami! You speak too quickly for me to understand all your words of English which I speak not so good, American soldier. Do you have a dirty face, or pain in your crotch? I'm no Doctor, but I look at it if you would like, soldier." Sergeant Regina Raphael offered seriously.

"Yeah baby, that's it, I got me a stinking pain right in my stinking crotch area alright, and only your sweet French lips sucking on my shaft will ease the damn pain for me, baby. It's time you gimme a real close short arm inspection, wit your stinking lipstick on my dickstick will do."

"Ohhhh... I understand what you want from me now, soldier. I'm afraid I don't do that sex stuff please. At least not until I get to know you some much better, American soldier... err...?"

"Frenchie that jerk over there with his stinking dick locked in his effing hand is known as the Mutt." Mother Flanagan Sergeant Richard Flanagan called out as he rolled a joint for the group.

"God dammit Mother, I fucking told you none of that crap until we know what the fuck we're doing in sand land, man. This one and no more buddy or I'll kick ya in the can." Walker warned.

Sergeant Barbara Meyerhoff, known to the other soldiers from the elite Unit of soldiers as Fun Bags, and she was the Mutt's girlfriend, saw him waving his dick in front of the new female fighter as she joined the others and she immediately complained at him. "Jesus Mutt, every time I see you lately, you have that damn black snake of yours in hand, and you're always trying to get some poor girl to suck on the damn thing for you, buster. When are you ever going to learn?"

"Never happen baby, I don't learn nuthin too good you know baby." The Mutt grinned at her.

"You got that right Homes. He don't know nuthin." Someone else called from the group.

"Mon ami, what kind of name is the Mutt for a soldier? You American soldier have very peculiar names for each other I see. I'll never get use to the funny names you soldiers call each other." The female French Sergeant placed her hand on the side of her face, and then she stared at the Mutt's dick being wiggled right in front of her face.

"Hey Frenchie, he got the stinking name of the Mutt, cause he has a white mother and a sambo father, making him a mutt to both stinking races baby." The soldier branded the Roach Sergeant David Burgwald called out as he popped a beer and then joined the rest of the group.

"Ohhhh... I see why you call soldier the Mutt, mon ami. You are what we call in France... err... White Chocolate, no?" She offered as she flashed a smile that would have melted butter.

Walker laughed as he clapped his hands together and called out to the other soldiers. "White Chocolate! I fucking love it man. What a stinking name for a mixed breed fucked up ass like you Mutt. Christ, I don't know what name I like betta now. The stinking Mutt or White Chocolate."

"Hey man you can call me any shit you wanna, as long as this Frenchie does the dirty to me."

Fun Bags moved close enough to grab the Mutt's member, and she drew it into her mouth and ran her tongue on the sides of it, before stopping when the shaft got as hard as it could get, and then she announced to the other soldiers standing in the group. "If anyone's going to put a damn lip lock on that colorful shaft of his, it's going to be me and me alone people. Unless we're partying together that is, wiseguy. Now put that damn thing away before a seagull dive bombs down and takes it for a small worm and bites the damn thing off on you, stupid."

"Small?" The Mutt cried as he repeated again. "Small! Whatdaya fucking mean by calling my King Cobra snake here small for crap sake? I'll show you how small it is little sister. C'mere and suck on it again and see how small it is, or how large you can make it with your stinking mouth."

"Small," Fun Bags repeated and added. "That's why they called it a short arm inspection fool."

"How the hell am I gonna get my damn black snake back inside my stinking pants while it's hard like this, baby? You gotta C'mere and take care of it for me, or big Jim and the stinking twins will hang out until someone else steps up and does me right and proper baby." The Mutt again waved his member back and forth as he looked at his girlfriend with pleading eyes.

"Oh please Barb you have to do something with that damn thing of his now. I don't want to see him dragging his black snake on the floor in front of the rest of us for the rest of the day, girl. If you don't do something with the damn thing, he's going to try to shove it in my mouth. Or between the lips of us other girls from the Unit until someone takes pity on his ass and does him." Sergeant Ramirez stared at Fun Bags as she gave her friend a smile and wink of her eye.

"You saying I'm only good for a pity fuck now, huh bitch? What the hell's going on around here all of a sudden." The Mutt griped as he turned to Ramirez and gave her a heated stare.

"I hate to burst your bubble on you stupid, but that's all you were ever any good for, just a pity fuck stupid." Sergeant

Ramirez added to her bitch at him as she grinned and wiggled her hips.

"I'm stunned, I'm really hurt by that last remark Raz. Look at my stinking puss, see the hurt in my damn eyes? Nevertheless, I'm turned on by the offer anyway, Raz. You game for a pity blowjob?" the Mutt turned his head and put on the stupidest smile, trying his best to look hurt.

"Hey Mutt, the only thing that could ever hurt your stinking feelings, is not being able to get it up." Sergeant Ramirez laughed as she turned her back, and she said over her shoulder at the soldier. "Will you please put that damn thing away, it's ugly as hell you know, Mutt."

"Why? Does it offend you all of a sudden, honey?" The Mutt grumbled back at her, not knowing for certain if Ramirez was really serious with her bitch at him.

Sergeant Ramirez suddenly spun around as if she was really angry at the Mutt, carrying out her joke a little further by barking at him angrily. "Now you look here you ugly, lazy, half breed, filthy, dirty, stupid, smelly, inconsiderate, self centered, unthinking, maniacal, uncouth, animal, you. You either put that damn thing away, or I'm going to cut it off on you, mister. Then you]can hold it in your hand all day long mister." With that, Sergeant Ramirez pulled her razor sharp K-bar blade out, and she made a threatening motion towards the exposed member with it.

The Mutt stared at Ramirez for a few moments, and then he mumbled barely over a whisper back at her. "Uncouth! Whaddaya stinking mean saying I'm fucking uncouth baby? I wash my stinking hands before I eat any one or thing you know, Raz."

The soldiers broke up as the Mutt continued to wave his dick in his hands, now at Ramirez. It was still hard, and the Mutt was enjoying exposing himself to the women. It was at this point that Fun Bags suddenly grabbed the Mutt's member, and then she tried to shove it back in his pants.

"Yeeeooowww, wow, wow, take it easy with it will ya huh, you're fucking killing me here dammit." He cried as he jumped up and down and put his hands on the bench, and shoved himself in the air while Barbara continued to try and force his member back inside his pants. "C'mon, you can't do it that way for tripe sake. You gotta do the right thing and take care of it so it'll go soft, and I can then get it back in my pants. C'mon, C'mon, you gotta suck on it like you were drowning in the deep blue, and my dick was the only source of oxygen you could get."

"Look you clown, I'm not going to do you in front of the new girl until I get to know her a little better first, stupid." Fun Bags warned him as she finally got his dick back in his pants.

The Mutt jumped up and started to walk around like he had a load of shit in his pants, trying to make everyone believe a rupture was stopping him from walking right.

"Sit down stupid, you're not hurt you big baby you. You're making a spectacle of yourself as always, mister." Barbara snapped, not offering the slightest bit of sympathy towards her beau.

Sergeant John Kirkpatrick allowed the joking to go on before ordering the troops in the gym.

"C'mon Mutt, I'll take you over to the parallel bars and teach you a few things about them if you want." Barbara offered as the troops followed the Sergeant into the gym.

"Man, you can't teach me nuthin about a pair of stinking bars you know baby. I spent half my life in stinking bars, baby." The Mutt grinned as he followed her into the building.

Walker waited until the doctor was in step with him, he smiled at the surprised newcomer.

"Is it always like this Lieutenant Walker?" The doctor asked him with concern.

"Like what Doc? Everything I see seems normal enuf for my ass, Doc." Walker remarked.

"Like this sir, this wild, this crazy, with women giving oral satisfaction to the male soldier right in front of the other soldiers in the group sir. I'm forty two years old and I never witnessed such a spectacle perpetrated on that soldier a few moments ago in my life, Lieutenant."

"Well Doc according to the stinking Mutt, he didn't get the satisfaction he was looking for from his main squeeze you know, sir. Did it offend you to see that shit go down, Doc? I can't believe you're so fucking old and never once watched a woman give her lover some stinking head, man. Whatsumatter Doc, you stinking eggheads don't engage in group sex where your ass come from, my new friend?" Walker laughed as they started to lag behind the group.

"Heavens no Lieutenant. Group sex is the breeding grounds for AIDS, and every other sexually transmitted disease plaguing the world."

"C'mon Doc, don't knock it till you fucking tried it, man. We're all clean, and we have regular checkups every other month, and we use protection when we fuck outside the stinking group, Doc. Besides Doc, if we keep it all in the stinking family, no one hasta worry about them damn bugs sneaking in on our stinking group man. Say Doc you didn't answer my uther question man. Did the act of her giving some head in sight of the other pukes offend ya stinking ass, man?"

"I must admit it Lieutenant Walker, I found it rather exciting and I hate to admit it to you that I was a little turned on by the act as well, sir. I was also intrigued by it, and I was wondering how it'd feel to get what you call some head from a lady one day, sir."

Walker stopped walking and he turned and stared at the civilian doctor before remarking. "Jesus, don't tell me you never enjoyed a stinking blowjob? I can't believe that shit, egghead."

"That's a contradiction of terms I believe, Lieutenant. If you were being given a blow job, theoretically you wouldn't be as you so crudely put it, fucking, Lieutenant Walker."

"Stop trying to analyze everything I say to you man, as if you're some kinda fucking space aged computer man, and fricking answer the damn question I just asked ya, Doc. You never had a stinking blowjob in your wasted life, have you Doc? Tell me the truth man."

"To be quite honest with you, I'd have to answer no to that question, Lieutenant."

"Holy shit man, you just said you were forty two years old, and you're still a fucking virgin to the head thing, Doc? I can't believe that shit for a stinking minute, Doc. You stinking eggheads do live in a fucking sheltered life, sir. Looks like I'm gonna hafta do something about you getting your first stinking blowjob while you're part of our outfit, Doc." Lieutenant Walker grinned as they both started walking again, so they could catch up to the other soldiers.

"Please Lieutenant, this is most embarrassing to me, sir. I hope you don't intend to announce to the rest of your criminals that I never experienced a blowjob. I hate that word, it's so crude."

"Believe me Doc once you get your first bit of head, you won't care how crude the stinking word is, sir. You'll get use to it real quick buddy, and you'll try to get your stinking dick stuck between the lips of your girlfriend, more than you try to get laid by her, man. You have been laid in your stinking life right Doc? I mean you're not a complete fucking virgin, are you Doctor?"

"I might be a little old fashioned in your eyes Lieutenant Walker, but even us eggheads as you seem to like calling me engage in sex. Normal sex that is I add to you, sir."

"Doc, that normal sex is about to come to a sudden halt on your ass, sir. You're about to engage in a night of sex like you have never lived through in your entire wasted life, sir. Tonight, you'll get laid in ways you only dared to dream about." Walker stopped speaking as they entered the gym. He leaned closer to the doctor and added. "Hey Doc, I'd never embarrass your ass by letting these uther nuts know you never had a BJ, sir. But after tonight, it'll be academic, because you'll get some stinking head. I have to warn ya though, it'll change your life dramatically."

"How will this take place, I have to share my sleeping quarters with Colonel Leadbetter you know, Lieutenant." The doctor asked, kind of getting turned on by what Walker was telling him.

"I'll fix that easy enuf fur your stinking ass, Doc. I'll just tell him I wanna go over some of the items you're after inside the damn Iranian complex, sir. That should do the trick for us, sir."

"What if the Colonel wants to sit in on the so called briefing, Lieutenant Walker?"

"He's good, but he's not that stinking good, Doc. The stinking Colonel likes his sleep, he'll let you out so he can get his eight hours in as usual, man."

"I hope you're right Lieutenant Walker. After hearing what you were telling me, I'm afraid I'm kind of looking forward to tonight's offered festivities, sir. A new experience is something to surely look forward to, as long as you're certain the female's free of any illness sir."

"Not to mention a stinking blowjob at the same stinking time, Doc." Walker added as he jabbed him in the ribs, and then headed for the free weights.

The Mutt followed Fun Bags over to the mat covered section of the gym. She went to the parallel bars, grabbed them and jumped up, pointed her toes and then glided low between them. She then kipped up and straightened her arms until her hips were even with the bars.

"What's this crap you're doing baby?" the Mutt complained at his girlfriend.

"These my dear Mutt, are what's known to us normal folks as a pair of parallel bars, mister." Barbara grunted as she powered her way into a hand stand on the bars in front of him.

"Huh, these damn things are the fucking parallel bars you were talking to me about, baby? I fucking thought you were taking me to a pair of stinking drinking bars built right next to each uther baby." The Mutt complained seriously at her and refused to crack a smile.

Barbara laughed so hard she had to let go of the bars and jump down to the mat. She started to chase him around the mats until she finally tackled and pulled him to the floor. They rolled over with the Mutt coming to rest sitting on top of her chest, threatening her with his member again.

"Now bitch, you're gonna give me that fucking blowjob you owe me." The Mutt warned her.

"I'm warning you mister, if you take that damn thing out again and try to stuff it in my mouth, I'm going to bite it off on you, mister." She warned as she glared up at him this time.

"Yeeeooowww, I bet that'd hurt some baby." The Mutt said as he grinned down at her.

"Damn right it'll hurt, more than you can possibly imagine, buster." Fun Bags pushed up with her chest and flipped the Mutt off the top of her and she grumbled at him. "Besides big guy, it's your turn to do me, right?" Barbara straddled Mutt's face and lowered herself across his mouth.

The Mutt stuck his tongue out and made it vibrate as he gave her a Bronx cheer, not only making Fun Bags wet between her legs, but causing her to jump and offer. "Wow that felt real good dog man, remind me to have you try that when it really counts mister."

"Your wish is my command, mistress of the olive green drab uniform." The Mutt replied.

Lieutenant Walker called out waiting for a different apparatus to be freed up. "It's a damn good thing you two birds broke that crap off before it got outta hand on you guys. I was about to crack out the stinking fire hose, and douse down you two dogs in heat off."

The Mutt gave Walker half a peace sign before chasing Fun Bags around the bars again.

The soldiers had a good workout for themselves, with each one pushing the other to get the best possible benefits from the hard work out. Once done, the soldiers attacked the showers as if the enemy. Soldiers, men and women shared showers together, a few guys grabbed hand full's of the females bathing next to them, but this did not stop the women from returning the favor by grabbing the men between the legs as their reply to their attacks on them. Everything was cool, as long as respect was shown to the women. Each trooper knew what would happen if they overstepped the bounds. Before being dumped from the group, the perpetrator would find out what it meant to betray a trust. He would be lucky to get out of this with his balls still intact.

Once finished bathing and changing, the soldiers headed for the mess. Walker found the doctor bathing between Ramirez and the Frenchie, who they were about to dub Blind Date. He smiled as he noticed the doctor taking sneaky little peeks at the two naked women. He knew he had the doctor's attention, and he was sure he was going to cement this attention once he talked the female French soldier into living up to her obligation of fun night, by having sex with the doc. Usually, fun night consisted of a few girls taking care of the NCO's all night. But since the doctor was a FnG (Fucking new Guy) and so was the French fighter. He decided to allow the two to go at it together. He knew once the doctor received his first taste of the beliefs of the unit, he would be more than willing to join a future so called gang bang parties with the other soldiers.

Walker waited for the civilian doctor to finish with his shower. He then went over to Ramirez, who automatically began to play with him in front of the French fighter and he offered to his lover. "Hey baby, I want you to inform the stinking Frenchie if she wants in our outfit, she has certain obligations she hasta fulfill before we can allow her to join our little group of criminals and misfits. I have something I want her to do so we can welcome her into the Unit, baby."

"What? Are you and the Mutt going to take her on?" Ramirez snapped as she straightened up.

"No, calm down and don't let your tits get in an uproar. I'm not gonna tap her ass, leastwise not now. She'll be welcomed in the Unit later the right way, once we're sure she's gonna make the grade. Raz, I want her to take care of the Doc. Between you and me, he never had head."

"He never had any head? Oh the poor thing, how did he ever survive in this world without one, Walker?" Ramirez offered as she looked in the direction of the doctor who was shyly trying to dry himself off with a towel and she added. He's not that bad looking you know, especially for a Doc, Bobby. I guess he never hooked up with the right kinda girl, that's all lover."

"That bit of news is just between us. Don't let it out or the ass will never live it down."

"Okay Bobby I won't embarrass him I promise you." Ramirez offered to her soldier.

"Whaddaya think? You've been with the French babe since she first arrived to the group baby. Do you think she'll do the egghead good and proper if you asked her to?" he asked as he reached out and cupped her breast, and then drew her nipple in his mouth and sucked on it.

"No prob there, you just leave her to me Bobby. By the time she's finished with the Doc, he'll never walk straight again, and he'll be trying to stick his dick in the mouth of every female egghead he works with, the poor square babes." She replied with a grin and a wink of the eye.

"I knew I could depend on you baby." Walker offered as he patted her lightly on the rearend.

"When do you want her to do him?" Ramirez asked the Lieutenant.

"Err... I figure tonight will be good enuf, before we turn in. But it has to be in public, so everyone knows the Doc's got four sharp edges on him, and the Frenchie's cool."

"I'll let her know what she's in for tonight, Bobby." Ramirez offered to her lover and soldier.

"Let's get going with this stinking act then Raz." Walker added as he grabbed a towel. She stopped him by getting on her knees in front of her lover and taking him into her mouth, but not before saying. "Hey big boy, is this what you want her to do to the egg man, Walker dear?"

Raphael saw the act going down out of the corner of her eye, and she continued her shower until Ramirez polished off Walker good and proper. She was turned on by the sex display, yet shocked by Sergeant Ramirez's lack of concern over who watched her do him. Every soldier, male and female in the shower area, stopped what they were doing and watched Ramirez do Walker off in the shower. Some of the soldiers goaded Ramirez on, offering other suggestions of what they believed would increase Walker's pleasures for him. Raphael could not help herself and she now openly stared as everyone else was doing as Ramirez finished off Walker.

When they was done, the soldiers filed out of the showers and took off for the mess. The group ate, many going over the simulated attack using their fingers to draw it out on the surface of the table. It was almost mayhem in the mess with so many of the soldiers speaking at the same time.

GENERAL JOHN WHITE'S OFFICE AT THE PENTAGON

Before heading out for their meeting with the President, the Chairman of the Joint Chiefs of Staff, General White along with the CIA Director Raincloud discussed the report they had just received from the Agent Sand Star operating in Iran. After they finished reading the report, Director Raincloud, knowing Sand Star was waiting for a reply, asked to use General White's communication console. His fingers danced across the keyboard as the message was broken down into a series of numbers, letters, dots, dashes, and other confusing symbols, to confuse anyone who might intercept his message. The computer stored the items until its memory was full, and then sent it on its way in a rush of confusing electronic static to the operative.

Sand Star was getting a little anxious over the amount of time it was taking for his controller back on the states to reply to his report. He was just about ready to disassemble his radio when the buzz started. He waited for the miniature computer in his radio to sort out the mess, and then the words clearly showed up printed out properly on his display.

/\/\/\ BIG BOY TO SAND STAR /\/\/\
/\/\/\ COMPANY COMING. STOP... TRUST YOU CAN TAKE CARE
OF VISITORS ON THEIR ARRIVAL. STOP...
SURE TRUST YOUR FRIEND'S HELP? STOP...
VISITORS WILL EVALUATE FRIENDS AND TAKE PROPER
MEASURES TO ASSURE SUCCESS OF OPERATION. STOP...
VISITORS WILL ARRIVE YOUR AREA BY MEANS OF
LAV-25 (LIGHT ARMOR VEHICLES) AND BRADLEY M-2 IFV
(INFANTRY FIGHTING VEHICLE) FOR INSERTION FORCES
PROTECTION. INSERTION FORCES WILL ARRIVE YOUR
POSITION VIA AAV-7-A1 AMPHIBIOUS ASSAULT VEHICLES
PULLING TROOP SLEDS. STOP... AS STANDS, EVERYTHING
IN ORDER, MEETING WITH BOSS TO GET FINAL NOD ON
MISSION.STOP...
AFTER ASSAULT COMPLETED, WILL EXTRADITE YOU FROM
DUTY. STOP...

LOOKING FORWARD TO MEET YOU...
BIG BOY OUT..... /\/\/\

Ahmed Hussein al-Shamarral, looked over Mohammed Boua Bdellah's shoulder and read the report as it appeared on his computer screen and then he remarked. "By the Almighty Allah Himself, the ones you consider your control seem to be having trouble believing any Persian is willing to help your country, son. I'll pray to Allah for His guidance, what's it we Persians have to do to show your government not every Persian's uncivilized, or unable to be trusted?" the old man was disturbed, he was being threatened by American troops who were not in his country yet.

"I pray to the Almighty Allah you'll be more seeing than the ones running my government, father of the desert. If I did not trust you, I'd not have allowed you to look over my shoulder and read my message. Once I speak to my troops, I promise your desert fighters will be safe. Al-Shamarral, I cannot carry off my orders without the help of you and your desert children. You must be patient with my foolish people, because how many years has it been since they tried to approach your people in a trusting environment, father of time everlasting."

"That environment of trust would've been established long ago, if your government was willing to trust more than they offer us. I'm sorry to speak these words of disrespect, it's far from my heart's belief, but in all of the Middle East. The only ones your people have displayed any trust in, are the hated Jews, the Jews are a hard lot to live with my son."

"As are the Persians, father." Bdellah added, trying to break the tension.

"Yes, as are the Persians is true, my faithful new son, but it's the Arab and Persian's land the Jews have stole, and are unwilling to return those sacred lands to their rightful Arab owners." Al-Shamarral's face flashed red for a quick moment as he spoke words of hatred, they escaped his lips and there was no way to retrieve them now.

Bdellah quickly wrapped his radio up after the computer erase the message, he stared at the old man, trying to judge if this old beggar was a friend to be trusted. If his mind was so involved over the Jew problem, was he a secret member of Hamas, Hezbollah, or the Fattah Hawks?

Al-Shamarral noticed the look on Bdellah's face, and he read the Americans thoughts and remarked. "No my son, I am not a member of any Arab or Persian hate groups. I think if the Jews were easier to communicate with, if they would once live up to the agreements the leaders of old agreed to, I see Arab and Persians and Jews living and working together in the name of peace. We Persian and Arabs are a simple and trusting people, who believe if we're treated in an honest manner, we'll respond as such. I have listened to the many cries of the children of the desert, and heard how they cried to have respect from the Jews and Americans alike. In this world, you cannot command respect without first giving it, my foolish son.

"I'm not a well educated politician, I'm but a poor beggar willing to help the American soldiers free my country from madmen who control my lands. I once asked if you believe in destiny, because that is what I believe brought us together. But I'm not an old fool who ambles about the desert, nor am I a man who would stick my head into the mouth of the lion, to prove a point without protecting myself first my son. I'd make sure that lion is not hungry, before I trusted it with my foolish head. In the case of working with your soldiers. I'll protect myself by having my desert fighters prepare for any possibilities. We Persians have an old saying, 'one must place his trust in Allah, but remember to tie up your camel.'" Al-Shamarral looked at his fighters he surrounded himself with. His eyes ended up resting on a slim, young female warrior.

"Sayeh, you may come forth to your honorable father's side, my lovely daughter!"

The beautiful woman came from the group and crouched down alongside the beggar in silence.

"My lovely daughter, praise Allah for delivering this foreign freedom fighter to my midst. Mohammed Bdellah, I'll introduce you to one of my Generals involved in the struggle against the tyrants of my country. Bdellah, this fighter is my beloved daughter Sayeh Rahimi, and she commands forty fighters faithfully. She's my backbone, every time I find myself in trouble, she and her ones are there to see me out of it. Sayeh, my daughter, this man is known as Bedouin's Mohammed Boua Bdellah, and he has been sent to us by Allah, destiny, and the United States."

Sayeh barely nodded at the American, showing no support for him whatsoever as she courteously eyed Bdellah. Al-Shamarral picked up the look and laughed as he rested his hand lightly on her knee and said to her. "Sayeh, this is not the man responsible for the death of your parents and brothers. He was not in Iran at the time of the great takeover. He's a trusted friend sent to us by Allah in our time of most need of assistance. Sayeh, show respect for the one sent to enable us to rid Iran of the cursed fools driving Iran to the very gates of hell."

When still no reaction came from the female fighter, al-Shamarral felt compelled to continue. "Mohammed Bdellah, of course she's not deliciously fat as I enjoy a woman, but she's a tested warrior proven her worth time and again in our many battles for freedom. She's worthy of assisting us, and I'm placing her in charge of your safety. Be not so foolish as to believe this woman fighter would place your welfare over mine, or the welfare of my other children." Al-Shamarral waved his hand over the fighters crouched on their haunches staring at Bdellah.

"I'll utilize Sayeh and her great desert fighters to my advantage. If your soldiers are so foolish as to think they want to eliminate my useless existence before my time is called by Allah's breath. Everyone of your soldiers will be slaughtered to the last before their dead eyes gaze upon my person. As I told you, my desert fighters and myself will help the American soldiers succeed in their plight to rid Iran of these cursed weapons of mass destruction. If America does not want our help, my children will disappear in the dunes from whence they came. Attack one of my children and you attack all, and your soldiers will pay for their foolishness with their foul heads.

"Their mothers will cry as their bones bleach white in the harsh desert sand. It's up to you my son Bdellah. I have planned to allow you to meet with the American soldiers coming to free my country first, before I dare approach them. If the foolish American soldiers intend to eliminate myself, you must signal me and my children will leave, and then your soldiers will be allowed to continue with their orders by themselves. But if your soldiers dare to try and attack us as their enemy, they'll die uselessly I warn you, my son." Al-Shamarral took a quick breath as he continued to stare the young American spy in the eyes as if he was trying to read his thoughts.

"Follow the Vulture and he'll surely lead you to death. I have not spent many years in the unforgiving desert since the Iranian fools drove the old Shah fleeing from his country, to meet my death at the hands of what I believe could be our liberators. No Bdellah, this will not happen, I'll engage your soldiers if they attack my children of the desert. If you join your soldiers if they attack my children, the whites of my eyes will be the last you see, before you kiss the feet of Allah. The decision, the destiny of your proud soldiers is locked within your hands, squander what could be a chance to trust the Persian world, and America will never step foot in Iran.

"I'm not very prone to threats and unfulfilled words of anger. If you're unable to talk your proud young warriors into working with us, you must warn me before my children come out to die needlessly. Why do I take these precautions you may ask me? This is necessary, because the United States has decided not to trust the Persian peoples. Stupid, foolish, a waste of time and is unnecessary. Someone has to break the cycle of mistrust developed between your country, and the rest of the Arab and Persian world, and that someone might as well be you my son."

Al-Shamarral stopped speaking and rested his hand on the hilt of the deadly Jambiya blade. His movement to his knife did not go unnoticed by the desert fighters surrounding Bdellah, and they did the same, ready to spring at the stranger over the slightest provocation.

Bdellah saw this action and knew his life was worthless if he did not make the American soldiers work with these Persian fighters. He looked at the flames from the fire dancing before his eyes, they disappeared into the darkness of night as he offered to the old man. "My father of the desert sands, I'll make the soldiers of my country know your children are here to help them. If they're so pig headed that they're still unwilling to accept the help you offer to them. I'll signal you to make sure your children can flee before they encounter any of the American troops. What would you like me to use as a signal they are a threat against your children of the sands?"

"Hmmmm... it's a shame trust and help must be dealt in such a useless and foolish manner, Allah be praised. One day, with Allah's help maybe the United States can find it in their hearts to trust the Persian peoples again. When you speak with the soldiers from your country, if they're unwilling to trust my desert children, scratch your piles and spit on the sand. By the time the sands absorbs your spittle, my fighters will be far away from your soldiers not to be a threat or threatened by them. But enough of mistrusting and these sorrowful questions and offerings my son." Al-Shamarral bellowed as he slammed a disfigured hand on Bdellah's shoulder.

"Come, and accompany me to my humble tent for some much needed refreshment my son. The night is long, and the desert will be cold and we must keep up our strength if we're expected to fight for our convictions against the evil that stalks the people of Iran. We'll eat good on this dark night, my son. Bring us food to enjoy my children of the sand world!"

A number of Persian women suddenly appeared from behind a low sand dune while carrying baskets stuffed with food, a cooked goat, dates, and fruits. Breads appeared next before him, and Bdellah realized this must have cost al-Shamarral a vast sum to prepare for them. It was rare to see full goats roasted by the poor of the desert. Bdellah did not know if he should offer the American cash to the old man to pay for the food they are sharing on this night.

"Ahhh... my foolish child, you look suddenly confused for some unknown reason. What troubles you so on this night of enjoyment my son?" Al-Shamarral offered, as he took a hank of goat meat and then gnaw on it, making terrible noises as he enjoyed the meat.

"I am confused my father, you see my government gave me much cash, and I used very little of it as yet. I know your desert fighters are in need of cash, but I fear of insulting your kindness if I was to offer it to you my father of protection." Bdellah informed the old man as he smiled at him, hoping he was not insulting him by his offer to give him some of the American cash he had.

Al-Shamarral bellowed with laughter as he held out a grease covered paw. "My foolish son, you'd not insult me if you offered me this useless money you say you have no use for. Cash to a beggar is never an insult. Allow me to relieve you of this burden you carry upon your person."

Now it was Bdellah who laughed as he fished in his pockets, and removed the money and gave it over to the old beggar. Bdellah held back enough cash to buy his freedom, or enlist the aid of other Iranians to help him escape Iran, if the commando's assault collapsed.

Al-Shamarral dropped the hank of goat meat on the cloth as his eyes opened wide, and he stared at the thick roll of cash and he announced while trying to catch his breath. "Praise the Almighty Allah for His unending love and great wisdom, this is more money here than my eyes have seen in their many years of life." The beggar scooped up the cash and in an instant, it disappeared between the many folds of his Howli, but not before he held up the cash and called out to his protectors. "My Bedouins brothers and sisters of the land of vast sand dunes, you see, it's as I told you. At long last, Allah, in His infinite wisdom, has sent this man to our midst, to help shed the ties that bind our thinking and our lives. With this cash, we'll buy the supplies needed to make our fight true. Then we can begin the war between the lowly jackals and win our cause." The old man grinned at the fighters as he dropped down on his rearend after hiding the cash, and went back to his eating his goat meat as if nothing had just transpired.

Bdellah scanned the many faces staring at him as they stuffed their mouths. It seemed like everyone in the tent was now pleased with his presence, all but Sayeh. When his eyes found her, he noticed she was not eating, she was just staring angrily at him. He could not figure out if the stare was threatening, or if she might have been interested in him. He shook his head as he looked down, and returned to eating his dinner. When the wine came, it helped to lessen the tension even further with the group. Twice during the feast, Bdellah tried to engage Sayeh in some conversation, but she refused to respond to any of his questioning words aimed at her. She just kept staring at him as if she was angry and ready to harm him.

When the feast ended, al-Shamarral stood and raised his hands for attention. "My desert wanderers it's late, and I feel it's time for each to hunt the place in which to wait the American soldier's arrival. Don't allow yourselves to be discovered by any security guards. If you are discovered, dispatch the locator at once and then assume his post. Be careful my children, the days of totalitarianism are fast coming to an end, I feel it here." The beggar pounded his chest.

The Persian fighters stood as one and they all bowed to the old man. Then as silently as the breeze, they quickly disappeared into the darkness of the night. In the background, Bdellah heard the angry protests coming from the angry camels being disturbed from their sleep.

Sayeh moved over to Bdellah's side, she chose not to speak with him. All the desert fighters in her command, circled protectively around her. Even though he did not feel threatened, Bdellah wanted to be free of them because they were all standing much too close to him. He tried to walk through them, but the group would not move out of his way an inch. He looked to al-Shamarral, who merely shrugged and then he looked to Sayeh to see what she was going to do next.

Bdellah got the meaning of the movement, and he turned back to the stunning Iranian beauty.

She was so near to Bdellah he actually felt her breath on the back of his neck as she whispered angrily at him. "Filthy American spy, you might have fooled that old man, but you'll not fool me for one cursed moment. You dare to step over that line in the sand, if you dare to betray him and his faithful followers, it'll be I who you'll deal with. American, I despise the poisonous breath of the United States and its military presence here in the Middle East and Persian Gulf.

"Betray that old man and I'll make your death a long and very painful ordeal to endure. I do not like you, I'd rather fight you and your cursed soldiers, than fight other Persian peoples. But since al-Shamarral has ordered me to protect your worthless life, that's what I'll do. Dog of an unbeliever, no harm will ever come to you as long as the old man's protecting your worthless life. If anything happens to him, if I believe it was a trap set by you and your hated soldiers, my eyes will be the last thing you'll ever see before you die the death of a thousand cuts. I must go now before I soil my hands with the blood of an unclean fool such as you, evil one."

Bdellah was stunned by the ferocity of the threat coming from this Iranian beauty, all he could do was grin dumbly back at her. When his senses returned, he gave her the once over. Sayeh was five foot five tall, and he figured she weighed about one hundred and five pounds. Her skin had that beautiful golden hue and was absolutely flawless, adding to her beauty. Her nose was perfect, and the angry black eyes were circled with the faintest hint of eye liner. Her chin was pointed and her teeth perfect and white, her head was crowned with beautiful, long black curly hair like a halo. Her neck was long, and her shoulders contested to the fact she did not have a very easy life, they were large. Her breasts were ample, and she possessed a narrow waist, making her rearend seem a little larger than it should be.

Sayeh wore tight pants, the only drawback he detected of her body was her waist was so narrow it made her backside look larger. He notice she moved like a cat, ready to pounce on all her enemies, her moves were well calculated before she committed herself to them. He believed this woman was extremely dangerous, and not to be taken very lightly. If she said something, she would die trying to carry it out what she had offered.

Sayeh picked up the American looking over her body, she was insulted by his exploration of her body as she hissed with venom in his face. "Filthy pig, your evil eyes burn my body, it's only because my father al-Shamarral has ordered I allow you to remain alive and draw breath. If you dare to look at me in lust ever again. I'll pluck out your god cursed insulting eyes and leave them for the creatures of the sand to cleanse. It's as I have warned you, the only thing on a filthy American's mind is sex. I hate you, I hate all god cursed untrusting Americans."

Bdellah did not flinch, and this made Sayeh all the more angry at him. But her anger did not go unnoticed by the old beggar, who softly called out to her. "Sayeh, come over to my side my lovely daughter, I wish private words with you."

Without taking her eyes off Bdellah for a moment, Sayeh threateningly stood and walked over to al-Shamarral. They whispered together, "Sayeh, this man's needed by our people. If you're unable to separate yourself from your ill feelings towards him and his soldiers, I'll have you replaced as protector and appoint someone who can behave properly with him."

"I hate all Americans, great father of mine." Sayeh hissed through clenched teeth.

"I understand your ill feelings towards this man, but you have to separate yourself from this terrible hatred. It's the sign of a true leader to be able to control one's emotions, and all your thoughts are working for the needs of your people, Sayeh." Al-Shamarral cautioned her.

"I'll try my best to accomplish what you have just suggested to me, father of kindness." Sayeh replied as she bowed politely at the old man smiling at her.

"You'll do better than your best Sayeh! For this is my order to you my daughter."

Sayeh nodded, and then she lowered her head in respect of the old man's angry words.

"That's much better my daughter of the desert sands, we'll move out to the deep desert shortly. You'll station your faithful fighters all around him for his protection, and then we'll wait for his friends to arrive to free us. I have decided to wait with him Sayeh."

"I must protest this most unwise decision of yours, father. I feel you have not given this thought enough time. You'll expose yourself to great danger needlessly I fear. I must ask you to reconsider this suggestion you have just offered to me my father." Sayeh snapped in a low voice.

"Sayeh, although I know you have my nothing but my best interests in your heart and mind at all times, but it's as I have just offered to you my lovely daughter. We have to begin to trust the Americans, and hopefully, some day in the future they'll return this trust. For trust is the true foundation that'll cement our new government with the United States. Because without their support, I fear Iran will soon dry up in the unforgiving sands of the vast desert much in the same way Egypt's great past had disappeared from the face of the earth. We have to prove to the Americans as much as we need them, they need us also. I'm willing to lay down my worthless old life in that quest to trust. History warns us any advance in civilization was always filled with countless dangers, but the strides were still taken by the daring.

"Sayeh, you must remember this for all your coming years, no matter what happens to this old and worthless body of mine, you must protect this foolish American warrior with every breath that is held within your young body. No harm must to come to him, no matter the outcome of this attack against the fools who have stepped upon our throats and fill our mouths with the burning sands of the vast desert. You must promise this with your heart, and with your soul to me, my lovely daughter." Al-Shamarral looked deeply into Sayeh's eyes.

"I am sorry to offer this to you father of countless ages past, but alas I cannot promise what you have requested from me in good faith, my father. If his foul soldiers kill you, I'll take his worthless life if it's the last thing I do upon this earth. I have sworn this to Allah, my father. I'm honor bound by my blood oath to carry out my threat again this loathsome American spy." Sayeh growled while leaning a little closer to the old beggar.

"I don't care one grain of worthless sand what oaths you might have shared with Allah. That's between you and Him to deal with my daughter. Sayeh, I'm ordering you to place all your hatful anger aside, and listen to my words of wisdom. Your honor means absolutely nothing to me, what matters the most to me is the future of Iran and her faithful children, without the American's help, there'll be no future for us and our country, my daughter. Promise me you'll not allow anything to happen to this young American fool."

Sayeh hesitated for a moment as she continued to stare at the old and proud man.

"I'm waiting for your reply my always angry and most upsetting young daughter!" Al-Shamarral demanded hotly of her as he continued to stare at her as he waited for her reply.

"I promise it'll be as you have requested of me, my father of time past. I shall agree even though I despise this man so." Sayeh gave in as she lowered her head.

With tenderness in his actions, the old beggar reached out and placed a finger under Sayeh's chin, and he lifted her head with his finger until their eyes met again, and then he offered to her. "Thank you my faithful daughter. May Allah give you a tent full of healthy male children, and a loving and most kind husband to protect you in the way you'll protect this young American fool. Perhaps, if you truly believe in destiny, you might be looking at your future husband standing before you, Sayeh." The wise beggar said with a twinkle in his eye.

"I'd rather lie with the devil than share my bed with the filthy American spy, my father."

Anger instantly clouded over al-Shamarral's eyes as he stared at Sayeh and then he nastily barked at her in a low voice. "My foolish young daughter, if I believed those words true for one moment of time, I'd have you stripped bare before all, and then lashed with the whip of truth to within an inch of your life until all this foul evil has left your soul. Even if it meant beating you to death for your terrible sin you have just voiced against Allah's faithful words. There's no greater enemy in all the world than the devil for us to fear and hate, and though the Americans were regarded as such, they are not. Be gone from my worthy eyes before I carry out my threat against you my wayward daughter who speaks without using her mind to control her foolish words. Pray Allah He forgives your most unwise words, and does not strike your tongue from its vile mouth." The old man reached out and actually struck Sayeh across the face.

There was a gasp from the other fighters standing around the camp, as all eyes went to Sayeh to see why she was just struck by their father. The slap was nothing more than a slight glancing blow, but the ramifications of the slap was as bad as if being stoned to death for a sin.

Sayeh did not dare rub the side of her cheek as she stood, and then she bowed towards the old man, she motioned to her fighters who moved even closer to her, all confused by what they had just witnessed, and moving Bdellah with them.

Mohammed Bdellah looked to the old man with a look that betrayed his fear and concern.

"Bdellah, my son, do not fear anything within the borders of Iran as I offered you, go with my faithful daughter and her Persian fighters. You'll be well protected by them, as well protected as I am in their presence. She'll not allow anything bad to happen to you while she still breathes life in this world of mass confusion and unending mistrust. We'll meet before your proud warriors arrive in Iran to help set us free from the cursed fools who rule Iran's faithful children. I'll stand with you and greet your proud young warriors as they arrive to assist us in our times of need, my son." Al-Shamarral gave Bdellah a simple wave of his hand as a dismissal, the anger he displayed towards Sayeh, robbed him of his strength, and he knew he dared not try and stand at this time. Striking her unsettled him more than it did Sayeh.

CHAPTER TWENTY

THE PORT CITY OF BANDER BEHESHI, IRAN

The receding tide was at its lowest point by the time the second Iranian submarine was loaded with the two Russian made missiles and nuclear warheads. It was then Colonel Muhsin Abu Marzuk noticed more of the destroyed submarine lying half in half out the deeper part of the channel. The Iranian Officer bellowed for the dock engineer to come over to him. Once there, Marzuk pointed to the destroyed submarine and then demanded. Of the worker "Fool of a camel's arse, is the carcass of that cursed submarine blocking the route of my other submarines?"

The Dock Master quickly scanned the mangled remains of the destroyed boat, and then he responded to the Colonel's question. "I'm sorry for not realizing this sooner, Colonel Marzuk. When civilian shipping was ordered not to approach the channel, this threat has completely slipped my mind, and I didn't detect this situation before this time, Colonel Marzuk..."

"I don't need any god cursed polite words, I need answers fool. Is that destroyed submarine blocking the escape route of my other submarines?" Colonel Marzuk repeated angrily.

"Yes, it's completely blocking the route out to the sea for all shipping now trapped at port, whether it be civilian or military in nature, Colonel Marzuk."

"Fear Allah's great wrath, what the devil am I supposed to do now, you camel eating fool? It'll take a week to remove all the debris of that destroyed submarine from the foul channel, dunce."

"I'm sorry Colonel, but when the tide returns to the channel. The draft will be deep enough to allow your submarines to sail over the remains of the destroyed one safely. But they'll have to leave the channel with no ballast in their hulls, Colonel Marzuk." The dock engineer reported.

"A curse be upon your worthless mustache, traitor to my work and needs. Don't be so happy with yourself old fool. If you were doing your duties in the first place, you would've brought this situation up to my attention before I realized it for myself, fool." Colonel Marzuk glared at the old man as his hand removed the pistol. He shot the engineer right in the face, and allowed his body to remain where it fell as he went back to supervising the loading of the missiles inside his submarine. The fuming Iranian Colonel knew he had at least twelve hours to load this submarine before the tide returned to its fullest. Angrily, he resided himself to allow his other submarines to sail out of the harbor at the same time. The only peace he could possibly derive from this latest problem was an age old saying 'in numbers there is strength'. He wondered if it was not wise to have his submarines wait for the last one to be loaded before allowing them to make for the open sea. He suddenly roared at the Heavens. "Ahhhh... Allah works in the strange ways."

THE OVAL OFFICE AT THE
WHITE HOUSE, WASHINGTON D.C.
4:03 P.M, EST, SATURDAY, NOVEMBER 9th, 1998

President Albert Cole waited in the Oval Office until General John White and CIA Director John Raincloud arrived for the meeting. The President was flanked by his female Vice President, the Secretaries of State, Defense, Navy, Airforce and Army, along with the National Security Director, and the Deputy Secretary of Defense. The civilian advisor, Raymond Manning was also allowed to attend the special and latest military briefing, before the elite Special Forces troops entered Iran to destroy the supposed secret Iranian complex.

General White nodded to everyone in the office except for the civilian advisor, as he took his seat and made himself comfortable. Director Raincloud sat next to the General as always.

President Cole clapped his hands, getting everyone's attention. Then he picked up a pencil and twirled it between his fingers. "We better get going. General, do you have anything to report?"

"Yes Sir I certainly do Mr. President Sir, it was reported to command that one of the mined Iranian submarines had exploded right in the center of the narrow channel, and the submarine's shattered remains has successfully trapped the other three submarines at port."

"Does this mean the last three Iranian submarines are no longer a threat to our operation, General?" Ms. Hernandez asked, excited the threat of the submarines might be academic.

"I'm sorry to say this Maria, but the boats are only slightly out of the question at this time, Ma'am. All the Iranians have to do is wait until the tide reaches its fullest, and the now trapped submarines can then make it out of the channel. But either way, once the missiles are loaded on board the remaining Iranian submarines, they can launch the nuclear tipped missiles at any target they may chose, even the United States if they decide to launch one of them at us, Ma'am."

"But these remaining three Iranian three submarines are already mined, am I right to believe this General White Sir?" Vice President Mary Hirshfield asked the military officer.

"As far as we believe, yes Ma'am. But we don't know what other precautions the Iranian defenders might have adopted after the first submarine exploded on them. The latest satellite intelligence reported a horde of Iranian dock workers doing nothing out of the ordinary with the remaining submarines, Ma'am. It seems their driving force is to load the missiles on the last three submarines, and that's about all, Ma'am. I don't know for certain if there were any divers put over the side to check the remaining submarine's hulls, but from what we can see. It looks like the Iranians are reacting as if the submarine's destruction was from natural causes..."

"What natural causes could there possibly be for it that would've lead to the destruction of a nuclear powered submarine, General White?" The Defense Secretary requested sarcastically.

"There are a few situations that could cause that type of situation to take place with destroying one of their submarines. I tend to believe the Iranians are accepting the destruction of the boat was caused by actions of the Captain of the boat. Before the explosion, the Captain had to do some rather fancy maneuvering around the port to avoid a tanker bearing down on his boat. We picked it up as it unfolded on the video from a satellite feed. It was quite a scene to witness. The explosion destroyed a few buildings, and it crippled some of the civilian shipping ported in..."

"I'm going to see this tape, am I right General White?" the President interrupted cautiously.

"Yes Sir by all means Mr. President, I have a copy of the tape with me sir. We believe this is why the dock workers and military aren't reacting as if we had anything to do with the sinking of their damn boat, sir. We're keeping a close eye on everything still taking place on and around the docks of the port, and as of yet we haven't noticed any divers going over the side, sir. I can't wait to see their damn faces when the other submarines explode on their asses, Mr. President."

"General White Sir, what's the status on the submarines that made it to sea before our SEAL Teams were able to place their charges on the other boats?" Secretary of State Hernandez asked.

"I'm not in the position to make that report intelligently for you Ma'am. I believe the Secretary of Navy is in a far better position to answer that question for you, Ma'am." The General turned to the Secretary and gave him a nod and he threw the ball on his court this time.

Admiral Richardson immediately replied as he rose to his feet. "Ms. Hernandez, the two boats in the sea lanes of the

Persian Gulf waters are being monitored at all times by BGSRSAT that's our Blue/Green Specter Radar Satellite system, Ma'am. The missing two Iranian submarines positions are available to us both day and night, Ma'am. Each boat is also being tailed by a pair of Guided Missile Frigates equipped with Sea Sprite LAMPS systems, and two Sikorsky Seahawk LAMPS III attack helicopters we refer to as submarine killers, Ma'am. Each Frigate carries one of these specialized helicopters on board, but in this case we decided to load them with a number of extra machines. When word comes to attack the Iranian submarines, the life expectancy of these two submarines will be less than the time it takes to flush the damn head, Ma'am."

"Will the two Iranian boats have a chance to launch their missiles before the end comes for their damn submarines, Admiral Richardson Sir? I don't want them to be able to launch any of their missiles at anyone or thing, sir." National Security Director, Norm Griffin inquired.

"Not a chance in hell will they have a chance to launch their damn missiles before we send the two damn things down to the bottom of the sea, Director Griffin Sir. The second the boats are reported opening their launch hatches, the trailing Frigates have their orders and they'll attack the two submarines in question, even if the main action on the installations hasn't been augmented as yet, sir. I have no intention of allowing any god damn nuclear tipped missiles to become airborne sir. Heaven knows who the damn missiles will be targeted against, and I believe the Iranians won't hesitate for one second to launch the damn things, that's why my ships have standing orders to attack these two submarines, if they detect launching hatches being open to the sea."

"It's a good belief to adopt over this present situation I must say Admiral Richardson Sir, and I agree with your decision as you just stated, sir." The worried President offered as he nodded to the Secretary, pleased he showed the initiative in dealing with the missing two boats.

"What about the ground forces then?" The Secretary of Defense next asked the General.

General White offered with a sort of snap in his voice. "The soldiers are completing their tune up operations, and tomorrow they'll be boarding their assigned aircraft sir. By night they'll enter Iran and within the first seven hours of Monday morning, November 10th, the troops will end their assault against the complex, and the surviving troops should be out of Iran and back in Pakistan by this time, sir. I'm hoping to have the soldiers out of Pakistan on Monday night. By Tuesday, the attack should be history. Then the President's problems will begin in earnest sir."

There was a slight chuckle because everyone understood what the General's words meant. Once the attack in Iran was over with, the President's problems would begin because he would be forced to deal with the irate Iranians, and the other Arab nations who had agreed with the Iranians that the United States had invaded Iran needlessly. There would be plenty of naysayers to go around no matter how honorable the actions of the United States were, there were always nations just waiting to pull those actions apart of the United States.

"General White Sir, I know you went over this subject in the past for us. But please forgive an old woman and allow me to ask this question of you sir. I promise I'll commit it to my memory this time, General White Sir." Ms. Hernandez mumbled while flashing her smile at him.

"Please Ma'am, you may ask any question of me as many times as you care to ask them of me, Ma'am. I always have time for you young lady." General White retorted pleasantly.

"Oh, aren't you polite today General White Sir. I really appreciate that, but I forgot how long this operation was going to last for our troops operating in the Iranian desert, sir."

"Ms. Hernandez, our troops are scheduled to jump off for action at exactly Twenty One Hundred Hours on Sunday morning, while entering Iran at this time stated, Ma'am. The assault's marked to begin at exactly Zero, Four, Thirty Hours, and should be completed, with our troops pulling out of the Iranian desert by Zero, Six, Thirty Hours, Ma'am. So the time on target for our ground forces should be no longer than the two hours of action as stated, barring any unforeseen complications that is, Ma'am." General White took a quick breath as he smiled.

"Director Raincloud, what's the present status of your operative working in Iran, sir?"

"Mr. President Sir, my operative's in position to intercept our troops as they enter Iran and then help guide them to the complex. Evidently, the operative was able to enlist a number of Iranian freedom fighters, who offered help and they're willing to join our troops sir."

"That's great, we can sure use the help. What did you say to the help offered by the Iranians?"

"Mr. President, I gave word we weren't to use their help sir. In fact sir, I believe the General has issued orders to eliminate the helpers for the sake of the security and success of the damn operation sir. I believe it's a good call on the General's part to make that call and..."

President Cole's head snapped in the direction of the General, as he jumped up and began to pace behind his desk as he went deep in thought, he stopped his pacing and then rested his hands flat on his desk and growled at his military officer. "Dammit to hell and back General White Sir! I can't believe you're so damn willing to give the order to eliminate the Iranian freedom fighters because you don't trust them, sir. That way of thinking is in the can as of this moment, General. I'm ordering you to inform the MNRRF that they're to utilize the Iranians help to the fullest, to the fullest I say General White. Enlist their help, it's the opening I've been searching for all along sir. I want those damn Iranian fighters side by side with our troops, do you understand General?"

"Yes sir, I'll send word our people are to linkup and use them, Mr. President Sir."

"That's better, Christ I can't believe you, General. What's it they say about an angry dog biting its wounds? I hope you're not thinking with the idealism that caused this rift between the United States and the Islamic nations, General White." The President snapped at his military officer.

"I certainly hope the President isn't referring to me as a angry dog here, sir?"

"Don't be so foolish General White, that's the furthest thing from my mind I assure you sir. But I feel it's about time we look at some of these other nations for a change, and their freedom fighters in a different light, that's all I meant by that statement General. We have to start enlisting the aid of anyone, and I mean anyone who's willing to come to our aid. General White, is there anything else you have to add to this conversation, before I conclude this meeting sir?"

"No Mr. President, not at this time. This about covers all I have and need to know for now."

"Fine General White, it was a detailed and rather enlightening report, and it seems you have covered everything of concern to me, sir. Sunday, my schedule's heavy General, and I'm engage in a number of scheduled meeting, but after eight p.m. I'll be free and looking to be kept in the loop. If you'd like to, you can set up headquarters in the White House, that way I'll be informed of the progress of our troops in Iran much quicker, sir. If I can't be with the troops in battle, the least I can do is to lose some sleep with them." The President looked right at the General calmly.

"Mr. President that'll do just fine for all my needs sir. I can easily set up shop in the FBI room on the first floor of the White House, sir. The FBI Units working there have all the computers and hookups I'll have need of in order to get Intel transferred to there, sir."

"Fine. Err... Director Raincloud Sir, I trust that I'll be seeing you at the General's side working when the troops enter this operation for us, sir?"

"Yes by all means sir, all the time the troops are on the ground, I'll be working closely with the General, Mr. President Sir." Director Raincloud offered with a grin to his Commander in Chief.

"Fine, that about covers it all then for myself as well." The President said as he loudly clapped his hands together, and then he waited for the General and Director Raincloud to stand, and as they did he offered. "Thank you gentlemen for your diligence to this operation and the success of our troops, I have other things to discuss with my cabinet. You're dismissed."

Both the General and Director Raincloud snapped to attention and saluted the President, and then they turned and left the Office. Once in the hallway out of ear shot of the President, General White bitched. "Say Director, are you able to make contact with your damn Sand Flea yet sir?"

"Not until noon Iranian time can I communicate with him General White, that's when he's to monitor his radio to check if we're transmitting new orders. I know what you want me to send."

"You bet you know, I want you to clue your damn operative in that he's not to take any aggressive actions against the Iranian fighters he made friends with in Iran, sir. Inform him we're to make use of their help, he's to regard them as part of this mission at this point forward, Director." General White opened the door of his staff car, and allowed the Director to enter it.

Once seated, General White growled at the Marine driver of his staff car. "Son, get me over to the Pentagon pronto, and keep yourself available for the rest of the day and night as well mister. We'll be going back and forth to the Pentagon and White House. Get moving young man!"

CAMP LEJEUNE, JACKSONVILLE NORTH CAROLINA. TWENTY, THIRTY HOURS EST NOVEMBER, 9th, 1998

After eating mess, Lieutenant Robert Walker and the rest of his group headed for the barracks and down tome for the rest of the night. Doctor Joel Russbinder followed Sergeant John Kirkpatrick in silence back to Colonel Bruce Leadbetter's private office and living quarters and his temporary sleeping quarters. Once in the room, the Colonel offered the doctor a beer, but he refused it saying he was too exhausted to enjoy it, and he wanted to catch up on his sleep.

"That's a good idea Herr Doctor. Tomorrow's a rather big day in your once well adjusted fucking lifestyle, sir." Colonel Leadbetter snarled sarcastically as he sucked on a can of beer.

Doctor Russbinder crawled onto the cot and he laid down and stared up at the ceiling while waiting for whoever was going to be sent out to retrieve him. No sooner did he get comfortable then there was a loud knock on the Colonel's door.

"Enter!" The Colonel barked, not even bothering to look up from the report he was reading.

The Mutt strolled in the office wearing a smile and walking like he owned the world.

"You, the next time you knock on my fucking door, you better knock like you have a fucking pair, mister. I had a mind to leave your sagging ass out there until the next coming of the Christ Child. What the fuck do you want in my god damn office anyway, spudhead? And why the hell aren't you back in your barracks, sleeping dog man?" the Colonel hissed at the young soldier.

"Colonel Leadbetter, Lieutenant Walker sent me to fetch the civilian dude, sir. He has a few uther questions for him, and the Lieutenant wants to speak to the Doc about them, sir." The grin continued as the Mutt stared at the cautious looking Colonel with the same look of mistrust.

"What the fuck do you think the Doctor is, a well you're going to fetch a pail of water out of, puke?" Colonel Leadbetter growled as he sat back and then slowly stroked his chin as he carefully studied the face of the young soldier before saying to him. "What the fuck are you pack of god damn wahoos up to now buster? What the hell are you puds going to do to my Doctor?"

"Not a stinking thing Colonel Leadbetter Sir, I swear it sir. Lieutenant Walker just has a few stinking nagging questions for the Doc, that's all sir. Nuthin funny is gonna happen to his stinking ass, I assure you Colonel Sir." The Mutt pleaded with is commanding officer.

"In a pig's fricking ear you people don't have something up your damn sleeves, buster. You'll have to wake up much earlier in the fucking morning than that to pull the shit cloud over my damn eyes, shithead." Colonel Leadbetter hissed while continuing to study the soldier's face.

"Sir, and just what time might that be, Colonel Leadbetter Sir?" the Mutt asked with a smirk.

The concerned Colonel suddenly leaned forward and he rested his elbows on the desk and held a pencil in a threatening manner as he pointed it right at the Mutt's chest and warned him in no uncertain words this time. "Don't be too fucking funny with my ass sucka, or I'll turn you inside fucking out and see if you're mixed assed colored inside as well outside your damn body, buster. Sergeant Kirkpatrick! Get your ass in here on the double quick mister!"

When the Sergeant did not appear, the Colonel got up and he went to the outer office looking for the Sergeant. His chair was empty and he growled. "Where the hell's the damn Sergeant at?"

"Beats the shit outta my stinking ass sir." The Mutt snorted as he shrugged at the Colonel.

"Don't tempt me half breed, I just might do that to your damn ass for the fun of it, mister."

"He wasn't at his desk when I came in the building, Colonel." The Mutt offered the Colonel.

"Convenient for your fucking ass I guess, buster. I have a good mind to come along with you and the damn Doctor and listen to these fucking questions Lieutenant Walker has for this pain in the ass civilian puke, dammit." Colonel Leadbetter then cast a wary eye at his desk covered to overflowing with unread reports and lists and other problems he had to look after. He knew he had a pile of paperwork to catch up on. With a disgusted sigh, he gave in and called out.

"Doctor Russbinder, I hate to disturb you at this time sir. It seems that Lieutenant Walker has a few questions for your ass sir. I'd like you to go with Lieutenant Hall here, he'll see you arrive at Walker's barracks safely, sir. If he doesn't, I'll have his balls for a damn tie tack. I want you back here in one hour, no later sir. If Walker needs you any longer than that, have him send me a runner. By that time, I should be done with most of this damn paperwork, and I'll sit in on the rest of the briefing with the Lieutenant and yourself, Herr Doctor."

Colonel Leadbetter then turned to the Mutt, pointing his finger at him threateningly and then he warned angrily. "This thing better not be a fucking sham, or I'll skin both you butter bars (Lieutenant) alive, and enjoy myself while I'm at it. You pukes better remember the Doc's health is my responsibility. You guys damage him and I'll double that damage on your ass. Got me?"

"Hear ya loud and clear sir." The Mutt offered as he watched the doctor get out of his rack.

"Shut that fucking butthole of yours up tight and wait for the damn Doctor, dog man."

"Colonel Leadbetter, I thought this was America and I had freedom of speech, sir." The Mutt offered with a smirk, still trying to dig the angry Colonel anyway he could think of.

"Arrrr... you're going to keep screwing with my ass I see, until I finally react huh wiseguy? What the fuck makes you think you have freedom of speech around here, buster? This is no democracy here, I'm running the fucking show and you speak when I allow it to be done by you spudhead. Besides puke, freedom of speech in this country works only as long as you're not making enough noise to be heard by others." Colonel Leadbetter growled at the young soldier.

The Mutt stiffened to attention, and he saluted the Colonel as he replied loudly. "Yes sir."

"You saluting my ass now buster? Whoa boy, now I know you pack of shitbirds are up to no good tonight, that's the first time you ever saluted me correctly. What's Walker up to buster?"

"Questions sir, that's all it is bout Colonel Leadbetter Sir, just some stinking extra questions for the Doctor, sir. If you think we're up to no good tonight, all the Colonel has to do is not allow the damn Doc to come wit me sir. But if the questions Lieutenant Walker needs answered, aren't answered by the Doc, and the missing information leads to the operation's failure sir. How would the Colonel feel then, sir?" the Mutt placed the big shit eating grin back on his face again.

"Whoa ho, now I know I'm in trouble when you try to argue any fucking logic with my damn ass, dog man. I didn't even know you knew how to pronounce the fucking word, let alone what it meant. Okay shitbird, you can take the damn Doc with you, but remember buster. If anything happens to the damn puke, if one fucking feather's out of place when he returns, you and your damn sidekick will never see the States again. If I catch any damn flack over this meeting, I'll eat the both of ya alive. Take the prick and get the fuck out of my sight. I'll send the Sergeant to Walker's barracks when he returns. I better not find you birds were responsible for his leaving."

"Me Colonel Leadbetter Sir?" the Mutt cried as he pointed to himself with his thumb.

"Don't try any of that innocent poor little me crap on my ass, it's wasted buster. The only way you pudheads will even be able to pull the shit cloud over my eyes, is by coming up with something I haven't done myself, and I done everything you shitbirds can possibly think of, and a few you can't think of mister. Get the hell out of my sight, your face turns my guts. Get back to your Kami Kazi friend and give him my warning, I'm watching the pack of ya damn shitbirds."

"Yes sir. Doctor Russbinder, follow me sir. Lieutenant Walker's waiting back at the barracks for us sir." The Mutt stepped aside and allowed the doctor to walk out the door first.

"You better not return the bastard too crippled up on me, or you'll rule the fucking day you were born, dog man." Colonel Leadbetter snapped as an afterthought at the soldier.

"I assure you sir, I'll get him back to you in one stinking piece, Colonel." The Mutt smirked.

"I bet, wiseass." The Colonel took his eyes off the report he was holding, and watched the two heading for the other barracks. He was pleased his troops allowed the doctor in their ranks. It was important both sides accepted the other, it added greatly to the potential success of the operation. Colonel Leadbetter shook his head slowly as the two people quickly disappeared in the night. "Poor bastard, I wonder what the hell those mad men have in store for ya stinking ass mister."

"What's that sir? You said something and I didn't catch all of it, Colonel Leadbetter."

The Colonel turned his head and saw Sergeant Kirkpatrick standing in the doorway and he immediately barked hotly at him. "Where the hell were you a few moments ago mister? I needed you, Walker just kidnapped the damn civilian puke on me, and I wanted you to accompany the dumb shit to make sure he's being treated properly by them damn wahoos. He sent his mad dog partner with a cock-n-bull story about going over some points of interest with the Doc.

Those bastards are up to no good, and I want you to protect the damn Doc from them pains in the ass."

"Sorry sir, I was taking a dump, Colonel Leadbetter Sir. If you really want to know what Walker's planning for the Doc, all you had to do was ask me sir." Sergeant Kirkpatrick grunted.

"Do you know what the fuck those damn sleazebags are up to tonight, mister?"

"Colonel Leadbetter Sir, what the hell type of Sergeant would I be if I didn't know what my people are up on base at all times, sir. The soldiers are planning to get the civilian puke his first BJ, sir. They're using the stinking French hen to get the, errr... for a lack of a better word, job done for them sir. I heard it said they're going to initiate both of them into the group at the same time. I didn't see any harm or I would've reported it to you sooner, or stopped it. Sorry sir."

The surprised Colonel suddenly laughed aloud as he shoved his chair away from the desk and then he placed his feet on top of it and he bitched at his Sergeant. "Why the lousy sonsofbitches, so they're going to coarsen up the poor Doc a little on me huh? The dopey bastard needs some messing up, the damn pussy wipe's such a fucking whoosh. I can't believe he never enjoyed a blowjob in his damn life. Man, he's going to be looking to stick that damn thing between the lips of any bitch that'll open her mouth for him after tonight. I remember my first one, wow. I spent the next week trying to get as many as my dick could take." The Colonel rubbed his stiffening dick through his pants and he complained. "The lucky little bastard doesn't know what the hell he's in for tonight with them crazy ass people of ours. I sure hope the damn fools leave enough of him left in one piece to carry out his orders on this upcoming fucking operation, Sergeant."

"You want I should sort of hang around Walker's barracks, to make sure it doesn't get too out of hand on them, sir?" Kirkpatrick asked, showing some concern for the doctor's well being.

"Naw... fuck the damn Doc in the ass. He's a big boy and he should be more than able to take care of himself. If he can't live through a fucking blow job, what fricking chance does he have making it through the damn mission then mister? Besides Sergeant, it'll make the Unit tighter, and more willing to protect the lousy bastard on the mission. Go back to your office, or you can turn in if you want. I'll keep an eye on the time, and if the Doc's gone too long, I'll go get the little bastard. Maybe there's a chance I can get in on some of the action myself. Some of those babes are hot, and I wouldn't mind taking a tumble with one of them. Good night Sergeant." Even though the Colonel joked about joining in the festivities, he would not dare. It was against regulations to experience sexual relations with any female soldier under his command.

"Good night Colonel Leadbetter, if you want any company, wake me sir." Sergeant Kirkpatrick snapped to attention and then he saluted the Colonel.

LIEUTENANT ROBERT WALKER'S BARRACKS

Lieutenant Robert Walker and Sergeant Dorothy Ramirez were keeping an eye outside the barracks, and when they spotted the Mutt and the doctor heading for the barracks, they told everyone to get ready. Ramirez spent an hour talking the beautiful French warrior to participate in the fun and games. She informed the French fighter this was one way the Unit indoctrinated new members in the group. After assuring her she and the other females had to do this and more, she agreed to do the doctor. At first she balked at doing it before the others, but when Ramirez told her it was the only way the soldiers would believe the act took place, she relented.

The Mutt dragged the shaking and worried doctor into the darkened barracks, once inside he made the doctor move further into the room until he stood right center of the building. The beds were all moved around to form a rough circle where the doctor ended standing when the light was turned on. Ramirez slid a chair up behind the doctor, and then she, Fun Bags, Baby Tee, Hand Full, Snow Flake, and Jail Bait took turns stripping the doctor. Hoots and yells came from the other soldiers in the barracks as they all watched with envy as the girls made a big thing of stripping the egghead doctor naked in front of all of them.

Everyone was enjoying themselves, all but Danko. Walker noticed right off that Danko was looking angry as hell and he called out to him from across the room. "Hey Danko, what the hell gives with you anyway man? You look like you're fucking pissed off at the stinking world man."

"Fuck the damn world man." Danko growled, refusing to join in on the fun.

Walker made his way over to the warrior and asked him again. "What the hell's up your stinking ass Homes? I can't have you down on the fucking world before we go in an action, Homes." Walker snapped as he leaned ever a little closer to Danko, Sergeant Christopher Danko.

"You wanna know what's bugging my ass? I'll tell ya, it's this country Walker. We're such a smart bunch of shitheads over the past years we allowed many good paying Union jobs to jump the damn borders. Why? Because of greed, the pay next door was cheaper than our workers, and now their workers are going on strike to make their pay half ass comparable to ours, man. The suck ass part of this damn mess is when those bastards strike, they put our workers here on the unemployment lines. It's shit, we're so damn smart aren't we? The big businesses save money hand over foot using cheaper workers, yet the prices of the cars and uther crap's skyrocketing.

"We go off and grin with pride when the big three brag they're enjoying windfall profits. While the poor bastards have to do the give back acts, and suffer cutbacks in pay and benefits to keep their jobs, now they're ending up eating shit, and were eating shit from the other countries. And where am I, I'm preparing to defend my country against these damn assholes waiting to get to fucking Paradise, and my father's unemployed because the workers in Canada wants to picket GM. Don't get me wrong, I have nothing against Unions, my father's been in one all his life, but this is the first time he's being forced to stay away from work because of non American workers.

"Everyone dumps on the damn Union workers, saying their pay's so high. Look what's happened to the United States since we started dumping on the damn Unions. Now, all you read about is corporate cut backs, people being laid off and no more job security. Over educated Americans are being forced to accept menial work and pay, because we did nothing but export our better paying jobs to poor countries to save corporate America some big fucking bucks. If Unions woulda remained strong, and the slobs who said they hated fricking Unions, and Unions were destroying the country woulda joined damn Unions in the first place rather than buck them. I bet you the asses would have jobs, and their companies would still be here in the States.

"One thing you don't see, with cutbacks and lesser pay our citizens are forced to accept, you don't see taxes and prices for crap coming down. That's the only thing they didn't export to the other countries. In fact, they did nothing but give these hot shots tax breaks, and we hafta make up the difference in the till. I'm tired of it, I'm so sick I feel like telling the service to go to hell, and get the bastards keeping my old man from working to defend their shores. I'd like to know who's running our country. They tell us to vote, but what good does it do, once the fucks are in office they do everything in their power to sell out the workers. It don't make any sense, it sucks. Non American workers causing our workers to stay home and not get paid, it don't make sense."

"I know what you're saying, maybe the man in the big seat will stay to his promises he made when running for the Presidency, and make some things right again for all of us. Who the fuck knows, but I agree with your gripes man, it don't make any sense. Something I do know, you're not gonna solve any of the stinking problems facing the United States by refusing to do your duty. C'mon pal, lean back and enjoy the festivities, tomorrow we jump off and you can work out your frustrations on the asses of those damn sand buggers. Whose got a bone going?"

"I thought you said none of that crap until our mission is done with man?"

"What the hell are you, a fucking parrot now, dammit? I know what the hell I said, but I'm countermanding that order as of now. Who's holding the damn blunt?"

Wacko, waiting for the French fighter to make her first appearance in the center of the group, announced proudly to the Lieutenant. "I got a stick wit me Walker."

"Shoulda fucking known it'd be you who would be holding the shit, Wacker. Well light the damn thing up buddy and get it going around the clock, beginning with me." Walker growled.

"Why starting with you Homes?" No Neck grumbled as he put out his massive mitt.

"Because I'm the badest dog in this fucking barnyard, that's why tree trunk. You can have the third hit from the damn thing." Walker was handed the joint and took a pull from it, and then he passed it to Danko. "Take a second hit from it man. It'll make you feel a whole lot betta."

When Walker was certain Danko was loosen up some, he took the joint and headed for the naked and thoroughly embarrassed civilian doctor. Sitting half ass tied to the chair with his own tie. Walker offered the grinning and high as a kite doctor the bone as he held it for him, and then he waited for the drunk doctor to take the bone from his hand.

"What's this stuff you're offering me, Lieutenant Walker Sir?" The doctor asked the grinning Lieutenant as he tried to focus his eyes on the officer and what he had in his hand.

"It'll make you feel a helluva lot betta and help you relax some at the same time, Doc. Try it, you'll like it good, man." He offered as the last female warrior finished playing with the wasted doctor. Fun Bags was having a great time rubbing her breasts in front of the doctor's face, making him turn red with embarrassment.

"I know what this is, this is that marijuana stuff, isn't it Lieutenant Walker?" the doctor cried.

"Never mind any fucking questions Doc, and take a hit from the damn thing will ya. You're letting it burn up for nuthin man." Walker leaned closer to the drunk civilian and whispered. "C'mon man, you're fucking embarrassing the shit outta my stinking ass here, Doc. I stuck up for you, you wanna be accepted by the uther troops into our group don't ya? Then you're gonna hafta live by the fucking rules we go by man." Walker shoved the doctor's arm with his hand.

The doctor took a drag and almost instantly, his head started to spin.

"C'mon Doc, you can't fly with one fucking wing you know man. Take a good stinking hit this time round will ya and it'll make it all good with yourself, sir."

As the doctor drew in the smoke, the other soldiers started to clap.

"Hold the smoke in for a sec Doc. There, that's it, let it do its thing fur ya." Walker coached.

"My head's spinning Lieutenant, I doubt if I could walk straight right now sir." The doctor cried as he choked on the harsh smoke filling his lungs.

"Now your flying like a fucking Eagle, Homes." The Mutt called out from his position as he added to his words. "Take another fucking hit from the damn thing and really get up in the damn clouds man. It'll make the game really feel good fur ya Homes."

As if right on cue, French Sergeant Regina Raphael came strolling out of the head dressed in a black bra, nylons, and garter belt and nothing else. The Frenchie had her reddish blonde hair up in a bun, so everyone would see what she was doing to the doctor when the fun began.

Walker looked at the female fighter as she seductively swayed her way over at the drooling doctor. He looked at Doctor Russbinder and saw he was as hard as a nail, and offered him another hit from the joint. "Here you go Doc, it looks like you're gonna really need it, pal."

The civilian doctor took a double drag of the roach avariciously, without even thinking or complaining. His eyes were glued to the swaying breasts dancing just inches away from his face.

The grunts were egging the Frenchie on, giving her a number of suggestions on how to do the doctor good and proper. But when she placed her feet on both sides of the chair, and then she straddled the doctor's face, the grunts hollowed with laughter and continued to call out to her.

"C'mon Doc, you gotta lick that thang as if it was a watermelon. You know what they say about a hair pie being shoved in your puss. If you don't eat it, you don't fucking need it Homes."

Caps flew across the room, many striking Buckethead's body for his crude comment he just made, with Walker adding as he got on the huge soldier's case. "A fucking watermelon? Now we know where your stinking head's at, asshole."

Baby Tee next called out. "Hey Frenchie, you have to remember a man's like a kitchen floor. If you lay it right the first time, you can spend the rest of your life walking all over it, honey."

The women clapped over Baby Tee's words of wisdom to the French fighter.

"Hey Doc, once you get passed the stink, you got it fricking licked, man." The Roach Sergeant David Burgwald called out this time and was turned on by the women standing next to him.

To everyone's surprise, the civilian was starting to really get into the act as he struggled to free his arms from the loosely tied bonds. But when the French fighter got off his face, and then she lowered herself down on his shaft, the poor soul started to wiggle like a fish out of water.

"Hey Frenchie, don't forget you hafta finish him off with your face." McNip offered with a grin from ear to ear as he took the joint going around the group and took a hit from it.

The French soldier did not lose her rhythm as she flipped the bird at McNip, Sergeant David Nirajima without looking at him, staying on the doc's shaft and making the group laugh more.

When Regina felt she had the doctor thoroughly excited, she got off his lap and drew his shaft into her mouth. With just a few strokes, the doc erupted like Mt. Saint Helen. The Frenchie did a good job, keeping on his shaft as he shot off. The group shouted, clapped and cheered, and then a chorus of 'oorahs' suddenly broke out until the Unit's call was almost deafening.

Walker kept a close eye on the action going down before him, and when he was sure the doctor was empty, he rushed in and pulled the Frenchie up to her feet, holding one hand over her head as he announced. "Listen up assholes, I wanna introduce you to the newest member of the stinking Unit. Sergeant Regina Raphael, from this moment on, known to us as Blind Date."

Blind Date wiped her mouth and chin with the back of her hand, and flashed a huge grin of victory. She was overjoyed to be part of the elite Unit, to be accepted into the tight knit group.

The group clapped as they shoved each other, with some soldiers calling out at the new member. "Hey Blind Date, I'm next honey. Do me next huh pretty baby?"

"You gonna do me as good as you did the dopey Doc over there?" Another soldier called out.

"Can the shit." Walker growled as he turned to the doc who was passed out on the chair, and asked the group as a whole. "What are we gonna do with this flaming asshole over here? We can't return him to the damn Colonel in this condition. He'll have all our friggin heads."

"Arrr... I say we leave his dopey ass right where it is and make this a military operation."

"No can do that, the slob's one of us now people. He earned the right to wear the split eagle wings." Walker groaned as he lightly kicked the doctor's foot. No sign of life was displayed.

"Hey Walker, you betta check the dumb shit out, maybe the fuck's deada than a fucking door knob on us man. It's be just like the egghead to crap out on us over a stinking blow job, man."

"Fat chance of that shit happening, the asshole's still fucking breathing people. But if you think about it, what a friggin way to go to the next world." Walker grunted back at the group.

"You should have one of the girls try to blow him up again Walker. Maybe that'll bring the dopey pud back to life for us, Homes." Another soldier called out from the group.

"I glad offer me service you Lieutenant." A voice heavily laden with a Russian accent offered.

All eyes went over to the female Russian soldier branded Siberia. Sergeant Taras Zarugnaya walked into the lighted circle, and then she knelt down before the doctor, and sucked his limp shaft into her mouth. This did the trick, almost instantly he was wiggling in the chair again. When the doctor was rock hard and aware of what was happening to him, Siberia simply stopped what she was doing to him and she merely turned and walked away from the man.

"You're not gonna finish him off now you got him standing at attention again?" The Mutt asked, shocked the Russian would go so far and then left the poor guy with a standing member.

"You want finish off, you do youself big shot boy soldier. I offer bring him to sense back. I no never say anything about, I err... how you say, finish off him please." Siberia hissed as she rejoined the other two female Russian soldiers standing away from the rest of the group.

"Is that what you're gonna do to me when I cash in on that fucking blowjob you owe my ass, Siberia?" the Mutt growled as he moved a little closer to the center of the makeshift circle.

"Man, that's a real cold fucking bitch there man. That's colder than the uther side of the damn pillow, baby." Walker griped as he went to the doctor and told him he better get dressed.

The doctor did as he was told, but he asked for another hit from the joint. By the time he was half dressed, he was way out there feeling real great and swaying back and forth on his feet.

"Here Homes, you betta have a cold one, we don't want the stinking Colonel thinking you're high on grass." Walker warned as he popped the top and offered the beer to the swaying doc.

"Thank you Home." The drunk doctor mumbled back at Walker as he took the offered beer.

"No Doc, and that's Homes, get it right now you're one of us stinking pukes here, Doc."

"I reallllly dig youuuu Lieutenant Walker." The doctor grinned at Walker.

"Whoa Doc, you gotta dump the old time dig shit, if you wanna be one of the guys, man."

"I hearrrrr you, fuuuuck it Walkerrrrr." The doctor said as he staggered backwards, and then he almost fell backwards over the chair they used to get the doctor off on.

"Now ya got it friggin right Homes. By the time we return you to the stinking egghead world, you're gonna be one real hip hop fucking hot ass stinking Doc, man. I can't wait to see those stinking stuff shirt female Doctors when they get a load of your new rhythm, man. You're gonna hafta fart the bitches offa your stinking back then, Homes." Walker grunted at the man.

"Yeah maaaan this is greatttt stuffff you gave me hereeeee, Lieutenanttttt." The doctor slurred and then leaned back and grabbed his crotch, and wiggled his dick through his pants.

"C'mon Doc, I'll bring you back to the stinking Colonel before he has a fucking puppy."

"Arrrr... fuuuuck him where he breathes, I waaaant some more pot, and I waaaaant another one of them blowjobs." The doctor blurted out as he belched and farted, causing the group to roar.

"You got it now Doc. You're sailing way out there." Casper called out as he lit another joint.

"C'mon go light on that damn crap will ya, Casper. Dammit to hell, I know I said you can light them up tonight, but I don't want anyone over doing it now, dammit. We got a job ahead of us, and I don't need anyone bleeding from the fricking eyes out in the stinking field, people." Walker warned as he took the doc by the arm and then lead him from the barracks.

"Come on myyyyy newwww fucccking soldier friendddd, and let oooone of the girlssss suck onnn my caduceus again." The high doctor cried while rubbing his crotch again through his half zipped up pants.

"No Doc, I believe that's suppose to be wand. It's 'let the girls suck on your wand, your mean stick, Doc. You'll catch on betta the longer you hang round with the rest of this group of slugs, Doc. C'mon Homes, you had enuf shit for one night man." Walker led him down the five steps.

"But I waaaaant to have another sucking off jobbb. It was soooooo good, I never experienced annnnything like it befooore, Lieutenant. I can't believe all thaaaat I beeeen missing for so loooong." The civilian doctor cried as he did his best to walk with Walker out of the barracks.

"Man Doc, you're really embarrassing the stinking shit outta my lousy ass, dammit. You gotta straighten up some man, or the stinking Colonel's gonna have both of us hanging from the damn yardarm." Walker warned the egghead as he guided the staggering doctor to the Colonel's office.

"Fuckkkk him, he's such a tight collar all the timeee with meeeee. Always threateningggg to beat me up, telling meeeee what he's going to do to my boooody if I don't pay close attention to himmmmm." Another belch from the doctor as he pitched forward, and almost threw up.

"Yeah Doc, I know, but he's the top fucking banana man. So we gotta pay attention to all his stinking orders. Once I get you out in the field, things will go a lot lighter on ya ass. C'mon, it's getting late, and the Colonel's probably eating the furniture by now waiting for you to get back to him. I'm surprised he didn't send his little henchman over to make sure you're still alive, Doc."

"Fuckkkk him I saidddd." The doctor slurred as he allowed Walker to push him forward.

Walker stopped walking just outside Colonel Leadbetter's office, and he swallowed when he notice the lights were still on in the room. He knew the Colonel was up and obviously waiting for the doctor to return and he warned the doctor. "C'mon Doc, might as well give him some raw meat to chew on for the rest of the stinking night man." Walker led the still staggering doctor up the steps, and then he slammed his palm loudly on the side of the building.

"Enter!" Colonel Leadbetter growled from inside the office.

Walker pushed the doctor through the door. The Colonel stared at the doctor's condition as he stood behind his desk. With his mouth hanging open as he eyes darted up and down the length of his disheveled, slouching form of the civilian. The doctor was a mess, his shirt buttoned wrong, and outside his pants on one side. The collar of the shirt half turned in, and his undershirt obviously pulled up, maybe one of the Doctor's arms missed the sleeve. One of his pant legs was hanging over his untied shoe, while the other pant leg rode up his leg. One sock was missing, and his shoes were untied, and his suit jacket miss buttoned and hung wrong on his shoulders.

"Christ Almighty, look at you Doc, you look like a fucking wreck left on the side of the damn road after being hit by a damn car." The Colonel's eyes darted to Walker, and he glared at him.

"C'mon Doc, I'm gonna get you to bed before you pass out on your damn feet sir."

"Fuckkkk that, I want another head job Walkerrrr." The doctor cried to the young officer.

"How many times I gotta tell ya, it's a stinking blowjob Doc." Walker corrected him as he tried to get the doctor moving towards his rack so he could relieve himself of the drunk civilian.

"Fuck you Walker! You stand there with that hole buttoned tight on your damn ass, mister. What the fuck have you done to this pain in the ass on me, dammit? I told you not to break the sonofabitch on me, stupid. Stand at attention while I assist him over to his damn rack. I'll handle your ass once I get this damn butt wipe to his fucking rack." Colonel Leadbetter moved from behind the desk and he took the doctor's arm and then lead the doc over to his rack.

"I want another blow head job Lieutenantttt Walker." The doctor mumbled at him.

"Yeah yeah Doc, get in your damn rack will ya stupid. Be careful dammit, I don't need you getting hurt in my damn office now asshole." Colonel Leadbetter warned the drunk.

"Youuuu going to get me my head job Colonel?" the doctor slurred his words again.

"I'm not going to blow your ass, get on the damn bed Doc so I can settle up with Walker."

"Fuckkkk you Mr. Big shottt, you'll do nothingggggg to that young man, Colonellll. He has opened my eyes to new pleasures I haveeee been denyinggg myself because I was a Doctor, sirrrr. You leave him alone Colonel, or I plant my foot up your ass for youuuuu." The doctor pitched forward, and then he heaved on the floor, passed out and sagged down to the floor himself.

Without saying a word to the plastered doctor as he glared at Walker. Colonel Leadbetter hoisted the limp man up on his shoulder, and then walked the few feet to the doctor's rack and unceremoniously dumped the unconscious civilian on it. Colonel Leadbetter covered him with the sheet, making certain he could breathe, in case he heaved again. The last thing he needed was for the doctor to choke to death on his own vomit. He then turned his attention to Walker and he snarled savagely at him. "Hey fuck face, what the fuck have you done to my god damn Doctor, you little prick you? I warned you before about him for fuck sake mister."

"I got his sagging ass laid good and proper, that all Colonel." Walker smirked as he grinned at the officer who looked like he was going to take his head off his shoulder on him. The smile was wasted on the angry Colonel as he snarled at the Lieutenant. "You fucked him up real bad on me mister. God dammit, I thought I told you I didn't need him messed up when I return the dumb sonofabitch back to the President. Christ sake and miracles, I can see the Boss now, when the damn Doc let's out with a string of fucking obscenities. I told you I didn't need the lousy bastard walking in the President's office and taking a dump on his precious carpet. The way the prick looks, he's liable to do just that, dammit. You and your shit filled assholes had to fuck him up on me, didn't you? You couldn't leave well enough a fucking lone, damn you to hell, Walker."

Walker smiled at the steaming Colonel as he replied. "My people took good care of the little puke, and nothing woulda happened to him. Besides Colonel, most of them had nothing to do with it. If you wanna hang this rap on someone's ass, hang it on my ass, Colonel Leadbetter."

"Fuck you Walker, most of your god damn people couldn't pass the god damn drug test, so don't gimme any of that shit about them being innocent bystanders, mister. None of your god damn soldiers are innocent of anything that goes wrong around here, mister. They should all be stood before a fricking wall and then shot on general principles, buster. Get the hell out of my office before I skin your ass alive and laugh as I do it, buster. I swear to hell and back again Walker, the god damn Doc better be back to fricking normal tomorrow morning, or it's your ass that's going to be pitched into the damn blender, mister. Well Lieutenant, what more can I add to this messed up conversation? What the hell's done is done I guess, buster. I swear to everything that's Holy mister, if I get hell over this new damn attitude of the damn Doc, you're going to catch more Pandemonium than a little bit at the same damn time, Lieutenant.

"Christ sake Walker, I can't believe you just couldn't leave the lousy sonofabitch alone, you just had to fuck with him on my ass, dammit. I should've known when you got hold of his fag ass, his stinking life was going to change drastically forever for crap sake. Shit and damnation Walker, it was like allowing the god damn wolf to play around with the damn lambs. Get the hell out of my face before I forget I'm a gentleman, and I make a fool of myself by beating on your ass, mister. We'll continue this little conversation of ours when we return from the mission."

Walker allowed the largest, shit eating grin to slowly cross over his lips as he turned on his heels while laughing inside as he started to leave the Colonel's office. He left the Colonel's office without showing the slightest bit of concern over his terribly threatening words.

CHAPTER TWENTY ONE

The last full day at the massive Marine Base flew by with the special operations troops spending their remaining hours packing equipment, and covering their preparations for the upcoming attack on Iran. The special ops troops were scheduled to depart the base early morning on Sunday. The C-17 Globemaster transport planes were already on the ground, and the air crews began loading the Bradley fighting machines, along with the amphibious assault vehicles, sand sleds and light, fast moving LAV-25 assault vehicles. While the assault teams were sleeping, most their military equipment and weapons were loaded on board the C-17 transport planes.

Colonel Bruce Leadbetter fell asleep after dumping on Lieutenant Robert Walker for getting Doctor Joel Russbinder stoned, but he was awakened at three a.m. by Sergeant John Kirkpatrick who informed the groggy Colonel the aircraft were loaded with the troop's gear. The Colonel woke in a worse mood then when he went to sleep, and his first thought was to wake Walker, and make him standby him while he made certain all aspects of the troop's needs were covered by command. After thinking about it further, he changed his mind. He was not really that pissed off at Walker or the doctor for that matter. There was no way of telling if everyone was going to make it back alive, and he decided not to anger the troops before a mission.

The Marine Colonel had everything ready to go the day before, and the only things left for the troops to look after, was their personal equipment. The body armor had been removed from the barracks the night before, and placed on board the planes with their extra ammunition and heavy weapons they would need for the mission. This left the soldiers responsible for only their own personal weapons that they had with them at all times, and the ammunition for the weapons.

Lieutenant Walker was dead to the world when Colonel Leadbetter and Sergeant Kirkpatrick came storming into the barracks while beating on the metal racks with wood batons, and also screaming at the top of their lungs as if they had stubbed their toes. A barrage of pillows launched in the air, not only striking the Colonel, but the troops already out of their racks. Curses replaced orders from Colonel Leadbetter telling the grunts to get up. Showers ran as the women rushed in to take their final shower in the States, before the men took over the head and messed it up on the women fighters. Singing soon replaced the many curses and complaints.

Lieutenant Walker walked up to Colonel Leadbetter naked, saluted him as he took a second to listen to the women singing, and the light hearted jokes and complaints being bantered about by his elite warriors and he offered to his commanding officer. "It sure looks like my people are in a pretty good fucking mood for the stat of this stinking operation, sir. But make no mistake about it Colonel Leadbetter Sir, we're ready to kill on first enemy contact, sir."

"That's just fucking peachy, mister." Colonel Leadbetter snapped, he was sorry it was not Walker's fault he had a shitty night's sleep. He could not rest all night long, worrying about how the loading of the C-17s was going for his troops. The Colonel was worried if the Loadmaster made certain the troop's specialized equipment made it on board the aircraft safely and completely. He knew he would be in a world of shit if any military equipment was left behind.

"Still pissed off at me I see huh Colonel?" Walker smirked as he grinned at the officer.

"Naw you P.O.S.. (Piece Of Shit) I kind of half expected you to fuck up the Doc one way or the other on me. I knew you couldn't leave well enough alone, and it was only a matter of time before you fucked him up on my ass. What's that shit I smell, you birds smoking grass? Didn't I tell you to have the bastards lay off that crap until after the fucking mission's done, Lieutenant?" Colonel Leadbetter grunted, and turned to the troops pouring out of their racks and milling about.

"You pussy sniffers better get a fucking move on it, or I'm going to start kicking some ass and taking numbers around here, dammit." The Colonel snarled at the soldiers seemingly taking their time getting ready as he kicked at a pillow lying at his feet, sending it flying across the room.

"Does that go for me too Colonel?" Baby Tee called out in a sweet, sexy tone as she added to her question. "I'm not too interested in pussy myself, but I'm kind of fond of dicks, Colonel."

Her words made the group break up, and the shoving and laughter replaced the tedious job of stuffing their worldly belongings into their fieldpacks. Another barrage of pillows were launched.

"Enough with the fucking pillows already for fuck sake, dammit." Colonel Leadbetter bitched as he snatched one in flight, and he threw it to the floor as if he was angry at it. Then he looked at Baby Tee and barked at her. "Don't go fucking around with me at this time, Tee. I'm not in the fucking mood for you screwing around with me, sister. There's too much to get done, and little fricking time to get it done, dammit. You better start to move it to lose it Tee."

Some of the female warriors strolled out of the showers naked, and this made Colonel Leadbetter all the more angrier and he ordered the female soldiers. "You damn bitches better get some god damn uniform on that bare skin of yours, or I'm going to bite off any fucking parts sticking out further than your damn noses."

Sergeant Dorothy Ramirez stopped walking and she jiggled her breasts right in front of the steaming Colonel, just daring him to do what he just threatened the female warriors with.

Colonel Leadbetter glared at her and then he snapped his teeth, causing her to run from him.

The soldiers laughed as Ramirez made like she was scared the Colonel was going to bite her.

Colonel Leadbetter hung around the barracks until most of the specialized soldiers were dressed and packed and then he growled at them. "Okay you damn tent pegs, the transport aircraft are loaded up with your heavy gear, all that's left is your personal crap you damn Squids want to take along with you people. When we get on board, I want a few of you pack rats to check the equipment stowed away. I want to make certain nothing's left behind before we liftoff. Walker, you can appoint the ones who'll double check on the Loadmaster's work I'm sure."

"Got it covered Colonel, hey Mother, (Sergeant Richard Flanagan), you and Neck (Sergeant Robert Abbott), check on the crap stowed on board our damn aircraft, while CoCo-G and Poncho Villa checks the equipment on the second aircraft. Dock Rat, you and Lipman, check out the crap on the third transport, while Jungle Bunny and Jail Bait check out the shit stowed on the fourth plane. Make sure the important stuff's on board the damn things, as long as all the vital crap's there, fuck the rest of the shit if it doesn't make it on board the damn aircraft."

"Countermand that last order, dammit. Fine fucking orders you just issued to these damn sweat hogs of yours, Walker! What the hell's wrong with your damn head anyway, Lieutenant? I want all the god damn equipment we need for this damn operation on board the fricking junk haulers, period mister. Your people will make certain all, and I mean every bit of our god damn military equipment's stored on board those fucking planes." Colonel Leadbetter hissed as he actually slugged Walker on his arm for caring so little about their equipment.

The chosen soldiers grumbled their response to their added orders and duties from the angry Colonel on checking on their equipment on board the aircraft.

Colonel Leadbetter then leaned close to Lieutenant Walker and complained at him. "Christ sake Walker, didn't I tell you to change the tag name on that one you branded Jungle Bunny for crap sake? Shit, if the higher ups ever hear that one's tag name, someone's liable to end up with a foot sticking up his ass sideways for shit sake. I want that one's name changed now!"

"Sorry, no can do Colonel Leadbetter Sir. It'll take nothing short of an act of Congress to changed the name now, sir. Besides, the jerk doesn't mind the tag in the least sir. Each name given our people, are given with the utmost of respect sir. If it crosses over lines of racism, who gives a fuck, because that's not what the names were given out for. In our ranks, there's no such thing as racism and disrespect sir. Here, everyone's the same color, and treated with the same respect, or lack thereof sir, whether he's white, black, red, or pink, or if he's a male or a female, or if we're not sure either way. He, she or it, is to be treated as everyone is, equal and I'm not changing Jungle Bunny's fucking name for anyone but him on his request, Colonel Leadbetter."

"You know, you're getting to be a real pain in the fucking ass Walker. One of these days."

"Understood Colonel Leadbetter Sir." Walker grinned at the angry acting officer.

"Yeah, but don't say I didn't warn you about the god damn tag name for that stinking soldier mister, or the damn trouble you could get your ass in over it, asshole. I have to see if I can wake the damn Doc, he's still out like a fucking light thank you very much, buster. I was trying to give him as much time as possible to sleep a little longer mister. His damn time just ran out on his sagging ass, Lieutenant. I sure hope he has his god damn head screwed on tight, we're really going to need him on this damn operation, sir. Keep on your damn people Lieutenant, get them hot, when they're finished, have them assemble outside my damn office for further orders."

"You got it Colonel." Walker bitched back at the Colonel.

Colonel Leadbetter gave Lieutenant Walker a half hearted salute, and then he left. Sergeant Kirkpatrick left and went to the second building to wake the other soldiers sleeping there.

When the Colonel left, the Mutt moved over to Walker's side and complained at him. "Well whaddaya gonna do with the three stinking Russian babes, man? You want I should have them linkup with Mother Flanagan's stinking Unit to give them a home for this operation, Homes?"

Walker growled back at the Mutt. "Naw, they're betta off hanging with us, dog man. I don't know if we can trust them damn bitches yet buddy. We're gonna hafta keep an eye on them until we're certain they're part of our unit, and not operating under a preconceived agenda, man."

"I hear that man. Preconceived agenda huh? Walker, those damn Lieutenant bars are starting to make you a helluva lot smarter than you look, man. Soon, I'm gonna hafta start carrying a damn dictionary, so I know what the fuck you're talking about, my friend. I'll have the Russian babes move their asses to our plane, and I'll have Boot Camp and Repeat keep an eye on them. I'll tell the rest of the guys if they see the Ruskies screwing up, and doing shit that goes against our best interests, they're to become casualties of our invasion." The Mutt's face broke out in a grin.

"Fuck casualties huh, they're to become friggin fatalities if it seems like they're working against us on this damn operation, buster. If they're not working for us then they're working against us and that'll cost them their asses. Have Boot and Repeat take them out if they think the damn

Russians are going against us man. No if, ands, or buts bout it, you got it Homes?"

"No prob, I'll clue them in on the order." The Mutt warned as he waved Boot Camp to him.

The soldier branded Boot Camp, (Sergeant Fred Moorehouse) was packed up and ready to ship out. He looked at the Mutt, and then grinned as he held up a hand with all fingers sticking up but one, the athletic digit, the finger used to give the bird. This sign was the street way of flashing the 'fuck you' signal. He slung his ruckpack over his shoulder as if it weighed nothing, and then he picked his way through the other soldiers cluttering the walkway of the barracks on him.

"Yeah, you and me are gonna take care of that computer worm, keep his fat ass outta any stinking trouble on this one. I kinda like the stuffed collar, he seems like a square deal for a stinking egghead." Walker allowed a slight chuckle as he remembered the doctor's face when he was coming. "Yeah Mutt, I want Blind Date to be in our outfit as well man. I want you to take her under your damn wing. I want that one to make the grade and stay in our outfit for the duration. I think she'll be use to us in more ways than one if you catch my stinking drift Homes."

"Fuck you, I know you better than you do man, you want her to give you a blowjob, Walker."

"So! You got a problem with that thought, dog man?" Walker asked him with a smirk.

"So nuthin Bro. I kinda like the thought myself man." The Mutt snapped as Boot Camp placed his hand on his shoulder and asked the soldier."What's up Mutt?"

"Here's what's up, you and Repeat are to keep an eye on the damn Russian babes. If they're not following orders to the tee, take them out and leave their stinking bodies for the goat eaters."

"Really Homes? You're not fucking doping me right man? You really want me to take the three stinking Russian chicks out if they fuck up any while out on the operation, man?" The large black soldier asked the Lieutenant like he could not believe the last order.

"Deader than a fucking door knob that quick, Homes." The Mutt warned Repeat angrily.

"Easy order to follow I guess if that's what you really want man. Whaddaya want me to do with their stinking equipment if we hafta take them out on the operation Mutt?"

"They're carrying Russian junk, just leave the crap with them. Maybe it'll help confuse the stinking Iranians and make them believe their Commie friends were in on this fucking raid."

"Out fucking standing thought, I couldn't have come up with a betta solution myself, Mutt."

"C'mon Mutt, I know Leadbetter wants to be airborne by seven a.m. We betta get the rest of the damn grunts moving." Walker grumbled as he went to check on his equipment.

COLONEL BRUCE LEADBETTER'S OFFICE

Colonel Leadbetter entered his office just as the doctor was swinging his legs off his rack, and he asked the civilian with concern. "You okay Doc? You look like shit warmed over you know."

"Arrrr... my fucking head's thumping to beat the band, and my eyes hurt, and my mouth feels like someone took a dump in it, sir." The doctor complained as he ran his tongue around his lips.

Colonel Leadbetter winced when the doctor continued to use the curse words he obviously been taught by Walker and the rest of his crew of misfits as he offered."Here you go Doc, take a good pull of this crap. It'll sort of help with the nasty taste in your damn mouth, sir. I was hoping you'd forget the damn street language when you came back to your senses again, Herr Doctor. Obviously, that training session you went through last night stayed with ya stinking ass, sir. Herr Doctor, you better be careful, I don't need you slipping in front of the Boss using our lingo."

"There's no problem with that, Colonel. I know how to speak before the President at all time sir. What's this Colonel?" Doctor Russbinder moaned while holding on his head.

"It's a damn Pepsi, it'll help with the shit taste in your trap, and might even help a little with the pounding in your noggin, Doc." Colonel Leadbetter smirked as he handed him the soda.

"It's so early in the morning, I haven't had anything to eat and you want me to drink this?"

"Stop analyzing everything and just do what I tell you to do will ya, Doc.? Take my word for it, it'll help you get over the bad effects of last night, sir. Then we're going to grab something to eat and get the troops airborne. Herr Doctor, we have thirty minutes to get ready, eat, and pack up the crap you want to take along with you on the fucking operation, sir. Then we have to ship out for the Iranian target sir. You going to be able to accomplish everything in that short a time mister?" Colonel Leadbetter growled as he watched the shaky doctor drain the Pepsi.

A belch followed the pull of soda, and then Doctor Russbinder held the can at arm's length as he studied it for a moment, and then he placed the cold can against his forehead and grumbled at the colonel. "Huh, this stuff really works sir. My head's feeling a little better already, Colonel." He tried to stand and fell back, paying for the attempt as he closed his eyes as stars blasted in his mind. This was followed by intense pain going off inside his skull. It was as if someone had placed a mule inside his head, and prodding it to kick the sides and back of his eyes.

"Whoa, not that many miracles I'm afraid. The rooms spinning crazily on me Colonel."

"First time you been drunk in your fucking life huh, Doc?" Colonel Leadbetter asked him.

"No. But it's the first time I smoked some of that cannabis stuff with the troops, Colonel."

"Cannabis huh Doc?" Colonel Leadbetter stared at the still drunk civilian.

"Yes, I believe the soldiers called it a cooking pot, or something like that if I remember right last night sir. I can't remember the exact words they called the stuff though, Colonel."

"You mean to tell me someone was cooking off a bone inside the fucking barracks, Doc?"

"Yes that's what they called it alright Colonel." The shaky civilian doctor said as he tried to hold his head in both his hands to try and stop it from pounding so bad on him.

"I can't believe those scumbags gave you some damn grass sir. Wait till I get my hands on that fucker's neck. I'm going to kill that sonofabitch yet dammit. I'll squeeze Walker's neck until his eyeballs pop out of his damn head and roll around the floor. I thought all they were going to do was get you high and let some broad get your rocks off for ya. Who did you last night anyway?"

"Did me Colonel?" The civilian asked the Colonel, confused by his last words.

"Yeah Doc, C'mon man and be square with me for crap sake. Who got your damn rocks off last night, Herr Doctor?" Colonel Leadbetter smirked as he cast a wary eye at him, thinking he was trying to deny he had sex with one of the female soldier's last night.

"I see no harm telling you what I remember. The soldiers had the French woman do me."

"Holy shit, you mean that hot new number from France did ya last night, Doc?"

"Yes, I guess so sir. It was easy for me to understand her because I speak French, Colonel."

"Geeeesus Keerist Doc, how was she sir. She looks hotter than a fucking match stick. I've been keeping my eye on her ever since she first joined the group. What did she do to you Doc?"

"She was naked, and I remember her straddling me and shoving her private parts in my face, Colonel. Then she sat on me, and she used her mouth and made me..."

"She gave you a fucking blowjob Doc. Right on front of all the other shitbirds?" Colonel Leadbetter interrupted as he leaned closer to the civilian so he could hear his response better.

"Yes Colonel." He moaned as he rubbed his burning, painful eyes with both hands.

"So that's what you meant by a fucking blow head last night, huh Doc. I thought so sir."

The doctor laughed and then he immediately grabbed his head again, after paying the price for the slight chuckle and he mumbled. "Is that what I called it sir? I must have really been drunk, sir." He moaned while continuing to hold his head as if in danger of it breaking on him.

"That's what you called it Doc. How was it man?" Colonel Leadbetter asked with a grin.

"From what I can remember of it Colonel Leadbetter. It was really great, absolutely great sir. I intend to have a lot more of them before I'm put to rest in the grave I can assure you sir."

Colonel Leadbetter sat back on the doctor's rack, clapping his hands as he laughed and then announced. "Say Doc, enough of this crap until we get back to the States, sir. We have to get ready to go sir. Are you going to have any trouble getting ready in thirty minutes, Doc?"

"No not at all Colonel Leadbetter Sir. Most of the equipment I need was already packed up, and I believe it's all been loaded on one of the transport aircraft. I supervised the packing of my equipment myself before I arrived on base, Colonel. As far as I know, my apparatus might be already in Pakistan. Now I remember, I recall someone saying they were going to ship it through a private carrier, to ensure its safe arrival where I'll need it. Someone said the private handlers will toss it on their planes underhand, instead of the military's usual mode of packing everything up with machines and heaving boxes packed every which way, Colonel Leadbetter sir." The still suffering doctor drew in a breath while trying to cope with the pounding in his head.

"I'm glad to see someone's using his damn head for more than a fucking hat rack around here lately, Doc. That was most wise on your part to send your crap via private handlers, sir. It'll help with the Unit's security at the same time sir. C'mon Doc, we have to get a move on it, or we'll never liftoff on time sir." Colonel Leadbetter led the way to the mess

BANDER BEHESHI, IRAN. NOVEMBER 10ᵗʰ, 1998

It was late afternoon, the Iranian Colonel Marzuk breathed in a sigh as the last nuclear tipped missile stowed in the submarine was secured, and the launch hatch closed and locked in place. Colonel Marzuk looked down the narrow canal, the tide was rising rapidly, and soon it would be high tide again, and his remaining submarines would be free to prowl the seas in search of the American warships. The Iranian Colonel turned to his aide and grumbled at him. "At long last Jawad, the dreams of our country of becoming a nuclear entity will finally be realized. With the launching of these four submarines, we'll become as powerful as the once feared United States, and the nations of the world will fear us as they should, and listen to our words of warning.

"It'll be only a matter of time before the teaching of Islam is the only religion followed in the Middle East and then the world. I believe the tide is high enough for my submarines to begin their sacred mission to sterilize the Middle East of all American warships. Soon my friend, we'll have enough missiles, warheads and submarines to stop all commercial shipping in the entire Middle East. Praise the all powerful Allah for giving us the will to carry out his bidding.

"It's not I who makes these decisions; it's the will of Allah. I'm merely the instrument in which He uses to see His will is carried out faithfully. Allah has ordained Iran will train the faithful and eliminate all non-believers from the face of the earth. My brother, it's time we launch the weapons that'll free Iran from the oppressive yoke of Satan. At last, we'll be free of American criminal influences, we'll be free to pursue the interests of Iran in the manner of the leaders of the Persian world. We'll move the holy place of Mecca to the soil of Iran, making Iran the center of Islam. The Eye of Allah shall shine brightly over the lands of Iran and her satellites forever. May Allah be with you and guide you on your faithful mission. Allah Akbar Jawad!"

The dock workers gathered on the deck of the submarine, repeated Colonel Marzuk's prayer.

"Allah Akbar, Allah Akbar, Allah Akbar." Over and over the workers repeated the prayer. The excited soldiers on the dock emptied their weapons in the air. Civilian ships moored in port blew their powerful air horns, as the dock crews stopped their work and joined the prayer.

More weapons fired, soon, the dock was becoming a dangerous place as spent shells returned to earth. Colonel Marzuk held his hands in the sign of silence. It took a few minutes for sanity to return to the work area. When the Iranian Colonel was certain he could be heard, he issued more orders. "Captains, on this day you've been entrusted with the fate of Iran's future. I order you to start your boat's engines, the tide's high for you to navigate the canal safely, and make for the open sea. I'm proud of the dock workers who toiled under pressure long hours to prepare my submarines for action, before the hated American warplanes had arrived to destroy them. I'll make sure there's a place of honor for all of you in the new Iranian government."

At the mention of the American warplanes attacking them, all eyes of the workers immediately started to scan the sky in search of the first of the attacking American planes of war.

"Captains of the submarines, you're free to set sail on your sacred mission to..."

A second aide suddenly rushed up to Colonel Marzuk's side and handed him a dispatch. The Colonel realized it was a communiqué from military headquarters. He swallowed at the fear rising in his stomach. His first thought was the report was warning him American fighter aircraft were on their way, and would arrive before his submarines made it to sea. Silently, he cursed as he unfolded the dispatch. He knew the worst thing he could do was display fear before his men.

Colonel Marzuk let out his breath in a rush as he barked. "What's this you bring to me, you great dung eating fool you?" He held the communiqué out, and then he waved it angrily at the aide and added to his complaint against him. "This foul report is still written in code, by Allah's great wrath. I'm unable to understand this paper. You'll have the dispatch translated it to a form I'm able to read, fool. I should have your head on a stick for insulting me this way, bringing me a report in this gibberish. You'll have this report translated in seconds, or your family will not see the coming sunrise." The angry Iranian Colonel shoved the paper in the aide's hand.

The Colonel angrily trapped his foot, not knowing how to react. He wanted his submarines sailing in the ocean, free to carry out their threat of nuclear retaliation if Iran was attacked by Americans, or any of her allies. Colonel Marzuk understood he could not send them on their way, to be caught in the middle of the narrow channel and then sunk on him, while trapping the civilian shipping at dock if the Americans started their attack. His mind raced, trying to figure out what to do, he decided and ordered as he raised his hand to get everyone's attention. "Captains, you'll build power in your machines to full, but you'll remain at port until I read what command has just sent to us. Then we'll decide on the next course of action to take."

Colonel Marzuk lowered his hand and waited for his aide to return with the report. His temper grew until he could barely control it any longer. The workers who wanted their heads to remain on their shoulders, gave the angry pacing Colonel a wide berth for him to walk off his steam.

The door to the communication building smashed open, and the aide ran as fast as he could run back to Colonel Marzuk's side. With a trembling hand he offered the now readable page. The Colonel roughly pulled it from his hand and barked at the aide again. "Leave my sight before I have you flogged to within an inch of your worthless life, lowly jackal. You'll thank Allah I don't force your wife to service of our fighting men, and have your sons sold to the slave world."

The aide dashed off as Colonel Marzuk read the page. 'Colonel Marzuk, it's my duty to inform you that a number of American warships are shadowing the two submarines launched to the Indian Ocean. After consideration, it's suggested you'll wait for darkness before launching your remaining submarines. It's hoped by retraining the boats until night, the submarines shall elude the pursuing American warships stationed in the Persian Gulf. We're extremely disappointed to hear one submarine came to end before chance engaging the American ships, or their allies throughout waters surrounding the Middle East. We hope the other boats will not suffer same fate. You know what it means if you're unsuccessful in this endeavor, Colonel Marzuk. You, and your family will pay with your foolish lives, and your relations will live on, but under terrible circumstances. They'll live, but will curse your name forever with their lips as they pray to die.

'Colonel Marzuk, we have not detected any American warships sailing towards your direction. It's believed the hated Americans have no intention of attacking the Bander Beheshi port. There's been no military activity in the region, Colonel. It's believed Bandar-e-Abbas will be primary

American target for attack against our nation when they open hostilities against our country. It's been reported large number of American and ally warships steaming towards that port, and the American airbases stationed in Saudi Arabia and Kuwait were placed on full alert. We ordered our warplanes to the north to save them from the same fate that was endured by Iraq during their war against the god cursed United States, Colonel Marzuk.

"Believe the American lead attack on Iran will be mainly diversions, designed to force us to rejoin the worthless organization of the god cursed United Nations. Then they'll waste more of their foolish time trying to bend the non-bending of Iran's will to their worthless beliefs. We're willing to tie up the great American war machine by bantering empty words about that useless organization, until their time has all but ran out on the great fools. By time the worthless fools will realize what we're doing to them and their words wasted, we'll be in position to defeat the hated American soldiers on any front they may choose to engage us on, Colonel Marzuk.

'Of course, this great feat would not be possible for the nation of Iran to realize, if not was not for your ability to buy and then arm those god cursed Russian submarines with nuclear missiles. Colonel Marzuk, you have served Iran well in her time of great need, to defeat all the hated infidels of the world, and you'll be well rewarded when successful in this war with United States, and all who support them is realized, and we'll then reshape the entire Middle East region to our beliefs, and you'll be an intricate part of that reshaping, Colonel Marzuk. Remember Colonel Marzuk, everything hinges on launching those nuclear powered submarines, and their success under the sea against all the enemy of Iran. If the submarines fail their mission then you have failed, and as great as Iran will become because of these submarines, her wrath will be boundless on your families heads if they fail their orders. Colonel Marzuk, we understand threats are not founded in the truth, but must be offered to ensure success.

'Colonel Marzuk, we must do everything in our power to guarantee the complete success in this battle for Iran's survival. A battle that'll drive the great Satan, and all Satan's foolish allies from every Arab and Persian land, and allow us to organize all the Islamic nations in a united stand against all those who dare attack us and do not believe as we do. May Allah be with you, and protect you from all harm, Colonel Marzuk.' The communiqué was signed by General Abdel Aziz Abdul Ahmed, the Supreme Commander of all Iran land forces.

Colonel Marzuk crumbled up the report and turned to Jawad and coldly announced. "Son of a filthy dog, you'll have this paper burned before my eyes, fool. I don't want any trace of it left when done with it. I'll wait until you have accomplished this feat, before I address my troops."

Jawad held the paper like it might explode in his hands, and then he called for a metal pail. He had to ask two dock workers before he located a match. He tried to light the balled up paper, and after three failed attempts, Colonel Marzuk's patience left and he snarled at his aide. "Stupid jackal swill, untwist the god cursed paper, you jackal you. If you hope to burn it before I grow old watching you foolishly toil like this. I pray Allah I am surrounded by lowly infidels."

Jawad untwisted the paper which burned much easier this time. Within seconds, it was burned up to ash, Jawad then poured the ashes on the ground and with his heel, he ground the ash into the sand until nothing but a slight ash stain remained in the sand. Which was then blown away by the slight breeze blowing through the port.

Colonel Marzuk glared at the cowering aide, he enjoyed the fear his mere glaze cause the strongest of Iranian soldiers, as he snapped at the submarine commanders. "My Captains, we have to wait for our proper time of truth to arrive a while longer I fear. The devils of Satan have successfully located our sister submarines in the open seas, and their worthless warships are trailing them. We're now ordered to wait for the cover of darkness before we head out to the open sea with our four remaining submarines. The time will not hurt us, the tide will be with us, and it might aid because it'll be going out. It'll make navigation the channel easier. Although we're forced to wait before we start our mission of freedom for Iran, we'll make good use of this time to make certain our submarines are prepared for the battle with the hated Satan warships.

"Crew members will make certain all the torpedoes are primed and ready for use against the god cursed American and their allied warships. Missile crews will check and recheck their missiles and launch systems, deck workers will clean and check the outside of the submarines. Dock workers will secure the entire area, soldiers will check all their anti aircraft weapons and missiles, and even construct more fortifications to better protect this Naval Base from possible attack by the hated American warplanes. I want the submarine pens secured, and made ready to accept my submarines when they return from their glorious mission against the lowly infidels of the world. We have to pour concrete that'll protect my submarines, and protect the new ones we'll soon construct inside the submarine pens. Iran will be greater than she is now!" Colonel Marzuk bellowed as he raised his hands over his head, and then emptied his pistol in the air.

THE WHITE HOUSE, WASHINGTON D.C., NOVEMBER 10th, 1998

The American President was seated in the Oval Office when the dispatch from General White arrived, along with the latest pictures of the attack areas spread throughout Iran. The report from the powerful General was short and right to the point. "Mr. President with all due respect sir, the MNRRF has loaded and is on its way to Pakistan. With God's help and protection, we'll be successful on this latest mission, and suffer light causalities at the same time sir."

President Cole passed the report on to Ms. Hernandez, the Secretary of State. They both waited for word to come in the special ops troops were on their way for the operation. "I see the General sent some pictures with this report Al, do you mind if I have a look at them?" The Secretary asked after reading the letter as she reached out flashing a warming smile at her dear friend.

"I'm sorry Maria, I should've handed the pictures to you without your asking me for them. This mess has my mind in a such state and I'm forgetting my manners. Our General's keeping us well informed of the situation." President Cole looked at the pictures then passed them to her.

The latest satellite pictures covered the Iranian complex constructed right in the middle of the deep desert outside the Iranian town of Iranshahr. Even though the thought to be secret complex was hard to distinguish, with most of the buildings almost covered over completely by sand, but the structures were able to be detected by the pictures. Of the earth, this was the perfect place to build the complex. The second set of pictures covered the port of Bander Beheshi.

The President saw the three nuclear powered submarines still moored at the Iranian dock. General White placed a circle on a few pictures, to better mark out where the carcass of the destroyed submarine lay half sunk in the flow of the narrow channel. A third set of pictures clearly showed where the dock workers were constructing the new concrete submarine pens at the port. The pens would house up to ten submarines, undoubtedly nuclear powered, and able to act as launch platforms for nuclear missiles. President Cole passed them over to Maria.

"One thing I don't understand Albert. Why are these troops driving to the Iranian complex? I thought we should have them parachute in, in the interest of saving some time and expense, sir."

"That's because to drop the soldiers in by parachute, would require three long range C-130 transport aircraft, and the Iranians would detect the planes coming in by radar, and know we're aware of their supposed secret complex. This problem was discussed about inserting the troops by air, and also a helicopter insertion, Ma'am. But it was pointed out by General White that the troops would be detected long before reaching their objective. I didn't want the Iranians to have any advance warning of this attack. I want our troops to catch them with the complex intact, and the evidence we need still in the damn buildings that's why the ground insertion. In case our troops capture some Russian technicians working with the Iranians, or the troops come under fire. I ordered a wing of Apache fast attack helicopters to stand by. They'll be ready to protect the troop's withdrawal, along with a wing of A-60 Blackhawk helicopters for air extraction."

"What about the troop's equipment and supplies, what happens to them Albert?" Maria asked with concern, as she tried to shift her weight in the wheelchair while trying to get comfortable.

"The troops have orders to abandon all their equipment where it is, if the troops have to be air evacuated out of Iran. They were instructed to destroy the machines left behind. I don't want the Iranians ending up with any of our equipment intact Ma'am." The President replied.

"I see Albert, I just hope we don't lose too many of our nation's children on this operation, sir." The Secretary replied to his words calmly.

"Maria, we have to stop the damn Iranians before they finish constructing their damn missiles and nuclear warheads for the damn things. These pictures show the width and breadth of the ambitions of the latest Iran's government, to develop these damn weapons of mass destruction. Judging by their actions in the past, we have to believe the damn Iranians will use the weapons once they have them in their possession. The only action that would be left open to our pursuit is obvious, and the time to react is now. I thank the diligence of both Director Raincloud and General White, for discovering this new world threatening situation before the damn Iranians had a chance to complete their plans in secrecy. We know it's much easier to destroy the missiles before they're fully developed. Look at what happened in Iraq when we hit them, Ma'am.

"We thought we had successfully destroyed all their weapons of mass destruction in the Desert Storm Operation. But when Libya attacked Chad, Iraq hit Israel first and when the Iraqi's were beaten back by our forces, they reduced the Jewish State to ash with nuclear weapons. Iraq's decision to employ nukes in that war forced to us to respond with our own nuclear weapons. In one action and reaction, half of the entire Middle East was wiped from the face of the earth. I thought, at least I hoped we would've learned from that damn lesson. But since that exchange occurred, we found ourselves in how many different military actions?" The President had to think for a moment while he counted up the engagements his forces were involved in.

"Yes, the first action was in North Korea when the rebel Russian Colonel tried to launch a number of nuclear missiles at China to start a nuclear exchange between Russia and China. Then the action inside Russia, where our troops had to stop this same Russian Colonel from getting his damn hands on a number of intercontinental long range missiles, and threatening not only China, but ourselves in the process. Then, it was the action in South Africa where we had to beat back the latest challenge against the black lead government from the whites, there was a possible threat of nuclear weapons there as well, Maria. Then the damn military action with China and the Island of Taiwan, when we drove the Chinese out of Taiwan, and the fighting stopped when China threatened to unleash her own nuclear weapons if we tried to invade their country.

"Yes Maria the first action I was involved in before becoming the President, was the action with Cuba, where their new military government after killing Castro, found the nuclear missiles he hid on the Island after all those years. That's five military engagements I was involved in with these damn weapons of mass destruction, Maria. And here we are again, trying to do it one more time. This shit has to stop, I can't have our boys be the world's police, someone else has to step up to the plate and take a couple of swings at the ball in the dirt for a change, Ma'am."

President Cole's shoulders sagged while sitting behind his desk as he drew in a breath in an exhausted sigh, and then stopped speaking while trying to collect his thoughts. The President wanted to continue with Maria, because it was taking pressure off his mind by speaking to someone over the serious problems he's been facing since becoming America's Leader. The President slowly lifted his head and looked at the Secretary of State, and she started speaking.

"Everything you say is absolutely correct Albert." The Secretary of State replied as she shook her head slowly, and then she added to her words. "But Albert, we'll fail our post if we ever allow any other nation in the world to get control of these weapons of mass destruction, and these other nations might be irresponsible enough to use the damn things against their neighbors. I fear the outcome for the world if this ever takes place on us, sir. I fear what might be left of the earth once a nuclear exchange of this sort and size is ever released on the planet. I shudder to think of the outcome for all of us, Albert. Please, don't get me wrong over what I'm offering you sir, I see no other alternative with the actions you're carrying out since becoming the President.

"We have to keep engaging any and all of these god damn extremely unpredictable and wild troublemakers of the world where they live, and take their damn weapons of mass destruction away from them before they use the damn things, no matter what the cost to our children and our country, Albert. We just have to stop the spread of these so dangerous world destroying and threatening weapons, even if we have to shoulder the responsibility completely by ourselves. I'm quite certain that once the world sees the threats arising from these implements of uncountable death, they'll be much more responsive and the nations responsible enough to join forces with us. In the interest of world peace, and the security of the world, they'll have to fight alongside us to keep these damn weapons out of the hands of those who don't know how to control them, or the devastating power that they could unleash upon the earth and her children.

"Look at what's happening just today Al. It's beginning as we sit here speaking together. Our Rapid Response Force soldiers created from many other countries filling its ranks. It's like I just stated, the other nations are slowly becoming aware of the terrible threat these damn missiles and nuclear warheads pose to world peace, and these other nations are willing to do something about them now rather than later. Even the nations who haven't sent us any of their soldiers to help us guard against the spread of these mass destruction weapons. They're sending money to support this elite group of soldiers we put together. I'm looking forward to the future Al, and the way I see it. It's only a matter of time before the other nations of the world, come together over this terrifying situation, and they do something about the weapons and terrorists once and for all."

The Secretary of State reached out with tenderness and she lightly rested her hand on the President's hand on his desk. With his other hand, the President covered her hand and gently patted it. President Cole could see the pain etched deep in her eyes, and was not sure if the pain was from the disease eating away at her body and strength. Or if it was from the knowledge that soon, more American children might die in the heat of the desert, fighting a new batch of terrorists to keep the United States and the world, free.

With a deep sigh, the President replied as he smiled gently at his favorite. "Yes Maria, I see what you mean. I never noticed this until you have brought it to my attention young lady. Perhaps I was wrong, perhaps there's some hope after all for this mixed up crazy ass world, Maria. I wish to hell this crap didn't happened on my watch though. I'm getting more than tired with sending our soldiers to their deaths. Because some backassward country is too stupid to control the spread of these damn weapons of mass destruction on their own, Ma'am. Or somewhere, some other ambitious fool decided he wants his country to become a nuclear threat against the world.

"For Christ sake Maria, I curse the damn day we have ever learned to split the atom, and created these dangerous weapons of mass destruction so feared by the world at large. What a day that was for humanity, splitting the damn atom gave us the power to erase the world from its orbit. Now we can destroy the world instead of just a few nations who start wars on the globe."

CHAPTER TWENTY TWO

CAMP LEJEUNE, NORTH CAROLINA.
NOVEMBER 10th, 1998. ZERO,
SIX HUNDRED TEN HOURS EST

A mind shattering roar coming from the powerful engines of the C-17 Globemaster transport aircraft as the machine raced down the makeshift runway, deafening the soldiers trapped inside the bowels of the massive aircraft. Adding to the anxiety and excitement of the troops was the landing strip, the transports were using a wide dirt road for their runway. Whatever the plane went over while building takeoff speed, made the aircraft sway and bounce and buck along the road. Every time the plane was tossed from side to side, the movement beat up the troops inside its vastness. As the first aircraft struggled to liftoff, a cry was heard from a woman fighter.

Lieutenant Walker looked over his shoulder to make sure everyone was okay. Colonel Leadbetter leaned over and whispered to Walker. "I hope the French broad makes it."

"From what I seen of her so far sir, she'll do well, Colonel." Walker snapped just as the plane lifted off. In no time, the craft was cutting through the clouds and leveled off.

Once the Globemaster was on level flight, the troops relaxed and began chatting with each other. Walker unbuckled his seat belt and went and checked on the French fighter sitting near the Mutt. He used the excuse of having to speak to the Mutt to check on her condition. He stood with his hand resting on the Mutt's shoulder as he looked at the green looking young woman fighter sitting to his left, and then he asked her. "Hey Blind Date, you okay baby? You gotta hang in there for us baby girl You gonna make it alright I promise honey?"

Fighting the need to upchuck by covering her mouth with the back of her hand, Sergeant Regina Raphael mumbled to the concerned Lieutenant. "Yes."

"When this mission's done with, you come down to my place in the stinking Keys and relax some with us and catch an all over tan baby." Walker offered, taking Regina's mind off the turbulence causing the aircraft to buck and dip in the air.

"Hey man, I'm heading for fucking Disneyland when I get back, Walker." The Mutt offered.

"You are fucking Disneyland, asshole." Walker retorted with a grin.

"Where is it you say you live in United States, Lieutenant Walker?" Regina asked, forgetting the plane's activity already. Fun Bags seated next to the Mutt smiled at Walker as he leaned around the Mutt and offered to the French fighter. "You'll just love the stinking Keys, it's like Heaven on earth down there baby."

"Keys, what are Keys? Do you live on a big lock, Lieutenant Walker?"

"Oh you're dead wrong there baby. The Keys are a bunch of small Islands off, over a hundred of them at the very end of Florida." Walker offered as he glanced at Fun Bags, to see if she was alright with inviting the French women down to their little Island and world.

"I know of this Florida place you speak of. I have read about that country, I always wanted to visit it if I ever came to America, sir." The female French fighter offered in an excited tone.

"It's not a country, it's part of the United States. The Keys are separate from the main land but they're still part of the United States. Most grunts on this flying pipe live on Marathon, or Big Pine Key. The uther soldiers are spread out on a few of the uther Keys nearby." Walker grinned.

"How large is this Marathon Key Island you live on Lieutenant Walker Sir? I saw many pictures of the United States, and I don't remember seeing land after end of Florida, sir."

"Marathon Island's more than six miles long, and less than a mile and a half wide. But it's one helluva place to live and have fun on." Walker offered to the beautiful French female warrior.

"You are not afraid of this Key Island you live on sinking into the Ocean? It does not seem to be much land you live on I'm afraid, sir. What do you do for night life on this Island you live on sir? What kind of night life could such small Island offer to keep your interest, Lieutenant?" Blind Date asked, she was still a little confused as to why anyone would want to live on such a small land mass as Marathon seemed to be.

"Night life! The stinking Island's alive with it, baby." Fun Bags replied as she leaned forward to see around the Mutt who seemed bored to death with the conversation as she added. "There's bars like Dock Side that have live entertainment every night, and you can drink at the bar, or on the dock overlooking Boot Key Harbor, and there's a shrimp bar that'll make a basket of fried shrimp for you right at the bar. Then there's Porkies, that's a great place to eat and the people are great, you can watch the sunset that can't be matched anywhere in the rest of the world, and drink if you like. Another place to enjoy the local flavor of the Island and meet good friends is Herbies, and on Wednesday they have this thing called Hump Day, which means you made it over the hump of the week, and it's all downhill from there baby.

"There's one person you have to meet on the Island, he's dubbed the unofficial Mayor of Marathon. I don't know his real name, but he goes by the name of Rocket man. He's a real character, a one man band, comedian, and all around good puke. He knows everything there is to know about the place, and he'll help anyone, and loves the Island and its people. The crime's about nonexistent, the Sheriff seems to have everything under control. This was the main reason I headed down there with my baby." Fun Bags took hold of the Mutt's hand and gave a squeeze as she went on. "If living was any better down there, it'd be illegal honey. There's so much to see, but the biggest thing's the weather. It's Paradise, warm, with a constant breeze and sunny. Yes Blind

Date, if there's an Eden, a touch of Paradise on the earth, it has to be there honey."

"That seems great, how are the people who live on this Island you moved to, Lieutenant Walker?" Blind Date asked, displaying more interest about the Island now.

"The people are really something else. A few local fishermen showed me where the best fishing holes are. That's something I thought they woulda guarded like the crown jewels, and take to their death. Hell, some of them took the time to show me how to dive and catch critters."

"Critters?" The female French soldier asked, confused by what critters were.

"Yep critters. They're Florida lobsters you can snatch by hand, or using a stinking net and a tickle stick to walk them out of their damn holes, baby. They're great eating, and you can catch up to twenty four a day. The most I ever caught was twelve, but they're worth all the effort. Yeah, the people on Marathon are something to be with and around." The Mutt offered as he got into the conversation as he turned to look at the French soldier.

"Oh... it's so nice you speak with me like this White Chocolate." Blind Date purred sweetly at the Mutt as she smiled at him.

"Don't call me that fucking name, my tag's Mutt." He snapped as he glared angrily at her.

"Ahhh... will you not allow me to call you White Chocolate please? I like that name better than the Mutt. It fits you better than that other terrible name does." Blind Date smiled sexily.

"You keep doing that to the big dumb jerk, and you'll cause him to come in his pants, sweetheart." Fun Bags smirked as she sat in her uncomfortable metal framed chair.

The Mutt ignored her as he concentrated on Blind Date, and what she was doing. "If you wanna get my attention then you're rubbing the wrong thing there baby."

"Tell me what you want me to rub for you, and I'll be pleased to do it, if you allow me call you White Chocolate, Mutt." Regina got up and she actually sat on the Mutt's lap and she rubbed her rearend in his lap, knowing what she was doing to the always horny soldier.

Walker saw everything was fine with the French fighter, so he left the three soldiers.

"Hey Blind Date, most us girls call the Mutt, Don Juan, honey." A female called out.

The French soldier turned to Ice and she asked her. "Why you call him Don Juan?"

The Mutt shrugged, this was a new name to him.

"Because most us girls Don Juan anything to do with him." Ice turned to Fire, and held her hand aloft, as they both slapped hands together. Laughter filled the plane.

The Mutt ignored the joke at his expense, he was enjoying what Blind Date was doing to him. "Little darling, you can call me anything you heart desires, as long as you keep doing your act."

"Can I call you White Chocolate if I sit on your lap and wiggle my ass?" Buckethead asked.

"Fuck you Charlie, and the horse you rode in on tree trunk. My name's Mutt to the rest of you shits, and don't any of you shitbirds forget it a second. Got it Homes?" the Mutt growled at him.

"Unless you're a bitch offering up favors to ya, huh Mutt?" Blood Clot called out, causing the rest of the soldiers to break up over his reply to the Mutt's threat.

"You got a problem with that, blood sucker?" the Mutt steamed at the unit's medic.

"No, no, not really come to think of it Mutt." Blood Clot offered, scared of the Mutt.

"Blind Date, if you get bored with that little game you're playing with that mixed breed jackass, I'm offering free mustache rides over here if you're interested baby." Casper offered as he tweaked the end of his lip whiskers.

"What does that soldier mean by mustache ride? I'm not familiar with his words soldier."

Fun Bags got up and whispered in Blind Date's ear what Casper wanted her to do on his face.

Someone called out. "Hey stupid, he wants you to sit on his stinking face so he can do his act."

Blind Date turned red and got off the Mutt's lap and stretched. She turned to Casper and ran her tongue over her teeth and lips and then wiggled her ass at him, causing the rest to egg him on.

"Okay assholes, you had your little bit of fun on this god damn flying garbage truck, listen up people this is important." Colonel Leadbetter growled as he removed his seat straps, and then he stood and moved to the center aisle where he addressed the soldiers.

"C'mon Colonel, not now. We wanna see Casper lick the foreign snatch." Someone called.

"I told you shits to knock the crap off and pay attention, god dammit. There's a written test on this shit later on." Colonel Leadbetter snarled at the soldiers and then informed them. "First I'll give you a last minute run down on the fly boys delivering us to target. The C-17s are attached to the SA-ALC, that's Site Activation Task Force, out of San Antonio Air Logistics Center for the ones who can't tie their own fucking shoe laces, or think for themselves. They're part of the 23rd Air Force, SADML-1st SOW, the 2nd Air Division Military Lift in command of the 1st Special Operations Wing for the... The Colonel would have continued speaking, but he was cut off by some of the other soldiers as they bitched at him.

"Yeah yeah, we know, for the dumb ones who can't tie their own fucking shoes, Colonel Leadbetter." The troops recited to their commanding officer.

"Funny, you shits are a bunch of real Jerk Benny's I see. Enough screwing round here dammit, time to get fucking serious, people. As you pack of wingnuts are aware, we're using working for the Army Core of Engineers as a cover for our damn mission. So save the black face (face paint) until we're in the fucking desert, and act like construction men when we land..."

"How do we accomplish that feat, pray tell Colonel?" Snatch asked the officer.

Colonel Leadbetter scanned the many faces of the soldiers staring at him, and he immediately settled on one of them and offered to the group. "Look like fucking Buckethead over there if you want to see the look like a construction man."

All eyes went over to the giant of a soldier. It looked like Buckethead was trapped in a lost land. He barked out at the soldiers staring at him now. "What! What!"

"That's the dumb look I want from the rest of you asses. If you look that dumb, no reporters on the face of the earth are going to give you a second look, or waste their damn time asking you any fucking questions. Walker, here's the GPP (Global Positioning Point) coordinates where CIA Director Raincloud's spook's supposed to wait to linkup with your troops, mister." He handed the coordinates over to Walker and waited for him to secure the paper, and then he continued with his orders to the troops. "You do understand you're supposed to eat that paper if you're in danger of being overrun, and possibly taken prisoner. I don't want Director Raincloud's fucking operative compromised on this mission, because you're clumsy enough to get your ass caught."

"Jesus Christ Colonel, you coulda used a smaller slip of paper then sir."

"There's a simple solution to that problem, stupid. If you don't want to eat the damn thing then don't get caught by the fucking enemy, mister. If I had my way, I would've put each word on a separate page, at least you would be full if taken prisoner. Remember," Colonel Leadbetter snapped at the soldiers. "the final word on these bastards, the friendly Persians are to be treated with respect, with kid fucking gloves. Trade them ammo, knives, anything they want except for personal weapons until after the damn mission's completed. This damn Persian spook's supposed to have fuel stowed somewhere for our machines for the return trip home, along with some extra food and water in case we run low on any of the crap while we're working.

"If we're lucky enough to take any fucking Russian prisoners on this mission, the helicopters from the 1st Operations Wing will rendezvous with us, and take the prisoners and wounded off our hands. If we come under attack, we're to abandon our military equipment after rendering it useless to the damn enemy, and then we're scheduled to be air E-vaced out of sand land by air. Err...there's one thing I want every grunt on this mission to memorize. I don't want any of you slugs being an asshole about this damn mission, don't think for one moment the fucking Iranians are a beaten bunch of soldiers incapable of forming a counterattack after the initial attack started. These sonofabitches aren't fucking Iraqi soldiers scared of their own god damn shadows.

"These lousy bastards are damn good fighters, more than capable of taking it to us if given half a fucking chance to. Selling the stinking Iranian soldiers short is bad thinking that's not only asinine, but it'll lead you to becoming confident and sloppy on this damn mission. You pack of nincompoops know what these two sins will lead to without my going into it with you asses. We're heading on this mission with the belief the damn Iranian defenders are prepared for our attack against them. If we know it's coming, you can rest assure they know we're coming after them. It's the only way to think and prepare properly for the damn attack. Don't forget, the only way we'll be successful on this damn mission is to achieve our objectives, get what we want out of the dump, and then leave the rest of the shit behind and get the fuck out of sand land. I don't want any of you assholes weighing yourselves down with any Iranian trinkets. Leave any damn souvenirs where they are, they'll cost you your life if you waste time looking for them.

"Walker, I take it you're aware three of your men speak Arabic, Iranian, that's Farsi, Iraqi, and some of the off shoot dialects of this damn language. Anytime you're dealing with the damn spook, which I don't trust for a fucking second, or any of his friends I trust even less. I want one of these grunts standing by your side. Prowler, you're one of the pukes, stay close by Walker when he speaks to these pukes, and pay close attention to every word spoken by the damn shits. If any of the fucks are setting us up, kill the lot of them including Director Raincloud's spook, our mission will be compromised and we'll get the hell out and let the Birdmen (pilots) take out the complex. One thing else, once we begin, nothing this side of judgment day will stop us.

"There's nothing worst for an attacking Unit than to get pumped up for the kill, only to be forced to stand down because something changed on you. You know damn well no matter how hard you try, you'll never get to that same level achieved preparing for the original attack." Another breath by the Colonel before he went on. "You people will follow every one of my orders as if they came from the Almighty. I don't care if Jesus Christ comes down from the cross and tries to change your mind. Follow my orders, or you'll wish Christ did come to save your asses from my wrath. Remember ladies, if you think these damn Iranians are the only ones you have to worry about, you better change your way of thinking double quick. I'm the dark shadow that's lurking in the woods you have to fear. Now that bit of crap's settled, let's go over our orders. So I know you shitbirds know what you're supposed to do once you're in sand land."

"Captain Wilson's Unit's responsible for mining roads leading to our target, continuing the mining for a hundred yards off the road on either side. Wilson's Unit has the duty of delaying any fucking Iranian reinforcements from reaching the target until Lieutenant Walker's Unit's are able to carry out their responsibilities inside the complex, you're responsible for security. You're free to use any diversion you deem fit, to deny any Iranian troops the luxury of concentrating their forces from reinforcing the target. Remember Captain, all we want from your Unit is for these sonofabitches to hesitate long enough for us to get our foot in the door, we'll own the dopey bastards." Colonel Leadbetter shot a glare at Wilson who nodded back at him.

"Colonel Salsiccia, the same thing goes for your Unit sir. We have to be afforded the fucking time needed on target to get inside the complex, before being forced to defend our action against any Iranian reinforcements who might be attacking our flanks. Use the planes if needed, have them expand the mine area if necessary. Only use the damn aircraft as a weapon's platform as a last resort, Colonel. Our word's few causalities to ourselves, and the Iranian soldiers as well." Colonel Leadbetter next turned to the Lieutenant, and barked at the young soldier. "Walker, I believed you assigned troops to special duties, you want to take it from here, sir?"

Colonel Leadbetter stepped aside and allowed Walker to take his position in the aisle.

Lieutenant Walker started to speak. "Mother, your stinking teams are to eliminate any enemy trapped inside and around the damn complex. Deny them the ability to regroup and then start a counterattack against us. You'll accomplish this by spreading your forces out around the damn complex, taking up positions and covering any and all exits and garage doors once we're inside the damn dump. Kill any swinging dicks that comes out of the place, or enters the complex on us. Anyone who shows up are to be considered a threat and dealt with quickly..."

"How the hell am I supposed to know which one of these lousy pukes are a threat to our asses, Walker?" Mother Flanagan wanted to make sure he had his orders straight.

"It's fucking simple if you think about it for a minute, Mother. Anyone coming in or out of any fucking doors that doesn't have our uniform on, is a fucking threat against the damn Unit, stupid." Walker glared angrily at Mother Flanagan before continuing.

Mother Flanagan crossed his eyes and stuck out his tongue, trying to look as stupid as he felt.

Walker ignored Mother's clowning around as he went on. "Nintendo, both you and McNip will control the stinking fly boys for this mission. If any Units find themselves cut off by enemy troops, you're to call in air until we enter the complex, and receive orders from either me or the Colonel. Keep some tabs on those flying asses, I don't want them shooting up the friggin place on us until we're the fuck outta the damn area. The stinking planes are armed with air to ground and anti tank weapons, and they have cannon fire ready at your..."

"How come they get all the stinking tit jobs for this stinking operation, man?" Buckethead grumbled as he went on with his complaint. "I can handle the stinking radio good Walker."

Walker stared at him and then barked. "Because they're the smartest of you pack of high school fucking dropouts and criminals I have. That's why Bucket."

"Whoup, whoup, whoup, Oorah." Was chanted by the soldiers inside the plane.

"Enough crap, everyone here know who's coming inside the damn complex?"

The troops picked to follow Walker's lead, responded yes to his words.

"Good, you're to be the first off this stinking plane, and then you're to assemble at the lead AAV7-A1s and sand sleds. You passed the Fit Rep, (Fitness Report) so no one's allowed to drop off unless he's bleeding, or fucking dead. I don't want anyone getting fucking killed on this mission because if you die, I'm gonna get stuck with a shitload of stinking paperwork, and everyone of you tent pegs knows how I hate fucking paperwork. Everyone's in this for the long haul, and you'll pull your fucking weight on this mission. Once we linkup with the damn Persians, we'll be led to the complex, but we control the stinking operation from start to finish.

"Once the damn complex is in view, I'll send Casper and the Hunter to scout out the area to make certain Director

Raincloud's stinking spook spotted everything we need to know about, and if the damn Iranians didn't change their security on our asses at the stinking complex before we hit the dump. We're operating in twelve man hit teams, this will enable us to develop concentrated fire power if needed if we run into any serious resistance inside the complex.

"It should be more than enuf to get any bogged down Unit's outta trouble and escape any possible ambushes. It should work out well for us, unless the trapped Unit finds itself severely outnumbered, and then they're to go Nine, One, One. Remember, this is no SLAM (Search, Locate and Annihilate Mission) deal we're on, but I don't want any stinking surprises along the way on this mission. When the point people report back, we'll begin our attack on the complex. I don't want any of that body line shooting from the damn hip crap when we go active, you hear that Mutt? You aim and fire, keep the causalities down. I don't want any Rambo's or Pambos on this attack. In fact Mutt, I'm making you sniper for this one. Yeah, that's what I'm gonna do with your lousy ass, you pick up a Barrett fifty caliber sniper weapon, and stay close to my ass.

"CoCo, you're coming inside the dump with me, you and Payback arm yourselves with twelve gauge Ithaca thirty seven shotguns. You two birds are to take the legs of any attackers out, if we come under attack once we're inside the damn complex. If anyone finds him or herself engaging a powerful enemy force, resort to S&S (Shoot & Scoot), keep engaging the enemy, but in a running battle and keep the enemy busy, and they'll not be able to hit a second Unit who might not be prepared for an attack against them." Walker took a second to gather his thoughts and make certain he had his troops knowing where he wanted them inside the Iranian complex.

Body line firing was when a soldier held the stock of his MP-5, 9 mm Heckler & Koch submachine gun, or M-16 to his guts, and sprays the area with rounds without aiming.

"Oh yeah, I forgot. The Russian babes will accompany me inside the complex, along with Blind Date, Baby Tee, Bouncer and Jail Bait. The rest of you people will divide up in uther Units and carry out your orders to the best of your abilities people. Nothing personal, but those are the bounces of the ball for this operation. AK, you come with me as well I guess. That's about it, the rest of you people are gonna hafta play it by fucking ear. Good luck people, whoa I almost forgot someone. Doctor Russbinder, you're to stick to my stinking ass like a second fucking skin, buddy. If I hafta go looking for your ass, I'm gonna be an extremely unhappy fella, and you don't wanna be the cause of my being unhappy on a mission, mister." Walker glared at the civilian.

"You got that right Homes? We were all there at least once in our lives, and none of us would ever want to end up there for a second time, Doc. Walker's not a very friendly person when he's really pissed off at ya, Doc. Hope you never hafta find out how he is when he's pissed off." One of the soldiers called from the rear of the plane, causing the soldiers to make obscene noises.

"Whatdaya fucking mean by that load of crap you people are spouting off here. Walker's never a nice person to be around day or night. He's always pissed off at everyone or thing around him." Another soldier called out from the rear seats of the plane.

Walker let the comments slide as he plopped down in his chair and then strapped himself in again. The Mutt leaned over to Walker and grumbled at him. "Guys in suits give me a stinking rash between the fricking legs man." He nodded at the doctor.

"Arrr... he's a square deal I guess, so lay offa the dumb fuck man. I don't want you screwing him up with the rest of the soldiers, got that buddy." Walker warned the Mutt.

"This thang ain't gonna fucking work Homes." The Mutt complained as he stared at Walker.

"Why say that crap Mutt?" Walker growled back at him.

"No fucking reason, I was just trying to build the suspense on ya ass, that's all man."

"Fuck you farly and the horse you rode in on, buddy." Walker growled low at the Mutt.

The Mutt laughed as he rose and offered the rest of the troops inside the aircraft. "Listen up people, I wanna offer a stinking toast to you pukes before we jump off and do these stinking Iranian slugs in on this operation." He removed his canteen and held it high as he added. "I drink to fucking water." He took a good pull from the canteen.

The soldiers were quiet, as they stared at the dog man. They were all expecting something a lot better coming from the crazy Mutt than that.

"Hey, someone betta check that prick's damn canteen, he musta put something uther than water in the damn thing, or he's going nuts and he's trying to rust his plumbing from the inside out. Maybe get himself a Section Eight while he's at it, look at that sucka drink water man." A soldier called out, causing the rest of the group of soldiers to break up.

When the Mutt finished his drink, he wiped his mouth with the back of his hand and added. "You can get just as drunk on water as you can get on the fucking land."

A roar filled the plane, as the troops realized the Mutt was okay.

The Mutt dropped in his chair with Walker growling. "You hadta set them off, didn't ya?"

"Let them laugh, it's fucking good for them shits, it keeps them relaxed Homes."

"Colonel Leadbetter, these people are the best soldiers I ever saw. I can't believe how they follow orders thrown at them without hesitation, without regard to their own safety. It's fantastic to see them in action, working as one sir." Doctor Russbinder said to the resting Colonel.

"Damn straight Herr Doctor! What you see before you are the necessities created by world situations with one thought in mind. To stop any aggression before it's allowed to grow into a world threatening problem. This action's classified as low intensity situation at this time, and it's up to us to keep it that fucking way, Doctor. These damn kids are highly motivated at all times, and they have mastered the skills required for a successful stint behind enemy lines, without the luxury of supplies reaching them. They're trained on how to live off the damn land, foraging for needed food and fucking water and if they run low on ammunition, they will find ways to get some. Doc, these kids are prepared to eat and drink things that'd make most civilized people heave with the mere thought of having to eat these same damn things, and be repulsed in horror.

"We don't expect an ammunition drops once we're on the ground, so we trained the soldiers in the art of replenishing themselves by attacking any enemy patrols they happen across, and taking their weapons and ammunition for use in further battles. The soldiers will use these to replace the ones they lost or used up in an engagement." Colonel Leadbetter took a second to catch his breath, and then he went on with his conversation. "Herr Doctor, these kids are the very best. I'll break it down a little further for ya so you understand where I and the soldiers are coming from.

"You give me a puke sitting on his stinking ass because he thinks he's tired, or he feels done in. You can't do a thing with him once he makes up his mind he's out of the operation. This puke isn't the type of soldier I'm looking for, and he or she wouldn't be allowed to join my Unit no matter how hard he or she tried to correct this major deficiency. He's no good for anything but a frontal fucking charge, and some DPW. (Dumb Private Work) On the other hand, each of these soldiers inside these trash haulers, are different type of grunts you're accustom to seeing. When one of these soldiers thinks he's tired, he'll push himself on no matter how tired he or she feels. They'll push on because of their specialized training, their inner strength and they work on their sheer guts and desire for carrying out a successfully mission for their country.

"This group of elite soldiers will keep going no matter what the circumstances facing them, because of their self-discipline and high degree of motivation they have adopted from their specialized training and inner self. Something no stinking enemy soldier, or natural forces could ever possibly overcome. These stinking pukes are so well trained, they fear nothing living on the face of this earth, and they shy away from absolutely nothing, and will do anything asked of them to accomplish their mission successfully, sir."

"I was unaware they were this well trained, Colonel Leadbetter. I guess I only saw the surface of their training." The doctor offered as he turned to see Colonel Leadbetter easier.

"Herr Doctor, you don't know the half of what these fucking troops have been trained, or are capable of accomplishing on any mission they're sent out on. Their training consisted of cliff and mountain assaults, survival training under the harshest of weather conditions. These soldiers learned not only to take on the enemy, but how to handle weather and living conditions so they won't pose a threat or discomfort to the soldiers. They're schooled in the art of close combat using rifle, pistols, knives and even piano wire for garroting purposes, Doc.

"These soldier's extensive education in hand to hand combat that is the soldier's last line of defense. We try to have them not resort to this form of protection on any missions. I don't know if you ever been involved in a street fight with your fists, Doc. But I assure you, no one comes out of a fucking fight in one piece. I saw hand to hand fighting affect a soldier's condition for the rest of his life. You never really get over them Doctor." Colonel Leadbetter stopped speaking at this point in order to give the civilian doctor a chance to ask him any questions, and when none came he continued with his explanation of his troop's training.

"Doc, these soldiers struggled through a variety of detailed assault and defense courses, which painstakingly cover every scenario, covering assaulting terrorist held friendly embassies and buildings, attacking various types of compromised aircraft, like civilian airlines, and most types of military aircraft. We carried out work-ups involving the President and Air Force One. These kids are educated in an action involving the White House, where terrorists breached security of the building. We moved in to root out the bad guys before they're able to get at the President. Not many people are aware, but the White House is equipped with a room the President and his wife enters under times of threat or attack. They'll be safe until we naturalize the terrorists, sir."

The doctor's eyebrow raised slightly, showing he was impressed by the Colonel's words.

Colonel Leadbetter continued, pleased he was able to brag about the troops training. "Doc, these kid's training covers assaulting Naval ships and aircraft, and communication centers, a civilian school, and certain government buildings. We tried to cover everything..."

"Then your troops aren't just used for a military application, Colonel Leadbetter?"

"No way in hell, we're prepared to go wherever we're needed throughout the world, and accomplish anything put before us. Whether it be military or civilian in origin sir. Hell Doc, we even ran a number of attack scenarios covering a civilian university some place in Maine if I remember correctly, sir. We did a number of mock up assaults carried out in the middle of the night in summer months, when most universities are closed for vacation. The assault I like the most was the mock attack on the New York Stock Market building sir. That was a very challenging action for my troops to carry out successfully, Herr Doctor."

"Why would anyone want to attack such an institution, Colonel Leadbetter?"

"Why? For fuck sake, cause Doc if a terrorist cell disrupts the flow of money involved in the damn stock market. They would severely cripple the economy of the United States that we might never get over. Lives would be completely destroyed, companies destroyed, states would go bankrupt and belly up in a flash. It'd deal a deadly blow to the all the States. That's why we ran assaults against terrorists taking over the damn stock market, fella. But this is only half my people's specialized training, my troops are well versed on the procedure of swift water river crossing, and attacking from the river bank taking enemy fire and causalities. Other sections of their ongoing training cover live fire crossings in darkness, without light from the moon. We ran a number of mock situations covering a nuclear reactor installation occupied by terrorists. We used the Indian Point nuclear power structure in New York for this work-up.

"This exercise consisted of freeing a number of hostages, locating, and taking out the supposed terrorists, and locating and disarming any demolition charges planted by the terrorists by our EODT. (Explosive Ordinance Disposal Teams) It was quite an operation we carried out, covering many different ways any fucking terrorists could possibly take over one of our nuclear installations throughout the United States, and neighboring nations." Colonel Leadbetter took a second to shift his weight in the uncomfortable pipe formed chair, and went on.

"Most of these specialized soldiers are schooled in placing explosives in strategic positions to destroy a building, or harm enemy soldiers engaging our troops. To cause the greatest amount of damage to a selected target, or to erase it from the face of the earth. We studied where to place these charges where they'll cause the enemy shock and disorientation. This action is designed to confuse and cause fear in any terrorist cell. Doc, the skills of my people can't be compared to, or defeated by any enemy soldiers on this earth. As I said Doc, these damn kids are the best, more than capable of overcoming any possible obstacle before them by nature or man. Each one of these kids are consummate professionals, perfect in every detail."

A pause and then Colonel Leadbetter went on. "Herr Doctor, our beliefs, our religion isn't to deal with a terrorist cell, but to kill them with extreme malice. To serve as a warning to any other fucking fool who tries to attack United States civilians, or property, or our interests overseas. Our motto is 'Just don't try it, or you'll die in the fucking attempt' and our eleventh commandment is, Thou shall not die. Doc, team work's our main driving force on any operation we're sent out on. My people work together, live together, love together, and they even fucking die together sir. We're all one and god damn proud of it at that, Herr Doctor. Make no mistake about it in the damn least Doc. We're killers of the worst kind, animals if you will, and we're just as proud of that as well, as we are of our first born child.

"Doctor Russbinder, our specialized Unit's training covers all possible aspects of guerrilla warfare, assaulting entrenched terrorists or enemy soldiers, controlling targets during peace time, and low level operations as the one we're working on today is, sir. Now there's a contradiction of terms if I ever said one, using our troops during a peace time operation sir. If my troops are ever employed, peace is the last thing that'll take place where we're operating from, Doc." Colonel Leadbetter allowed himself a quick chuckle over his last statement.

Then the Colonel leaned a little closer to the doctor and offered. "You know something bugging the shit out of my ass, Doc. I'm having a much easier time recruiting hogs for my Special Forces, than most police departments have recruiting Officers. That's fucking nuts, sir."

"Why is that Colonel Leadbetter?" the doctor asked the Colonel with concern.

"Why, I'll tell you why? Jesus Doc, are you walking with your head in the damn sand? Arrr... fuhgedaboutit, I'm getting a little off the fucking point I was trying to make with you. I'll tell you this much. We've been adopting a new course of action in our training lately, Herr Doctor, and little by little we're leaning our training more towards a number of civilian operations to be carried out in the streets of most major cities and towns having trouble with fucking street gangs, rioters looters and assholes who hate our country and the such, Doctor Russbinder. I believe in the near future we might even be let loose in a number of American cities and towns whose police departments can't keep up with criminal activities destroying those cities, sir."

"Don't tell me we're about to unleash these special operation soldiers, these what you call trained killers as you say. Patrol the streets of the inner cities, Colonel Leadbetter Sir?" the stunned doctor cried as he stared in disbelief at the grinning Colonel.

"Doc, lately things are getting so fucking bad in some major cities and towns, in case you didn't know. It's getting so damn bad when a cop ends up having to employ lethal force in the streets, a stinking riot breaks out. Whatever the fuck happened to, 'you do the crime, you do the time'. I was taught when I was a kid if I break the law, I better be man enough to accept the outcome of my stupid actions. Even if I ended up bleeding to death on the streets. Arrr shit... getting back to your question Doc. I don't think it'll ever come down to deploying my specialized troops on streets of the United States. One thing you have to remember about my Units, any time we go in, it's nothing but all out warfare, and anything goes in that warfare for us to carry out a successful operation. As in this case Herr Doctor, we're trying to keep the damn death toll down, but if the shit hits the fan, it's going to be all out hell for anyone attacking my troops.

"We answer to God, and our moral sense of duty. In both cases Doc, they're sound asleep during any operation in progress. Once the operation's completed, it's a different story, and we learn to cope with this problem in our own ways. We insert from the air and water, as well as what we're doing here, coming in by fucking land, and most operations begin in the middle of the damn night, using the darkness as cover for our military actions sir. We're more than capable of entering a compromised target any time of the day or night, under any fucking circumstances we're forced to engage enemy forces, under any weather conditions, and against all odds stacked against us, no matter how bad they're stacked.

"I have instilled the makings of a fearless and best possible trained soldier. His unwavering love for his Unit boosts his power and belief, and fighting spirit, the kind of spirit that made the United States the world power she is today. I make each soldier an independent highly polished weapon, I give the soldiers discipline, build their integrity, and then I give them firm belief of righteousness. The most important virtue I teach these god damn soldiers is loyalty. Loyalty for his chosen God, his country, and his Unit in that order. We're the meanest bunch of shits to ever walk the face of the earth, and we love it that way sir. Right you pukes on his trash haulers?"

"Whoup, whoup, whoup, oorah." The troops replied as pone as they all raised their black gloved hands with the missing fingers in the air. The soldiers sitting around the doctor and Colonel Leadbetter listened to his every word. They were proud by the way the Colonel described, and how he felt about them.

Sudden turbulence bounced the transport plane, and some soldiers cheered.

The Mutt reared back and yelled. "Yeehawwwwwwwwww man, what a fucking rush."

Colonel Leadbetter looked over his shoulder at the man as if he had two heads. Then he shook his head slowly, knowing the Mutt was as nuts as he looked.

"Colonel Leadbetter, how long until we get to Iran, sir?" the doctor asked the Colonel.

"We're not going directly to Iran, Doctor Russbinder. Didn't you listen to any of the fucking briefing you attended back in the States, dammit? We're heading for Pakistan."

"Forgive me I made a mistake, I assure you Colonel, I paid close attention at all the briefings I attended, Colonel Leadbetter. That's why I'm accompanying you sir. I should have my head examined, I don't know what the hell I'm doing with these psychopaths you call soldiers, sir."

"It's too late to get cold fucking feet on me now, Doc. If you want out of this stinking mission, it's a long first step out the fucking aircraft, mister. If you really want to know what the fuck you're doing here, I'll tell you Herr Doctor. You're stopping the spread of nuclear weapons to a country that's not afraid to use them against any country. Look at it this way, Doc. You might be stopping a nuclear exchange, or a third World War, Doctor. One that would surely erase all living things from the face of the earth. These fucking popinjays who have these nuclear missiles, aren't afraid to go to a fiery end, as long as they can take a part of the United States with them. The Iranians believe they're carving out their niche in Paradise by hurting the United State, and it's time we prove they're fucking mistaken. Doctor, you in this mission or what?"

After a few moments of silence then Doctor Russbinder replied with one word to the anxious military officer staring him right in the eyes. "Yes."

"Out fucking standing Herr Doctor. I knew I could count on your stinking ass to do what's fucking right for our country and Unit. Pleased to have you on board with us, sir." Colonel Leadbetter said as he slammed the doctor on his shoulder for replying in the right fashion.

CHAPTER TWENTY THREE

THE PERSIAN GULF

The two American Frigates, Joseph Hewes and Vandegrift, were assigned to trail the two Russian made Iranian submarines that got free of their port, sailing in open waters. The Hewes passed the Horn of Oman in the Persian Gulf, when the alarm sounded on board the ship.

"Radar to Conn, Captain Wimberley!" the radar operator called out.

"Conn, what the hell's up Johnson?" the Captain snapped from in the tower.

"Captain Wimberley, I'm picking up a number of fast moving bogies on the screen sir. They're coming straight at us a high rate of speed, sir." The sailor reported to his Captain.

"I'm on my way to CIC." The Combat Information Center, was the very heart of the ship.

The Captain rushed down a ladder and entered the CIC chamber. He headed right for his radar operator, rested his hand on his shoulder and shared his scope as he asked the operator.

"How many targets are you picking up coming at us son? Are the targets still coming directly at my god damn ship, mister?"

"It's hard to tell at this time, sir. All targets are riding in tight formation, Captain. I'm picking up at least two blimps changing shape and size number of times on us, sir. It could be just two targets, or even up to four possible targets coming at us, sir." Johnson replied.

The Captain gave the upset sailor's shoulder a slight squeeze as he warned the operator. "Calm down a little for me son. I don't need you scaring the rest of my people on board the ship, mister. Boatswain, sound GQ sir."

"Aye sir." The Boatswain Mate went over to the ship's intercommunication system and snapped it on, and then blew his whistle three times. "General Quarters, General Quarters. All hands many your battle stations. General Quarters, General Quarters. This is not a drill, I repeat, this is not a drill, all hands man your battle stations. All fire watch personnel man your stations. Damage control to their assigned stations." He repeated the order a second time.

Instantly, the lights inside the CIC chamber, went from a bright white, to a soft red hue, as a number of excited sailors rushed around in all directions, taking their assigned battle positions. The ship's intercom came alive with sailors reporting in that their battle stations were manned and ready for immediate action.

"Gun Emplacement One. Manned and ready for immediate action, Captain."

Gun One was the five inch rapid fire cannon stationed on the bow of the craft.

"Gun Emplacement Two manned and ready for action, Captain Wimberly." These were the 20 mm cannons mounted on either side of the ship in mid-ship.

"ASROC section armed and ready for action sir." ASROC was an anti-ship system which consisted of eight tube launchers. These fired a compact missile which homed in on its target.

"Torpedo launcher armed and ready for action, Captain Wimberly."

"Heliport. Manned and ready for action and launch, sir."

The Captain ignored the reports flooding in as he continued to stare at the radar scope.

"There Captain Wimberley, there's another craft, I make the count five, with a possible sixth target trailing the third craft, sir." He pointed at his screen as singled out the crafts in question.

"That's the way I see it as well son, five targets still coming directly towards my ship. Boatswain, order the helicopter to spool up, get some men on the damn thing and arm them with heavy machine guns. I want it airborne immediately, we're under attack, and I want these god damn five shits stopped, before they come anywhere close to my ship. Open communications with the Vandegrift. I want to speak to Captain Peters STAT." The Captain turned his attention to the speed boats still being displayed on the radar scope rapidly closing in on his ship.

"Captain Wimberley, there are six crafts not five sir. I just got a good look at the one shadowing the group a second ago, sir."

"Keep your eyes glued to the rotten bastards. Are their positions being fed into the aiming systems of our on board weapon systems, mister?"

"Constantly, with all corrections going to the combat computers as they happen, Captain."

"Good, keep them updating at all times until we handle this latest threat aimed at my ship, dammit." The Captain picked up the mike and barked in it. "CIC to Weapons."

"Weapons here sir. Go with your traffic Captain Wimberley Sir." The speaker replied in the radio confidently.

"These six speed boats are still too far off for a shot across their damn bow. But I want you to lay down a blanket of warning rounds before them, make it ten in rapid succession. Let these damn clowns know what they're in for if they try to get any nearer my ship."

"Aye sir. Out of the tube, Skipper."

From inside the CIC, the Captain heard the ten five inch rounds being pumped out by his main mount one after the other.

"Any change in their god damn positions and direction…" The concerned and excited Captain of the Hewes started to ask, and he was cut off.

"Sir, I have Captain Peters on the horn as requested, sir. He's waiting to speak with you Captain." The Boatswain Mate bellowed at the Captain.

"Have him hold on for a minute. Johnson, any change on the speed boat's direction, son?"

"Negative on that last sir, they're still holding their course straight and true towards the Hewes, Skipper."

"Shit. Boatswain, I'll take Peters call now." The Captain growled.

"Aye sir. I'm having the call transferred over to your console, Captain Wimberley Sir."

"Joe, how you doing sir? Fine, I have six bogies closing in rapidly on my ship, sir."

"I know Doug, I've been marking them myself sir. What do you want to do about them sir?"

"Joe, keep on the submarines, this action might be a diversion to make us break off our contact with the damn things, sir. I think when we break off, these popinjays will break off, sir. Then we'll be hard pressed to pick up that sneaky bastard again, sir."

"I concur, I'll keep on the submarines, good luck with your inbound bogies, sir. Doug, why don't you pull in our air cap, and let the fly boys handle the attackers for ya, sir?"

"Shit, I forgot all about the ready air cap out of Dhahran, sir. I'll use them to whittle down these bastards a little for us, thanks for reminding me and good luck on the submarines, Joe."

The second the Captain got off of the horn with the Captain from the Vandegrift, he immediately placed a call to Air Cap Command out of Dhahran. "This is the Commander of the Joseph Hewes. Captain Douglas Wimberly to United States Air Command, Dhahran. This is an emergency call in and request sir. Over."

"Go Joseph Hewes, Commander Plantenberg. What state emergency sir? Over Captain."

"Commander Plantenberg, the position of the Joseph Hewes is Three, Three, One, in G sector Red. We've been trailing an Iranian submarine in the Persian Gulf for three hours, sir. We have six, I repeat, six rapidly moving sea going bogies, rapidly closing in on my ship. It's believed their intentions are hostile in nature, and I'm requesting your ready air cap to check out the situation for me and then react accordingly, sir. Over Commander."

"Roger on that request sir, will advise on our reply Captain Wimberly. Over sir."

"You better make that advisement real quick, mister. They'll be within range in the next five minutes, sir. Action will begin at that time with or without your assistance, sir. Over."

"Roger, copy that last Captain Wimberly. Will advise. Over."

Captain Wimberley pitched the mike at the console as he growled over the response from air command. "Will advise, he can stick his fucking advisement up his fucking ass for all I care, I want air cover dammit. Christ, where are those incoming boats, Johnson?"

"Twenty degrees off our port bow, fifty thousand yards out and closing fast on us, sir."

"What's the god damn situation on the helicopter, son?" the Captain demanded.

"She's up sir. The helo should be engaging the bogies within the next fifty five seconds, sir."

"Air Command Dhahran, Commander Plantenberg to Commander Frigate Hewes. Over sir."

The Captain lunged for the mike and barked. "Yes Commander, this is Wimberly. Over sir."

"Yes Captain Wimberly. Be advised we just diverted a pair of F-18 Hornets on way your current position, sir. Their call name's Slap Three and Four. They should be over your position in seven seconds. Only problem Captain Wimberley is, the aircraft are equipped for air to air combat only, and will only have aircraft's cannons to aid in your situation, sir. I'm refitting four other Hornets for air to ship combat. The second wing of Hornets should be over position within ten minutes, sir. Sorry about the slight delay, it's the best I can do for you Captain. Over."

"Commander Plantenberg, what the hell good will the other Hornets do in ten minutes, sir? By then everything will be over with sir. But I'll take what I can get and run with it sir. Out."

"Very good Captain Wimberley Sir, good luck sir. Sorry I couldn't be more help sir. Out."

"Johnson!" the Captain bellowed for his radar operator over his shoulder.

"I got them sir. I got the Hornets coming in sir, they're closing in from the south at nine hundred knots sir."

"What about the god damn Iranian speed boats? What the hell are they up to, mister?"

"Still holding course straight at us sir. There goes the helicopter, it's beginning its attack path on the lead speed boat, Skipper. The other bastards are scattering in all directions, sir."

"Outstanding, keep me informed of what's taking place out there, mister." The Captain replied to the latest information on the attackers of his ship.

HELICOPTER STOKER ONE

The Seahawk LAMPS helicopter dispatched from the Frigate Joseph Hewes, started its attack run on the lead Iranian speed boat, while the other small boats broke off their formation in defensive maneuvers. The SH-60B Seahawk, whose role was anti-submarine warfare, attacked the boats. It banked to her portside to allow the door gunners to open fire on the speed boat.

The instant the Iranians realized this was not an attack helicopter, they quickly regrouped and concentrated their 50 mm machine fire on the attacking American helicopter.

FRIGATE JOSEPH HEWES

"Captain Wimberly Sir, the Seahawk's running an attack angle on the lead inbound Iranian speed boats, sir."

"Give me the damn mike! Captain Wimberley to Seahawk Commander. What the hell does it look like out there sir?" the Captain nearly screamed his words in the radio.

"Seahawk to Hewes, the six speed boats are definitely Iranian crafts Skipper, armed with 50 cal. machines guns on the bow of each watercraft, sir. Captain Wimberley Sir, they must be doing sixty knots, they're out of their minds, sir. Beginning my approach on the lead boat now."

"Be careful, remember you're not made for boat attacks, and I don't want you to get knocked out of the air, mister. But you have to keep them off us until the damn Hornets take over, sir."

"Understood orders, sir. Beginning my attack on unfriendly inbounds, Captain Wimberly sir." The Commander of the helicopter reported to his Captain.

The extremely excited and concerned Captain kept the mike open, he held it in a death grip as the Seahawk helicopter descended on the first inbound target. The telltale signature of two M-60 machine guns could easily be heard over the open radio. The Captain turned to the radar scope as he listened to the fighting on the ocean.

"There he goes, he's started his attack run on the inbound small watercraft, sir." Johnson said as he pointed at his radarscope. The Iranian fire could also be heard over the open mike. The stunned helicopter pilot's words filled the CIC chamber next.

"Holy shit, the damn speed boats have turned back on us, and they're now concentrating their full weapon fire power on my craft, sir!"

The co-pilot's excited voice came in next over the open mike. "Captain, bank the god damn helo to starboard side, and get us the hell out of here before they zero in on us, sir. Jesus, they're ripping us apart sir, we're dead in the air, sir. Oh sweet Jesus help us."

The sounds of bullets ripping through the metal skin of the helicopter informed the Captain how violent the return enemy fire was. Kimberly squeezed the mike and yelled. "Seahawk, break off, get out of there! Break off, break off. That's a direct order. Break off immediately."

Captain Wimberley's orders were drowned out by the Captain of the helicopter as he screamed in his cockpit of the helicopter. "Jesus, they're ripping us a fucking part, Captain. My helicopter's coming apart under heavy weapon fire."

The co-pilot's voice came in over the radio next as he reported to the Captain of the helicopter. "Fire, we have fire in the rear compartment of the helo, both gunners and navigator are dead. We're spinning out of control, we're going down. I repeat, we're going down."

The pilot's voice overrode the co-pilot. "Mayday, mayday. This is flight One, One, Three. We're on fire, going down. Coordinates are. One, five.............. The radio went dead.

The radar operator yelled out. "Holy shit sir, I just lost the helo Skipper."

"Whaddaya mean you just lost the damn thing?" the Captain snarled at the operator.

"She's gone from my scope sir. She's no longer in the air, Captain Wimberly Sir."

"Bullshit! Bullshit on that crap! One, One, Three, this is Captain Wimberly. Come in. I order you to report in, dammit!" Captain Wimberley let go of the mike button, nothing but static filled the CIC center.

"I repeat One, One, Three! This is the god damn Captain Wimberly of the Hewes! I order you to come in and report your condition immediately, dammit!"

Again nothing came back to him from the missing helicopter but static.

"Shit, I have to believe she's down, god dammit." Captain Wimberley grumbled while holding onto the receiver, and then he ordered. "Okay people let's make plans to pick up any possible survivors, is Angel's Helper available to assist in a sea rescue?"

"Roger that Captain Wimberley, Air Command Dhahran has informed me she monitored the loss of our helo, and reporting she ordered an emergency launch of her rescue helicopter, sir. It's on the way out to the last known reported position of our down helo, Skipper. I was informed it'll take the Angel flight over forty five minutes for her to get to the point of the crash site, sir."

SLAP THREE

"Slap Three Leader to the Commander Joseph Hewes. Come in sir. Over."

The pilot's words made Captain Wimberley actually jump as he barked in his radio. "Captain Wimberley here, Slap Three Leader Sir."

"Captain this is Slap Three Leader along with a second Slap Wingman, sir. I've been informed you have a slight problem with a number of small Iranian speed boats you want taken care of. Point me at them and consider your problem eliminated, sir. Over."

"Slap Three Leader this is no fucking joke, mister. Those lousy sonofabitches just killed my god damn helicopter. They're responsible for American blood, and I want their asses kicked all the way back to their own god damn country. Do you understand my desire, Slap Three? Over."

After a few seconds of silence. "Understood orders sir. Will comply as ordered sir. Out."

Captain Wimberley rushed over to the window in the CIC chamber in time to see the two Hornets go to afterburners in flight as their aircraft sliced through the air.

"Go get them bastards, dammit!" he mumbled loud enough to be heard in the CIC chamber.

In a second, the Hornets were on top of the six fast moving Iranian speed boats.

"Slap Three Leader to Commander of the Hewes, am over said targets, sir. The first kill's for your helicopter sir. Over."

Slap Three Leader changed his radio frequency to in-flight guard communications, so he could coordinate his attack with his Wingman without being overheard by any enemy targets.

"Slap Three Leader to Slap Four. Come in. Over Commander."

"Roger Three. Go with your traffic Flight Leader. Over." The second pilot replied.

"Slap Four, I'm going in from the north at Angels Three (Three thousand feet) sir. You're cleared to come in off my right for your opening attack on the enemy contacts, sir. I'll take on the first three bogies, your responsibility is the other three Zappers, sir. Good hunting Four. Out." The leading pilot of the Slap fast attack team informed his Wingman.

"Roger, copy last Three. Good hunting Leader. Over." The second pilot reported.

Both Hornet pilots banked to their portside, and then they lined themselves up on the rapidly dispersing Iranian speed boats. Slap Three ordered his Wingman to leave his mike open, so the Frigate Commander could hear what was taking place in the air.

"Slap Three, I'm on the lead inbound watercraft, commencing my attack on the lousy bastard sir. Over." A low growl of cannon fire was heard on the Hewes that cause the sailors manning the inside of the CIC chamber to cheer. The Captain allowed them to vent their anger over the loss of his helicopter.

The cannon fire ended with the pilot announcing. "Splash one target. Over."

Another cheer from the CIC chamber arose, louder than the first one.

"Slap Four, splash another Iranian target. We have four more targets to take care of. Over." The second pilot reported over his radio.

Slap Three Leader lined up next on the second fleeing enemy target, he reported to his Wingman and the Commander of the Hewes at the same time. "Commencing my attack on the second bogie." A second growl of cannon fire was heard, followed by a thunderous explosion, and the voice of the Slap Four pilot reporting.

"Eeeyyyooowwweee, good God Almighty what a helluva pop that one was. That lousy bastard had very evil intent in mind sir. If that boat got anywhere near one of our ships and detonated, he would've knocked our ship right out of the damn water. Slap Three Leader check it out, that explosion was so strong it took two of his pals out with it."

"Roger that last, we still have two other enemy target remaining alive, and still moving towards the Hewes, sir. Over." The Wingman replied to the leader of the flight.

"I got him covered. His ass is grass and I'm the damn lawn mower, sir. This bastard have just ran out of time to live, dammit. Over."

"Slap Three Leader to Slap Four, you have him in your sights sir. Take your shot sir. Over."

"Roger that, am commencing my attack on my bogie. Over." The pilot of the second plane reported to his flight leader as he attacked the last Iranian speed boat as the Slap Three Leader took out his target at the same time.

ON BOARD THE FRIGATE JOSEPH HEWES

"Captain Wimberly Sir, I have four more fast moving bogies coming in at us from the southeast, sir. I don't know how the hell they got so close on us so damn quickly sir, but they're there, and we have to do something about them immediately, Captain Wimberly Sir." The radar operator yelled out from his seat in an excited tone of voice.

Captain Wimberley, standing near the window was able to see the massive explosion off his port bow, pushed off the side of his ship and he ran over to the radar operator as he barked at the young Seaman. Where the hell are the damn things at, dammit?"

"Here, here, here, and here sir." The operator pointed out the new targets to the Captain.

"Are you feeding their god damn positions to coordinates and weapon's control of the ship?"

"Yes Sir Captain Wimberley Sir, the weapon's control system's receiving their position right now from us, sir."

"Good, right full rudder, all ahead full, dammit." The Captain ordered for his ship.

"Aye sir." The helmsman replied to his new orders from the ship's Commander.

"Are the speed boats in range of weaponry?" the Captain demanded from his radar operator.

"Every one of them are at this time, sir." The operator reported to the Captain.

"Okay. CIC to Weapons." The Captain bellowed into his mike.

"Weapons aye sir. Go with traffic, Captain Wimberly Sir."

"Weapons, you're free to engage all enemy targets on water surface. Fire, fire, fire." The Captain snarled into his radio as he glared at the Iranian speed boats heading for his ship.

"Aye aye sir. Weapons free, commencing fire, on their way out the tube, Captain Wimberly."

"Left rudder, full ahead, Helmsman." The Captain growled, trying to save his ship from possible attack by the inbound Iranian speed boats. He started his ship on a zigzag maneuver in an effort to make the ship a much more difficult target for the speed boats to concentrate on. The Captain was employing every trick in the book for his ship's survival.

The steady drum beat from the five inch main gun mount of the Hewes echoed throughout the Hewes, as it pounded out round after round at the attacking speed boats. The 20 mm cannons opened up next, adding to the racket thundering below deck assaulting the Captain and sailors.

Captain Wimberley listened to the sounds of his ship, and smiled the instant he heard the ASROC system pressed into action. The Captain knew every sound, and what that sound meant to his ship's safety. A violent explosion occurred off the Hewes' stern, nearly lifted the Frigate's tail end completely out of the water. The Captain rushed outside the CIC on the catwalk, to see if his ship had been dealt a lethal blow by the speed boats, and their explosive cargo on board the small attacking watercrafts.

A dark cloud churned in the sky one hundred and twenty yards off his stern to the starboard side. He heard a sailor say it was a speed boat that received a direct hit from the five incher.

Captain Wimberley turned his attention to his five inch cannon main mount on the bow of the ship, and he watched as it pumped more rounds out at the attacking Iranian speed boats. He looked to the sea and picked up two speed boats trying to make it through the wall of heavy cannon fire. A second huge explosion ripped in the air much closer to his ship this time, and the Captain noticed the speed boat explode in fragments. Then it turn into nothingness as the ship's cannon fire turned on the other speed boat still barreling down on his ship.

A third large explosion occurred some fifty yards from the bow of the ship. This target was hit by his CIWS, Close In Weapons System, the 20 mm Phalanx gun that zeroed in on the rapidly approaching watercraft, and it ripped it apart. But the size and nearness of the explosion, cause some minor damage to the Hewes, and showered her deck with a rain of sea water.

Radar was down, and a number of small fires broke out when shorts in the electrical systems sparked to flames. Ten sailors were slightly injured from the powerful explosion, and large cloud flying debris and fighting fires. The Captain stuck his head back inside the CIC and barked at his radar operator. "Johnson, where the hell are those damn Hornets at for God sake mister?"

"I don't know Captain Wimberly Sir. I'm currently down across the board at this time, sir."

"Shit, are the damn guns going to be able to keep on those remaining speed boats, mister?"

"No prob sir. The weapon's support locked on the speed boat's coordinates, and they're still tracking the remaining inbound watercraft, sir. There's no way in hell any of the remaining speed boats will be able to out maneuver our guns on us, Captain."

The Captain pulled his head back out of the CIC, and he looked in the direction his guns were firing off in. His hat suddenly blew off his head, but he did nothing to try and retrieve it as it landed in the boiling foam his ship was sailing on. The angry American Captain picked up the last speed boat traveling recklessly in the boiling sea, zigzagging as the driver tried desperately to avoid the hail of weapon's fire being aimed at him from the American Naval ship. The water around the small craft rose feet in the air as the rounds worked towards the approaching boat.

Heavy flack rounds exploded above the small watercraft, but the speed boat kept coming at a fast rate of speed. The Frigate's 20 mm side weapons were pouring out lethal rounds, trying to hit the recklessly moving boat. But it was not until the CIWS finally opened up, the small boat exploded with the same force as the others when they were hit by the rounds.

The Captain's face was slightly burned from the heat of the massive fireball as the boiling flames churned and rolled in on themselves, as the raging holocaust climbed three hundred feet into the air. A roar came from within the chilling fireball as it quickly broke up in the air. Small pieces of speed boat showered down on the Hewes deck, injuring some of the sailors as they checked for any damage to the ship.

The Captain rushed back inside CIC and picked up the mike and demanded. "Damage report!"

"Engineering! Generator three's down and out of action Captain, along with bilge pump one, Skipper. Generators one and two are on line and working sir. We have a small fire developing in the engine room, it's being contained Captain. Boiler one's down to fifty percent steam pressure, that's because we lost a pressure valve on her side, sir. Nothing serious to report from here though Captain. We'll be back on line at full capacity in ten minutes, Captain Wimberley Sir."

"Fire Control! Captain Wimberley Sir, we have a number of small fires in the mess area, one is working its way above bulkhead Three, One, Niner, sir. We're getting them under control sir. There's another fire in ladder way Section Seventeen, Skipper. I have a number of fighter fighters on their way to that fire, it's been reported not a serious one, sir. Other than those few fires, we're in relatively good shape, Captain Wimberly Sir."

"Electrical Control to CIC. Captain Wimberley Sir, we have numerous shorts and minor fires in a few fuse cross over boxes in six areas throughout the ship, sir. Nothing major to report in sir. We'll be back on line at a hundred percent in a few seconds, Captain."

"Sick Bay. Captain Wimberley Sir, I have fifteen male Sailors, and two women Sailors down, suffering from a series of minor bumps and bruises sir. One broken arm to report sir, and maybe one possible concussion, sir. No major injuries reported, Captain Wimberly Sir."

"Outstanding, we weathered that mess pretty well considering what was being thrown at our ship, people. Okay people, get those damn fires out, report all damage to me immediately. I want to linkup with the Vandegrift." The Captain turned to Johnson and asked the radar operator. "How soon before you're restored and full back on line, mister?"

"Ten minutes or less Captain. It's nothing mechanical that's the problem, Skipper. The radar mast has been knocked down due to the proximity of the explosion of the speed boat sir. The repair crews have the mast standing and workers are hooking lines up to the radar units, sir."

"Great, okay son raise me a secured line out to the Vandegrift, STAT mister. I want to coordinate my linkup with the other Captain, so we can get back on that damn submarine we were tracking before we had to deal with those damn speed boats that just attacked my ship." The still extremely upset Captain ordered his radio operator, as he stuck his head outside the CIC chamber, to observe the condition of his ship.

Everything the Captain looked at, informed him his ship was in good condition, and was not in any danger of sinking. With a deep sigh of relief, he let out his breath and then allowed himself to relax for the first time since the two separate groups of Iranian speed boats showed up on his radar scope, and they began their attack on his ship.

The Captain of the Hewes hated the speed boats with a passion, because he was in command of a Destroyer when the Iranians used the small boats to open fire on the oil tankers during Iran's war with Iraq. This marked the second time he was forced to go against the maneuverable fast attack speed boats used to attack civilian tanker ships sailing on the Persian Gulf water.

THE C-17 TRANSPORT PLANES

The C-17 Globemaster transport aircraft loaded with Colonel Bruce Leadbetter and the rest of his highly trained elite troops on board, circled the civilian airbase in Pakistan. The Marine Colonel had no idea of any military action taking place in the Persian Gulf between the American Frigates, and the two groups of Iranian speed boats, nor did it concern him either. The Colonel's main objective and only concern, was to get his troops out and in the Iranian desert, to carry out his part of this operation, and then get his troops out of Iran before the soldiers were forced to tangle with Iranian reinforcements. Anything else was another service's or politician's problems.

The transport aircraft's intercom sparked to life, with the Commander of the aircraft ordering the soldiers to secure their seat belts for immediate landing. Colonel Leadbetter stood and ordered his troops. "Okay people, you heard the fucking order, buckle them seat belts and secure any lose equipment for landing. I don't want anyone eating a chunk of crap, because one of you assholes forgot to secure the damn thing before we landed. Let's look like what we are, fucking professional ladies." Colonel Leadbetter took a second to secure his own rucksack, along with any other items he had on board the aircraft, which he dug into several times during the flight, before sitting down and securing himself back in his seat.

The huge aircraft dipped to the starboard as the nose of the craft dropped. The constant whine and pitch from the plane's powerful engines changed, and the motors controlling the flaps and rudder operated, adding to the noise on board the aircraft. The landing gear engaged, causing the plane to vibrate from the wheels going down and locking in landing position.

"Okay people look a fucking live, we're touching down." Colonel Leadbetter yelled as the wheels struck the tarmac. The screaming engines slammed in reverse, making them scream even louder in protest over the terrible strain placed on them for breaking. The aircraft bucked down the badly neglected runway, spotted with pot holes and a number of cracks running the full length of the crumbling tarmac strip. The plane slowed and Leadbetter bellowed out at his troopers.

"Lieutenant Walker, get the troops assigned to your Unit organized, mister. I'll make certain the damn vehicles are where they're supposed to be by the time your troops are ready to mount the damn things. Colonel Salsiccia, assemble your people behind the last aircraft, because your troopers are the rear guard Unit for this damn operation. Captain Wilson, you know what the fuck you have to do, so get it done for me sir. I want everyone on board this damn trash hauler to look like fucking professionals, but remember, dumb looking fucking professionals. If any news reporters show any interest in you people, make it like you don't understand their fucking lingo. If anyone gets your attention, make sure they leave believing you're stupid as sin, and working for the damn Army Core of Engineers."

The Colonel removed a small note pad from his pack and flipped through it. He check the list, making certain he covered everything needing to be cared for before his troops moved out of the four massive transport aircraft. When he was sure he covered everything, he waited for the tail ramp to finally lower. Before the plane stopped, the ramp began to lower with a deafening screech. The rush of fresh air instantly revived the exhausted specialized troops trapped inside the bowels of the huge plane, and increased the level of activity of the soldiers.

As the Globemaster rolled to a stop, the first Marine AAV7-A1s drove down the tail ramp of the aircraft. It was followed by the Bradley fighting machine, and this was followed by the second machine in the first C-17 plane, it was another AAV7-A1's.

The second Globemaster taxied alongside the first aircraft while Lieutenant Walker moved his troops over to the first AAV7. The second C-17 had five loaded sand sleds of the troop's military equipment, and one AAV7. There were few troops inside the second aircraft because of the load of military equipment. The AAV7 pulled the light weight aluminum sand sleds with ease, and move them over to where they could be hooked up to one of the other tracked AAV7s. Each piece of military equipment bore the stamp of the Army Core Of Engineers. The only thing that could be a mystery to anyone was the appearance of the Bradley fighting machines.

Lieutenant Robert Walker had his people make a sloppy ring around the idling Bradley's, actually trying to shield them from any reporters hanging around the airport. He eyed a number of reporters make their way over to them as the third transport aircraft touched down, and he growled. "Hey Mutt, take Buckethead and Neck and cut off those nosey shits before they get over here buddy." He pointed at the two civilians walking towards the troopers.

"You got it man. Buckethead, Neck, you two assholes follow me double quick like." The Mutt and the two largest soldiers in the Unit moved out together.

The one not carrying a camera stopped and he immediately called out to the three soldiers he spotted walking towards them. "Hey bud, what's happening over there Mac?"

"Nothin's happening nowhere Homes. We're here to work on the earthen Dam that's supposed to stop the next stinking storm from ripping this backasswards country apart, man. Between you and me fella, there's no way in hell anything we do is gonna stop any fucking storm from wrecking this lousy dump of a country apart, man. We're just blowing fucking smoke in the air, that's all pal. But the United Nations picking up the stinking tab for this stinking mess, so we're gonna do what they want and we're gonna grin all the way to the stinking bank, man."

"Is that so soldier? Mind if we get some shots of your men as they go about their business of unloading those aircraft, soldier?" The second reported asked.

"Tell you what you should go and do buddy. Why don't you wait till tomorrow when we start to work on this stinking Dam to get your stinking shots of us guys working. I'll fix it wit the Colonel, and he'll allow you shitbirds to come over to where we'll be breaking ground, man. We kinda don't want any you guys hanging round us while we're unloading our crap, man. You know, you guys might get hurt by some of the moving machines and uther crap, and we also hafta worry bout the stinking security of our equipment, and all that uther crap that goes..."

"Why all the weapons if this is supposed to be a civilian situation soldier? The Bradley's, and those crazy looking landing craft?" The first reporter asked him as he shifted his eyes towards the idling war machines, and he tried to aim his camera at them at the same time.

"They're wit us because there's been a shitload of scuttlebutt about some god damn trouble making Indian Shiitiates, who might plan to make a stinking raid on us while we're working here, fella. They let it be known they don't like us being in their damn country, Homes"

"What the hell are you taking about soldier? Talk English to me if you will."

"Man, you're dumber than you even look for stinking news shits pal. You know damn well who I'm talking bout, those flaming nuts who attacked the busses and shopping spots a few month ago fella. Killing and eating everyone they fucking capture, buddy."

The reporter laughed as he realized who the soldier was speaking about. Smelling a much better story than the one they were pursuing with these newly arriving American troops. The first reporter asked The Mutt while smiling at him. "Hey soldier, do you know where the hell these attacks are supposed to take place against your people, mister?"

"Dunno for sure man. But I'm ordered to move the soldiers, and the damn Bradley's where they're gonna begin constructing the new water processing plant, pal. Wherever the hell that might be, buddy. As you can see man, I'm the new kid on the fucking block, sir."

The reporters spoke among themselves for a few moments and they ignored the Mutt.

"What do you think about this line of shit these assholes are trying to hand us here, Bill?" One of the reporters asked the other.

"I don't see a good story happening with these pack of slobs who can't even talk right for Pete's sake. If this bird doesn't hear his name twice a day, I believe he'd forget the damn thing. We should head over to the water tower and hang around there for a little while. Just in case an attack does takes place against these assholes, Joe." The reporter replied to the first one.

"Good idea Bill, I'll clear it with the network bigwigs." The reporter turned back to the Mutt and offered the soldier who was picking his nose, and then checking out what he just pulled from his nose. "That'll be fine soldier, we'll look for you tomorrow, once you and the rest of the engineers are settled in and ready to start your work. Thanks for all the help, soldier. Looking forward to interviewing you and some of the other soldiers with you, when you guys are working on this new project. Thanks again for all your help, soldier."

"Yeah, sure Homes, anything you fucking say, Mac." The Mutt snapped as he watched the reporters rush over to the water tower and he mumbled at them. "Go ahead Homes, and you think I'm the fucking dumb one around here, huh bub? Hope you get fricking heatstroke waiting for the stinking boogie men to arrive. C'mon grunts, let's get back to our people."

Lieutenant Walker looked up just as the Mutt returned to the group and he barked at him. "Well buster? Don't make me ask you what went on over there, buddy."

"Well shit man! We got rid of those stinking pukes nice and easy for your ass, man. They're gonna hang round that stinking water tower until after Christmas looking for a stupid story that ain't gonna happen, Homes." The Mutt smirked as he popped a hard candy in his mouth.

Walker laughed as he closed the distance separating him from the machines. By the time he reached them, the military equipment needed for the operation was already stored on the sand sleds, to make room for the soldiers who had to hitch a ride on them. The AAV7-A1s were hitched up to the sand sleds and ready to go. The Lieutenant gave them the once over, making sure everything was secured and once satisfied, he checked his watch next.

CHAPTER TWENTY FOUR

Lieutenant Robert Walker smiled as he realized his soldiers were ready to move out for their beginning operation inside Iran. Rather than blow his whistle that would immediately draw the attention of any reporters hanging around the area to their actions, he gave a number of quick hand signals in order to avoid creating any problems for the soldiers. He planned to parallel the Iran, Pakistan border until they came across their assigned insertion area. As he jumped on the side of the sand sled, he quickly checked the map. They were five miles away from their scheduled insertion point. A number of soldiers from the Pakistani Army cleared any civilian stragglers away from the position, so Walker was not too concerned about anyone seeing his Unit crossing into Iran when they opened their attack against the country.

The machines pulled out in a sloppy column, the roar from their powerful vehicles caught the attention of the reporters hanging around the water tower. But when the first two reporters told the rest they were heading off on a boring surveying expedition for a new Dam location. The reporters lost all interest in the soldiers moving off into the night. The newsmen noticed the seal of the Army Core on the sides of the machines and accepted the other reporter's explanation.

Lieutenant Walker's convoy traveled at a slow pace, the modified Bradley's fighting machines increased their speed up to sixty six km/h. Usually, AAV7s would travel at seventy three km/h. The soldiers on the sand sleds covered their faces because of the clouds of dust and sand being raised by the vehicles. Colonel Leadbetter informed Lieutenant Walker the action against Iran was scheduled to start at exactly Zero, One, Fifty Hours on Monday, November 11th. The attack on the Iranian submarines, and coordinate with the attacks by fighter planes from the Aircraft Carrier Washington, on the Iranian port cities of Bandar-e-Abbas and Bander Beheshi. The action was to start forty minutes before the attack on the complex, in an effort to draw attention away from Walker's team. He did not like this part of the plan, he felt the attack on Iran should begin with an assault on the complex, but those people running the operation saw things otherwise.

The lead AAV7s rumbled on, the night was pitch black and the wind picking up, even the stars seemed like they were afraid to come out tonight. Buckethead, manning the portable Prick 77, (AN/PRC77 Field Radio dubbed the Prick) leaned to Walker and mumbled. "Hey Road Kill, I got the latest weather report for the target. There's a good blow ahead, and it looks like we'll be eating sand on this whole mission. I can't believe how this shit's starting to blow already, man."

"Whaddaya expect stupid, a fucking picnic buddy? We're moving on sand, so you betta be prepared to eat some, Alpha Hotel. (slang for Ass Hole) I got word it's blowing harder near the stinking target, big man." Walker grumbled, uncomfortable as he sat on a wood crate on the sled. He never expected it to be such a rough ride, it seemed like everything stuck him in the ass, or jabbed him in the ribs. It was amazing, the instant the soldiers worked their way into the vast desert the mission began, and so did the slang and attitudes of the troops as did their survival instincts that would keep them alive throughout the low intensity engagement in Iran.

"Man, I saw ZDT (Zebra Dark Thirty, slang for early in the morning) before, but this shit takes the fucking cake I tell ya people." The Mutt mumbled as he shifted his weight on the sand sled alongside Walker, trying to see where they were going in the pitch darkness.

"Betta get fucking used to it Tent Peg, it's always our stinking way of life, Homes." Walker growled, fighting to get comfortable. Tent Peg meant Stupid Soldier in the world of the military.

"Fuck you up your damn ass, Homes." The Mutt shot back angrily at Walker.

"Mon ami, don't upset White Chocolate so, Lieutenant Walker Sir. I don't like him when he's angry, sir." Blind Date called out unseen from the other side of the sand sled.

"Fuck you bitch. Why the hell can't you get it through that thick French noggin of yours, my fucking name's the Mutt, got it right honey?"

"Road Kill, does your friend always get so uptight while on a mission?" Blind Date asked.

"Only when he has people busting his stinking horns like you're doing, or if he's fucking hungry, sister." Walker snarled, and was instantly sorry for his nasty outburst aimed at the French soldier. He let the conditions of the mission to already get under his skin.

Colonel Bruce Leadbetter, who was riding in the second large AAV-7, radioed Walker and bitched at him. "Lieutenant, when we cross into fucking Iran, I'll have the convoy stop so we can get in our damn body armor. I know this will add to the uncomfortable conditions of this damn mission, but it'll help with making room on the damn sleds, and it'll also serve to keep your body heat in. The temperature's going to reach 120 degrees Fahrenheit when the sun's up, and drop like it's doing now to around 60 degrees at night. It'll be cold as a damn witch's tit by the fucking time we finally reach our objective, Walker."

"Got it sir, how long before we stop then Colonel?" Walker asked the other military officer.

Colonel Leadbetter checked his watch and asked the driver for their location. Once receiving it, he checked the GPS and then he informed Walker. "We'll reach our insertion point in five minutes or so, another five to Iran, and then we'll come to a section of wild scrub brush."

"You got it sir. I'll keep my eyes open for that spot sir." Walker offered and then he handed the radio back to Buckethead and informed the rest of his soldiers of the plan.

The bouncing continued then a harsh turn to the right, and the AAV-7 instantly increased its speed. The Lieutenant looked to the two Bradley's struggling to keep pace with the faster moving machines, and he realized Colonel Leadbetter must have ordered the AAV-7s to increase their speed so they would have the time to change into the body armor, while the Bradley's caught up to the rest of their column. The soldiers riding in the AAV-7s were already dressed in their full body armor, and the sand blew into everything, stinging any exposed skin of the troops.

The lead AAV-7 machine slid to stop before a small forest of weeds and thick scrub brush. Colonel Leadbetter was out of his machine and already barking at the rest of the soldiers. "Get off them damn sleds and get in your damn body armor. Unass yourselves, move it people."

The soldiers piled off of the sand sleds, and they started unloading their gear they opened boxes to remove their body armor. They stripped out of their uniforms, leaving the specially designed ribbed underwear on, the troopers then clamped the body armor around their bodies. The women warriors complained, because the design pinched their breasts and rearends. The man who invented the protective armor, had not taken into account women might be wearing the armor. Most of the women fighters breasts were being crushed in the heavy Kevlar armor coating.

Once the soldiers were dressed in their armor, the boxes were pitched in the thick scrub brush, the troopers covered over all traces of their covert entry into Iran. Walker agreed with Colonel Leadbetter's decision to have the soldiers dress in their body armor, now the soldiers were more comfortable riding on the sleds because of the extra room, and they were also a lot warmer for their night time ride into the vast desert.

The machines continued to ramble through the desert with the blowing sand stinging any exposed skin of the elite soldiers. The lead vehicle stopped, and Colonel Leadbetter growled. "Walker, get your damn Vampires out and working. (Vampire was slang for sniper) Infrared's picking up a soft target dead ahead of our damn column, mister. I want him taken out before the sonofabitch gives out the damn alarm about us being in this fucking desert. I don't want the dumb fuck creased, (wounded) I want you to way his ass cold out flat, understand?"

"Understood my orders Colonel Leadbetter, Mutt, unass your fucking self and get out there. We have a detected soft target, and the stinking Colonel wants him taken outta the damn picture toot sweet. I'll be slack man and you take the point on this one, Mutt."

Slack man was military slang for the soldier behind the point or lead man.

The Mutt picked up his weapon and then he quickly moved out, complaining all the way as usual. "Hey Walker, this stinking mission shoulda been handled by the fucking Bird Shit (Paratroopers) pukes for crap sake. I hate riding them damn sled things man."

"It coulda been a helluva lot worse than it is, Homes." Walker warned the bitching Mutt.

"Zat so man, how the hell is that Walker? The only way this stinking mission could be worst was if it rained or snowed on our asses, man. I have working in snow buddy." The Mutt snapped because Walker interested in how it could have been any worse than it was and he added.

"We could also be making our stinking way to target by ankle fricking express, man."

"I hear that buddy." The Mutt retorted with a grin to Walker's words, thinking how hard it would have been on the soldiers if they had to walk to their intended target.

"Let me get the stinking position on our fucking soft target, man. Walker to Leadbetter. Where the hell's my stinking target hanging at, sir? I can't locate the lousy fuck in this darkness and my night vision isn't picking up the scumbag yet, sir."

"Walker, snap on your Nine, One, One beacon, so I know where the hell you are out there, mister." The 911 beacon was a handheld unit that sent out a low and constant frequency signal the soldiers used when lost, or if they needed any air support or evac.

"I got ya Walker, your soft target's about seventy yards left of your present position, sir."

Walker slammed his hand on the Mutt's back. Getting his attention, he pointed. "Go red."

The Mutt switched his infrared scope on, and he immediately picked up a human form doing something in the sand off to his left, some seventy yards away from his position.

"Do him Mutt faster than quick!" Walker ordered the Mutt in a commanding tone.

"I got the stinking sonofabitch dead to rights, if the scumbag tries to run on us, he'll only end up dying fucking tired, man." The Mutt smirked as the silent report from his weapon made a sound like someone spitting. Walker was employing his infrared field glasses and he also picked up the person as his body suddenly pitch forward violently, and then he drop down to the ground in a clump. He watched the target go down and then kept the target under observation until all movement of his body stopped, and he then scanned the surrounding area for any signs of other targets hiding in the sand dunes near the dead guy. Spotting no one hanging round or moving in the area, he signaled the Mutt with his hand to move out. They had to get out to the downed body and check it out to see if this was an Iranian soldier, or just some desert wander. Either way the Lieutenant was comfortable with the stranger's death.

The Mutt held his weapon at the ready as they both worked their way over to the soft target lying face down in the sand. At one point the Mutt griped at Walker. "Hey man, he was no fun, all the dumb shit did was fall and squirm around a bit. I didn't have to lead him any."

Walker ignored the Mutt's foolish comment as he moved nearer to the downed body. He stopped and dropped down to a knee and flipped the dead man over on his side. The Mutt laughed, the poor bastard was obviously taking a piss when he did him in.

"I wondered what the scumbag was doing out here all by his damn lonesome, man?" Walker mumbled as he continued to check out the body for any identification.

"Who the hell gives a shit man. Whaddaya wanna do with his ass Walker?" the Mutt snapped.

"I guess we gotta bury the damn asshole. We can't allow anything to possibly give away our presence out here in this stinking desert, man." Walker grumbled as he removed a small shovel from his fieldpack, and began making a hole in the soft sand.

"Oh man, I really hate this stinking part of the shit detail Walker." The Mutt bitched as he rested his rifle on the body, and then he removed his shovel and helped Walker dig in the sand. They had no way of knowing, but they just killed one of the desert children sent out by al-Shamarral to protect them on their journey to free Iran.

The two soldiers hustled back to the AAV-7 vehicle, and the machine moved off. Walker did not have a chance to get comfortable before Buckethead handed him the radio receiver.

"Yeah Colonel the piece of shit was alone, sir. Yes sir, I'm positive he was alone sir. I have no idea what the fuck he was doing out there all alone, sir. I do know what the dumb slug was doing when the Mutt tagged his stinking ass, sir. The asshole was taking a fucking leak sir. Yeah, that's the last piss he'll ever take. No Colonel Leadbetter Sir, I'm sure of it. I didn't see anyone else hanging around out here, and we really checked out the surrounding area before we headed back to the convoy and the uther troops, sir. I'm sure no one was hiding anywhere near the uther guy we just iced, sir. Relax will ya Colonel, you're gonna have a stinking apoplexy, sir."

Tensions relaxed when the soldiers did not come across any other travelers in the desert as the caravan worked deeper into the vast desert. At one point, the American military vehicles were stopped and the soldiers had to take cover as an aircraft was spotted, but the plane stayed well east of their position, and the aircraft had no chance of detecting the machines the way they were parked. Once the aircraft was out of sight, Colonel Leadbetter started the vehicles forward again.

Lieutenant Robert Walker and Colonel Bruce Leadbetter checked their watches to make certain they both operating on the same time. It was close to the time the attack was scheduled to begin against the Iranian complex. Colonel Leadbetter kept a close eye on the troop's progress and he was pleased with it, even though the soldiers had to make two stops along the way. The elite troopers made better time than expected. The modified Bradley fighting machines were keeping up pretty well with his faster AAV-7's, because of the adaptations on the engines, and the added fuel tanks. The Bradley's were not expected to have much trouble making it out to the target, carrying out the mission and getting back to the extraction point on the Iranian coast, that had been changed after the Colonel received word from command.

THE USS CARRIER GEORGE WASHINGTON ON STATION IN THE INDIAN OCEAN

Twenty Four, Fifteen Hours, the deck of the Aircraft Carrier George Washington was a beehive of activity. As the massive ship prepared to go into an Alfa launch of their complete compliment of on board F-18 Hornets, and the new YF-22 Raptors for the bombing mission against the Iranian ports and submarines. The warplanes waited by the foul line on the Carrier deck while building up engine power before being led over to the catapults for launch.

Two fighter/bomber aircraft were launched in rapid succession from the flight deck. Once the warplanes were airborne, the aircraft marshaled off the fantail of the Carrier, waiting for the other planes to be airborne and linkup with them. Crews from the Aircraft Carrier Abraham Lincoln also went into an Alpha launch of their full complement of warplanes for the joint attack effort. Fighter aircraft from both Carriers were supposed to linkup twenty miles off the coast of Iran. Then attack in a combined effort against the Iranian ports, and the civilian shipping trapped there.

THE AMERICAN FRIGATES VANDEGRIFT AND THE HEWES

The paid of American Frigates assigned to trail the two Iranian submarines received orders through command to kill the enemy. The Vandegrift and the Joseph Hewes immediately increased their speed and closed the gap separating the warships from the submarines they have been trailing since the boats left port. Anti submarine missiles were loaded on the submarine attack helicopters on the two Frigates, and then the game of cat and mouse truly began.

OPERATION SANDSTORM

Lieutenant Robert Walker's Unit was operating under the code name of Sandstorm. Lighthouse was the control for his Units working in the desert. The soldiers reported to Lighthouse in communication with General White, Director Raincloud, and the President of the United States. Lighthouse was being controlled on board the Mount Whitney, an Amphibious Command Ship capable of controlling the action going down in Iran. The Mount Whitney was stationed seventy three miles off the coast of Iran sailing in the Indian Ocean. She was the target assigned to the submarine leaving its mooring at Bander Beheshi.

Colonel Leadbetter checked his watch and then checked the time against the schedule of attack, and he placed a call to the young Lieutenant. "Hey Walker, the fricking aircraft are in the air, and the ships trailing the two Iranian submarines are rapidly closing in on the bastards. The shit's going to hit the fan any second on us now. Have your people keep their damn eyes glued to the sky, in case there's an increase in Iranian aircraft activity, sir. I don't want to get caught with my damn dick in my hands, mister. I'm sure as hell once the damn attack begins, the Iranians will have their military equipment running all over the damn country, Lieutenant."

"Roger that last Colonel." Walker replied to his new orders.

"Walker, don't forget, we have a ready air cap five minutes out at all times, sir. We get hit by any Iranian soldiers, help's a piss and hop, skip, and a fricking jump away from our asses. Those damn Birdmen are chomping at the bit to make some fucking kills, so hang in there sir."

"I hear you there and I have no problem, this is just another shit magnet mission as far as I'm concerned, Colonel Leadbetter Sir. Nothing more, nothing less sir."

"Fine Walker, we should be linking up with that damn Persian spook of Raincloud's within the next hour and fifteen minutes or so, sir. So keep your damn eyes open for the lousy little turd. I just wish to hell we could see where the frig we're going in this shit. I hate walking in the damn sand and not able to see a foot in front of my stinking face."

THE IRANIAN PORT OF BANDER BEHESHI

Iranian Colonel Muhsin Abu Marzuk watched as the pair of remaining submarines carefully worked their way up the channel in preparation to turn and make their way to the open sea. The three submarines were having some minor problems because of the civilian shipping trapped in the channel, there was a tight passageway leading to the submarine's freedom. Although he expected an attack from American warplanes at any time. The Iranian Colonel had no feeling of any pending disaster befalling him at this time. He stood on the furthest point of the dock, and grinned as the three crafts wove their way between the massive fuel tankers at port. Air horns blew as the submarines passed by the moored ships, and sailors fired weapons in the air.

OPERATION SANDSTORM

Lieutenant Walker counted the minutes as they ticked off, the inserted soldiers were to linkup with CIA Director Raincloud's operative at around the same time as the aircraft and warships attacked their assigned targets in Iran. Mile after mile of unending oceans of blowing sand spread out to the ends of the horizon. The Lieutenant had no problem seeing through the clouds of sand with his night vision glasses, because there were no obstacles between him and the ends of the earth. His vehicle slowed and then came to a complete stop when the driver poked his head out of the machine and called out to his commanding officer. "Hey Lieutenant, I'm picking up a weak infrared signature of a lone tent peg sitting atop a stinking sand dune way out there man, and the dumb slug's waving his arms like he has a bee trapped in his fucking drawers, sir."

"That's gotta be the stinking sand slug we've been out here looking for ever since we first began this fucked up operation, man. Where the hell is he at Roach?"

The soldier branded the Roach pointed in the direction of the signature he picked up.

Walker pointed his night vision glasses in the direction pointed by Roach, and he instantly picked up the Persian standing with one hand resting on his hip, while holding a long rifle in the other and he was waving it over head at his machine. He adjusted the glasses, all he could see was the one man and churning clouds of sand. He snapped on the inter squad radio in his Kevlar helmet and reported to Colonel Leadbetter. He blew in the mike crystal twice to open the link.

"Go Walker!" Colonel Leadbetter said as he searched for the Lieutenant out before him.

"Colonel Leadbetter, I'm picking up a lone soft target and he's doing nothing to try and avoid our detection of the dumb shit, sir. I got a good MOE, (Mark One Eyeball) on the dopey slug's ass, Colonel. I believe the asshole's actually trying to signal us, sir. The sand's blowing so damn hard out there the stupid jackass had to drop down and cover his ass, Colonel. I believe he's the stinking sand flea we're ordered to linkup with for this operation, sir."

"You mean he's the fucking spook we've been looking for, Lieutenant?"

"If he ain't, he has to be the one representing the dopey bastard then, sir."

"Are you willing to stake your damn dick on that assumption, mister?"

"What uther friggin choice do I have but to agree with that crap, Colonel? There's no way in hell we'll be able to sneak up on the dumb shit with the position he has adopted to keep us under his constant observation, unless the dumb sonofa fucking bitch turns to stone on us, Colonel. The damn shit has to know we're out here, sir. Thinking about it a little longer sir, I have to say yes, he's the one we're looking for sir. I'll stake my stinking dick on it he's the one."

"I concur with your assumption Walker." Colonel Leadbetter stretched his neck so he could see who Walker was referring to further out in the desert. He used his night vision glasses and once he picked up the target he reported back to his Lieutenant. "Walker, sashay your ass up there and see what this lousy prick has on his mind, mister. Take that homicidal maniac along with you, along with Buckethead. He's sure to scare the shit out of the damn Persian once he see the size of that big jerk. I want you to take two others, your choice and linkup with this nut.

"Walker, I'll keep your ass covered from here, the first sign of any trouble drop down to the ground and I'll do the rest. If everything's cool with the prick, wave your right arm and I'll move the column up to ya ass." Colonel Leadbetter hated the Persians with a passion, that's why he was always referring to them in derogatory and insulting terms, and encouraged his troops to do likewise by using sand nigger, or sand flea, or worst words they had for Arabs or Persians.

"Roger that last Colonel Leadbetter Sir, we're moving out now sir. Mutt, Buckethead, McNip and Mother, you people are with my ass. We gonna see if this little prick's on our fucking side or what." Walker jumped down from the sand sled, and then he and the other soldiers quickly worked their way out to the motionless figure still sitting out in plain sight. The Lieutenant was flanked by the other soldiers he ordered to go with him. Sergeant Dorothy Ramirez got off the sled and she stared at Walker's back, hurt he had not picked her to go along with him. Walker decided to take McNip, because he understood some Arabic and Persian language.

Colonel Leadbetter had his snipers fan out and take up positions of protection for Walker's team. The Hunter set up Mother's M-60 machine gun with his, in case Walker was walking into a possible trap. A pair of MK-19-3 40 mm grenade launchers were also set up on the side of the machine to cover any retreat Walker's people might have to execute. The wise Marine Colonel wanted his fire power at the ready in case the shit curtain fell on him. Once his defenses were deployed, the Colonel turned to the small group of soldiers making their way out to the man sitting on the top of the sand dune waiting for them to reach him. He watched the group as Walker and the Mutt walked right up to the stranger. He shook his head as he marveled at the

Lieutenant's moxie. He knew this young man was afraid of no one or thing in this world.

As Walker reached the stranger he immediately put out his hand to the man still sitting on the sand, but the stranger did not respond to Walker's greeting. He had to actually tap the Persian on the foot with his foot to get the Bedouin's attention. Displaying the least bit of concern, the Persian looked up at Walker, and then he grinned as he reached in one of the folds of his filthy Howli, looking for something he had hidden in it.

With the movement of his hand in his robes, the Mutt instantly dropped down and aimed his weapon right at his chest, daring him to pull a weapon on Walker, or the other soldiers. The Persian ignored the threatening display as he pulled out a slip of paper. The words on the paper were written in English, and the Persian spoke the only English word he knew. "Americans?"

"Yeah! Americans fucker!" Walker growled back at him as he took the paper from the Persian.

Colonel Leadbetter picked up the Mutt's sudden move aimed at the Persian the soldiers were to linkup with, and he immediately warned the other soldiers of the mission. "Look alive people, I think it's a fucking trap. The stupid Mutt's got the lousy bastard covered, if he fires, I want a blanket of suppressing fire laid out to protect Walker's retreat."

Walker unfolded the paper and read it, it stated. "American soldiers, this is CIA Operative Sand Star, I work for the United States government. My cover numbers are, 1145-A6, if you wish to corroborate my identity, contact NORASATCOM at 334R and insert cover numbers, and then you'll receive confirmation of my person, sir. I believe by now you have confirmed my identify. I ask you to follow this faithful Bedouin back to my camp. You'll treat this

Persian with the greatest of dignity and respect at all times while you're in his presence. Any disrespect displayed against this man, will be dealt with by our Command and myself, the first chance I have to deal with the situation, sir. I have sent this man out to intercept you, so you'll find my encampment easier and safely. I'm looking forward to hearing an American voice again. 1145-A6 out.

Lieutenant Walker said nothing to the Persian as he handed the paper to Mother. Flanagan quickly disappeared, heading back to report to Colonel Leadbetter. He was going to need the SATCOM radio to check the identity of the one who wrote the paper. Walker kept the Persian covered until Mother Flanagan returned and he announced. "Hey Walker, the little prick's the real deal here, sir. Command confirms this is the dopey slug on the paper we're ordered to linkup with man. The stinking Colonel told me to warn you to watch the little prick though, man. That man don't trust anyone who wears an Arab robe and headdress anywhere in the world."

Walker smiled at the Persian who nodded while he removed a pack of cigarettes, and offered him one. The Iranian increased his grin as he took the smoke, and clamped his hand around the pack of smokes and pulled it from Walker's hand. Instantly, the pack disappeared into a fold of the robe. Then the Iranian removed a bullet and bit the lead, and then he handed it to Walker.

The concerned Lieutenant stared at the round until Mother Flanagan barked at him. "Take the damn thing stupid. He's paying you a stinking compliment with the fucking round. Give the little rude dude one of your fucking rounds in turn, asshole."

Walker took the shell and put it in his pocket, he then removed the clip from his Heckler & Koch and pulled a round out, he bit a dent in it and then handed it to the Persian who was shaking his head yes so rapidly that Mother thought he was going to knock his brains loose inside his noggin. The round instantly disappeared into a fold of his robe along with his smokes.

Walker was trying to keep the good will going and he offered the Persian one of his melted candy bars, and placed his hand on the Iranian man's shoulder and waved back to the other soldiers waiting for them by their machines. To display was to show the Colonel and the rest of the troops that everything was cool. He then lead the Persian and the other soldiers down the sloping sand dune. McNip talked to the Persian in his native tongue of Farsi the best he could speak it, and the Persian nodded at McNip. Walker allowed McNip to handle the translation, because the two were getting along pretty well. Just as long as McNip spoke to the Persian, he did not seem to care where he was being led to by the other American troops.

The Colonel had the forward vehicles moved out to meet up with the small group of soldiers and the Persian helper, but he ordered a stop to the advance when Walker was near them. The machines stopped and the Lieutenant went up to Colonel Leadbetter and informed him the American spy Bdellah sent this Persian, so he could lead them to the spy's encampment.

Colonel Leadbetter shot back he was aware of that, he read the paper. The Colonel turned to the soldier branded McNip and ordered him. "Find out how fucking far this damn supposed friendly camp of Iranian assholes is from where we're hold up, stupid." Colonel Leadbetter glared at McNip, and watched the trooper as he spoke to the Persian.

"Already did that sir. He reports the encampment's under two Klicks to the east from us, sir."

"Fine, we'll leave the fricking machines parked here, and we'll sneak up on the damn spook, just in case he's being held prisoner, and they're using him as bait to ambush our asses. Walker, lead the way but keep the damn Persian's ass tight with you, when we get near the fricking camp we'll put the ass eating prick in custody and then contact the damn spook."

"Are you sure you wanna put this damn sand digger under arrest, Colonel Leadbetter Sir? He looks harmless enuf to me, and I don't wanna insult the damn sand eater, or any of his damn friends, sir." Walker asked the Colonel as he stared at the officer waiting his reply.

"Where's your fucking brains at, mister! In your damn shoe or something, asshole? If you think for one fricking moment that this little scumbag is harmless, pull open his damn robe and see what's staring back at your ass, Walker." Colonel Leadbetter warned the new military officer as he held him in his angry stare.

Walker reached out and pulled the grinning Persian's robe open, and instantly noticed the hilt of the deadly Jambiya blade and he remarked to his commanding officer. "Shit man, I'd sure hate like hell to be jabbed by that friggin tooth in the damn guts, Colonel. Christ Colonel Leadbetter, how the hell did I ever get talked into taking a bunch of shits on a mission like this one, with me being the biggest asshole of the fucking bunch, sir. I didn't see that one coming at my ass, we disarmed him of his stinking rifle, sir." Walker smiled at the Colonel.

"You better remember this shit the next fucking time you gripe about anything, Lieutenant. That there pig sticker could've been shoved in your damn guts before you knew what was happening to your ass. Remember, the higher you go up on the flagpole you go, the more exposed your damn ass becomes. Next time you think one of these Persian bastards are harmless friends, stupid. Remember that there pig sticker. Walker, I don't want you to trust any of these shit filled Persians while on this or any other mission we're ordered on involving these people. None of them can be trusted for a fucking moment, sir. The only thing you can depend on when dealing with any A-rabs or Persians, is they'll eat your hand off up to the damn elbow. I got a mind to pop a cap in his damn ass, and leave him behind and let him bleed out. Do I hate these bastards? I hate everything about and dealing with them." Colonel Leadbetter sneered at Walker as he shoved the Persian before him with his forearm, and followed him to the machines.

CHAPTER TWENTY FIVE

Lieutenant Robert Walker was taking nothing for granted any longer, and he was actually using the Iranian as a sort of shield as they climbed through the desert over one sand dune and down the other. He was amazed the Iranian guide was able to see so well through the darkness and still blowing sand. When the Persian stopped moving forward, and he suddenly pointed to a soft glow in the dark about two thousand yards ahead of them, Walker gave a quick set of hand signals, and two troopers grabbed hold of the Persian. The Iranian offered no resistance whatsoever against the two American soldiers treating him so roughly.

He had no way of knowing their Persian hostage was acting on orders from al-Shamarral to offer no resistance if the Americans did not trust him. The beggar's fighter was told to do as ordered by them. Walker watched as the Persian was hustled to the rear of the column, his body disappearing in the darkness. He dropped down to a knee as his troops gathered around him. He waited for Colonel Leadbetter to catch up to them before addressing the troops around him.

Colonel Leadbetter was out of breath when he dropped down to his knees by Walker's side as he drew in huge gulps of sand coated air. The Colonel stabbed his razor sharp K-bar blade deep into the soft sand as if it was his enemy, and then he snapped at his young Lieutenant. "Walker, what the hell do you want to do next?"

"Colonel Leadbetter Sir, I wanna take ten men and circle round them asses. I'm gonna make sure I'm not walking into a stinking ambush before I go strolling out in the open with any of these pricks." Walker pulled the knife out of the sand and handed it back to the Colonel.

"Sounds like a fucking idea to me mister. Get it done then Walker." Colonel Leadbetter warned the military officer.

Walker looked at the staring faces, and then barked. "Mutt, Mother, CoCo-G, McNip, Ramirez, Buckethead, Neck, Boot Camp, Wacko, Sun Tan. You guys are with me let's move."

The Mutt took his time getting in gear which prompted Walker to snap hotly at him. "You better get a fucking move on it or I'm gonna hop you right in the ass Homes." Walker gave the Mutt a kick in his Kevlar protected ass as he went by him.

"Yeah, you kick me now fucker. But if my big brother was here, I bet you wouldn't have done that crap my so called friend of mine. He woulda banged you upside the stinking head, that's what he woulda done to you okay." The Mutt smirked back at Walker.

"You shoulda kicked him in the damn slats instead of the end zone, Walker. He doesn't have any feeling there, Bobby." Sergeant Ramirez offered as she smiled at her lover.

Walker saw the look in her eyes and stopped her by grabbing her arm. He pulled her to the side. "Relax, everything's gonna be fine. It's just another mission, nothing more, nothing less."

"I know that, but these buggers are better trained than the ones we usually go up against." Ramirez moaned, for once in her life she was worried about the mission and getting home alive.

"Trust me baby, the only time you gotta be scared of anything in this stinking world, is when you're a single woman, and your period's over due." Walker smirked at his girlfriend.

Ramirez ignored the crude remark Walker shot at her as she purred after wiggling her armor plated rearend at him. "Yeah, like I trusted you once before, big guy. What was it you once told me, oh yeah I remember. You said trust me honey, and you wouldn't come in my mouth. Are you fibbing to me again, big boy?" Ramirez smiled at her lover as she stared deeply into his eyes.

Walker laughed over Ramirez's remark as he shoved her forward, and then he followed her in the direction the Mutt and the other soldiers headed off in. The small group of soldiers moved in two by two standard formation while working their way towards the Persian. It took the team fifteen minutes to work to a position where they could see the man standing by himself on the surface of the sea of unending sand.

AL-SHAMARRAL'S IRANIAN FORCES

Ahmed Hussein al-Shamarral argued many minutes with Mohammed Boua Bdellah, as Bdellah expressed his want to go and greet the soldiers alone. He was afraid the soldiers might attack the Iranians protecting him. After a heated debate, al-Shamarral realized further words were wasted and relented, allowing Bdellah to climb to the top of the sand dune alone. He was pleased the wind was blowing so hard, al-Shamarral knew the desert well and understood with the wind blowing the sand this hard, Bdellah would be a hard target for the soldiers to hit.

As Bdellah walked off to greet his soldiers, al-Shamarral sent his children out to protect his new son. One hundred Iranian fighters worked their way into the surrounding desert. Some of them were masters of deception, digging holes in the sand with their hands and feet, and pulling their Howlis over them, knowing the blowing sand would completely cover over them. It was easy for them to hear everything going on the surface of the sand. Sayeh trailed behind the man she was ordered to protect with her life. She followed him until Bdellah stopped walking and then he sat down on the sand. Silently, she worked her way in the sand using her Howli to cover herself, and allowing her the ability to breathe under the sand. With one finger, she kept a small opening in the desert dress to allow her to not only see Bdellah while he waited for the American soldiers to arrive, but to be able to breathe under the sand as well. Sayeh was hunkered down at least twenty feet to his rear, and Bdellah had no idea she was there.

Sayeh was in the strategic position to come to the aid of Bdellah, should anything go wrong with his meeting the American soldiers. She was armed with an AK-47 assault rifle and an extra five clips for the weapon. As much as she hated the Americans, she was fascinated by them and their strong fighting spirit. She admitted she was looking forward to fighting alongside the feared foreign soldiers, to see how good they were at the art of waging war and surviving.

LIEUTENANT ROBERT WALKER'S UNIT MOVING OUT TO GREET BDELLAH

Lieutenant Walker's people closed the gap separating them from the waiting spy. As he moved to the base of the sand dune, his helmet radio suddenly squawked. "Leadbetter to Walker."

"Yeah Colonel." Walker snapped back in his radio mike.

"What the hell's going on out there for crap sake? Can you see any sign of the lousy puke?"

"Just about, visibility's going to hell in a handbag quick as shit, sir. If it wasn't for the infrared system, I wouldn't have any stinking idea where the damn sand rat was lurking, Colonel."

"Keep going, I have your back mister. You'll keep me informed." Colonel Leadbetter broke off the communications with Walker, and tried to see his movements through the darkness.

Walker did not reply to the Colonel's last words, instead he blew into his helmet mike, making a god awful sound on the other end, but it was another way of signing off. He then gathered his troops round him, and using a number of sign language and heated words, he positioned the soldiers where he wanted them as he left them and moved up the tall sand dune. Traveling was tough, every step he took up the side of the dune sand rushed out from under foot, causing him to walk more on his knees and hands than his feet. With the blowing wind and biting sand stinging his eyes, he cursing everything alive and dead, wishing he resigned his commission, and was back in the States sitting on the beach on Marathon. At least that way he would be able to take a dip in the cool water if he had to do so much dancing on the hot sand in this heat.

The sound of the footsteps on the hard packed sand crest reached the ears of Bdellah moments before the outline of the American soldier looming out of the darkness, was a sight to behold. Bdellah was surprised he was able to hear the footsteps over the wind, and other sounds of the desert. At first, he tried to locate the soldier, but with the disorienting conditions, he had to wait until the soldier came out of the darkness as he had done right before him. He noticed the first soldier, he straightened and placed his hands on his hips waiting for the Americans to greet him.

With much effort on his part, Lieutenant Walker breached the crest of the sand dune and found walking much easier on the harder packed sand crest. He was surprised to be standing just a few feet away from his target. He lowered his Heckler and Koch weapon and aimed it directly at the robe covered apparition, not able to see his face or eyes. He stood ready to blow the stranger's head off his shoulders at the first sign of an altercation. He relaxed when he picked up the shadow do a movement, and a bare hand come out from under the heavy desert robe.

"Are you the man I'm supposed to meet up with, buddy?" Walker growled at him, allowing the hand to remain suspended until the Persian answered his demand first.

"Yes, and I must caution you to keep a civil tongue in your vile mouth while in Iran, Soldier. The Persian people don't think very kindly of men who use vile and threatening words against them." Bdellah replied as he forced his body to stand tall before the soldier.

"Yeah, sure fine, impress me buddy. Give me the fucking word! If it's wrong, you're fucking history sucka." Walker snarled while keeping his weapon leveled on Bdellah's chest.

"Grasshopper's egg." Bdellah replied with a smile after he allowed the fold of his robe covering his mouth to slip down a little, exposing it to Walker for the first time.

Neither man was aware Sayeh had crawled out from under her protective sand cover, and when she picked up the soldier approach and aim his weapon at Bdellah. She immediately lined Walker up in her sights, and she was ready to shoot him in the head if he dared to fire on Bdellah. She fought to refrain herself from shooting this arrogant acting soldier standing before Bdellah like he was going to shoot him, dressed in a strange looking uniform that made him look as if he came from outer space. She found herself filled with fear of the threatening specter.

Walker smiled when the spook gave the correct response and he replied. "Okay buster, the name's Robert Walker, Lieutenant, my friends call me Road Kill, buddy." He lowered his weapon, and then he put out his hand and took Bdellah's and shook hands.

Sayeh moved nearer Bdellah's side, drawing the attention of the other soldiers with the speaker. Bdellah fished for his pistol and aimed it at the shadowy figure lurking behind him. Walker dropped down to his knee and aimed his weapon at the slender shape coming at them.

Bdellah recognized the shape and put up his pistol, and held up his hand as he stopped Walker from spraying her with a veil of death as he begged the soldier. "No Lieutenant Walker, she's a friend. Obviously sent here to protect me by my father. Sayeh, come out of the darkness so we can see you, and I'll introduce you to the soldiers who came to our country to save us."

Cautiously, Sayeh walked up behind Bdellah, staring at the soldier dressed in the strange uniform. She slung her weapon over her shoulder to show everyone she was no threat.

"Come, he will not bite you." Bdellah offered when he saw her let down her guard.

"Don't be too sure of that buddy." Walker snorted as he glared at the shapely form.

"My sister Sayeh, this soldier's name is Robert Walker, he's an American Lieutenant. Say hello to him politely Sayeh." Bdellah ordered the pretty female Iranian warrior.

Instead of speaking, Sayeh reached out not to shake hands but to touch the metal skin cover.

"That's Kevlar baby, it's armor body protection from small arms fire and shrapnel, honey."

"Lieutenant Walker, again I must caution you to pay the utmost of respect to the women of Iran, or I'll not be able to protect your life while you're in their country. The Persian people are a strange lot who offer their women little in the way of equal rights, but they'll take the head of anyone who they feel is insulting them or their women, Lieutenant." Bdellah warned Walker.

"I'll remember that the next time man, thanks for the stinking warning pal. Now err..."

"Bdellah will do fine for the time we're working together in the desert, Lieutenant Walker."

"Okay Bdellah, we have a stinking job to accomplish fella. I guess you'll lead the way for me and my troops, right fella?"

"Correct as you have stated to me, Lieutenant Walker." Bdellah replied to Walker.

"Then do it asshole, I'll have the rest of my troops move out after us when we start moving, Bdellah. Walker to Leadbetter. Come in Colonel. Over."

"Leadbetter here, go with your traffic mister. What the fuck do you have going on over there for crap sake? Is this Raincloud's god damn spook or what Lieutenant?"

"Yeah, this is the stinking dude we're out here looking for Colonel, and he's gonna take the lead for us, and we're gonna follow the little puke to the Iranian nest of workers."

"Roger that, what about the rest of his Iranian fucking friends supposed to be with him out here in this damn desert mister? Where are they?" Colonel Leadbetter asked over the radio.

"Dunno but I got one of his lousy sand fighters in my face, Colonel. Bdellah, where the hell's the rest of your fighters hiding at fella?"

"Al-Shamarral placed them about in the desert to aid our mission against the fools who want to construct weapons of mass destruction. If we lose our way, they'll be there to lead us to target."

"The you betta take the stinking lead for us Bdellah. Walker to Leadbetter. Colonel, he states his friggin friends are set up all over the stinking desert to help us if we get lost out here sir. I don't see any of the slugs hanging round where I can pick them up, but I can sure as hell feel the friggin shits lurking round me, my dick's hard sir."

"One of these days that damn dick of yours is going to get all of us in some serious trouble we won't be able to fuck our way out of, mister. Walker, I want you to keep your damn eyes out for the rest of these Iranian fighters who are supposed to help us on this damn operation. I want a number on them so I know what we might be up against if they turn no us, Lieutenant." Colonel Leadbetter snapped in the radio as he gave hand signals for the rest of the troops to head out

"Understood sir, leaving now Colonel." Walker said as he looked a Bdellah.

"Roger that, we're behind your ass all the way, Lieutenant."

THE AMERICAN FRIGATE THE HEWES

At the same instant Lieutenant Walker shook hands with the Persian Operative, the Frigate Joseph Hewes engaged the Iranian submarine they have been trailing for the better part of the week now. The Captain of Vandegrift allowed the privilege of the kill to go to the Hewes crew, to repay her for the loss of her helicopter and its crew when it attacked The Iranian speed boats. The Vandegrift took up picket duty, while the Hewes rapidly closed in on the enemy submarine. The Hewes used the heavier Sikorsky Seahawk LAMPS III helicopter she borrowed from her sister Frigate ship, the Ingraham who was on picked duty in the Indian Ocean.

The helicopter spooled up to full power before lifting off the Hewes swaying deck.

"Revenge One Flight airborne and moving in for the kill Captain."

"Revenge One Flight, Captain Wimberly. Go get that sonofabitch for us sir! These bastards have drawn first blood, and I want their blood for killing my damn helicopter and her crew." The Captain ordered as he watched the helicopter slowly lift off his ship's deck.

"Roger that Captain Wimberly Sir, will do as ordered sir." The pilot of the helicopter replied as he guided his helicopter away from the tail end section of the Hewes.

"Johnson, keep a close eye on the damn helo mister. I want to know her every move as soon as she maneuvers in on that Iranian submarine."

"Captain, I have the helicopter on the scope sir, she's five hundred yards off our portside stern, sir. She's dropping a number of sonar buoys on target, trying to bring the submarine up to the surface of the water sir. They're working on an active signal sir, there goes another buoy, looks like they're getting ready to drop the torp on the submarine, Captain. They have the submarine well blanketed with buoys, Captain. I was right, there goes the torp sir."

The Captain dashed outside the CIC room in time to see a water spout raise in the air where the torpedo had just entered the water, and then it went after the submarine.

"Captain Wimberly, the torp's in the searching mode, she's pinging away, uh oh, the torpedo's homing in on the damn Iranian submarine. The submarine's making enough racket to wake the dead as she's trying to our run our torp, sir. Huh, the Iranian skipper just launched a number of counter measures in an attempt to confuse the torp, sir. It didn't happen, the torp has her dead and is closing in for the kill. Bingo, bingo, bingo, the torp got the submarine sir."

There was a deep rumbling from under the water and on the surface was whipped into a frothy turbulence of white spray as the submarine was destroyed by the torpedo.

"Revenge One to Hewes. Enemy found, enemy sank. Confirmed kill on target. Over."

The Captain of the Hewes looked to Johnson and waited until he answered what was being reported over the radio by the revenge flight. "He's right Captain, I hear heavy hull popping and grinding metal. She's dead and going for a visit to the deep six, sir. It's a confirmed kill sir."

"Outstanding. Give the helo crew a well done, and then order them to do a victory flyover the Vandegrift's fantail. Let them rub it in. We have to get some pleasure out of this nightmare."

"Aye sir. Will do as ordered Skipper." The radar operator replied to his Captain of the ship.

Moments later, the Captain of the Hewes heard the five round salute Vandegrift paid to his revenge flight helo crew as they flew over the heart of the other Frigate. He breathed a deep sigh of relief, knowing he paid back the Iranians for killing his helo and the crew.

"Johnson, what about the other damn Iranian sub, mister?" The Captain demanded hotly.

"Captain Wimberly Sir, the other two Frigates are working the bastard over good and proper sir. There she goes, they're reporting a confirmed kill as well, sir. Scratch two nuclear powered Russian made Iranian submarines, Skipper."

THE IRANIAN PORT OF BANDER BEHESHI

At the same time the two Iranian submarines met their deaths by the American Frigates, the first flight of American F-117 stealth fighters neared their intended target of Bander Beheshi. As the almost invisible aircraft done in the Iraqi war, the fifteen F-117's were operating to take out all radar and communications stations at the Iranian port, rendering them blind to any further attacks against the port and ships moored there. Although the United States was knocking every piece of Iranian communications out of the air, the Iranians were still trying to make their aiming radar's come back up on line. The F-117s assembled and lined up on their ordered targets.

Colonel Muhsin Abu Marzuk stared as his second submarine caught up to her sister boat making their turn and avoiding the civilian shipping still moored along the narrow channel inlet. There were too many civilian ships in port to use the docking facilities. Colonel Marzuk's heart jumped when a second cargo tanker slipped its mooring, and the massive ship drifted into the path of his three moving submarines. The ship's Captain saw what was happening and moved his ship out of the submarine's way. The Iranian Colonel Marzuk was furious his submarines were in such danger in the inlet channel as he roared at dock workers near him. "Give me a radio so I may communicate with my submarines, you god cursed fool you."

Colonel Marzuk's aide handed him a portable radio and keyed the mike for him.

The Colonel pulled the mike from the aide's hand and growled, taking it for granted the scared aide handed him the radio ready to use.

"Captain al-Basandwad, you'll get those god cursed submarines out of the channel before the civilian tankers run over you. Or I'll have your families brought to the slums to service the unclean infidels. Your duty's to get the submarines out to the open sea, and attack all American shipping you come across in the Persian Gulf. Remember Captain, your primary targets are the prized American Aircraft Carriers the worthless dogs are so proud of. You'll hit them with one of your missiles, and the second one will be aimed at the American puppet government ruling Saudi Arabia. You'll succeed with your orders, because we're acting with the mighty hand of Allah resting upon our shoulders. May Allah be with you for this sacred mission for Allah."

Colonel Marzuk held the mike locked in his hand, but he stopped speaking as he stared at the lead submarine, as it carefully lined itself up with the narrow inlet channel. He was not going to be satisfied until the submarine increased her speed as ordered to navigate the channel. Once this was accomplished, the Iranian Colonel relaxed and handed the mike back to his aide.

The sleek Russian built submarine cut through the shallow waters of the port creating a fine wake of its own. Her ballast tanks were absolutely emptied, so the submarine would ride high in the water and avoid colliding with the remains of the sunken submarine destroyed within the channel. The lead craft increased her speed from three up to five knots. Once reaching five knots, Captain al-Basandwad ordered his speed increased to eight knots, the fastest speed he dared to travel within the channel. Even at this slow speed, he was placing his submarine in danger of running aground in the inlet, or having a collision with one of the civilian ships moored in the channel. Al-Basandwad was upset Colonel Marzuk forced him to take risks with his submarine.

Captain al-Basandwad stood over his navigator with his hand resting lightly on the navigator's back as they stared at the submarine's speed and he grumbled. "I hate this, the god cursed fool of a Colonel should be in command of a fleet of garbage scowls, rather than ordering our submarine to travel at this dangerous speed within this worthless narrow inlet channel."

"Captain, we have another civilian tanker moored fifty yards off to our portside, sir. She's real close to where we have to sail to get out of the port safely, sir."

"Will we clear it?" Al-Basandwad growled, not taking his eyes from the navigator's scope.

"Yes Captain, but only if we stay on present course sir. We cannot deviate one degree from it, or we'll run aground to the starboard, or collide with the moored tanker to the portside, sir?"

"Where's the other god dom submarine at?" the upset Captain asked his navigator with some concern lacing his voice.

"The other one is one hundred yards off our stern, Captain al-Basandwad. She just increased speed sir, and is now pacing us very closely sir."

"Hold your course true until otherwise ordered by me. Make certain we're well clear of all this civilian shipping for the rest of the way out of this god cursed narrow channel." The Captain grumbled as he happened to glance at the speed gauge as it clicked from five to six knots.

Colonel Marzuk stood on the dock with his hands resting on his hips as the submarine sailed passed him. He allowed a grin to cross his lips as he noticed the smooth wake his submarines were creating in the water. He knew the Captain listened to him and was pushing his submarine onward towards the open sea. Just as he allowed his shoulders to relax a bit, the wood dock under his feet suddenly shook to its very foundation by a thunderous blast that came from his nuclear submarine he was staring at as it exploded, and then began to rip itself apart with a number of secondary explosions on the boat. Huge chunks of the destroyed submarine rose in the air, it tumbled over itself and returned to the earth as a pile of scrap metal and flames.

The stunned Iranian Colonel Marzuk was forced to raise his hands over his eyes to protect himself from the tumbling debris returning to the ground. The Iranian Officer stared in stunned disbelief as a second of his prized submarines continued to rip itself apart a mere hundred yards away from where he stood on the dock. He could not believe he just lost a second submarine before the boats even had a chance to engage any of the enemy ships sailing on the waters of the Persian Gulf. The fuming Colonel's eyes were forced to the air, searching the skies for the hated American warplanes he felt were surely the cause of his submarine's sudden death. Although Colonel Marzuk searched the sky, there was no sign of any aircraft. He did not know how, but he was certain the Americans had something to do with the death of his submarines. He could not understand how the Americans were able to destroy his submarines like this, he wondered foolish thoughts maybe they had an invisible weapon able to kill any ship from far off.

The Iranian Colonel's mind was spinning with wild thoughts, he now believed maybe the Americans had their agents working in the port, and they were responsible for the destruction of his submarines. Colonel Marzuk rubbed his eyes as he tried to gather his rampaging thoughts, but the Americans did not give him the luxury of time to sort them out long, as they pressed the attack on the burning port lit up by a number of raging fires from the destroyed submarine.

Colonel Marzuk's eyes ripped away from his search of the sky as the trailing submarine suddenly erupted in an explosion that shook the port for a second time. The magnitude of the blast literally ripped the craft into three large sections of twisted, mangled steel no longer resembling the sleek craft it was a few moments before, as the torpedoes stored in the bow of the boat cooked off, and then added to the continuing explosions ripping apart the third submarine. Again, Colonel Marzuk found himself staring in stunned disbelief at the catastrophe that had just befallen his once mighty submarine fleet. More destroyed submarine fell from the sky, killing dock workers who had not make it safely to cover. Persian soldiers fired anti aircraft weapons into the empty sky, causing more heated steel to fall onto the burning port facility.

The Iranian Special Agent was frozen in the place he stood, his body shook with fear, anger, and hatred. Colonel Marzuk raised his hand to the heavens and bellowed. "If Allah is truly in Paradise, why are you allowing the destruction of my submarines before they had a chance to carry out your divine will? I curse all for allowing this disaster to happen to meeee! I served you faithfully in my worthless life, and I don't deserve this foul fate you have rested upon my shoulders on this endless and foul day. You have allowed my death as sure as you caused the death of my family. I'll curse the hated Americans with my dying breath. I wil...." Colonel Marzuk's cursing of everything he held dear to myself, was interrupted by the screams of the workers who came out from under their shelter to look after the injured.

"Americans! The American warplanes are attacking our complex!!!" An excited Iranian dock worker cried out as he point towards the sky and then covered his head with his hands.

While holding his arm to the Heavens, Colonel Marzuk looked in the direction the scared dock worker pointed. He made out the twin tongues of flames coming from the exhaust of an unseen plane in the blackness of the night. His anti-aircraft and missiles fire deafening him, and forced him to place his hands over his ears and hunch his shoulders for added protection. He could not see the attacking aircraft, but the scream from the fins of the bomb coming at his base was clearly heard over the heavy cannon fire. Explosions were going off all over the port, hitting strategic positions and military installations, instantly crippling them. The ground he stood on, trembled violently as the Colonel actually lost his footing and was violently tossed to the ground. Dust filled his nostrils as the bombs fell so near where he stood a second ago. He struggled back to his feet and scanned the area once a busy seaport in search of his one remaining submarine.

His last remaining submarine was dead in the water, flames lapping at her ripped apart deck. Certain buildings and dock facilities were also destroyed and reduced to burning piles of rubble, it was a precision bombing raid taking place against his port. Colonel Marzuk saw the areas now under attack and knew the American warplanes cut the eyes and ears off his war making machines. He looked to the sky again and noticed the dots of flames from the departing and still unseen enemy planes as they climbed into the sky. They were nothing like the flames from his aircraft when they flew in the night. He stared at the departing American aircraft, awed by the simplicity of how they had just turned his entire port into a twisted mess of death and flames.

Colonel Marzuk was not allowed time to observe this carnage for long, as suddenly as the planes departed, a second wave of American aircraft took their place. But these were different from the first wing of aircraft that attacked. The flames exhausted from the rear of these planes stretched across the horizon. They were much noisier and easily seen as they lined up to attack.

The words, "Americans", resounded across the all but destroyed Iranian port.

The attacking planes seemed to be using Colonel Marzuk's body as their alignment point for the bombing run on the burning port, and when he picked up the attacking aircraft were coming directly at him, the Iranian Colonel decided to run for his life. As he ran for cover, his mind screamed at him. The first wave of planes were more than likely the American stealth fighter bombers, these new planes coming to attack his port were the devastating bomber aircraft.

The Colonel was correct with his thoughts, the first planes were the F-117 stealth fighters, the second wave were a combination of F-111 bombers, and the F-18 Hornets equipped for ground bombing runs. The Hornets came from the Aircraft Carriers, they hooked up with F-111, Eagles and Falcon aircraft from the 71st Tactical Fighter Squadron stationed in both Saudi Arabia and Kuwait. The planes were prepared for their bombing runs, there was an air cap of Tomcats and Hornets, from the Carriers and a second squadron of F-16s from Saudi Arabia for fighter intercept operations and protection of the bombers. These aircraft were the ones ordered to engage any enemy planes trying to get at the attacking bombers hitting the Iranian Naval Port.

Colonel Marzuk crawled below a forty foot steel shipping container when the first bombs hit the base. It seemed the attacking warplanes were concentrating most of their efforts on his under construction concrete submarine pens. Again, he staring in awe as he was sure the bombs were hitting the pens, but strangely there were no immediate explosions from his facility. Instead he heard the bombs impacting the concrete and ground, but still no explosion. For the first time since the first attacking American aircraft appeared over the port, Colonel Marzuk smiled. He grinned as he slapped the air around him and then announced proudly to the air surrounding him. "Duds, the American fools are attacking us with dud bombs."

The Iranian Colonel actually laid on his back while bellowing with laughter as he thought his submarine pens were being spared the terrible onslaught of the American bomber aircraft. While on his back, he suddenly felt the earth beneath him start to tremble again. Then, the entire area once his submarine pens violently erupted in a mass of flying earth, flames and smoke, slabs of broken concrete, salt water and twisted steel were tossed high in the air, as the delayed fuses of the ground penetrating two thousand pound bombs went off one after the other some twenty feet under the ground. Within seconds, the submarine buildings was nothing more than a pile of rubble, death and waste.

Once the submarine pens were completely destroyed, the attacking American aircraft turned their attack loose on the civilian ships blocking the channel. A few ships attempted a dash out of the channel for the open sea, but when the shipping plowed into the destroyed hulks of the three submarines, the ship's hulls were damaged and the ships took on water, and the Captains stopped their effort to try and escape the trap they were mired in. This action served to close the channel down completely on the civilian ships, trapping the rest of the ships at port. The attacking planes of war then began to pick and chose their targets, taking out any and all Iranian, Libyan, and Iraqi flagged shipping, leaving the rest to survive for the time being.

A number of moored fuel tankers erupted into a boiling roar out of control flames reaching hundreds of feet in the air, illuminating the other targets still trapped at the Iranian port for the attacking aircraft to concentrate on. All ships thought to be carrying any possible military equipment were singled out by the warplanes flying about the shipping much the same way bee's swarms about a sea of blossoming flowers. The ships thought to be carrying military supplies were attack no matter whose flag they were sailing under.

The Iranian Colonel ducked low as the wood dock disappeared under a large wave of water and flying splinters and other debris, after receiving a direct hit from the incoming bombs. The full length and width of the dock was skillfully being worked over by the aircraft until the once active port was reduced to nothing more than waste. Fuel tankers lay resting on their sides, their hulls ripped apart by powerful secondary explosions, and roaring fires burning unchecked on the bodies of the ships. Smaller supply crafts were blown in halves, sinking in the shallow water of the narrow inlet. After each wave of attacking warplanes flew the length of the channel, more civilian ships were left broken and burning. Nothing of the port and many of the ships were left intact. Colonel Marzuk pulled his head out from under cover, trying to see where his anti-aircraft weapons were, and what they were doing to protect his port. He angrily cursed when he saw the double guns lying twisted, the soldiers once manning them nowhere to be seen.

Colonel Marzuk realized his Naval Port was now totally helpless and unable to be defended itself against attack and all was lost to him. For the first time since the American warplanes began to attack the port, he allowed his mind to wander. It did not take very long to figure out what was happening, and what the planes would next attack. He knew if the Americans were so prepared to attack his port, their command had to know of his secret nuclear plant constructed in the deep desert near the small Iranian town of Iranshahr. He would be a fool not to believe the hated Americans knew of the complex. His eyes searched the terrible destruction of the port, looking for the aide who just moments ago handed him the radio.

BANDAR-E-ABBAS

The larger Iranian port of Bandar-e-Abbas was the Naval Port that originally moored the six nuclear powered submarines brought by the Iranian government in 1993 from Russia. This port received much the same treatment as Bander Beheshi suffered from the attacks on the installation by the attacking Coalition Forces. Bandar-e-Abbas was in the process of being assaulted by one hundred and twenty American, English, Italian, French and Russian bombers, backed by a good number of light fighter escort aircraft from three American Aircraft Carriers and military bases stationed in Saudi Arabia, Kuwait and Qatar. In a matter of seconds, the large Iranian Naval Port was reduced to nothing more than a mass of flaming, twisted rubble and destroyed military and civilian shipping. Most of the civilian and military shipping caught moored in the port was sunk, or left disabled and in flames. A third wave of Coalition bomber and escort aircraft lined up on the port to finish off anything that was left intact from the first bombing raid on the port.

CHAPTER TWENTY SIX

THE IRANIAN PORT OF BANDER BEHESHI

The fuming Iranian Colonel Muhsin Abu Marzuk, was finally able to locate the aide with the radio receiver hiding under a parked fork lift truck. At first, he was afraid to leave his protection and tried to ignore the angry man. But when the Colonel pulled out his pistol and aimed it directly at his face, the young and scared aide relented. Crawling on his hands and knees over the rubble covered ground while dodging bullets and flying debris, he made his way over to the fuming Marzuk. When he reached him, the Colonel pulled the radio savagely out of his hand.

It did not work, so the angry Colonel Marzuk kicked the aide in the face with the heel of his boot as he hissed at the young dock worker. "Stupid god cursed lowly infidel, this worthless radio does not work, fool of an unbeliever and son of a jackal! You'll fix it in a hurry for my use, or I'll shoot you where you lay, you great dung eating dog of a fool!"

The trembling aide took the radio and quickly examined it. He was embarrassed when he discovered he handed the angry Colonel the radio switched off and he offered. "Please, forgive this foolish man Colonel Marzuk, because I have failed to turn the radio on for your use, sir. Here, it'll work properly now for you sir, I swear by Allah's Almighty hand sir."

Colonel Marzuk was furious at the young aide, his hand trembled with anger as he glared at him while figuring out the punishment for his failure to serve him properly. He aimed the pistol at the aide's eye and fired. The aide's head shot back, taking the rest of his body with it, as blood and bone flew everywhere.

"Thus is the god cursed fate of all who have failed to serve me correctly at my times of need." Colonel Marzuk growled at the body of the dead dock worker. He then keyed the mike and he yelled into the radio. "Colonel Marzuk to command! Come in!"

"Command. Colonel Marzuk, I meant to contact you sooner than this time sir. How are things going in Bander Beheshi? Were you successful with the launching of your submarines?"

"Command! We're under heavy attack by many cursed American planes of war! They have completely destroyed the entire port, and the enemy aircraft are continuing their attack on the base with no interference from our own warplanes or defensive systems."

"Praise Allah, I assure you this attack is nothing to be overly concerned with Colonel Marzuk. Be brave about you, this is not as though it was unexpected, god curse all infidels and jackals and their foul souls. Colonel Marzuk, I have already asked you and I'll repeat that request to you. Did you successfully launch your submarines before the hated enemy planes attacked the port?"

"Command! I don't care one grain of worthless sand about my submarines at this time. The American dogs are about to attack the complex at Iranshahr." The excited Iranian Colonel bellowed as he was forced to duck more debris from his destroyed Naval Port.

"Praise the Almighty Allah, Colonel Marzuk! You must have sand in your foolish brain. How could the Americans have possibly known of the existence of the nuclear complex? You speak utter nonsense to me. Your mind must have become confused by the shock of the attack you're suffering. What do you mean you're not concerned about your submarines, Colonel? They're your only responsibility and should be your only thought, fool. Have you launched them yet?"

"Listen to me! I said the god hated Americans know of the complex at Iranshahr, and they're about to attack it! You have to listen to me, believe me, they know of the complex's existence, and they will attack it soon, fool." Colonel Marzuk bellowed, his voice dripping with sarcasm.

"Colonel Marzuk, how could this be possible? You must be mistaken, I fear the shock from the attack on your port is robbing you of all your foolish senses and courage, foul one. I urge you to think before you speak again to me because it could cost you your worthless life, Colonel."

"How is this possible you asked of me, fool?" Colonel Marzuk yelled uncontrollably into the handheld radio, and then added to his warning to the Iranian Command. "How is it possible for the god cursed lowly infidels to destroy my submarines while still moored at port without using any of their worthless warplanes or weapons? How is this possible I ask you, fool?"

There was dead silence on the other end for several long moments, and then the calm and controlled voice growled at the Iranian Colonel. "Marzuk, your submarines are destroyed?"

"Yes! All four of them have been destroyed in this attack on the port."

"Marzuk, even the ones that made it to the open sea?" The voice demanded.

"Yes, I'd have to believe those submarines are likewise destroyed by the American warships reported trailing them, Command." The fuming Colonel replied to his commanding officer. "If the hated American aircraft is able to so completely destroy my port, then yes, I have to believe the lowly Americans know of the secret base constructed out in the deep desert of our country.

Another pause, and then command's reply to their Colonel. "Marzuk, you'll place your gun up against your worthless head, and then you are ordered to pull the trigger to pay for your failures to Iran and your government. You have let down your government, and you and your family will pay dearly for this failure to your duty. Your death will be only the beginning of your pain."

There was no reply from Colonel Marzuk.

COLONEL MUHSIN ABU MARZUK
BACK TO HIDING UNDER THE CARGO CONTAINER

Colonel Marzuk was silent as death as his attention picked up the rapidly approaching enemy warplane hurtling at him at near supersonic speed. The troubled Iranian Colonel noticed the heavy wrack of bombs slung under the wings of the aircraft, and the pair of white painted stars on her wings. Everything taking place seemed to be happening in slow motion to him at this point. Suddenly he could not move a muscle, as if he was frozen in place as he stared in dumb struck awe at the plane streaking directly at him. He swallowed, his mouth dry as the desert sand as he witnessed the incoming aircraft release the bombs hurtling at the earth and screaming.

Slowly, Colonel Marzuk quickly worked his way out from under the heavy protection offered him by the large metal cargo container, and then he stood out in the open with his arms resting at his sides, his whole being was strangely calm and relaxed. He was at peace with the world, mesmerized by the scream of the bombs as they tore through the air right at him. Colonel Marzuk followed the path of the bombs until they hit a mere few feet away from where he stood. The ground beneath his feet instantly erupted in a heaving and boiling plot of earth, splintered wood and chunks of steel. His body was lifted in the warm air amidst the churning earth and burning debris. He was aware of his body tumbling end over end, but strangely he suffered no pain from the explosions. Just a warmth and horrifying, blinding light from the bomb blasts.

"Is this what it is meant to die?" Colonel Marzuk bellowing in the madness of this manmade hell storm on the earth he was trapped in. Demanding from himself, the answer his mind knew would never come. Reality quickly answered as his call, as it set in once the shock of the bomb blasts wore off, and the shrapnel started to rip his exposed body apart.

Shearing, all consuming unbearable pain, instantly embraced the tumbling and breaking bones in his battered and torn body, replacing the once warmth and light of the terrible blast. The bright cloud of rolling mayhem rapidly closed in around him, robbing the very breath from his burning lungs. The once bright cloud darkened when his lungs burst from the scream he emitted, as he continued to tumble end over end in the air.

Pain, Colonel Marzuk's body was a mass of burning, searing pain as parts of it were violently ripped asunder from the blast. The rapidly spreading darkness increased around his body, until there was nothing but total darkness surrounding him, and his life left his mangled and twisted body. Colonel Marzuk's body was then deposited unceremoniously as a crumbled up, broken heap of humanity laying on the rubble once his once prized port dock.

The radio once locked in his hand fell to the earth just inches away from the shattered head of the Iranian Colonel, still clutched by his severed hand. It worked, and the voice from command continued to bellow at him. "Marzuk, you will blow your foul head off your worthless shoulders for failing your government in our greatest time of her need. Marzuk! Marzuk! You have failed your mission, and you'll answer to me for that failure, and do as I have just ordered you to do, fool. Marzuk! Speak, reply to me at once you cursed fool you, there is no place you can possibly hide on the face of this earth from my wrath. Marzuk! I command you to kill yourself, fool!"

SANDSTORM

The complex constructed near the Iranian town of Iranshahr was built like a concrete fortress, with a profile close to the ground except for the one center section of a building that reached three stories in height, to enable the construction of the missiles. Inside the main structure, there were two narrow sets of windows. These were on the second floor to the side Walker and a number of his troops were gathered, and he saw two skylights on the roof. Another section of the neatly hidden complex held five large steel garage doors leading into the interior of the complex.

Walker's troops were spread out to their positions where they would surround the structures. He tapped his radio and then whispered. "Ghost, you and Hunter do a creep, get out there and scout the damn place out good. I want a few people to get over by those damn garage doors, I need Intel. That spot might offer us an easy entry in the stinking dump. Take out any soft targets (enemy soldiers) you come across silently. Hardon, you and Snatch will work your way over to the Army Barracks, I want you guys to lob in a coupla crash bangs (stun grenades) and bye-byes (sleeping agent grenades). I don't want any of them damn pukes pouring outta their beehive once we attack the damn complex and get in our flanks. Take Scrap Iron and Sticks with you for some extra support on your assault of the barracks. Make certain you get all the stinking targets, if any shits aren't affected by the knock out gas and stun grenades, send them for the big dirt nap.

"Once you're sure the damn gas done its job, get in there and handcuff the swinging dicks still alive, so they're outta the action without having to kill the damn tent pegs outright. Remember, keep your damn eyes open and your asses close to the stinking ground, keep checking for any possible planted gut rippers, (anti-personnel mines) and mantraps set up against us. They could be set up anywhere in the area of this dump. I'm sure they're here. Wacko, get your ass up here with that damn IF-484 Unit, so we know what we're going up against inside the damn place."

The IF-484 Unit was a powerful, portable, handheld, thermal read, infrared system that enabled the user to detect any heat signatures being emitted by any soldiers hidden inside the shadows of a building, or a civilian working inside the structure. The powerful IF-484 Unit gave a complete 3D layout of the interior of the building, pinpointing the whereabouts of anyone working inside it, or defending the building against attack.

The Mutt worked his way over to Walker and then plopped down on his rearend and offered him a hit of water as he complained at the Lieutenant. "Hey man, this fucking place is dryer than a stinking popcorn fart, Homes. I thought you might need a slug of water buddy."

Walker took the half empty bottle of water from the Mutt and drew a good pull, and then he passed it along to the next guy sitting on his rump to his right.

"Man, I wish this job was being handled by those dirt dart creepers we got working for us, man. I think this one woulda been much betta handled by them damn dirt (slang for Ranger paratroopers) eating pukes, pal." The Mutt moaned at him.

"Fuck that shit man, we're the best America has to offer Homes. Whatsumatta pal, you getting soft on me or what?" Walker snarled as he looked into his lifelong friend's eyes for the answer.

"Hey man, I'm not here for a long time, I'm here for a good time. So don't go apeshit on my stinking ass, I ain't going soft on no one, fucker. I was just stating my opinion, that's al..."

Their conversation was interrupted by the soldier branded Wacko Sergeant Salvatore Tomassi, who joined the two soldiers hunched over by the side of the building. He carried the small IF-484 Unit slung over his shoulder, and was completely out of breath by the time he reached the two Lieutenants. He smiled at Walker who immediately barked at him.

"Get that fucking thing set up as quick as you can, Wacker. I wanna know how many stinking bad guys we're going up against inside there man." The Lieutenant snapped as he picked some grains of sand bothering him out of his teeth with his fingernail. The wind stirred up new clouds of whipping sand that was getting into everything the soldiers carried or ate and drank.

"Man Road Kill, visibility's really getting fucked to hell and back again on us, sir. I sure hope this damn Unit's gonna work as it's supposed too in all this crap man. This is a very sensitive machine not meant to be operating in a sea of stinking sand like this." Wacko bitched as he quickly set up the machine, trying to shield it the best he could from the windblown sand.

"Wacker be damn glad for the stinking sand kicking up like this, man. If we're having this much fricking trouble with trying to spot the damn bad guys in all this stinking crap, think of all the fricking trouble they'll have with trying to pick up our damn asses when we go after the stinking suckers without the equipment we have at hand, buddy. If they spotted us first, we'd be dick deep in screaming, crazy ass acting Iranian soldiers.

"Yeah, I guess you got a good point there dog man. I never looked at it that way man." Wacko agreed with the Mutt who took over speaking with him from Walker.

Walker stretched his neck while trying to get a fix on what Casper or the Hunter was up to. He smiled when he found no trace of the two soldiers in the dark. They were good he thought while trying to locate them. His radio suddenly squawked to life, it was Casper and he offered. "Walker, I'm getting something happening over here I though you should know about, man."

The Mutt snapped back. "Well rub the damn thing and maybe it'll go away fur ya man."

Walker glared at the Mutt as he warned him in an angry voice. "Can the fucking jokes asshole. Can't you be fricking serious for one second in your stinking life, man? I got a mind to slap you upside that block of concrete you call a fucking noggin, dog man."

Casper, pissed off at the Mutt butted in by snarling at him. "Ha fucking ha butt nugget. That wiseass hadta be the fricking Mutt sticking his damn nose where it doesn't belong again. Hey Walker, you betta get a damn leash on that pet dog of yours, before he fucks up the mission."

"Am I gonna start having some trouble with you too, now, dammit? Christ sake, I wish I knew how I ever allowed myself to be roped into this cockamamie operation with you stack of stinking shitbirds. Whaddaya got going down out there you wish to report to me about, Homes?"

"Err... Walker, I think I'm picking up something coming in from one of the..."

The Hunter cut Casper's report off in mid stream and he reported to Walker.

"Walker, I'm picking up..." Casper stared to report to Walker.

"Hunter, hold your damn pee pee for a minute will ya man. I got Casper on the line."

"Sure thing Homes. Remember I'm here and I need to talk with ya real fast Lieutenant."

"Go Casper, whaddaya got for me soldier?"Walker asked the Ghost.

"Walker, I have a pair of organ donors lurking about a Soviet 120 mm 2B16 towed howitzer, sucking ass and pulling their damn puds, man. Whatdaya want me to do about them things?"

"What the hell are they doing by the damn thing?" Walker demanded of him.

"Just kinda hanging about the fucking wind counting off time to get out of the damn service I'd guess. It looks like the dopey little bastards are drinking something man. The assholes show no stinking sign of knowing we're stalking their damn asses out here, Walker."

"Casper hang tight for the time being, I'll assign the Goat and Short Cut to take them out when we start our go against the damn complex. Now you Hunter, whaddaya got for me Homes?"

"Walker, I have a pair of Russian T-72 tanks hooked up to portable generators, they don't look like they're operating any too good. The machines look like they're suffering from a severe lack of attention and maintenance, but there's one brand fucking new T-80H 125 mm main mount muthafakka working under her own stinking power, and it looks like she's ready to go at the drop of a fricking hat, man. The big ass mutherfucking thing is so new it looks like it's still got some of its protective packaging wrapped around its infrared aiming system man. Walker, we'll have to shit O rings if we're gonna go up against that fucking machine in full operation, buddy."

"Sssshit! Well we'll have to make sure the big bastard's dead before we jump off, right Hunter? Where's that damn spook hiding at anyway?" Walker growled over his shoulder.

"Yes? I am here by your side Lieutenant Walker." Bdellah replied to Walker asking for him.

"Bdellah, how come you didn't report this new fucking Russian T-80 tank in your initial fucking report to your damn control back in the States, buster? That damn thing's gonna give me a stinking apoplexy if it gets loose in my fucking troops ranks on us, fella."

"I'm sorry about that err Lieutenant. That's because the Iranians must have moved the new tank in position after I had made my original observation of the complex, and reported so to my control. Surely, you cannot hold me responsible for any possible changes the Iranians and their Command carried out, after I had made my first report to control, Lieutenant?" Bdellah moaned in his defense, showing Walker he was bored with this conversation as they spoke together.

"Walker! Walker! I found an old man hiding back here sir." Blood Clot offered.

"Where the hell is he, and who the hell is he Blood Clot?" Walker growled into the radio.

"He's with me Lieutenant Walker. I took him in custody, and I'm sitting on his smelly ass until you give me word on his stinking fate man." Blood Clot moaned into his helmet radio.

Walker looked at Bdellah, and merely shrugged.

"Lieutenant Walker, that old man you speak of has to be al-Shamarral. I was wondering when he was going to show up. You have to order your men to treat him with the greatest of respect at all times sir. He's the one who controls the desert fighters helping us on this mission, Walker."

"Don't get a fucking mind cramp on my ass buster. Your stinking Iranian pals haven't been too much stinking help to us so far you know mister. We still have a horde of fricking Iranian soldiers up the stinking wazoo we're gonna hafta deal with when we finally hit this complex."

"I beg to argue that point with you, Lieutenant Walker Sir. I fear now is not the time to get involved in that conversation. I'll argue this much with you Lieutenant. You and your soldiers have arrived in the desert alive, did you not sir?" Bdellah asked with a smirk on his lips.

"Don't tell me it was because of this old fucker we now have in custody, Bdellah?" Walker growled as he tried to rub his balls through the thick body armor.

"Please Lieutenant, when speaking of this old man, you must show him the proper respect at all times as if your very life depends on him. Because your life and the lives of the rest of your soldiers does depend on him, and yes Lieutenant. You're here only because he has allowed you the privilege of traveling through his desert safely and without any harm, Lieutenant."

"Yeah, right, okay Bdellah whatever you say man." Walker spat some sand out of his mouth, and then he tapped his helmet mike and ordered. "Blood Clot, he's the man we're looking for. Treat him like a God, but keep him back there until you hear otherwise from my ass, man. Okay, satisfied my friend?" Walker snapped as he turned back to face Bdellah again.

"Yes, thank you Lieutenant Walker. You have honored him properly I offer you sir."

"Mother, have you found anything on your side of this stinking dump? I haven't hear jack shit coming from your ass yet through this mess, buster. What's going on over there pal?"

"Yep, I found the three machine gun embrasures. They're where right where they were marked out on the damn map by our little spook friend, two are on the damn roof of the main structure of the stinking complex. Tell your damn spook friend he did real well with marking them out for us, sir. He has made our part of this damn operation a little easier to carry out, man."

"Embrasures? What the fuck are you talking about damn embrasures, sucka? Did you get college edufuckingcated all of a sudden on me or what, buddy? Embrasures, they're fucking machine emplacement or nests. Mother, I don't want you hanging around that damn civilian Doc any longer buddy. He's starting to screw you up on me, dammit. Next thing you know, I'll be needing a damn dictionary to communicate with your stinking ass. The damn machine guns are your responsibility to deal with, they're the first to go when we hit this damn dump, buster. You got it? Embrasures, geeesss." Walker snarled then added. "Can you get at them easy enuf?"

"Easy man, consider them out of the fucking picture when we go bang." Mother bragged.

"Okay Mother, get your people on the roof then. You lead the group, repel up the err..."

"The east side of the stinking building's gonna offer us the best possible protection, and easiest access to the damn gun emplacements stationed up there on us man." Mother offered.

"That's fucking betta, at least I can read you again, use the east side of the stinking building to get on the roof, and take them damn guns out toot sweet. Get it done for me Mother, I'm relying on your ass doing what's ordered of ya man. Once the guns are out of the picture, penetrate the damn building from the roof, and then work your way down the building to linkup with us on the first floor of the dump. Make sure your personal IFF (Identify, Friend or Foe) system's turned on, buddy. I don't wanna lose any of you tent pegs to friendly fire on this one." Walker snapped.

"You got that straight Walker, IFF's are on and transmitting loud and clear. The building looks like it's made of poured concrete, at least a foot thick in some places, Walker." Mother Flanagan replied as he gave a quick series of hand signals, and his people moved out with him.

"Walker, I have a soft target moving near your position. The dopey marmaluke's moving from north to south, forty feet away from your forward position. He seems to be armed with an AK, and the target's making moves like he's an ever loving fucking soldier." Prowler cut in.

Walker immediately checked the area around him, and he easily picked up the lone Iranian soldier doing something too close to his position for comfort. The alert Lieutenant looked over his shoulder and barked an order to his other Lieutenant. "Hey Mutt, you gotta take this stinking spudhead out nice and quiet like for us, Homes? He's too damn close to us to leave the lousy prick roaming round alive. Until the enemy soldier ends up with dumb luck and stumbles over our asses out here. Get him and take him out of the equation toot sweet but silently Mutt."

Without a word, the Mutt moved out and worked his way towards the top of the sand mound he was using for cover. He then unslung his sniper weapon and lined up his shot on the enemy breather. He held his breath as he carefully aimed at the head of the enemy soldier. The soft report of the silenced weapon sounded louder to Walker than it was.

Walker looked over the Mutt's shoulder, and he picked up the enemy soldier as he grab at his neck, and then he drop like a rock to the sand. But he was able to tell the target was still moving and he grumbled at his sniper. "Christ sake Mutt! You only creased the fucking speed bump, dummy. Sheesh, hit the damn puke again before he gives out the god damn alarm against us, stupid." Walker punched the Mutt on the armored back and glared at him angrily.

A second low report made the Iranian guard's body jump again, and then it quickly settled down in his death's sleep.

"Christ sake Mutt, two stinking rounds to take one slimeball out, some fucking sniper you make, dickhead. The next time I need someone put down fast, I'll get me a real stinking sniper to do the damn job correctly, man." Walker moaned at the Mutt as he studied his handiwork on the dead soldier. It was a decent hit for being so dark, and the movement of the enemy soldier.

"Hey man what the hell can I tell ya man, the stinking sun musta been in my fricking eyes, man." The Mutt offered the Lieutenant with a grin.

"It's the middle of the fucking night grunt? Some sun in your eyes tent peg, you use the same excuse, betta think up another one, pest. Arr… fuhgedaboutit, Baby Tee, you and Siberia get out there and drag that lousy puke's ass back here so we can hide his body, and then man the forty."

The soldiers watched as the two women fighters struggled with the soldier's limp body, once they dragged it behind their forward line, they dumped it on the sand like a sack of potatoes. Walker gave a number of hand signals that informed the soldiers they were about to move out against the complex. Before moving out, the Lieutenant contacted his two working Vipers or snipers, and ordered them to take out any enemy targets they can line up in their sights.

There were a series of soft pops by the Iranian tanks, and Walker saw the puffs of smoke raising, telling him the grenades been dropped inside the iron coffins, and all inside the tanks were dead. He eyed the T-80 and smiled when he noticed smoke billowing out from its gun port. He hoped the ammunition would give him time to carry out his opening attack against the complex with surprise, before it cooked off and then exploded from the fire inside the tank.

The young Lieutenant turned his attention to the Iranian military barracks. He picked up three of his troops pitching a number of stun and chemical grenades, containing a quick acting sleeping agent inside the barracks. His soldiers then charged inside the smoke filled enemy barracks while wearing their gas masks, their silenced weapons held at the ready.

He barely heard more stun and chemical poppers going off inside the barracks. There was no return fire against his people attacking the barracks, and when the original attackers left their positions, and they entered the barracks as if out on a Sunday walk. The concerned Lieutenant knew instantly the barracks was secured, and the enemy troops were all dead, or under his troop's control. He kept his eyes glued on the entrance of the barracks, and waited until one of his people came out, and he gave him the thumbs up signal.

"The barrack is secured, we only have the sleazbags still inside the complex to contend with. Wacker, how are you doing with that image enhancing thing?" Walker looked at Wacko.

"Fine man, it's working out okay. I was able to locate four soft targets on the first floor in the room to the left of the main doors, Walker. I'm also picking up two soft targets hanging around in the main corridor area. All hot traces are acting like soldiers standing guard. Left of those few traces, I'm picking up two more targets standing at the head of another corridor, but shorter than the first one. I'm got another room with at least six traces inside it. There's a shitload of activity from these traces in this one room, sir. I believe these creeps are workers doing their stinking act, Lieutenant. I have three other traces inside maybe another lab type room, just off to the right side of the main corridor, sir. I take these uther targets to be more of the Iranian civilian workers man. Walker, I'm not picking up enough traces inside the stinking dump I'd designate as civilian technicians and workers. That means there has to be another structure somewhere else in the damn complex housing those uther pukes we know are working at the site, Homes."

Walker scanned the outside of the complex until he settled on the building left of him he felt was capable of housing the horde of doctors, and technicians, and he ordered the soldier to concentrate the Image Enhancing machine on that structure. "Wacko, scan the stinking building to the left of the main structure, and tell me what you pick up inside there, man."

"Whew Lieutenant." Wacko moaned as he added a low whistle to emphasize what he just found inside the other building in question. "There's plenty of fucking traces I'm picking up in there, sir. I think you just found your mother lode of stinking civilian technicians and workers."

"Wacko, get on the main building again and work over the second floor of the dump." He demanded, and then ordered the soldiers who attacked the barracks, to do their act on the building marked Three on the map, where they located a mess of hot traces inside that building.

Wacko adjusted the sight of the machine back on the main building again, before working over the second floor of the structure, he did a quick scan of the area he left to go to the other building, and complained to his commanding officer.

"Yeeeooowww Walker, the fucking area of the first floor to the right is one hot spot of Iranian pricks doing crap in there, dude."

The concerned Doctor Russbinder moved over to Walker's side, and he listened to Wacko's report, and then he replied. "Lieutenant Walker, that has to be the area where the workers must be constructing the nuclear warheads for the missiles, sir. Mr. Soldier, what you're system's picking up is radiation contamination inside the room. From what your description's reporting, it sounds like the work area's filthy. We in the field of nuclear research commonly refer to this area as a Hot Spot, there's radioactive contamination released inside this lab area. I'm at a total loss as to why the Russian technicians are accepting these terribly life threatening conditions to work under. They must know they're placing their lives in deadly danger. I think they're committi..."

"Not to mention ours lives as well, Doc." Walker interrupted hotly.

"Yes, quite right sir. Not to mention our lives will be in danger as well in there, Lieutenant."

Walker shook his head slowly and then spat on the sand in sheer disgust, knowing he had no other alternative but to continue on with his mission, even though he was placing his troop's lives in danger of radiation contamination and poisoning. Who knew what the crap would do to their bodies once exposed to the deadly crap. The worried Lieutenant looked the civilian dead in the eyes and then barked at him hotly. "Is there enough crap in there to kill us, Doc?"

"I won't know that for certain until we're inside the building, and I get a look at the readings on the amount of radiation that's being released inside the work lab. I seriously doubt it's enough to kill us outright, but we don't want to hang around needlessly inside the lab if we don't have to, sir. Lieutenant, in light of this latest discovery, I'd suggest you allow only the soldiers needed to secure the complex, to enter the lab area in question sir. Outside, the radiation's registering far less dangerous, and it's a lot less of a threat against our bodies Lieutenant."

The doctor held up a Geiger counter and studied the gauge, he then warned the young military officer in no uncertain terms. "Gees Lieutenant Walker, I'm picking up nine hundred milirenkons an hour outside the complex structure. That's not enough to hurt you, unless you spend the entire day in the hot zone sir, and even that much wouldn't do much permanent damage to your body." The doctor took a quick breath, and then he continued with his warning to the military officer. "Lieutenant Walker, I didn't take into consideration the possibility of carrying out our mission under highly radioactive contaminated conditions, sir. I suggest we make haste, complete our orders as quickly as possible, and then get out of the structure to allow your soldiers to completely destroy the building before it becomes a serious threat to the ecology of the desert."

"Doc, all of a fucking sudden I'm damn glad you came along on this damn mission with us, sir." Walker then turned to Wacko and used the doctor's term of addressing him. "Mr. Soldier, would you scan the second floor of that stinking dump like I ordered you to do, so I can get my people in gear and hit this damn place and then get the hell outta stinking town."

Wacko turned his scope towards the second floor of the structure, and he immediately picked up twenty traces scattered about the interior of the building, and he reported this to Walker.

"That brings the total of assholes working inside the stinking complex up to thirty seven targets we'll have to deal with inside the stinking dump..."

"At the least Lieutenant, I'm still picking up an awful lot of ground clutter floating around inside the stinking dump, and all this damn clutter could be hiding a number of other targets from my probe of the place, man. The shit could be coming from the fluorescent lights or the stinking radiation inside the building, Walker. There's a good possibility some of these fucking traces are overlapping each other, and this could also hide them from my view. I'd go under the assumption of at least forty five or more targets could be inside the structure to be on the safe side, Walker."

"Good thinking on your part, and I'll do just as you have suggested to me Wacko. I'll inform the other troops of the numbers of targets we picked up in there, man."

Just as Walker was about to clue the other soldiers in on what they had discovered, his helmet radio suddenly squawked on him. "Walker, I have some suspect enemy activity going down by door one, artillery pieces." The female Russian soldier branded Caviar, reported.

"That hasta be my people moving around out there, Caviar. They shoulda destroyed those damn things by this time, dammit."

"Negative on that Walker. If you people, what do they come outside complex for then?"

"Good point there sister. That's not my people moving around out there then. Shit! Hey Hardon, you and your people anywhere near the damn artillery pieces yet, mister?"

"I'm right here, shoot man." Hardon, Sergeant Leslie Horner replied to Walker who called him over the radio.

"Don't fucking tempt me, I have enuf target to shoot at as it is, man. Hardon, I have a shitload of activity going down near those damn cannons, and my people haven't successfully destroyed the fucking things yet. They must be bogged down for some reason. Can you get at them and give them a stinking hand if they're in any trouble over there? Then destroy those fucking cannons."

"Easy, too easy man, consider them damn things already naturalized, Homes."

"What the hell are you waiting for, screwball? Do them damn things in now dammit!"

"You got it Walker. I'm on my fucking way to the other troops, man." Hardon snapped as he waved back at the Lieutenant as he picked him up in his field of vision.

IRANIAN CENTRAL COMMAND

The Iranian Command carefully weighed Colonel Muhsin Abu Marzuk's words, and the Commander decided to take his warning seriously. He ordered a pair of companies of troops to secure the complex, just in case Colonel Marzuk was correct, and the complex was about to come under attack by American foot soldiers. The Commander checked his map, and discovered he had a few well seasoned companies of troops in the vicinity of the complex. The Iranian soldiers were twenty miles away from the complex, and they were under control of General Ghelamerza Ardebili. The Commander remembered the General, and knew the troops would be well trained and highly disciplined, but he cursed his luck because neither company was an armored company. They had old tanks and artillery pieces in the units, but that was all.

The Iranian Commander reached for the phone and discovered the Americans were still scrambling all incoming and outgoing calls, he called his aide over to his side and ordered him to send a plane out to General Ardebili's position. As an afterthought, he ordered the aide to scramble two Russian built Mig-31 Foxhound interceptors to do a pass over the complex.

SANDSTORM'S POSITION

Lieutenant Robert Walker prepared himself and the rest of his troops to move out when he received the first call from his ready air cap.

"Razor Blade Leader to Sandstorm Commander. Come in sir. I wanted to inform you that I have an active air cap over your troops and if you guys run into any trouble, we're here for you sir. Over." The Flight Leader called to speak with Colonel Leadbetter.

Colonel Leadbetter cut in and he growled. "Go Razor Blade, this is Sandstorm Commander. Over." The Colonel diverted his eyes towards the night sky, in an attempt to see the plane he was talking to the pilot of. It was no good, he could not pick up any sign of the aircraft.

"Sandstorm Commander, be advised that I'm instructed to inform you I have six Razor Cuts in my Flight Wing, sir. I'm assigned to your ready air cap and air to ground support cover, Colonel. If you guys run into any trouble with the damn Iranians down there sir, all you have to do is send me a quick 911 call, and we'll be there in a flash, Sandstorm Commander. I have three Razor's armed for air to ground combat, the rest of my Wing are armed for possible air to air response, sir. Over." The Commander of Razor Flight offered to the ground Colonel.

"Razor Blade Leader. I read you loud and clear, glad to have you pukes over us, sir. Thanks for the help, we're getting ready to engage the enemy. Will keep you advised. Sandstorm Out."

"Roger that Sandstorm. Will standby if needed, we have enough fuel to offer you forty minutes of ready air cap cover. We'll not move off until a second Wing of aircraft is overhead. Out."

Walker turned to the Mutt and asked him if he was keeping an eye on Mother's progress.

"Mother Flanagan and the rest of his people got over the top of the stinking roof. I believe he took out one of the damn guns already, and he's moving against the other one as we speak, man. The gun emplacement on the ground is already knocked out of commission, Walker."

"Good fucking deal, there's nothing for us to do now but get this stinking show on the fucking road." As Walker spoke the words, automatic weapons fire suddenly broke out by the artillery emplacements. Both Walker and the Mutt ducked down as the concerned Lieutenant growled into his helmet radio. "What the fuck's that shit going down? Who the fuck's firing dammit?"

The soldier branded the Goat yelled out. "Walker! We just ran into a fucking ambush man. These fuckas were lying in wait for our stinking asses man. They have a pair of machine guns setup out of sight, and they're working us over good and proper. I'm cut off and nailed down to the fucking ground, Walker. I can't move a stinking muscle without getting my damn dick shot off out here, man. I need some stinking help down here, and I need it real fast like, Walker."

A series of explosions by the main building went off next, and Walker picked up the three Iranian tanks ripping themselves apart, as their ammunition cooked off inside the burning machines. He ignored the explosions as he complained to the soldier over his helmet radio. "Hey Goat, they were lying in wait against you because you musta made fucking noise while working your way over to them, you hadta alerted them fucks somehow, dammit. Sit tight, help's on the way, man. There's no fricking sense with trying to keep our stinking presence secret any longer, our fucking mission's been compromised. The lousy fuckers know we're here, and this mess is turning into a shit storm. Listen up people, anyone who can get a shot at those pukes, take it."

Walker was correct, the Iranian defenders knew the American troops were there, because three search lights suddenly snapped on, and they began to scan the sand dunes for any signs of the intruders. One light concentrated its strong beam on the exploding tanks for a few moments, and then it joined the other two searching for the attackers.

"Goat, where the fuck's Casper, and what the hell's he doing out there, dammit?"

"Dunno man fur sure man. But I do know where he's not, and that's with us Walker."

"Ghost here, what's up Walker?" Casper asked Walker over the radio.

"What's up? I'll tell you what's up buster. Where the hell are ya at man? Take out those damn Christmas lights for me, or we're gonna end up sitting ducks out here, dammit."

"Hang onto your stinking wanker before you bust a damn gut, Walker. I got the lights man."

Walker stretched his neck out as rounds were fired at the powerful search lights, the first light instantly went dark. Two more rounds, and the other two lights exploded and went down.

"Easy. Real easy man." Casper whispered into his mike to the Lieutenant.

"Too easy Ghost. Can you get up to the Goat and give him a hand? I haven't heard jack shit from his ass in the past few seconds, Casper." Walker ordered the soldier.

Small weapons fire was erupting from a number of different locations within the complex area. Someone was shooting at Walker's people from inside the main part of the structure.

"Shit, there's no sense moving to his location, Walker. I can see Goat's down and outta it from where I'm stationed man. He looks like he has been cut in fucking half by machine guns, he doesn't need any fucking help from us any longer Walker."

"Shit! Okay, delay that last order then buddy. What about Short Cut, Casper? Do you see him out there anywhere? He was supposed to be with the Goat."

"Yeah, he's lying right next to the Goat, Walker. He's not moving any, but he might not be dead, at least he's still in one fucking piece as far as I can tell from here, man. Walker, if you're gonna do some of that soldier stuff, you betta start doing it real quick like man, before the shit falls hot and heavy on our stinking asses, buddy. The damn Iranian's are loading up the cannons still operational, and they're preparing to fire the damn things at your troops, sir. Red tip shit, that's anti-fucking personnel rounds man." Casper warned Walker over the radio.

"I read your last Casper. I'll have the Bunker Busters and 40 mm grenade launchers open up on the lousy bastards and their damn artillery pieces man."

Bunker Busters were light weight and disposable man portable guns fired once, were discarded by the soldiers. The weapons were a single round container weapon weighing eighteen pounds, with an effective range of two hundred meters, and the report hit with the power of a mortar.

Walker gave the order and the troops went in action, working over the area where the artillery pieces were dug in. The bunker busters joined the action, ripping apart the Iranian soldiers manning the artillery pieces. In seconds, the cannons were turned into useless weapons to the defenders of the complex, but not before they got three rounds off at Walker's troops. Each round fell well short to the ground harmlessly a hundred yards away from Walker's forward position.

Casper's voice came in on his radio again. "Hey Walker, the stinking artillery pieces are stinking history man. Tell them fucking trigger happy assholes with those damn hell poppers to hold their friggin fire while I check on the Goat and Short Cut."

"Get it done for me." Walker snarled at the complaining Casper over his radio.

CHAPTER TWENTY SEVEN

INSIDE THE ONCE SECRET IRANIAN COMPLEX

The thirty five Iranian security guards defending the inside of the complex, quickly surveyed the situation erupting outside the structure. The defenders armed the twenty two Russian and Iranian technicians, and stationed them inside the stairwells and doorways of the interior of the structure. The guards then constructed roughly put together defensive bunkers in the interior of the complex, to repel the unknown invaders they believed were about to attack the structure. The guards piled up a number of desks and file cabinets one on top of another, and all around them. Then the guards waited for the invaders to attack. Other guards took up defensive positions in the shadows of the interior, waiting for the invaders to begin their attack against them.

Lieutenant Walker held off his opening attack on the complex until he found out the condition of his two downed soldiers. A soft blow in the helmet radio followed by Casper's voice reporting while speaking low into the radio as not to give away his position to the defending Iranian soldiers. "Hey Walker, the Goat's down and out of it. He's taking the long dirt nap man."

"I know that man. What about Short Cut, Ghost? What's his condition?" Walker asked.

"I'm checking him now, shit, he's still alive, but he's really fucked up bad, man. He's hit in the neck and blood's pumping out of him like a fucking oil well, Walker."

Walker looked over his shoulder and then called out. "Hey Blood Clot, get your ass over to Casper, Short Cut's hit real bad, man."

"Moving out!" Blood Clot left al-Shamarral with the rear guard as he worked to Short Cut.

The Mutt rapped Lieutenant Walker on the armored leg and then warned him. "Hey man I think it's time we go into our stinking act against these slugs, Homes."

"You got that right buddy." Walker then raised his hand to give the signal, as his arm went up, weapons fire suddenly erupted from the windows on the second floor of the complex, pinning down most of his troops, as the Iranian defenders sprayed bullets in all directions.

"Hey man, someone around here is being awful careless with fucking firearms man. Do you think they're fucking shooting at us Walker?" The Mutt laughed at him.

Walker spun around and stared at him for a moment before shaking his head and then grumbling at the soldier. "You know Mutt, you're really fucking nuts man."

"You got that right buddy, but at least I'm fucking happy." Mutt said with a grin to Walker.

"Yeah, you're really happy with yourself, aren't you Mutt?" Walker snapped back at him.

"Say Walker, what the hell's going on up there for crap sake? I have fucking soldiers and aircraft bunching up all over the damn place on us mister. You have to start the damn attack right now buster, or we're going to really fuck up the time schedule on ourselves, Lieutenant." Colonel Leadbetter bitched into the helmet radio in an effort to get Walker moving.

"Colonel, I have heavy weapon fire coming from every stinking windows of the complex."

"Well take them asses out and get your ass inside the place. We're falling behind schedule."

"Roger that last Colonel, moving out si..." Walker's words were cut off by the pilot.

"Razor Blade to Sandstorm Commander! Come in sir. Over."

Colonel Leadbetter decided to allow Walker to take this communication from the pilot.

"Now what?" Walker moaned as he tapped his mike and then asked the Commander of the ready air cap. "Sandstorm here. What's up Razor Blade Flight Leader Sir?"

"Sandstorm, am picking up two fast moving inbounds heading your position as of..."

"What the fuck are these damn contacts you're picking up for crap sake, and what the hell are they up to, Razor Blade Leader? Are they a threat to my troops, and if so, do your damn act up there against them and take them out before they fuck us up but good down here. Over!"

"Sandstorm Commander, I make the two inbound contacts to be the Russian made Mig-31 Foxhounds by their radar signature return. Over." The lead pilot reported back to Walker.

"Then go fox hunting man. You gotta keep those lousy fuckers offa my stinking ass down here, or I'm gonna abort this damn mission, and make my bird from this place. Over."

"Understood last as received Sandstorm Commander. Suggest you stay real low to the ground until we eliminate the twin inbound contacts. Over."

"No shit Sherlock. Get it fucking done for my ass man. Over." Lieutenant Walker growled, and then he opened communications for the rest of his troops and warned them. "Okay people listen up, we have two enemy fighter aircraft rapidly closing in on our position fast. Hunker down until I give the all clear signal out. Who's manning the fucking forties?"

"Baby Tee here along with Sergeant Ramirez, Lieutenant. We got the forties covered and hot and ready for immediate action, honey."

"Baby Tee, send Raz up here, have One Finger man her forty for her. I want you to work over those damn windows on the side of the complex. I can't have my stinking people move out under this much enemy fire. Silence those damn guns for us man!" Walker shouted.

"You got it, all you had to do is ask and you shall receive from the Lord above, my son." Tee purred sexily. Instantly, a number of 40 mm grenades started to pound away at the side of the Iranian building, a number of them got in through the shattered windows. One enemy machine gun stopped firing, but the other one continued to fire at the American troops.

Sergeant Dorothy Ramirez worked her way up to Walker's side as ordered, and then she slapped him on his armor plated rump. Walker barely took any notice of her as he concentrated his full attention on the target and then bitched at her. "Hey Raz, you and Fun Bags linkup with Boot Camp and the three Russian babes. Keep your eye on them stinking foreign bitches for me, and take them out if you think they're trying to fuck us over any. Once we're inside the damn complex, you come with me wherever I go inside the damn dump." Walker warned his lover.

"Oh C'mon Walker, I can't believe you still don't trust them female Russian fighters?"

"No I don't! I might never trust the three damn Commie bitches, Raz."

"Wow, what a grouch you're getting to be lately Walker." Ramirez snapped back at him.

"Don't fuck with me right now will ya. I ain't in no fucking mood for any goofing around, kid. I lost one grunt and another one is bad hurt on this stinking operation already, Raz." Walker pointed his finger at Ramirez's nose and then he added. "You betta be damn careful and be serious. I don't want anything happening to that little ass of yours." Walker allowed a smile.

RAZOR BLADE FLIGHT LEADER

"Razor One to trailers Razor Two and Razor Three, line up on my wing. We have to do a little fox hunting before these bastards give our ground pounders any trouble down there. Over." The Commander of the Razor Blade Flight warned his wing personnel.

Razor Flight Leader waited until his Wingmen were on both sides of his wings thirty yards behind, and sixty feet below his position. The sleek F-18 D twin seat aircraft soared in the dark sky. The flames from their twin engines in afterburner lightening up the sky behind their aircraft like shooting stars blazing their way through the heavens.

Razor Leader spoke to his weapons officer or Wizzo in his rear seat of the plane. "Arty, keep me informed on the damn inbounds positions. I have to know where the creeps are and their speed if I want to defeat the bastards. Can you identify them as Russian Foxhounds yet?"

"Phil, the inbounds are coming at us at Angels Fifty Seven, at Nine Hundred Knots. Their course and speed indicates they are a pair of Foxhounds, sir. I'll confirm with Big Eye, sir."

Big Eye was the AWACS (Airborne Warning And Control System) aircraft controlling flight information for this mission.

"Razor One to Big Eye. Need a confirmation of speed, altitude, and identification on the twin enemy inbounds our area. Over." The lead rear pilot offered to the AWACS Commander.

"Big Eye to Razor Blade Leader. Positively confirm the pair of inbound bandits are Russian Mig-31 Foxhound bandits, sir. Repeat, the twin inbound bandits are identified as Mig-31s. Information's confirmed with your read as first reported sir. Do you wish me to give you a quick rundown on your requested information for the inbound bandits, sir? Big Eye Over."

"Razor Flight Leader to Big Eye. Negatory on that request, will rely on own information on inbounds. Keep monitoring my output, and make certain my information's correct. Out."

"Roger that Razor Flight Leader. Will keep you advised as requested sir. Big Eye Out."

"How are they flying Art?" The pilot asked his weapon's officer.

"Close formation, good shape for inbounds. They must be experienced fighter pilots. Or..."

"Or what?" Phil snapped back in the mike. "Now's not the time to go thick on me pal."

"Phil, the twin inbounds could be being flown by a lair of fucking Russian pilots, sir. I heard some scuttlebutt a few weeks back about many defecting Russian pilots offering their services to Iran, and Iraq, with Libya, and any other Arab nation willing to pay the asking price for their services, sir." The Wizzo replied to his pilot.

"Shit. Yeah, right, okay, we're going to go under the damn assumption the two inbounds are Russian pilots flying those damn things then, and we'll act accordingly against them if and when we make contact with the two inbounds, Art. Razor Two, Flight Leader, you'll be my Wingman for this engagement. Razor Three, you're our safety air cap. Get up to Angels Fifty, and stay in the sun, if we get in any trouble on this engagement, drop down and engage the enemy's Six."

"Roger that last Razor Leader." Razor Three immediately peeled off and climbed into the sun.

"Art, where the hell are those two bastards hiding on me out there for Christ sake?"

"Coming in from the north, northeast, increasing speed to nine, twenty, three, and beginning their drop down on us. They're down to Angels Forty and still dropping. Thirty miles out, sir."

"Do you think they know we're hanging around out here, Arty?"

"You can bet the damn farm they know we're out here sir." His Wizzo warned him.

"Then why the hell aren't they preparing to engage us for Pete's sake? What the hell are these two bastards up to, dammit?" The pilot asked.

"No idea. Maybe they think we're on their side or something."

"Any hits from their IFF or radar tags, Arty?" The pilot asked his Wizzo.

"Nope. Not a peep coming from either of the two enemy inbound aircraft, sir."

"Fine, we'll act like some dumb Iranian pilots then until they decide to challenge us. Keep their location and speed coming in for me Arty. John, are you reading this crap with me?"

John was the pilot of Razor Two. "That's a Roger on last. Loud and clear sir. Over."

"Okay, go master arm but don't tickle any warheads just yet sir. I want to try and bluff these two jokers as long as I can, Arty." The pilot ordered his Wizzo.

"Roger that, master's armed and ready for action sir. No report from the warheads, ready to engage the twin enemy inbounds on your command. Over." Arty informed his pilot.

"Here we go. Increasing speed to max, let's go ballistic on the lousy bastards and see if that move wakes up their lazy asses." Phil moved the throttles of his Hornet up to the stops, and the Hornet ripped through the air at over one thousand one hundred and ninety knots, or Mach One point Eight as the excited pilot announced. "Beacon on, set double pulse mode."

"Roger that last Captain. Beacon's set on double pulse mode sir. Over."

The second the two sleek F-18's went to Mach One point Eight, the two Russian pilots immediately realized these two aircraft could not possibly be Iranian pilots coming at them.

They probed the unidentified and rapidly approaching aircraft with their own IFF system, and when the aircraft did not respond to the probe, they instantly took evasive action.

"Phil, I have an IFF probe. Shit, I have a lock on radar pulse, they're hunting us now sir, dammit. The bastards are trying to lock us up sir. Over." Razor Two reported to Razor Leader.

"Dammit, how far out are they, Arty?" The pilot snorted in the radio.

"Eighteen miles out and closing fast on us sir." Arty replied as he checked them.

"What's the latest scoop on their lock on radar beacon? I need some words man."

"Our jamming's playing pure havoc with their radar and lock on abilities, every time they burn through it, our boys change the channel and they have to start all over again, sir."

"What about our own damn radar systems? Are we picking up any of this interference?"

"Were working just fine sir. I have a strong target signature and response from our lock-on abilities as well, sir. Should I arm the warheads sir?" Arty replied to his pilot.

"Launch, launch, launch, I have a positive launch missile from the right Mig. Second launch, I have a second launch from Mig two." The Wizzo from Razor Two reported in a high pitch tone.

"Arty, God dammit! Talk to me man!" The pilot screamed in his radio.

"I have positive missile launch from both inbounds sir. I make the weapons to be long range Russian R-33 SARH air to air missiles sir. The two enemy inbounds have to be firing blind at this point, I know they can't see us through our heavy electronic haze we're pounding them with. They're trying for dumb luck shot against us sir, the missiles have been unable to lock on."

Suddenly, the F-18 Hornet's threat warning signal blurred to life and the Wizzo screamed out excitedly. "I can't believe this shit, somehow the god damn R-33 missile has successfully locked on us, take evasive action Flight Commander. Dive and break right. Dive! Dive!"

"Christ Almightily, how the hell did those pieces of Russian built shit successfully lock on to our fucking ass, dammit?" Phil growled as he did as ordered, dropping his aircraft several thousand feet and then breaking off hard to his right, and then pulling back hard on his stick and sending his aircraft shooting almost straight up in the air.

"Dumb luck, break left. Climb, it's getting a good run on us Captain. Climb, I'm firing off hot bags and flares. Break right, level flight." With a noticeable sigh, the Wizzo reported. "There it goes sir, the missile's locking onto the hot bag. She's dropping down to the earth blind."

"I'm finished playing around with these fucking birds. It's time to engage the bastards and show them who the hell's who, and who's going to kill who in the air, dammit. Art, where the hell are the two bandits, and what are they up too?" The pilot of the Hornet asked his Wizzo.

"Both enemy inbounds are flying six miles off our starboard side and dropping down to Angels Ten. It looks like that shot was to serve as a warning for us to back off them sir. It seems like the two inbounds have a mission in mind, and they won't deviate from it until it's done."

"That's good, we'll have the upper hand on the dopey bastards then. Razor Two, Razor Leader. Come in. Over." The lead pilot called his second in command.

"Razor Two. Go with traffic Razor Flight Leader. Over." The second plane's pilot replied.

"Razor Two, I'm going to attack the two enemy inbounds from Six, Six, Three, at Angels One, Four. I'll be coming at them from the sun. Going in with AIM-9W, arming long range Sidewinder missiles. I'm singling out the lead bandit of the two sir. The other bandit's your responsibility to eliminate, sir. Beginning my run on the damn inbound aircraft. Over."

"Roger that last, good hunting Razor Leader. Beginning my attack on remaining bandit."

The two American Hornets dropped down to fourteen thousand feet, and they aligned up with the glare from the sun blotting out their approach on the two enemy aircraft. The American pilots waited for the inbounds to line up on their original course and speed. Once they were certain the two enemy inbounds were ignoring them, the pilots began their attack on the Iranian planes.

Razor Blade Leader dipped his aircraft into a steep roll maneuver as he lined his aircraft up on the first enemy inbound aircraft. The attacking American pilot refrained from locking up the enemy inbound on his attack radar until the last possible moment. The pilot knew the instant he painted the enemy craft with his tracking and lock-on radar system, the bandit would immediately begin evasive maneuvers against his attack. When his F-18 was less than two thousand yards from the tail feathers of his target, the pilot flipped on his arming radar that instantly locked up the bandit with the sidewinder's homing warhead. The bandit realized he was about to die, and the pilot placed his aircraft in a hard vertical dive, and then tried a number of radical evasive maneuvers, jinxing his plane up and down and from left to right. But it was all for naught, the sidewinder missile was like a pit bull once she locked on this close.

The inbound enemy aircraft tried popping off some flares and hot bags in a last ditch attempt to try and fool the rapidly closing in sidewinder missile, but nothing the Russian pilot did would change the sidewinder's mind, as it continued to close in on his aircraft. With a flash of flames and smoke, the tail end of the Mig erupted in a small ball of fire as the aircraft began to break up while still in flight from the explosion on the rear of the plane.

Phil then immediately placed his aircraft into a tight victory roll off to his left, as he climbed and increased speed, searching for his wingman and the other inbound enemy Zapper.

The voice of the pilot of Razor Three filled the radio next. Ralph was excited as he spat out orders to Razor Two's pilot. Phil leveled off at Angels Fifteen and started searching for Razor Two's aircraft, spotting him below his aircraft, he began to direct his attack on the remaining Iranian plane flying just above him.

"Razor Two, get a lockup on the sonofabitch. Lock the bastard up, or he's going to do you in. Don't pay attention to his evasive actions. Ignore that other crap he's doing and stay glued to his tail feathers like a fly on shit, and lock him up and take your shot at the bastard, pilot."

"I missed him. Dammit, I couldn't pull on his fucking ass. I didn't get a solid lock on tone from the target before he was able to veer off on me." The Razor Two pilot complained as he stared at the Russian plane leave his attack sights.

"Forget about the miss pilot, your target's getting away on you sir. He's heading north at Angels Seven. Heads up, he's banking hard, he's turning back on you. Here he comes right at you! Razor Two, get down on the hard deck sir! Get down on the damn deck! Your bandit's traveling at five hundred knots. Get right, get right and go vertical." The lead pilot warned.

Razor Two placed his aircraft in a hard dive as he slammed the throttles home, and the Mig fighter aircraft shot passed him on level flight with his Gsh-6-23 23 mm 6 barrel cannon blazing, one hundred and twenty rounds missed their target of the Hornet's tail feathers. As the faster F-18 shot towards the earth like an out of control rocket to save the life of the aircraft.

"High Cover, High Cover, get in there or that fucking Zapper's going to ace John." Phil growled, all the while he was cursing himself for being caught out of position to help the younger pilot of the flight group. He watched out of his cockpit as the High Cover Hornet dropped down, and began efforts of trying to get on the Six of the Iranian plane dogging his other pilot's aircraft.

Ralph went vertical in flight, charging wildly after the enemy Mig fighter aircraft. In an all out effort to try and cut him off as the Zapper tried to get on John's Six again. (Tail)

The bandit was so intent on locking up the fleeing and more inexperienced Hornet pilot, he completely ignored the other two American warplanes in the vicinity. Twice he got a weak lock-on tone on John's fleeing F-18, but due to a series of hard banking turns and jinking, John broke off the lockup of the enemy missile on his plane.

Ralph was able to finally get his Hornet on the bandit's tail without much trouble, and then contacted Razor Two to inform him of his position. "Razor Two, I have your Six. This Zapper's mine, keep jinking until I lock him up. Hang in and don't let him get the best of you sir."

Ralph worked his way up on the inbound bandit's backside until he had good position on the enemy aircraft, and he instantly locked him up with his attack radar in a effort to have him back off the tail end of the Hornet he was trying to engage and destroy. Razor Two heard the report in his radio as the other pilot offered his attack set up.

"Fox One, I have a good positive lock-on tone on the enemy target, taking my shot. Fox One away. Missile's in good flight and detection. Missile has locked onto the damn bandit." A second later, another report from the Razor Three pilot. "Got the bastard. Splash one Russian Mig aircraft, he's on his way to Paradise. Razor One and Two, let's get the hell out of here, and back to our air cover over the ground pounders, and assist their damn mission if they run into any trouble down there. Over." The lead pilot warned the second pilot over his radio.

"Roger that Razor Three. Over." The Razor Two pilot replied as he dared a look behind him in time to see the Mig aircraft breakup while in flight from the missile hit on the tail of his plane. The body of the aircraft went into a flat spin, and the pilot hit an unsuspected air pocket, and the plane began to tumble end over end. An explosion engulfed what was left of the disintegrating aircraft, and it turned it into a free falling fireball of death, heading towards the earth.

"Razor Flight Leader to Razor followers, see any chutes from the enemy pilots?" The lead pilot asked the other two pilots. He was out of position to enable him to see behind his aircraft easily. So he was relying on the other pilots to report chute bloom from the destroyed plane

"Razor Two to One. No sir. I see no chute plum at this time sir. Over."

"Razor Three to Razor One. No, I don't think the pilot was lucky enough to get out of the mess in time to save himself, sir. Over." Razor Three pilot reported in a low tone.

"Shit, I didn't want that to happen dammit. I didn't want to take the damn pilot's life. I just wanted to destroy his damn aircraft or drive him out of the area. Well there was no other way out of this mess than death for the enemy pilot. I wish his family well, he was a brave fighter. Over."

"Agreed. Over." The other two American pilots added to their leader's words over the radio.

The two Hornets formed up in a tight formation on Razor Blade Leader's wings, and the three aircraft headed back to their responsibility zone to support the ground troops engaging the Iranian complex security units, as they continued to attack the complex constructed in the very heart of the deep Iranian desert.

THE SANDSTORM GROUND FORCES

Lieutenant Robert Walker stared at the flaming debris of the destroyed aircraft as it tumbled towards the ground. Once he was certain the Iranian planes were done in, he ordered the attack to begin against the complex and defenders. "Walker to troops, go active. We're hot, so let's get this damn thing over with so we can get the hell out of sand land and back to the real world."

Walker was the first soldier to jump up and charge towards the Iranian complex emptying his MP-5 at the windows where the enemy weapons fire was coming from, as he ran at the building. No return fire came from inside the complex at this point. The young Lieutenant ran until he dropped down to the ground, and then he tumble up against the side of the structure. Leaning against the cement wall, he waited for the rest of his troops to catch up to him. Half of his group split up and went to either side of the main doors of the structure. The Lieutenant peered in the plate glass doors and was surprised to see the shutters closed on the inside, and he growled at his troops. "EOT get up here, the bastard closed some kinda door on the inside of the dump."

"On the way up to your position ns with the rest of my team, Lieutenant."

Walker looked to Buckethead and CoCo-G, both soldiers were out of breath and leaning up against the wall gulping air. "Can either of you slugs see anything moving around in there?"

Buckethead moved over to take a better look through the slit between the shutters in the complex, and dropped on his ass when two rounds struck the glass where he was trying see through, and he grumbled at his commanding officer. "Christ Almighty Walker, the fucking assholes have a god damn wall of crap stacked up in front of them, and they're shooting at us from behind it at anything that moves out here man."

"How many targets didja see inside there when you looked, Buckethead?"

"How the fuck am I supposed to know the answer to that question, man? I didn't take the time to count any heads while they were trying to blow my fucking noggin offa my damn shoulders, sir." Buckethead ran a paw over his helmet, and felt the dent in it from where the bullet struck it. Then he complained again. "They tried to take my head off, look." Bucket held his helmet out.

"If they tried to hurt that damn block of yours you call your noggin, they woulda needed one of those damn artillery pieces to get you attention, buddy." Neck grunted from behind the grinning Walker. The soldiers bunched up with Walker laughed over Buckethead's complaint.

The Explosive Ordinance Team made it up to Walker's side, and then waited for orders.

"I want a bunker bag (C-4 satchel explosive) placed up against those damn doors. Check it out, but be damn careful while you're at it guys. We have a coupla bad asses in there, and they're head hunting anything that moves out here. Do you think one stinking charge will be enuf to blow this mess the hell outta the way for us?" Walker grumbled at him.

The soldier branded Wild Card, Sergeant Edein S. Casillas checked out the doors and barrier constructed behind it. After studying it for a moment, the soldier decided to add a second charge to his efforts, just in case the enemy placed heavier objects in the mess he could not see clearly.

Walker agreed with his decision to add the second charge against the doors, he wanted to create as much shock and awe as possible against the Iranian defenders now trapped inside the complex. He was hoping the second charge would knock most of the fight out of the Iranians. He gave Wild Card the nod and then ordered his troops to the left of the door to pull around the other side of the building for their safety. The Lieutenant and the other troops with him stayed with the EOT until the charges were set, and then he made sure his people were well out of the way, he gave the nod to the explosive team as he joined the other soldiers on the side of the building.

The EO team gave Walker time to get out of the way, before they pulled the fuses of the explosive charges. Then the team rushed behind the protection offered by the building to join Walker and the other soldiers hunkered down with him. For what seemed like a lifetime, the fifteen seconds ticked away, and then a set of heavy explosions took place. The charges went off so close together one could not tell two charges just went off.

Lieutenant Walker noticed charades of shattered glass and chunks of concrete, with parts of the iron shutters fly by his face. He leaned against the side of the building and felt it tremble from the force of the twin explosions. He then lifted his weapon to firing position, and cautiously worked his way towards the main doors. Buckethead, and the soldiers with him, moved up from the other side of the complex. When Walker got to the corner of the structure, he looked to see if anyone might give him any information on what was going on inside the hall they just blasted through. Scanning the troops, he spotted Baby Tee with the grenade launcher. He then tapped his helmet mike, and whispered in it at the female soldier. "Walker to Baby Tee."

"Go ahead sugar. I'm here for you as always honey." Baby Tee replied to Walker's call.

"Tee, can you see inside the shattered doors?"

"Easy enough Walker. From where I'm positioned, I can see pretty well inside the structure."

"Great baby girl. See if can you spot anyone moving around in there for me, girl?"

"Lemme see sugar. Yes, I see two Iranian soldiers armed with AK's hiding behind a wall of desks and other crap sir. Do you want me to place a few grenades inside to soften them up?"

"Can you lob a few in and not hit us while you're firing at the structure, sister?" Walker asked.

"Easy Walker, if I wanted to hit you, I'd hit you real easy baby." Tee warned Walker.

"Then do it and stop clowning around with my stinking ass will ya little sister." The Lieutenant growled at the smallish female soldier as he glared at her.

"Wow grouch consider them on the way sugar." Tee fired five grenades in rapid succession, once she finished she waited until the smoke settle down. When she could see inside the building clearly again, she scanned the barrier of desks. She located an Iranian soldier lying in the middle of the twisted mess, the soldier was obviously dead and she reported. "Tee to Walker."

"Go Tee. What do you have for me sister?" Walker asked the pretty female fighter.

"Lieutenant, I see one organ donor, he's down and dead. There's no sign of the other one I spotted inside the building though. You want me to fire another set of rounds off to make certain the second one's done, Walker dear?" The female warrior asked her commanding officer.

"Don't ask just do it, dammit. I'm going in right behind the last grenade going off, I'll count."

"Then I'll fire slow so you can keep a better count on the rounds fired. On the way Walker."

As the three new grenades blew up inside the building, Walker moved nearer the main doors. He removed a grenade from his Alice strap, seeing Buckethead standing on the other side of the doors, he pitched the grenade to him, and then he held up three fingers. He then removed a second grenade from the harness and pulled the pin and then waited for Buckethead to do the same with his grenade. He then counted to three using his fingers and mouth movements to show Buckethead the count, and then he pitched the grenade inside the hallway of the complex, Buckethead did the same with his grenade then ducked down a bit.

The second the grenades popped off inside the hall of the Persian complex, Walker and Buckethead immediately jumped in the shattered doorway, their weapons blazing on full as they attacked the structure. Bullets ripped into the pile of upturned furniture, making metal and wood splinters fly in the air as the bullets tore into the mess. The spent cartridges fell to the floor in a musical tone, making walking dangerous on the attacking American soldiers. Walking on spent cartridges was like trying to walk on a floor covered with marbles. The Lieutenant ejected an empty clip, and then he slammed another one home, he cocked his weapon and again fired wildly into the jumble of destroyed office furniture and other items the Iranians had stacked up.

An enemy round suddenly punched Walker in the shoulder, but it did not penetrate the body armor. It let him know he was just hit by a round though. He roared a curse and dropped to the ground and searched where the round was fired from. In the shadows of the hall, he noticed a slight movement and he pumped seven rounds into the void. A body fell out barely twitching. Buckethead saw the movement and he fired at the falling body also, making it dance along the floor as the rounds tore through the body. Behind the soldiers, the rest of the troops poured into the building and they quickly fanned out in the long hallway, covering their fellow soldiers as they moved deeper into the structure. They added their fire to Walker and Buckethead.

The second Lieutenant Walker disappeared inside the building, Colonel Leadbetter contacted Nightwind. This was the Wing of F-117 stealth fighters standing by, he ordered these aircraft to mine the roads and flats reinforcing Iranian troops might use to make their way to the besieged Iranian structure. After giving the orders, the wise Colonel then checked the sky for the stealth aircraft moving to carry out their new orders.

Within mere moments, the first of the wing of Nightwind aircraft swooped in and dropped the Lazy Dog II CBU-75 cluster bomb containers on the road's surface. The twin canisters seemed to glide over the sand packed road until it popped open, depositing seventy five miniature anti tank and personnel mines, until it fell empty out of the sky and landed off the side of the road Walker ordered mined by the aircraft. A second and then third stealth fighter dropped their Lazy Dogs ordinates, and as fast as they appeared over the roads leading towards the complex. The almost completely invisible aircraft disappeared in the darkness protecting them from enemy attack. The only thing seen were the canisters as they sprayed the mines out on each side of the road.

The same process was carried out on every flat area and sand road surrounding the entire Iranian complex. The instant the mines were laid down, the soldier branded Poncho Villa, Sergeant Robert Lopez put his computer on, and it instantly linked up with the mine field laid down in his sector of responsibility. When the mines checked in with his computer, they were immediately activated. It gave Poncho the power to set off certain sections of the mine field while holding the other charges in reserve. This would enable him to head off any frontal assault from possible reinforcing of the trapped personnel inside the complex. The mines were set off in the conventional way, by having pressure placed on their detonation prongs. On the other hand, he second Poncho's computer lost contact with the mines, they would automatically detonate on their own. This was to ensure the troops would not leave an active mine field behind when they pulled out of the area, or leave anything useful to the enemy at the same time.

According to United Nations decorate of 17789593, this was the only way any land mines would be allowed to be employed in any military action taking place anywhere in the world. A nation using the old style land mines that would not self detonate when their military operation was over, and it remain active after the opposing troops had pulled back, would suffer the wrath of the world for leaving behind an active land mine field for civilians to wander into.

Once Colonel Leadbetter was certain he had all possible approaches to the Iranian complex covered with man power and land mines, he turned his attention back to Lieutenant Walker's part of the operation. Overhead, a constant hovering pair of Spectre AC-130 A/H Gunships circled over Colonel Leadbetter's position, to add their massive fire power to the defense that the ground forces might have to employ against any possible Iranian reinforcing troops, or the defenders trapped inside the complex.

THE IRANIAN MAIN COMMAND CENTER

General Ghelamerza Ardebili ordered his light armor companies in gear. He was in command of a modern Tank and Motorized Rifle Company consisting of ten outdated Russian built T-72 tanks, ten BMP-3 armor troop carriers armed with 100 mm gun, a 30 mm gun, a pair of ATGMs (Anti Tank Guided Missiles) and one hundred well trained Iranian soldiers. His second company consisted of five outdated T-64 light tanks, nine ancient and rusting BTR-50P track machines built in 1957, armed with 12.7 mm MG with a speed of twenty five mph and forty five ground troops. The Iranian Officer had a unit of soldiers on a training mission, and he ordered them to form up and support the complex from the south side. The heaviest weapons these troops had was a pair of American made M-60 machine guns. The Iranian soldiers were armed with an array of M-16s, AK-47s and old British bolt action rifles and other weapons of no importance.

The Iranian General was satisfied he had a third force of soldiers already marching on the complex from the south. He hoped this would enable him to catch any possible invading American soldiers between his three forces, and easily annihilate them before they had a chance to destroy the installation. He was concerned no word was received from the two fighter aircraft sent out by command to check on the situation possibly taking place at the complex. He did not like going into a battle blind. He took the lead and gave the signal, and the column of military machines followed the road leading towards the complex, whose location was known only by the General. He knew his troops coming in from the south would reach the complex well before his troops did, because of the slower BTR-50Ps he used, and he gave orders to report to him what they found once they arrived at the complex, so he would know better what he was up against.

CHAPTER TWENTY EIGHT

THE AMERICAN SANDSTORM'S FORCES INSIDE IRAN

Lieutenant Robert Walker's progress was being hampered by the heavy return fire he was receiving from the Iranian defenders inside the structure. Many times his troops were forced to stop their advance to pound the defenders with small arms fire and stun and fragmentation grenades. Every time he thought they were getting the upper hand on the defenders, return fire came from every nook and cranny inside the building, and from every shadow, stairway and door, completely stopping his advance until they took out the resistors.

The American troops were trying to work their way into the labs where the heavier radioactive contamination was being registered on their equipment. The doctor working with the American troops took up the rear position with the huge soldier branded No Neck. Walker was ten feet away from the stairway leading up to the second floor of the complex. He estimated there were at least five defenders blocking the stairway against them. He emptied a clip at the stairwell, and then ordered Buckethead, the three Russian female soldiers along with Boot Camp and Sun Tan, to secure the second floor. The Lieutenant made certain Sergeant Ramirez linked up with him, and allowed Fun Bags to go off with the splinter group aiming at the stairway.

Talking through the gas mask was a pain, and it forcing the Lieutenant to scream at the soldiers to be heard by the other troops as he called for more stun grenades to be lobed into the stairway area. He had to lift the mask to be heard properly by the troops. The radiation inside the complex was screwing with the radio communications on the invading soldiers.

Walker, along with the Mutt, Ramirez, McNip, Wacko went with Neck and the doctor armed with an AR-18, even though the Lieutenant knew the civilian doctor was unfamiliar with using the weapon. But this gave the unit another weapon to draw fire from, though it was doubtful the doctor would hit any enemy he fired at inside the complex. The young Lieutenant felt it would also give the civilian doctor something to do besides being dragged all over the complex by hand by his troops. Ali Baba, Snatch, Danko, CoCo, Dago, and Smith and Wesson accompanied Walker and the other soldiers on the assault on the complex.

No Neck, Sergeant Robert Abbott, had a number of sleep grenades on his person, and Walker instructed him to lob the grenades at the Iranian defenders he could not get at from his present position. Neck immediately tossed the two grenades as if they were oranges and the defenders lurking inside the stairwell and they began choking on the knock out gas. But they did something Walker did not count on, instead of dropping to the ground and going out, the Iranian defenders made a suicide charge at him and his troops. With AK's blazing, the five defenders charged Walker, forcing both him and Sergeant Ramirez to hunt for cover. They were caught out of position and had to drop down behind some destroyed furniture.

This forced Neck and the other soldiers to step up and take over the attack as they hit the enemy defenders with heavy return fire. Six enemy soldiers were dropped before they could reach the pinned down Walker and Ramirez. He poked his head out from a sideways lying desk, Ramirez was stuffed inside the foot well by the Lieutenant who forced her into the cramped area for her own safety when the defenders began their attack against them.

The Mutt was extremely excited as he quickly checked on his friend's condition, seeing him with Ramirez's rearend stuck in his face, he retorted at the Lieutenant. "Man, that's what I needed to see, another bad fucking habit for me to pick up, buddy. Walker, don't you think of anything other than eating out some pussy man? You gotta do that crap even on a mission, huh?"

Walker was relieved the action ended so quickly as he picked up a broken chair leg and tossed it at the Mutt who easily brushed the wooden missile aside with a shoulder movement. The friendly moment ended abruptly when renewed enemy fire came from the steel and lead lined doors of the main lab, forcing the soldiers to jump for cover for a second time. The Mutt ended up sitting on Walker's chest and he grumbled at his commanding officer. "Dammit, how many of these lousy fucking pukes are there still alive inside this damn dump, man?"

"Enuf to keep us busy I'd say Mutt. Buckethead, the stairway looks clear enuf for you to start up for the second floor. Keep your eyes open for Mother's group, they should be working their way down from the roof area by now. Jesus, I wish I had Casper or the Hunter in here, dammit."

"They're here Walker, they took up positions by the doors behind us, man."

Lieutenant Walker let out his breath in a rush as he blew in his helmet mike, and was surprised it still worked with all the battering his helmet was taking. "Casper, stop beating your stinking meat back there and get your stinking ass up disway, man. I need you, you got eyes like a stinking cat in the dark, maybe you can see through this crap for us. I can't afford to have these damn Iranian pukes roaming round in the damn dark, and coming at us when we least expect it. Whatsumatta, don'tcha wanna play around with these lousy sleazebags a bit, buddy?"

"I'm on my way up to your position Walker. And yes, I like dancing around with any dumb shits who want to be off on their stinking way to Paradise, man. Aim me at the bastards Lieutenant." Casper replied as he moved forward to Walker's position.

"I got a stack of stinking enemy defenders up the fucking wazoo over here, and you wanna stay back there and play cards with the stinking Hunter." Walker griped as both Casper and the Hunter quickly moved alongside him and the Lieutenant added to his gripe. "Whatdaya fucking people have carrying with you two love birds?"

"Stunners, but no sleeper grenades, Walker. I don't like the damn things. I like an instant reaction to my attack, man. I don't like to hafta wait until the bastards fall asleep on me man."

"Good, can you pitch the damn things through those damn doors, wiseguy?"

Casper looked at the doors, and then he replied to his commanding officer. "No way in hell Jose, them damn doors aren't open enuf to get the right angle for me to get the damn grenades in them, sir. Someone's gonna hafta blow them damn things open for us, or we're gonna find our asses bogged down for who knows how the hell long, man."

The first floor hall of the complex had been bathed in red light ever since Walker's people blew the power source for the entire structure. In an effort to stop the loss of computer memory, the building was placed on backup battery systems. The soft lights, combined with the thick smoke from grenades going off in the area, along with the fires still raging throughout half of the building, added to the terrible working conditions inside.

The Mutt looked over Casper's shoulder and grumbled at the Lieutenant. "Hey man I happen to agree with the stinking Ghost on this one, Walker."

"Who asked you for your two fucking cents in this conversation, buster?" Walker snapped before realizing what he just said to his lifelong friend and fellow soldier.

"Wow man, take about someone with a wild hair up his ass." The Mutt shot back at him.

Walker felt embarrassed over the way he barked at the Mutt and held up his arm and the Mutt banged arms with him as he replied. "It's cool Homes. This shit sucks the big one for all of us."

"Right O Mutt. EOT, I need you people up here with some stinking crash bangs."

"Moving up to your position Walker." The two man EOT moved up from their rear position. Walker's helmet radio blasted in his ear, it was Colonel Leadbetter, and he was already bitching at the Lieutenant. "Walker, what the fuck's taking you so damn long to secure the interior of that fucking building? You shoulda been completed with your mission by now, buster."

"I know that shit for Christ sake! Clear the fucking net Colonel! I need an open line so I can communicate with the rest of my troops working inside this stinking rat hole sir. I'll report back to you when we get the situation under fucking control, sir. We'll pick up the lost time when we get a handle on the damn defenders in here sir." Walker cleared the Colonel off his net.

"Who was that busting your stinking horns over the damn radio man? We're kinda busy to be wasting our time on the radio man." The Mutt grunted at Walker.

"Whatsisface is bugging my stinking ass, Homes. He wants this damn operation over with ten minutes ago." Walker grumbled at the Mutt.

"What the fuck did the stinking asshole want from your ass, Walker? You know something man, the stinking Colonel's getting real good with fighting any engagements we're set out on from the fucking cheap seats always behind our damn asses, man. If he wants to push us like he is, maybe he should come up here where the fighting's happening, and take some of the fucking heat for himself. Maybe then he'd get offa our stinking asses a little."

"Arrr... he's pissing and moaning that we're falling behind schedule on this stinking raid dog man. I told him to clear the fucking line, and we'll pick up any lost time later on, Mutt. I do hear your gripe and I agree with your bitch, Mutt." Walker replied and smiled.

"Fuck him where he breathes from man. If he wants us to move any fucking faster, like I said, let him get his stinking ass up in here and take some of the fricking heat from these damn Iranian snipers tearing us new assholes." The Mutt growled as he looked over his shoulder to where he believed Colonel Leadbetter was hold up and running the operation from their rear as he added to his gripe. "I gotta good mind to send a few rounds down his way for the hell of it, to let him know what it's like up here, dammit. Maybe then he'll get offa our case."

Walker ignored the Mutt's continuing complaining as he pointed towards the doors of the lab and ordered the EOT. "I want them fucking door outta there so we can get at the hairy motherfuckers we have trapped in there."

"Easy enuf from here, Lieutenant Walker." The EOT leader dragged his satchel charge bag over to his knees, and he removed a smaller shape charge. He cleared it, pulled the pin and then lined the bag up with the half open door and waited. All the while he waited, the smoke from the fuse whisked softly from the charge locked in his hands.

Neck stared at the sack charge, and then he placed some distance between him and the nut with the explosive, as he griped at the man. "Throw the fucking thing before the damn thing blows up in your fucking face, asshole. It's getting close to going off in your damn hands."

The EOD team soldier who was branded Zippo smiled at the other soldier, he was chewing on a four oh Mercury cap used to detonate a stick of TNT. Neck could see the number of small dents on the blasting cap from his teeth, and he moved ever further away from the mad bomber. The Neck was smart enough to know the proper pressure placed on the detonation cap would set it off, and the charge was powerful enough to easily take Zippo's head off his shoulders, and harm anyone near the charge at the same time.

"Hey pal, don't let your stinking shit get fucking hot on ya man, there's plenty of time left on the damn fuse. We don't need the bad guys grabbing our charge, and then pitching the damn thing back in our faces on us, do we now Homes?" Zippo complained at the Neck.

"Yeah, and we don't need you holding that fucking thing until it goes off in our stinking faces either you know, chum. Just throw the damn thing will ya, man." Neck warned as he lowered his weapon in a better firing position and then aimed it right at Zippo.

"Relax big man, everything's under control here buddy." Zippo smirked as he gave the charge a hard shove. It slid across the highly polished floor and stopped a foot before the two doors.

"If you're scared of a little pop, you betta put your head down between your legs and suck your dick right about now, Neck." Zippo hunched his shoulders just as the charge went off in the hall with the sound of thunder echoing. The blast made the soldiers lined up in the corridor ear's ring, as a few of them choked on the smoke that filtered into their masks. Walker heard the coughing and bitched at the soldiers behind him. "Who doesn't have their damn mask on right for crap sake? I see anyone without a fucking mask on, I'm gonna stick my foot so far up your ass, the water on my knee is gonna quench your fucking thrust."

"Walker, Zippo's fucking nuts man. You betta keep that madman far away from my stinking ass. Or I'm gonna snap him in half, and use his skinny ass legs as stinking toothpicks man." Neck warned Walker as he shifted his weapon across his chest, and then held it in a much more threatening manner at the grinning soldier branded Zippo.

"Don't start something you can't fucking handle big guy. One day you just might be taking a dump, and your fart's gonna end up carrying your ass right to the fucking moon, if you're not more careful with your damn threats aimed at my ass, fella." Zippo warned in a heated tone as he stared at Neck and his weapon pointing at his chest.

"You threatening my fucking ass buster? You betta go home and grow yourself bigger fucking pair of balls before you go off threatening my stinking ass like that, you little pissant."

"Enuf, cut the shit out before I hop the both of ya in the ass. In case you two shitbirds don't understand it, the stinking enemy's thataway people. They're the ones you're supposed to be fighting." Walker pointed towards the set of double doors hanging off their hinges.

"I'll lead the charge fur the rest of you slobs." The Mutt offered as he started to stand.

"Mutt, once you're inside the damn lab, drop off to your right and stay low. I'll be right behind your ass, and I'll go to the left and stay high. That way we'll catch any Iranian assholes in a cross fire. Raz, you follow me in and go off to my left, and remain standing to get a better bead on any pud fucker's firing at us. Dago, you follow the stinking Mutt in and go to the right and stay high as well. The rest of you people will follow and head down the gut of the damn lab, we'll give you cover fire from our positions. We have to secure the lab in a hurry it up, so the damn Doc can do his thing in there. Doc, you stay here until I send for your stinking ass. Stay behind that desk."

"Okay Lieutenant Walker." The doctor replied as he ducked lower.

"I don't believe this shit for one stinking second man. A stinking book worm anyway on a fucking military operation is nuts man." The Mutt snapped at the civilian, pissed they had to take the doctor with them as he pulled his weapon up and charged the destroyed doors. Casper and the Hunter pitched in a few extra stun grenades before the other soldiers ran into the lab.

The Mutt roared, screaming when he hit the ground inside the lad, and then he rolled to his side until he ended up behind a heavy metal filing cabinet. He took a defensive posture, and then he quickly scanned the interior of the room, using the barrel of his weapon as a pointer. To draw his attention to where he was aiming his weapon, and he bellowed for the follow on forces to hear. "Clear on the stinking right!"

Walker followed the Mutt in and went left. Scanning the area before replying. "Clear left!"

The grenades went off a second before both soldiers charged the lab. The flash, and shock wave and smoke created by the grenades served to disorient the Mutt for a quick moment. He had to shake the cobwebs from his head. He checked on Walker who ended up behind a cabinet, while aiming his weapon in the center of the lab. Both specialized soldiers spotted no one they classified as enemy moving around anywhere inside the room for the time being.

Walker thought he saw something move and he fired in that direction, causing the Mutt to respond with a few rounds of his own hitting the same area Walker just fired on. Seeing nothing in the room, Walker was trying to draw enemy fire to find their positions. No return fire came from within the lab, and he slowly stood and scanned the interior a lot better this time. He easily spotted six bodies, he gave a number of quick hand signals, and the other soldiers with him moved forward and they checked the down people. Two of the defenders were dead, another one was in bad shape, while the other three were just sort of stunned from the grenades.

Dago worked on the stunned workers, and realized the three of them were Russian technicians and he reported to the Lieutenant. "Hey Walker, I got me three shit filled Russian bastards here."

"Are they still alive stupid?" Walker snarled at Dago over his helmet radio.

"Yeah, but they're really shook up some man, you want me to talk them out of their misery and waste them?" As Dago mumbled the word stupid under his breath and shot a glare at Walker.

"No stupid, just hook the sonofabitches up and get the lousy bastards the hell outside and bring them over to the sled and hold them there."

'Stupid again huh?' Dago complained to himself as he began to follow Walker's orders.

Walker blew in his helmet mike and barked. "Colonel Leadbetter, I have three Russian technicians alive and in custody, sir. They're beat up some but they're still alive sir. Suggest you move the machines up so we can load the stinking prisoners and uther crap the civilian puke's gonna want taken outta this lousy shit filled dump, sir."

"It's on the way, is the complex fully secured Walker?" Colonel Leadbetter demanded.

"No Sir Colonel! Just the stinking lab we wanted to check out is fully secured at this time, sir. There are still a number of small wars going off in the halls and upstairs of this stinking dump, Colonel." Walker reported to the commander of the operation.

"You need any extra help in there securing the complex, Walker?" Colonel Leadbetter asked.

"Naw Colonel, we'll handle things just fine for ourselves, get the machines up here sir."

Colonel Leadbetter did not reply to Walker's last comment. Instead, he contacted the Roach, Sergeant David Burgwald who was left behind in order to protect the AAV-7s, sand sleds and the pair of Bradley fighting machines. "Leadbetter to Roach."

"Roach here. Shoot Colonel." The Roach offered, he was prepared to lend help to the soldiers.

"Move all the damn machines up, we're ready to load some shit in the damn things."

"It's about time, man. Moving them up to your position now, Colonel Leadbetter."

"Colonel, some of the damn Iranians supposed to be helping us, are moving out like their assholes are shitting out sparks, sir." Moss interrupted and reported.

"What the hell are they up to, dammit?" Colonel Leadbetter snarled back in his radio.

"Dammed if I know Colonel Leadbetter, all I do know for certain at this point is I'm picking up a helluva mess of small arms fire popping off in the direction the damn Iranian helpers are heading off in a fast hurry it up sir. You want me to head out and check it out and see what the devil the dumb shits are up to out there sir?"

"Yes. Check it out for me Moss. I want to know what those damn popping jays are up to out there. I don't need them hitting our stinking flanks on us." Colonel Leadbetter ordered the female fighter, and then he got back in communication with his Lieutenant.

"Leadbetter to Walker. Step it up in there for crap sake mister! We're about to run out of fucking time out here Lieutenant. I believe our Iranian friends just ran across an enemy patrol not too far away from the damn complex, and they're busy engaging the patrol, Walker. Moss is reporting small arms fire popping off in the direction the sucka's just took off in sir."

"I copy and I'll try and pick it up as much as I possibly can in here, Colonel. Doc, time's a resource we have very little of at this point, and we're about to run outta what we have left sir. We gotta step it up real quick in here, Doc. Or we might just get stuck leaving some of this crap you want behind, whaddaya want my fucking people to do fur ya, Doc?" Walker growled at the concerned looking civilian doctor as he held him in his angry gaze for the moment.

"Lieutenant Walker, have your people move to that bank of computers over there. I'll show you what the soldiers have to do to the machine to retrieve the information I need from them. In the interest of saving some time for us, have your people remove the cover of the computers like this, these four screws hold the cover in place. Then they have to reach in the computer and disconnect this stalk of wires from the hard drive, by removing the side clips holding the wires in place like this. Have the soldiers remove this screw holding the hard drive in place, remove it like this and carefully remove the hard drive like this, it's that easy Lieutenant.

"Then you have to tell your soldiers they have to be very careful doing this, once they have the hard drive free of the computer, they're to give it to me and I'll take care of it from there sir. Another thing you have to remove from this lab, over there resting on that stainless steel table is a nuclear warhead still under construction. We have to place it in that travel case on the floor by the other table, and get it and the other warheads sitting next to it, and get them loaded on the sand sleds for me, sir. That's the hard evidence we've been sent out to find by the President. With those warheads, and the evidence stored on the hard drives and inside the file cabinets, we'll have more than enough evidence to hang the Iranians in any court of law, sir."

The doctor was going to drain the information on the hard drives from the computers by using a portable Zip drive system and portable computer. Once he gleamed the information, he was prepared to load a virus into the computers, to destroy any terminal hooked up to try and retrieve the information he was going to bury deep within the computers. Being they were running out of time to carry this wish out, the doctor changed his mind, adding to this change was the fact he discovered the amount of radiation released inside the lab the soldiers were working in.

A grenade suddenly popped off on the second floor, drawing everyone's attention.

Walker looked at the ceiling as if he was trying to see through it, and moaned at his soldiers. "Shit, I wish to fuck I knew what the fuck was going on up there." He growled as he explained to the soldiers watching the doctor remove the first hard drive. The soldiers were concentrating on how to remove the covers, and identify and remove the hard drive a second time from the heart of the computer, to make sure they understood what they were supposed to do with the machines.

"Lieutenant Walker, what we have to collect here in the lab is more important than what's going on upstairs, sir." The civilian doctor hissed as he moved to the second computer, and skillfully removed the cover and worked on the wire harness hooked up to the hard drive.

"Doc, you telling me my stinking people upstairs are expendable for this stinking operation, mister?" Walker glared harshly at the doctor.

"Totally, as are all of us, Lieutenant. I need the hard drives from this bank of computers. I want, no, correct that

Lieutenant, I demand your people grab those file cabinets in the corner of the lab. I'm not going to waste any time with trying to find out what's important, and what's not stored inside the cabinets. I want everything removed and go with us, and we'll sort it out later. This place is as hot as they come, and I want everyone out of here in ten minutes, or I can't be held responsible for their health after that time Lieutenant." As if to emphasize his point, the doctor held up the Geiger counter and the gauge went off the scale.

Walker stared at the Geiger counter until he understood what the machine was warning him and bellowed. "CoCo-G, let McNip, Nintendo, and Raz work on the hard drives, the rest of you people are too heavy handed and might screw things up on us, dammit. You and Neck get those three warheads packed up and outside this dump pronto. The rest of you carry those file cabinets outta the stinking lab, we gotta get outta here PDQ. EOT, set charges, I want this dump to fall in on itself. Use enuf pop to do the job right, I don't want anything left to be of use to anyone."

Everyone carried out orders as received, with Walker's people giving the EOTs a wide birth. So they could set their charges without anyone getting in their way.

The follow on forces trailing Walker's group cleaned out the rest of the rooms and labs on the first floor. More weapons fire filled the first floor as the follow on forces located a number of hiding Iranian soldiers and quickly eliminated them. The new soldiers charged into every side room and closet on the first floor in their search of any enemy and information on what they were searching for inside the structure. The more pressure the Americans placed on the defenders, the more they reacted in turn, carrying out suicide charges. The fire on the first floor forced the bulk of the defenders up to the second floor as they setup against the American soldiers.

It was Buckethead and his group receiving the heaviest resistance from the Iranian defenders still trapped inside the building. Buckethead's group was forced to fight their way up the staircase and once on the second floor, they had to go room to room rooting out any resistance. Buckethead was not interested in weeding out the Russian technicians and taking them prisoners, he had his people enter the rooms while firing at anyone found inside. He believed there was no difference between the Iranians and Russian workers. Most of them were armed with MP-5s.

The three Russian women fighters were bogged down by nine defenders, firing at the warriors from behind a half wall. It took the combined fire power of Buckethead's group to beat back the resistance the invading soldiers were encountering, none of the defenders chose to give up.

Outside the building, the Roach and the other drivers moved their vehicles in place outside of the main doors of the Iranian complex. Walker's people loaded up the nuclear warheads on board the first sand sled, along with five of the twenty file cabinets they were taking from the complex. The way the cabinets were loading on the sled made it impossible for many of the American troops to have enough room to sit comfortably on the sled. This time they would be forced to stand while heading towards their extraction point.

Inside the complex, Walker kept screaming at his troops, trying to get them to move a little faster than they were moving. But nothing he threatened them with made them move any faster. They were moving as quickly as their jobs would allow them. The fuming young Lieutenant stood behind the doctor while he was shaking his arm where he was just tagged by a round. It was the second hit he took since the action started inside the complex. The pain was strong, and he was certain there was a cracked bone in his arm. He took his eyes from the doc and checked on the Mutt who was struggling mightily with a heavy file cabinet and bitched. "Hey Snatch, give the stinking Mutt a hand with that damn thing will ya before he drops a friggin nut on the damn thing. He's gonna bust a fucking nut if he tries to hump it by himself."

Walker's words were still echoing inside the lab when a shot suddenly rang out, and he saw the doc go down who was standing almost right in front of him. "Jesus!" He bellowed as he turned his weapon in the direction of the shot and emptied the clip. His rounds tore into a filing cabinet that was about ten feet away from where he was standing.

The Mutt, McNip, and Snatch also fired in that direction, their bullets destroyed one of the file cabinets, a body of a defender hiding behind it tumbled dead to the floor. The Mutt tagged the sniper once more in the head to make sure he was done for.

Walker rushed over to the doctor's side, and checked him out. The doctor was hit dead center of the chest plate body armor. There was a good size dent right over his heart area. The doctor was breathing hard and his eyes were pressed tightly closed and he was biting his lip, and he was drooling and crying like a baby who just received a spanking.

"Oh God, I'm hit, I'm hit, I'm going to die. Oh sweet Jesus I'm going to die. Lieutenant, where are you. I need your help sir. I'm wounded and I'm going to die, Lieutenant." The doctor began to cry as he held his eyes closed, afraid to open them because of what he might see.

"I'm right with ya Doc. So put a fucking sock in it will ya Doc! You're not gonna fucking die from that slight wound, you big baby you. Damn civilians anyway for crap sake." Walker hissed as he made sure the bullet did not penetrate the doc's body armor and he added. "C'mon Doc and be a fucking man about it will ya huh. The damn thing didn't even make it through your fucking armor, you shit filled spudhead. I know it hurts like hell Doc, but you gotta take the fucking pain and finish what you started in here man. Or we're gonna get fucked up real bad."

"It hurts like hell Lieutenant, I can feel blood running down my chest sir. I'm hurt Lieutenant, I'm going to die sir." The worried doctor still refused to open his eyes for Walker.

"Yeah Doc, you're right, you're hit man. As I told ya, the bullet didn't make it through your fucking body armor. You might be bleeding, and you might even have a stinking broken rib or two. But I assure you Doc, you're not gonna fucking die so stop crying like a little pussy. C'mon you big girl you, you gotta take the fucking pain, suck it up Doc and get back to your stinking job in here, buster. Or I'm gonna hop you right in the fucking ass, and then leave it behind for the Iranians to cook and eat once we're the fuck outta here." Walker warned the civilian doctor.

The doctor struggled to get his breathing and pain under control, and asked the Lieutenant. "You're not lying to me, are you Lieutenant? The bullet didn't make it through the body armor?" The doc moaned as he got control, he did not know he pissed himself. Slowly, the civilian felt the dent in his armor with his trembling finger, feeling no hole he breathed a little easier and offered. "Wow Lieutenant, it hurts like the bullet went right through the armor."

"Bet your ass it does Doc. But it hurts a lot less than being hit by a round without the plating on your ass. You gonna be okay to finish the crap you need from the computers and other shit?"

"Yes, I'll be fine in a little while sir. Give me a few seconds to try and collect my bearings though, Lieutenant." The doctor offered as he drew in a breath, and then let it out slowly.

"Sorry, but you don't have the stinking time to get friggin right again, Doc. You gotta get back to fricking work even though you're still suffering from the stinking hit, Doc. We gotta get the hell outta here before any stinking Iranian reinforcements arrive and we end up in a firefight." Walker smirked as he helped the doc to his feet and asked. "Are you sure you're okay Doc?"

"Yes sir, I guess I'll be fine in a few moments. I wish I could get in there and rub the pain from my ribs though, Lieutenant." The hurting doctor replied as Walker released his arm and allowed the civilian to stand on his feet. The Lieutenant stood at the ready to catch him if he fell from the pain still assaulting his body.

"Look Doc, tell ya what I'm gonna do fur ya sir. When we get back to the real world, I'm gonna fix it so some young hen will suck the pain outta your stinking body by the end of ya dick. Whaddaya say to that offer Doc?" Walker slapped him on the back and gave him a wink.

The doctor smiled and started to work on the next to last computer on the desk. He was still in a lot of pain, but he was doing his best to finish his job.

Ramirez moved over to Walker's side and she asked him with concern lacing her voice. "Have you heard anything from Fun Bags?"

"Not since she went upstairs with Buckethead, and the Russian babes, Raz."

"I wonder what's going on up there lover. There's still an awful lot of firing still going on up there you know Walker."

"I'll check it out for you if you want me to." Walker offered with a slight smile.

"Please, I'm really worried about her, she told me this was going to be her last operation. She wanted to settle down and have a few of the Mutt's babies. She's scared to death of this mission, she told me she had a gut feeling she wasn't going to make it through this one, Walker."

"I know how she feels, we're all getting too old for this shit, Raz." Walker moaned and then he blew softly into his helmet radio and warned. "Walker to Buckethead."

Buckethead was busy firing at a number of the well dug in Iranian defenders, armed with AK's and the small group of defenders seemed to know how to use the weapons. They were hiding in a doorway that seemed to be leading onto a second floor landing overlooking the lab on this floor. Buckethead ducked down and allowed Boot Camp and Sun Tan to replace him while he checked in with Walker to see what he wanted from him.

"Yeah Walker, what's up man?" Buckethead offered in his radio.

"I'm checking on how you're doing up there, buddy. You need any extra people up there to help ya out any, buddy?" Walker asked the big man then waited for his reply.

"Naw man, I'm doing lovely, just fucking lovely up here Homes. We got ourselves in one helluva shit storm with these fricking bad guys, Walker. I think every sonofabitching Iranian bastard who can carry a stinking weapon is on this damn floor, and they're mad as hell at me. Twice we were hammered by the damn defenders trapped up here, and it took our combined fire power to break up the trap they setup against us, man. The Russian babes are doing real great Walker, they're holding up their part of this stinking deal, and I think they're cool to work with. Walker, you're really off base about them babes. I believe we can trust them with our backs, pal." Buckethead offered as he cast a glance at the Russians doing their part for the mission.

"I don't give a stinking rat's ass about them Russian bitches! What about Mother and the rest of his people? They shoulda linked up with you by now. They were supposed to work their way down from the roof and assist you. Any fucking sign of them up there yet Buckethead?"

"No, but I hear a shitload of weapon's fire still going down at the uther end of the stinking hall where there's a set of stairs leading up to the next floor of this dump I believe, man. Hey Walker, it seems that every fucking Iranian bastard who was once stationed on the first floor of this dump, has ended up here, and I think Mother's people stopped them from making it up to the third floor of the complex. I believe once we get all the bastards done in on this floor, the stinking building should be completely secured, man." Buckethead broke off his communication because a swarm of bullets ripped into the jumble of office furniture he was using for shelter and cover.

"Bucket come back, are you all right up there Hoss? You need any fucking reinforcements up there to help you out any, big fella? I can hear the shit going down up there big guy. I can shake a number of grunts loose to give ya a stinking hand if you feel you might need it. Come back Bucket or we're coming up in fucking force." Walker bellowed into his helmet radio.

Buckethead checked to see what was going on in the battle they were locked in, and he picked up Sun Tan, Caviar, and Boot Camp pulling a number of dead enemy soldiers out from behind the long half wall they were hiding behind and firing from. With a deep sigh he spoke on the radio to his commanding officer again. "Naw Walker, I don't think I need any more fucking people up here to secure this stinking floor, thanks for the offer though man. It fricking looks like we're finally getting the upper hand on this fucking mess going down up here sir. I have three more stinking rooms I still gotta check out, and then the second floor should be completely secured. Hang on a sec Walker, something's up at the uther end of the hall."

Buckethead stretched his neck up, and saw Mother and three other soldiers assigned to him break out of the stairwell from the third floor, and the soldiers dove behind a different half wall. Buckethead continued to watch as they checked out the room nearest them. Weapons fire filled the hall and then Mother Flanagan came out of the room while lighting up a smoke, and he gave Buckethead the thumbs up signal. He then hung three fingers towards the ground. Buckethead waved to the soldier and then reported to Walker.

"Walker, Mother and the rest of his people just broke out and they're working on this floor, and they just erased three enemy shits from this action sir. Mother and his three soldiers are now working their way over to the next to last room not checked ou..."

"Just three fucking troopers are with him Bucket?" Walker interrupted his report.

"That's right Walker just three soldiers are with him, why man?" Buckethead asked.

"God dammit! That means he musta lost one of his guys upstairs, for crap sake."

Sergeant Ramirez tapped Walker lightly on his armor protected arm because she wanted to remind him about finding out how Fun Bags was doing on the second floor of the complex.

"Hold on a sec will ya Bucket. I got someone busting my horns again, man." Walker complained as he turned and looked at Ramirez.

"Sure thing man, it looks like we're starting to securing the fucking floor anyhow, sir. The rest of my people just entered the last room on this floor to be checked out. I don't hear any shit coming outta the room they just entered, man." Buckethead reported to Walker as he took a second to catch his breath and check on his people.

"What's up babe?" Walker asked Sergeant Ramirez.

"What about Fun Bags, Walker? That's why you made contact with Buckethead in the first place, Bobby." Ramirez looked at her man with tears building in her eyes.

"Oh shit yeah, I forgot all about her already. Hey Bucket." Walker said in his radio.

"Yeah go Walker, I'm still here man. It's really coming to an end up here man." Buckethead replied as he tore his eyes from what his people were doing to reply to Walker.

"Bucket, how's Fun Bags doing up there, buddy? Is she working or is she just looking good up there, big man?" Walker asked Buckethead as he kept his eyes glued on Sergeant Ramirez's face while making certain she was holding up to the fighting they we doing inside the complex.

"Dunno for certain man, I haven't seen much of her lately since all the heavy fighting started to take place, Lieutenant. She was right behind me a little while ago. But I'm sure she's fine wherever the hell she is at, Walker. I've been trying to keep her well out of the line of fucking fire up here while we contend with these lousy fucks still active here, Walker." Buckethead said as he looked behind himself, trying to see where Fun Bags might be at.

"I really appreciate that big man, thanks a shoe full for the concern for her. Bucket, the second you secure the fucking floor, check on Fun Bags and have her make contact with Raz before she has a stinking baby on me man. She's worried sick about her down here, Homes."

"Hey, what the devil's all of the worry down there about little old me for. I'm doing just fine up here thank you, big sister." Fun Bags voice came in over the squad radio to Walker.

Walker smiled when he picked up the relief etched in Ramirez's eyes once she heard her best friend was okay upstairs.

CHAPTER TWENTY NINE

REINFORCING IRANIAN TROOPS

The well seasoned and highly trained Iranian soldiers under command of the Iranian General, finally reached a point where the soldiers could make out the complex in the desert by Iranshahr. The Iranian Commander ordered his armored personnel carriers and foot soldiers to drop back, and allow his main battle tanks to take the lead of his advance units towards the complex, in case something wrong was happening there, and he did not know it.

The cautious Iranian General lead the column of foot fighters along with the T-64 tanks, fearing he might be heading into a trap. He held back the few newer Russian built T-72 tanks, to better defend himself in case he got his troops involved in a rear guard action, while trying to save his forward troops from slaughter. The wise Persian General allowed the older tanks to open up a thousand foot gap as they headed directly for the complex.

Captain Wilson was in command of the American forces designated as the northern security force for the operation. The Captain had his troops well dug in, and had the M-252 81 mm mortars set out for both attack and defense. He was sort of day dreaming when a trooper bellowed into the squad mike at him. "Jesus Captain, I have a number of fucking Iranian tanks coming in at us from Victor, Victor, Charlie, Alpha, November, Whiskey, One."

The Captain jumped to his feet as he quickly scanned with his infrared unit to the reported area of concern. His vision plate was filled with many obvious enemy signatures. And he grumbled "Dammit, it looks like the whole fucking Iranian Army is out there and coming at us." He changed to Colonel Leadbetter's frequency and blew in the mike. "Red Leader to Gold."

"Leadbetter here! Go Captain Wilson. What's happening with your troops, sir?"

"Colonel, I have at least a full company of advancing Iranian troops coming down the main road directly for the complex. It looks like a whole fucking Army of them, Colonel." Wilson reported as he continued to stare at the advancing Iranian troops closing in on his position.

"Whaddaya mean a whole fucking Army, Captain? What the hell's coming at us, soldier? Report, are they foot soldiers, and do they have any armor with them, dammit.

Shit, I knew we were fast ruining out of fucking time on target, dammit."

"Tanks Colonel Leadbetter! I see an enemy column of tanks rapidly moving in on us."

"Tanks! How fucking many of the damn things are coming at us for Pete's sake, Captain? What kind of damn tanks are they at that Captain? Report to me man."

"Colonel Leadbetter Sir, it's like Grand Central Station out there sir. Tanks, old ones, they look like the old and outdated Russian built T-64s, I count five, at least two hundred yards from my present position, and they're moving like they're expecting trouble. I'm picking up trailing armor units behind the first tank column. Some reserve tanks looks like the T-55's, maybe ten or more of the god damn things sir. There's more armor behind the second wave of armor I'm spotting, they could be APC's (Armor Personnel Carriers) and a heavy number of foot breathers, near as I can tell from my present position, Colonel. Over a hundred, maybe closer to a hundred and fifty enemy foot soldiers. I also have a number of APC's shitting out soldiers from their rears. It looks like they're taking a page from the Germans, and attacking with their armor first."

(APC-Armored Personnel Carriers, breathers is military slang for foot soldiers.)

"Got ya Captain, how soon before the leading elements tangle with the damn mine field sir?"

"Right about now Colonel! They're just about to enter it sir." The Captain reported.

"That should slow the lousy bastards down some for us, Captain. Okay Captain, keep me informed, I want to put as much real estate between us and them as possible. I'll see if I can free up a pair of Hornets, or a few F-22 Raptors for ground support. I'll have them thin out the enemy soldiers and armor for us, Captain. Leadbetter to Walker, you just ran out of fucking time in there mister. You have to get the fuck out of there right now soldier. I have an armor company of damn Iranian reinforcements rapidly closing in on the mine field double quick, Walker. I'm going to make contact with our air cap, and see if the birdmen can thin them out a little for us, before we have to tangle with the suckas. Hang in there Lieutenant, I'll be back to you."

"Roger that last Colonel. Am wrapping things up in here as we speak as quickly as possible, sir. Should be done and the fuck out of here momentarily, Colonel. You hafta keep those fucking Iranian reinforcements offa my can so we can get the hell out of here sir."

"Moss to Colonel Leadbetter. Come in sir. Over." The female fighter requested over her radio,

"Go Moss! What's going on with our supposed Iranian helpers, dammit?"

"Colonel, they're engaging a powerful Iranian Unit in the south sector of the complex area, sir. I think they should be able to hold them off until we can break out of here on our own, sir."

"Good deal Moss. Get back here on the fucking double, we're pulling out as soon as the other troops are out of the damn complex. Walker!"

"I heard that report, and I'm ending my part of this mess right now Colonel. What we have will have to be enuf for the Boss. Walker to all penetrating troops, time's up, wrap up what the fuck you're doing, and then get the hell out to the damn sleds. We're ordered to shove off in fifteen seconds. Any shits who miss the fucking boat, will have to swim back to the States. Check in or I'm coming out looking for anyone who don't report in."

"Mother here Walker, I have a shitload of stinking files I still gotta fucking account for, man. I'm scooping the damn things up now, and then me and the rest of the troops with me will be heading downstairs, Homes." Flanagan reported to Walker.

"Buckethead to Walker, I have a crap load of people spread out all over the damn place up here. It'll take me a bit longer than just ten seconds to organize them, and then carry the crap we located outta here, and get everyone together and accounted for, man. There's still a helluva mess of files, computer disks and video tapes we got Lieutenant, and we're still having some minor problems with a number of defender stragglers hitting us every time we try and enter a secured office sir. It's still fucking nuts up here, Lieutenant." Buckethead complained.

"Buckethead, listen close to me will ya, man. I don't give a flying fuck what you mighta found up there that you think is important, grab what you can and get your troops the fuck down here on the double quick, mister. Or some of you damn slugs are gonna be eating Iranian fucking sand and spending a helluva vacation in the notorious Evin Iranian prison for the next twenty fucking years, buddy. You do understand what I mean by those damn words, right Homes?" Lieutenant Walker warned the huge soldier as he again glanced up towards the ceiling, trying to see what Buckethead and the other soldiers were doing on the next floor of the complex.

"Yeah, I got ya good enuf Walker. I'm finishing up now, most of my people have already passed the office I'm in, and they gave me the thumbs up that they're ready to shove outta this stinking shit hole. I have to check on a few other troopers, get what they found, and then I'll be downstairs before the fucking train leaves the damn station, Lieutenant."

"Get it done for me Bucket." Walker replied, and then he added to his warning to the large soldier. "I won't wait too damn long for ya stinking ass to get down here you know buddy."

Outside the complex, Colonel Leadbetter made contact with ready air cap. "Sandstorm Commander to Razor Blade Leader. Come in sir. Over."

"Razor Leader. What's up Sandstorm Commander? Over." The pilot asked the Colonel.

"I have a shitload of Iranian tanks and ground troops working their way towards my position from the northwest, sir. I suggest you thin the lousy bastards out a little for us, before we have to engage the remainder of the stinking enemy troops and armor in battle. Get it done sir. Over."

"Roger that last Sandstorm. We just topped off our fuel tanks. Make sure your people have their personal IFF systems switched on and working. Lower your heads, and we'll do the rest for you, Colonel. Beginning our attack on the enemy armor and ground troops now sir. Out."

Razor Blade Leader looked behind him, there he saw the three assigned ground attack aircraft making up his Flight Wing and he ordered his three Wingmen. "Razor Flight Leader to Razor's Four, Five and Six. Our ground below pounders need some of our help down there. Switch over to infrared and then hit any enemy armor caught in the open on main road leading to the complex in the northwest area of our attack zone."

"Razor Three to Razor Leader. Roger that last, am arming my master switch, missiles communicating with my computer, I'm hot and heavy. Beginning my attack. Out."

"Roger last, good hunting Razor Three. Out.

IRANIAN GENERAL ARDEBILI GHELAMERZA'S REINFORCING TROOPS AND ARMOR

The short hairs on the back of the well feared Iranian General Ghelamerza's neck stood on end, and he could not understand the reason for this unusual reaction. But the Persian Officer could not fight off the terrible feeling that his armor column was about to come under heavy attack by some unforeseen forces lurking in the darkness of the night. The Persian General knew the powerful American forces were attacking a number of different installations throughout his country, but he never dared to dream the American forces would attack so deep into his country, no matter what the target was for them to destroy.

At one point, the Iranian General was in the lead of the column of armor, but he decided to be a little cautious, and he allowed his armor carrier to slowly drift back in the formation of tanks and other armor vehicles advancing. Until his machine was between the lead tank, and his follow up tank column a hundred yards behind his lead machines. The wise General stared into the night with his field glasses, which offered him very little if any help.

The overwhelming feeling and fear of being attacked by the unseen enemy American forces still weighed very heavy with the Iranian General, until he finally reached inside his machine, and he took a cigarette to help calm down his rattled nerves. He placed the cigarette in his mouth, and used the hot wire lighter to ignite it. He then drew in a huge lung full of air and smoke, and just as he was about to exhale it, his leading tank suddenly exploded in a ball of flames and sparks right before his vehicle's nose. General Ghelamerza actually choked on the smoke still trapped in his lungs as he stared in stunned disbelief as his exploding machine, when three other explosions ripped more of his tanks open, as if some unseen can opener was hard at work against him, while the cigarette fell from his fingers.

Iranian General Ghelamerza shook his head, and then he blew out the smoke as he took his radio and screamed in it for his tanks to stop all forward progress towards the complex. As he gave out the order, a forth older tank exploded with the same fury as the first three exploded moments before. This time two explosions ripped off the track, and opened the tail section of the tank to expose the massive engine spewing out raw fuel, oil, smoke and flames.

"By Allah's Almighty hand and great wisdom, what have I stumbled my cursed troops into?" The fuming Iranian General asked himself as he stared at the other leading tanks. One of his tanks tried to turn, its tracks dragging over five mines which exploded, and caused the tank to erupt into a wall of sparks and roaring flames. The violence of the explosions caused the damaged tank to spew fuel and explode in hell's fury.

Once again, the General found himself asking what was happening to his war machines. He looked towards the sky and saw no aircraft, and then it hit him. Mines! The American troops thought to place an active mine field out before my tanks, and they must be smiling and pleased with themselves as we destroy our own machines in the field. "Damn them cursed animals to the eternal fires of hell. We have stumbled into a cursed mine field." He yelled at no one.

The General ripped out his map and checked for any possible marked old mine fields in this section of Iran. Finding no trace of any past mine fields, he came to the only conclusion he could come to to this situation. He was correct with his assumption that this mine field had to have been laid down recently by the hated American forces invading his country. He lifted his infrared glasses to his eyes and quickly scanned the sector out before the complex. His tanks stopped, waiting further orders from the Iranian General in command.

General Ghelamerza picked up a number of American ground soldiers running in all directions around the complex. The steaming Persian General checked the building and noticed a number of known American machines parked before the main entrance to the complex. More soldiers were loading machinery he never saw before, on their track machines. The Iranian Commander took hold of his mike and gave orders for his main mounts to open fire on any American machines and troops operating in front of the complex they could hit from their positions.

The older tanks found themselves trapped right in the middle of the mine field, fired at the American machines they were able to pick up. The first rounds fell well short by some twenty yards of the invading soldier's position, and were off to the right by thirty yards more. General Ghelamerza picked up the American soldiers drop to the sand to protect themselves. Then a series of white/yellow flashes came from the American position, and his tanks trapped in the open in the mine field, started to explode in a wall of flames and smoke. One of the turrets of his tanks tumbled in the air, and came to rest lying on its side some fifteen feet away from the destroyed hull of the tank. The Commander was still at his post inside the destroyed turret, half his body hung out of the open hatch, with the turret resting on the Commander's head.

One of the General's troops climbed on his idling APC, and he reported anti tank missiles were being fired by the

American soldiers, and they were what just destroyed the tanks.

THE AMERICAN SANDSTORM FORCES

Colonel Bruce Leadbetter realized the Iranian tanks were going to open fire on his troops, and he immediately called up his Javelin anti-tank squads to the front lines. Four troopers fired on the trapped enemy tanks, and the birds roared true to target. The Colonel turned to the building as he cursed the Hornets, and smiled as he noticed Walker's men pouring out of the complex. Some of the AAV-7's were loaded, and the troops were hanging onto anything they could get their hands on. As the machines started to move away from the front of the complex, as quickly as they could travel on the soft sand. Two of the Bradley fighting machines opened fire on the reinforcing Iranian forces, while trying to work over the breathers (enemy soldiers) they picked up fanning out against them, and taking pot shots at the soldiers coming out of the building.

Colonel Leadbetter looked to the sky and he bellowed angrily at the clouds. "Where the hell are those god damn birdmen for the love of God!"

GENERAL ARDEBILI GHELAMERZA'S
IRANIAN REINFORCING TROOPS

The fuming General Ardebili Ghelamerza knew he had to hit the American troops who were attacking his country. But he dared not move his tanks any closer towards the complex, for fear of losing more of his armor to the land mines. In his mind he knew where the safe distance of the anti tank weapons was, and since the American soldiers had no real armor with them, he chose to have his newer tanks attack from safer positions. He planned to allow the tanks to eat up the invading enemy force, and when he felt there was no fight left in the American soldiers, he would then send in his ground forces to slaughter every invader alive. As the General raised his arm to commence his attack, a soldier screamed as he ran frantically away from his vehicle.

"Americans! American planes! General, American warplanes are attacking us sir!"

The Persian General looked in the direction the running soldier pointed in, and he quickly picked up the twin tails of flames from the first American warplanes lining itself up to attack his armor. He counted six cones of flames lighting up the night sky, and he realized three American fighter warplanes were preparing to attack his armor column. He grabbed his mike and ordered his tanks to pull back and head off the road, and then they were ordered to take cover in the sand dunes before the enemy warplanes destroyed them.

The Iranian General's tanks and armor vehicles had no prayer of surviving the vicious attack by the American aircraft as the Hornets launched missiles at the fleeing armor. Six AGM-65D Infrared guided Maverick missiles instantly locked on six Iranian targets, each T-72 tanks tried evasive maneuvers. The General noticed the three warplanes coming in, and he ordered his driver to get his vehicle out of the line of fire. He knew the warplanes were going after the tanks, and decided he did not want to be anywhere near them as he witnessed the attacking planes do a high end over end loop, and end up in another attacking profile, even before the first missiles found their targets. The fuming Iranian General looked over his shoulder in time to see the first missiles turn his rapidly fleeing tanks into molten metal and roaring flames. Three tanks blew up, flames replacing the outline of the once feared Iranian tanks.

The enraged General stared as the attacking warplanes lining up for a second attack against his remaining tanks and armored vehicles, launch another wave of air to ground missiles at his armor. His APC was moving further away from the target area at full speed, trying desperately to place distance between himself, and his doomed tanks and other armor vehicles. In less than a heartbeat, his remaining tanks and two armor vehicles turned into flaming, burning wrecks. His vehicle came to a stop on his orders when he realized the warplanes were suddenly pulling back. Now, his driving force was to reorganize his remaining troops and armor, and prepare them for an all out ground attack using his foot soldiers, and remaining armor as support. The moment his machine pulled back in the lead of the remaining armor, his officers contacted him. The surviving armor moved even closer to their commanding officer's lead machine, and the foot soldiers quickly organized and tried to catch up to the moving armor.

The Hornets moved to their ordered standoff position, and the aircraft waited as they allowed the Psy-Ops helicopter to move in and warn off the Iranian troops before they dared to attack the American forces on the ground. The deadly AC-130H Spectre gunship continued to circle overhead, waiting to be ordered in to attack the enemy positions.

The operative inside the Psy-Ops helicopter spoke to the Iranian troops in Farsi, warning them in no uncertain terms, if they tried to continue their attack against the American troops, they would suffer a terrible fate. To add emphasis to his warning, the operative called in the Spectre gunship, and had him lay down a show of force fifty yards from the lead Iranian armor vehicle.

Many rounds from the two 20 mm Vulcan cannons viciously ate up the soft sand near General Ghelamerza's APC, and the weapon fire made him flinch and duck a bit. A number of heavier rounds from the one 40 mm rapid fire Bofor cannon, and the tail mounted 105 mm howitzer, ripped up more of the desert sand before the Iranian General's vehicle.

General Ghelamerza stared with his mouth hanging open in stunned disbelief, he had never saw such awesome fire power coming from the stars above him. His mind listened to the words from the enemy helicopter hovering just above his vehicle, but well out of range of his weapon fire, a quick glance behind him informed him how his troops felt about their sudden situation and warning coming from the dark sky above them.

Most of the Iranian ground troops had pulled back away from his lead machine. Every once in a while, one round from the unseen aircraft hit a mine, setting it off and adding to the growing fear gripping the General's ground troops. The Iranian Commander looked for his armor, and noticed the machines were pulling further away from his position as well. His shoulders sagged as he realized nothing he did, would allow him to successfully attack the American troops on his soil, and live through that attack. Giving up all hope, he reached inside his machine and took the mike and gave the order to pull back to his secondary line of armor, he added he wanted his snipers out to pick off any Americans they could sight up on. Even though he knew he was not going to attack the main force of enemy soldiers, at least this way some of his snipers would avenge this insult to Iran and him and his troops. By killing a number of the enemy soldiers they could reach from this far a distance away from the enemy troops.

The endless rain of heavy rounds from the sky fired from the Spectre gunship finally stopped, and the desert was once again strangely quiet and at peace. The soldier in the helicopter bellowed at the Iranian troops, ordering them not to try and go any further than they were towards the complex. Or they would be slaughtered to the last before they could do any damage against the American soldiers operating on the ground.

General Ghelamerza's frown turned to a wicked smile as he watched more than just his snipers moving out to try and engage the American troops on the ground. Seconds later he heard his soldiers firing on the enemy troops. But the smile quickly left his lips, every time one of his soldiers fired on any of the invader soldiers, a hailstorm of rounds returned, killing the sniper who had no place to hide on the sand. Slowly, the rounds fired by his troops ended, with none of the them willing to take another shot at the American soldiers for fear of reprisals.

THE AMERICAN SANDSTORM FORCES INSIDE IRAN

Colonel Leadbetter smirked when he watched the power displayed by the Specter gunship. He watched the enemy troops rushing for cover offered by the countless dunes, and picked up the enemy troops settle down and open fire on his troops. He grinned as Baby Tee fired the 40 mm grenade launcher, ripping apart the sands where the weapon fire just came from. The 60 mm machine guns added to the destructive power possessed by the invasion troops. Colonel Leadbetter turned to Lieutenant Walker's group, once he felt he had successfully neutralized the Iranian reinforcements. Three specially designed sand sleds were packed full with file cabinets and other equipment removed from the complex, topping off the load were the troops. The Colonel tried to locate Walker in the group, not seeing him he growled in his radio. "Walker! Walker! Where the fuck are you mister? I told you your time's up, dammit."

Lieutenant Walker was still working in the lab in the main building of the complex, he and the civilian doctor were making one final sweep of the entire area, to make certain they did not over look some vital pieces of equipment, paper, or other form of information they needed to help their President convince the world of what Iran was up to in this part of the desert. He had no way of knowing Buckethead, and a few of the other soldiers with him, were still working on the second floor of the enemy complex.

He let out with a disgusted sigh as he replied to Colonel Leadbetter's angry words. "Colonel, I'm still inside the fucking building, sir. The Doc and I are doing a final sweep of the lab, to make sure we didn't overlook anything vitally important for the people back home, sir."

"That's all fine, well, and good buster, but I already told you to fuck anything you left behind and get your damn troops the hell out of the god damn building so we can head for the EZ and get the devil out of this godforsaken country, mister." (Extraction Zone)

"As far as I know Colonel Leadbetter Sir, we're the last people still working inside this stinking dump, sir. The rest of the fucking troops should be outside the damn building and loading up the stinking sleds with the crap we took from this fucking place, sir. So we can get the hell outta here double quick once I'm satisfied we got everything the stinking civilian Doc wants from this miserable place, sir, Colonel."

"Well I have a fucking news flash for ya ass, mister. I scouted the outside of the damn complex, and don't see half of your damn people outside the dump, Lieutenant. Where the hell are your missing soldiers at, Walker?" Colonel Leadbetter snapped in his headset as he angrily eyed the soldiers pouring outside the structure.

"What about the fucking enemy reinforcements reported to be hanging round out there and hitting us every once in a while, Colonel? What's going on with them fucking Iranian bastards, sir?" Walker fired back at the Colonel as he scanned the lab, looking for any other troops still inside the Iranian building. His eyes ended up resting on the Mutt's face, which was standing right behind him and grinning at him.

"What the hell are you still doing in here for crap sake Mutt? Don't you know it's dangerous in here, you asshole." Walker growled at his lifelong friend.

"I do what the little voices in my head tell me to do man." The Mutt smirked back at Walker.

"You're driving me fucking batty here, pal." Walker hissed back at the Mutt.

"Hey man what the hell can I tell ya friend, I'm just making sure you don't get your stinking ass lost inside here, man. Just in case you don't know it yet buddy. There's a shitload of fricking Iranian defenders still operational in here, and I didn't want your sagging ass to get tagged, unless I'm here to see it happen to ya, man. Anyone whose stupid enuf to get tagged twice on the same stinking mission, has to be protected from himself of he's not gonna make it outta here alive, pal. You know these stinking monkey suits are only good for stopping so many rounds. Sooner or a later, one of the damn things are bound to get through it." The Mutt shifted his weapon and made like he was trying to ignore Walker glaring at him.

Walker let out his breath in a laugh as he replied. "Thanks a fucking lot for your concern Mutt. We're about wrapped it up in here, so why the fuck don't you get your half breed ass outside, and make sure the rest of the slugs out there are done packing up the damn sand sleds."

"Fuhgedaboutit man, I'm gonna stick like glue to your stinking ass, Walker. Knowing how you are my friend, you're liable to find some hot looking fox hiding in here, and I'll be out in the cold with my dick in my hand while you go off and play patty cake with the Iranian hen." The Mutt replied as he flashed a quick smile.

"You win Mutt, huh, wait a minute Mutt, what was that Colonel?"

"Whatsumatter with you, you not paying attention to my damn orders mister? I just told you the damn enemy reinforcements are out of the picture out here for the time being, Walker. But I don't know how long they intend to remain sitting on their damn fingers and spinning, asshole. You have to wrap it up in there damn quick Walker. Now! Dammit soldier!"

"Understood Colonel, I'm about done in here. We'll be out of here in a coupla seconds..."

"Walker! Walker! Buckethead man." The soldier said into his radio excitedly.

"Wait a minute Colonel. Buckethead, what the fuck do you want from me, dammit?"

"Can you clear the fucking net for me man? I have a serious problem up here and I need to talk to you about it in private Walker." The worried sounding soldier reported.

"You still inside the fucking building stupid? I told you to clear out your people, big man."

"Yep, but you gotta clear the fucking net for me before we talk. It's that important man."

"Why Bucket, what the fuck's got ya buddy?" Walker growled at the huge man.

"Not until you clear the fucking channel for me first Walker! I have to speak to you without any other soldier hearing what I have to tell ya, man. It's that fucking important man." Buckethead snapped back in the mike.

The Mutt, standing by Walker's side and listening in on Buckethead's transmission, laughed as he offered his commanding officer. "Hey man, I wonder what's up his stinking ass, Walker? I never heard the big man get angry over anything. It must be something real serious that's eating at him Walker. You betta do as he asks and clear the fucking channel, buddy."

Walker barely glanced at the Mutt as he sighed, and then he snapped in his radio at the rest of the soldiers on the mission. "Okay boys and girls you heard the big man, shut down all radios until further notice." Walker waited a few seconds, and then looked at the Mutt and warned him. "What's up with you buster? You think you're somethin' special round here, buster? You too shithead. Shut it down, shut it down now."

"Me man?" the Mutt shot back as he pointed to himself with his finger and stared at Walker.

"Yes you. Shut it down double quick Mutt." Walker repeated at him.

Once Walker was certain everyone was off the squad channel, he keyed his mike and bitched at the large soldier still working on the second floor of the complex. "Okay Bucket, you have my undivided attention, man. This betta be fucking real important, or I'll bitch slap you on top of that god damn gob you call a head. What's up Bucket?"

Bucket's tone was dry, deathly serious as he asked his commanding officer. "Walker, are you sure everyone's offa the fucking channel? This is fucking important man."

"Yeah, whaddaya want me to do, swear on a stack of Bibles for your ass. You have the net all to yourself, big man. What's got your balls tied up in a fucking knot?"

"Is Mutt anywhere near you Walker?" Buckethead asked the Lieutenant.

"Bucket, I'm sure you didn't want me to clear the fucking channel to find out if the stinking Mutt was with me. I'm getting tired of this crap buster. Where the hell did you think he'd be, stupid. If this ain't fucking important, I'm gonna fuck you to death, Bucket. Now, what the fuck's up with you chum? We have to get the fuck outta this building as of five minutes ago. Colonel Leadbetter's threatening to leave any soldier who doesn't hook up with the rest of the troops outside, behind for a meal for these damn Iranian soldiers to enjoy."

"Walker, it's Fun Bags, Barbara's down." Bucket's voice almost broke on him.

"Christ! Bad?" Walker was stunned as he gave the Mutt a quick sideways glance.

"She's out of it man, she's down for the stinking count." Bucket reported to Walker.

"Dead!" Walker replied barely over a whisper to the Bucket.

"Sorry man, yeah, I think she's dead Walker. She took one right in the fucking neck, Lieutenant." Bucket replied as he tried to control his emotions.

"Christ sake, I thought everyone was going to pull outta this shitting thing in one fucking piece, dammit. Where's she at Bucket?"

"She's up here with me Walker. I wouldn't leave her for a stinking second in this fucking dump, man." Buckethead replied as if he was insulted by Walker's words.

"That's good, I'd expect that from everyone. I'll be right up, hang tight friend."

"Walker, you gonna control the fucking Mutt for me? I don't want him fragging my stinking ass because Barbara got tagged on this stinking operation, man. I don't need him blaming me for not keeping my eyes on her betta. It's not my fault she got tagged."

"Don't sweat it I'll control the Mutt. I'll be right up man. Walker to Leadbetter."

"Go Walker. What's up Lieutenant?" the Colonel barked in the radio.

"Colonel Leadbetter, I have a major fricking problem on my hands and I need some personal down time to handle it before it gets outta hand on me, sir." He reported to the Colonel as he kept his eye on the Mutt at the same time.

"I heard the fucking report. You do whatever you have to do, and I'll stand behind ya all the way, Lieutenant. I'll make sure everyone's ready to go by the time you get her body the hell out of there sir." Colonel Leadbetter replied to young soldier.

Lieutenant Walker took off his helmet and threw it across the litter covered floor of the lab. The civilian doctor stared uncomfortably at Walker and then he warned him in no uncertain terms. "Lieutenant Walker that was an extremely bad move on your part sir. It's far too dangerous to remain inside this building any longer than we have..." The doctor shut up when he saw the look Walker gave him, and he read the warning the way it was delivered.

"Mutt, take off you fucking helmet. We gotta talk man."

The Mutt did as he was told, and snapped at Walker. "Yeah? What's up man?"

"Mutt, I want you to get a hold of yourself dude. I don't what you flying offa the fucking handle on me my friend. I have some heavy shit I gotta lay down on your ass, and it's gonna suck big time." Walker placed his hand on his friends shoulder and looked him in the eyes.

The Mutt stared at Walker as he waited for him to tell him what was bothering him.

"Mutt, it's Barbara, she's down. I'm afraid it's bad, real bad brother."

"Fuck you, that's a piss poor fucking joke you just made, fuck head! I have a fricking mind to stick my foot up your ass for it man." The Mutt hissed, searching Walker's eyes for the sign of this being a bad joke.

Walker saw the terrible look that slowly cloud over the Mutt's face when he realized he was not joking with him. Lieutenant Frank Hall heaved his helmet on the cement floor, and his weapon followed it across the room as he tried to push his way past Walker to get to his lover.

"Hey man, it's nobody's fucking fault Mutt. It's one of those shitty things that's bound to happen to any soldier on a fucking mission, man. No one's to blame for what happened to Barb. Mutt, I don't want you to go off half cocked and hurt any other troops over this shit, man." Walker warned his friend as he tried to keep some kind of control over the fuming wild man.

"Where the fuck is she at Walker? God dammit man, where the fuck is she Walker! Is she still with that fuckup Buckethead upstairs of this fucking dump, Walker"

"Mutt!!!" Walker bellowed into the face of his hurting friend as he tried to maintain his attention as he tried to tell him what was going down.

"Where the fuck is she at, god dammit Walker? Don't make me rip this muther fucking place apart with my bare hands looking for her, man. Where the fuck is she?" the Mutt demanded as he spun around and stared dead angrily in Walker's burning eyes.

"She's upstairs Mutt, Bucket's with her, he wouldn't leave her side for a fucking second."

The Mutt did not wait for Walker to finish his words, he shot out of the lab and flew up the stairs, taking two steps at a time. "Barbara!!!" He bellowed over and over again.

"In here Mutt." Buckethead called out cautiously to the young soldier.

Lieutenant Frank Hall headed for the voice who just called out to him. He caught up to him and followed the Mutt in the nearly destroyed room. Buckethead looked at the Mutt, he was close to tears. "Hey Mutt, I'm real sorry man. I tried to keep her in the rear of the fucking action to keep her out of the hell zone, man." He took a step back like he was actually afraid the Mutt was going to beat on him.

The Mutt stared at the big man and then slapped him on the shoulder as he dropped to his knees and he pulled Barbara's head close to his armor plated chest. He swallowed as he noticed a bullet nearly ripped her head from her shoulders and he cried as he stare at her bloody face. "Oh man, I shoulda fucking listened to you on this one baby. You didn't want to come on this fucking mission, baby girl. I was the one who talked you into coming with me dammit. I shoulda knocked you up like you wanted, that way I woulda had something of yours to live with for the rest of my stinking life. Arrr... Christ, this shit sucks, baby."

The Mutt pulled Barbara's body close to his and he hugged her head to him for dear life. Tears ran down his cheeks unashamed, and some of them landed on Barbara's grime covered, blood splattered face, and he softly wiped them off her with his fingers.

There was a slight commotion behind Walker and he turned to see Sergeant Dorothy Ramirez standing directly behind him, tears rolling down her face and she was staring at the Mutt and Barbara on the floor. She tried to rush by Walker, but he intercepted her and pulled her close to him. She buried her head against his armor plated shoulder and cried. Other soldiers poured in the hall, everyone trying to get in the room with the Mutt and Barbara. There were no secrets between the specialized soldiers. It was a tight knit group who looked after each other as if they were all they had. Men, soldiers, big men, strong women, men who thought nothing of taking another person's life, were leaning against each other, trying to find their own private way of accepting the death of one of their own. Some of the troopers were openly crying, while others leaned against each other for closeness and comfort. The women soldiers tried to console the shaken men as they coped with their loss.

Ramirez pulled free of Walker's grasp, and then she moved over to the Mutt's side and she knelt down beside him. He turned to her and she pulled his head to her chest and kissed.

CHAPTER THIRTY

Colonel Bruce Leadbetter followed Bdellah as he walked up to the old man, whose Howli was covered with blood, sweat and grime. The old man looked thoroughly exhausted, as he tried to stand tall before the American military officer and agent.

"Salam Alaikum father of the vast desert sands. (Peace be upon you) May Allah keep you safe in your worldly travels. Are you all right, father of the great deserts of Iran?" Bdellah asked with concern lacing his tone, as he reached out his arm while staring at the old man. His Khafia, the red and white checkered head dress was stained crimson, his Howli was ripped in many different places, and the old man looked as if he was going to drop to the ground any minute.

Al-Shamarral took Bdellah's arm, gripping his arm with his hand he replied in an exhausted voice to him. "Yes my son, do not concern yourself about this old desert wanderer. I am fine, but there shall be no more enemy reinforcements coming to aid the rest of these great fools doing the devil's work in this foul place of death. It was a bloody fight on this dark night, and I lost many faithful fighters to this combat against a band of jackals. I'm afraid there shall be many weeping sad hearts at our camp fire for many nights to come."

"May Allah be praised and give you many fine and healthy sons to carry on your bloodline, my father. Your great desert fighters fight like no others I have ever witnessed in all my life. Al-Shamarral, this American soldier standing by my side is Colonel Leadbetter. Colonel Leadbetter, this great leader who stands before you is named Ahmed Hussein al-Shamarral. He's the leader of the desert fighters who came to our aide, and they made our operation the success it was."

Al-Shamarral took his eyes away from Bdellah's face, and he allowed them to rest on the American Colonel's face. He reached out and shaking arm and shook his hand in the ways of the Bedouin.

Colonel Leadbetter smiled as he announced to the old man. "Glad to meet you sir. It's because of your losses that my mission is a success, sir." The Colonel bowed his head slightly towards the old man whose chest swelled with pride over the outstanding compliment being paid him by this American warrior dressed in metal looking skin.

"Tonight, you have taught me a very valuable lesson. Tonight, I have learned not all Arab or Persian peoples are my country's enemy. I have learned there are many good

Arab and Persian people living in the Middle East who we can trust and believe in and hopefully, live in peace with them." The Colonel offered to the old man with sincerity lacing his tone.

Al-Shamarral's grin grew even larger as he replied to the American military officer. "Colonel whose last name I'll not dare try and pronounce for fear of insulting you for saying your name wrong. I cannot begin to tell you how long I have waited to hear those blessed words being spoken by an American, any American. I'm happy I have been able to change your mind over my people's intention. Perhaps, there's hope for a lasting peace in the Middle East after all, Colonel. Because is not the foundation of peace based upon trust, my son? But one thing you have to remember. We in Iran are not Arabs, we are Persians and proud of it."

"Yes sir. Perhaps peace will come to all of the Middle East at that my all seeing father. I fear both you and your people have a long road to hoe, before peace and freedom can come freely to your nation of Iran. Good luck in your future quests during your allotted time on this earth from Allah, father of the desert sands. If you even have need of my help, contact me at Camp Lejeune, and I'll try and help you." Bdellah offered to the old man as he picked up the conversation from the Colonel.

Behind al-Shamarral stood the young and very beautiful Sayeh, and she moved out of the shadows like a cat stalking her prey, and she stood by the beggar's side. She smiled that certain smile to Bdellah, and his knees went weak on him as he nodded to her. He forced his eyes from the Persian beauty, and turned to Colonel Leadbetter and informed him. "Colonel Leadbetter Sir, I have made up my mind to stay in Iran. My work here is not done. I feel I can better serve my country by remaining behind and working with these people of the desert, Colonel. I'll make contact with my control at the prescribed time as ordered, and explain my actions to him."

"What!!! Personally, I think you're nuttier than a squirrel's turd, mister. Arrr... okay, suit yourself Bdellah. What can I tell ya, I still think you're nuts, but if that's your decision, so be it and I'll respect it and you, my friend. Err... I suggest we leave, because in a few minutes this place is going to erupt like a super nova."

Bdellah looked to al-Shamarral, and got the slight nod he was looking for and added. "Yes Colonel Leadbetter, I am staying in Iran. I feel there is much more I can do for this country and besides, it seems I have another reason to remain here, sir."

Sayeh moved over to Bdellah's side to stand proud with him.

"I see what you mean my friend. Okay, it was good meeting and working with ya. You have save some of my people's lives, and for this I'm forever beholding to ya, Bdellah. I hope we'll meet sometime in the future, I owe you a drink or two for your help with this operation, sir." The Colonel put out his hand and they shook, and he looked at al-Shamarral who nodded at him.

Colonel Leadbetter spun around when he felt he had nothing else to add to the Persians who had assisted his troops. The Colonel charged for his Bradley fighting machine and climbed aboard in a hurry. The EOD Team made it to his machine at the same time, and they jumped on the side of the vehicle as Colonel Leadbetter scurried to the top of the machine, and he poked his head inside the iron beast and roared at the driver. "Let's get the hell outta here on the double quick before we're in the middle of the god damn explosion. The EODT are on board this damn thing, and

Bdellah is remaining behind to continue his work with these people."

The rest of his troops were already a full mile ahead of his machine. Colonel Leadbetter's once lead machine was carrying the linkup to the mines separating them from the Iranian reinforcements still trapped on the other side of the large mine field. The Colonel kept his head bent, while trying to look at the complex as they drove away from the structures.

He had no idea if they would leave the area of control over the mines before the building finally exploded. He hoped to keep the Iranian troops held at bay until after the explosion occurred, and the structures were gone from the face of the earth. His Bradley was traveling at fifty miles an hour when he took one last look at the Iranian complex. He picked up the Iranian troops carefully trying to work their way through the mine field. The commanding officer of the operation cursed, hoping they would not reach the buildings in time to disarm the explosive charges he left behind.

Zippo, the leading soldier of the EODT noticed the look from the Colonel, and he knew what was bugging the officer and he offered. "Colonel Leadbetter Sir, the explosives will pop long before any Persian soldiers can get through the mine field and disarm them on us sir. If the Iranians are lucky enough to reach the charges before they go off, their luck will still run out on them. Because the second they go fucking around with any of my charges, they're going to pop off right in their damn faces, sir. I tampered proofed the charges, sir."

Colonel Leadbetter nodded at Zippo as he remained staring at the structures. In what looked like a scene right out of a nightmare, the Colonel watched as the series of heavy explosions took place in rapid succession. The ground over eight miles away from the source of the explosions, shook under his tracked machine as roaring flames and columns of smoke engulfed the complex in a blinding light. The blast was so bright and powerful that it lit up the Iranian troops working through the computer controlled mine field.

Colonel Leadbetter kept staring at the destruction eating its way through the entire Iranian complex. When his Bradley traveled ten miles away from the concrete structures, a series of small explosions took place where the Iranian General's troops were trapped in the mine field. Many of the surprised Iranian soldiers were cut down by the shrapnel from the exploding mines automatically going off, as they self destruct from lack of computer signals to remain stable. The General did not understand what was happening around him and his troops, and out of fear and confusion, the Iranian Officer ordered his troops to pull back, opening the gap between his troops and fleeing American forces. This wide a gap made it completely impossible for the Iranian and his troops to catch up with the fleeing Americans before they were extracted from his country.

Colonel Leadbetter had to climb in his machine, because of the speed it was traveling. It was then the radio came to life as his Bradley caught up to the other vehicles in his column.

"Sandstorm, this is USSOC." United States Special Operations Command, Tampa, Florida.

"This is Sandstorm. Go Commander." Colonel Leadbetter replied in an exhausted tone.

"Colonel Leadbetter Sir, your orders have been altered sir. We have just received information the Iranian government has moved a number of ground forces and military equipment along the coast of their country. It's believed they're preparing to fend off an invasion attempt of their country mounted by us or our allies, sir. This move has compromised your original EP. (Extraction Point) So it's been decided to make a land extraction of your troops, sir. Your new ER (Extraction Rendezvous) is stationed at GPP (Global Positioning Point) November Three, Three, Five, Whiskey, by Sierra Seven, One, One, Three, Echo, Colonel Leadbetter.

"By the time you reach this new position for the extraction of your troops. I'll have a wing of V-22 Osprey Vertical takeoff and landing aircraft waiting for you and the rest of your troops, Colonel. You'll have your troops, along with the items removed from the complex, and any small items of equipment absolutely needed to be removed from the machines, loaded on board these aircraft. Then you're instructed to have your EOD people plant charges on any military equipment left behind, Colonel Leadbetter Sir. I want everything left behind, destroyed before you leave the area. I'll have a wing of F-117 Stealth fighters overhead, and the second you get in the ring, they'll drop Lazy Boy mining bombs around your abandoned equipment to keep you safe until your people are in the air. Then we don't care what the Iranians do. Are these orders clear, sir?"

"Yes sir. I understand my orders as received, thanks for the added backup support sir."

"Very well Colonel Leadbetter. I'm looking forward to seeing you. Good luck sir and coagulations on a mission well done. You're further ordered to give your troops a well done, and this order's coming from your Commander in Chief, the President of the United States, sir."

"Yes sir, and I'll give my soldiers a well done from their President, sir." Colonel Leadbetter broke off his communication with USSOC, and then gave his driver the new position for their extraction point. It took his column fifteen minutes to reach the new location. The Marine Colonel saw the waiting V-22s as his machine skidded to a stop. He bellowed at his troops, ordering them to load up the file cabinets and warheads and computer information in the first two V-22s. Then he watched as his troops loaded the wounded and dead from the unit onto another plane as the exhausted, battered and bloody soldiers piled in the other five planes. Both Colonel Leadbetter and Walker watched as the EODs set the charges on their abandoned military equipment, and then they piled into the last aircraft, and they marveled at how the plane lifted off the ground straight up.

Lieutenant Robert Walker kept a close watch out of the window until the Bradley's, along with the AAV-7s and sand sleds, erupted in balls of flames. Then he sat back by Sergeant Ramirez, and took her hand in his and patted it gently and smiled at his lady warrior. The empty seat to Walker's right, was the Mutt's, who was in the aircraft behind theirs carrying the dead and injured from the unit. The Mutt decided to kept Barbara's body company back to whatever base they were to be deposited on. Walker looked at Ramirez and smiled again, she finally smiled at him, but a tear ran down the side of her cheek as he kissed her hand and announced. "It's over baby, we're on our way home."